About the Author

Carol Marinelli recently filled in a form asking for her job title. Thrilled to be able to put down her answer, she put 'writer'. Then it asked what Carol did for relaxation an[illegible]th—'writing'. The third quest[illegible] Well, not wanting to look o[illegible]gers an[illegible]ered 'swimming'– but, given [illegible]n the pool does terrible things to her highlights, I'm sure you can guess the real answer!

The Rumours
COLLECTION

July 2019

August 2019

September 2019

October 2019

November 2019

December 2019

Rumours: The One-Night Heirs

CAROL MARINELLI

MILLS & BOON

First Published in Great Britain 2019
By Mills & Boon, an imprint of HarperCollins *Publishers*
1 London Bridge Street, London, SE1 9GF

RUMOURS: THE ONE-NIGHT HEIRS

ISBN: 978-0-26327675-6

1219

MIX
Paper from
responsible sources
FSC™ C007454

This book is produced from independently certified FSC™ paper to ensure responsible forest management.

For more information visit: www.harpercollins.co.uk/green

Printed and bound in Spain
by CPI, Barcelona

THE INNOCENT'S SECRET BABY

For Lena, my mum.

You were wonderful as both
and I will love you for ever.

Until we meet again…

PROLOGUE

SURELY NOT?

As Raul Di Savo thanked the mourners who had attended his mother's funeral a figure standing in the distance caught his attention.

He wouldn't *dare* to come here!

Not today of all days.

The tolling of the bell in the small Sicilian church had long since ceased, but it still seemed to ring in Raul's ears.

'Condoglianze.'

Raul forced himself to focus on the elderly gentleman in front of him rather than the young man who stood on the periphery of the cemetery.

'Grazie,' Raul said, and thanked the old man for his attendance.

Given the circumstances of Maria's death, and fearing Raul's father's wrath, most had stayed away.

Gino had not attended his wife's funeral.

'She was a whore when I married her and she goes into the ground the same.'

That was how he had broken the news of her death to his son.

Raul, having been told of a car accident involving his mother, had travelled from Rome back to Casta—a town on the Sicilian wild west coast—but he had arrived only to be told that she had already gone.

He had been too late.

Slowly, painfully, he had pieced together the timeline of shocking events that had led to Maria's death. Now Raul performed his familial duties and stood graveside as the line of mourners slowly moved past him.

Condolences were offered, but small talk was strained. The events of the last few days and the savage condemnations that were now coursing through the valley made even the simplest sentence a mockery.

'She was a good…' A lifetime family friend faltered in his choice of words. 'She was…' Again there was hesitation over what should be said. 'Maria will be missed.'

'She will be,' Raul duly replied.

The scent of freshly dug soil filled his nostrils and lined the back of his throat, and Raul knew there was no comfort to be had.

None.

He had left it too late to save her.

And now she was gone.

Raul had studied hard at school and had done so well in his exams that he had received a scholarship and, as he had always intended, been able to get out of the Valley of Casta.

Or, as Raul and his friend Bastiano had called it, *the Valley of Hell.*

Raul had been determined to get his mother away from his father.

Maria Di Savo.

Unhinged, some had called her.

'Fragile' was perhaps a more appropriate word.

Deeply religious until she had met his father, Maria had hoped to join the local convent—an imposing stone residence that looked out on the Sicilian Strait. His mother had wept when it had closed down due to declining numbers, as if somehow her absence had contributed to its demise.

The building had long stood abandoned, but there was not a day Raul could remember when his mother hadn't rued the day she had not followed her heart and become a novice nun.

If only she had.

Raul stood now, questioning his very existence, for her

pregnancy had forced Maria into the unhappiest of marriages.

Raul had always loathed the valley, but never more so than now.

He would never return.

Raul knew his drunken father's demise was already secured, for without Maria's care his descent would be rapid.

But there was another person to be taken care of.

The man who had forced this tragic end.

Raul had made a vow as he'd thrown a final handful of soil into his mother's open grave that he would do whatever it might take to bring him down.

'I shall miss her.'

Raul looked up and saw Loretta, a long-time friend of his mother's who worked in the family bar.

'No trouble today, Raul.'

Raul found himself frowning at Loretta's choice of words and then realised why she suddenly sounded concerned—he was looking beyond the mourners now, to the man who stood in the distance.

Bastiano Conti.

At seventeen, Bastiano was a full year younger than Raul.

Their families were rivals.

Bastiano's uncle owned most of the properties and all of the vineyards on the west of the valley.

Raul's father was king of the east.

The rivalry went back generations, and yet their black history had been ignored by the young boys and, growing up, the two of them had been friends. They had gone through school together and often spent time with each other during the long summer breaks. Before Raul had left the valley he and Bastiano had sat drinking wine from the opposing families' vines.

Both wines were terrible, they had agreed.

Similar in looks, both were tall and dark and were opposed only in nature.

Bastiano, an orphan, had been raised by his extended family and got through life on charm.

Raul was serious and mistrusting and had been taught to be fickle.

He trusted no one but said what he had to to get by.

Though different in style, they were equally adored by women.

Bastiano seduced.

Raul simply returned the favour.

There had been no rivalry between the young men—both could have their pick of the valley and the fruits were plenty.

Yet Bastiano had used his dark charm on the weakest and had taken Maria as his lover.

Pillow talk had been gathered and secrets had been prised from loose lips.

Not only had Maria had an affair—she had taken it beyond precarious and slept with a member of the family that Gino considered his enemy.

When the affair had been discovered—when the rumours had reached Gino—Loretta had called her to warn her Gino was on his angry way home. Maria had taken out a car she didn't know how to drive.

An unwise choice in the valley.

And Raul knew the accident would not have happened but for Bastiano.

'Raul…' Loretta spoke softly, for she felt the tension rip through him and could hear his ragged breathing. She held on to his hand, while knowing nothing could really stop him now. 'You are Sicilian, and that means you have a lifetime to get your revenge—just don't let it be today.'

'No,' Raul agreed.

Or did he refute?

Raul's words were coming out all wrong, his voice was a

touch hoarse, and as he looked down he could see the veins in his hand and feel the pulse in his temples. He was primed for action, and the only thing Raul knew for sure was that he hated Bastiano with all that he had.

He dropped Loretta's hand and brushed past her, then shrugged off someone else who moved to try to stop him.

'Raul!' The priest shot him a warning. 'Not here—not now.'

'Then he should have stayed away!' Raul responded as he strode through the cemetery towards the man who had sent his mother to an early grave.

Raul picked up speed—and God help Bastiano because hate and fury catapulted Raul those last few steps.

'Pezzo di merda...' Raul shouted out words that did not belong in such a setting.

Any sane man who saw murder approach would surely turn and run, but instead Bastiano walked towards Raul, hurling insults of his own. 'Your mother wanted—'

Raul did not let him finish, for Bastiano had already sullied her enough, and to silence him Raul slammed his fist into Bastiano's face. He felt the enamel of Bastiano's tooth pierce his knuckle, but that was the last thing he felt.

It was bloody.

Two parts grief, several belts of rage and a hefty dose of shame proved a volatile concoction indeed.

Raul would kill him.

That was all he knew.

Yet Bastiano refused to go quietly and fought back.

There were shouts and the sounds of sirens in the distance as the two men battled it out. Raul felt nothing as he was slammed against a gravestone. The granite tore through the dark suit and white shirt on his back with the same ease that it gouged through muscle and flesh.

It didn't matter.

His back was already a map of scars from his father's beatings, and adrenaline was a great anaesthetic.

Only vaguely aware of the wound that ran from shoulder to flank, Raul hauled himself up to stand, took aim again and felled his rival.

Yet Bastiano refused to submit.

Raul pinned Bastiano and slammed his fist into his face, marring those perfect features with relish, and then he held him to the ground and told him he should have stayed the hell away from his mother.

'Like *you* did!'

Those words were more painful than any physical blow, for Raul knew that he had done just that—stayed away.

CHAPTER ONE

ROME AGAIN… ROME AGAIN…

The City of Love.

Wrapped in a towel, and damp from the shower, Lydia Hayward lay on the bed in her hotel suite and considered the irony.

Yes, she might be in Rome, and meeting tonight with a very eligible man, but it had nothing to do with love.

There were more practical matters that needed to be addressed.

Oh, it hadn't been said outright, of course.

Her mother hadn't sat her down one evening and explained that, without the vast and practically bottomless pit of money that this man could provide, they would lose everything. *Everything* being the castle they lived in, which was the family business too.

And Valerie had never *said* that Lydia had to sleep with the man she and her stepfather were meeting tonight.

Of course she hadn't.

Valerie *had*, however, enquired whether Lydia was on the Pill.

'You don't want to ruin your holiday.'

Since when had her mother taken an interest in such things? Lydia had been to Italy once before, on a school trip at the age of seventeen, and her mother hadn't been concerned enough to ask then.

Anyway, why would she be on the Pill?

Lydia had been told to 'save' herself.

And she had.

Though not because of her mother's instruction—more because she did not know how to let her guard down.

People thought her aloof and cold.

Better they think that than she reveal her heart.

And so, by default, she had saved herself.

Lydia had secretly hoped for love.

It would seem not in this lifetime.

Tonight she would be left alone with him.

The towel fell away and, though she was alone, Lydia pulled it back and covered herself.

She was on the edge of a panic attack, and she hadn't had one since…

Rome.

Or was it Venice?

Venice.

Both.

That awful school trip.

She had said yes to this trip to Rome, hoping to lay a ghost to rest. Lydia wanted to see Rome through adult eyes, yet she was as scared of the world now as she had been as a teenager.

Pull yourself together, Lydia.

And so she did.

Lydia got up from the bed and got dressed.

She was meeting Maurice, her stepfather, at eight for breakfast. Rather than be late she just quickly combed her long blonde hair, which had dried a little wild. She had bought a taupe linen dress to wear, which had buttons from neck to hem—though perhaps not the best choice for her shaking hands.

They are not *expecting you to sleep with him!*

Lydia told herself she was being utterly ridiculous even to entertain such a thought. She would stop by for a drink with this man tonight, with her stepfather, thank him for his hospitality and then explain that she was going out with friends. Arabella lived here now and had said they should catch up when Lydia got here.

In fact…

Lydia took out her phone and fired off a quick text.

Hi, Arabella,
Not sure if you got my message.
Made it to Rome.
I'm free for dinner tonight if you would like to catch up.
Lydia

And so to breakfast.

Lydia stepped out of her suite and took the elevator down to the dining room. As she walked through the lavish foyer she caught sight of herself in a mirror. Those deportment classes had been good for something at least—she was the picture of calm and had her head held high.

Yet she wanted to run away.

'No, grazie.'

Raul Di Savo declined the waiter's offer of a second espresso and continued to read through reports on the Hotel Grande Lucia, where he now sat, having just taken breakfast.

At Raul's request his lawyer had attained some comprehensive information, but it had come through only this morning. In a couple of hours Raul was to meet with Sultan Alim, so there was a lot to go through.

The Grande Lucia was indeed a sumptuous hotel, and Raul took a moment to look up from his computer screen and take in the sumptuous dining room that was currently set up for breakfast.

There was the pleasant clink of fine china and a quiet murmur of conversation and, though formal, the room had a relaxed air that had made Raul's stay so far pleasurable. There was a certain old-world feel to the place that spoke of Rome's rich history and beauty.

And Raul wanted the hotel to be his.

Raul had been toying with the idea of adding it to his portfolio and had just spent the night in the Presidential Suite as a guest of Sultan Alim.

Raul hadn't expected to be so impressed.

He had been, though.

Every detail was perfection personified—the décor was stunning, the staff were attentive yet discreet, and it appeared to be a rich haven for both the business traveller and the well-heeled tourist.

Raul was now seriously considering taking over this landmark hotel.

Which meant that so too was Bastiano.

Fifteen years on and their rivalry continued unabated.

Mutual hatred was a silent, yet daily motivator—a black cord that connected them.

And Bastiano would be arriving later today.

Raul knew that Bastiano was also a personal friend of Sultan Alim. Raul had considered if that might have any bearing on their negotiations but had soon discounted it. Sultan Alim was a brilliant businessman, and his friendship with Bastiano would have no sway over his dealings, Raul was certain of that.

Raul rather hoped his presence at the hotel might cause Bastiano some discomfort, for though they moved in similar circles in truth their paths rarely crossed. Raul, even on his father's death, had never returned to Casta.

There had been no respects to pay.

Yet Casta had remained Bastiano's base.

He had converted the old convent into a luxury retreat for the seriously wealthy.

It was actually, Raul knew, an extremely upmarket rehab facility.

His mother would be turning in her grave.

Raul's black thoughts were interrupted when the portly

middle-aged gentleman sitting to his right made his disgruntled feelings known.

'Who do you have to sleep with around here to get some service?' he muttered in well-schooled English.

It would seem that the tourists were getting impatient!

Raul smiled inwardly as the waiter continued to ignore the pompous Englishman. The waiter had had enough. This man had been complaining since the moment he had been shown to his table, and there was absolutely nothing to complain about.

Raul was not being generous in that observation. Many of his nights were spent in hotels—mainly those that he owned—and so more than most he had a very critical eye.

There were certain ways to behave, and despite his accent this man did not adhere to them. He seemed to assume that just because he was in Rome no one would speak English and his insults would go unnoticed.

They did not.

And so—just because he could—Raul gestured with his index and middle fingers towards the small china cup on his table. The motion was subtle, barely noticeable to many, and yet it was enough to indicate to the attentive waiter that Raul had changed his mind and would now like another coffee.

Raul knew that his preferential treatment would incense the diner to his right.

From the huff of indignation as his drink was delivered, it did.

Good!

Yes, Raul decided, he wanted this hotel.

Raul read through the figures again and decided to make some further calls to try to get behind the real reason the Sultan was selling such an iconic hotel. Even with Raul's extensive probing he could see no reason for the sale. While the outgoings were vast, it was profitable indeed. The crème de la crème stayed at the Grande Lucia, and it was here that their children were christened and wed.

There had to be a reason Alim was selling, and Raul had every intention of finding out just what it was.

Just as Raul had decided to leave he glanced up and saw a woman enter the dining room.

Raul was more than used to beautiful women, and the room was busy enough that he should not even have noticed, but there was something about her that drew the eye.

She was tall and slender and she wore a taupe dress. Her long blonde hair appeared freshly washed and tumbled over her shoulders. Raul watched as she had a brief conversation with the maître d' and then started to walk in his direction.

Still Raul did not look away.

She made her way between the tables with elegant ease, and Raul noted that she carried herself beautifully. Her complexion was pale and creamy, and suddenly Raul wanted her to be close enough so that he could know the colour of her eyes. She lifted a hand and gave a small wave, and Raul, who was rarely the recipient of a sinking feeling where women were concerned, felt one now.

She was with *him*, Raul realised—she was here to have breakfast with the obnoxious man who sat to his right.

Pity.

The blonde beauty walked past his table, and he could not help but notice the delicate row of buttons that ran from neck to hem on her dress. But he pointedly returned his attention to his computer screen rather than mentally undress her.

That she was with someone rendered her of no interest to him in that way.

Raul loathed cheats.

Still, the morning scent of her was fresh and heady—a delicate cloud that reached Raul a few seconds after she had passed and lingered for a few moments more.

'Good morning,' she said as she took a seat, and unlike her companion's the woman's voice was pleasant.

'Hmph.'

Her greeting was barely acknowledged by the seated Englishman. Some people, Raul decided, simply did not know how to appreciate the finer things in life.

And this lady was certainly amongst the finest.

The waiter knew that too.

He was there in an instant to lavish attention upon her and was appreciative of her efforts when she attempted to ask for Breakfast Tea in schoolgirl Italian, remembering her manners and adding a clumsy *'per favour'*.

Such poor Italian would usually be responded to in English, in arrogant reprimand, and yet the waiter gave a nod. *'Prego.'*

'I'll have another coffee,' the man said and then, before the waiter had even left, added rather loudly to his companion, 'The service is terribly slow here—I've had nothing but trouble with the staff since the moment I arrived.'

'Well, I think it's excellent.' Her voice was crisp and curt, instantly dismissing his findings. 'I've found that a please and a thank-you work wonders—you really ought to try it, Maurice.'

'What are your plans for today?' he asked.

'I'm hoping to do some sightseeing.'

'Well, you need to shop—perhaps you should consider something a little less beige,' Maurice added. 'I asked the concierge and he recommended a hair and beauty salon a short distance from the hotel. I've booked you in for four.'

'Excuse me?'

Raul was about to close his laptop. His interest had waned the second he had realised she was with someone.

Almost.

But then the man spoke on.

'We're meeting Bastiano at six, and you want to be looking your best.'

The sound of his nemesis's name halted Raul and again the couple had his full attention—though not by a flicker did he betray his interest.

'*You're* meeting Bastiano at six,' the blonde beauty responded. 'I don't see why I have to be there while you two discuss business.'

'I'm not arguing about this. I expect you to be there at six.'

Raul drained his espresso but made no move to stand. He wanted to know what they had to do with Bastiano—any inside knowledge on the man he most loathed was valuable.

'I can't make it,' she said. 'I'm meeting a friend tonight.'

'Come off it!' The awful man snorted. 'We both know that you don't have any friends.'

It was a horrible statement to make, and Raul forgot to pretend to listen and actually turned his head to see her reaction. Most women Raul knew would crumble a little, but instead she gave a thin smile and a shrug.

'Acquaintance, then. I really am busy tonight.'

'Lydia, you will do what is right by the family.'

Her name was Lydia.

As Raul continued to look at her, perhaps sensing her conversation was being overheard, she glanced over and their eyes briefly met. He saw that they were china blue.

His question as to the colour of her eyes was answered, but now Raul had so many more.

She flicked her gaze away and the conversation was halted as the waiter brought their drinks.

Raul made no move to leave.

He wanted to know more.

A family had come into the restaurant and were being seated close to them. The activity drowned out the words from the table beside him, revealing only hints of the conversation.

'Some old convent…' she said, and the small cup in his hand clattered just a little as it hit the saucer.

Raul realised they were discussing the valley.

'Well, that shows he's used to old buildings,' Maurice said. 'Apparently it's an inordinate success.'

A baby that was being squeezed into an antique high chair started to wail, and Raul frowned in impatience as an older child loudly declared that he was hungry and he wanted chocolate milk.

'Scusi…' he called to the waiter, and with a mere couple of words more and a slight gesture of his hand in the family's direction his displeasure was noted.

Noted not just by the waiter—Lydia noted it too.

In fact she had noticed him the moment the maître d' had gestured to where her stepfather, Maurice, was seated.

Even from a distance, even seated, the man's beauty had been evident.

There was something about him that had forced her attention as she had crossed the dining room.

No one should look that good at eight in the morning.

His black hair gleamed, and as she had approached Lydia had realised it was damp and he must have been in the shower around the same time as her.

Such an odd thought.

That rapidly turned into a filthy one.

Her first with the recipient in the same room!

She had looked away quickly as soon as she had seen that he was watching her approach.

Her stomach had done a little somersault and her legs had requested of their owner that they might bypass Maurice and be seated with *him*.

Such a ridiculous thought, for she knew him not at all.

And he *wasn't* nice.

That much she knew.

Lydia turned her head slightly and saw that on his command the family was being moved.

They were *children*, for goodness' sake!

This man irritated her.

This stranger irritated her far more than a stranger should, and she frowned her disapproval at him and her neck felt hot and itchy as he gave a small shrug in return and then closed his computer.

You were already leaving, Lydia wanted to point out. *Why have the family moved when you were about to leave?*

Yes, he irritated her—like an itch she needed to scratch.

Her ears felt hot and her jaw clenched as the waiter came and apologised to him for the disruption.

Disruption?

The child had asked for chocolate milk, for goodness' sake, and the baby had merely cried.

Of course she said nothing. Instead Lydia reached for her pot of tea as Maurice droned on about their plans for tonight—or rather, what he thought Lydia should wear.

'Why don't you speak to a stylist?'

'I think I can manage. I've been dressing myself since I was three,' Lydia calmly informed him, and as she watched the amber fluid pour into her cup she knew—she just knew—that the stranger beside her was listening.

It was her audience that gave her strength.

Oh, she couldn't see him, but she knew his attention was on her.

There was an awareness between them that she could not define—a conversation taking place such as she had never experienced, for it was one without words.

'Don't be facetious, Lydia,' Maurice snapped.

But with this man beside her Lydia felt just that.

The sun was shining, she was in Rome, and the day

stretched before her—she simply did not want to waste a single moment of it with Maurice.

'Have a lovely day...' She took her napkin and placed it on the table, clearly about to leave. 'Give Bastiano my regards.'

'This isn't up for debate, Lydia. You're to keep tonight free. Bastiano has flown us to Rome for this meeting and housed us in two stunning suites. The very least you can do is come for a drink and thank him.'

'Fine,' Lydia retorted. 'But know this, I'll have a drink, but it's not the "very least" I'll do—it's the most.'

'You'll do what's right for the family.'

'I've tried that for years,' Lydia said, and stood up. 'I think it's about time I did what's right by *me*!'

Lydia walked out of the restaurant with her head still high, but though she looked absolutely in control she was in turmoil, for her silent fears were starting to come true.

This wasn't a holiday.

And it wasn't just drinks.

She was being offered up, Lydia knew.

'Scusi...'

A hand on her elbow halted her, and as she spun around Lydia almost shot into orbit when she saw it was the man from the next table.

'Can I help you?' she snapped.

'I saw you leaving suddenly.'

'I wasn't aware that I needed your permission.'

'Of course you don't,' he responded.

His voice was deep, and his English, though excellent, was laced heavily with a rich accent. Her toes attempted to curl in her flat sandals at its sound.

Lydia was tall, but then so was he—she didn't come close to his eye level.

It felt like a disadvantage.

'I just wanted to check that you were okay.'

'Why wouldn't I be?'

'I heard some of what was said in there.'

'And do you *always* listen in on private conversations?'

'Of course.' He shrugged. 'I rarely intervene, but you seemed upset.'

'No,' Lydia said. 'I didn't.'

She knew that as fact—she was very good at keeping her emotions in check.

She should have walked off then. Only she didn't. She continued the conversation. 'That baby, however, *was* upset—and I didn't see you following him across the dining room.'

'I don't like tantrums with my breakfast, and the toddler is now throwing one,' he said. 'I thought I might go somewhere else to eat. Would you like to join me?'

He was forward *and* he lied, for she had seen the waiter removing his plates and knew he had already had breakfast.

'No, thank you.' Lydia shook her head.

'But you haven't eaten.'

'Again,' Lydia replied coolly, 'that's not your concern.'

Bastiano *was* his concern, though.

For years revenge had been his motivator, and yet still Bastiano flourished.

Something had to give, and Raul had waited a long time for that day to arrive.

Now it would seem that it had—in the delicate shape of an English rose.

Raul was no fool, and even from the snippets of conversation he'd heard, he had worked out a little of what was going on.

Bastiano wanted Lydia to be there tonight.

And Lydia didn't want to go.

It was enough to go on—more than enough. For despite her calm demeanour he could see the pulse leaping in her throat. More than that, Raul knew women—and knew them well.

There was another issue that existed between them.

She was turned on.

So was he.

They had been on sight.

From her slow walk across the dining room and for every moment since they had been aware of each other at the basest of levels.

'Come for breakfast,' he said, and then he remembered how she liked manners. *'Per favore.'*

Lydia realised then that every word she had uttered in the restaurant had been noted.

It should feel intrusive.

And it did.

But in the most delightful of ways.

Her breath felt hot in her lungs and the warm feeling from the brief touch of his hand on her arm was still present.

She wanted to say yes—to accept this dark stranger's invitation and follow this dangerous lead.

But that would be reckless at best, and Lydia was far from that.

There was something about him that she could not quite define, and every cell in her body recognised it and screamed danger. He was polished and poised—immaculate, in fact. And yet despite the calm demeanour there was a restless edge. Beneath the smooth jaw was a blue hue that hinted at the unshaven, decadent beauty of him. Even his scent clamoured for attention, subtle and at the same time overwhelming.

Raul had her on the edge of panic—an unfamiliar one.

He was potent—*so* potent that she wanted to say yes. To simply throw caution to the wind and have breakfast with this beautiful man.

She didn't even know his name.

'Do you always ask complete strangers for breakfast?' Lydia asked.

'No,' he admitted, and then he lowered his head just a fraction and lowered his voice an octave more. 'But then you defy the hour.'

CHAPTER TWO

THEY DEFIED THE HOUR, Lydia thought. Because as they stepped outside the hotel surely the moon should be hanging in a dark sky.

It was just breakfast, she told herself as his hand took her elbow and guided her across the busy street.

Yet it felt like a date.

Her first.

But it wasn't a romantic Italian evening, for the sun shone brightly and Rome was at its busy rush hour best.

Yet he made it so.

The restaurant he steered her to had a roped-off section and the tables were clearly reserved, yet the greeter unclipped the rope and they breezed through as if they were expected guests.

'Did you have a reservation?' Lydia asked, more than a little confused as they took their seats.

'No.'

'Then…' Lydia stopped, for she had answered her own question—the best seats were permanently reserved for the likes of him. He had a confident air that demanded, without words, only the best.

Coffee was brought and sparkling water was poured. They were handed the heavy menus, but as the waiter started to explain the choices he waved him away.

Lydia was grateful that he had, for there was a real need for the two of them to be left alone.

He was an absolute stranger.

A black-eyed stranger who had led and she had followed.

'I don't know your name,' Lydia said, and found she was worried a little that it might disappoint.

'Raul.'

It didn't.

He rolled the *R* just a little, and then she found herself repeating it, *'Rau—el...'* Though it did not roll easily from her tongue.

She waited for his surname.

It didn't come.

'I'm Lydia.'

'I had worked that out.' He glanced down at the menu. He never wasted time with small talk, unless it suited him. 'What would you like?'

She should be hungry. Lydia hadn't eaten since the plane, and even then she had just toyed with her meal.

She had been sick with nerves last night, but now, though still nervous, the feeling was pleasant.

'I'd like...' Lydia peered at the menu.

Really she ought to eat something, given that breakfast was the reason she was here.

But then she blushed while reading the menu, because food was the furthest thing from her mind.

'It's in Italian,' Lydia said, and could immediately have kicked herself, for it was such a stupid thing to say—and so rude to assume it should be otherwise.

But he did not chide her, and he did not score a point by stating that Italy was, in fact, where they were.

He just waited patiently as she stumbled her way through the selections till she came upon something she knew. But she frowned. 'Tiramisu for breakfast?'

'Sounds good.'

Perhaps he hadn't heard the question in her voice, because Lydia had assumed it was served only as a dessert, but Raul was right—it sounded good.

The waiter complimented their choice as he took their orders, and very soon she tasted bliss.

'Oh…' It was light and not too sweet, and the liquor made it decadent. It really had been an accidental perfect choice.

'Nice,' Raul said, and watched her hurriedly swallow and clear her mouth before speaking.

'Yes.' Lydia nodded. 'Very.'

'I wasn't asking a question.'

Just observing.

He looked at her mouth, and Lydia wondered if she had a crumb on her lip, but she resisted putting out her tongue to check.

And then he looked at her mouth, and the pressure within built as still she resisted that simple oral manoeuvre. Instead she pulled her bottom lip into her mouth and ran her tongue over it there.

No crumb.

Her eyes met his and she frowned at his impertinence as they asked a question—*Are you imagining what I think you are?*

Of course she said no such thing, and his features were impassive, but those black eyes offered his response.

Yes, Lydia, I am.

Had she had her purse with her, Lydia might well have called for the bill and fled, because she felt as if she were going insane. She looked around. Almost certain that the spectacle she was creating would have the world on pause and watching.

Yet the waiters were waiting, the patrons were chatting, the commuters were commuting and the word was just carrying on, oblivious to the fire smouldering unchecked in this roped-off section.

And so too must Raul be—oblivious, that was. For his voice was even and his question polite. 'How are you finding Rome?'

Lydia was about to nod and say how wonderful it was, or

give some other pat response, but she put down her spoon, let go of the end of her tether and simply stated the truth.

The real reason she was in Rome.

'I'm *determined* to love it this time.'

'Okay…' Raul said. His stance was relaxed and he leant back in the seat, seemingly nonchalant, but in his mind he was searching for an angle—how to get her to speak of Bastiano without too direct a question.

Lydia was terribly formal—very English and uptight. One wrong move, Raul knew, and he would be the recipient of a downed napkin and he'd have to watch her stalk off back to the hotel.

She was so incredibly sexy, though.

A woman who would make you *earn* that reward.

Lydia did not flirt, he noted.

Not a fraction.

No playing with her hair, no leaning forward, no secret smiles and no innuendo.

Really, the way she was sitting so upright in the chair, he could be at a breakfast meeting with Allegra, his PA.

Except Raul was aroused.

He was here to garner information, Raul reminded himself, and took his mind back to their conversation.

Or tried to.

'How long are you here for?'

'Till Sunday,' Lydia answered. 'Two nights. How about you?'

'I'm here for business.'

Raul should not be taking this time now. He had a very packed day. First he would meet with Alim and his team. Then, if time allowed, he would drop in unexpectedly on the other hotel he owned in Rome.

But he always made Bastiano his business.

'When do you leave?' she asked.

'When business is done.' Raul's jet was in fact booked for six this evening, but he did not share his itinerary with anyone outside his close circle. 'So, you've been to Rome before?'

'Yes, I came to Italy on a school trip and had a rather miserable time. I don't think my mood then did the place justice.'

'Where did you go?'

'Rome, Florence and Venice.'

'Which was your favourite?'

Lydia thought for a moment. 'Venice.'

'And your least favourite?'

Oh, that was easy—Lydia didn't have to think to answer that, even if he didn't understand her response. 'Venice.'

He *did* understand.

So much so that Raul again forgot that he was trying to steer the conversation. Even though Bastiano was the reason Raul was there, for now he left Raul's mind.

He thought of Venice—the city he loved and now called home.

Not that he told *her* that.

Raul gave away nothing.

Then suddenly he did.

For as she looked over she was rewarded with the slow reveal of his smile.

And his smile was a true and very rare gift.

She saw those full dark lips stretch and the white of his teeth, but the real beauty was in eyes that stared so deeply into hers she felt there was nowhere to hide.

And nor did she want to.

'Venice,' Raul said, in that deep, measured voice, 'can be the loneliest place in the world.'

'Yes,' Lydia admitted. 'It was.'

It was as if she was seventeen again, walking alongside the Grand Canal alone and wanting to be in love with the city.

To be in love.

Of course nearly every schoolgirl on a trip to Italy secretly hoped for a little romance.

But on that day—on that terribly lonely day—Lydia would have been happy with a friend.

One true friend.

Raul was right. Lydia had felt utterly alone then, and for the most part she had felt the same since.

She was looking at him, but not really, and then his voice brought her back.

'And you forgive her because how could you not?'

'Her?' Lydia checked, her mind still on friendships that had failed.

'Venice.'

'I wasn't there long enough to forgive her,' Lydia admitted.

'What happened?'

'Just being a teenager…'

She could easily dismiss it as that, but it had been more. Oh, she didn't want to tell him that her father had just died and left behind him utter chaos, for while it might explain her unhappiness then, it wasn't the entire truth—it had been more than that.

'Schoolgirls can be such bitches.'

'I don't think it is exclusive to that age bracket.'

'No!' Lydia actually laughed at his observation because, yes, those girls were now women and probably still much the same.

She glanced at her phone, which had remained silent.

Arabella hadn't responded to her text.

Neither had she responded to Lydia's last message.

And suddenly Lydia was back in Italy, hurting again.

'What happened in Venice?'

Raul chose his moment to ask. He knew how to steer conversations, and yet he actually found himself wanting to know.

'We went to Murano…to a glass factory.' She shook her head and, as she had then, felt pained to reveal the truth.

It felt like a betrayal.

Money should never be discussed outside the home.

'And…?' Raul gently pushed.

Why lie? Lydia thought.

She would never see him again.

It wasn't such a big deal.

Surely?

'My father had died the year before.'

He didn't say he was sorry—did not offer the automatic response to that statement.

It was oddly freeing.

Everyone had been *so* sorry.

If there's anything I can do... The words had been tossed around like black confetti at his funeral.

Yet they had done nothing!

When it was clear the money had gone, so had they.

'I'd told Arabella, my best friend, that my mother was struggling financially.' Lydia was sweating, and that wasn't flattering. She wanted to call the waiter to move the shade umbrella but knew she could be sitting in ice and the result would be the same.

It wasn't sexy sweat.

Lydia wasn't turned on now.

She felt sick.

'I told Arabella that we might lose the castle.'

She offered more explanation.

'The castle was in my mother's family, but my father ran it. I thought he had run it well, but on his death I found out that my parents had been going under.'

Raul offered no comment, just let her speak.

'He took his own life.'

She'd never said it out loud before.

Had never been allowed to say it.

'I'm sorry you had to go through that.'

And because he hadn't said sorry before, now—when he did—she felt he meant it.

'I still can't believe he left me.'

'To deal with the fallout?'

He completed her sentence, even though Lydia thought she already had. She thought about it for a moment and nodded.

'Things really were dire. My mother kept selling things off, to pay for my school fees. The trip to Italy was a compulsory one. I got a part-time job—saved up some spending money. Of course it didn't come close to what my friends had. They were hitting all the boutiques and Arabella kept asking why I wasn't buying anything. In the end I told her how bad things were. I swore her to secrecy.'

He gave a soft, mirthless laugh—one that told her he understood.

And then they were silent.

In *that* moment they met.

Not at a breakfast table in Rome but in a bleak, desolate space a world away from there.

They met and he reached across and took her hand, and together they walked it through.

'At the factory, after a demonstration, everyone was buying things. I held back, of course. There was a table with damaged glassware and Belinda, another friend, held up a three-legged horse and suggested it was something that I might be able to afford. I realised then that Arabella had told everyone.'

She could still feel the betrayal.

Could still remember looking over to her best friend as everyone had laughed.

Arabella hadn't so much as blushed at being caught.

'She suggested that they all have a whip-round for me.'

'So you walked off?' Raul asked, impatient to know and understand her some more.

'Oh, no!' Lydia shook her head and then sighed. 'I used up all my spending money, and the money I'd been given for my birthday, and bought a vase that I certainly couldn't afford.'

It was that response in herself she had hated the most.

'How shallow is that?'

'People have been known to drown in shallow waters.'

'Well, it's certainly not easy to swim in them! Anyway, I didn't see them much after that…'

'You left school?'

'I went to the local comprehensive for my final year. Far more sensible…but hell.'

Everything—not just the fact that she was a new girl for the last year, but every little thing, from her accent to her handwriting—had ensured she didn't fit in from the very first day.

Raul knew it would have been hell.

He could imagine *his* schoolmates if an Italian version of Lydia had shown up in his old schoolyard. Raul could guess all she would have gone through.

'I was a joke to them, of course.'

He squeezed her hand and it was the kindest touch, so contrary to that time.

'Too posh to handle?' Raul said, and she nodded, almost smiled.

But then the smile changed.

Lydia never cried.

Ever.

Not even when her father had died.

So why start now?

Lydia pulled her hand back.

She was done with introspection—done with musings.

They hurt too much.

Lydia was somewhat appalled at how much she had told him.

'Raul, why am I here?'

'Because…' Raul shrugged, but when that did not appease her he elaborated. 'Maurice was getting in the way.'

Lydia found herself laughing, and it surprised her that she could.

A second ago she had felt like crying.

It was nice being with him.

Not soothing.

Just liberating.

She had told another person some of the truth and he had remained.

'Maurice is my stepfather,' she explained.

'Good,' Raul said, but she missed the innuendo.

'Not really.'

Lydia didn't respond to his flirting as others usually did, so he adopted a more businesslike tone. The rest they could do later—he wanted information now.

'Maurice wants you to be at some dinner tonight?'

Lydia nodded. 'He's got an important meeting with a potential investor and he wants me there.'

'Why?'

Lydia gave a dismissive shake of her head.

She certainly wasn't going to discuss *that*!

'I probably shan't go,' Lydia said, instead of explaining things. 'I'm supposed to be catching up with a friend—or rather,' she added, remembering all he had heard, 'an acquaintance.'

'Who?'

'Arabella.' She was embarrassed to admit it after all she had told him. 'She works in Rome now.'

'I thought you fell out?'

'That was all a very long time ago,' Lydia said, but she didn't actually like the point he had raised.

They hadn't fallen out.

The incident had been buried—like everything else.

She conversed with Arabella only through social media and the odd text. It had been years since they had been face-to-face, and Lydia wasn't sure she was relishing the prospect of seeing her, so, rather than admit that, she went back to his original question—why Maurice wanted her to be there tonight.

'The family castle is now a wedding venue.'

'Do you work there?'

Lydia nodded.

'Doing what?'

'I deal with the bookings and organise the catering...' She gave a tight smile, because what she did for a living was so far away from her dreams. When her father had been alive she had loved the visitors that came to the castle. He would take them through it and pass on its rich history and Lydia would learn something new every time.

'And you still live at home?'

'Yes.'

She didn't add that there was no choice. The business was failing so badly that they couldn't afford much outside help, and she didn't get a wage as such.

'Bastiano—this man we're supposed to meet tonight—has had a lot of success converting old buildings... He has several luxury retreats and my mother and Maurice are hoping to go that route with the castle. Still, it would take a massive cash injection...'

'Castles need more than an injection—they require a permanent infusion,' Raul corrected.

All old buildings did.

It galled him that Bastiano had been able to turn the convent into a successful business venture. On paper it should never have worked, and yet somehow he had ensured that it had.

'Quite,' Lydia agreed. 'But more than money we need his wisdom...' She misinterpreted the slight narrowing of Raul's eyes as confusion. 'A lot of these types of venture fail—somehow Bastiano's succeed.'

'So why would this successful businessman be interested in *your* castle?'

Lydia found she was holding her breath. His question was just a little bit insulting. After all, the castle was splendid indeed, and Raul could have no idea what a disaster in business Maurice had turned out to be.

'I'm sure Bastiano recognises its potential.'

'And he wants you there tonight so he can hear your vision for the castle?'

Lydia gave a small shake of her head. The truth was that she was actually *opposed* to the idea of turning it into a retreat—not that her objections held much weight.

'Then why do you need to go?'

'I've been invited.'

'Lydia, I have had more business meetings than I've had dinners.' Raul spoke when she did not. 'But I can't ever remember asking anyone—*ever*—to bring along their daughter, or rather their stepdaughter.'

She blushed.

Those creamy cheeks turned an unflattering red.

Lydia knew it—she could feel the fire, not just on her skin but building inside her at the inappropriateness he was alluding to.

'Excuse me?' she snapped.

'Why?' Raul said. 'What did you do?'

'I mean you're rude to insinuate that there might be something else going on!'

'I know that's what you meant.'

He remained annoyingly calm, and more annoyingly he didn't back down.

'And I'm not *insinuating* anything—I'm telling you that unless you hold the deeds to the castle, or are to be a major player in the renovations, or some such, there is no reason for this Bastiano to insist on your company tonight. '

'He isn't insisting.'

'Good.' Raul shrugged. 'Then don't go.'

'I don't have any excuse not to.'

'You don't need one.'

It was Lydia who gave a shrug now.

A tense one.

She was still cross at his insinuation.

Or rather she was cross that Raul might be right—that he could see what she had spent weeks frantically trying *not* to.

'Lydia, can I tell you something?'

She didn't answer.

'Some free advice.'

'Why would I take advice from a stranger?'

'I'm no longer a stranger.'

He wasn't. She had told him more than she had told many people who were in her day-to-day life.

'Can I?' Raul checked.

She liked it that he did not give advice unrequested, and when she met his eyes they were patient and awaiting her answer.

'Yes.'

'You can walk away from anyone you choose to, and you don't have to come up with a reason.'

'I know that.'

She had walked off from breakfast with Maurice, after all.

It wasn't enough, though—Lydia knew that. And though Raul's words made perfect sense, they just did not apply to her world.

'So why don't you tell your stepfather that you can't make it tonight because you're catching up with a friend?'

'I already have.'

'But you don't like Arabella,' Raul pointed out. 'So why don't you meet me instead?'

She laughed a black laugh. '*You're* not a friend.'

He wasn't.

'No,' he answered honestly. 'I'm not.'

She was about to take a sip of her coffee when he added something else.

'I could be for tonight, though.'

'I don't think so.' Lydia gave a small laugh, not really getting what he had just said—or rather not really thinking he meant it.

'Do you have many friends?' she asked, replacing her cup. Perhaps her question was a little invasive, but she'd told him rather a lot and was curious to know about him.

'Some.'

'Close friends?' Lydia pushed.

'No one whose birthday I need to remember.'

'No one?'

He shook his head.

'I guess it saves shopping for presents.'

'Not really.'

Raul decided to take things to another level and tell her how things could be. In sex, at least, he was up front.

'I like to give a present the morning after.'

Lydia got what he meant this time.

She didn't blush. If anything Lydia felt a shiver, as if the sun had slipped behind a cloud.

It hadn't.

He was dark, he was dangerous, and he was as sexy as hell. Absolutely she was out of her depth.

'I'm here to sightsee, Raul.'

'Then you need an expert.'

Lydia stared coolly back at this man who was certainly that. She wondered at his reaction if she told him just how inexperienced she was—that in fact he would be her first.

Not that it was going to happen!

But *what* a first, Lydia thought.

She went to reach for water but decided against it, unsure she could manage the simple feat when the air thrummed with an energy that was foreign to her.

He was potent, and Lydia was tempted in a way she had never been.

She glanced down to his hand, and that was beautiful too—olive-skinned and long-fingered with very neat nails. And it was happening again, because now she imagined them inside her.

Oh!

She was sitting at breakfast, imagining those very fingers in the filthiest of thoughts, and she dared not look up at him for she felt he could read her mind.

'So what are your plans for today?' Raul asked.

His voice seemed to be coming from a distance, and yet he was so prominent in her mind.

She could take his hand, Lydia was certain, and be led to his bed.

Oh, what was *happening* to her?

'I told you—sightseeing, and then I'm shopping for a dress.'

'I wish I could be there to see that.'

'I thought men didn't like shopping.'

'I don't, usually.'

His eyes flicked to the row of buttons at the front of her dress and then to the thick nipples that ached, just *ached* for his touch, for his mouth. And then they moved back to her face.

'I have to go,' Raul told her, and she sat still as he stood. With good reason: her legs simply refused to move. Standing would be difficult…walking back over to the hotel would prove a completely impossible feat.

Please go, Lydia thought, because she felt drunk on lust and was trying not to let him see.

He summoned the waiter, and though he spoke in Italian he spoke slowly enough that she could just make out what was being said.

Hold this table for tonight at six.

And then he turned to where she sat, now with her back to him, and lowered his head. For a moment she thought he was going to kiss her.

He did not.

His breath was warm on her cheek and his scent was like a delicious invasion. His glossy black hair was so close that she fought not to reach out and feel it, fought not to turn and lick his face.

And then he spoke.

'Hold that thought till six.'

Lydia blinked and tried to pretend that she still felt normal, that this was simply breakfast and she was somehow in control.

'I already told you—I can't make it tonight.'

Then he offered but one word.

'Choose.'

CHAPTER THREE

WHAT THE HELL was happening to her?

Lydia watched him walk across the street and then disappear inside the hotel.

He did not turn around. He didn't walk with haste.

She wanted him to hurry, to disappear, just so that she could clear her mind—because in fact she *wanted* him to turn around.

One crook of his finger and she knew she would rise and run to him—and that was so *not* her. She kept her distance from people—not just physically but emotionally too.

Her father's death had rocked every aspect of her world, and the aftermath had been hell. Watching her mother selling off heirlooms and precious memories one by one, in a permanent attempt to keep up appearances, and then marrying that frightful man. Finding her friends had all been fair-weather ones had also hurt Lydia to the core. And so she held back—from family, from friends and, yes, from men.

She was guarded, and possibly the assumption made by others that she was cold was a correct one.

But not now—not this morning.

She felt as if she had been scalded, as if every nerve was heated and raw, and all he had done was buy her breakfast.

She sat alone at the table. There was nothing to indicate romance—no candles or champagne—and no favourable dusk to soften the view. Just the brightness of morning.

There had been no romance.

Raul had offered her one night and a present the following morning. She should have damn well slapped him for the insult!

Yet he'd left her on a slightly giddy high that she couldn't quite come down from.

Sightseeing as such didn't happen.

When she should have been sorting out what to do about tonight she wandered around, thinking about this morning.

But finally she shopped, and accepted the assistant's advice, and stood in the changing room with various options.

The black did not match her mood.

The caramel felt rather safe.

But as for the red!

The rich fabric caressed her skin and gave curves where she had few. It was ruched across her stomach and her hand went to smooth it before she realised that was the desired effect—it drew the eye lower.

Lydia slipped on the heels that stood in the corner and looked at her reflection from behind. And then she looked from the front.

She felt sexy, and for the first time beautiful and just a touch wild as she lifted her hair and imagined it piled up in curls. And *his* reaction.

It wasn't Bastiano's reaction she was envisaging—it was the reaction of the man who had invited her out this evening.

Only that wasn't quite right.

He hadn't asked her out on a date.

Raul had invited her to a night in his bed.

'Bellisima...'

Lydia spun around as the assistant came in, and her cheeks matched the fabric as if she had been caught stealing.

'That dress is perfect on you...' the assistant said.

'Well, I prefer this one.'

She could see the assistant's confusion as she plucked the closest dress to hand and passed it to her.

Caramel—or rather a dark shade of beige.

Safe.

Bastiano was *not* a safe option.

Raul knew that as fact.

'I trust you were comfortable last night?' Sultan Alim asked when they met.

Raul had met the Sultan once before, but that had been in the Middle East and then Alim had been dressed in traditional robes. Today he wore a deep navy suit.

'Extremely comfortable,' Raul agreed. 'Your staff are excellent.'

'We have a rigorous recruiting process for all levels.' Alim nodded. 'Few make it through the interviews, and not many past the three-month trial. We retain only the best.'

Raul had seen that for himself.

Alim was unhurried as he took Raul behind the scenes of his iconic hotel. 'I have had four serious expressions of interest,' Alim went on to explain. 'Two I know have the means—one I doubt. The other…' He held his hand flat and waved it to indicate he was uncertain.

'So I have one definite rival?' Raul said, and watched as Alim gave a conceding smile.

Both knew Raul was a serious contender.

He didn't have to try hard to guess who the other was—not that Alim let on.

Raul had done his homework, and he knew that Alim was not just an astute businessman but very discreet in all his dealings.

He would have to be.

Allegra, Raul's long-suffering PA, had found out all she could on him.

Sultan Alim was a playboy, and his palace's PR must be on overtime to keep his decadent ways out of the press.

Alim kissed but never told, and in return the silence of his aggrieved lovers was paid for in diamonds.

And in business he played his cards close to his chest.

The latter Raul could attest to, for Alim did not bend to any of Raul's mercurial ways.

By the end of a very long day Raul was still no closer to finding out the real reason for the sale.

Alim had dismissed his team and was taking Raul for one final look around.

'I haven't seen Bastiano,' Raul commented as the elevator arrived to take them down to the function rooms. When Alim did not respond, Raul pushed. 'I see that his guests are already here.'

Still Alim gave nothing away. 'I shall take you now to the ballroom.'

Raul had no choice but to accept his silence.

He knew that Alim and Bastiano were friends, and in turn Alim would know that Raul and Bastiano were business rivals and enemies.

So, instead of trying to find out more about Bastiano, Raul returned his mind to work.

'Why?' Raul asked Sultan Alim as they walked along the lush corridors. 'Why are you selling?'

'I've already answered that,' Sultan Alim said. 'I am to marry soon and I am moving my portfolio back to the Middle East.'

'I want the real reason.'

Alim halted mid-stride and turned to face Raul as he spoke.

'You have several hotels throughout Europe that you aren't letting go, yet this jewel you are.'

'You're correct,' Alim said. 'Hotel Grande Lucia *is* a jewel.'

As Raul frowned, Alim gave a nod that told Raul he would explain some more.

'Come and see this.'

They stepped into the grand ballroom, where a dark-haired woman, dressed in a dark suit that was rather too tight, was standing in the middle of the dance floor.

Just standing.

Her shoes must be a little tight too, for she was holding stilettos in one hand.

'Is everything okay, Gabi?' Alim asked her.

'Oh!' Clearly she hadn't heard them come in, because she startled but then pushed out a smile. 'Yes, everything is fine. I was just trying to work out the table plan for Saturday.'

'We have a large wedding coming up,' Alim explained to Raul.

'And both sets of parents are twice divorced.' Gabi gave a slight eye-roll and then chatted away as she bent to put on her shoes. 'Trying to work out where everyone should be seated is proving—'

'Gabi!' Alim scolded, and then turned to Raul. 'Gabi is not on my staff. *They* tend to be rather more discreet.' He waved his hand, but this time it was to dismiss her. 'Excuse us, please.'

Alim, who had until now been exceptionally pleasant with all his staff, was less than polite now. Raul watched as a very put-out Gabi flounced from the ballroom.

'She is a wedding planner from an outside firm,' Alim said, to explain the indiscretion. '*My* staff would *never* discuss clients that way in front of a visitor.'

'Of course.' Raul nodded as the huge entrance doors closed loudly, and he resisted raising his eyebrows as the crystals in the chandeliers responded to the pointed slam.

It was actually rather spectacular to watch.

The reflection of the low, late-afternoon sun was captured by several thousand crystals, and for a moment it was as if it was raining sunbeams as light danced across the walls and the ceiling and the floor—even over their suits.

'It's a beautiful ballroom,' Raul commented as he looked around, though he was unsure exactly why Alim had brought him here instead of to a meeting room, when it was figures that Raul wanted to discuss.

'When I bought the hotel those had not been cleaned in years,' Alim said, gesturing to the magnificent lights. 'Now they are taken down and cared for properly. It is a huge undertaking. The room has to be closed, so no functions can be held, and it is all too easy to put it off.'

Raul could see that it would be, but he did not get involved in such details and told Alim so.

'I leave all that to my managers to organise,' Raul said.

Alim nodded. 'Usually I do too, but when I took over the Grande Lucia there had been many cost-cutting measures. It was slowly turning into just another hotel. It is not just the lighting in the ballroom, of course. What I am trying to explain is that this hotel has become more than an investment to me. Once I return to my homeland I shall not be able to give it the attention it deserves.'

'The next owner might not either,' Raul pointed out.

'That is his business. But while the hotel is mine I want no part in her demise.'

Raul knew he was now hearing the true reason for the sale. To keep this hotel to its current standard would be a huge undertaking, and one that Raul would play no major part in—he would delegate that. Perhaps he'd do so more carefully, given what he had been told. But at the end of the day managers managed, and Raul had neither the time nor the inclination to be that heavily involved.

'Now you have given me pause for thought,' Raul admitted.

'Good.' Alim smiled. 'The Grande Lucia deserves the best caretaker. Please,' Alim said, indicating that their long day of meetings had come to an end, 'take all the time you need to look around and to enjoy the rest of your stay.'

Sultan Alim excused himself and Raul stood in the empty ballroom, watching the light dancing around the walls like a shower of stars.

He thought of home.

And he understood Alim's concerns.

Last year Raul had purchased a stunning Venetian Gothic *palazzo* on the Grand Canal.

It required more than casual upkeep.

The house was run by Loretta—the woman who had warned his mother of Gino's imminent return home all those years ago.

She ran the staff—and there were many.

Raul looked around the ballroom at the intricate cornices and arched windows.

Yes, he knew what Alim was talking about. But this was a hotel, not a home.

Raul would play no part in her demise.

He was going to pass.

So there was no need to linger.

His mind went back to that morning and he hoped very much that Lydia would be there to meet him tonight—not just to score a point over Bastiano and to rot up his plans.

Raul had enjoyed her company.

His company was not for keeps.

Lydia knew that.

She sat in her button-up dress in the hairdresser's at four and asked for a French roll, but the hairdresser tutted, picked up a long coil of blonde and suggested—or rather, *strongly* suggested—curls. After some hesitation finally Lydia agreed.

Whatever had happened to her this morning, it was still occurring.

She felt as if she were shedding her skin, and at every turn she fought to retrieve it.

Her lashes were darkened, and then Lydia opened her eyes when the beautician spoke.

'Porpora...'

Lydia did not know that word, but as the beautician pushed up a lipstick Lydia managed, without translation, to work out what it meant.

Crimson.

'No.' Lydia shook her head and insisted on a more neutral shade.

Oh, Lydia wanted to be back in her cocoon—she was a very unwilling butterfly indeed—but she did buy the lipstick, and on her way back to the hotel she stopped at the boutique and bought the red dress.

And then she entered the complex world of sexy shoes.

Lydia had bought a neutral pair to go with the caramel dress and thought she was done. But…

'Red and red,' the assistant insisted.

'I think neutral would look better.'

'You *need* these shoes.'

Oh, Lydia *was* starting to take advice from strangers for she tried them on. They were low-heeled and slender and a little bit strappy.

'It's too much,' Lydia said, but both women knew she was not protesting at the price.

'No, no,' the assistant said. 'Trust me—these are right.'

Oh, Lydia didn't trust her.

But she bought them anyway.

For *him*.

Or rather to one day dress up alone to the memory of him.

As she arrived back at the hotel Lydia looked at the restaurant across the street, to the roped-off section and the table he had reserved for them.

Of course he wasn't there yet.

Yet.

Knowing he would be—knowing she *could* be—made tonight somehow worse.

Her mother called, but she let it go to voicemail.

A pep talk wasn't required.

Lydia didn't need to be told that everything hinged on tonight. That the castle was at the very end of the line and that it would come down to her actions tonight to save it.

She had a shallow bath, so as not to mess up her new curls, and as she washed she tried to remind herself how good-looking Bastiano was.

Even his scar did not mar his good looks.

He had been attending a wedding when they'd first met.

Maybe this time when he kissed her she would know better how to respond.

Try as she might, though, she couldn't keep her focus on Bastiano. Her thoughts strayed to Raul.

With a sob of frustration Lydia hauled herself out of the bath and dried herself.

In a last-ditch attempt, Lydia rang Arabella. Searching for an excuse—any excuse—to get out of this meeting tonight.

'Lydia!' Arabella was brusque. 'I meant to call you. You didn't say it was *this* weekend you were in Rome.'

Of course Lydia had.

'I've actually got a party on tonight,' Arabella said.

'Sounds good.'

'Invitation only.'

And of course Lydia was not invited.

And there she sat again, like a beggar beside the table, waiting for Arabella's crumbs.

'That's fine.'

Lydia rang off.

Maurice was right. She had no friends.

Arabella was her only contact from her first school, but

she kept her at arm's length, and there hadn't even been a semblance of friendship at the other school.

Lydia could remember the howls of laughter from the other students when she had shaken hands and made a small curtsey for the teacher at the end of her first day.

It was what she had been taught, but of course *her* norms weren't the norms of her new school.

She didn't fit in anywhere.

Yet this morning Lydia had felt she did.

Oh, Raul had been far too forward and suggestive, but when they had spoken she had felt as if she were confiding in a friend—had felt a little as if she belonged in the world.

But all Raul wanted was sex.

Lydia had hoped for a little more.

Not a whole lot, but, yes, perhaps a little romance would be a nice side dish for her first time.

Wrong dress, Lydia thought as she looked in the mirror.

Wrong shoes, Lydia thought as she strapped on her neutral heels.

Wrong man, Lydia knew as she walked into the bar and saw Bastiano waiting.

Oh, he was terribly good-looking—even with that scar—and yet he did not move her. But perhaps *this* was romance, Lydia thought sadly, for he was charming as he ordered champagne. He was the perfect gentleman, and on the surface it was all terribly polite.

As was her life.

She thanked him for his generous hospitality. 'It's so lovely to be here. We've been looked after so well.'

'It is my pleasure,' Bastiano said. 'Are you enjoying Rome?'

'Absolutely.' Lydia smiled and thought of her far more honest response this morning with Raul.

It was after six, and she knew—just knew—that Raul wouldn't wait for very long.

And that she would regret it for ever if she missed out on tonight.

'I was thinking,' Bastiano said, 'that for dinner we might—'

'Actually…' Maurice interrupted, and put his fingers to his temples.

Lydia knew he was going to plead a headache and excuse himself from dinner. Leaving her alone with Bastiano.

It was seven minutes past six and she made her choice.

'Oh, didn't Maurice tell you?' Lydia spoke over Maurice, before he could make his excuses and leave.

Out of the corner of her eye she saw Maurice clench the glass he was holding, and she could feel his eyes shoot a stern warning, and yet Lydia spoke on.

'I'm catching up with a friend tonight—we're heading off to dinner soon. I wanted to stop by and say thank you, though.' She gave Bastiano her best false smile, but it wasn't returned. 'I don't want to get in the way of your business talk.'

'I don't think you could ever be in the way.' Bastiano's response was smooth.

'Oh, you're far too polite!' Lydia offered a small laugh to a less than impressed audience.

It sank like a stone.

'I'll leave you two to talk castles.'

She placed her unfinished drink on the table and said her farewells, and simply ignored the fury in Maurice's eyes and the muscle flickering in Bastiano's scarred cheek.

Oh, there would be consequences, Lydia knew.

But she was prepared to bear them.

For now she was free.

She wanted the red dress and the lipstick to match. She had, Lydia acknowledged, bought them for this moment, after all.

But there just wasn't time.

He could be gone already, Lydia thought in mild panic as she swept out through the revolving door.

When she glanced across the street she felt the crush of disappointment when she saw that Raul wasn't there.

But then she heard him.

'You're late.'

Lydia turned and there he was, tie loosened, tall and gorgeous, and, yes, she had made her choice.

'For the first time in my life.'

He was going to kiss her, she was sure, but she walked on ahead.

'Come on,' Lydia said quickly, worried that Maurice might follow her out.

They walked briskly, or rather Lydia did, for his stride beside her seemed slow and more measured. She felt fuelled by elation as they turned into a side street.

'Where to now?' Raul asked, and they stopped walking and she turned.

'You're the expert.'

Oh, he was—because somehow she was back against the wall with his hands on either side of her head.

She put her hands up to his chest and felt him solid beneath her palms, just felt him there for a moment, and then she looked up to his eyes.

His mouth moved in close, and as it did so she stared deeper.

She could feel heat hovering between their mouths in a slow tease before they met.

Then they met.

And all that had been missing was suddenly there.

The gentle pressure his mouth exerted, though blissful, caused a mire of sensations—until the gentleness was no longer enough.

Even before the thought was formed, he delivered.

His mouth moved more insistently and seemed to stir her from within.

Raul wanted her tongue, and yet he did not prise—he never forced a door open.

No need to.

There it was.

A slight inhalation, a hitch in her breath, and her lips parted just a little and he slipped his tongue in.

The moan she made went straight to his groin.

At first taste she was his and he knew it, for her hands moved to the back of his head, and he kissed her as hard as her fingers demanded.

More so, even.

His tongue was wicked, and her fingers tightened in his thick hair, and she could feel the wall cold and hard against her shoulders.

It was the middle of the city, just after six, and even down a side street there was no real hiding from the crowds.

Lydia didn't care.

He slid one arm around her waist to move her body away from the wall and closer to his, so that her head could fall backwards.

If there'd been a bed she would have been on it.

If there'd been a room they would have closed the door.

Yet there wasn't, and so he halted them—but only their lips.

Their bodies were heated and close and he looked her right in the eye. His mouth was wet from hers and his hair a little mussed from her fingers.

'What do you want to do?' Raul asked, knowing it was a no-brainer.

It was a very early bedtime and that suited him fine.

But the thought of waltzing her past Bastiano and Maurice no longer appealed.

A side entrance, perhaps, Raul thought, and went for her neck.

She had never thought that a kiss beneath her ear could make it impossible to breathe, let alone think.

'What do you want to do?' he whispered to her skin, and then blew on her neck, damp from his kisses. He raised his head and met her eye. 'Tonight I can give you anything you want.'

'Anything?' Lydia checked.

'Oh, yes.'

And if he was offering perfection, then she would take it.

'I want to see Rome at night—with you.'

'It's not dark yet.'

He could suggest a guided tour of his body—a very luxurious one, of course—but then he looked into her china-blue eyes.

'I want some romance with my one-night stand.'

'But I don't *do* romance.'

'Try it,' Lydia said. She didn't want some bauble in the morning and so she named her price. 'For one night.'

And Raul, who was usually *very* open to experiments, found himself reluctant to try.

Yet he had cancelled his flight for this.

And she had had the most terrible time here on her last visit, Raul knew.

The bed would always be there.

And he *had* invited her to state her wants.

He had known from the start that Lydia would make him work for his reward.

'I know just the place to start,' Raul said. 'While it's still light.'

CHAPTER FOUR

THIS WAS ROME.

He would have called for a car, but she hadn't wanted to go to the front of the hotel and risk seeing Maurice.

And so Raul found himself in his first taxi for a very long time.

He would not be repeating it!

Still, it was worth it for the result.

He took her to Aventine Hill. 'Rome's seventh hill,' he told her.

'I know that,' Lydia said. 'We came past it on a bus tour.'

'Who were you sitting with?' Raul nudged her as they walked.

'The teacher.'

'They really hated you, didn't they?'

But he put his arm around her shoulders as he said it, and it was something in the way he spoke that made her smile as she answered.

'They did.'

And then they stopped walking.

'This is the headquarters of the Order of the Knights of Malta,' he told her. 'Usually it is busy.' But tonight the stars had aligned, for there was a small group just leaving. 'Go on, then.'

'What?'

And she waited—for what, she didn't know. For him to open the door and go through?

They did neither.

'Look through the keyhole.'

Lydia bent down and did as she was told, but there was nothing to see at first—just an arch of greenery.

And then her eye grew accustomed to the view and she looked past the greenery, and there, perfectly framed in the centre, was the dome of St Peter's.

He knew the moment she saw it, for she let out a gasp.

It was a view to die for.

The soft green edging framed the eternal city and she bent there for a while, just taking it in.

It was a memory.

A magical one because it made Rome a secret garden.

Her secret garden.

By the time she stood there were others lined up, all waiting for their glimpse of heaven, and her smile told them it would be worth the wait.

Raul refused to be rushed.

'Don't you want a photo?' he asked. Assuming, of course, that she would.

'No.'

She didn't need one to remember it.

Even if Raul took her back to the hotel now, it would still be the best night ever.

In fact if Raul were to suggest taking her back to the hotel she would wave the taxi down herself, for he was kissing her again—a nice one, a not-going-anywhere one, just sharing in her excitement.

He did not take her back yet.

They walked down the hill, just talking, and he showed her the tiny streets she would never have found. He took her past the Bocca della Verità sculpture—the Mouth of Truth—though he did not tell her the legend that the old man would bite off the hand of liars.

For perhaps she might test him.

Though Raul told himself he did not lie.

He just omitted certain information.

And he continued to do so, even when the opportunity arose to reveal it.

They were now sitting on a balcony, looking out to the Colosseum, and a waiter placed their drinks down on the table.

Cognac for Raul and a cocktail that was the same fiery orange as the sky for Lydia.

He didn't assume champagne, as Bastiano had.

Like this morning at breakfast, she let her eyes wander through the menu selections.

She chose hers—he knew his.

Raul gave her choice at every turn, and that was something terribly new to Lydia.

Finally she had good memories of Rome.

'Salute,' Raul said, and they clinked glasses.

Wonderful memories, really.

It wasn't the sight of the Colosseum that brought a lump to her throat but the fact that *now* there were candles and flowers on the table, and that at every turn Raul had surprised her with his ease and enjoyment.

He did not sulk, nor reluctantly trudge along and put up with things before taking her to bed.

Raul led.

But she must remember it could never—for her—be the City of Love.

Raul didn't do love.

'How did Bastiano take your leaving?' Raul asked, and his question caught her by surprise, for her mind had long moved on from the hotel.

Raul himself had only just remembered the real reason he was there.

'He was fine,' Lydia replied. 'Well, he was polite. I can't blame him for being fed up—anyone would be, stuck with Maurice for the night.'

He was about to say that he doubted Bastiano would hang around anywhere he didn't choose to be, but stopped himself.

For the first time since they had met Lydia looked truly relaxed. The conversation flowed easily, and quite simply he did not want to take the chance of ruining a very nice night.

But he did need to know more. And he did not need to delve, for a very at ease Lydia was now talking.

'I know he can't stand Maurice.'

'How do you know that?'

'Because Bastiano told me.'

She was stirring her drink and didn't see the sudden tension in his features. It dawned on Raul that Bastiano and Lydia might already be lovers for all he knew.

'There was a wedding at the castle one weekend,' Lydia explained. 'It was a very good one. Of course Maurice had been through the guest list, and he made a bit of a beeline for Bastiano. He'd found out that he'd converted an old convent into a retreat, and Maurice wanted to hear his thoughts on doing something similar with the castle.'

Raul gave a disparaging laugh, and Lydia assumed it was in reference to Maurice's gall at approaching a guest.

But Raul was mocking Maurice's ignorance—Bastiano would never part with his knowledge for free.

'Bastiano wasn't interested,' Lydia said.

'Maurice told you that?' Raul checked.

'No, Bastiano did.' Lydia gave a soft laugh and looked out onto the street as she recalled that night. 'I was serving drinks, and Bastiano made some comment about saving him from the most boring man… I laughed. I knew exactly who he was referring to. But then I felt guilty, as if I ought to defend my family, and so I told him that Maurice was my stepfather.'

And there was the difference between them. Raul felt no guilt in not admitting the truth.

Perhaps a slight niggle, but he easily pushed that aside.

'You told Bastiano that Maurice was your stepfather?' he asked.

'Yes.' Lydia nodded. 'Bastiano apologised and said he would speak with him again and pay attention this time.

'And that was it?' Raul checked.

'Sorry?' Lydia frowned.

'That was all that happened between you two?'

She went pink.

'Excuse me,' Raul said. 'That is none of my business.'

The thought, though, did not sit well with him.

But then she told him.

'Just a kiss.'

She screwed up her nose as Raul breathed out in relief that they had never been lovers.

Then the relief dissolved and he loathed the fact that they had even shared a kiss.

'Come on,' he said, confused by the jealousy that arose in him. 'It's dark now.'

Oh, it was.

And busy and noisy.

It was everything Rome should be.

The Trevi Fountain had kept its promise, because she had made a wish to be back under better circumstances and now she was.

They walked for miles, and though the cobbled streets weren't stiletto-friendly Lydia felt as if she were wearing ballet slippers—the world felt lighter tonight.

'Where are we now?' Lydia asked.

'Citta Universitaria—my home for four years.'

'I would have loved to have gone to university,' Lydia said. 'I wanted to study history.'

'Why didn't you?'

'I failed my exams.'

Another truth she rarely told.

She hadn't decided to go straight into the family business, as her mother often said.

Lydia had failed all her exams.

Spectacularly.

'I messed up,' Lydia admitted.

She offered no reason or excuse although there were so many.

He knew that.

'I had to repeat some subjects after my mother died,' Raul told her. He rarely revealed anything, and certainly not his failings, yet it seemed right to do so now. 'I hit the clubs for a while.'

His honesty elicited both a smile and an admission. 'I wish that I had.'

'I moved here from Sicily to study under great protest—my father wanted me to work for him. Filthy money,' he added. 'Anyway, after my mother died for a while I made it my mission to find out how wild Rome could be at night.'

'Where in Si—'

'I lived there,' he said, pointing across the street.

She had been about to ask whereabouts in Sicily, Raul knew, but she had mentioned the convent a couple of times and perhaps knew its location. Certainly he didn't want her knowing that he and Bastiano were from the same place. So he interrupted her and gave more information about himself than he usually would.

Raul pointed upwards and Lydia found herself looking at a hotel. It was far smaller than the one they were staying at, but it was beautifully lit and from the smart cars pulling up and the guests spilling out it seemed rather exclusive.

'How could a student afford to stay in that hotel?' Lydia asked.

'It was flats back then. In fact they were very seedy.'

'And then the developers came along?'

'That was me.'

And she stared at a hotel—in the centre of Rome, for goodness' sake—and found out that he owned it.

'How?'

But Raul did not want to revisit those times.

'Come on…'

It was late—after midnight—and he'd had enough of taxis to last a lifetime, and so, despite the hour, he texted Allegra and very soon a vehicle appeared.

It wasn't a taxi!

She sat in the back and he climbed in and sat so he faced her.

It was bliss to sink into the seats. 'My feet are killing me,' Lydia admitted. 'These shoes really weren't made for walking.'

'Take them off, then,' Raul said, and he leant over and lifted her foot and placed it in his lap.

Lydia could feel his solid thigh beneath her calf, and though she willed herself to relax her leg was trembling as he started to undo the strap.

He ran his hand along her calf and found the muscle was a knot of tension. He worked it with deft fingers.

The muscle did not relax.

In fact it tightened.

And when her toes curled to his touch he placed her foot so that she could feel his desire for her.

She ought to tell him she was a virgin.

But she rather guessed that Raul wouldn't find her innocence endearing.

His fingers continued to work on the tense muscle till it loosened. High in her thigh she contracted, and then he removed the sandal and lifted her naked foot.

'Please don't,' she choked as he lifted it towards his mouth. 'I've been walking…'

'Dirty girl.'

He kissed the arch of her foot, and she tried again to pull away, but only because the wicked sensation his tongue delivered shot straight between her legs.

'Raul…' She pronounced it correctly for the first time—it simply rolled off her tongue. 'Someone might see.'

'They can't see in.'

She could see, though.

For that moment Lydia felt as if she could see inside herself.

And she was…

The feeling was so unfamiliar it took a second for Lydia to recognise just what it was.

She was happy.

Just that.

'We're here,' Raul said, and released her foot, and that tiny glimpse of carefree happiness was over.

Just like that.

For she saw him—Maurice—standing outside the hotel.

He was smoking a cigar and on his phone—no doubt to her mother.

'We'll use the side entrance.'

Raul went to the intercom to inform the driver, but her hand stopped him.

'No.'

It was over.

The windows were dark and she knew that Maurice couldn't see in—neither would he be expecting her to return in such a luxurious vehicle.

'I need to face things.'

'Tomorrow,' Raul said.

And she looked at this man who chose not to get close enough to anyone to remember a birthday.

A man who did not live by the rules.

She did.

'I think it would be better dealt with tonight. It might be a little more difficult to take the moral high road about Bastiano with my knickers in my purse.'

'Lydia…' Raul started, but then halted. He had no qualms

over a one-night stand, but he conceded with a nod that she made a valid point.

'Go and tell him to get the hell out of your life, and then come to my suite.' He gave her the floor and the number, while knowing the night *he* had planned was gone. 'Will you be okay?'

'Of course I will.' Lydia gave a scoffing laugh. 'I'm twenty-four—he can hardly put me on curfew.'

'Will you be okay?' Raul asked again.

'Yes.' Lydia nodded. 'This needs to be dealt with.'

It did.

He asked his driver to move a little way down the street, and in that space of time Raul did something he rarely did. He took out a card.

Not the one he generally gave out.

'This is my number—you'll get straight through to me. If there is any problem…'

'There won't be,' Lydia said, but he opened her purse and put in the card.

This was it—both knew.

Though both hoped otherwise.

'Remember what I told you this morning,' Raul said, and she nodded.

He went to kiss her, but she moved her head to the side. It really wasn't a turn-on, knowing that Maurice waited.

And she should never have let Raul take her shoe off, because now there was all the hassle of getting it back on.

And happiness seemed determined to elude her as she climbed out of the vehicle.

'Where the hell have you been?' Maurice asked as she approached.

'Out,' Lydia snapped.

'Your mother is worried sick,' Maurice said as they walked briskly through the foyer, though he waited until they were in the elevator to say any more. 'I'm trying to save *your* family's business and you walk out on the one person who could help do just that.'

'I came for a drink.'

'He wanted to take us both to dinner. I've said to Bastiano that you'll be there tomorrow.'

'Well, you shouldn't have,' Lydia retorted.

They got out of the elevator and Lydia headed for her suite. 'I'm going to bed.'

'Don't you walk away from me,' Maurice told her. 'You'll be there tomorrow night, with a smile on, and—'

'Maurice, *why* do I need to be there?' She pointed out what Raul had this morning. 'I don't hold the deeds to the castle—my mother does. And I don't actually *like* the idea of turning it into a retreat. There's absolutely no reason for me to be there.'

'You know there is.'

'But *why*?'

Say it, Maurice, Lydia thought. *Have the guts to voice it out loud.*

'Because Bastiano wants you.'

'Then you need to tell him that I'm not part of the deal.' Her voice was shaky. The truth, even if deep down she'd already known it, was actually very difficult to hear said out loud. 'In fact you can tell Bastiano that, as of now, I no longer live or work at the castle.'

'Lydia, he's a charming man, he's extremely wealthy, and he's very interested in you.'

'Well, I'm not for sale! I've told you—I'm leaving.'

'And where are you going to go? Lydia, you've got no qualifications, no savings…'

'Odd, that,' Lydia responded, 'when I've been living at home and working my backside off for the last six years.'

She was done, she was through, and she dug in her purse for her keycard and let herself into her suite.

Maurice knocked loudly.

Oh, my God.

She could not take even another night of this.

She didn't have to, Lydia realised as she recalled Raul's advice.

'You can walk away from anyone you choose to and you don't have to come up with a reason.'

She had *many* good reasons to walk, Lydia thought, and started throwing her possessions into her case.

'Your mother is going to be very upset…' Maurice called through the door, but he fell silent when it was opened and Lydia stood holding her case.

'I'm leaving.'

'What the hell…? Lydia…'

Lydia could see a bit of spittle at the side of his mouth, and she could feel his anger at her refusal to comply.

When she always had in the past.

For the sake of her mother Lydia would generally back down when things got heated—but for the sake of herself she now stood her ground.

It was as if the blinkers had been lifted, and she could now see the control and the pressure he exerted.

And she would play the game no more.

No, she could not save the castle and, no, she would not meekly comply just to keep his mood tolerable. She could almost feel the eggshells she had walked on dissolving beneath her feet.

She marched to the elevators and he followed. He reached for her as she reached the doors and suddenly she was scared.

Raul had been right to be concerned.

She *was* scared of Maurice and his temper.

Oh, she wasn't running to Raul—she was running away from hell.

Maurice slapped her.

He delivered a stinging slap to her cheek and pulled at her hair, raised his other hand—but somehow she freed herself.

Lydia ducked into the elevator and wrenched the doors closed on his hand.

'Thank you,' she said. With the gate safely between them she spoke in a withering tone. 'Now I know for a fact what an utter bastard you are.'

She did not crumple.

Lydia refused to.

And she refused to waste even a single tear.

She was scared, though.

Scared and alone.

And she would have run into the night.

Without Raul, absolutely she would have run.

But instead of going down Lydia pressed the elevator button that would take her to his floor.

CHAPTER FIVE

RAUL STEPPED INTO his suite, unexpectedly alone.

Allegra had, of course, rung ahead, and everything had been prepared for Raul to return with a female guest.

The suite was dimly lit, but Raul saw champagne chilling in a bucket. He bypassed it. Throwing his jacket on a chair, he poured a large cognac and downed half in one gulp, then kicked off his socks and shoes, wrenched off his tie and removed his shirt.

In the bathroom Raul rolled his eyes, for the sight that greeted him seemed to mock. Candles had been lit and the deep bath was filled with fragrant water. But Raul would be bypassing that too—perhaps a cold shower might be more fitting.

He soon gave up prowling the penthouse suite dressed for two and lay on the bed. He took another belt of his drink and considered extending his stay for another night in Rome.

Unlike before, when he had actually wanted to flaunt Lydia under Bastiano's nose, Raul suddenly had a sense of foreboding.

Yes, Lydia might have stood up to her stepfather tonight, but for how long would that last? She was strong—Raul had seen that—but her family clearly saw Lydia as their ticket out of whatever mess they were in. And Bastiano, Raul knew, didn't care *what* methods he used to get his own way.

It wasn't his problem.

Over and over Raul told himself that.

He was angry with Bastiano rather than concerned about Lydia, Raul decided.

Only that didn't sit quite right.

Tomorrow he would be out of here.

Raul had rescheduled the jet for midday tomorrow. He would soon be back in Venice and this trip would be forgotten.

Raul didn't even want the hotel now—Sultan Alim's words had hit home. The Grande Lucia was far too much responsibility. He wanted investments he could manage from a distance. Raul wanted no labour of love.

In any area of his life.

Raul managed to convince himself that he was relieved with tonight's outcome.

Well, not relieved.

Far from it.

He was aching and hard, and was just sliding down his zipper, when he heard knocking at the door.

Good things, Raul realised as he made his way to the door, did come to those who waited. For just when he had thought the night was over, it would seem it had just begun!

He didn't bother to turn on the lounge light—just opened the door and Lydia tumbled in.

She had a suitcase beside her, which would usually be enough to perturb him, but there were other concerns right now.

She was shaking while trying to appear calm.

'Sorry to disturb you…'

Her voice was trembling.

'What happened?'

'We had a row,' Lydia said. 'A long overdue one. Anyway, I don't want to talk about that now.'

Oh, it wasn't just that she knew the price for a night in his room—Lydia wanted to go back to feeling happy.

Preferably now, please.

She wanted the oblivion his mouth offered, not to think of the turbulent times ahead.

He was naked from the waist up and her demand was sudden. 'Where were we?'

And her mouth found his and her kiss was urgent.

He tasted of liquor, and he was obviously aroused when she pressed into him.

Yet for once Raul was the one slowing things down.

His body demanded he kiss her back with fervour, that he take her now, up against the wall, and give her what she craved.

Yet there was more to this, he knew.

'Lydia…'

He peeled her off him and it was a feat indeed, for between his attempts to halt her he was resisting going back in for a kiss. He was hard and primed, and she was desperate and willing.

An obvious match.

Yet somehow not.

'Slow down…' he told her. 'Angry sex we can do later.'

Raul never thought of 'later' with women and was surprised by his own thought process, but his overriding feeling was concern.

'I'm not angry,' Lydia said.

She could feel his arms holding her back as he somehow read her exactly and told her how she felt.

'Oh, baby, you are!'

She was.

Lydia was a ball of fury that he held at arm's length.

She was trying to go for his zipper. She was actually wild.

'Lydia?'

He guided her to a chair, and it was like folding wood trying to get her to sit down, but finally he did.

Lydia could hear her own rapid breathing as Raul went over and flicked on a light, and she knew he was right.

She was angry.

He saw her pale face and the red hand mark, and Raul's

own anger coiled his gut tight. But he kept his voice even. 'What happened?'

'I told Maurice that I shan't be his puppet and neither shall I be returning home.'

He came to her and knelt down, and his hand went to her swollen cheek.

'Did he hit you anywhere else?'

'No.' She shook her head. 'I'm fine. Really I am.'

Raul frowned, because there were no tears—it was suppressed rage that glittered in her eyes.

'Do you want me to go and sort him out?'

'I would hate that.'

He rather guessed that she would.

'Please?' he said, and saw that she gave a small smile.

'No.'

He would do so later.

Right now, though, Raul's concern was Lydia. He stood and looked around. There was a woman in his hotel suite, and for the first time Raul didn't know what to do with her.

Lydia too looked around, and she was starting to calm. She saw the champagne and the flowers, and the room that had been prepared for them, and cringed at her own behaviour. She had asked for romance and he had delivered, and then she'd thrust herself on him.

'Can we pretend the last fifteen minutes never happened?' Lydia asked.

'You want me to go back to licking your feet?'

Lydia laughed.

Not a lot, but on a night when laughter should be an impossible task somehow she did.

She felt calmer.

Though she was shaken, and embarrassed at foisting herself upon Raul, now that she had stood up to Maurice she felt clearer in the head than she had in years.

'Do you want a drink?'

She nodded.

'What would you like?'

And she could see his amber drink and still taste it on her tongue.

'The same as you.'

'So, what happened?' Raul asked, and she answered as he crossed the suite.

'A necessary confrontation, and one that's been a long time coming,' she admitted. 'I've hated him since the day my mother first brought him home.'

'How long after your father died?'

'Eighteen months. Maurice had all these lavish ideas for the castle—decided to use it for weddings.'

'I hate weddings,' Raul said, taking the stopper off the bottle and pouring her a drink. 'Imagine having to deal with one every week.'

'They're not every week—unfortunately. Sometimes in the summer…' Her voice trailed off mid-sentence and Raul knew why. He was minus his shirt, and with his back to her, therefore Lydia must have seen his scar.

She had.

It was the sort of scar that at first glance could stop a conversation.

A jagged fault line on a perfect landscape, for he was muscled and defined, but then she frowned as she focused on the thinner lines.

A not so perfect landscape.

Oh, so badly she wanted to know more about this man.

But Lydia remembered her manners and cleared her throat and resumed talking.

'In the summer they used to be weekly, but the numbers have been dwindling.'

'Why?' Raul asked, and handed her the drink. He was grateful that she had said nothing about the scars. He loathed it when women asked about them, as if one night with him meant access to his past.

And it was always just one night.

Lydia took a sip. In truth it had tasted better on his tongue, but it was warming and pleasant and she focused on that for a moment. But then Raul asked the question again.

'Why are the numbers dwindling?'

'Because when people book a luxury venue they expect luxury at every turn, but Maurice cuts corners.'

He had heard that so many times.

In fact Raul had made his fortune from just that. He generally bought hotels on their last legs and turned them into palaces.

The Grande Lucia was a different venture—this hotel was a palace already, and that was why he was no longer considering making the purchase.

'Maurice is always after the quick fix,' Lydia said, and then stilled when she heard the buzzing of her phone.

'It's him,' Lydia said.

'I'll speak to him for you,' Raul said, and went to pick it up.

'Please don't.' Her voice was very clear. 'You would only make things worse.'

'How?'

'You won't be the one dealing with the fallout.'

And, yes, he *could* deal with Maurice tonight, but who would that really help? Oh, it might make Raul feel better, and Maurice certainly deserved it, but Lydia was right—it wouldn't actually help things in the long run, given he wouldn't be around.

'Turn your phone off,' Raul suggested, but she shook her head.

'I can't—he'll call my mother and she'll be worried.'

Raul wasn't so sure about that. He rather guessed that

Lydia's mother would more likely be annoyed that Lydia hadn't meekly gone along with their plans.

He watched as her phone rang again, but when she looked at it this time, instead of being angry she screwed her eyes closed.

'Maurice?'

'No, it's my mother.'

'Ignore it.'

'I can't,' Lydia said. 'He must have told her I've run off.' Her phone fell silent, but Lydia knew it wouldn't stay like that for very long. 'I'll ring her and tell her I'm safe. I shan't tell her where I am—just that I'm fine. Can I…?' She gestured to the double doors and it was clear that Lydia wanted some privacy to make the call.

'Of course.'

It was a bedroom.

Her first time in a man's bedroom, and it was so far from the circumstances she had hoped for that it was almost laughable.

It had been an almost perfect night, yet it was ruined now. Lydia sat on the bed and cringed as she recalled her entrance into his suite.

Lydia was very used to hiding her true feelings, yet Raul seemed to bring them bubbling up to the surface.

Right now, though, she needed somehow to snap back to efficient mode—though it was hard when she heard her mother's accusatory voice.

'What the hell are you playing at, Lydia?'

'I'm not playing at anything.'

'You know damn well how important this trip is!'

A part of Lydia had hoped for her mother to take her side. To agree that Maurice's behaviour tonight had been preposterous and tell her that of *course* Lydia didn't have to agree to anything she didn't want to do.

It had been foolish to hope.

Instead Lydia sat there as her mother told her how charming Bastiano was, how he'd been nothing but a gentleman to date, and asked how she dared embarrass the family like this.

And then, finally, her mother was honest.

'It's time you stepped up…'

'Bastiano doesn't even know me,' Lydia pointed out. 'We've spoken, at best, a couple of times.'

'Lydia, it's time to get your head out of the clouds. I've done everything I can to keep us from going under. For whatever reason, Bastiano has taken an interest in you…'

Lydia didn't hear much of the rest.

For whatever reason…

As if it was unfathomable that someone might simply want her for no other reason than they simply did.

It was Lydia who ended the call, and after sitting for a few minutes in silence she looked up when there was a knock at the door.

'Come in,' Lydia said, and then gave a wry smile as Raul entered—it was *his* bedroom, after all.

'How did it go with your mother?'

'Not very well,' Lydia admitted. 'I'm being overly dramatic, apparently.'

'Why don't you have a bath?'

'A bath!' A laugh shot out of her pale lips at his odd suggestion.

'It might relax you. There's one already run.'

'I'm guessing I wouldn't have been bathing alone, had I come up the first time.'

'Plans change,' Raul said. 'Give me your phone and go and wind down.'

'You won't answer it?' Lydia checked.

'No,' Raul said.

Her family was persistent.

Raul, though, was stubborn.

The phone continued to buzz, but rather than turn it off Raul went back to lying on the bed, as he had been when Lydia had arrived.

And that was how she found him.

The bath *had* been soothing. Lydia had lain in the fragrant water, terribly glad of his suggestion to leave her phone.

It had given her a chance to calm down and to regroup.

'They've been calling,' Raul told her by way of greeting.

'I thought that they might.' Lydia sighed. 'I doubt they'll give up if Bastiano hasn't. Apparently Maurice has said he'll meet him tomorrow and I'm supposed to be there.'

'And what did you say?'

'No, of course—but it's not just about dinner with Bastiano…'

'Of course it's not,' Raul agreed.

'I think he wants sex.'

'He wants more than sex, Lydia. He wants to marry you. He thinks you'd make a very nice trophy wife. Bastiano wants to be King of your castle.'

He watched for her reaction and as always she surprised him, because Lydia just gave a shrug.

'I wouldn't be the first to marry for money.'

And though the thought appalled her it did not surprise her.

'I doubt my mother married Maurice for his sparkling personality,' Lydia said, and Raul gave a small nod that told her he agreed. 'Would *you* marry for money?' Lydia asked.

'No,' Raul said, 'but that's not from any moral standpoint—I just would never marry.'

'Why?'

'I've generally run out of conversation by the morning. I can't imagine keeping one going with the same person for the rest of my life.'

He did make her smile.

And he put her at ease.

No, that wasn't the word, because *ease* wasn't what she felt around him.

She felt like herself.

Whoever that was.

Lydia had never really been allowed to find out.

'You'd have to remember her birthday,' Lydia said, and sat next to him when he patted the bed.

'And our anniversary.' Raul rolled his eyes. 'And married people become obsessed with what's for dinner.'

'They do!' Lydia agreed.

'I had a perfectly normal PA—Allegra. Now, every day, her husband rings and they talk about what they are going to have for dinner. I pay her more than enough that she could eat out every night…'

Yes, he made her smile.

'Do you believe in love?' Lydia asked.

'No.'

She actually liked how abruptly he dismissed the very notion.

It was so peaceful in his room, and though common sense told her she should be nervous Lydia wasn't. It was nice to talk with someone who was so matter-of-fact about something she had wrestled with for so long.

'Would you marry if it meant you might save your family from going under?'

'My family is gone.' Raul shrugged. 'Anyway, you can't save anyone from going under. Whatever you try and do.'

The sudden pensive note to his voice had her turning to face him.

'I wanted my mother to leave my father. I did everything I could to get her to leave, but she wouldn't. I knew I had to get out. I was working a part-time job in Rome and studying, and I had found a flat for her.' He looked over at Lydia briefly. 'Next to the one I told you about. But she wouldn't leave. She said that she could not afford to, and that aside from that she took her wedding vows seriously.'

'I would too,' Lydia told him.

'Well, my mother said the same—but then she had an affair.' It was surprisingly easy to tell her, given what Lydia had shared with him. 'She died in a car accident just after the affair was exposed. I doubt her mind was on the road. After she died I found out that she'd had access to more than enough money to start a new life. I think her lover had found that out too.'

He wanted to tell her that his mother's lover had been Bastiano, but that wasn't the point he was trying to make, and he did not want to make things worse for her tonight.

'Lydia, what I'm trying to say is you can't prevent anyone from going under.'

'I don't believe that.'

'Even if you marry him, do you really think Bastiano is going to take advice from Maurice? Do you think he will want to keep your mother and her husband in residence?'

He took out all her dark thoughts, the fears that had kept her awake at night, and forced her to examine them.

'No.'

'Take it from me—the only person you can ever save is yourself.'

Strong words, but clearly she didn't take them in, because when her phone buzzed Lydia went to pick it up.

'Leave it,' Raul said.

'I can't do that,' Lydia admitted. 'I might turn it off.'

'Then they'll know you're avoiding them. Just ignore it.'

'I can't.'

'Yes, you can—because I shan't let you hear it.'

She had thought Raul meant he would turn the ring down, but instead as the phone started to ring again he reached for her and drew her face towards him.

Nothing, Lydia was sure, could take her mind from her family tonight.

She was wrong.

His kiss was softer than the others he had delivered.

So light, in fact, that as she closed her eyes in anticipation all he gave was a light graze to her lips that had her hungry for more as his hand slid into her hair.

Kiss by soft kiss he took care of every pin, and Lydia found her lips had parted, but still he made her wait for his tongue.

She had tasted him already, and her body was hungry for more.

Yet he was cruel in attack for he gave so little.

He undid the knot of her robe with the same measured pace he had taken in dealing with her hair and then pushed it down over her arms so that she sat naked.

Lydia felt something akin to panic as contact ceased and he ran his gaze down her body. It *wasn't* panic, though, she thought. It was far nicer—because as the phone buzzed by the bed she was staring down at him, watching his mouth near her breast, and she would have died rather than answer it.

'Do you want to get that?' Raul asked, and she could feel his breath on her breast.

'No…' Her voice had gone—it came out like a husk.

'I can't hear you,' he said, and then he delivered his tongue in a motion too light, for she bunched the sheet with her fingers and fought not to grab his head.

'No,' she said, and when his mouth paused in delivering its magic, she added, 'I don't want to answer.'

'Good.'

He sucked hard now, and she knew he bruised.

Raul gave one breast the deep attention that her mouth had craved, and she fought not to swear or, worse, to plead.

She should tell him that he was her first, Lydia thought

as he guided her hand to his crotch and she felt his thick, hard length through the fabric.

But then her phone buzzed again and the teasing resumed, for he stood.

'Do you want me to get that?'

'Turn it off,' Lydia said.

'Oh, no.'

He slid down his zipper and the buzz of the phone dimmed in her ears when she saw him naked.

Yes, that would hurt.

Oh, she really should tell him, Lydia thought as she reached out to hold him. But then she closed her eyes at the bliss of energy beneath her fingers and the low moan that came from him as his hand closed around hers.

He moved her slender fingers more roughly than she would have. She opened her eyes at the feel of him.

She could hear their breathing, rapid and shallow, and then his free hand took her head and pushed it down, and she tasted him just a little as her tongue caressed him.

And for Raul, what should have been too slow, the touch of her tongue too light, somehow she owned the night.

The slight choking in her throat closing around him brought him close to release, so that he was grateful for the sudden buzzing and it was Raul who was briefly distracted.

Lydia wasn't.

She was lost in the taste of him when for the second time that night—but for a very different reason—she felt a tug on her hair and looked up.

Now when she licked her lips it was to savour the taste of him.

And Raul, who did not want this to be over, put her to bed.

On top of it.

Raul was decisive in his positioning of Lydia, and her loose limbs were his to place.

He knelt astride her and put her arms above her head, held them one-handed as the other hand played with the breast he wasn't sucking.

'Raul...' She was about to tell him about her virginal status, but her phone buzzed again and he thought that was her complaint.

'Shush...'

And then he moved so that he knelt between her legs, and reached to the bedside drawer for a condom, and she lay there watching as he rolled it on.

'Raul...' Her voice was breathless, but she should say it now—she was trying to.

'You talk too much.'

She had said two words and both had been his name. She went to point that out but lost her thought processes as his head went down between her legs and she lay holding her breath and nervously awaiting his intimate touch.

He kissed her exactly as he had the first time.

Raul's mouth lightly pressed *there*, and then there was the tease of his tongue. Slowly at first, as Lydia had been slow, for he thought she had been teasing him at the time.

'Please...' Lydia said, not sure if she was asking to speak, asking him to slow down or asking for more.

His jaw was rough, his mouth soft and his tongue probing. It was sublime.

His mouth worked on and she started to moan.

His tongue urged her on.

Lydia's thighs were shaking and she fought to stay silent. And then she gave in, and he moaned in pleasure as she orgasmed. He kissed her and swallowed as she pulsed against his lips.

And then he left them.

She was heated and twitching, breathless and giddy and perfectly done as he moved over her and crushed her tense lips with his moist ones. His thigh moved between her legs and splayed her, and even coming down from a high, with the feel of him nudging and the energy of him, Lydia knew this would hurt.

'Slowly,' she said, but her words were muffled, so she turned her head. 'I've never—'

He was about to aim for hard, fast and deep, when he heard those two words that were so unexpected.

'Slowly,' she said again.

He could do that.

An unseen smile stretched his lips at the thought of taking her first, practically beneath Bastiano's nose. And then the thought of taking her first made his ardour grow.

But then, just when bliss appeared on the menu, the stars seemed to collect and become one that shone too bright. And, like a headmaster grabbing an errant student by the shoulder, he suddenly hauled himself back from the edge.

Everything went still.

All the delicious sensations, gathering tight, slowly loosened as his weight came down on her rather than within her.

And then he rolled off and onto his back and lay breathless, unsated, both turned on and angry.

He told her why. 'I don't do virgins.'

There was so much she could protest at about that statement.

Do?

And her response was tart, to cover up her disappointment and, yes, her embarrassment that he had brought things to a very shuddering halt.

'What, only experienced applicants need apply?'

'Don't you get it?' He ripped off the condom and tossed it aside, and ached to finish the job. 'There's nothing to apply *for*, Lydia. I like one-night stands. I like to get up in the morning and have coffee and then go about my day. It's sex. That's it. There are no vacant positions waiting to be filled in my life.'

'I wasn't expecting anything more.'

'You say that *now*.'

And *now* Raul sulked.

He had heard it so many times before.

Raul didn't *do* virgins, and with good reason—because even the most seasoned of his lovers tended to ask for more than he was prepared to give.

'I mean it,' Lydia insisted.

'Do you know what, Lydia? If you've waited till you're twenty-four I'm guessing there's a reason.'

There was—she'd hardly had men beating down the door.

But a small voice was telling her that Raul, as arrogant as his words were, was actually right—making love *would* change things for her.

Then again, since she had met Raul everything had already changed.

'Go to sleep,' he said.

'I can't.'

'Yes, Lydia, *you* can.'

His voice was sulky, and she didn't know what he meant, but as she lay there Lydia started to understand.

She felt a little as if she was floating.

All the events of the night were dancing before her eyes, and she could watch them unfold without feeling—except for one.

'What happened to your back?'

Her voice came from that place just before she fell asleep. Raul knew that.

Yet he wished she had not asked.

Lydia had not asked about one scar but about his whole back.

He did not want to think about that.

But now he was starting to.

CHAPTER SIX

'It's your mother's funeral,' the priest admonished, but only once Raul had been safely cuffed and led away.

Raul and Bastiano, the police decided, should not be in the same building, so Raul was taken to the jailhouse to cool down and Bastiano was cuffed to a stretcher and taken to the valley's small hospital.

A towel covered Raul's injury, and he sat in a cell until a doctor came to check on him.

Raul loathed anyone seeing his back, due to the scars his father had put there, but thankfully the doctor didn't comment on them. He took one look at the gaping wound and shook his head.

'This is too big to repair under a local,' the doctor informed him. 'I'll tell the guards to arrange your transfer to the hospital.'

'Is Bastiano still there?' Raul asked, and the doctor nodded. 'Then you'll do it here.'

The thought of being in the same building as Bastiano tonight was not one he relished, and a hospital was no place for his current mood.

'It's going to hurt,' the doctor warned.

But Raul already did.

The closure of the wound took ages.

He felt the fizz and sear of the peroxide as it bubbled its way through raw flesh, and then came the jab of the doctor's fingers as he explored it.

'I really think…' the doctor started, but Raul did not change his stance.

'Just close it.'

Deep catgut sutures closed the muscles and then thick silk finally drew together the skin.

He was written up for some painkillers to be taken throughout the night when required, but he did not bother to ask the guards for them.

Nothing could dim the pain.

It was not the wounds of the flesh that caused agony, more the memories and regret.

He should have known what was going on.

His mother's more cheerful disposition on his last visit was because she'd had a lover. Raul knew that now.

And there was guilt too—tangible guilt—because she had called him on the morning she had died and Raul had not picked up.

Instead he had been deep in oblivion with some no-name woman and had chosen not to take the call.

Raul lay on the hard, narrow bed and stared at the ceiling through the longest night of his life.

There would be many more to come.

Light came in through the barred windows and he heard a drunk who had sung the night through being processed and released.

And then another.

Raul was in no rush for his turn.

'Hey.'

The heavy door opened and a police officer brought him coffee. He was familiar.

Marco.

They had been at school together.

'For what it's worth, I'm on your side,' Marco told Raul as he handed him a coffee. 'Bastiano's a snake. I wish they had let you finish the job.'

Raul said nothing—just accepted the coffee.

God, but he hated the valley. There was corruption at every turn. If memory served him correctly, and it usually did, Bastiano had slept with the young woman who was now Marco's fiancée.

Just after nine Raul signed the papers for his release and Marco handed him his tie and belt, which Raul pocketed.

'Smarten up,' Marco warned him. 'You are to be at the courthouse by ten.'

Raul put on his belt and tucked in his shirt somewhat but gave up by the time he got to his tie. One look in the small washroom mirror and he knew it was pointless. His eyes were bruised purple, his lips swollen, his hair matted with blood and he needed to shave.

Groggy, his head pounding, Raul stepped out onto the street into a cruelly bright day and walked the short distance to the courthouse. Raul assumed he was there to be formally charged, but instead he found out it was for the reading of Maria Di Savo's last will and testament.

His father, Gino, was there for that, of course. And he sat gloating, because he knew that apart from the very few trinkets he had given her in earlier years everything Maria had had was his.

Raul just wanted it over and done with, and then he would get the hell out.

He was done with Casta for good.

But then, for the second time in less than twenty-four hours, the man he hated most in the world appeared—again at the most inappropriate time.

'What the hell is *he* doing here?'

It was Gino who rose in angry response as an equally battered Bastiano took a seat on a bench. His face had been sutured and a jagged scar ran the length of his now purple cheek. Clearly he had just come from the hospital, for he was still wearing yesterday's suit.

And then the judge commenced the reading of the will.

This was a mere formality, and Raul simply hoped he might get the crucifix Maria had always worn.

That wish came true, for he was handed a slim envelope and the simple cross and chain fell onto his palm.

But then out slid a ring.

It was exquisite—far more elaborate than anything his mother had owned—rose gold with an emerald stone, it was dotted with tiny seed pearls and it felt heavy in his palm. Raul picked it up between finger and thumb and tried to place it, yet he could not remember his mother wearing it.

He was distracted from examining the ring when the judge spoke again.

'Testamona Segreto.'

Even the rather bored court personnel stood to attention, as suddenly there was an unexpected turn in the formalities.

Raul stopped looking at the ring and Gino frowned and leant forward as all present learnt that his mother had made a secret will.

More intriguing was the news that it been amended just a few short weeks ago.

A considerable sum had been left to Maria on the death of her brother, Luigi, on condition that it did not in any way benefit Maria's husband.

Luigi had loathed Gino.

But Luigi had died some ten years ago.

Most shocking for Raul was the realisation that his mother had had the means to leave.

Raul had been working his butt off, trying to save to provide for her, when she could have walked away at any time.

It made no sense.

Nothing in his life made sense any more.

And then Raul felt a pulse beat a tattoo in his temples as the judge read out his mother's directions.

'The sum is to be divided equally between my son Raul Di Savo and Bastiano Conti. My hope is that they use it wisely. My prayer is that they have a wonderful life.'

Raul sat silent as pandemonium broke out in the courthouse. Money was Gino's god, and *this* betrayal hit harder than the other. He started cursing, and as he moved to finish off Raul's work on Bastiano, Security were called.

'He gets nothing!' Gino sneered, and jabbed his finger towards Bastiano. 'Maria was sick in the head—she would not have known what she was doing when she made that will.'

'The testimonial is clear,' the judge responded calmly as Gino was led out.

'Bastiano used her. Tell him that we will fight…' Gino roared over his shoulder.

Raul said nothing in response—just sat silent as his mother's final wishes sank in.

She had chosen Bastiano as the second benefactor and had asked that her money be divided equally…

Oh, that stung.

He looked over at Bastiano, who stared ahead and refused to meet his gaze.

Why the hell had she left it to *him*? Had Bastiano known about the money and engineered the entire thing? Had he sweet-talked her into changing her will and then deliberately exposed their affair, knowing that the fragile Maria could never survive the fallout?

Gino was still shouting from the corridor. 'I stood by her all these years!'

Raul sat thinking. He knew he could contest this in court—or he could wait till he and Bastiano were outside and fight. This time to the bloody end.

He chose the latter.

Outside, the sun seemed to chip at his skull and he felt like throwing up—and then Bastiano stepped out, also wincing at the bright afternoon sun.

'So,' Raul said by way of greeting, 'the gossip in the valley was wrong.' He watched as Bastiano's brow creased in confusion, and then he better explained. 'As it turns out—*you* were the whore.'

The court attendees spilled out onto the street, the guards hovered, and a police vehicle drove slowly past. Raul saw that Marco was at the wheel.

As it slid out of sight Raul knew that if Marco was summoned to a fight outside the courthouse the response time would be slow.

They stared at each other.

Raul's black eyes met Bastiano's silver-grey and they shared their mutual loathing.

'Your mother…' Bastiano started, and then, perhaps wisely, chose not to continue—though that did not stop Raul.

'Are you going to tell me to respect her wishes?' Raul sneered. 'You knew she had this money—you knew…' He halted, but only because his voice was close to faltering and he would not allow Bastiano to glimpse weakness.

He would beat Bastiano with more than his fists.

Raul cleared his throat and delivered his threat, low but strong, and for Bastiano's ears only. 'Collect promptly… pay slowly.'

It was an old Italian saying, but it came with different meaning on this day.

Bastiano might have collected promptly today, but he would pay.

And slowly.

Their eyes met, and though nothing further was said it was as if Raul had repeated those words and he watched as his threat sank in.

Raul would keep his word—the vow he had made by his mother's grave.

Every day he would fight Bastiano—not with fists but with action, and so, to the chagrin of the gathered crowd, who wanted the day to end in blood, Raul walked away.

Bastiano might have got a payout today, but Raul would take his mother's inheritance and build a life from it far away from here.

And in the process he would destroy Bastiano at every opportunity.

Revenge would be his motivator now.

CHAPTER SEVEN

LYDIA KNEW EXACTLY where she was even before her eyes had opened.

There was constant awareness of him, even in sleep. Hearing his deep breathing and feeling his warm, sleeping body beside her, Lydia thought it was the nicest awakening she had ever had.

She chose not to stretch, or pull herself out of this slumberous lull. The mattress felt like a cloud, and the room was the perfect temperature, because even with the bedding around her waist she was warm.

Raul's back did not make pleasant viewing.

Oh, it was muscled, and his shoulders were wide, and his black hair narrowed neatly into the nape of his neck. All was perfect except for the scars.

And there were a lot of them.

There was the ugly, thick vertical one that was untidy and jagged and ran from mid-shoulder to waist.

But there were others that ran across his back.

Thin white lines…row upon row.

She had asked him about his back last night.

Lydia lay there trying to recall his answer.

There hadn't been one.

And she did not ask with words this time—instead with touch, for while she had been looking at his back her fingers had inadvertently gone there.

Raul felt the question in her touch and loathed the fact that he had fallen to sleep on his side, and he rolled onto his back.

'I'm sorry I asked,' Lydia said.

'Then why did you?'

'Because when I'm with you I seem to forget to be polite.'

A phone rang, and this time it wasn't Lydia's. The battery had finally given out.

Raul reached over and swore, even before he had answered the call and then he spoke for a few minutes and lay back down—but this time he faced her.

'We overslept.'

'What time is it?'

'Midday.'

Lydia's eyes widened in surprise. 'Did you miss your plane?'

'No, it is missing me. That's why Allegra rang. She's going to reschedule.'

He stared at her and Lydia found out then why she had thrown herself at him last night.

It was the correct response to those black eyes, Lydia realised, because her desire was still the same.

'Sorry I didn't tell you I was a virgin.'

'It's a miracle you still are.'

She didn't want to be, though.

How heavenly to be made love to by him, Lydia thought, though she said not a word.

He reached out a hand and moved her hair back from her face, and still nothing was said. Lydia liked sharing this silent space with him.

No demands—just silence.

He thought again of all she'd told him—how she had sat at breakfast yesterday and given him that dark piece of her past.

And they were back in that place, together again, only this time it was Raul who spoke.

'I got into a fight at my mother's funeral. At the cemetery.'

'Oh, dear.'

She smiled—not a happy one, just a little smile at their differences.

And he gave a thin smile too.

'With whom?' Lydia asked.

'Her lover.'

And it was at that moment, when he didn't name Bastiano, that Raul, for the first time, properly lied.

Oh, last night it had technically been a lie by omission. She had been angry and confused and there had been good reason for him not to disclose. But now they were in bed together, facing each other and talking as if they were lovers, and Raul knew at his base that he should at that moment have told her.

Yet he did not want her to turn away.

Which she would.

Of course she would.

'When did you find out that your mother was having an affair?' Lydia asked.

'Right after she died,' Raul said. 'I didn't believe it at first. My mother was very religious—when she was a girl, growing up she had hoped to be a nun…'

'Why didn't she?'

'She got pregnant at sixteen.'

'With you? By your father?'

'Of course.' Raul gave a nod. 'It wasn't a happy marriage, I knew that, but I was still surprised…' He didn't finish.

'To find that she cheated?' Lydia asked, and watched his eyes narrow at her choice of words.

'I think my mother was the one who was cheated.' He thought of Bastiano's slick charm and the inheritance that he had ensured was signed over to his name.

'Or,' Lydia pondered out loud, 'maybe she fell in love.'

'Please!' Raul's voice was derisive, but more at Lydia's suggestion than at her. And then he told her something. 'She was used. I hate that man.'

'Do you ever see him?' Lydia asked. 'Her lover?'

'On occasion,' Raul admitted. 'I have made it my mission to take from him, to get there first, to beat him at everything…' It was the reason he was here at the Hotel Grande Lucia. Usually he would be ringing Allegra, drafting an offer to put to Alim.

Yet he had slept until midday.

And that need to conquer had been the real reason for pulling back last night.

Lydia deserved far better than that.

And it was there again—the chance to tell her just who Bastiano was, here and now, in bed, during the most intimate conversation of his life—for Raul never usually discussed such things.

But he didn't tell.

There was no need for that.

And anyway she would be gone soon. So Raul kissed her instead.

It was a different kiss from last night—they knew more about each other now than then—but it did not last for long.

Raul knew his own reputation, and that it wouldn't be changing any time soon, and so he pulled back.

She was dismissed.

Yet still they lingered in bed.

'What are you going to do with the rest of your day?' he asked her.

'I'm going to head home while I've still got one. I'll see if I can transfer my flight to today,' Lydia said. 'I want to tell my mother—away from Maurice—that I'm moving out.'

'Good,' Raul said. 'You need to…' He halted. It was not his place to tell her what to do.

'I know what I need to do, Raul.'

She closed her eyes for a moment and thought of the mountain in front of her that she was about to climb—walking out on the family business, forging a career of her own, finding somewhere to live with nothing.

Yet there was excitement there too.

It was time.

And that made her smile.

'What will *you* do today?' Lydia asked.

Raul thought for a moment—the weekend spread out before him, and really he could take his pick.

Allegra was waiting for Raul to call with his amended schedule.

There were parties and invitations galore—particularly as he was known to be in Rome. And yet whatever he chose Raul knew it could not top last night.

'I'll go home,' Raul said.

'And where's that?' Lydia asked.

'Venezia.'

Venice.

Lydia gave a wistful sigh, but then, so contrary were her memories from there, she screwed up her nose just a fraction—and he saw that she did.

To cover herself, and because she could not take him delving deep this morning, she quickly chose laughter and gave him a dig in his ribs.

'You never told me that you lived there.'

'Why would I?'

'When I was talking about it you never let on…' And then she halted, remembering that Raul owed her no explanations—they danced on the edge of the other, revealing only what they chose. 'I'm not very good at being a one-night stand.'

'No,' he agreed with a wry smile, 'you're not.' And then his smile dimmed, but still his eyes held hers and Raul asked a question. 'Would you have regretted it if we had slept together?'

'No.' Lydia shook her head. 'Raul, you seem to have

decided that just because I haven't slept with anyone I'm looking for something permanent. By all accounts I could have had that with Bastiano, but I chose not to. He's not…' Lydia faltered and then, rather than finishing, swallowed her words down. Raul didn't need to hear them. The truth was she had no feelings for Bastiano.

None.

Yet she did for Raul.

'Not what?' Raul asked.

He's not you would be her honest response.

But rather than say that Lydia was far more evasive. 'He's not what I want.'

'What *do* you want?'

'I wanted what every woman wants, a bit of romance while I was here. I'm not shopping for a husband.' She gave a shrug and pulled one of the tangled sheets from the bed to cover herself. 'I'm going to have a shower.'

And it was in the shower, with space between them, that Lydia pondered what she had been about to say.

He's not you.

With Bastiano there was no attraction. Had it been Raul whom her family were trying to match-make her with she'd have been embarrassed, yes, and annoyed, perhaps, and yet there would have been excitement and trepidation too.

She liked Raul far more than it was safe to let on.

And Raul liked Lydia.

A lot.

That feeling was rare.

Mornings were never his strong point—generally he preferred women who dressed in the dark and were gone. He wasn't proud of that fact, just honest, as he examined his usual wants. Yet this morning he was lying listening to Lydia in the shower and trying to resist joining her.

And again she had surprised him.

Lydia was tough.

There had been no tears, no pleas for help or for him to get involved. In fact she had actively discouraged it when he had offered to step in and deal with Maurice.

There was a level of independence to her that he had seen in few and he did not want her to be gone.

And, more honestly, he wanted to be her first.

It had nothing to do with Bastiano.

In fact Raul wanted her well away from here.

He was wondering if he could give Lydia what she wanted.

The romantic trip to Italy she craved.

He could do that for a day, surely?

Raul didn't look over at her when Lydia came out from the bathroom and went through to the lounge. There she found her case and pulled out an outfit.

Lydia chose the nice cream dress she had brought for sightseeing and some flat sandals.

Her hair was a bit of a disaster, but she had left her adaptor in her hotel room, so there was no point dragging out her straighteners.

Lydia made do and smoothed it as best she could. She could hear Raul making some calls on his phone and commencing his day.

She had been but a brief interlude, Lydia knew. And so she checked that her sunglasses were in her purse and then walked back into the bedroom—and there he lay. He was even more beautiful now than when she had met him.

Then Raul had been in a suit and clean-shaven.

A mystery.

Now he lay in bed with his hands behind his head, thinking. She knew, because she had lain beside him all night, that he was naked save the sheet that barely covered him. He was unshaven and his eyes seemed heavy from sleep as he turned and looked at her.

And the more that she knew, the more of a mystery he was.

This was regret, Lydia thought.

That he could so easily let her go.

And how did she walk away? Lydia wondered.

How did she go over and kiss that sulky mouth and say goodbye when really she wanted to climb back into bed?

How did she accept that she would never know how it felt to be made love to by him?

But rather than reveal her thoughts she flicked that internal default switch which had been permanently set to 'polite'.

'Thank you so much for last night.'

'I haven't finished being your tour guide yet.'

He stretched out his arm and held out his hand, but Lydia didn't go over. She did not want to let in hope, so she just stood there as Raul spoke.

'It would be remiss of me to let you go home without seeing Venice as it should be seen.'

'Venice?'

Oh, she repeated his offer only because she was mystified. She'd been preparing to leave with her head held high, but then, when she had least expected it, he'd offered more.

So much more.

'I like to call it by its other name—La Serenissima,' Raul said. 'It means the Most Serene.'

'That's not how I remember my time there.'

'Then you have a chance to change that. I'm heading there today. Why don't you come with me? Fly out of Marco Polo tomorrow instead.'

There was another night between now and then, and Lydia knew that even while he offered her an extension he made it clear there was a cut-off.

Time added on for good behaviour.

And Raul's version of 'good behaviour' was that there

would be no tears or drama as she walked away. Lydia knew that. If she were to accept his offer, then she had to remember that.

'I'd like that.' The calm of her voice belied the trembling she felt inside. 'It sounds wonderful.'

'Only if you're sure,' Raul added.

'Of course.'

But how could she be sure of anything now she had set foot in Raul's world?

He made her dizzy.

Disorientated.

Not just her head, but every cell in her body seemed to be spinning as he hauled himself from the bed and unlike Lydia, with her sheet-covered dash to the bathroom, his body was hers to view.

And that blasted default switch was stuck, because Lydia did the right thing and averted her eyes.

Yet he didn't walk past. Instead Raul walked right over to her and stood in front of her.

She could feel the heat—not just from his naked body but her own—and it felt as if her dress might disintegrate.

He put his fingers on her chin, tilted her head so that she met his eyes, and it killed that he did not kiss her, nor drag her back to his bed. Instead he checked again. 'Are you sure?'

'Of course,' Lydia said, and tried to make light of it. 'I never say no to a free trip.'

It was a joke—a teeny reference to the very reason she was here in Rome—but it put her in an unflattering light. She was about to correct herself, to say that it hadn't come out as she had meant, but then she saw his slight smile and it spelt approval.

A gold-digger he could handle, Lydia realised.

Her emerging feelings for him—perhaps not.

At every turn her world changed, and she fought for a

semblance of control. Fought to convince not just Raul but herself that she could handle this.

They were driven right up to his jet, and his pilot and crew were waiting on the runway to greet them.

'Do you always have a jet on standby?' Lydia asked.

'Always.'

'What's wrong with first class?' Lydia asked, refusing to appear too impressed.

'When children are banned from first class, then I'll consider commercial flights.'

He wouldn't!

Raul liked his privacy, as well as his own staff.

Inside the plane was just as luxurious as the hotel they had come from, and very soon there was take-off and she looked out of the window and watched Rome disappear beneath them.

Lydia felt free.

Excited, nervous, but finally free.

'I travel a lot.' Raul explained the real reason for his plane. 'And, as you saw this morning, my schedule is prone to change. Having my own jet shaves hours off my working week.'

'How did you do all this?' Lydia asked.

'I received an inheritance when my mother died.'

'Your family was rich?'

'No.'

He thought back to Casta. They had been comfortable financially, compared to some, but it had been dirty money and always quickly spent.

Neither the Di Savo nor the Conti wineries had ever really taken off.

And then he thought of him and Bastiano, drinking the wine together and laughing at how disgusting it tasted.

They had been such good friends.

In the anger and hate that had fuelled him for years, Raul had forgotten that part.

It would serve him better not to remember it now.

Bastiano was the enemy, and he reminded himself of that when he spoke next.

'My mother had some money from her brother. She left half to her lover and half to me. It was enough for me to buy the flat I was renting. Then I took out a mortgage on one across the floor and rented it out. I kept going like that. You were right—developers did come in, and they made me an offer that I should not have been able to refuse.'

'But you did?'

'Yes. If they could see the potential, then so could I. One of the owners upstairs had done some refurbishing, and I watched and learnt. By then I had four studio apartments, and I turned them into two more luxurious ones… It had always been an amazing location, but now it was a desirable address. A few years later the other owner and I got the backing to turn it into a hotel. I bought him out in the end. I wanted it for myself. That was always the end game.'

'You used him?'

'Of course,' Raul said. 'That's what I do.'

He didn't care if that put him in an unflattering light.

Better that she know.

'Do you go back often?' Lydia asked. 'To Sicily?'

Raul shook his head. 'I haven't been back since my mother's funeral.

'Don't you miss it?' Lydia pushed.

'There is nothing there for me to miss.'

'You didn't go back for your father's funeral?' Lydia checked.

'No. He was already dead to me.'

'But even so—'

'Should I pretend to care?' Raul interrupted.

Lydia didn't know how to answer that. In her family appearances were everything, and there was a constant demand to be seen to do the right thing.

Raul lived by rules of his own.

'No,' she answered finally.

Her response was the truth—she could think of nothing worse than Raul pretending to care and her believing in his lies.

Better to know from the start that this was just temporary, for when he removed her from his life she really would be gone for good.

'Do you want to change for dinner?'

'Dinner?' Lydia checked, and then she looked at the sun, too low in the sky. The day was running away from them already.

And soon, Lydia knew, it would be her turn to be the one left behind.

CHAPTER EIGHT

LYDIA HAD BEEN in two different bedrooms belonging to Raul.

One at the hotel.

The other on his plane.

Tonight would make it three.

Raul was wearing black pants and a white shirt—dressed for anything, she guessed.

Lydia opened her case, and there was the red dress she had bought with Raul on her mind.

It was too much, surely?

Yet she would never get the chance again. She thought of where she'd be tomorrow—rowing with her mother and no doubt packing a lifetime of stuff into trunks and preparing to move out of the castle.

A bell buzzed, and Lydia knew she had to move a little more quickly.

Simple, yet elegant, there was nothing that should scream 'warning' in the dress, and yet it hugged her curves, and the slight ruching of the fabric over her stomach seemed to indicate the shiver she felt inside.

On sight he had triggered something.

Those dark eyes seemed to see far beyond the rather brittle façade she wore.

She didn't know how to be sexy, yet around him she was.

More than that—she wanted to be.

She added lipstick and wished she'd worn the neutral shoes.

Except Lydia felt far from neutral about tonight.

It was too much.

Far, far too much.

She would quickly change, Lydia decided.

But then there was a gentle rap on the door and she was informed that it was time to be seated.

'I'll just be a few moments,' Lydia said, and dismissed the steward. But what she did not understand about private jets was the fact that there were not two hundred passengers to get strapped in.

'Now.' The steward smiled. 'We're about to come in to land.'

There was no chance to change and so, shy, reluctant, but trying not to show it, Lydia stepped out.

'Sit down,' Raul said.

He offered no compliment—really, he gave no reaction.

In fact he took out his phone and sent a text.

Oddly, it helped.

She had a moment to sit with her new self, away from his gaze, and Lydia looked out of the window and willed her breathing to calm.

Venice was always beautiful, and yet today it was even more so.

As they flew over on their final descent she rose out of the Adriatic in full midsummer splendour, and Lydia knew she would remember this moment for ever. The last time she had felt as if she were sitting alone, even though she had been surrounded by school friends.

Now, as the wheels hit the runway, Lydia came down to earth as her spirit soared high.

And as they stood to leave he told her.

'You look amazing.'

'Is it too much?'

'Too much?' Raul frowned. 'It's still summer.'

'No, I meant…' She wasn't talking about the amount of skin on show, but she gave up trying to explain what she meant.

But Raul hadn't been lost in translation—he had deliberately played vague.

He had heard Maurice's reprimand yesterday morning and knew colour was not a feature in her life.

Till today.

And so he had played it down.

He had told her to sit, as if blonde beauties in sexy red dresses wearing red high heels regularly walked out of the bedroom of his plane.

Actually, they did.

But they had never had him reaching for his phone and calling in a favour from Silvio, a friend.

Raul had been toying with the idea all afternoon…wondering if it would be too much.

But then he had seen her. Stunning in red. Shy but brave. And if Lydia had let loose for tonight, then so too would he.

'Where are we going?' Lydia asked.

'Just leave all that to me.'

Last time she'd been in Venice there had been strict itineraries and meeting points, but this time around there was no water taxi to board. Instead their luggage was loaded onto a waiting speedboat, and while Raul spoke with the driver Lydia took a seat and drank in the gorgeous view.

Then she became impatient to know more, because the island they were approaching looked familiar.

'Tell me where we're going.'

'To Murano.'

'Oh.' Just for a second her smile faltered. Last time Lydia had been there she had felt so wretched.

'Sometimes it is good to go back.'

'*You* don't, though,' Lydia pointed out, because from everything she knew about Raul he did all he could not to revisit the past.

'No, I don't.'

She should leave it, Lydia knew, and for the moment she did.

There was barely a breeze as their boat sliced through the lagoon. Venice could never disappoint. Raul had been right. It heightened the emotions, and today Lydia's happiness was turning to elation.

In a place of which she had only dark memories suddenly everything was bright, and so she looked over to him and offered a suggestion.

'Maybe you should go back, Raul.'

He did not respond.

They docked in Murano, the Island of Bridges, and Raul took her hand to help Lydia off the boat. The same way as he had last night in Rome, he didn't let her hand go.

And in a sea of shorts and summer tops and dresses Lydia *was* overdressed.

For once she cared not.

They walked past all the showrooms and turned down a small cobbled street. Away from the tourists there was space to slow down and just revel in the feel of the sun on her shoulders.

'I know someone who has a studio here,' Raul said.

He did not explain that often in the mornings Silvio was at Raul's favourite café, and they would speak a little at times. And neither did he explain that he had taken Silvio up on a long-standing offer—'If you ever want to bring a friend…'

Raul had never envisaged that he might.

Oh, he admired Silvio's work—in fact his work had been one of the features that had drawn Raul to buy his home.

He had never thought he might bring someone, though, and yet she was so thrilled to be here, so lacking in being spoilt…

'Silvio is a master glassmaker,' Raul explained. 'He comes from a long line of them. His work is commissioned years in advance and it's exquisite. There will be no three-legged ponies to tempt you.'

And Lydia had never thought she could smile at that memory, yet she did today.

'In fact there is nothing to buy—there is a waiting list so long that he could never complete it in his lifetime. People say that to see him work is to watch the sun being painted in the sky. All we have to do this evening is enjoy.'

'You've never seen him work?'

'No.'

But that changed today.

It was the great man himself who opened a large wooden door and let them in. The place was rather nondescript, with high ceilings and a stained cement floor, and in the middle was a large furnace.

Silvio wore filthy old jeans and a creased shirt and he was unshaven, yet there was an air of magnificence about him.

'This is Lydia,' Raul introduced her.

'Welcome to Murano.'

'She has been here before,' Raul said. 'Though the last time it was on a school trip.'

The old man smiled. 'And did you bring home a souvenir?'

'A vase.' Lydia nodded. 'It was for my mother.'

'Did she like it?'

Lydia was about to give her usual smile and nod, but then she stood there remembering her mother's air of disdain as she had opened the present.

'She didn't seem to appreciate it,' Lydia admitted.

It had hurt a lot at the time.

All her savings and so much pain had gone into the purchase, and yet Valerie had turned up her nose.

But Silvio was looking out of the windows.

'I had better get started. The light is getting low,' he explained.

'Too low to work?' Lydia asked.

'No, no…' He smiled. 'I do very few pieces in a fading light. They are my best, though. I will get some coffee.'

Silvio headed to a small kitchenette and Lydia wandered, her heels noisy on the concrete floor.

There was nothing to see, really, nor to indicate brilliance—nothing to pull her focus back from the past.

'My mother hated that vase,' Lydia told Raul as she wandered. 'She ended up giving it to one of the staff as a gift.' God, that had hurt at the time, but rather than bring down the mood Lydia shrugged. 'At least it went to practical use rather than gathering dust.'

The coffee Silvio had made was not for his guests, Lydia quickly found out. He returned and placed a huge mug on the floor beside a large glass of water, and then she and Raul had the privilege of watching him work.

Molten glass was stretched and shaped and, with a combination of the most basic of tools and impossible skill, a human form emerged.

And then another.

It was mesmerising to watch—as if the rather drab surroundings had turned into a cathedral. The sun streamed in from the westerly windows and caught the thick ribbons of glass. And Lydia watched the alchemy as somehow Silvio formed two bodies, and then limbs emerged.

It was like witnessing creation.

Over and over Silvio twisted and drew out tiny slivers of glass—spinning hair, eyes, and shaping a slender waist. It was erotic too, watching as Silvio formed breasts and then shaped the curve of a buttock.

Nothing was held back. The male form was made with nothing left to the imagination, and the heat in her cheeks had little to do with the furnace that Silvio used to fire his tools and keep the statue fluid.

It was sensual, creative and simply art at its best. Faces formed and pliable heads were carefully moved, and the kiss that emerged was open-mouthed and so erotic that Lydia found her own tongue running over her lips as she remembered the blistering kisses she and Raul had shared.

It was like tasting Raul all over again and feeling the weight of his mouth on hers.

Lydia fought not to step closer, because she didn't want to get in the way or distract Silvio, yet every minuscule detail that he drew from the liquid glass deserved attention. She watched the male form place a hand on the female form's buttock and flushed as if Raul had just touched her there.

Raul was trying not to touch her.

It was such an intimate piece, and personal too, for it felt as if the energy that hummed between them had somehow been tapped.

And then Silvio merged the couple, pulling the feminine thigh around the male loin, arching the neck backwards, and Lydia was aware of the sound of her own pulse whooshing in her ears.

The erotic beauty was more subtle now, the anatomical details conjoined for ever and captured in glass. And then Silvio rolled another layer of molten glass over them, covering the conjoined beauty with a silken glass sheet.

Yet they all knew what lay beneath.

'Now my signature…' Silvio said, and Lydia felt as if she had been snapped from a trance.

He seared his name into the base, and smoothed it till it was embedded, and then it was for Raul and Lydia to admire the finished piece.

'I've never seen anything like it,' Lydia admitted as she examined the statue.

How could glass be sexy? Yet this was a kiss, in solid form, and the intimate anatomical work that had seemed wasted when the forms had been merged was now revealed—she could see the density at the base of the woman's spine that spoke of the man deep within her.

'It's an amazing piece,' Raul said, and Lydia couldn't believe that his voice sounded normal when she felt as if she had only just returned from being spirited away.

'There are more…' Silvio said, and he took them through to another area and showed them several other pieces.

As stunning as they all were, for Lydia they didn't quite live up to the lovers' statue. Perhaps it was because she had witnessed it being made, Lydia mused as they stepped back out into the street.

It was disorientating.

Lydia went to head left, but Raul took her hand and they went right and he led her back to the speedboat.

The driver had gone, on Raul's instruction, and it was he who drove them to San Marco.

Raul took great pride in showing her around this most seductive of cities.

They wandered through ghostly back streets and over bridges.

'It's so wonderful to be here,' Lydia said. 'It was all so rushed last time, and it felt as if we were just ticking things off a list.'

'And the obligatory gondola ride?' Raul said, but her response surprised him.

'No.' Lydia shook her head. 'Some of the girls did, but…' She stopped.

'But?'

'Sitting on the bus with the teacher was bad enough. I think a gondola ride with her would have been worse somehow.'

She tried to keep it light, as Raul had managed to when

they had been talking about her lonely school trip in Rome. She didn't quite manage it, though.

Raul, who had been starting to think about their dinner reservation, steered her towards the canal.

'Come on,' he said. 'You cannot do Venice without a gondola ride.'

Till this point Raul had, though.

Raul's usual mode of transport was a speedboat.

But there was nothing like Venice at sunset from a gondola, as both found out together.

The low boat sliced gently through the water and the Grand Canal blushed pink as the sun dipped down. He looked over as she sighed, and saw Lydia smiling softly as she drank it all in.

'You don't take photos?' Raul observed.

'My phone's flat,' Lydia said, but then admitted more. 'I'm not one for taking photos.'

'Why not?'

He was ever-curious about her—something Raul had never really been before.

'Because when it's gone it's gone,' Lydia said. 'Best to move on.'

The gondolier took them through the interior canals that were so atmospheric that silence was the best option.

It was cool on the water, and there were blankets they could put over their knees, but she accepted Raul's jacket.

The silk was warm from him, and as she put it on he helped her. The only reason he had not kissed her before was because he'd thought it might prove impossible to stop.

But Raul was beyond common sense thinking now—and so was she.

He took her face in his hands and he looked at her mouth—the lipstick was long gone.

'I want you,' he told her.

'And you know I want you.'

Lydia did.

His mouth told her just how much he wanted her. She watched his eyelids shutter, and then he tasted her. Lydia did the same. She felt the soft weight of him and her mouth opened just a little as they flirted with their tongues. There was tenderness, promise and building passion in every stroke and beat. Yet even as they kissed she cared for the view, and now and then opened her eyes just for a glimpse, because it was like spinning circles in a blazing sky.

His hand slipped inside the jacket. First just the pad of his thumb caressed her breast, and then—she had been right—the dress drew his attention down.

His hand was on her stomach, just lingering, and Lydia felt his warm palm through the fabric. Her breathing stilled and he felt the change and pulled her closer, to taste and feel more.

They sailed under ancient bridges and he kissed her knowingly. So attuned were they no one would guess they weren't lovers yet.

There was just the sound of the gondolier's paddle and the taste of passion.

She was on fire, and yet he made her shiver.

Soon Raul knew the gondolier would turn them around, for the canal ended soon. They were about to pass under the Bridge of Sighs and the bells of St Mark's Campanile were tolling.

Which meant, according to legend, that if they kissed they would be granted eternal love and bliss.

Which Raul did not want.

But their mouths made a fever—a fever neither wanted to break—and anyway he didn't believe in legends.

They pulled their mouths apart as the gondolier turned them around, but their foreheads were still touching.

Lydia was breathless and flushed, and though Raul had

made so many plans for her perfect Venetian night he could wait no more.

They should be stopping soon for champagne, and then a canalside dinner at his favourite restaurant. Except his hand was back between them, stroking her nipple through velvet, and her tongue was more knowing.

His best-laid plans were fading.

Lydia pulled her mouth back, but he kissed her cheek and moved his lips towards her ear, and his jaw was rough and delicious, and his hand on her breast had her suddenly desperate.

'Raul…' Lydia said.

Oh, she said his name so easily now.

And he knew her so much more, because there was a slight plea in her voice and it matched the way he felt.

He pulled back his own mouth, only enough to deliver the gondolier an instruction.

The sky was darker as they kissed through the night, and soon they were gliding back towards the Grand Canal, and now Raul wished for an engine and the speed of his own boat.

The gondolier came to a stop at a water door and said something. It took a moment for Lydia to register that they had stopped and so had the kiss. Realising that she was being spoken to, she looked around breathlessly, staring up at yet another *palazzo* and trying to take in her surroundings.

'It's beautiful!' Lydia said, trying to be a good tourist while wishing they could get back to kissing.

Raul smiled at her attempt to be polite when she was throbbing between the legs.

'It's even more beautiful inside,' Raul told her. 'This is my home.'

Lydia almost wept in relief.

He got out first and took her by the hand, and then pushed open the dark door.

She entered his home an innocent.

Lydia would not be leaving it the same.

CHAPTER NINE

THROUGH THE ENTRANCE and into an internal elevator they went, but Lydia prayed there would be no fire in the night, for she did not take in her surroundings at all—their kisses were frantic and urgent now.

His body was hard against hers, and his hands were a little rough as Raul fought with himself not to hitch up her dress.

The jolt of the old elevator was barely noted—there was just relief that they could get out.

They almost ran.

Raul took her hand and led her with haste through a long corridor lined with ancient mirrors and lit with white pillar candles.

And at the end, as if she were looking through a keyhole, there was the reward of open wooden doors that revealed a vast bed.

She would wake up soon, Lydia was sure.

She would wake up from this sensual dream.

Yet she did not.

There were colours that rained on the walls and the bed, yet she was too into Raul to look for their source.

And was she scared?

No.

Shy?

Not a bit.

Raul stripped, and then no words were needed, no instruction required, as naked, erect, he dealt with her dress.

Lydia held up her hair as he unzipped her.

She shook as he removed the dress, then her bra.

And she moaned as he knelt to remove first her shoes and then the final garment between them.

Raul slid the silk down and probed her with his tongue. Lydia stood and knotted her fingers in his hair, and as Raul gently eased in two fingers, though it hurt, it was bliss.

She parted her legs as he licked and stretched her, and ensured she was oiled at the same time.

He turned away from her then, reaching for the bedside table.

'You're on the Pill?'

Lydia nodded, a touch frantic. She wanted no pause for she needed him inside her.

Lydia had the rest of her life to be sensible and behave.

Just this night.

He took her to his bed and they knelt upon it, kissing and caressing each other. Gliding their hands over each other's body. His muscled and taut…hers softer. They recreated the scene from earlier, at the glassblower's, because it had felt at the time as if they were watching themselves.

'Since we met…' Raul said, and kissed her arched neck.

And her breasts ached for him, but not as much as between her legs.

His erection was pressed against her stomach, nudging, promising, and he wanted to take her kneeling but was aware that it was her first time, and he had felt how tight she was with his fingers.

Raul tried to kiss her into lying down so that he could take things slowly.

She resisted.

And he was glad that she did.

He raised her higher, hooked her leg around him and held himself. And she rested her arms over his shoulders and then lowered herself.

A little.

It hurt, but it was the best hurt.

Raul's eyes were open, and they were both barely breathing, just focused on the bliss they felt.

'Since we met…' he said again, and his voice was low, rich and smoky.

And she lowered herself a little more, and he felt her, tight and hot.

She wanted him so badly but could not see that last bit through. 'Raul…'

There was a plea in her voice again, and he heeded it and took control and thrust hard.

Lydia sobbed as he seared into her. Everything went black, and not just because she'd screwed her eyes closed. She thought she might faint, but he took her hips and held her still and waited as best he could for her to open her eyes.

They opened, and she thought she would never get used to it—ever—but then her breathing evened. And when she opened her eyes again, as she had on the canal, this time they met his.

Raul's hand went to the very base of her spine. His touch was sensual and she moved a little, slowly, acclimatising to the feel of him within her.

She was sweaty and hot as his hands moved to her buttocks and he started to thrust.

'Raul…'

She wanted him to slow down, yet he *was* moving slowly.

And then Lydia wanted him never to stop.

Pain had left and in its place was a craving, an intense desire for more of what built within.

His hands had guided her into rhythm, but now she found her own. And it was slower than they could account for, for their bodies were frantic, but they relished the intense pleasure. Raul felt the oiled and yet tight grip of her, and each thrust brought him deeper into the mire, to savour or release. Lydia was lost to sensation. His breath in her ear was like music as it combined with the energies concentrated within her.

Her calf ached, but she did not have the will to move it, and then her inner thighs tensed as she parted around him.

The centre of her felt pulled so tight it was almost a spasm, and then she was lost for control and he held her still. And then, when she had thought he could fill her no more, Raul swelled and thrust—rapid and fast.

Lydia screamed, just a little, but it was a sound she had never made before and it came from a place she had never been.

Her legs coiled tight around him, her body hot and pulsing as he filled her.

'Since we met,' he said as she rested her head on his shoulder and felt the last flickers of their union fade, 'I've wanted you.'

'And I you,' Lydia said, for it was the truth.

And then he kissed her down from what felt like the ceiling.

'Res…' Raul said, and then halted and changed what he had been about to say. 'Rest.'

And she lay there in his arms, silent.

Lydia knew there could be no going back from what had just taken place.

And it had nothing to do with innocence lost.

How the hell did she go back to her life without him?

CHAPTER TEN

A GORGEOUS CHANDELIER, creating prisms of light in every shade of spring, was the first thing Lydia saw when she awoke.

There was a long peal of bells ringing out in the distance, but it was a closer, more occasional, deep, sonorous chime that held her attention. It rang low, soft and yet clear, till the sound slowly faded. When it struck again she remembered gliding underneath the Bridge of Sighs with his kiss.

Lydia knew the legend.

She had stood by the bridge with one of her school friends and struck it from her study sheet.

Eternal love and bliss had not applied to her then and it could not now, Lydia knew.

And so she stared up instead and remembered her vow to not show the hurt when it ended.

Pinks, lemons and minty greens dotted the ceiling, and she saw that the beads were actually flowers that threw little prisms of light across the room.

He was awake.

Stretching languorously beside her.

Lydia relished the moment.

His hand slid to her hips and pulled her closer, and rather than ponder over the fact that soon she would be gone, Lydia chose to keep things light.

'I never pictured you as a man who might have a chandelier in the bedroom.'

Raul gave a low laugh.

He was a mystery, but not hers to solve, and so she did her best to maintain a stiff upper lip.

'A floral chandelier at that,' Lydia added. Her eyes could

not stop following the beams of light. 'Though I have to say it's amazing.'

'It drives me crazy,' Raul admitted. 'When I first moved in I considered having it taken down, or changing the master bedroom, but the view of the canal is the best from here.'

'Oh, you can't have it taken down,' Lydia said.

'Easy for you to say. I feel like I am having laser surgery on my eyes some mornings.'

Lydia smiled and carried on watching the light show.

She never wanted to move.

Or rather she did, but only to the beat of their lovemaking.

His hand was making circles on her stomach and he was hard against her thigh.

Lydia didn't want to check the time just to find out how little time they had left.

'I love your home.'

'You haven't really seen it.'

And she was about to throw him a line about how she could live in just his bedroom for ever, but it would come out wrong, she knew.

He watched the lips he had been about to kiss press together.

Raul saw that.

Then he thought of what he'd been about to say last night.

Restare.

Stay.

He should be congratulating himself for not making such a foolish mistake by uttering that word last night.

Yet the feeling was still there.

And so Raul, far safer than making love to her, as he wanted to, told her how he had come by his home.

'There is a café nearby that I go to. I sometimes see Silvio there, and we chat. On one occasion he told me that this *palazzo* had come on the market. He was not interested in purchasing it but had been to view it as some of his early work was inside.'

I don't care, Lydia wanted to say. *I want to be kissed.*

Yet she did care.

And she did want to know about his home and how he had come by it.

She wanted more information to add to the file marked 'Raul Di Savo' that her heart would soon have to close.

And his voice was as deep as that occasional bell and it resonated in every cell of her body.

She wanted to turn her mouth to feel his, but she lay listening instead.

'Half a century ago it underwent major refurbishment. Silvio made all the internal door handles with his grandfather. But it was the chandelier in the master bedroom that he really wanted to see.'

And now they both lay bathed in the dancing sunbeams of the chandelier as he told its tale.

'It was created by three generations of Silvio's family, long before he was born. I knew that I had to see it, so I called Allegra to arrange a viewing, and then, when I saw it, I had to own it.'

'I can see why.' Lydia sighed. 'I'm back in love with Venice.'

And then she said it.

'I never want to leave.'

It was just what people said at the end of a good trip, Raul knew, but silence hung in the air now, the bells were quiet, and it felt as if even the sky awaited his response.

He needed to think—away from Lydia. For the temptation was still there to say it, to roll into her and make love to her and ask her to remain.

It was unfamiliar and confusing enough for Raul to deal with, let alone her. And so he tried to dismiss the thought in his head that refused to leave.

And Raul knew that Lydia needed her heart that was starting to soar to be reined in.

'People love their holidays,' Raul said. 'I know that. I study it a lot in my line of work. But there is one thing I have consistently found—no matter how luxurious the surroundings, or how fine the cognac, no matter how much my staff do everything they can to ensure the very best stay…' he could see tears sparkle in her eyes and he had never once seen her even close to crying before '…at the end of even the most perfect stay most are ready to go back to their lives.'

'Not always.' Lydia fought him just a little.

And they *both* fought to keep the conversation from getting too heavy, but they were not discussing holidays—they both knew that.

'I know,' Lydia persisted, 'that when I've had a really good holiday I want more of it…even just a few more days…' She lied, and they both knew it, because Lydia had never had a really good holiday, but he kept to the theme.

'Then that means it was an exceptional trip—a once-in-a-lifetime experience. A guest should always leave wanting more.'

He saw her lips turn white at this relegation and tempered it just a little as he told her they could never be. 'I'll tell you something else I have found—if people do return to that treasured memory it is never quite the same.'

'No.' Lydia shook her head.

'True,' Raul insisted. 'We have couples come back for their anniversary and they complain that the hotel has changed, or that the waterways are too busy, or that the restaurant they once loved is no longer any good… And I know they are wrong, that my hotel has got better since they were there and that the restaurant retains its standard. I know that the waterways of Venice are ever beautiful. It is the couple who have changed.'

'How arrogant of you to assume your guests have no cause for complaint.'

'They don't.'

And as she fought for her belief that all things might be possible, that their slice of time might lead to more, his words thwarted her.

'Why risk spoiling something wonderful?' Raul asked, but when Lydia didn't answer he lay there asking himself the same thing.

Why would he even risk suggesting that she stay?

But didn't guests extend their stays all the time?

Only Lydia wasn't a guest.

He climbed from the bed and attempted to get life back to normal.

'I'm going out for a little while,' Raul told her. 'I'll bring back breakfast.'

Only 'normal' seemed to have left—for Raul never brought back breakfast, and he certainly didn't eat it in bed.

But he had made plans yesterday when she had walked out in that dress. He had sworn to give her the best of Venice, and now it was time to execute that plan.

Then things could get back to normal—once she had gone his head would surely clear.

Lydia, he decided, *wasn't* a guest—she was in fact a squatter who had taken over his long-abandoned heart.

'You'd better call soon to transfer your flight.'

'I will,' Lydia said, glad that he was going out for breakfast. She just needed the space, for the air between them had changed. And she was cross with Raul that he should be able to see her off on a plane after the time they had shared.

And he was cross that he was considering otherwise—that he was *still* considering asking her to stay.

Raul shot her an angry glance as she watched him dress, but she didn't see it. Lydia was too busy watching as he pulled on black jeans over his nakedness.

He looked seedy and unshaven, and he was on the edge of hardening again, and she fought not to pull up her knees as lust punched low in her stomach.

He pulled on black boots, although it was summer, and then turned to reach for his top. She saw the nail marks on his scarred back and the injury toll from yesterday started to surface.

She was starting to feel sore.

Deliciously so.

'Go back to sleep,' Raul suggested.

He went to walk out, but his resident squatter did what she always did and niggled at his conscience. And so, rather than stalk out, he went over and bent down and gave her a kiss.

They were arguing, Lydia knew.

And she *liked* it.

His jaw scratched as he fought with himself to remove his mouth and get out, and then her tongue was the one to part his lips.

And that perfunctory kiss was no more.

Hellcat.

She made him *want*.

He was dressed and kneeling on the bed, kissing her hard, and she was arching into him.

His hand was rough through the sheet, squeezing her breast hard, and she wanted him to whip the sheet off.

Her hand told the back of his head that.

Lydia wanted him to unzip himself and to feel rough denim.

And so he stopped kissing her and stood.

Raul liked her endless wanting.

And he liked it that he wanted to go back to bed.

And *that* was very concerning to him.

Yes, he needed to think.

'Why don't you go back to sleep?' Raul suggested again, his voice even and calm, with nothing to indicate the passion he was walking away from.

Apart from the bulge in his jeans.

She gave a slightly derisive laugh at the suggestion that she might find it possible to sleep as he walked to the door.

Raul took the elevator down and, as he always did on a Sunday, drove the speedboat himself. He took it slowly. The sky was a riot of pink and orange, and there was the delicious scent of impending rain hanging heavily in the air.

Her gift would be arriving soon, and Raul badly needed some time alone to think.

Restare.

Stay.

He had almost said it out loud last night but had held back, worried that he might regret it in the light of day. Yet the light was here and the word was still there, on the tip of his tongue and at the front of his thoughts.

Usually he would take breakfast at his favourite café and sit watching the world go by, or on occasion chat with a local such as Silvio.

Not this morning.

He wanted to be home.

On a personal level Raul had never really understood the pleasure of breakfast in bed. He always rose early and, whether home or away, was dressed for the first coffee of the day and checking emails before it had even been poured.

On a business level Raul had both examined and profited from it. There was a lovers' breakfast served at his hotel here in Venice, and a favourite on the menu was the *baci in gondola*—sweet white pastry melded with dark chocolate.

Raul was at his favourite café and ordering them now—only this time he was asking them to be placed in one of their trademark boxes and tied with a red velvet ribbon.

It was to be a true lovers' breakfast, because he did not want maids intruding, and he wanted his coffee stronger and sweeter than usual today.

Raul wore the barista's eye-roll when he also asked for English Breakfast Tea.

'Cinque minute, Raul,' the waitress told him.

Five minutes turned into seven, and he was grateful for the extra two, but even when they had passed still the thought remained.

Restare.

He wanted a chance for them.

Lydia lay, half listening to the sounds of Venice on a Sunday morning, and thought of their lovemaking.

It was still too close to be called a memory.

Yet it would be soon.

Unless she changed her flight times.

What if she told him she couldn't get a flight out of Venice until tomorrow?

Lydia got out of bed and pulled on a robe and found her phone. Even as she plugged it in to charge it Lydia knew she was breaking the deal they had made—simply to walk away.

Only it wasn't that simple.

This felt like love.

It was infatuation, Lydia scolded herself.

He was the first person who had shown an interest…

Only that wasn't so.

There had been others, but she had chosen to let no one in.

'Signorina...'

There was a knock at the door and Lydia opened it and smiled at the friendly face of a maid, who said her name was Loretta.

'You have a delivery.'

'Me?' Lydia checked. 'But no one knows that…' And

then her voice trailed off, because the name on the box was indeed hers, and as she took it Lydia felt its weight.

There were stickers saying 'Fragile' all over the box and Lydia was trying to reel herself in.

The word was the same in both Italian and English, and she wanted to peel the stickers off and place them on herself.

She was too fragile for this much hope.

Lydia took the box out to the balcony to open it.

It didn't matter that it had started to rain. She needed air, she truly did, because as she peeled back layers of tape and padding, the hopes she had been trying not to get up soared, for there, nestled in velvet, was the art they had seen made.

It was exquisite.

Dark gold it was shot through with colour, red and crimson, and she ran her fingers along the cool glass and recalled the way Raul had held her last night.

It was more than a gift, and far more than the once-promised morning-after present, surely—it felt like a diary of *them*.

The kisses and caresses…the oblivion they had found… the melding of two bodies. It was the most beautiful thing she had ever seen, let alone been given.

How could she even hope to hold on to her heart? Lydia thought, and then she looked out on the canal and there he was, steering the boat with ease, the man she loved.

Loved.

Her own admission scared her.

Raul didn't want her love.

She felt that if he so much as looked up he might read her, so Lydia gathered the box and the statue and went back into the room and attempted to reel herself in.

It was a gift.

An exceptionally generous gift.

It didn't necessarily mean that he felt the same and she had to remember that.

She was trying to hold on to that thought so hard that when her phone rang, unthinkingly Lydia took the call.

'You fool.'

That was how Maurice greeted her, and Lydia pulled the phone back from her ear, about to turn it off, because she refused to let him ruin this day.

But, having called her a fool, Maurice then asked her a question.

'What the hell are you doing with Raul Di Savo?' Maurice asked.

'That's not your concern.'

He'd never told her his surname, though she had seen it on the business card he had given her.

More concerning was how Maurice had known. But, unasked, he told her. 'There are pictures of the two of you all over the Net.'

'Us?'

'Have you *any* idea of the fire you're playing with? He's using you, Lydia.'

That much she knew wasn't true.

Lydia looked at the statue he had bought her, the most beautiful gift ever given, and she recalled not just Raul's touch but how even without words he made her feel good about herself.

Even if their time was to be fleeting, for once in her life someone had truly liked her.

That was the real gift.

'He isn't *using* me,' Lydia sneered, utterly confident in that statement.

She had gone willingly, after all.

And then everything changed.

'He just wants to get at Bastiano.'

She was so sick of hearing that man's name. 'What the

hell does Bastiano—' And she stopped, for in that second Lydia answered her own question.

Even before Maurice told her outright, Lydia already knew.

'They were friends until Bastiano had an affair with his mother. Raul has sworn to make him pay slowly… Screwing you was mere revenge.'

Hope died silently, Lydia found out as she stood there.

No protest.

No flailing.

For Maurice's filthy term matched her thoughts.

She *had* been screwed.

It made sense.

Well, better sense than that she might ever be loved for herself.

She ended the call and looked for the photos Maurice had alluded to. Her heart was thumping…she knew that soon Raul would be back.

There was only one photo she could find—they were in that Rome café, drenched in the morning sun, and he was holding her hand.

She had been innocent then.

And Lydia wasn't thinking about sex.

She had been innocent of the level of hurt he might cause, for she had sworn she would let no one close ever again.

Oh, she was a fool—for she had.

So, *so* close.

Lydia wanted to retch as she thought of their lovemaking, and she held in a sob as she had a sudden vision of herself coming undone under his expert ministrations.

Had he been laughing on the inside?

Everything was tainted black.

Her phone rang again, and Lydia saw that it was Arabella.

She must have seen the photos.

Lydia was no doubt popular now.

'Hey…' Arabella said. 'When are we going to catch up? How about tonight?'

'I can't make it.'

'Well, soon?'

'No, thank you.'

'When, then?'

'I've got to go.'

Lydia gave no reason.

Raul had taught her that much at least.

She ended the call and ran to the balcony and stood there dragging in air and trying to fathom how to face the man who had destroyed her.

Would he be like Arabella and barely flinch when he found he'd been caught out?

All her confidence was shredded.

She was no butterfly emerging, Lydia knew, but a dragonfly.

Didn't they spread their wings for just one day?

Her wings were gone now, torn and stripped, and it hurt to be bare.

She stood clutching the stone balcony in the rain and wondered if she had time to pack and get out. But it was too late. She looked down and saw the empty speedboat and knew he must be on his way up.

Leaving without tears, leaving with pride, wasn't just a wish but an imperative now—Raul must *never* know the hurt he had caused her, Lydia vowed.

Not one tear would she give him.

She would have been better off with Bastiano!

At least there she had known the score.

A whore, albeit with a ring on her finger.

And then it came to her—Lydia knew how to hurt Raul now.

CHAPTER ELEVEN

'HEY...'

She turned and saw him. His hair was wet, and had she not found out, Lydia knew they would have been naked soon.

Why did he have to be so beautiful?

How she wished there had been just another day till she'd found out.

'Why are you standing in the rain?' Raul asked.

'I was just taking in the view before I go.'

'About that...'

'I called and they can transfer my flight, but I have to leave soon.'

'You don't.' Raul shook his head. He had a jet on call, after all, but more than that he wanted to say it.

Stay.

'Come and have breakfast and we can talk.'

'No, thanks,' Lydia said, and she wondered herself how she did it, because she actually managed to smile.

She had at her father's funeral as she had thanked the guests for coming.

And she had smiled at Arabella that awful day in Murano as she had purchased the vase.

No one knew her, and now she would make sure no one ever did.

Yes, her innocence was gone.

In every sense.

'I have a lot to sort out, Raul. I need to get home and face things.'

'I know that, but it can wait a few days. Come inside—I brought breakfast.'

And Lydia knew she wasn't that good an actress. She could not lie in bed and eat. And so she shook her head. 'I need to go, Raul.'

He kissed her to change her mind.

And she let him.

Desperate for the taste of him just one more time.

He nudged with his hips, he cajoled with his tongue, and he nearly won.

'Come on.'

He led her inside, but instead of going to bed Lydia reached for her case and placed it on the bed and started to pack.

'I don't get why you're leaving,' Raul said. He did not understand her mood.

'Wasn't it you who said I don't need to give an excuse or a reason?'

Indeed it had been.

And so he watched as she put the red shoes into the case, and the underwear he had peeled off last night, and selected fresh for today.

Her robe was clinging and her nipples were thick, and Lydia, as she went and unplugged her phone, did not understand how she could both hate and want.

'Can we talk?' Raul said.

'And say what?' Lydia asked, and there was strain to her voice.

'I don't want you to leave yet.'

A few moments ago she would have knelt at his feet for those words, now she turned angrily.

'Oh, sorry—were you hoping for a morning shag because you bought me a statue?'

Oh, it wasn't her wings growing back—it was nails. Thick steel nails that shot out like armour.

'Raul, thank you so much for your hospitality. I had a wonderful time.'

'That's it?'

And she did know how to hurt him!

'I think we both know I was never going to be leaving Italy a virgin. It was you or Bastiano. I chose you.'

He stood there silent, Raul did not ask why, yet Lydia answered as if he had.

'Bastiano isn't what I want.'

'And what is?'

'Money.'

'He has that.'

She screwed up her nose. 'I want old money.'

'I see.'

'If I'm to marry for money I'd at least like a title.'

'You're a snob.'

'I have every right to be.'

'And a gold-digger,' Raul said.

'Yes!' Lydia smiled a black smile. 'I'm a snob *and* a gold-digger, and some Sicilian who just made good doesn't really do it for me.'

'You make no sense, given the way you screamed last night.'

'We're talking about Bastiano,' Lydia said. 'As you pointed out—he wanted marriage and a nice trophy wife. I, on the other hand, wanted sex.' She ran a finger along his jaw and taunted him and it felt so good. 'For a one-night stand, you were the far better option. What I *really* want is a gentleman.'

'Well.' He gave a black smile and removed her hand from his face. 'I don't qualify, then.'

'No.'

He dropped all contact, and as she turned and walked away suddenly Lydia wasn't so brave.

As she bent to retrieve her red dress and picked it up from the floor, it felt as if she was waving a flag to a very angry bull, though Raul did not move.

His hackles were up. Raul could fight dirty when he chose—and he was starting to choose to now.

He looked at her slender legs and her hair falling forward and knew she could feel his eyes on her body as she pretended to concentrate on folding the dress as she bent over the open case.

She was pink in the cheeks and her ears were red, and as his eyes took in the curve of her bottom he knew she was as turned on as he was.

Tension crackled between them and she could almost picture his hands pulling up her robe.

It was bizarre.

He made filthy thoughts mandatory, gave anger a new outlet, and she recalled his promise that angry sex could wait.

'You know,' he said, 'once you leave, you're gone. I don't play games, and I don't pursue...'

'I'm not asking you to.'

He walked over—she heard him but did not turn around. She must have folded that dress twenty times when his hand came to her hip. Just a small gesture, almost indicating that she should turn to him, but Lydia resisted.

'Hey, Lydia,' he said, and he bent over her and spoke in that low, calm voice, while hard against her bottom. 'When you find your suitably titled Englishman, don't think of me.'

'I shan't.'

'It would not be fair to him.'

'You really—' She stopped, and she dared not turn around, for now one hand moved to her waist and the other to her shoulder, and there was a desire in Lydia for the sound of his zip, but it never came.

'When you're in bed,' Raul said, and she held on to the bed with cheeks flaming, 'and he says, "Is that nice, darling?" or "Do you like it like that?"' He put on an affected tone. 'Try not to remember that I never needed to enquire.

And,' he added cruelly, 'when you lie there beside him, unsated, and you *do* think of me…'

'I told you—I shan't.'

'Liar.'

He pressed into her one more time and then pulled back and let her go and she straightened up.

She was a bit breathless.

Oh, and still angry.

She pulled off her robe and he did not avert his eyes. He watched as she pulled on knickers, and watched as she put on her bra.

And he watched as she pulled on the taupe dress—the one with the buttons.

Bloody things!

As she struggled to dress he walked over—but not to her. This time he picked up the statue and tossed it into her case.

'I don't want your stupid statue.'

'I thought you were a gold-digger,' he pointed out. 'Sell it.' Raul shrugged. 'Or hurl it out of the window of your turret in frustration when your fingers can't deliver.'

'Oh, *please*,' Lydia sneered. 'You think you're *so* good.'

'No,' Raul said. 'I *know* that we were.'

He did.

For he had never experienced it before—that absolute connection and the erotic bliss they had found last night.

She snapped her case closed and, rather annoyingly, set the security code on the lock.

As she bumped it from the bed he kicked off his boots and got on. Raul lay on the rumpled sheets and reached for his cake box and took out his phone.

She could see herself out, Raul decided.

The private jet was closed.

Lydia stood there for a moment. It was hard making a dignified exit when you didn't know the way out.

'Is there a street entrance?' Lydia asked, and watched as he barely glanced up from his phone.

'Yep.'

Raul opened the box of pastries and selected one, took a bite as he got back to his phone.

Lydia could find it herself.

'You can see yourself out.'

CHAPTER TWELVE

ALL ROADS LED to Rome.

But today Raul hoped that Rome would lead him to Lydia.

Raul could not get her out of his mind.

Disquiet gnawed and unfinished business reared up and he simply could not let it go.

Summer was gone.

As he walked past the café where they had shared breakfast Raul looked up to the dark clouds above and it looked as if the sky had been hung too low.

It had felt like that since Lydia had gone.

Autumn had arrived, and usually it was Raul's favourite time of the year.

Not this one.

He missed her, and Raul had never missed anyone, and he just could not shake off the feeling.

It was something he could not define.

Even if the tourists never really thinned out in Venice, La Serenissima had felt empty rather than serene. Here in Rome the locals were enjoying the slight lull that came with the change. Back in Sicily the vines that threaded the valley would be turning to russet…

Raul never went back.

Not even in his head.

Yet he was starting to now.

Lydia had been right—perhaps he should go back.

If this visit to the Grande Lucia did not work out as he hoped, then Raul would be making his first trip back to Casta since the will had been read.

The doorman nodded as Raul went through the brass

revolving door, and he stood for a moment remembering their brief time there.

But that was not right. It didn't *feel* brief—if anything it was the most examined part of his life.

Lydia was the most contrary person he knew.

Cold and guarded…warm and intense.

And, although they had both agreed to a one-night stand, he still could not make sense of that morning.

That kiss before he had left to get breakfast had held promise, but Raul had returned to a stranger and he *had* to know why.

But he didn't even know her surname.

Raul knew some of the darkest most intimate parts of Lydia, and yet her full name he did not know.

Nor where she lived.

Usually those details did not matter to him.

Oh, but they did now.

He had searched, and so had Allegra.

There were a surprising number of castles in England, and there were many that were used for weddings.

They had got nowhere.

Allegra was working her way through them all and had flown over to England three times.

And now Raul was in Rome.

Back at the Grande Lucia, where it had all started.

Now that Raul was showing no interest in purchasing the hotel he was having trouble getting through to Sultan Alim.

And so he was here in person.

But trouble remained in the shape of the young receptionist.

'Sultan Alim is only available by appointment.'

'Call and tell him that Raul Di Savo is here.'

'As I said, he only sees people by appointment. We don't disturb him with phone calls.'

She was as snooty and as immutable as he demanded that Allegra should be if someone—anyone—tried to invade Raul's time.

'Is he even in the country?' Raul asked, but that information was off-limits.

'He would prefer that we do not discuss his movements. I shall let him know you were here.'

Now what?

Did he sit in the foyer and wait for a royal sultan who might already be back in the Middle East? Or warn the poor receptionist that if she valued her job she should let Alim know…

And then Raul saw someone who might be able to help.

She was walking through the foyer carrying a huge display of roses.

Gabi.

The indiscreet wedding planner!

'Hey,' Raul said.

'Hi.'

He had forgotten how to flirt—even for gain.

'Gabi?'

'Oh!' She stopped. 'You were in the ballroom when Alim…' Her voice trailed off.

There had been something going on that afternoon. Raul knew it. He hadn't given it much thought until now.

'I'm hoping to meet with him.'

'Good luck!' Gabi rolled her eyes. 'He's back home.'

'Oh!'

'For his wedding.'

'I see.'

'I'm planning it, actually.'

She looked as if she were about to cry.

'Can you let him know I need to speak with him?'

'I'm a wedding planner,' Gabi said. 'I don't get access to the Royal Sultan.'

And neither would he, Raul thought as Gabi flounced off.

So that left Bastiano—and Raul already knew where *he* was.

Casta.

His jet landed at Cosimo airport, and though it was warmer the sky still seemed to be hung too low. Raul put on his shades and transferred to the helicopter he had arranged to take him to the old convent.

To afford the nuns seclusion it had been made accessible only by horse or helicopter.

Of course Raul chose the latter.

The convent was an ancient sprawling building that no one could get to, set on the crest of the valley overlooking the wild Sicilian Strait.

Its inaccessibility made it the perfect retreat, and Raul had to hand it to Bastiano for his foresight.

Not that he would admit that.

Raul boarded the helicopter and saw his orders had been followed. There was a bunch of lilies there, which, after meeting with Bastiano, he would take to Maria's grave.

He would arrive unannounced.

Raul had sworn never to return.

Only for Lydia he did.

It would be kinder, perhaps, not to look out of the helicopter window and at first he chose not to. The last time he had been home it had been on a commercial flight and then a frantic taxi ride to the valley.

Raul had been eighteen then, and he recalled the taxi driver asking him to pay the fare in advance before agreeing to take him.

Different times.

Same place.

He looked, and the view was starting to become familiar. Even if he had never seen it from this vantage point, the lie of this land was etched on the dark side of his soul.

There were the fields that the Contis and Di Savos had fought over for generations, and yet the wine had never made either family their fortune—and Raul's palate now knew it never would.

His stomach turned in on itself, and it had nothing to do with the sudden banking of the chopper, more the view of the schoolyard, and beyond it to what had been his family home.

He could hear his childish lies to his father.

'Mamma has been here all day.'

Or…

'I think she went to breakfast with Loretta.'

And now perhaps he understood why Lydia did not take photos, for there were memories you did not want to see.

Raul hadn't lied just to save himself.

He had lied to cover for his mother.

Over and over and over.

And then he recalled her more cheerful dispositions. When she would sing and start to go out more, and Raul's lies to his father would have to begin again.

There was the church, and to the side the tombstones.

Raul's history stretched beneath him and there was nothing he wanted to see.

But he made himself look.

The ocean was wild and choppy, crashing onto jagged rocks, and then he saw it.

Far from falling into disrepair the old convent now stood proud, and he remembered his mother's tears when it had closed down.

Had it really been her dream?

The chopper landed and Raul climbed out.

He thought Security might halt him, but he walked

across the lush lawn and towards the gateway without confrontation.

There was a sign for Reception and Raul headed towards it. He walked past a fountain and then ignored the bell and pushed open a heavy arched door.

There were downlights—a modern touch that softened the stone walls—and at a desk sat a young woman wearing what looked like a dental nurse's uniform.

'Posso aiutarla?'

With a smile she asked Raul if she could help him.

'Si.' Raul nodded. 'I am here to speak with Bastiano.'

No frown marred her Botoxed brow, but Raul could see the worry in her eyes as she checked the computer, even though her smile stayed in place.

'May I have your name?'

'Raul Di Savo…'

She must be just about due to have her anti-wrinkle injections topped up, for now a line formed between her brow and the smile faded.

Oh, that name—even now—was known in the valley.

'Do you have an appointment?'

'No,' Raul responded. 'He isn't expecting me…'

'On the contrary.'

Bastiano's voice arrived before he did, and Raul looked up as he emerged from the shadows of the archway. A glint of sun captured the scar on his cheek, and Raul thought he looked like the devil himself appearing.

'Bastiano.' Raul didn't even attempt to keep the ice from his voice. 'I would like to speak with you.'

'I rather thought that you might,' Bastiano said, his response equally cool. His indubitable charm would never be wasted on Raul. 'Come this way.'

Raul followed him through the arch and they walked along a cloister that looked down on a quadrangle where a small group were sitting in the afternoon sun, talking. They glanced up at the two dark-suited men, for there was a foreboding energy about them that drew attention.

Even the receptionist had followed, and stood watching as they disappeared into the old refectory.

The darkness was welcome, and the windows were like photo frames, setting off a view of the Sicilian Strait that roared in the distance.

'Take a seat,' Bastiano offered.

It would be churlish to stand, Raul knew, when he was here for a favour, so as Bastiano moved behind his desk Raul sat at the other side.

'There is something I need from you,' Raul said. 'I would have preferred not to just land on you, but you refused to take my calls.'

Bastiano didn't say anything, but Raul saw the smile of triumph that he attempted to contain. Of course he would not take Raul's calls—he would far prefer to witness him beg.

'I didn't return your calls because I don't think I can help you, Raul,' Bastiano answered, and his manicured hand gestured to some papers on the desk before him. 'Alim said you have been trying to reach him. I know how badly you wanted the hotel, but a deal has been reached—the contracts are awaiting my signature.'

Bastiano thought he was here about the Grande Lucia, Raul realised.

But then why *wouldn't* he think that?

A few weeks ago that had been all that had mattered to Raul—acquisitions, pipping Bastiano to the post and amassing the biggest fortune.

'I'm not here about the hotel,' Raul said, and he watched as Bastiano's contained features briefly showed his confusion.

But he righted himself quickly.

'So what is it that you want?'

'You were considering investing in a property in the UK.' Raul attempted to be vague, but it did not work.

'I have many investments there.'

'It was a castle.'

Raul knew the exact second that Bastiano understood the reason for his visit, for now he made no effort to contain his black smile as he spoke. 'I don't recall.'

'Of course you do.' Raul refused to play games. 'If you could give me the details I would be grateful.'

'I don't require your gratitude, though.'

He had been mad to come, Raul realised.

But then mad was how he *had* been of late.

And now he sat in front of his nemesis, asking him for help.

Worse, though, there were other questions he wanted to ask him. Bastiano held some of the keys to his past.

A past Raul did not want to examine.

Yes, this was madness, Raul decided.

No more.

He stood to leave and did not even bother making the right noises, for there was nothing even to pretend to thank Bastiano for.

But as he reached the door Bastiano's voice halted him.

'There is something I want.'

Raul did not turn around and Bastiano continued.

'If you return the ring I'll give you the information.'

Still Raul did not turn around, though he halted. He actually fought not to lean on the door, for he felt as if the air had been sucked out of the room. He was back in the courtroom, staring at that emerald and seed pearl ring and wondering from where it had come.

Gino had given his mother nothing other than a thin gold band that might just as well have been a ball and chain, for in Maria's eyes it had held her to him for life…

Not quite.

She had been unfaithful, after all.

Then Bastiano spoke. 'I gave it to your mother the week before she died. It belongs in my family…'

'Why did you give her the ring?' Raul turned.

'She said that she wanted to leave Casta and be with me. The ring secured our plans.'

'You expect me to believe that you two were in *love*?' Raul sneered.

'I thought so for a while.' Bastiano shrugged. 'It was really just sex.'

Raul was across the room in an instant, and he reached out to upend the table just to get to Bastiano, but somehow the bastard had him halting, for he held out a pen as if it were a knife.

'I want my ring,' Bastiano said.

And the pen in his hand was the only thing preventing Raul from slamming him against the stone wall and exacting his final revenge.

'You'll get it.'

Bastiano wrote down the details, but, as he did, he said something that a few years ago would have had Raul reaching again for his throat.

Now it made Raul feel sick.

'Don't make her a saint, Raul,' Bastiano said. 'She was far from that.'

Raul felt as if his head was exploding as he walked out.

The helicopter's rotors started at the pilot's sight of him and Raul ran across the ground.

It took minutes.

Barely minutes,

And he was standing at his mother's grave.

It should feel peaceful—there was just the sound of birds and the buzzing of his phone—but the roar in his ears remained.

It had never left.

Or rather it had dimmed in the brief time he and Lydia had shared.

Now he turned off his phone, and it felt as if even the birds were silent as he faced the truth.

Bastiano had not been the first affair.

He had been the last.

And there had been many.

Raul had been taught to lie—not just to save himself but to cover for his mother.

He looked back to the convent and remembered her tears when it had closed and her misery. Then he recalled her being more cheerful, when her mood would lift for a while. And while it would make most children happy to see their mother smile, Raul had known that if he were to keep her safe, then the lies had to start again.

Maria Di Savo.

Unhinged, some had called her.

'Fragile' was perhaps a more appropriate word.

At least it was the one Raul chose.

But with more open eyes than the last time he had stood here.

'Rest now,' he said to the stone, and he went to lay the lilies.

But then he divided them into two.

And he turned to the grave of Gino Di Savo.

There was someone he had never considered forgiving—it had been so far from his mind as to be deemed irrelevant.

It was more than relevant now.

Was Gino even his father?

Sixteen and pregnant in the valley would have been a shameful place to be.

Had the younger Gino been kinder?

Had he lived with the knowledge of constant infidelity?

Perhaps Raul would never know.

He understood the beatings more, though.

And maybe there were some respects to be paid.

'Rest now,' Raul said again, and he put the remaining lilies on Gino Di Savo's grave.

CHAPTER THIRTEEN

'IT'S A VERY recent piece.'

The valuation manager had called in the director. And Lydia was starting to get a glimpse of just how valuable the statue was.

'Three months,' Lydia said, but they didn't look over at her.

For the first morning in a very long time Lydia had held down some toast and decided it was time to be practical and deal with things.

Lydia had returned to the castle expecting anger and recrimination, and had been ready to get the hell out.

Instead she'd returned to her mother's devastation.

It wasn't only Lydia who hadn't cried on her father's death.

Valerie too had held it in, and finally the dam had broken.

'I'm sorry!' She had just slumped in a chair and cried. 'I've told him he's never to come back.'

Of all the hurts in Lydia's heart, Maurice didn't rank, and so instead of fighting back or getting out Lydia had done what Raul had done. She'd poured her mother a drink and stayed calm.

She'd been her practical self, in fact, and had put her own hurts aside.

Lydia pulled the castle as a wedding venue and then dealt as best as she could with what was.

There was no money and very little left to sell.

Last week she had suggested that Valerie go and spend some time with her sister.

Lydia needed to be alone.

She was pregnant.

But she did have her mother's practical nature and had decided to find out what the statue was worth.

Not to save the castle.

Raul was right—it would require a constant infusion.

The proceeds of the sale of the statue might at least go towards a deposit on a house.

But then the valuation manager had called for the director and numbers had started to be discussed between the men.

Lydia realised she had far more than a deposit.

In fact she could buy a home.

It was worth that much and very possibly more.

She could provide for her baby and Raul didn't even need to know.

'Are you thinking of the New York auction?' the manager was asking his senior.

'That's a few months off.'

He glanced over to Lydia and offered her an option.

'I have several collectors who would be extremely interested—we could run a private auction. This piece is exquisite.'

And she loved it so.

It was just a piece of glass, Lydia told herself.

There was a reason she didn't take photos—going over old memories hurt too much.

She would be better rid of it, Lydia knew, and yet it was the only thing she had ever loved.

Apart from Raul.

He wasn't a thing—he was a person.

An utter bastard, in fact.

But the statue spoke of a different time, before it had all fallen apart, and Lydia could not stand the thought of letting it go.

Over and over she dissected each moment with him.

At every minute her mind was back there, peeping through the keyhole he had once shown her and seeing them.

Every moment was captured, and yet she had no photos, bar the one of them holding hands that was smeared all over the internet.

Apparently the great Raul did not usually stoop to holding hands, so the press had been interested.

She'd been telling him about her father then.

Confiding in him.

And he had been playing her all along.

All she had of him was this statue.

No, Lydia corrected, in six months' time she would have his baby.

And Raul needed to know.

The director finally addressed her. 'With your permission I'm going to make a few phone calls, and then perhaps we'll be able to see more where we're at.'

'Of course,' Lydia agreed.

And so must she make some calls.

Lydia was shown to a comfortable waiting room that was more like a lounge and offered tea.

'No, thank you,' Lydia said as she took a seat. 'Could you please close the door?'

The door was closed and from her purse Lydia took out the business card he had given her.

It had been three months since Lydia had heard his voice.

The business card had had many outings, but always she'd bailed before completing his number.

Today Lydia held her breath as she was finally put through.

He didn't answer.

It was just a recording—telling her to leave a message. *'Lasciate un messagio...'*

An anti-climax, really, and yet the sound of his voice had her folded over in the chair.

Not because of what she had to say to him, but because of what she wanted to.

That even while she was so terribly angry with him, it was the hurt of not seeing him, not hearing him, not touching him that refused to heal.

She didn't know what to do.

How did you tell a man who would have a baby removed from a restaurant for crying that you were pregnant with his child?

Raul would think she was calling for money.

How could he not, given she had looked him in the eye and *told* him she was a gold-digger?

And a snob.

Oh, she had to play the part now. But she couldn't and so rang off.

Straighten up, she told herself, and reminded herself of the terrible things he had done.

Raul had used her so badly.

He had sunk to such depraved lows and she must always remember that.

Always.

Panic was starting to build, but Lydia took a deep breath and told herself to be practical and deal with things.

So she straightened up in the chair and repeated the call.

'Lasciate un messagio...'

'Raul, this is Lydia.'

She refused to cheapen herself by giving him dates and further details. If Raul was such a playboy that he didn't remember her, then she wasn't going to make things easier for him.

'I'm pregnant.'

She had said it too fast and too soon, Lydia knew that, but better that than to break down.

'I've had a few weeks to get used to the idea, and I'm actually...' She let out her first calm breath—maybe because she'd told him now...maybe because she was speaking the truth. 'I'm fine with it. We'll be fine. The baby and I, I mean.'

And she knew that had sounded too brusque.

'What I'm trying to say is that I'm not calling for support, neither on an emotional nor financial front. We both know you don't do the former, and I've had the statue valued and it covers the latter…'

Not quite.

Yes, no doubt she could squeeze him for half of his billions, but it was not the route she wanted to take. The thought of lawyers and acrimony, of whether or not he believed her, were the last things she wanted.

'If you need to discuss things, then give me a call back.'

Lydia ended the call and sat staring at her phone for a very long time.

His reaction she could not fathom, and, for the first time since arriving back in England, Lydia felt grateful for the distance between them.

He knew now.

CHAPTER FOURTEEN

SHE WAS IN a holding pattern now of her own making.

Awaiting his response.

Once home, Lydia had replaced the statue by her bed.

She had decided that it was not for sale.

Some things *were* more important.

For now.

She did not want to be like her mother, holding on to a castle she could not afford to keep, but she was not going to rush into selling it.

Lydia checked her phone for the hundredth time, but of course it hadn't rung.

So she checked her email to see if anyone had responded to her many job applications.

She'd had one interview at a museum, but there were four other applicants—no doubt all with qualifications.

And she had an interview next week to work at one of their rival wedding venues.

Joy.

Not.

The pregnancy would start to show soon.

Who would want to take her on then?

Lydia opened a window and leant out and looked over the land her mother's family had owned for ever.

The hills to the left and the fields to the right had been sold off some time ago, but if she looked ahead it was still theirs—for now.

And she understood her mother a little better, for she knew it hurt so much to let go.

Lydia heard the low buzz of a helicopter and looked to the sky.

It was a familiar sound in these parts—the well-heeled left for London in the morning and returned in the evening, but usually later than now.

Occasionally there was an air ambulance or a tourist.

Except this helicopter hovered over the castle and the buzzing sound grew louder.

She could see the grass in the meadow moving in the swirl the rotors created.

It was Raul who was descending, Lydia knew.

Not for *her.*

He'd had weeks and months to find *her.*

No, she had dropped the baby bombshell and he had responded immediately.

He was here about their child.

Her breath quickened as he climbed out. He was wearing a dark suit and tie and shades. He looked completely together as he strode across the land with purpose and she watched him.

There was no instinct to hide.

If anything her instinct was to descend the stairs and run towards him, but that would show just how much she had missed him.

Raul didn't need to know that.

And neither would she tell him that she knew about his long-running feud with Bastiano.

Yes, Lydia was far from innocent now.

Knowledge was power, and she would use it wisely.

And she would never reveal how deeply she had loved.

So she did not check her reflection, nor bother to don lip gloss. Instead she descended the circular stairs of the turret and walked through to the main entrance.

Neither did she go through the palaver of making him knock.

The door was heavy, but she opened it with practised

ease. The days of having staff to attend to such things were long since gone.

'Raul...' She hesitated, because unlike her earlier summation she saw he *wasn't* quite so together. There was a grey pallor to his face and his jaw was tense. His eyes remained hidden behind dark shades. 'I wasn't expecting you.'

'Then you don't know me.'

Those words sent a shiver of warning down her spine.

No, she didn't know him—but those words told her the news she had so recently broken to him was being taken very seriously indeed.

'Were you already in England?'

'No.'

Raul had been walking away from the cemetery when he had heard her message.

'Oh...' The speed of his arrival was rapid, but then she had only been privy to his casual use of his private jet but once.

'I'm sorry for the shock.'

'Nobody has died, Lydia.'

Raul was right. It was a pregnancy they were dealing with, after all, not a sudden death, and yet it was surely a shock to a man like him—a confirmed bachelor, a reprobate playboy.

Or maybe not, Lydia mused.

Perhaps he had illegitimate children dotted all over the world, for certainly he seemed to be taking rapid control.

'We need to talk.'

'Of course we do,' Lydia said. 'That's why I called. Come through and I'll make some tea.'

She would take him to the receiving room, Lydia decided. It was a little faded and empty, but it was certainly the smartest room. There she would ask him to take a seat, and then go and make some tea, and then they could calmly discuss...

Fool.

'I don't drink tea, Lydia.'

As she went to walk away his hand closed around the top of her arm, and Lydia actually kicked herself for thinking she could so easily dictate this.

'Coffee, then?'

She received a black smile in response.

'The helicopter is waiting to take us to my jet—we shall discuss this in Venice.'

'Venice?' She shook her head, her attempt to deal with him calmly, disintegrating. 'Absolutely not. We can talk here. My mother is at her sister's and Maurice is gone.'

His features did not soften.

'We can go out for tea if you prefer. If that makes you feel…'

She did not get to finish.

'You think we are going to sit in some quaint café and discuss the future of our child?'

'We could!'

'And what time does this café close?' He watched her jaw clench and then continued. 'We have a lot to sort out, dear Lydia.' The term was without endearment. 'Did you really think you could drop a message like that on my phone and expect us to go out for *afternoon tea*?'

'I thought we could calmly discuss—'

'I am calm.'

He didn't sound it to Lydia.

Oh, his words were calm, but there was an undercurrent, an energy that danced in the grand entrance hall and not even these ancient walls could contain it.

'We shall speak at my home.'

'No!'

'Okay, we'll talk at my office.'

'In Venice?'

'Of course.'

'No.'

'Lydia, what time to you have to be at work tomorrow?' Raul asked, guessing she probably hadn't bothered to get a job.

'That wasn't kind.'

'I'm not here to be kind.'

She glimpsed again his power and knew this man did not fight fair.

He proved it now.

'I thought you said you were leaving home and getting a job...' He gave a black laugh as he looked around. 'But you're still here, and of course you don't need to work now.'

'Raul...' She wanted to take back that gold-digger comment, but it was way, way too late. 'Please listen—it was an accident.'

'Of course it was!'

She could almost taste his sarcasm.

'Lydia, unlike you, I *do* have to work—however, I have set aside an hour tomorrow at eleven for us to start to go through things. If you don't want to fly with me, fine, but can you get yourself there, at least?'

'I'm not going to be there, Raul.'

'Then we do this through lawyers. Text me the name of yours.'

He was done.

Raul was not going to stand there and plead.

His head was throbbing.

The events of today—Bastiano, the revelations about his mother, his father, if Gino had even been his father, and now the fact that he himself was going to be a father...

Hell, Raul wanted a drink.

He did not want to be standing in some draughty old castle, rowing with a woman he wanted—even after the way she had left—to have all over again.

Lydia turned him on.

And, titled or not, he turned *her* on too.

Raul could feel it.

This day might end not in bed but on the floor, two minutes from now.

But sex had got them into this hot mess and it was time for him to get out.

'Lawyer up!' he said, and turned and left.

He was leaving, Lydia knew.

Leaving their baby in the hands of lawyers.

She ran out and grabbed his arm.

'I'll talk to you.'

He looked down at her hand and shook it off, because even minimal contact he could not keep to for long.

'Then go and pack,' Raul told her. 'If you're not ready in five minutes we leave it to the professionals to sort out.'

She packed—though five minutes didn't give her much time. Especially when she wasted two of them by sitting on her bed and wondering what she should do.

She could not bear to go back to Venice.

Yet Lydia knew she had to.

Somehow she had to get past the raw hurt and sort out the future of their child.

He had hurt her so deeply, though.

And he didn't even know.

Just like the jagged wound that ran down Raul's back, just like the savage scar on Bastiano's cheek, her pain ran deep.

She had been used for revenge.

It was a wound that could never properly heal.

And yet Lydia knew she had to be adult and somehow work out terms with this difficult and complex man.

There was the baby to focus on, and she would not be weakened by his undeniably seductive charms. The sexual energy between them had unnerved her—Lydia was still aware of her palm where she had grabbed his arm.

But she dusted her hands together and brushed it off.

No way!

Worried that her mother might return and sell the statue, Lydia wrapped it in a thick jumper and packed it. Trying as she did so to not remember the night when it had been the two of *them* melded and heated. She swore she would not allow herself to lose her head to him again.

No, she would not weaken.

Lydia walked down the steps and he didn't rush to relieve her of her case. Instead he stood impatient at the door.

'Hold on,' she said, and bent down. 'I forgot to lock it.'

'For God's sake!' he said, and went over and took it. 'Come on.'

'Raul…' Lydia stalled. She wanted to make things very clear. 'I'm going to Venice only to discuss the baby.'

'What else would I be bringing you there for?' he asked. 'Lydia, you've had what you wanted from me in the bedroom department.'

'I just want to make it perfectly clear. I don't want—'

'Lydia, let me stop you there,' Raul interrupted her. 'This isn't about your wants—we're going to be discussing our child.'

'Well, let's keep things civil.'

'Civil?' Raul checked. 'I thought you didn't consider me capable.'

'I meant businesslike.'

'That,' Raul responded as they walked to the waiting helicopter, 'I can clearly be.'

'Good.'

He might just as well have painted her gold and handed her a spade as he stalked ahead with her case.

And the last word was his.

'But then, you knew that right from the start.'

CHAPTER FIFTEEN

THERE WAS NO worse place to be lonely than Venice.

And for Lydia that theory was proved again.

Loretta, his housekeeper, walked her along the lovely mirrored hallway, but instead of going straight ahead, Lydia was shown to the right.

She walked along another hallway and through to an apartment within his home. Loretta brought her dinner, and it was served at a polished table on beautiful china, but though her surroundings were gorgeous Lydia ate alone.

Raul, of course, ate out.

Naturally she didn't sleep, and in the morning she spent ages trying to work out what to wear.

It wasn't just that she had no idea what she should wear to a meeting to discuss their child's future. Nothing was a comfortable fit.

Lydia had no choice but to settle for the taupe dress—the one with the buttons. Only now it strained across her breasts.

Instead of undoing a couple of buttons she put on a little cardigan.

It would have to do.

She loathed it that she had been pencilled in as some sixty-minute item on his to-do list.

And she certainly hadn't expected an audience to be in attendance!

But as she walked into the drawing room Raul sat relaxed and chatting with a very beautiful woman.

'This is Allegra,' Raul told her. 'My assistant.'

Lydia, with her hackles already up and perhaps a little

too used to her mother's handling of staff, gave Allegra a cursory nod and then ignored her.

Raul could see that Lydia was uncomfortable and he didn't blame her for that.

He had resisted discussing this at her home and was aware that he had the advantage, so he moved to the first point on his list.

'Would you be more comfortable in a hotel?'

'I don't intend to be staying very long,' Lydia replied coolly. 'The apartment is sufficient.'

Sufficient?

She had a six-room apartment within his home.

But Raul said nothing—just moved to the next point.

'There is a property less than a mile from here that has come onto the market. Allegra has arranged a viewing for you at two today.'

'Why would I need to see a property here?' Lydia asked. 'The baby will be raised in England.'

'But I shall be seeing my baby regularly. I assume you will want to be close when I do? Especially at first.'

'You assume correctly. However…'

But Raul had moved on.

'Allegra is going to look into the hiring of a nanny. It would appear good ones need to be secured early.'

That was an easy one, and Lydia dismissed it with a shake of her head. 'I shan't be hiring a nanny.'

It really annoyed her when Allegra wrote something down, and then she asked Lydia a question in a rich Italian purr.

'Will you want to sit in on the preliminary interviews, or would you prefer I do that and then we discuss the shortlist?'

'I just *said…*' Lydia was responding to Allegra as if she was speaking to a three-year-old with a hearing problem '…that I don't require a nanny.'

'We heard you the first time,' Raul said. 'But *I* need a nanny for the times when the baby is to be with me.'

Lydia, who had been glaring at Allegra, snapped her gaze back to Raul. 'Could we speak alone, please?'

'Of course.'

Allegra stood and walked out. Lydia sat with her back ramrod-straight and said nothing until the door behind her had closed.

Oh, but when it closed!

'You've been busy.'

'Yes,' Raul agreed.

And as she sat there she gleaned the fact that while she'd been eating alone last night Raul had been out to dinner, with Allegra, discussing her baby's future.

Of course he had.

Raul's time was heavily in demand, and a lot of his day-to-day stuff was delegated.

'Do you really think I have time to be wandering around looking at apartments for someone I spent a weekend with three months ago?'

Lydia opened her mouth to respond, but then closed it.

'You wanted businesslike, and you have made it clear you don't want to be in Venice for long, so I discussed things with my assistant…'

'Over *dinner*,' Lydia sneered. 'Have you slept with her?'

Oh, she hated it that she'd asked that—she really did.

'What the hell does that have to do with anything?'

And she hated his exasperated inevitable answer.

'Yes, but that was ages ago.'

And then he asked Lydia again.

'What the hell does that have to do with this?'

And she still couldn't answer, because really it should have *nothing* to do with this—yet it did.

'Lydia, I have a past—quite a colourful one. You really should choose your one-night stands more carefully.'

'I just don't like the fact…'

'Go on,' Raul said when she faltered, and he leant back in his chair to hear what she had to say.

'I don't like the fact that someone you've been intimate with is discussing my future and my baby.'

'*Our* baby.'

'Yes, but…' She tried to get back to the nanny point, because she was starting to sound jealous.

Which she was.

And irrational.

Which she wasn't.

Was she?

'Lydia, Allegra is very happily married.' He was annoyingly patient in his explanation. 'In fact I've already told you that. If you really think she's making bedroom eyes at me and we're still at it, then that's your issue. But we're not. I don't like cheats. Now, can we bring it back to business?'

'*It* is a baby.'

'Che cazzo!' he cursed.

'Don't swear.'

'The baby can't hear me!' Raul said.

'You discuss it so clinically.'

'You told me yourself to keep it businesslike. Come on, Lydia, tell me what you want. You've had three months to get used to the idea. I've had less than twenty-four hours. Tell me what you've decided and we can work from there.'

And she tried to tell him just that.

'There's no need for me to have an apartment here. Of course we'll visit often…'

A smile—a black smile—played on his lips, and she sat back as Raul chose his words.

'And where would you stay?' Raul asked. 'The guest wing?'

As she nodded that dark smile faded.

'Lydia, I don't want my ex, or rather one of my one-night

stands, as a regular guest in my home. I don't want someone who has already said that she disapproves of me dictating the relationship I have with my child.'

'And I don't want my baby to be raised by a nanny.'

'Tough.' Raul shrugged. 'Do you *really* see me getting up at night to feed it and…' He pulled a face.

And, no, she could *not* see it.

'Raul, I haven't made any plans…'

'Oh, I would say you set your plans in motion a long time ago,' Raul said. 'And I would suggest that when you "forgot" to take your Pill you thought you'd chosen carefully indeed.'

She frowned.

He enlightened her.

'I said I don't like children, and you decided I'd make a very good absentee father…'

'No!' she shouted.

'Correct,' Raul said. 'Because I shan't just be a cheque-book father—I'm going to be very hands-on.'

He dismissed her then—she knew it from the wave of his hand.

'We're getting nowhere. We can try again tomorrow if you would like?'

'You're going to schedule me in again?' Lydia asked in a sarcastic tone.

Raul ignored it but answered her question. 'If you want me to.'

And that was how they would be, Lydia was starting to realise.

Parents, but apart.

So, so far apart that she could not see across the void.

'Do you want to see the apartment?' Raul checked before he closed this disaster of a meeting. 'We should try to get as much as possible done while you're still here.'

'Fine.'

Raul heard the resignation in her voice and loathed it.

They had ended up fighting, and he knew he tended to win fights.

'I think perhaps we should do this through lawyers,' Raul admitted.

He didn't want to fight Lydia. He just wanted the details sorted. He would leave it to them and then sign.

'Raul, I can't afford a lawyer.'

It was a very difficult admission for someone like Lydia to make.

But he just sat there and leant back in his chair, and wondered just who she took him for.

'We both know that's not true.'

'Seriously, Raul. I know I live in a castle…'

'Lydia,' he told her as he sat there, and let her know himself how to nail him to the wall. 'Call a lawyer—the best you can find—and tell him my surname.'

'I can't afford to.'

'Try it,' he said. 'Tell them whose baby you're having and I guarantee they won't give a damn as to the current state of your finances. They'll probably offer to hold your hand in the delivery room.'

She stood.

'For their cut, of course,' Raul added.

He watched as she walked out, and usually he would be feeling delighted that a meeting had concluded early and he could get on to the next thing.

Yet she *was* the next thing.

When there was so much he should be getting on with Raul sat there thinking. Not even about the baby, but about her.

All roads did *not* lead to Rome.

But to Lydia.

Instead of thinking about the baby, which surely she should be, all Lydia could think about was Raul.

He was trying to get this sorted for both of them as best he could, Lydia thought as the realtor let both herself and Allegra into the apartment.

It was stunning, with crimson walls and drapes and a view of the canal.

In fact from one of the bedrooms she could see the balcony of his home.

'I missed that when I came this morning,' Allegra said when she looked to where Lydia's gaze fell, and again she wrote something down.

'Sorry?' Lydia checked.

'I'm sure you don't need a view of Daddy's home from yours! You'll want your own life…'

Allegra was trying too, Lydia realised.

Lydia was so used to everyone being the enemy.

No one really was here.

They were trying to do this without lawyers, and she was fighting them at every point, and Lydia knew why.

It wasn't the Venice apartment she wanted, nor the monthly payment dump in her account, or flights on his jet for time with Daddy.

It was Raul.

And for a tiny moment she had considered that desire attainable.

That was why she still held on to the statue—because when she'd opened up that box and looked down from the balcony for a second she'd thought it was possible that someone might actually *love* her.

Allegra was talking with the realtor, and then she excused herself to take a call on her phone.

From her affectionate tone, it was her husband, and from what Lydia could glean they were discussing what they would have tonight for dinner.

She almost smiled as she recalled for the millionth time one of her and Raul's conversations.

Only she couldn't smile.

Because if they were a couple she'd be texting him now, or telling him tonight, and they'd be laughing at their own private joke.

But they weren't a couple.

And in that same conversation he'd told her he never wanted marriage.

She looked out to the canal. She was back where she had longed to be, but she ached at the coolness between them.

Lydia didn't just want the parenting side of things to be sorted.

There was a reason she was resisting everything he suggested and she faced the lonely truth—

Lydia wanted Raul, herself and the baby to be a family.

CHAPTER SIXTEEN

'HERE.'

Loretta set down Lydia's dinner. Homemade fettuccini and a creamy sauce that smelt delicious. Finally Lydia's appetite was back.

'It looks lovely.'

'It is nice to have someone to cook for.' Loretta accepted the compliment. 'This is a recipe from Casta. I haven't made it for years.'

'You're from Casta?'

'I worked for Raul's father, and now for him. I know who I prefer.'

Lydia didn't respond at first. She assumed from that that Raul worked her too hard.

'I guess Raul must be demanding.'

'Raul?' Loretta laughed. 'No. I love working for him. It's been nearly ten years now, and I still pinch myself to make sure that it's true. I worked in his father's bar for more years than I care to count. Then Raul brought me to Rome and I used to take care of the apartments, and then I ran the housekeeping side of his first hotel.' She gave Lydia a smile. 'I'll leave you to eat.'

'Thank you,' Lydia said. Only she didn't want to be left to eat—she wanted to chat with Loretta, and she wanted to know more about Raul, but it wasn't her place to ask.

What *was* her place?

Lydia didn't know.

And so she ate her dinner and had a bath, and then pulled on summer pyjamas which were short and a bit too tight, then lay in her bed in the guest room while no doubt Raul headed out.

Perhaps for another dinner to discuss her and the baby.

His latest set of problems.

And all because he wanted to get back at Bastiano!

Lydia didn't have the energy to think about that right now.

She was hurting.

They had to talk.

And, no, she didn't care if she was running outside his schedule and it wasn't her appointed hour.

They were *going* to discuss this.

Properly.

Even the difficult things, like nannies and visiting times.

She had no idea where in the house he was.

But she'd find him.

And if he wasn't at home…

She would wait.

Raul was actually in his office.

He looked up as Allegra stopped by on her way home and told him what she had organised.

'I've arranged two other apartments for Lydia to look at tomorrow, and there's a courier coming tomorrow at nine.'

'A courier?'

'You said you had a package you wanted hand-delivered to Casta?'

'Oh, yes.'

'How did you find her in the end?' Allegra asked as she pulled on her coat. 'I think I visited maybe fifty castles and rang a hundred more.'

'She found me,' Raul replied.

Only that wasn't quite true. But he didn't run everything by Allegra, and he certainly wasn't going to discuss the meeting he'd had with Bastiano with her.

With anyone.

'Anything else?' Allegra checked.

'I don't think so.'

She was gone.

And Raul didn't blame her a bit.

Last night she had worked till close to midnight, trying to have things as prepared as possible for today.

And tonight he had kept her again past ten.

'Raul?'

He looked up and there was Allegra, still hovering at the door.

'Yes?'

'I just thought I should let you know I'm also looking for a nanny.'

'Maybe hold back on that till Lydia has got more used to the idea.'

'I meant for me.'

'Oh,' Raul said, though what he really wanted to say was *merda*.

What the hell was going on with everyone?

'You're supposed to say congratulations.'

Raul rolled his eyes.

'I'm going to be running a crèche—I can see it now. Go home.'

'I am going. Seriously, though, it's going to be difficult finding a nanny who works to your hours. I don't want Lydia to explode in temper, but we really do need to start making some enquiries.'

'Leave it for now,' he said, and as Allegra walked off he wearily remembered his manners and congratulated her on the news of her baby. *'Complimenti!'*

Allegra just laughed as she walked out.

She knew he didn't mean it!

And her care factor?

Zero.

She really was a most brilliant PA.

But Allegra was wrong about one thing, Raul thought—Lydia didn't explode.

She imploded rather than let out the rage she held on to.

He'd seen it himself.

Whereas *he*…

Raul poured cognac and it was well earned—especially when he recalled how he had held on to his temper when Bastiano had insulted his mother.

But, no, that wasn't right.

It had been the truth that had held him back.

Bastiano had thought it was love between them.

Yet he had been just seventeen.

His mother had been in her mid-thirties.

What a mess!

Raul went into his drawer and took out the ring and went to package it for the courier.

Usually, of course, his parcels and such were left for others to deal with.

Not on this occasion.

This was beyond personal, Raul thought as he looked at the ring.

It was like holding a ghost—and one he didn't even know.

Bastiano was an orphan.

Had this been his mother's ring?

What the hell had his mother been doing, taking such a ring from a teenager?

A kid, really.

They had been children then.

Sure, they had thought they were adults, but what the hell…?

His mind leapt to the defence of the seventeen-year-old Lydia.

He was furious at how she'd been treated by adults who should have known better.

And now he sat trying to do the hardest thing in his life—afford Bastiano the same feelings.

'Raul!'

This time it wasn't Allegra.

Instead a very pale Lydia stood in the doorway, in short pyjamas.

He could see all the tiny changes in her. Her hips were rounder, her breasts fuller, but he wasn't really noticing them in reference to her being pregnant.

Her hips were round and her breasts were full and she would never, *ever*, not turn him on.

And how the hell did he keep his distance?

How did he keep removing himself from want?

He saw her gaze descend to the ring he held.

'Don't worry.' He did his best to keep things level and dropped the ring back in the drawer. 'I wasn't planning a surprise. It isn't for you.'

And to her shame, to the detriment of her stupid heart, for a second she had hoped that she might have found someone who would never leave.

Fool!

And when Lydia was angry, when she was hurting, she was ice.

'Of course it isn't,' Lydia said in her most crisp and affected tone, but then it cracked, just a little, and she could hold it in no more. 'You never cared about me—not for a moment. You were too busy working out how to get to Bastiano…'

'Merda.'

This time he said it out loud as he realised that she knew.

'Lydia!' Raul stood—not in defence, more in horror.

'Don't!' she warned him. 'Don't you *dare* try to justify it.'

'I'm not. How long have you known?'

'*I* get to ask the questions—did you follow me out of that

dining room because you were interested in me or because you wanted to find out more about Bastiano?'

Before he could react, she took away the safe answer.

'And please don't say *both*, Raul—at least give me the truth.'

He owed her that.

'Bastiano.'

Absolutely the truth hurt, but she forced herself to speak on. 'And when you invited me for dinner was it to get to him? When you told me to choose…?'

She wanted to spit as she recalled it.

'Were you hoping to flaunt me in front of him?'

'Yes,' Raul answered, and he knew that the absolute truth was needed now. 'Because that's how I've always operated—that's how I have run my life. I lie to get by. I say what I have to. However—'

'I *hate* you!' Lydia shouted.

Oh, the ice hadn't cracked—it had split wide open. And fury was pouring out—years of it.

And it terrified her.

'You're the cheat, Raul! You say you hate them, but you're actually the cheat. You were lying all along.'

'Not all along.'

'Yes! You screwed me to get back at him!'

She walked out, and then she ran.

Back to her room.

The bed was turned down and the light was on and she wondered how it could look just as it had before, now he had told her himself the truth—he had pursued her to get back at Bastiano.

'Lydia.' He didn't knock, he just came in, and he was very calm.

'Get out.'

'No. We're going to talk about this.'

His head was actually racing—everything looked different now.

'When did you find out?'

'Does it even matter?'

Of course it did—and of course he knew when she had found out.

When everything between them had changed.

'You were right,' Lydia said, her temper rising. 'We'll do this through lawyers.' She meant it. 'I'm going to screw *you* now, Raul. I am going to make your life hell.'

'You couldn't.'

He took her arms and tried to calm her, but she was crying now—seriously crying.

'You couldn't make my life hell.'

Lydia took his words as a threat—that he was mightier, richer—but he meant it otherwise.

Hell was *not* having her in his life.

An angry Lydia he could deal with—was what he had waited for, in fact.

Because her fury was private and deep and finally she shared it.

Loudly.

'You lied.'

'I did,' Raul agreed. 'That's what my life was like until you came along.'

'You were using me.'

'At first,' Raul said, but then reconsidered. 'Actually, I wanted you on sight. I remember your buttons.'

'I don't take that as a compliment.'

'Take it any way you like. The floor is yours.'

His calm enraged her.

That he could just *stand* there when she'd exposed what he had done.

'I should never have told you about the baby.' She picked

up the statue. 'I should have just sold this and you'd never have known.'

'I thought you already had sold it.'

And it had hurt him that she had.

Like her blasted mother—taking heirlooms and passing them on to get through another week.

He loved that statue too, and now she was holding it in her hand and about to toss it.

Raul stood there, a little conflicted.

He could stop her, because he knew she'd regret it later.

But she was angry.

Not just at him—that much he knew.

And, hell, she deserved to show it.

Lydia did.

She threw it.

Not at him.

She threw it against the wall and heard it shatter and she did the same.

Because she loved it, and she had destroyed the nicest thing she had ever had.

Except for Raul.

Yet she had never really had him at all.

And she wanted him so much.

But he didn't want her.

So why was he kissing her? Why was he telling her he'd better lock up the china or they were going to have very expensive rows?

Why, when she was crying and kicking and, oh, so angry, did he contain her, yet let her be, and seem to want her at the same time?

They were frantic—tearing buttons and shredding clothes with their lips locked, because Raul wanted to be out of his head too.

Today had been hell.

Yesterday too.

And all the weeks before that.

He wanted her badly.

Raul kissed her hard, pushed her to the wall, and her bottom was bare in his hands, and her swaying breasts were stilled by his chest.

Lydia climbed him.

Even as Raul was preparing himself she was wrapping around him, and then she was safe in strong arms and being taken away.

It was rough and intense, and her face was hot and wet as he kissed her cheek on his way to finding her mouth.

And there was not a scream left within her as she climaxed—there wasn't even air in her lungs left to come out. Because he took everything she had and gave her more.

Everything raced to her centre as he thrust in deep and filled her. Her orgasm was so tight as he joined her in a climax that went on as hers faded.

She was calmed and coming down, watching the tension of his features and revelling in the feel of his final rapid thrusts.

And then thought returned, but the hurt did not.

At least not in the way it had been there before.

They were still kissing as he let her down. Standing in a war zone and yet safe and kissing.

And then she peeled back and peeked out and saw the glass on the floor.

'I broke our statue…'

Because that was what it was.

Theirs.

A diary of them.

And she had destroyed it.

'Why didn't you sell it?'

'I couldn't.'

And that meant so much to Raul.

She hadn't taken a single photo—Lydia, he knew, held on to nothing—yet she had been unable to let this go.

'And now I've destroyed it,' Lydia said, looking at all the shattered glass.

'No.' He picked it up from the floor and showed her that the beautiful couple were somehow intact, just minus the sheet.

'I hated that sheet,' Raul said. 'I didn't like to say so to Silvio. It's his art and all that, but I think he made a mistake.'

'He's a master of his craft!'

'Well, I think it looks better now.' Raul shrugged. 'Though the valuers might disagree.' He smiled at her. 'But you don't need them now, and we don't need lawyers.'

Lydia wasn't so sure.

She could not deal with Raul with her head.

One tryst and she craved more—one more night in his bed and she would be putty.

And she was scared to try to forgive him.

Lydia was scared of his lies—in that he was the master.

'Come to bed.'

She knew he meant his.

'Come on.'

And it scared her, not that she would take his crumbs…

But that she did.

CHAPTER SEVENTEEN

WRAPPED IN A sheet on Lydia's command, so as not to scare Loretta, they headed down the mirrored hall.

'She won't be here,' Raul said as they shuffled along with him holding the statue.

'Well, I'm not walking naked through your house.'

'*Our* house.'

Lydia ignored that. Instead she asked about Loretta.

'How come she works for you?'

'Because she was always good to me, and when my father died I knew she would be without work.'

'So you *do* have friends?'

'I guess.'

They were at his bedroom—back to where she had promised never to be.

It was even more beautiful the second time around.

'It's so gorgeous.'

'It's your room now.'

He saw her shoulders stiffen.

'I mean it.'

'Raul, can we talk about this tomorrow? There's still a lot to sort out.'

'It's sorted.'

'Raul, I'm here because you found out I was pregnant. I don't think that's an awful lot to base a relationship on.'

'Nor do I,' Raul agreed. 'I lived with my parents, after all. It's not just the baby.'

'Please don't just say the right thing. You're a liar, Raul.' She thought back to the plane, the first time they had flown here. 'I can't bear the thought of you *pretending* to care. That's what you've been doing all along…'

'Never.'

'You stand there and tell me you're speaking the truth and then straight away you lie.'

'When I held your hand I wasn't lying. When we took a taxi rather than my car I was caring for you then. And when we didn't have sex that first time…'

He thought back.

'For a second I considered how good it would feel to get back at him.'

And she let out a sob and a laugh, because he was being too painfully honest now.

'But then I stopped,' Raul reminded her. 'And by morning I could not let you leave.'

'You should have told me you knew Bastiano.'

'I know that,' Raul admitted. 'But I knew that if I did you'd leave. And you did.'

'Had you *told* me…' Lydia said, and then halted. He was right. Whichever way she might have found out, she'd have gone.

'I missed you so much.' Raul said.

Now she knew he was lying.

'So much that you did nothing to try to contact me until I called and told you I was pregnant?'

'Lydia, I didn't even know your surname. I've had Allegra scouring all the castles in England.

She didn't believe him and he knew it.

'Ask her.'

'She'll say what you tell her to.'

'I think,' Raul said, 'that I've finally found someone as mistrusting as me.'

'You had three months to find me, and yet on the same day I call you to say I'm pregnant suddenly you appear.'

'I was already on my way when I heard your message,' Raul told her. 'Here…'

He placed the now naked statue on the bedside table and

then went to his drawer and took out a piece of paper with her name and address written on it.

'That's Bastiano's handwriting. I went to Casta to ask him.'

He handed it to her and Lydia looked at the paper. And she thought she would keep it for ever, because it told her that she *had* been missed.

'You went to Bastiano just for this?'

'Well, it wasn't for his company.'

'Did the two of you fight?'

'No,' Raul said. 'Nearly. He said he wanted a ring that had been left to me by my mother.'

'The ring you were looking at before?'

Raul nodded and got into bed, patted the space beside him for her to lie down with him.

'Hasn't he had enough from you?' Lydia asked as she climbed in. She really could not fathom his mother leaving half her legacy to a very young lover rather than leaving it all to her only son.

'It was a ring that he gave to her, apparently.'

'Oh.'

'He wanted it back in return for your address. I think it might have belonged to his mother. He's an orphan.' He made himself say it. 'He wasn't my mother's first affair.'

'How do you know?'

'Because I had been lying to my father to save her since I was a small child.'

And he had been lying to himself to save her memory since she'd died.

'Bastiano was just seventeen—half her age. Back then I thought we were men, and I hated him as such, but now…'

It felt very different, looking back.

'We were good friends growing up.'

'Could you be again?'

Raul was about to give a derisive laugh, but then he thought for a moment. 'I don't know…'

And it was nice to lie in bed talking with another person, rather than trying to make sense of things by himself.

'I think that my mother had problems for a very long time. Perhaps even before she was married. I don't even know if I'm my father's son.'

'Does it matter?'

'I think it did to him.'

'Is that why he beat you?'

He had never told her that Gino had given him those scars on his back, but it was clear now and Raul nodded.

And when he examined those times without hate and with her by his side things were easier to see.

His hand was on her stomach, and he could feel the little bump. It was starting to sink in properly that he would be a father.

She felt his hand there and wondered at his thoughts. 'I'm not a gold-digger, Raul.'

'I know. I had to put that statue in your case, remember?' He had gone over and over that time.

'I don't think I took the Pill every day, even though my mother had insisted I should be on it. I had no intention of sleeping with Bastiano, and maybe I should have known I wasn't covered. I didn't think.'

'Lydia, you could have been wearing a chastity belt that night and I'd have rung for wire cutters. I could have insisted we use a condom. Have you told your mother about the baby?' he added.

'No.'

'When will you?'

'When I'm ready to.'

'I'm glad you told me first,' Raul said.

'She was a mess when I got back. I think losing my father finally caught up with her. She kicked Maurice out. She's staying at her sister's now. She's agreed the castle should go on the market.'

'Lydia. I'll look after your mother, but not *him*.'

Maurice he could never forgive.

Lydia lay in his arms and gave a soft laugh at the way he'd spoken of Maurice, but then she thought about what he'd just said about her mother.

'You don't have to do that.'

'Of course I do.'

'No, Raul, you don't.'

'We're going to be a family, Lydia. Marry me?'

She lay silent. She could feel his hand on her stomach and put her hand over his. Lydia knew how she felt about Raul. But she also meant what she'd said—a baby wouldn't save them.

'You don't even *like* children.'

'No, I don't,' Raul agreed. 'I'll like ours, though. Please believe that I'm not asking you to marry me because of the baby.'

'I know that.'

She *almost* did.

But by his own admission Raul was a manipulative liar, and there was still the tiniest niggle that he was simply saying the right things to appease her.

But then she thought of his look of horror when she had exposed him. So unlike Arabella, who hadn't even flinched at being caught.

He seemed so loath to hurt her.

She was scared, though, to believe.

And as her mind flicked around, trying to find fault with this love, Raul lay sinking into his first glimpse of peace.

That feeling—not quite foreboding, but almost—was fading. His constant wondering as to how she was had been answered. He thought of that first surge of jealousy when he'd thought that she and Bastiano might be lovers.

And now they lay there together and he looked at her. 'Were you jealous at the thought of Allegra and me?'

'Of course I was.'

'Are you now?'

'No.' She shook her head.

'She really was looking for you for weeks. And,' he added, 'I've just found out she's pregnant too.'

And then she knew she wasn't jealous any more, or suspicious of Allegra, because he answered a question she wasn't even thinking.

'It's not mine.'

'I would *really* hope not.'

And he smiled, and when he did, for Lydia it was easy to smile too, but he could see the little sparkle of tears in her eyes on what should be their happiest night.

'Marry me?' he said again.

'Raul…'

Oh, she knew he cared—and deeply. And she knew how she felt. But there was still a tiny part of her that was scared that he'd asked in haste.

That without a baby there wouldn't be any 'them'.

She would just have to deal with it, Lydia knew. She would just have to accept never quite fully knowing if they were only together for the sake of their child. Because in every other way it felt perfect.

Stiff upper lip and all that.

'I hated being without you,' Raul said.

'And me.'

'No,' Raul said, 'I mean it. I felt as if there was something wrong. The sky seemed hung too low.'

He had been trying to work out what was wrong for months, and now suddenly, just like that, he knew exactly what had been wrong.

Raul had never felt it before.

Lydia lay looking at the chandelier struck by moonlight.

The shutters were open and there was the sound of a gondolier singing beneath them on the canal.

And then she heard something.

Not a bell.

But something as clear as one.

And it struck right at her soul and she turned her face to the sound.

'I love you,' Raul told her.

It can be said many ways, but when it is said right it strikes so clear and so pure. And the sound and the feeling vibrates and lingers and lasts even when it must surely be gone.

It's never gone.

She had heard his truth.

This really was love.

EPILOGUE

THERE HAD BEEN one more lie that Raul had told her.

Raul *did* get up at night for his baby.

And he fed and changed her.

Serena had come into their lives four weeks ago, and so far it had proved the perfect name.

Yes, she was from Venice—or La Serenissima—but it was more for her nature that the name had been chosen.

They had been rewarded with such a calm baby.

Of course she cried—but she calmed easily when held.

And they loved her so much.

From her one blonde tufty curl to her ten perfect toes.

It was seven on a Sunday—Lydia knew that without opening her eyes because her favourite bell rang its occasional deep note and the others would join in soon.

Raul was speaking to Serena as they stood on the balcony, telling her she should go back to sleep.

It made Lydia's heart melt to watch the gentle way he held his daughter.

He was naked from the waist up and she could see his scars. She was grateful for them.

Sometimes she needed their reminder, because life felt perfect and the scars told her how far they had come.

Lydia closed her eyes as he turned around, pretending to be asleep.

'Shh…' Raul said as Serena let out a protest when he returned her to her crib.

Serena hushed, and after a moment of watching her sleep Raul got dressed.

Lydia wanted to protest and insist that he come back to bed.

Sunday was her favourite day.

Raul would go out from their room and return with the breakfast Loretta had prepared. They loved Sunday breakfast in bed.

Where was he going?

Lydia heard the elevator taking him down and then the engine of his speedboat.

Perhaps he had gone for coffee?

Raul did that now and then.

She had hoped he would not this morning.

She lay there listening to the bells and then rolled on her back and looked at the lights. Wherever he had gone she was happy.

So happy that she fell back to sleep and then awoke to his voice.

'Happy Birthday.'

He *had* remembered.

Lydia had dropped no clues and given no reminders.

She hadn't met a stranger that morning. Lydia knew she had met the love of her life. A man who had told her that there was no one in his life whose birthday he remembered.

Now he had two.

Raul held out a cardboard box tied with a red velvet ribbon which was vaguely familiar.

And then he told her where he had been.

'Baci in gondola,' Raul told her. 'Had you not chosen to walk out that morning you would have had these.'

He handed her the box and she opened it up.

'I was coming back to ask you to stay.'

'I know that now.'

And then she asked him something that she had not before.

'Would you have told me about Bastiano then?'

'No,' he said. 'Maybe later that night, but that morning I was definitely coming home to go back to bed with you.'

'Here.' He handed her the other box he was carrying. 'Your present.'

Lydia opened it up and she was reminded of just how much she was loved.

It was an album filled with stunning photos of the castle.

Exterior shots and also interior.

And as she turned the pages it was like stepping into each room and seeing it as it had once been when she was a child.

The castle would be opened to the public today.

With Raul's help, things had been turned around.

Valerie lived in a cottage on the grounds, and this afternoon would be taking the first visitors in a very long time through the glorious building.

But that wasn't all of Lydia's presents.

'We fly at ten,' Raul told her. 'Then we are having afternoon tea in the garden. You'll make a gentleman of me yet.'

He *was* one.

A thousand times over and Lydia still cringed a bit when she thought of the words she had said, right here in this bedroom, that awful day.

They had survived it.

Better than that, they had thrived.

Raul came into the bed and they lay there, listening to the bells and to the contented sounds of their baby.

'When are we getting married?' Raul asked.

It hadn't yet happened.

'Soon.' Lydia smiled.

'You keep saying that,' Raul grumbled.

The last six months had been wonderful, but crazy. Their love had hit like lightning, and Lydia kept waiting to come down from the dizzy high and get organised.

She was starting to accept that there was no come-down when Raul was close.

Their kiss was slow, and he kept telling her he loved her,

and then Raul rolled on top of her and told her that he was tired of waiting.

She felt him *there* and he smiled.

'I didn't mean for that.'

'I know you didn't,' Lydia said.

But it had been four weeks and she was ready now.

'You're sure?'

He was very slow and tender, and that was a side of Raul that even he was only starting to find out existed.

It was the best birthday she could have known. They made slow Sunday love and afterwards he stayed leaning over her and told her that there was another thing she did not know.

'Raul?'

'We get married today,' Raul said.

Lydia frowned.

They both wanted a small wedding and had thought about having it here in Venice.

Or Rome, where they had first met, perhaps?

Even Sicily, for together they had been back there.

'At the castle,' Raul said.

That had been but a dream, for it had been falling down around them when they'd first met.

It was beautiful now.

'Yes?' he checked.

'Yes!' Lydia said.

'Per favore?' Raul said, and took her right back to the day they had met.

'Yes, please!' Lydia said, and together they smiled.

She *had* chosen wisely, for Raul was the love of her life.

And he would be King.

* * * * *

BOUND BY THE SULTAN'S BABY

CHAPTER ONE

GABI DERAMO HAD never been a bridesmaid, let alone a bride.

However, weddings were her life and she thought about them during most of the minutes of her day.

From way back she had lived and breathed weddings.

Gabi was a dreamer.

As a little girl, her dolls would regularly be lined up in a bridal procession. Once, to her mother's fury, Gabi had poured two whole bags of sugar and one of flour over them to create a winter wedding effect.

'Essere nerre nuvole,' her mother, Carmel, had scolded, telling her that she lived in the clouds.

What Gabi didn't tell her was that at each wedding she made with her dolls, she pretended it was her mother. As if somehow she could conjure her father's presence and make it so that he had not left a pregnant Carmel to struggle alone.

And while Gabi had never been so much as kissed, as an assistant wedding planner she had played her part in many a romantic escape.

She dreamt of the same most nights.

And she dreamt of Alim.

Now Gabi sat, flicking through the to-do list on her tablet and curling her long black hair around her finger, trying to work out how on earth she could possibly organise, from scratch, an extremely rushed but very exclusive winter wedding in Rome.

Mona, the bride-to-be, stepped out of the changing area on her third attempt at trying on a gown not of Gabi's choice.

It didn't suit Mona in the least—the antique lace made her olive skin look sallow and the heavy fabric did nothing to accentuate her delicate frame.

'What do you think?' Mona asked Gabi as she turned around to look in the mirror and examined herself from behind.

Gabi knew from experience how to deal with a bride who stood in completely the wrong choice of gown. 'What do *you* think, Mona?'

'I don't know,' Mona sighed. 'I quite like it.'

'Then it isn't the gown for you,' Gabi said. 'Because you have to *love* it.'

Mona had resisted the boutique owner's guidance and had completely dismissed Gabi's suggestion for a bright, white, column gown with subtle embroidery. In fact, Mona hadn't even tried it on.

Gabi's suggestions were dismissed rather a lot.

She was curvy and dressed in the severe, shapeless dark suit that her boss, Bernadetta, insisted she wear, so brides-to-be tended to assume that Gabi had no clue where fashion was concerned.

Oh, but she did.

Not for herself, of course, but Gabi could pick out the right wedding gown for a bride at fifty paces.

And they needed this to be sorted today!

Bernadetta was on leave and so it had fallen to Gabi to sort.

It always did.

The bigger the budget, the trickier the brief, the more likely it was to have been put into the 'Too Hard' basket and left for Gabi to pick up.

They were in the lull between Christmas and New Year. The wedding boutique was, in fact, closed today, but Gabi had many contacts and had called in a favour from Rosa, the owner, who had opened up just for them.

Rosa would not push them out, but they had to meet Marianna, the functions co-ordinator, at the Grande Lucia at four.

'Why don't you try Gabi's suggestion?' Fleur, the mother of the groom, said.

It was a little odd.

Usually this trip would be taken with the mother of the bride or her sister or friends, but it would seem that it was Fleur who had first and last say in things.

Fleur was also English, which meant that, in order to be polite, Gabi and Mona did not speak in Italian.

Yes, it was proving to be a long, tiring day.

And they would be back tomorrow with the bridesmaids!

Reluctantly, *very* reluctantly, Mona agreed to try on Gabi's suggestion and then disappeared with the dresser.

As Rosa hung up the failed gown she saw that Gabi was looking at another dress.

Silver-grey, it was elegant and simple and in a larger size, and when Gabi held it up she saw the luxurious fall of the fabric. Rosa was a talented seamstress indeed.

'It would fit you,' Rosa said.

'I doubt it.' Gabi sighed wistfully. 'It's beautiful, though.'

'The order was cancelled,' Rosa said. 'Why don't you go and try it on? It would look stunning, I am sure.'

'Not while I'm working.' Gabi shook her head. 'Anyway, even if it did fit, when would I get a chance to wear it?' Her question went unanswered as the curtains parted and a smiling Mona walked out.

'Oh, Mona!' Gabi breathed.

The dress was perfect.

It showed off Mona's slender figure, and the bright white was indeed the perfect shade against her olive skin.

'If only she had listened to you in the first place,' Fleur muttered. 'We are going to be late for the hotel.'

'It's all taken care of,' Gabi assured her, checking her list on her tablet. 'We're right on schedule.'

Ahead of it, in fact, because now that the dress had been chosen, everything else, Gabi knew, would fall more easily into place.

Measurements had already been taken but fitting dates could not yet be made. Gabi assured Rosa she would call her just as soon as they had finalised the wedding date.

They climbed back into the car and were driven through the wet streets of Rome towards the Grande Lucia but, again, Mona wasn't happy. 'I went to a wedding at the Grande Lucia a few years ago and it was so…' Mona faltered for a moment as she struggled with a word to describe it. 'Tired-looking.'

'Not now it isn't.' Gabi shook her head. 'It's under new management, well, Alim has been…' It was Gabi who now faltered but she quickly recovered. 'Alim has been the owner for a couple of years and there have been considerable renovations; the hotel is looking magnificent.'

Even saying his name made her stumble a little and blush.

Gabi saw Alim only occasionally but she thought about him a lot.

Their paths rarely crossed but if Gabi was organising a wedding at the Grande Lucia and Alim happened to be in residence at the time then her heart would get a rare treat, and she was secretly hoping for one today.

'Let's just see how you feel once you've actually seen the Grande Lucia for yourself,' Gabi suggested. 'Remember, though, that it's terribly hard to get a booking there, especially at such short notice.'

'Fleur doesn't seem to think it will be a problem,' Mona said with a distinct edge to her voice, and Gabi watched as she shot a look towards the mother of the groom. From all Gabi had gleaned, Fleur had agreed to finance the wedding on the condition that it was held there.

'It won't be,' Fleur responded.

Gabi wasn't so sure.

Marianna, the co-ordinator, was rather inflexible at the best of times and they wanted this wedding to be held in just over two weeks!

They made good time as the streets were comparatively empty. The rush of Christmas was over and even the Colosseum was closed to visitors.

Gabi stifled a yawn, wishing that she could put up her own *Do not disturb* sign to the world for a while.

She had hoped to spend the Christmas break going over the plans for starting her own business. Instead, she had again been called in to work through her leave. She was tired.

Almost too tired to keep alive the dream of one day owning her own business.

She had started working for Matrimoni di Bernadetta when she was eighteen and had hoped that it would provide the experience she needed to one day go it alone.

Six years later, at the age of twenty-four, that prospect seemed no brighter.

Bernadetta had made very sure of that—there was barely time to think, let alone act on her own dreams.

Still, she truly loved her job.

Gabi looked up as the gorgeous old building came into view and they soon pulled up at the entrance.

The car door was opened for them by the doorman, Ronaldo.

'Ben tornato,' Ronaldo said, and Gabi realised that it was Fleur and not she he was welcoming back.

Fleur must be a guest. And a favoured one too from the attention that Ronaldo gave her.

As Gabi got out there was a flutter of excitement at the thought that she might soon see Alim.

He was always polite, even if he was somewhat aloof. She didn't take it personally. Alim was the same with everyone and maintained a certain distance. There was just an air of mystery to him that had Gabi entranced. An entire floor of the Grande Lucia served as Alim's residence when he was in Rome, and so, through the hotel industry grapevine, Gabi knew more than a little of his reputation. He loved beautiful women and dated as many of them as he could—though one night with him was all they would ever get.

Breakfast was definitely not included in this particular package. In fact, according to Sophie, a friend of Gabi's and a maid at the Grande Lucia, cold and callous were the most frequent words used to describe him by his lovers after they had been discarded.

That didn't seem right to Gabi for she always felt warm in his gaze, and when it came to business, his professionalism was never in doubt.

Still, Sophie had told her, for all the tears there were perks for, rumour had it the reward for time spent in Alim's arms came in the shape of a diamond.

It sounded crass.

Until you saw Alim.

He was completely out of her league, of course, and that was not her being self-effacing. He veered towards slender blondes of the supermodel kind, and women who definitely knew the ropes in the bedroom.

Apparently he had no inclination to teach.

Gabi didn't mind in the least that Alim was utterly unattainable, for it made it safe for her to dream of him.

There was no sign that he was there when she walked through the brass revolving doors and into the magnificent foyer of the Grande Lucia.

It was *almost* perfection.

Stunning crimson carpet and silk walls were elegant—even sensual, perhaps—and worked well against the dark wooden furnishings. The space was vast and the ceilings high, yet there was an intimate feel from the moment you walked in, alongside the lovely buzz of a busy hotel.

As a centrepiece, there was a huge, crimson floral display.

Yes, *almost* perfect.

Gabi had an eye for detail and this arrangement irked her. It never varied, or moved with the times. Instead, there was a perpetual display of deep red roses and carnations and it had become a slight bone of contention when Gabi had negotiated on behalf of her brides.

Marianna came to greet them and took the trio for coffee at one of several intimate lounges just off the foyer.

There they went through a few details and though Marianna was delighted to announce that there was an opening in just over two weeks, she was not going to make it easy for the bride.

'I do need to verify dates with the owner,' Marianna said. 'We're expecting some VIP guests at the hotel in January so security will be particularly tight. I'm not sure we'll be able to accommodate you then. Alim has asked to be informed before any dates are locked in…' She paused and looked up. 'Oh, there he—'

Marianna halted, causing Gabi to glance up. Alim had just entered the foyer with the requisite stunning blonde.

Gabi guessed, and rightly so, that Alim did not like to be disturbed with minor details every time he made an appearance so Marianna did not alert Mona and Fleur to his presence.

Yet such was his charisma, both women looked over.

And while Marianna might be doing her best not to disrupt Alim's day, Gabi's had just been turned on its head.

In the nicest of ways.

He wore a slim dark coat and there was such an air of magnificence about him that he simply turned heads.

Not just for his dark looks—there was more to him than that—but they were rather wonderful to dwell on. His hair was black and glossy and swept back. He stood tall and his posture was so upright he always made Gabi want to pull back her own shoulders.

There was a shift that ran through her body whenever he was near, an awareness that made it difficult to focus on anything other than him, for all else seemed to move to the periphery of her consciousness to allow Alim centre stage.

'Quanti ospiti?'

Marianna's voice was coming from a distance and as she asked how many guests for the wedding, it was Mona who answered instead of Gabi.

For Alim had looked over and met her gaze.

He was beautiful.

Always.

Effortlessly elegant, supremely polite, he was the calm, still water to Gabi's fizz.

She was a dreamer, which meant that though he was out of her league, he was not out of bounds to her thoughts; innocent in body she may be, but not so in her mind.

And as for those eyes, they were a dark grey with silver flecks that spoke silently of the night.

His gaze was a dangerous thing to be held in, Gabi knew, and she was trapped in it now. There was a fire crackling in the grate and there was heat low, low in her stomach and rising to her neck.

She wanted to excuse herself from the conversation and walk over in response to his silent command. She wanted work to be gone, for his lover to disappear, and for Alim to lower her down onto a silken bed.

Just that.

'Gabi…' Marianna intruded.

'Alim,' his lover called.

But he was making his way over.

'Va tuto bene?'

He asked if everything was okay, and though his Italian was excellent, it was laced in his own rich accent and rendered Gabi incapable of response, for she had not expected him to come over.

It was Marianna who responded and told him the preferred date for the wedding.

'That would be fine.' Alim nodded to Marianna and to the other guests and then he looked directly at Gabi; she found herself staring at his mouth as he spoke, for it was just a little safer than to stare into his eyes. 'How are you, Gabi?'

'I am well.'

'That is good.'

He turned and walked away and she held her breath.

It was nothing—just an exchange so tiny that the others had not even noticed its significance, yet Gabi would survive on it for weeks.

He knew her name.

'Perhaps you could take Mona to see the ballroom while I discuss details with Fleur,' Marianna suggested.

Details being money.

'Of course.'

Gabi stood and smoothed her skirt.

Oh, she loathed the black suit with a gold logo and the heavy, cowl-necked cream top. It was the perfect outfit for a funeral director, not a wedding planner.

If it were her own business she would wear a willow-green check with a hint of pink. Gabi had already chosen the fabric.

And she would not wear the black high heels that Bernadetta insisted on, for she felt too tall and bulky as she walked through the foyer alongside the future bride.

And then she saw Alim and Ms Blonde stepping into his private elevator, and Gabi scowled at his departing back, for she envied the intimate experience they were about to share. Ms Blonde was coiling herself around him and whispering into his ear.

Thank God for gated elevators.

They were excellent for regaining self-control, for they slammed shut on the couple and as the world came back from the peripheries Gabi recalled that there was a wedding to be arranged.

There were large double doors to the ballroom and Gabi opened them both so that Mona could get the full effect as she stepped in.

It truly was stunning.

Huge crystal chandeliers first drew the eye, but it was a feast in all directions.

'Molto bello...' Mona breathed, and it was a relief to

slip back into speaking Italian. 'The ballroom is nothing like I remember it.'

'Alim, the owner, had it completely refurbished. The floor was sanded back, the chandeliers repaired. The Grande Lucia is once again *the* place for a wedding.'

'I know it is,' Mona admitted. 'It is actually where James and I met. I was here for my grandparents' anniversary. James was here, visiting…' Mona stopped herself from voicing whatever it was she had been about to say. 'I just don't like it that Fleur is calling all the shots just because her…' Mona clapped her lips together. Clearly she didn't want to say too much.

Gabi, curious by nature, wished that she would.

Fleur was being very elusive.

From the draft guest list, the groom's side seemed incredibly sparse. Just a best man from Scotland would be flying in and that was all. There was no mention of James's father.

Gabi wondered if Fleur was widowed.

But Gabi wasn't there to wonder and her mind turned, as it always did, into making this the very best of weddings.

'Imagine dancing under those lights at night,' Mona said.

'There is nothing more beautiful,' Gabi assured her, and then pointed up to a small gallery that ran the length of the westerly wall and imagined the select audience watching the proceedings in days long gone.

'The photographer can get some amazing overhead shots of the dance floor from up there. A photographer I…I mean Matrimoni di Bernadetta regularly uses does the most marvellous time-lapse shots from the gallery. They are stunning.'

She could see that Mona was starting to get excited.

'When you say you were here for your grandparents' anniversary,' Gabi probed, because the thought of time-lapse photos had got her thinking…

'My grandparents were married here,' Mona told her. 'Sometimes they take out the record they danced to on their wedding night.'

'Really?'

'I even recognise the floor from their wedding photos. It's like stepping back in time.'

Yes, even the ballroom floor was stunning—a parquet of mahogany, oak and redwood, all highly polished to reveal a subtle floral mosaic.

'Your grandparents still dance to their wedding song…'

Mona nodded and Gabi could see that she was already sold on the venue.

There would be a string quartet, but Mona loved Gabi's suggestion that she and James dance their first dance to the same record that her grandparents had.

And a wedding, a very beautiful one, was finally starting to be born.

It was a rather more glowing bride-to-be who returned to the lounge area and now chatted happily with Fleur and Marianna about plans.

And it was a bemused Gabi who looked up and saw Ms Blonde angrily striding through the foyer; she didn't know why, but she would bet her life's savings that Alim had uncoiled her, unwilling, from his arms.

Then later, much later, when plans were starting to be put more firmly in place, Gabi called Rosa with the official dates.

'I'm already working on the dress,' Rosa said. 'She's cutting it terribly fine to wear one of my gowns, even ready-to-wear.'

And, after a long, tiring day taking care of others, Gabi did something for herself.

She was all glowing and happy from that tiny exchange with Alim. Of course his lover's departure could have nothing to do with her, but Gabi was a dreamer, and already her mind was turning things around.

'Can I come and try on the silver dress?' she asked.

It was wonderful to dream of Alim.

CHAPTER TWO

IT TRULY WAS a beautiful wedding.

Not that Gabi had a second to enjoy it.

Resplendent in his kilt, the best man was being actively pursued by the matron of honour and doing his best to get away. Fleur was tense and asking that they hurry. The little flower girls were teary and cold as they stood in the snow for photos and Gabi felt like a bedraggled shepherdess as she juggled umbrellas for the bridal party and tried to herd the guests.

She was wearing boots, but that was the only concession to the cold.

Finally they were all in cars and heading off for the reception as Gabi ensured that the choir had been paid.

Bernadetta sat in her car, smoking, as Gabi shivered her way down the church steps.

And then it happened.

Gabi slipped on the ice and bumped down the last three stairs in the most ungainly fashion imaginable.

Not that anyone came over to help.

She sat for a moment, trying to catch her breath and assess the damage.

From the feel of things her bottom was bruised.

Pulling herself to a stand, Gabi saw that her skirt was

filthy and sodden and, removing her jacket, she saw that it had split along the back seam.

To make things just a little bit more miserable than they already were, Bernadetta was furious, especially that Gabi had no change of clothes.

'Why haven't you got a spare suit with you?' she demanded. 'You're supposed to be a planner after all.'

Because you only give me two suits, Gabi wanted to answer, but she knew it wouldn't help. 'It's at the dry-cleaner's.'

And, of course, Bernadetta spitefully pointed out that no one else had one that would fit Gabi.

'Go home and get changed,' she hissed. 'Wear something...' And she took her hands and sort of exasperatedly pushed them together, as if Gabi was supposed to produce something that might contract her size.

And Bernadetta didn't add, as she always did to her other staff, *Don't outshine the bride.*

Gabi, it was assumed, hadn't a hope of that.

Oh, she wanted to resign, so very much.

Gabi was close to tears as she arrived back at her tiny flat and, of course, there was nothing in her wardrobe she could possibly wear.

Well, there was one thing.

The silver-grey dress made by Rosa's magical hands, though Bernadetta would consider her grossly overdressed.

Yet it was a very simple design...

Gabi undressed and saw that, yes, she indeed had a bruise on her bottom and on the left of her thigh.

In fact, she ached and was cold to the bone.

A quick shower warmed her up and Gabi was, by the time she stepped out of it, actually a lot more relaxed for the brief reprieve.

Wedding days were always so full on and it was actually nice to take a short break.

When she had her own business, Gabi decided, she would organise a rota so that all of her staff were able to take some time between the formal service and the reception. Perhaps there could be a change of outfit for them too…

Gabi halted.

She was back to hoping and dreaming that one day she might be working for herself.

How, though, when Bernadetta had her securely locked in?

Still there wasn't time to dwell on it now.

The dress had been a gift from Rosa but, feeling guilty simply accepting it, Gabi had splurged on the right bra to go with it and, of course, matching silver knickers, which she quickly put on before wriggling into the dress.

Rosa really was a magician with fabric—the dress was cut on the bias and fell beautifully over her curves.

And it deserved more effort than her usual lack.

Sitting at her small dressing table, Gabi twisted her hair and piled it up on her head, rather than leaving it down. She put on some lip-gloss and mascara and then worried that it might be too much because usually she didn't bother with such things.

Yet she didn't wipe them off.

Instead, she dressed to look her best.

Tonight she didn't want to be the dowdy funeral director version of Gabi, or the clumsy, fall-down-the-stairs, eternally rushed wedding planner she appeared at times.

It was a split-second decision, a choice that she made.

Gabi looked in the mirror. This was the person she would be if she worked for herself and was orchestrating a high-class function tonight.

This was actually the closest she had ever looked to the woman she was inside.

Gabi arrived back at the hotel, her stunning dress hidden by a coat and wearing boots with her pretty shoes held in a bag. Security was tight and Ronaldo, the doorman, even though he knew her well, apologised but said that she had to show ID. 'There are VIP's staying at the hotel,' he explained as he stamped his feet against the cold.

'There often are,' Gabi said.

'Royalty,' Ronaldo grumbled, because royalty in residence meant a whole lot of extra work!

'Who?'

'Gabi,' Ronaldo warned, for he was under strict instruction, but then smiled as he chose to reveal—it was just to Gabi after all! 'The Sultan of Sultans and his daughter.'

'Wow!'

Oh, she hoped for a glimpse of them—it sounded amazing!

Gabi handed over her coat at Reception and pursed her lips when she saw the large crimson floral display in the foyer.

The Grande Lucia was a wonderful hotel but it was like turning the *Titanic* to effect change at times.

Nervous, a little shy, and doing her best not to show it, Gabi returned to the wedding and walked straight into Bernadetta's spiteful reproach.

'If the bride had wanted a Christmas tree arrangement in the corner, I would have charged her for one,' Bernadetta hissed, and Gabi felt her tiny drop of confidence in her newfound self drain away.

'We need to check that the gramophone has been properly set up,' Bernadetta told her. 'And we need to find the key to the gallery for the photographer.'

'*We*' being Gabi.

She hit the ballroom floor running, or rather working away to make the night go as smoothly as possible for the happy couple.

Indeed, they looked happy.

Mona's dress was sublime and her groom was handsome and relaxed and…

Gabi frowned.

James reminded her of someone, but she could not place him.

Or was it just the fact that he was tall and blond, like his mother, that made him stand out a touch more amongst the many Italian guests?

There was no time to dwell on it, though, and no time to acknowledge the ache of disappointment that Alim was nowhere to be seen.

And she admitted it to herself then, as she let the photographer up to the gallery and walked back through the foyer.

The dress, the pretty heels, the hair and the make-up…

In part they had been on the off chance that Alim might see her.

Alim was, in fact, in the building, but for once his presence was low key.

'I *hate* that we can't be at the wedding,' Yasmin moaned for the hundredth time, and pushed her dessert aside unfinished.

Alim said nothing in response.

He was very used to his sister's histrionics.

'We are shooed away like vermin,' Yasmin snarled, and threw down her napkin.

'Hardly vermin,' Alim drawled, refusing to be drawn

in—they were sitting in the private area of the sumptuous restaurant at the Grande Lucia after all.

Their father did not join them for it would only draw attention, and that was everything Alim was doing his best to avoid.

At least for tonight.

The staff at the Grande Lucia were very used to esteemed guests but, Alim knew, they were starting to comprehend that Oman, the Sultan of Sultans, was in fact Alim's father.

Alim did not use his title in the workplace—Sultan Alim al-Lehan of Zethlehan.

Neither did he use it in his personal life, for it was a risqué personal life indeed. Diamonds paid for silence and there was the slick machine of the palace PR to wash indiscretions away.

Oman's main indiscretion was the reason they were here in the dining room tonight.

Close to the wedding but not present.

Tonight, when the happy couple headed to the bridal suite, Fleur, the groom's mother, would head to her own sumptuous suite of rooms.

Violetta, who dealt with palace PR and external arrangements, had taken over the arrangements of the guest rooms from Marianna.

Alim did not need to know, though of course he did, that Fleur's suite adjoined his father's.

Fleur was Oman's mistress of long standing.

She had borne the Sultan of Sultans his first son.

James had had a seemingly privileged life. He had been schooled at Windsor, had attended university in Scotland, and had a trust fund that would make most people's eyes water.

But his father's name did not appear on his birth certificate and he bore no title. To the people of Zethlehan he simply did not exist.

Yet he was Alim, Kaleb and Yasmin's half-brother, and they loved him so.

Kaleb, who was younger than Alim, would instead see the happy couple in Paris, where he currently lived.

The three of them together would turn heads indeed but subtlety was the aim on this night.

Yasmin, who lived a very sheltered life in Zethlehan, had pleaded to be a part of the proceedings.

Those fervent pleas from Yasmin had been declined by their father and so Alim had stepped in and offered to do what he could to enable Yasmin to observe the wedding from a distance.

Alim had arranged it so that he and Yasmin had been taking refreshments in the lounge when the bridal party had arrived back from the church, so that Yasmin could see the dress and everything.

Yasmin had enjoyed it immensely. 'What on earth is he wearing?' she asked about the best man.

'A kilt,' Alim explained. 'He's from Scotland.'

'Oh, it's so exciting,' Yasmin breathed.

A glimpse of the bridal party wasn't enough for her, though.

And though Alim had arranged that they eat the same meal and drink the same wines as the bridal party, it was a somewhat muted celebration.

The speeches would be wrapping up now, Alim explained, and he actually ached that he was not able to hear them.

'I want to see them dance.' Yasmin pouted.

She was very used to getting her own way.

But not in this, Alim promised.

There were volumes of intricate and ancient laws and,

until he himself ruled, Alim had no choice but to adhere to them.

Alim loved his country fiercely, and respected many of the traditions, yet from childhood he had seen the need for change.

For now, though, he tried to placate his young sister.

'You will see James and Mona tomorrow for breakfast; you can congratulate them then.'

'It's not the same, though!' Yasmin refused to be mollified. 'Why can't I slip into the ballroom for just a few moments and see them? You shall, Alim.'

'I shall only because I own the hotel and I often check in on functions. You would be noticed.'

Yasmin, like her brothers, had her share of the al-Lehan good looks and her entrance would be noted.

It would not take much for people to work things out.

Even so, Alim could not bear to see his sister unhappy—he knew how much Yasmin had been looking forward to such a rare occasion as a trip overseas.

'Listen,' Alim said. 'There is a viewing gallery in the ballroom.' He watched Yasmin's eyes widen. 'The photographer will be there now, setting up for photos, but after he comes down, you could watch things from there for a short while. I can give you a master key and you can go in a separate entrance from him and wait.'

'Yes!' Her eyes shone with excitement.

'Just for a little while,' Alim warned. 'The photographer will be back towards the end of the celebrations so keep an eye on him for when he leaves to come back up.'

'I shall.'

He gave her the key and further instructions and pretended not to notice that she swiped a bottle of champagne as they walked from the dining room.

Yasmin was very protected and afforded none of the freedom that Alim and Kaleb had been.

She deserved a little fun during her time in Rome, Alim thought.

So he led her to the stairwell and warned her *again* to stay low and to be quiet.

'Thank you, Alim!'

'Don't make trouble! Watch for a little while and then go to bed.'

Alone now, it was Alim who wanted to see his brother on this his wedding day.

And he also wanted to speak with Gabi.

Alim was a very astute businessman and he recognised Gabi's talent. He had worked very hard to bring the hotel up to standard but was aware that there was still much to be done. Marianna was very set in her ways and the more he thought about it, the more he wanted Gabi to be a part of his team.

Alim did not use the main entrance to the ballroom, for he wished to be discreet. Instead, he walked out through a courtyard and breathed in the cold air.

It was snowing and he stood for a moment listening to the applause as the speeches ended. The master of ceremonies was telling the guests that there had been another couple who had married here some sixty years ago and was leading into the first dance for the newlyweds.

Holding the wedding here and all that entailed had been the least he could do for his half-brother.

The staff might discover his royal status perhaps, but that was a small price to pay for being able to be somewhat involved in this day.

He wondered how his father felt, upstairs in the Royal Suite, as his eldest son married downstairs.

Alim walked in through the French windows and

looked over at Fleur, who sat, a part of the bridal party yet somehow remote.

Alim held nothing against her—in fact, he felt for her. She had been a good mother to James and had never caused any problems for his family.

He, himself, was causing problems for a certain someone, though.

His entrance, however unobtrusive, could not have come at a worse time for Gabi.

Of all the moments that Alim could have chosen to check on proceedings, Gabi would have preferred that it was not this particular one.

Often he arrived with an entourage, but on this night he had slipped quietly into the ballroom just as the happy couple were about to take to the floor.

And *that* was the problem.

An old-fashioned gramophone had been set up and a microphone discreetly placed over it so that in this delicious old ballroom history would tonight be repeated.

Of course, there was a back-up recording to hand should the needle skid across the vinyl or start to jump, or should the assistant wedding planner's hand be shaking so much just at the sight of Alim.

He made her a quivering wreck simply by his presence.

He came in from the cold and, though impossible from this distance, she felt as if the cool air followed him in, for she shivered.

Do not look over, Gabi told herself. *Just ignore that he has come in.*

Under Bernadetta's less-than-reassuring glare, Gabi placed the needle on the vinyl and the sounds of yesteryear crackled into life. It was not the bride and groom who took to the dance floor—it was the bride's grandparents.

Tenderly, the elderly man held his wife and it was the perfect pastiche as the younger couple joined them.

It was an incredibly moving passing of the baton and just so utterly romantic to watch the elderly couple and the newlyweds dance side by side that it brought a tear to Gabi's eyes.

Oh, it made all the sleepless nights worth it, just for this.

She glanced up and saw that the photographer was snapping away.

They would be beautiful photos indeed.

Gabi went through her list on her tablet and saw that for now she was up to date.

Everything really had gone seamlessly.

'Another Matrimoni di Bernadetta success,' Bernadetta said, and Gabi's jaw gritted as her boss came and stood by her side. 'I hope that I can trust you to take it from here.'

Bernadetta made it sound as if she was bestowing a great favour when in truth she was skiving off early and leaving it all to Gabi.

All of it had been left to Gabi.

Bernadetta had flown back from her vacation just this morning and had spent most of the day staying warm in her luxurious car.

Gabi stood there, biting back tears as Bernadetta waltzed off, though of course she took time to network. Bernadetta knew very well which side her bread was buttered on, and was sweet and charming to anyone who might assist her ascent. She walked up to Alim, and Gabi saw her put her hands up in false modesty as she no doubt accepted congratulations from Alim for another hugely successful wedding.

And Gabi stood there, dreaming of one day going it alone.

Just dreaming of the day when she could call a night such as this *her* success and be the one Alim congratulated.

And that was how he saw her.

Lost in a dream.

Alim walked towards her and as she turned and looked towards him he smiled. She felt that she shone.

Criticism and fault were gone when she was held in his gaze.

No man had ever made her feel like that, no man had ever made her feel as if there was nothing, but nothing, that she needed to change.

He did that with just one look.

'I was wondering…' Alim said in that smoky voice of his, and so lost in her dream was Gabi that she put down the tablet she held and stepped towards him on instinct.

'I'd love to.'

And then she wished the ground would open up and swallow her.

Of course his arms were not waiting for her. Gabi had thought, stupidly thought, that he was asking her to dance, but instead, as he sidestepped, it was just a cringe-inducing faux pas.

Of all the embarrassing moments she had lived through, this was Gabi's worst.

'We're working, Gabi,' Alim said politely.

But no matter how skilfully he deflected or made light of her gaffe, not even he could save her from her shame as he told her the real reason that he had approached.

Of course he hadn't been about to ask her for this dance.

'I was wondering,' Alim repeated, 'if I might have a word.'

CHAPTER THREE

OH, THE SHAME!

Gabi wanted the dance floor to open up and swallow her whole.

Instead, she stood there as Alim gestured with his head, indicating that they move out from the ballroom.

When Alim asked to speak with someone, they tended to say yes, even if they would have preferred to run.

'The bride might need me.' Gabi floundered for an excuse. 'Bernadetta just left.'

'I know that.'

Alim had a word with one of the staff as they made their way out and told them where they could be found. 'If anyone is looking for you, you will be told.'

She retrieved her tablet and he led them out of the ball-room to a table and chairs, and as she took a seat he put up his hand to halt a waiter as he approached.

This was business.

Yet her navy eyes were shining with embarrassed tears and there was a mottle to her chest from the mother of all burning blushes.

Poor thing, Alim thought.

He was terribly used to women liking him, even if it was a more sophisticated sandpit where he usually played.

Gabi would know that.

Surely?

'The wedding and the celebrations have gone very well,' Alim said.

'Matrimoni di Bernadetta put a lot of effort into it,' Gabi duly responded.

'I think we both know,' Alim said, 'that Bernadetta put precisely zero effort into this wedding.'

Gabi blinked at his forthrightness.

'Bernadetta isn't here,' Alim interrupted, 'so speak to me, Gabi.'

'Why?'

'Because I might be able to help. I appreciate hard work, I like to see talent rewarded.'

'I am well rewarded.'

He raised an eyebrow slightly.

The pay, they both knew, was terrible.

'I know that the gramophone was your idea,' Alim told her.

'How could you know that?'

'I know the groom. That is why I had to drop in and check that everything was going well.'

'Oh.'

'And he told me how impressed they were with you.'

Actually, the information hadn't been that forthcoming, James hadn't raced to tell Alim how wonderful the assistant wedding planner was.

Alim had specifically asked.

His success had come, not by accident, or by acquired wealth or by flouting his title. He kept his royal status as private as he could, and while his impossible wealth had been a starting point, it was his attention to detail that caused his ventures to thrive.

Alim did not merely accept findings, he dug deeper. And while he knew that Matrimoni di Bernadetta was amongst the top tier of wedding planners, he was very aware of the mechanics of the business.

Bernadetta had chosen well!

'Tell me.'

He could tell she was nervous.

'Why did you choose this career?' he asked.

'Because I love weddings.'

'Even now?' Alim asked. 'Even after...?' He asked a question. 'How old are you?'

'Twenty-four and, yes, I still love weddings. I always have, since I was a little girl.'

'And you've worked for Bernadetta for how long?'

'Six years,' Gabi said. 'Before that I worked for a local seamstress. And when I was at school...' She halted, not wanting to bore him.

'Go on.'

'I worked for a local florist. I used to work through Friday night to have the bouquets ready for weddings. I would get up to go to the markets before school...'

This was the passion Alim wanted in his staff.

'I was very lucky that Bernadetta took me on.'

'Why is that?' he asked.

'Well, I had no qualifications. My mother needed me to work so I left school at sixteen and Matromoni di Bernadetta has a good reputation.'

'So how did you get an interview?'

'I wrote to her,' Gabi admitted. 'Many times. After a year she finally agreed to give me an interview, though she warned me the competition was extremely tough. I had my friend Rosa make me a suit and I...' Gabi gave a tight shrug. 'I asked for a trial.'

'I see.'

'Bernadetta showed me a brief she had for a very important wedding and asked for my ideas.' Gabi gave him a smile. 'You've heard of fake it till you make it…'

'Fake what?' Alim asked.

'I pretended that I knew what I was doing.'

'But you *did* know what you were doing,' Alim said, and Gabi swallowed. 'You had already worked for a seamstress and a florist…'

'Yes, but…'

'And what happened with the ideas you gave her for this very important wedding?'

'She incorporated some of them.'

'So what part were you faking?'

Gabi frowned. 'I've learnt an awful lot working for Bernadetta.'

'Of course,' Alim agreed. 'She is at the top of her game. I have no hesitation recommending her. Still, I know that lately most of the credit should fall to you. Have you ever thought about moving out on your own?'

Her blush had all but faded and now it returned, though not to her chest. He watched as her cheeks darkened and her jaw tightened and Gabi was angry indeed, Alim knew.

'I can't.'

'Why not?'

'Alim…' Gabi shook her head. She was loyal, even if it was misplaced, and she had also got into trouble for dreaming out loud before.

'Talk to me,' he said.

'Why?'

'Because I may be able to help.'

'Bernadetta found out that I one day hoped to go out on my own, and she reminded me of a clause in my contract.'

'Which is?'

'That I can't use any of the firms that she does for six months after leaving. I'd have to make new contacts.'

'But you already use only the best.'

'Yes.' Gabi nodded, glad that he immediately got it. She had spent hours trying to explain it to her mother, who'd said she should just be glad to have a job. It was so nice to discuss it with Alim! 'Those contacts weren't all Bernadetta's to start off with.' Gabi had held it in for so long that it was a relief to vent some of her frustration. 'The bride tonight is wearing Rosa's creation. It was her lounge floor that I used to cut fabric on.'

'Tell me,' he urged.

So Gabi did.

'When I first worked for Bernadetta we had a bride to dress and she had only one arm. So many of the designers shunned her, they did not want her wearing one of their creations. I was furious so I suggested that Bernadetta try Rosa. She scoffed at the idea at first but in the end agreed to give her a try—Rosa made the bride a princess on her day. It was a very high-profile wedding and so in came the orders. Now Rosa works in the best street in Rome. Rosa is *my* contact but of course I did not think to get that in writing at the time.'

Alim watched as Gabi slumped a little in her seat.

Defeated.

And then he fought not to smile as her hand went to her hair and she coiled a strand around her finger.

For after a moment's pause she rose again.

Now she had started to air her grievances, Gabi found that she could not stop. 'The flowers today, the gardenias—it was the florist's idea to replicate the grandmother's bouquet.' Alim noted that Gabi did not take credit where it was not due and he liked that. 'The florist,

Angela, is the woman I worked with when I was at school. We used to work in a tiny store, now she is known as one of the finest bridal florists in Rome.'

'So the best contacts are off limits,' Alim said, and Gabi nodded.

'For six months after I leave—and I doubt I could hold off for that long. That is assuming anyone will hire me as their wedding planner. I doubt Bernadetta will give a good reference.'

'She'll bad-mouth you.'

He said it as fact.

He was right.

Alim had thought he had the solution.

Right now, he could be wrapping the conversation up with the offer that Gabi come and work for him.

It was rather more complicated now, though, and not just because she liked him. Alim was very used to that.

It was that he liked her.

He acknowledged it then. Just a little, he assured himself.

But, yes, for two years the hotel had seemed warmer when Gabi was here. For two years he had smiled to himself as she clipped across the foyer in those awful heels, or muttered a swear word now and then under her breath.

He had never allowed himself to acknowledge her beauty but he could not deny it now.

She looked stunning.

Her hair was falling from its confines, her dress shimmered over her curves and how the hell had he not swept her into his arms to dance? Alim pondered. But the answer, though he denied it, was becoming clearer the longer they spoke—he had been resisting her for a long time.

The other week his mood had not been great.

Christmas was always busy in the hotel industry but it wasn't just that that had accounted for his dark mood.

Issues back home were becoming more pressing.

But it wasn't that either.

There had been a vague air of discontent that he could not place, though admittedly he had avoided seeking its source.

Alim had not wanted to give voice to it.

So he hadn't.

Outside work he had been his usual reprobate self, but some time between Christmas and New Year he had walked into the foyer of the Grande Lucia and seen that Fleur had taken him up on his suggestion that they use Matrimoni di Bernadetta to plan the wedding. They hadn't held a wedding here in a very long while and Alim had found that he missed Gabi's presence. The air felt different when she was around.

He fought to bring his thoughts back to work.

'What would you do differently from Bernadetta?'

Gabi frowned, for it felt like an interview, but she answered his question.

'I'd ditch the black suit.'

'You already have.' His eyes did not leave hers as he said it but he let her know that the change from her usual attire had been noted.

Oh, it had.

It no longer felt like an interview.

Their minds actually fought not to flirt—Gabi because she did not want to make a fool of herself again, and Alim because he kept work at work.

'There was a wardrobe malfunction back at the church,' Gabi carefully answered.

'Malfunction?'

'I fell,' Gabi said. 'Thankfully it was after the bridal party had left, but I tore my suit.'

'Did you hurt yourself?'

'A bit.'

He wanted to peel off her dress and examine her bruises; he wanted to bring her now to his lap.

But still his eyes never left hers and the conversation remained polite.

'So you would ditch the black suit in favour of what?

'I've seen this fabric, it's a willow-green and pink check, more a tartan. It sounds terrible but…'

'No,' Alim said. 'It sounds different. Do you have a picture?'

Of course she did, and she took only a moment to bring it up on her tablet and hand it to Alim.

He looked at the picture of the fabric she had chosen. It was more subtle than she had described and, yes, it would be the perfect choice.

'What would you change here at the Grande Lucia?' he asked as he handed back the tablet. He expected her to flounder, given that she'd had no time to prepare.

Gabi though knew exactly what the first change would be.

'There would be a blanket ban on red carnations throughout the hotel.'

She watched the slight twitch of his very beautiful lips. Alim had many areas of expertise but flowers were not amongst them. 'I don't tend to get involved with the floral displays,' he said.

'I do.' Gabi smiled. 'I obsess about such things.'

'Really?'

'Really.'

'What would you choose?'

'Sahara roses are always nice, though I think it should

vary through the week, and at weekends I would change the theme to tie in with the main function being held.'

'Would you, now?'

'You did ask.'

'Are Sahara roses your favourite flower?'

'No,' Gabi said.

'What is?'

'Sweet peas.' She gave him a smile. 'Marianna would faint at the idea and deny that they are sophisticated enough for the Grande Lucia, but, honestly, when arranged right…'

Her face lit up and he smiled.

Gabi was all fresh ideas and the zing of youth, and coupled with Marianna's wisdom…

But it was getting harder to think of business.

Very hard.

'Would you like a drink?' Alim offered.

'I'm working.'

And there was a slight ironic smile that dusted his lips as she mirrored his own words from earlier.

'Gabi…' Alim said, and then halted.

He needed to think this through before he offered her this role; she had already been dragged over the coals. If she were to work for him, it could get messy. One-night stands were his usual fare and that was why he kept his personal life where it belonged.

In bed.

He wanted the best for his business and yet, rarely for Alim, he found that he wanted what was best for her, so he came up with an alternative.

'Have you thought of going into partnership with Bernadetta?'

'Partnership?' Gabi shot him an incredulous look. 'She would laugh me out of her office if I suggested it.'

'And when she had stopped laughing, you would tell her that you'd make a better partner than rival.'

It had never even crossed her mind.

'Or, if you continue to work for her you set your limits, you tell Bernadetta only what you are prepared to do. What works for you…'

He did not want to lose her though.

Oh, this could get messy, yet the closer he examined it, the more it appealed.

'There is another option…'

'Gabi!' Her name was said again and she turned as one of the waiters came over. 'The photographer wants to speak with you.'

'Excuse me,' Gabi said, and, ever the gentleman, Alim stood as she left.

Alim went back into the ballroom and looked up. He saw the westerly door open and smiled at the thought of Yasmin creeping in.

And then he turned and saw his brother.

There were no halves where love was concerned.

'Congratulations,' Alim said.

'Thank you.'

And that was all he could offer in public.

James's complexion and hair were lighter but standing side by side it would be hard to miss the similarities. They had to step apart before someone made the connection.

Alim took a call from Violetta and was told that the Sultan of Sultans would like to speak with him.

Things were already tense between Alim and Oman.

Oman resented Alim's freedom, and was bitter with his lot for Fleur was the love of his life. And, in turn, Alim, though respectful with words, was silently disapproving, for he loved his mother and loathed how she had been treated.

Alim bowed as he entered the Royal Suite and then told his father about the wedding's progress.

'Everything is going smoothly,' Alim informed him, though that knowledge did not make things better for Oman since he could not be there to see his son marry for himself.

'Where is Yasmin?' he snapped.

'We had dinner,' Alim calmly answered, 'and she is now in her suite. The reception will finish shortly; you will see James and Mona in the morning.'

No doubt, Alim thought, Fleur would be here soon.

He thought he would now be dismissed but, instead, Oman brought up an argument of old.

One that had never really left them.

'I want you home.'

Alim was in no mood for this but he did not show his irritation. 'I was in Zethlehan last month and I shall be back for a formal visit in—'

'I mean permanently.' Oman interrupted.

'That isn't going to happen.'

They had had this argument many times before.

Alim refused to act as caretaker to his country just so that his father could travel abroad more.

He would not facilitate the shaming of his mother.

Although he was happy for James and Mona and wished he could participate more in the celebration, tonight still felt like a betrayal to his mother.

'You are thirty-two years old, Alim. Surely it is time that you marry?'

Alim stayed silent but his eyes told his father that he did not need marriage guidance from a man who had a wife and a mistress. Alim never cheated. He was upfront in all his relationships, and there could be no confusion that what he offered was a temporary affair. Arrogant, some might say, but better that than leading someone on.

'I shall select a bride for you,' Oman said in threat. 'Then you shall have no choice but to marry.'

'We always have choices.'

The advice he had so recently given to Gabi had been tested over and over by Alim—he had long ago set his limits with his father and told him what he was and was not willing to do.

'To choose a bride without my agreement could only serve to embarrass not just the bride but our country when the groom does not show,' Alim warned. 'I will not be pushed into marriage,'

'Alim, I am not well.'

'How unwell?' Alim asked, for he did not trust his father not to exaggerate for gain.

'I require treatment. I am going to have to stay out of the public eye for six months at least.'

Alim listened as his father went into detail about his health issues and Alim had to concede grudgingly that there was a battle ahead.

'I will step in,' Alim responded. 'You know that.'

It wasn't the response his father wanted, though, and he pressed his son further. 'Our people need good news, a wedding would be pleasing for them.'

Alim would not be manipulated and stood up to his father just as he always had. 'Our people would surely want to see the Sultan of Sultans at such a celebration. A son's wedding without his father's presence would send the message that the father did not approve of his son's choice of bride, and this could surely cause our people anxiety.' Alim watched his father's jaw grit. 'Let us discuss this again when you are well.'

His father would have argued further, but suddenly

Alim sensed distraction as he saw Oman glance towards the adjoining door, and he guessed that his father's lover had just arrived.

'I shall see you in the morning for breakfast,' Alim said, and then bowed and left.

As he walked along the corridor, though outwardly calm, inside his mood was dark. No, he could not put off choosing a bride for ever, but he had no desire to live the life that his parents did—he thought of his mother alone tonight in the palace. Always she had put on a brave face and smiled at her children as if things were just fine.

How could they be?

Alim did not want a bride chosen for him by his father.

He wanted…

What?

The maudlin feeling would not shift. Alim reminded himself that his friend Bastiano would be in town next week and that would likely cheer him up. But Bastiano was just another rich playboy, and the casinos and clubs did not hold their usual allure for Alim.

In truth, he was tired of his exhausting private life. The thrill of the chase no longer existed, for after two years in Rome women sought *him* out.

He walked through the foyer and, sure enough, the last of the guests were leaving.

Alim went up the stairwell and, unlocking the door, he went onto the gallery.

There were no signs of his sister and Alim assumed she was safely in her suite. The photographer had left some equipment so Alim made a mental note to lock the door as he left.

Alim glanced down at the stunning ballroom.

The staff were clearing the glasses and tables away but most of it would wait for the morning.

It was done.

The wedding had been *his* gift to the couple and Fleur had engineered things so that it was held at the Grande Lucia. Yet he had not taken any significant part in the proceedings.

Yes, it had been a wonderful wedding but for Alim it had been a wretched day and night.

Apart from the time spent with Gabi.

He looked down at her standing in the now-empty ballroom.

Alim had been going to ask her to work for him but had decided that, given how he felt, at best it would be foolish to get overly involved.

Then he smiled when he recalled her blush when she had thought he was about to ask her to dance.

And, as of now, he was no longer working.

CHAPTER FOUR

GABI WANTED TO go home and hide her shame.

Over and over she replayed it in her head—that awful moment when she had thought the suave Alim had been asking her to dance.

She stood in the empty ballroom and surveyed the slight chaos that a successful wedding reception left in its wake.

The staff had been in and cleared the plates and glasses, the tables had been stripped and the chairs stacked away. All Gabi had to do tonight was take the old gramophone out to her car and safely put away the grandparents' vinyl record that the bride and groom had danced to.

It could wait a few moments, though, and Gabi paused to look around.

It was *such* a magnificent ballroom.

The chandeliers had been switched off and it was lit now by the harsh white downlights that had come on when the music had ended and it had been time for the guests to leave.

And, because she could, Gabi headed to the power box and one by one flicked the switches until all the lights were off.

She did not turn on the chandeliers.

They didn't need electricity to be beautiful, for the

moonlight came in through the high windows and it was as if the snow outside was now falling within. Even unseen trees made an appearance because the shadows of branches crept along the silver walls.

It was like standing in an icy forest, so much so that she could imagine her breath blowing white.

What had Alim been about to say to her?

It might be weeks or months before she was here at the Grande Lucia again.

Maybe she would never know.

Gabi heard the door open and turned, assuming it was one of the staff to clear the remnants of the wedding away.

Instead, it was Alim.

'I was just…'

Just what?

Thinking about you.

Gabi didn't say that, of course.

'It went very well tonight,' he said.

'Thank you.'

And now she should collect her things and go home, yet she made no move to leave.

She was one burning blush as he walked across the room, and she did not know where to go or what to do with herself as he approached the old gramophone.

And then she shivered.

Not because it was cold, for the air was perfectly warm; instead, she shivered in silent delight as she heard the slight scratch of the needle hitting the vinyl. The sounds of old were given life again and etched on her heart for ever as he turned around, walked towards her and, without a word, offered her a dance.

And, without a word, she accepted.

His embrace was tender but firm and, close up, the

heady, musky sent of him held a peregrine note that she could not place. But, then, nothing about tonight was familiar.

Usually his greetings were polite; tonight things had changed and, Gabi thought, even the suave Alim seemed to accept they were on the edge of something.

'Listen.' He spoke into her ear and his low voice offered a delicious warning. 'I am trouble.'

'I know that.'

He felt her head nod against his chest and her words were accepting rather than resigned so he made things clearer. 'If you like me, then doubly so.'

'I know all of that,' Gabi said.

The trouble was, right now, here in his arms, Gabi didn't care and she lifted her face to his.

Tonight was her night.

Gabi knew his reputation and accepted it would never be anything more than a night, yet she had carried a torch for Alim for years.

The consequences she could live with.

It was regret she could do without.

His body she had craved and imagined for so long, and she rested against it now. He was lean and strong and he moved her so skilfully to the music that for the first time in her life Gabi felt not just co-ordinated but light.

They stared deep into each other's eyes. She never wanted to leave the warmth of his gaze, and for now she did not have to.

They stared and they swayed and they ached within.

His whole life, Alim had fought to keep his business and personal life separate. It had seemed the sensible thing to do, yet nothing made more sense than the thoughts that were now forming in his mind.

One woman.

He thought of the many upcoming trips home and he thought of returning to the Grande Lucia and to Gabi in his bed.

Alim thought of them working together and still it did not deter him, for there would be benefits for them both.

His head lowered, his lips brushed hers, and on contact Gabi knew she would never regret this.

A gentle kiss had been her fantasy, perhaps one on the cheek that changed midway.

Yet his kiss was decisive as his mouth met hers and he delivered her first kiss. She melted at the sheer bliss of it.

It actually felt as if her lips seemed to know what to do, for they moved and melded to the soft caress of Alim's.

He was used to slenderness yet his hands now ran over luscious curves; he felt the press of her breasts against his chest and suddenly there was less reason for caution than he had ever known.

He wanted Gabi in bed—and not just for this night—so he moved his mouth from hers.

'Are you seeing someone?' he asked.

And though she was held in his arms, though he was hard against her soft stomach, his question was so matter-of-fact and so direct that it felt again, to Gabi, like an interview.

'When does a wedding planner get time for a social life?' she murmured, keen to get back to his kiss.

'So it causes problems in your relationships?'

He was fishing, shamelessly so.

She was honest.

And not to her detriment.

'There have been no relationships.'

Her words went straight to his groin, and Gabi felt him further harden in response to them while his hands on her hips moved her further in.

As he met her mouth again, she felt the odd sensation of panic devoid of fear.

The intimate taste of him was briefly shocking, the intensity and the thoroughness of his kiss was better in the flesh than in dreams. There, in imaginings, she did not know quite what to do, but here, with him, she held his breath in her mouth and swallowed it as he accepted hers.

They made hunger.

Illicit.

That was the taste they made.

The tip of her tongue was surely nectar for he savoured it, and the scratch of his jaw was a new hurt for her to relish.

Her breasts ached against fabric as his hands roamed her curves, and she felt the dig of his fingers in her hips and the grind of him against her.

Dignity was not Gabi's forte.

She slipped and fell on so many occasions.

Tonight, though, she danced with the man of her dreams.

It was just a dance, she told herself. Her body denied it.

Oh, it was so much more than a dance.

He moved her an inch, a dangerous inch for it felt as if their heat met and she was scared to let go, scared to misread the situation again, but it felt as if they were headed for bed.

As she opened her eyes to the coolness of his cheek Gabi was ready for more.

It was the eyes of insatiable heat that met his.

'What the hell was I thinking?' Alim asked, for he still could not believe he had sidestepped that dance.

She did not understand the question, and since he offered no clarification Gabi did not attempt a reply.

Alim spoke for both of them.

'Come to bed.'

CHAPTER FIVE

HE TOOK HER hand and led her from the dance floor but as they reached the double doors he dropped it.

'For this to work,' he told her, 'we must be discreet.'

Alim was talking of the weeks and months ahead while Gabi was thinking just of this night, but nevertheless she nodded. Her cheeks were flushed and her mind was flurried with hormones like a snow-globe, and so she was grateful that he could think of sparing her blushes in the morning.

His thoughtfulness spurred her to think of tomorrow also.

'I need to get my coat, or they'll know that I stayed the night.'

'Do so, then,' Alim told her. 'Just say goodnight and that you are collecting some dresses...'

He knew her routines for he *had* noticed her... Often, before she went home, Gabi would head up to the dressing suite, where bridesmaids and such got changed, and leave the hotel with her arms filled with tulle.

She blinked at the fact that he knew.

'I'll head up,' Alim said. 'I have a private elevator...'

'I know that you do.'

'I shall send it back down.'

Alim left the ballroom and a moment later so too did she.

It was like any other night.

He walked to his elevator and pulled open the antique gate as Gabi smiled at Silvia, the receptionist on duty tonight.

'I just have to get some dresses and then I'm done,' Gabi said. 'Can I just get my coat?'

'Sure.'

Gabi slipped behind the desk and into the small staff cloakroom, where she collected her coat and put it on.

And just like on any other night she walked through the foyer.

There was a loud couple by the lifts who Gabi recognised as guests from the wedding and as she turned her head she saw a polished group coming in through the brass revolving doors.

No one was looking at Gabi.

The doors to the elevator were heavy and for a moment they did not budge and she wondered if he had forgotten to unlock them.

She was almost frantic, but suddenly they slid to one side and she stepped in and closed them.

His exotic fragrance lingered in the air and she leant against the soft cushioned wall.

The light was dim and she took a second, or maybe ten, just to imprint this moment for, she knew, things between them could never be the same again.

Oh, she accepted this was just one night, but it would be the absolute night of her life and she would never regret it, Gabi swore.

She went to press the button but before she did so the elevator jolted, and she guessed Alim would have known she was inside and was impatient for her to arrive.

It *was* he who had pressed the summons.

For he *was* impatient.

Alim was an ordered person.

Even as the elevator lifted her towards him, he made plans. Tonight was not the time to offer her a position here at the hotel and as his lover; he would wait until tomorrow when his head was clearer.

For now, he would take her to the bedroom and make very slow love to her, for he knew she was inexperienced and deserved due care.

And for once there was tomorrow.

Yes, Alim made plans…but then he saw her. She was flushed in the face and her hands moved with his to open the gated doors. Their fingers met, and haste was born.

Gated elevators were not so good for self-control, for they started to kiss through the gates. Dirty, fevered kisses as their hands reached through the bars.

It was ridiculous—one second apart and they could open them and be together, but even a second apart felt too long.

For the greater good she stepped back as Alim wrenched open the gate and rather than behaving shyly and reticently, as in her dreams she had been, she simply toppled into his arms.

How, he wondered, had he resisted her for so long?

'I hated it when you came up here with her…'

They were jealous words but she felt free to say them and he knew exactly the time Gabi referred to.

'You will recall that I sent her back down,' Alim said as he kissed her hard against the wall.

'Why?' she demanded.

'I was at risk of saying your name.'

'Why?'

'You know why,' Alim said, and mid-hallway, a long

way from the entrance to his lounge, let alone the bedroom door, he recalled that incident. 'Because I was hard for you.'

He was hard for her now.

Her hands were in his hair and though she was unskilled in her kiss, so untamed and frantic was her mouth it was effort that was rewarded.

His hands dug hard into her bottom as they kissed; he felt her wriggle and Gabi let out an 'Ow' as he dug into her bruise.

'It's sore there,' she said, for all her senses felt heightened and she saw him frown in concern that he had hurt her. 'Where I fell,' she further explained.

Oh, yes.

His apartment might just as well be in Venice, for the corridor was simply too long for both of them; he would have to drag her, like a marathon runner across the finishing line. Oh, her determination was there but her willpower had gone at the same moment as his.

Still he kissed her hard against the wall, his tongue forcing apart her lips and his hands holding Gabi's wrists by her sides.

She ached to touch him, but he held her tight as he kissed her hard. Her arms attempted to flex, but his grip tightened and then suddenly released.

'Bed,' he said.

'Please,' she told him.

They fell through the door and were greeted by warmth and the scent of wood and pine and a fire lit in the grate.

It surprised Gabi, for she had expected opulence but not warmth.

He was behind her and the intention was bed but so

warm was the room and so wanting the flesh that his hand came to her zipper.

'Show me where you hurt,' he said.

Gabi screwed her eyes closed for she wanted pitch blackness before she was naked but her dress was already sliding down.

She had felt beautiful in it, but now she was scared that the unwrapping of the parcel might reveal less than delicious contents.

Instead, she heard a low moan as he ran a finger down her spine.

'Alim…' Gabi breathed as she felt his fingers in her knickers, sliding them down.

Then he knelt and she felt his breath on her bottom and then his mouth soft and warm, and she thought she might fold over.

Her thighs were shaking as she stepped out of her knickers.

His hands splayed her thighs so that she stood in her lovely high heels with her legs spread a little apart. He kissed the sensitive flesh of her inner thigh, then kissed the new purple bruise and it was bliss, but a bliss that could not last, for either of them, for more was needed for such pleasure to be sustained.

He stood then, undid her bra and turned her around.

He was completely dressed.

As if he had just come in to check on his staff.

You could not tell he had been on his knees between her thighs.

'I feel at a disadvantage,' she admitted, for she was naked apart from her shoes.

'Yet you have the complete advantage,' Alim said, for she could bring him back to his knees if she so chose.

Instead, she took off her shoes.

They made her unsteady—or was that Alim?—for his eyes never left her face as he shrugged off his jacket.

Gabi stood perfectly still, yet her breath came in pants as if she had been sprinting. His fingers reached for a nipple, taking it between finger and thumb, and then he looked down. Gabi swallowed as he lowered his head and took a leisurely taste; to steady herself, her hand went for his head.

But he removed it.

Her breast was wet and cool from his mouth as he removed his tie and shirt.

Oh, she had wanted to see him for so long. His skin was like burnt caramel and his chest was wide, his arms strong. She looked at the fan of hair and the dark puckered skin of his nipples, and she too wanted her taste. For a moment she resisted, for there were other feasts to be had.

She ran a hand along his upper arm and it was an unexpected move for Alim but he liked the soft touch of her hands and the slight pinch of her fingers.

Then she looked down at the snake of hair and the swell beneath and she bit on her lip because she knew tonight was going to hurt.

'I'll be gentle.'

'Really?'

And there was a dry edge to her voice, a smoky provocative edge that even Gabi had not heard in herself before.

She was stroking the crinkle of hair on his stomach and then her mouth went to his flat nipple; she licked the salty skin and this time it was Alim who held her head and moaned at the soft nip of her teeth. And it was Gabi who slid down his zipper.

Alim had anticipated reticence, yet her touch was eager.

They both stood naked now, so there was no disadvantage, not a single one.

She could see and feel and touch his desire, which she did, stroking him at first then abandoning him erect so that she could reclaim his kiss.

He was damp and hard against her stomach and she was burning on the inside. She had dreamed of being kissed on his bed.

Instead, they did not make it past the fire.

They knelt, though their mouths remained engaged, sharing hot, wet kisses as they sank back onto their heels. His body was magnificent, his shoulders were wide as she ran her hands over them.

Always, she had felt cumbersome.

Not tonight.

He felt her lips stretch into a smile.

'What?' he asked, and pulled his head back a fraction.

'You always make me want to sit up straighter.'

'Sit up straighter, then.'

She had to fight to do so because, as he traced her clavicle with his tongue, she wanted to fold in two. Then down to her breast and he tasted it again, only slowly and deeply while massaging the other, rolling the swollen nipple between finger and thumb.

'Sit up straight,' he warned, as she started to sink into his skilled caress, which crept lower and lower.

She rested her arms on his shoulders as his fingers slipped into her tight hollow; she let out a sob of both pain and pleasure as he stretched and probed her, readying her for him.

She could sit up straight no more so he laid her down on the floor, stroking her and kissing her all the while.

His fingers did not rush, though his hand was insistent.

She went to push it away at one point for he made her want to scream, but instead Gabi clenched her jaw. He spoke in Arabic and his words, though not understood, matched her urgent desire.

He was passionate, sensual and far from cold as he coached her those final steps home.

'Come,' he told her, licking his lips, and she felt that if she did not then his lips would ensure that she did. Gabi succumbed to the pleasure, simply letting go.

She was tight around his fingers as her thighs clamped and her bottom lifted. Watching her pleasure was intense for Alim, and he fought his urgent need to take her.

Alim too was breathless as she lay there, temporarily sated, her hand over her mound.

She had not lied as others had, for there was blood on his fingers as he removed them.

Now they would retreat to the bedroom, yet still his hand roamed her thighs. Unwittingly, Gabi parted them for him, her mouth awaiting his kiss.

He fought with temptation and lost.

A little way, he decided, because he ached for her.

'It's going to hurt,' Gabi said, torn between fear and desire.

'A little,' he accepted, but despite his size her wetness eased him in.

It was *nothing* like her imaginings.

In her dreams it was a seamless, tender dance as he gently took her while telling her he loved her. In reality it was the tearing of flesh and the rising of pain as he inched into her.

Gabi found that she preferred the latter.

'Gabi...'

He had sworn *just a little way in*, but the grip was too

inviting, the scent of sex urged him on and he thrust in deeply.

She sobbed, loudly, and he cursed his lack of care. Alim stilled. It took a moment for her to acclimatise, to regroup, and then she begged him to do it again.

Alim obliged.

Over and over.

They rolled and they kissed, they dragged from each other pleasure beyond imagining, and she, the virgin, pushed him to extremes, for he fought hard not to come.

His life, his identity, even his seed was always protected.

Yet his abdomen was tight and he was lifting.

He did not withdraw and she did not resist. Instead, she coiled her legs tighter around his loins, and this time, when Gabi came, it was around his thick length.

He felt the throb of her demand.

'Alim…' Her voice told him *now*, in fact it pleaded, and Alim bade farewell to restraint and rained deep into her.

The rush of his release and the moan he made procured a tiny cry from Gabi that abruptly died, for she was back to his mouth, being consumed by his kiss and a slave to their bliss.

They lay there a while, until both the room and their bodies were cool. But the fires of passion had not dimmed.

'Bed,' Alim said, and he stood and helped her up.

For still it beckoned.

CHAPTER SIX

ALIM HAD ALWAYS been careful.

Always!

Until now.

There was nothing about this night that compared with others, for they made love again and then, instead of sleeping, lay in his bed, talking, thirstily drinking iced sparkling water.

It was refreshing.

Even mistakes were forgiven.

'Tomorrow I shall arrange for a doctor to see you,' he told Gabi as they discussed the morning-after pill.

'I'll sort it,' Gabi said, for she was not seeing a doctor here!

'I apologise,' he told her.

'Please don't.'

She would not change it, or, if she could, Gabi would only have been better prepared and been on the Pill, but nothing could have forewarned her that on this night her dreams would come true.

She had craved Alim from a distance for years. Now he was here and it was better even than she had dreamt.

Gabi might be inexperienced but she knew enough about Alim to be surprised by their ease in conversation afterwards.

She had known that he would be a brilliant lover; the surprise was that afterwards she felt like she was lying with a friend, for they chatted.

And she had never imagined that might happen with Alim.

Yet they spoke about their lack of thought earlier and made plans to remedy it later that day.

'I will sort it,' she told him. 'Believe me, I have no intention of ending up like—' She halted.

'Like who?'

'My mother,' Gabi said. 'I don't mean that I don't want to be like her, I mean I don't want to resent…'

Whatever way she said it made it sound wrong.

'Tell me,' Alim said, just as he had when they had spoken outside the ballroom, only this time she was wrapped in his arms.

'I was an accident,' Gabi explained. 'One she still pays for to this day.'

'Surely not,' Alim said. 'What about your father?'

'I don't know who he is.' Gabi admitted. 'It doesn't matter, I don't need to know…'

But she did.

Often, the need to know was so acute that she could not bear it, yet she played it down as she always had.

'My mother had been accepted to study at university but had to give it up to raise me.'

'It is not your fault that she did not follow her dreams.'

'It feels like it,' Gabi admitted. 'If she hadn't had me…'

'Then she would have found another excuse.'

'That's harsh,' Gabi said.

'Perhaps,' Alim conceded, and he smiled as she looked at him.

'Are you always so direct?'

'Always.'

Now it was Gabi who smiled.

'So planning weddings is your dream?' he asked.

Gabi nodded. She told him about when she had been a little girl and the flour and sugar that had driven her mother wild. 'I would pick flowers at the park for the bouquet and spend the whole day making sure that everything was perfect.' She thought for a moment. 'I was so worried about this wedding. It was so incredibly rushed but when I saw James and Mona dance last night I knew that they'd be okay.'

'How did you know that?'

'You can tell,' Gabi said. 'She was a very difficult bride, but together they seem so happy.'

He liked hearing that, for Alim wanted happiness for his brother.

It was not something he sought for himself.

Alim did not believe in happy marriages. He had been raised with the model that marriage was a business arrangement and a duty, and that happiness was sought elsewhere.

Things were different, of course, for James for he did not have the burden of being his father's heir.

Yes, he admitted in that moment, at times it felt like a burden.

Night was fading but there was no real thought of sleeping as they lay together chatting, Gabi idly running her fingers in circles on his chest.

And for Alim it was very relaxing, too, as well as a bit of a turn-on. He liked her curiosity about his body and her conversation made him smile as she moaned about Bernadetta, and the hell of getting this wedding sorted. But then Gabi crossed the line.

'The groom's mother is paying.'

'Gabi!' he scolded.

'What?'

Alim was considering her for a very senior role, yet she dropped confidential information like a shower of rain.

'You should not discuss such things.'

'Oh, come on,' Gabi said. 'I'm not down at the bar talking about it, I'm in bed with the boss. And it's you she's paying, so you must already know.' And then she smiled and it was like a rainbow and Alim found himself smiling back.

'Okay,' he conceded, and he pulled her in so that she lay with her head on his chest.

'It *is* odd, though,' Gabi said, though she was more thinking out loud, and it was so easy to do so with his hand stroking her hair. 'Usually it's the bride's parents who pay, or half and half…'

Alim shrugged. 'Perhaps Mona's parents are not wealthy.'

'Perhaps.' Gabi yawned. 'Though Fleur clearly is. She intrigues me.'

'Who?'

'Fleur,' Gabi said. 'The mother of the groom.'

Alim said nothing.

'I can't work out if she's divorced or widowed or just single like my mother.'

'Does it matter?' Alim asked.

'Probably not.'

Of course it did, Alim thought. Or it soon would.

He knew how the staff gossiped and very soon Gabi would know his title and it would be clear that the royal guests in residence tonight were related to him.

Or perhaps it would be the wedding photos that would be his undoing when Gabi saw them, for they had made love now and had stared deep into each other's eyes.

Alim knew he was a darker version of James.

Gabi might well see it too.

She was perceptive enough that soon she might work things out.

Alim did not enlighten her now, though.

There would be time for all that tomorrow.

It was more than one night he wanted, yet he was aware that he needed to think things through carefully.

And anyway, for now, Gabi was sleeping.

The more he tried to talk himself out of the plans he was making, the more sense they made. With his father unwell, the months ahead would be trying—that much Alim knew.

He could not put off marriage for ever, but he could certainly delay things.

And what nicer delay than this?

Alim did not expect Gabi to be at his beck and call as he carried on in the usual way; he would be faithful.

A year, perhaps.

It would work for both of them.

Alim's assessment was based on practicalities. Away from Bernadetta, her career would only flourish, he would see to that. And, during this difficult year, he could come back to Rome and to Gabi. There would be no scandal for the palace to deal with, particularly when he began taking a more prominent role while his father sought treatment.

Alim was arrogant enough to assume that Gabi would have no issues with what he was about to propose; after all, women never said no to him, and he was offering more to Gabi then he had to any woman in his life before.

Aside from his commitment to his country, it was the biggest pledge he had made and Alim made it in the still of the night as she lay sleeping.

The sky was grey and silver as the sun rose on a very cold Rome and he thought of her dress on the floor in another room and the soft warm body he held.

Gabi felt the roam of his hands as she awoke and turned her face for a glimpse of Alim asleep but it was denied to her, for Alim was already awake and looking at her.

He watched her eyes flicker open and her face turn to him. He wondered if he would see a grimace or a startle of panic as she recalled their night, but instead he watched as a smile stretched her lips and her sleepy eyes met his.

'Best night,' she said.

It had been.

And those were exactly the words he wanted to hear, for there was no tinge of regret in her smile and no confusion in her eyes.

Only desire.

And Alim *still* felt the same.

During the hours Gabi had slept, Alim had been thinking.

Yes, he still wanted more than one night.

'Fleur did not pay for the wedding,' he said, and watched her frown at the odd choice of topic, wrapped as they were in each other's arms and a breath away from a deep morning kiss.

She did not get yet that this was the most intimate conversation in the whole of Alim's life.

'It was my gift to Mona and James.'

'Why?'

'Because James is my half-brother.'

Her frown deepened and she ran a tongue over her lips as she tried to work things out; now that he had said it, she could see that James and Alim were related.

Gabi had started to see that last night as she had watched the couple dance—or rather there had been something in James that had spoken to her.

Now that she knew, Gabi felt almost foolish that she had not seen it more readily.

'Fleur is my father's mistress,' Alim explained.

'I don't understand,' Gabi said.

'Listen to me.' Alim's eyes and his tone told her that what he was saying was very important. 'Fleur was my father's lover but his father did not consider her a suitable bride. When she got pregnant with James, my grandfather summoned my father home and arranged his marriage to my mother, even though my father loved Fleur.'

'Why did he agree to marry a woman if he loved another?'

'Because he had little choice. His father was the Sultan of Sultans and his word is law; now that title belongs to my father.'

He actually felt the goose-bumps rise on her arm. 'And so what does that make you?'

'A sultan, and one day I shall rule.'

'Why are you telling me this?'

'Because my father is here in the hotel and it won't be long before the staff work out our connection. Soon you would have too.'

'But why are you telling me now?' she persisted.

'Because things back home are changing. My father is unwell, so I am going to have to travel there a lot in the coming months…' Still she stared at him with a puzzled look in her eyes so he made things a little clearer. 'I want to spend more time with you when I am here in Rome. Last night I was going to ask you to work for me as the events co-ordinator at the Grande Lucia.'

It was the offer of a lifetime.

Stunning, in fact.

It was the gateway to a shiny future and, Gabi realised, she may well have blown it for one night in his bed.

But still, she thought, she would not change it for anything.

'Is that offer being reconsidered in the light of certain events?' Gabi asked.

He smiled. 'It is being amended.'

And seriously so.

'What about a one-year contract?' he said.

'One year?'

'That frees you from Bernadetta; you would make many contacts here during that time.'

'And is sleeping with me a part of that contract?'

'Gabi.' Alim heard her indignation but was calm in his response. 'I think from last night it is clear we are not going to be able to work together and keep things strictly business. Of course, we will be discreet in front of the staff but...'

'You've really got this all worked out, haven't you?'

'I've given it considerable thought, yes.'

Gabi had walked in here last night without a doubt that it would be over by the morning.

Certain of it.

Reassured by it, in fact.

For Alim was a self-confessed reprobate and her heart could not be dangled on elastic by him, waiting to be hauled to his bedroom one minute, ignored or discarded the next.

She was shaken, seriously so.

'What happens when someone else comes along?'

She was direct with her questions and he liked that.

'Alim, I take my career seriously...'

'And I admire that you do,' he responded. 'I shan't

mess with it. And,' he offered, which for Alim was a great concession, 'there will be no one else.'

'Why a year?'

'Because I will be called home to marry.'

How cruel that he held her as he said that.

'Gabi.' He had felt her stiffen. 'Please, listen to me now. When Fleur fell pregnant my grandfather invoked a pre-marital diktat on my father. It is a harsh law, one intended to bring a reluctant groom to heel. Once invoked there can be no lovers, save for in the desert.'

'The desert?' she asked. 'You mean a harem.'

'That is what it meant then; they could have worked around it, but Fleur refused to be his desert mistress.'

'I don't blame her for that.'

'By the time James was due to be born my mother was pregnant with me. Fleur gave birth in London; my father could not leave at the time. But later, once he had royal heirs, things were easier for them and my father was more free to travel…'

Gabi didn't want to hear it. She sat up and clutched the sheet around her 'This conversation is medieval.' She did not like what she was hearing—it unnerved her, in fact—but Alim calmly spoke on.

'Perhaps when you see the doctor this morning you should speak about going on the Pill. I can call and arrange for him to see you here…'

'I make my own appointments, Alim, and I don't need to be told what to ask for.' She shot him a look. 'I don't need to go on the Pill because I'm not going to be your mistress…'

'Lover,' Alim corrected, for they were two very different roles.

'I am not going to be your lover for a year until your father summons you home.'

'I have given it a lot of thought.'

'Have you, now?'

'I don't see the issue.'

'Your assumption, for a start.'

She got out of bed and headed for the shower.

Gabi was sore from last night and her head was whirling from all she had been told.

And he was wrong about not messing with careers, Gabi thought as she showered.

Wrapping a towel around her, she headed out and told him so.

'What about Marianna? She's given the Grande Lucia years of her life and you'd discard her like that.' She tried to snap wet fingers; it didn't work.

'She wants to wind down her hours,' Alim answered. 'I would offer her a consulting role.'

She looked at him and for a brief second he seemed not so ruthless but then his hand shot out, stripping off the towel, and she stood naked. He would be ruthless to her heart, she amended.

But her body craved him.

It would be foolish at best not to go on the Pill because all she wanted at this moment was to climb back into bed.

'I know it's a lot to take in,' Alim said. 'But at least give it some thought.'

He did not understand her anger; most women pleaded for more time with him after all. 'Would you prefer it to have been just a one-night stand?'

'Yes.' She actually laughed—somewhat incredulously. 'Yes,' she said again, for this was too much for her to deal with.

'Liar.'

She caught his eyes and her laughter died. Gabi swallowed, because he actually meant it, she was starting to realise.

No!

'A year at your bidding?' she mocked.

'It works both ways,' Alim responded. 'I would be at your bidding too.'

He watched the colour spread up her cheeks and across her chest as she attempted indignation. He watched as she stood to pull on her knickers then sat back down to put on her bra.

He sat up and did it up for her and then kissed the back of her neck.

His tongue was thorough and he moved so he sat naked behind Gabi and kissed her neck harder as his hands played with her breasts.

'Alim.'

She was hot in the face and unable to stand and he knew it. Now one hand came down and slipped into her knickers. She was sore and swollen from last night, and his fingers were not there with the intent to soothe.

This love would hurt.

And it would be love, it possibly already was, but a year at his beck and call would only cement that fact.

'Alim…' She wanted to turn in his arms, to wrap herself around him, but he just upped the beats of pressure and kept bruising her neck with his mouth as she came.

And then he released her.

Somehow Gabi stood.

'The offer's there,' he told her.

And the pleasure might have been hers, but Alim knew it had been worth the restraint from him, for now they ached for each other.

It was the greatest feat of her life to dress and leave,

yet she needed the ice of the winter morning just to learn how to breathe again, and somehow think.

But the confusion he'd spun her into was not yet complete.

Alim leant over and opened a drawer to his beside.

The rumours were true, for there, in a small dish, as one might display after-dinner mints, was a collection of diamonds.

They sparkled in the wintry light, they beguiled, and one alone could make the months ahead so much easier for Gabi.

'Choose one,' Alim said. 'And then tomorrow—'

'I shan't be your whore.'

'In my country the tradition is—'

'We're in Rome, Alim,' she interrupted, and her lips pressed together in anger. Gabi shot him a look and then walked into the lounge and straight to her purse.

He made her feel confident. She felt emboldened.

Somehow he gave her permission to be completely herself.

And that self was cross!

'Here…' She opened up her purse and emptied the entire contents onto the bed. It wasn't much—a lot of coins and a few notes—but she tipped them all out and made him the whore now. 'Treat yourself, baby,' Gabi said.

As she walked out, to the surprise of both of them, Alim laughed.

He never laughed, and certainly not in the morning, yet here he was doing just that.

And, as the door slammed, Alim knew but one thing.

He wanted her back in his bed.

CHAPTER SEVEN

'THE SULTAN OF SULTANS is ready to receive you.'

Alim thanked Violetta when she called to inform him that his father was finally ready for him.

He had showered and dressed in black linen trousers and a fitted white shirt and then impatiently awaited the summons.

Alim had been looking forward to breakfast with the newlyweds, to being able to speak more freely with them.

Now, though, he was also looking forward to the rest of the day.

To the upcoming year.

He knew he had overwhelmed Gabi and that it was all too much to take in, but once she had thought it through, Alim was certain there was hope for them.

Alim looked forward not just to the nights ahead but to the working days, for he had loved this hotel on sight. Shabby, cheaply renovated, he had poured much into it and breathed it back to life. With Gabi as the new functions co-ordinator there was much to look forward to on many levels.

Violetta was waiting outside the Royal Suite. She gave Alim a smile as he approached, then three short knocks on the door to announce Alim's arrival. He opened it and stepped in, expecting to greet his family, but instead there was only his father.

'Alim.' Oman's voice was not particularly welcoming.

'Where are James and Mona?' Alim asked once he had bowed.

'On their way to Paris,' Oman said. 'I asked that they join me a little earlier.'

'I am sure they would have appreciated the early morning call the day after their wedding.'

Sarcasm was wasted on his father, Alim knew.

Still, he had long since realised that if he wanted a relationship with James then he had to forge that for himself.

When Alim had found out he had a half-brother, instead of quietly ignoring it, as would have been his parents' preferred way of dealing with things, Alim had insisted that they meet.

He had kept alive the relationship with his brother with calls, messages and visits, and would continue to do so. Once the newlyweds were back in Rome, Alim would see them, or he might call in a few days and catch up with them in Paris.

It would be good to see Kaleb too.

'What about Yasmin?' Alim asked.

'Violetta told me that she is unwell,' Oman said. 'Apparently she has a migraine—too much excitement last night.'

Or too much champagne, Alim thought, but made no comment as his father spoke on. 'It is just as well for I wish to speak to you alone. With all I told you last night there is a lot to discuss.'

'Very well.'

A gleaming walnut table had been laid and a feast prepared. Alim looked over to where it stood waiting on a large silver trolley.

There were no staff present, Alim noted, as was the case when formal business was to be discussed.

Alim was not really in the mood for a breakfast briefing but given his father's illness he knew there would be a lot to sort out.

If they'd been in Zethlehan, there might be an elder present in case sensitive issues were raised, but for now it was just the two of them.

Alim first served his father and then himself.

Oman preferred fruit, and usually so too did Alim, but this morning he helped himself to a generous serving of *shakshuka*—baked eggs in a rich and spicy sauce. There were several chefs at the Grande Lucia, including two from Zethlehan that Alim had brought over. He made light conversation with his father as he sat down.

'The Middle Eastern brunch at this hotel is becoming increasingly popular. Now people have to book in advance.'

Oman made no comment; he did not approve of Alim having investments overseas, and he particularly loathed his son's passion for this one.

And then Oman said it.

He did not look up; he said it as easily as he might ask for more mint tea.

'For some time now I have been considering invoking the pre-marital diktat.'

Alim, who had anticipated many things for the year ahead, had never envisaged this.

Never.

His father loathed the diktat, since it had been forced upon him, and Alim could not believe that he would bring this harsh ruling to bear on his son.

'There is no need for that.' Alim kept his voice calm, though he was rarely unsettled.

'It would seem that there is. I have been asking to choose your bride for many years.'

'And I have told you—' Alim's voice was still silk, but laced with threat '—that I shall never be pushed into marriage.'

Alim stared at his father. Not only was this unexpected, it was vindictive. 'You loathe that diktat,' Alim pointed out.

'It has its merits. My father chose well for me—your mother is an exemplary queen and our people adore her. We have raised three heirs…'

'And you hate it that you could not marry Fleur.'

He'd said her name out loud.

Now was not the time for reticence.

'You hate that your first born bears no title and that the woman you love gets no recognition.' Alim tried to stare down his father but Oman refused to meet his glare. 'You cannot do this.'

'It is done,' Oman told him. 'I informed the elders this morning. As of now you are Sultan Elect.'

This meant Alim was a sultan in choosing.

From this point on he must remain celibate for he could bring no shame on any future bride. There could be no release save from discreet times in the desert.

Alim stood, his appetite totally gone.

'You cannot force me into marriage.'

He said it again, loudly this time, and Alim never shouted.

Ever.

But this morning he did.

Oman did not flinch. In fact, vindictive had been the right word to describe his father's mood for the Sultan of Sultans' smile was black when he offered his response.

'I can make single life hell for you, though. You've had your fun, Alim. It's time to grow up.'

A year.

Gabi had stamped her way home through the slush and cold, furious at his suggestion.

But her flat was cold when she entered and she thought of the warmth she had left and the bliss of last night.

It should be over with by now.

Right now, Gabi thought, she should be accepting that, though amazing, her time with Alim was done.

Yet her mind danced with the hope of more.

Even before she had made a quick coffee, Bernadetta called.

'I have a meeting with a bride this afternoon but my vertigo has come on and I'm not going to be able to get there…'

Gabi closed her eyes as Bernadetta dragged out one of her tired excuses.

'Can it be moved to tomorrow?' Gabi asked.

Aside from all that had happened with Alim, Gabi had worked through to midnight and still had a lot to get done today.

She had to take the gramophone and record back to the grandparents, which was a considerable drive, and there were the outfits to collect, and a hundred other jobs that would go unnoticed but ensured that yesterday's wedding was seamless for the family.

'I don't want to let down a prospective client,' Bernadetta said. 'Gabi, I really haven't got the energy for debate. It's a summer wedding to be held at the Grande Lucia; you're going to be there today anyway.'

'I don't have a suit,' Gabi reminded her boss. 'Bernadetta…' Gabi paused. She was about to say no to her,

Gabi realised. She had been about to stand up to Bernadetta and not just on the strength of Alim's offer this morning. Their conversation last night had resonated. She was tired of being pushed around and knew she was worth a whole lot more than the treatment Bernadetta served, but for now Gabi held her tongue.

Her next step required careful thought, and so, instead of standing her ground, Gabi brushed down her skirt and did the best repair job that she could on the torn seam of her jacket and then headed back to the Grande Lucia.

There was a lot of activity in the foyer as huge brass trolleys filled with expensive luggage were being moved out.

'Gabi!'

She turned and smiled when she saw that it was the photographer. 'How did things go with you last night?' Gabi asked.

'Probably not as well as you,' he said, and Gabi frowned as he held out one of his cameras. 'I left this running in the gallery,' he explained. 'I set it to take intermittent photos up until midnight.'

Now Gabi started to blush as she realised what might have been captured.

He held out the camera and Gabi could almost not bring herself to look at the screen, terrified what she might see. 'Not exactly part of the bridal package, though it's a very beautiful image.' The photographer said.

Oh, yet another gaffe! Gabi thought, cringing, but she forced herself to look.

And then all the magic of last night returned.

For it had been captured exquisitely.

On the stunning ballroom floor, there, swirling in Alim's arms, was Gabi.

It was as beautiful as any professional wedding photo,

though it was almost impossible to reconcile that this was their first night and that they had at that point not so much as kissed.

She knew the very second that the photo had been taken. It had been when Alim had warned her that he was trouble and she had lifted her face to his.

The moment had been captured perfectly, for she was looking up into his eyes and Alim was holding her tenderly but firmly.

'Would you like me to delete it?' the photographer checked.

'No.'

'I thought as much.'

They had worked together on many occasions and he had Gabi's contact details. 'I'll forward it to you.'

He headed off with all his equipment and Gabi wanted to call out to him not to forget to forward it, but instead Gabi caught sight of Fleur in one of the side lounges, giving her order to a maid.

The woman had always intrigued Gabi, but never more so than now.

Was it lonely to be Fleur? Gabi pondered.

Of course it must be, but Alim wasn't suggesting the same for her. This was a business plan almost, a manageable slice of time.

A year.

She said it again to herself, though with mounting excitement this time.

Gabi had never dated, but knew from her friends that most relationships didn't even last that long.

It was the way he had said it and the assumption that she would simply comply that had irked.

'Gabi!' Anya, the receptionist on today, called out to her, and as Gabi looked over she realised that the foyer had become very busy. 'Can I ask you to step back, please? We have some VIP's about to leave.'

'Sure.'

Some dark-suited men were walking through the foyer and Gabi knew they were the hotel's security.

And she was about to see the Sultan of Sultans, Gabi realised.

She watched as the entourage moved through the foyer.

There was a young woman with a long mane of black hair wearing a deep mustard-coloured velvet gown and jewelled slippers. She was very beautiful, Gabi thought, even if her eyes were hidden behind dark glasses.

And then she saw a man dressed in a robe of black with a silver *keffiyeh* and Gabi felt her breath burn as she held it in her lungs, for she knew it was Alim's father. He was a mature version of Alim and had the same air of authority and elegance.

The managing director was in the foyer to bid farewell to the royal guests.

Usually, of course, it would be the owner.

Except the owner happened to be his son.

It all made sense now.

Fleur's insistence on the venue, and the reason that there had been few guests on the groom's side.

And all too soon it was over.

The procession walked through the foyer and out to the waiting cars, and when the last of them had gone, Gabi looked over to the lounge and to Fleur, who sat dignified and straight but terribly, terribly alone.

Gabi watched as she reached into her purse and took out a handkerchief, pressing it to her lips for a moment to gather herself.

There had been no kiss goodbye, not even so much as

a glance aimed at her by the Sultan of Sultans. No public acknowledgement from the man to whom she had borne a son.

What Alim had proposed this morning was different, though, Gabi told herself.

It was a year of her life and until last night there had been no love life for her.

It had been work, work, work.

Which she loved, of course.

But for a year she could have both.

And then what?

She saw that Fleur was making her way to the elevators and for the first time Gabi saw this usually poised woman with her shoulders slumped.

Defeated.

But that would not happen to her, Gabi assured herself, for she knew exactly what she was getting into. And Alim himself had said she would be a lover rather than a mistress. She had been carrying a flame for Alim since she had first seen him; the difference now was that she would be not carrying it alone.

And then?

She could not think of that now.

She was going to say yes.

It hadn't taken days of consideration, just hours, to come to her decision, and now that she had, hope filled her heart.

And as if in answer to her decision she watched as the gated, private elevator that had taken her to his suite last night opened.

Alim stepped out and her heart squeezed in reaction.

He was clean shaven and immaculate. But instead of ignoring Fleur, as he had before, Gabi watched as he stood and spoke for a moment with the woman and the conversation appeared tense.

It was.

'I tried to stop him, Alim,' Fleur said, 'but we both know my word holds little sway.'

And Alim let out a mirthless laugh for he had just come off the phone with his mother, imploring her to try and change Oman's mind, but her response had been almost the same.

'You hold more sway than you know,' Alim said. 'You simply refuse to stand up to him.'

'You try, then!' Fleur said, and her voice was weary.

Oh, he would.

Alim respected his father's title but not always the man himself.

Yet he was the ruler and his word was law.

Alim had tried to tell himself that just because the diktat had been invoked it did not mean that *everything* had to change. He would take over more duties while his father had treatment, but his work could continue here. Then he saw Gabi, standing in the foyer, dressed in that awful suit, but now that he had bedded her, she looked more beautiful than ever before and he realised that *everything* had changed.

The true ramifications were starting to hit home.

It was not even just about sex, for there could be no intimate conversation, no working alongside a woman for whom he harboured such thoughts.

And perhaps, more pointedly, no hope of observing the laws when Gabi was around.

He could only hope that her mood with him was as dark as it had been when she had left his bed this morning, so there would be no need to speak.

Alim could only think in minutes at the moment, so

he focussed on getting through the next few and, ignoring her gaze, he walked across the foyer. He wanted to be outside and to walk the streets of Rome.

He had changed his mind by the time he reached the brass doors, for Alim did not, by nature, avoid issues. He turned and walked towards Gabi, and when he saw her smile Alim knew she was going to say yes to the chance for them.

He watched the smile die on her lips as he approached.

'That offer…' Alim said, and he hesitated. He had been right when he'd said it would be impossible to work alongside each other and not sleep together.

'Yes?'

Here was no place to explain the diktat, but they could not be alone. He thought of her in bed this morning, wrapping the sheet around herself when he had tried to explain the rules and how lovers could only be alone in the desert.

Medieval had been her word to describe it.

It would be kinder to simply end it now, Alim knew.

It was also necessary.

He could smell the slight apple scent of her shampoo and could see the soft swelling of her mouth, a remnant from last night's hot kisses. He thought of how swollen she had been in readiness for him, and he thought of the love they could so easily still make.

Their bodies were aware of each other, they were attuned and wanting but, as of this morning, they were forbidden.

And so he said it, simply ended any hope for them.

'The offer has been withdrawn.'

He watched the colour drain from her face. He watched her rapid blink, and there was nothing he could do to comfort her.

'I see,' Gabi said, even though she didn't.

Yet she fought for dignity.

And dignity felt like a trapeze that she must grab onto, only Gabi was no acrobat.

She had only just accepted hope, only just accepted the brief possibility of them, and now it had been snatched away.

By him.

Oh, she had known he would hurt her one day, but after the way he had treated her that morning Gabi had never thought it would be today.

She could not even ask why or demand an explanation for she was fighting not to break down. Her nails dug into her palms and her breath was so shallow it made her feel a little giddy.

'You'll take care of what we discussed?' Alim checked.

Gabi looked at him. He was a bastard to the core, she decided, for she would have happily settled for just one night, but he'd ruined that with the glimpse of a dream. So as the imaginary trapeze swung by, she grabbed onto it with one hand and hoped it would quickly carry her away from him and drop her where she could weep unseen.

'Of course,' she responded.

'Gabi…' His voice husked and he did not continue with whatever it was he had been about to say.

It was Gabi who filled the silence. 'I need to get on,' she said. 'Bernadetta has given me quite a list to get through today.'

And she completed it. Somehow she got through the first day. Gabi and Marianna met with the new bride-to-be and her mother.

'We have the last Saturday in July available,' Marianna informed them.

'No, I want August,' the bride-to-be said.

'I'm sorry.' Marianna shook her head. 'Summer weddings have to be booked a long way in advance.'

'It's more than six months away!' the bride insisted.

'You are lucky that we have this one available.'

And Gabi just sat there.

Usually she would make soothing noises to take the edge off Marianna's slightly scolding tone.

She had been about to throw in her job, Gabi thought in horror. So trusting had she been that she had almost given Bernadetta her notice.

The numbness was fading, replaced now by a burn of anger as she watched Alim walk through the foyer.

Elegant, beautiful, it looked as if he had not a care in the world.

The rumours were true. Cold and callous did suit him. Alim did not look in her direction. She had been, Gabi knew, dismissed from his life.

And then the anger faded as she began to feel bereft. Soon followed by fear.

CHAPTER EIGHT

GABI DID NOT take care of things as the Sultan had ordered.

Though not out of recklessness or spite.

The first few days had felt like a bereavement, though not one she could ring in to work and explain about.

What could she say? *Bernadetta, I slept with Alim and he promised me the world and then dumped me.*

At best, she was a fool to have believed at all. Yet his behaviour made no sense to Gabi, for he had not offered her anything in the heat of passion. It had all been in the calm coolness of the morning, after hours of thinking, he had said.

So Gabi had somehow remembered to breathe as she'd fought not to cry and had done her best to get on with her work.

And by the time the fog had if not lifted then parted enough to take care of anything other than the seconds ahead, she had gone to the *farmacia*, only to find out that she had left it too late.

Late.

It became her most used word.

She was a day late, but put it down to stress.

A week late, but that happened at times.

And then she was late for work two days in a row because even the scent of her favourite morning coffee had her hunched over the bathroom sink.

Terror was her new friend.

Not just that she was pregnant, but by whom.

The more she found out about Zethlehan and the more she discovered about the power of the royals there, the more acute her terror became.

'Pregnant?'

'Yes,' Gabi had said to her mother.

It was a gorgeous spring morning.

Gabi had come from a weekend at the stunning Castelli vineyard, where the wedding had gone off beautifully, and she had told herself it was time. It had taken three months for Gabi to finally find the courage to tell her mother.

'Who is the father?' Carmel had asked.

And when Gabi had not answered, her mother had slapped her cheek.

Carmel, herself a single mother, had never wanted the same struggle for her only child.

'There go your dreams,' Carmel had said.

'No.'

Gabi knew things would be difficult but she was determined that her dreams would continue. It was her lack of contact with Alim that felt like an insufferable loss.

She had not told him about the baby.

Her mother assumed that because Gabi did not say who the father of her child was, it meant that she did not know.

Now Gabi was almost glad that she had been unable to tell Alim.

She was scared.

Not so much of his reaction, more the repercussions.

Sultan Alim of Zethlehan.

Sultan Elect.

He was next in line to the throne and the more she read about his kingdom the more she feared him. Alim was more powerful than she could fathom. His country was rich, extremely prosperous, and the royalty adored. There was a brother and a sister. Alim was the eldest and one day he would be Sultan of Sultans.

Gabi did not know how an illegitimate baby would be dealt with.

Her only reference point was Fleur, and she would never allow herself to become her, Gabi swore.

Though perhaps she was doing Alim an injustice?

On several occasions, Gabi had walked past the Grande Lucia, trying to find the courage to go in. Sometimes she would speak with Ronaldo and pretend that she was merely passing.

A couple of times she had plucked up the courage to go in but now Alim's royal status was known, security around him was tighter.

'Is Alim here?' Gabi asked Anya.

'Do you have an appointment?' Anya checked, when once she would have simply nodded or shaken her head, or picked up the phone to alert him.

'No,' Gabi said. 'I don't.'

'Then I can see if Marianna is available.'

'It's fine.' Gabi shook her head and, turning, looked over to the lounge and thought of Fleur, sitting alone and unacknowledged, and she thought too of James.

She did not want that life for her child, though it probably wasn't even an option to them. The Sultan of Sultans loved Fleur, whereas Alim had coldly ended things the morning after a night in his bed.

He had also told her to take the morning-after pill, not once, not twice, but three times.

Gabi was scared but determined to cope, for now, alone.

And so the next person she had told was Bernadetta.

And Bernadetta's reaction had been one of pure spite.

She resented that she would be paying for maternity leave and decided to get her money's worth while she could.

Every wedding that Bernadetta could, she passed over to Gabi.

Each teary bride or stressed call from the mother of said bride, Gabi dealt with.

And the most recent couple had barely left the church before Bernadetta skived off. Gabi barely had time to think, she was so busy working as Bernadetta became increasingly demanding.

'I don't want you showing,' she said when Gabi asked about wearing a dress for work rather than the hated suit.

It was the middle of summer and the weight had fallen off Gabi—or rather she had not, to her doctor's concern, put any on. Always curvy, at close to seven months pregnant she barely showed, but that wasn't good enough for Bernadetta.

'Our clients want to think your mind is on the job, not on a baby.'

'It *is* on the job,' Gabi insisted.

But the heavy suit remained. The only concession was that she wore the cream cowl-necked top out of the waistband.

And concealing her pregnancy as best she could was perhaps wise, for all too soon it was the wedding at the Grande Lucia that she had taken on the day the bottom had fallen out of her world.

Not that Alim would notice her, and neither was she likely to see him.

He was barely around any more. Ronaldo had told

her that he had moved back to Zethlehan and, sadly, the Grande Lucia was now on the market.

The staff were all worried for their jobs.

It was still beautiful, though, Gabi thought as, on the Friday before the wedding, she went for a breakfast meeting with Marianna in her office.

First they spoke about the timings of the big day and the arrival of the cars and photographers and such things.

Gabi's main focus was the wedding.

For Marianna, although the wedding was important, she was also dealing with the comfort of the other hotel guests and ensuring that they were not inconvenienced too much.

Again, Gabi pushed for a change to the flowers in the foyer.

'No, there has always been a red floral display.' Marianna shook her head and refused to budge on the issue. 'Our return guests like the familiarity.'

'But don't you want to attract new guests?'

Marianna pursed her lips as Gabi pushed on. 'Some of the hotels I work with actually organise in advance for their floral displays to tie in with the bridal theme…'

'The Grande Lucia does not compete with other hotels,' Marianna said. 'We're already at the top.'

Thanks to Alim, Gabi thought.

And Marianna was arrogant in her assumption that just because they were successful they could ignore competition.

For a very long while, before Alim had taken over, the hotel had struggled. Mona had been right in her description—the hotel had looked tired and many a potential bride had turned up her nose when the venue had been suggested. Oh, it was because of Alim that the Grande Lucia was now thriving and everyone knew it.

'I hear it will soon be under new ownership,' Gabi said.

'Yes, Alim is bringing potential buyers through over the weekend.'

'He's here?' Gabi squeaked, and then quickly recovered. Her voice had sounded too urgent, her words a demand, and she fought to relax herself. 'I thought that he was back in the Middle East?'

'For the most part he is there,' Marianna agreed. 'But this an important weekend. Today Signor Raul Di Savo is in residence and has free rein to look around; tomorrow it will be Signor Bastiano Conti.'

Gabi felt her heart sink a little. Hotels often took ages to sell but these were two serious names in the industry. Matrimoni di Bernadetta had held many weddings at Raul's boutique hotel here in Rome, and Gabi knew that Bastiano was also a formidable player in the industry.

'If you come across either of them, please be polite,' Marianna said.

'Of course.'

'They may have questions for you.'

Gabi nodded.

'And, please, ensure that all deliveries are discreet and that there is minimal disturbance to our guests. Alim is soon to marry so he wants the Grande Lucia off his hands as quickly as possible.'

Gabi just sat there.

She had read about it, of course, but it hurt to hear it voiced.

Even Alim had said that they could only last for a year because he had commitments back home.

How she wished they had had that year.

Or maybe not, Gabi thought as she sat there, trying to fathom being closer to him than she had been that night, knowing him more, loving him more…

For, yes, despite the anger and pain, Gabi now knew that it was love.

At least on her side.

'Gabi?' Marianna frowned because it was clear their meeting was over yet Gabi had made no move to leave. 'Was there anything else?'

'I don't think so.'

There could be no hope for them.

It was a very busy day spent liaising with the florists and soothing a temperamental head chef when she informed him that there had been some last-minute food preferences called in.

'I already have the updated list,' he told her.

'No,' Gabi said. 'There are more.'

A lot more.

And the head chef was not happy, declaring, as if it were her fault, that the world had gone gluten-free.

The gowns and outfits arrived and it was for Gabi to organise that tomorrow they would be sent to the correct suites.

She spoke with the make-up artist and hairdressers too, ensuring that every detail for tomorrow was in place.

Oh, she was tired, and there was still so much to be done.

Gabi headed to the ballroom to check on the set-up.

'There are some more changes to be made to the seating,' Bernadetta said by way of greeting. 'The ex-wife doesn't want to be near the aunt…'

Gabi sighed; she had been working on the seating into the small hours of last night and the bride constantly rang in her changes.

'I'll leave you to take it from here,' Bernadetta told Gabi. She didn't even pretend now to be sick, or to be meeting with a client. She simply waltzed off and left it all to Gabi.

It was late Friday afternoon and most people were just finishing up for the weekend yet Gabi's work had barely begun. Bernadetta would appear tomorrow, around eleven, just as the guests started to arrive.

One benefit of Bernadetta being gone, though, was that she could take off her shoes, which Gabi did; the high heels were not ideal and after a day of wearing them her back was starting to ache.

This weekend would be, Gabi was sure, her last real chance to tell Alim she was pregnant before the baby was born. Matrimoni di Bernadetta did not have another wedding at the Lucia for three months. She would have had her baby by then and the Grande Lucia could well be sold.

Gabi honestly did not know what to do.

His power scared her and, if she was honest, Alim's cruel dismissal still angered her; furthermore, he had made it very clear that he did not want any consequence from that night.

A kick beneath her ribs made Gabi smile.

As tiny as her baby was, it certainly made itself known.

At her ultrasound, Gabi had chosen not to find out what she was having. Not because she wasn't curious, more she did not want the baby's sex to have any bearing on the conversation, if she told Alim.

If she told him.

She was still troubled and unsure as to what to do.

Gabi stood in the ballroom and looked at the shower of stars that the chandelier created and recalled the bliss of dancing right here, alone with Alim, and how deeply happy she had been that night.

It brought her such pleasure to recall it.

The photographer had not forgotten and indeed the

image of the two of them that night now lived on her tablet. It had been her screensaver for a while but that had proved too painful, so she had taken it down and now Gabi barely looked at it.

It had always hurt too much to do so, but time perhaps *was* kind, because Gabi hadn't really been able to recall, with clarity, the bliss of them together.

Until now.

But on this afternoon, with her baby wriggling inside her, she remembered how the shadows of the branches outside had crept across the walls, how Alim had, without a word, asked her to dance.

Yes, Gabi was a dreamer, but it was a memory that she was lost in now.

And that was how he found her.

It had been a busy day for Alim.

And a hellish few months.

His sister Yasmin had created her own share of scandal at the wedding all those months ago, and Alim had been trying his best to sort that out.

Also, he had known the moment that diktat had been invoked that it would be impossible to be around Gabi and not want her. He took the laws of his land seriously. Now he walked into the ballroom with the first of the potential buyers and there was Gabi, holding her shoes and gazing up.

It was safer, far safer that she be gone.

'Is everything okay, Gabi?' Alim asked her, and his words were a touch stern.

'Oh!'

She turned and for the first time since that morning she saw him.

He was wearing a dark navy suit and looked stunning

as usual; she had never felt more drab, standing barefoot in an ill-fitting suit.

He was with a man she recognised as Raul Di Savo.

Gabi pushed out a smile and tried to be polite but her heart was hammering.

'Yes, everything is fine. I was just trying to work out the table plan for Saturday.'

'We have a large wedding coming up,' Alim explained to Raul.

'And both sets of parents are twice divorced.' Gabi gave a slight eye-roll, and then chatted away as she bent to put on her shoes, trying to keep things about work. 'Trying to work out where everyone should be seated is proving—'

'Gabi!' Alim scolded, and then turned to Raul. 'Gabi is not on my staff. *They* tend to be rather more discreet.' He waved his hand in dismissal. 'Excuse us, please.'

Just like that he dismissed her.

He knew that he had hurt her, for that morning she had left there had been so much promise between them and now she looked at him with funeral eyes. Alim could see the pain and bewildered confusion there.

He wanted to wave his hand to Raul and tell him to get the hell out of the ballroom. He wanted to take her to bed.

She did not leave quietly.

Gabi slammed the door on her way out and Alim and Raul stood in the ballroom with the lights dancing in the late afternoon sun.

'What is the real reason you are selling?' Raul asked him.

Raul knew the business was thriving and he wanted to know why Alim was letting it go. And Raul knew too that Alim could so easily outsource the management of the hotel as he moved his portfolio back to the Middle East.

Alim had brought him here to give the true answer, and now he tried to drag his mind back to the sale, yet Gabi's fragrance hung in the air, along with the memory of their dance.

'When I bought the hotel those had not been cleaned in years,' Alim said, gesturing to the magnificent lights and remembering when the moon had lit them. 'Now they are taken down regularly and cared for properly. It is a huge undertaking. The room has to be closed so no functions can be held, and it is all too easy to put it off.'

'I leave all that to my managers to organise,' Raul said.

Alim nodded. 'Usually I do too, but when I took over the Grande Lucia there had been many cost-cutting measures. It was slowly turning into just another hotel. It is not just the lighting in the ballroom, of course. What I am trying to explain is that this hotel has become more than an investment to me. Once I return to my homeland I shall not be able to give it the attention it deserves.'

'The next owner might not either,' Raul pointed out.

'That is his business. But while the hotel is mine I want no part in her demise.'

'Now you have given me pause for thought,' Raul admitted.

'Good.' Alim smiled. 'The Grande Lucia deserves the best caretaker. Please,' Alim said, indicating that their long day of meetings had come to an end, for he needed badly to be alone, 'take all the time you need to look around and to enjoy the rest of your stay.'

Alim walked out of the ballroom and he was conflicted.

So badly he wanted to seek her out. More worryingly, though, he wanted to work out a chance for them. The only place they could speak was the desert.

He could just imagine Gabi's reaction if he suggested that!

He was informed that Bastiano Conti, who had flown in from Sicily, had just arrived at the hotel. They were, in fact, friends, and would often hit the casinos and clubs together. Those carefree days were gone now, yet they were not the ones Alim craved.

It was one woman, and the hope for one more night with her that could be his undoing.

Alim went and greeted Bastiano and was grateful to hear that he had plans for tonight and would be entertaining guests.

'We will meet tomorrow?' Bastiano checked, and Alim was about to agree.

The hotel had to be sold after all and Raul seemed set to decline.

Yet Alim's problems were greater than real estate, and he watched his friend and potential buyer raise a surprised eyebrow as Alim, usually the consummate host, rearranged their plans.

'Bastiano, I deeply apologise, but I am going to have to reschedule the viewing. I have to return to my country tonight.'

There was not a hope of being in the same country, let alone the same building, as Gabi, and abiding by the rules.

His rapid departure from the Grande Lucia was unnecessary, though, because Gabi was no longer in the building.

By the time his private jet lifted into the sky, she was in the infirmary.

She had closed the ballroom door loudly on Alim, and at first had thought it was the shock of seeing him and being treated so coldly that had her doubling over.

It was then that her waters had broken.

The staff at the Grande Lucia were more than used to slight dramas unfolding and to handling them discreetly, though Anya was clearly shocked.

'You're pregnant?' she asked in surprise.

'Is there anyone I can call for you?' she continued as she ushered Gabi into a small room behind Reception.

'Not yet.'

Oh, she would have to let Bernadetta know but Gabi could not even think of her now.

And, yes, she would have to tell her mother, but Carmel's anger and resentment had hurt Gabi so much already.

She just wanted to be alone now.

They waited for the ambulance to arrive and as they did, need spoke for her as inadvertently she said his name.

'Alim…' Gabi gasped.

'Don't worry,' Anya reassured her, assuming that Gabi was upset that she might have created a problem for the smooth running of the hotel, especially when he was showing potential buyers around. 'No one saw what happened. Anyway, he has already left.'

'Left?'

'He flew back to his country a little while ago. Do you want me to call Marianna and let her know what is going on?'

Gabi didn't answer.

She was just trying to take in the news that Alim had gone.

A part of her had hoped that having seen her again in the ballroom he might later seek her out.

It would appear not.

Alim could not make it any clearer that he had no interest in her.

The ambulance did not come to the main entrance,

for that might be distressing or cause disruption to some of the guests.

Gabi left by the trade entrance, to bear the child of both the owner of the Grande Lucia and Sultan of Zethlehan.

'It's too soon,' she pleaded to the doctor at the hospital as she fought not to bear down, but time was no longer being kind.

Like endless waves submerging her, there was no pause, no time to catch her breath and calm her racing mind.

Alim.

She wanted his presence and to be held once again in his arms.

Yet she had chosen not to tell him, and whether it would have made a difference or not, this night she gave birth alone.

As she screamed, her mind flashed to Fleur, who had taken this lonely journey also.

And she would never be her, Gabi swore.

Her daughter was born a short while later.

She was delivered onto her stomach and, instead of being whisked away, her little girl was vigorous and Gabi was able to hold her to her chest and gaze down at her daughter.

Oh, she was beautiful, with silky black hair and dark eyes that were almond-shaped, like her father's.

'We have to take her now to the nursery,' the nurse informed Gabi, and it physically hurt to let her baby go.

Soon, though, her mother arrived and it was comforting to make up.

'You have me,' Carmel said.

'I know.'

It felt good to know that, and there were other things to be grateful for.

The baby was strong. So strong, the nurse told her when Gabi got in to see her, for she breathed with just a little oxygen for assistance.

'Do you have a name for her?' Gabi was asked.

Gabi had thought she was having a son; she had been so sure that history was about to repeat itself, and that, like Fleur, she would bear the Sultan's firstborn son.

But history had not repeated itself.

Still, she was absolutely beautiful, a little ray of light, and Gabi knew in that moment what to call her.

'Lucia.'

'That's such a pretty name,' the nurse said.

It was the place where love had been made.

Alim needed to know that he had a daughter, Gabi was painfully aware of that. But not now, not when she was so emotional and drained. Gabi was scared of what she might agree to. When she was stronger, she would work out how on earth to tell him.

Her mother came into the nursery to see her granddaughter. It was close to midnight and Carmel had been running errands for Gabi—packing a case and also letting Bernadetta know that not only would her very efficient assistant wedding planner not be there tomorrow but that there had also been a lot left undone tonight.

'Bernadetta is not best pleased,' she told Gabi. 'She wants to know if you sorted out the table plan.'

'No,' Gabi said, and she got back to gazing at her daughter.

Bernadetta, for once, could sort it all out.

Lucia was Gabi's priority now.

And always would be.

Whatever the future held.

CHAPTER NINE

'THE CONTRACTS ARE *still* with Bastiano?' Alim frowned when Violetta gave him the news. 'This should all have been dealt with by now.'

Despite Alim's rapid departure, an offer on the Grande Lucia had been made and accepted, but nearly three months later the sale seemed to have stalled.

Alim needed the hotel gone!

He sat in his sumptuous office in the palace and tried to take care of business with a mind that was elsewhere.

Seeing Gabi again had proved to be his undoing.

Temptation beckoned more with each passing day but never more so than now.

A wedding was being held there this weekend and Matrimoni di Bernadetta was the company that had been hired for the event.

The itinerary was open on his computer and Alim scrolled through it, hoping for a glimpse of her name, or a note that she might have left in the margins, as Gabi often did.

There was none, though.

'Do you want me to contact his attorney?' Violetta asked, but Alim shook his head.

'I will speak with Bastiano myself,' Alim said.

He might even speak with him face to face.

Alim was sorely tempted to summon the royal jet, with the excuse of meeting with Bastiano, but really for the chance to see Gabi.

He was dangerously close to breaking the diktat.

'That will be all,' Alim said, and, having dismissed Violetta, he attempted to deal with the day's correspondence.

He didn't get very far.

It had been months since he had seen Gabi again but the feelings had not faded.

If anything, they had intensified for, despite the pressure his father and the elders exerted, Alim was no closer to agreeing to a wedding.

His mind was in Rome, rather than here in Zethlehan, where it should belong.

He thought of the days he had loved most at the Grande Lucia.

Gabi, arriving early in the morning, and how she would become increasingly frazzled throughout the working day.

And he thought too of the wedding nights, and how she would finally relax again and enjoy watching the show she had produced.

He missed her.

Not the risqué life he had once led, but the small moments that were now long gone—stepping through the brass doors and seeing her sitting in the lounge with Marianna. Knowing that there would be another wedding soon and the chance to see her again had brought him more pleasure than he had realised at the time.

His times at the hotel had been made better by her—the scent of flowers coming from the ballroom and Gabi directing brass trolleys laden with gifts and arrangements…

Alim missed those times.

And they would soon be gone for ever.

He had done all he could to sever his ties to Rome, yet it felt as if his heart had been left there.

He looked up as his mother knocked at his open office door and he shook his head.

'Not now,' Alim said.

'Yes, now,' Rina said and came in.

He had always been polite—if a little distant—with others, though now he was stone cold.

The vast palace felt too small, and there was no company that he wished to keep.

Unless it was Gabi's.

'How are you, Alim?'

Alim didn't even bother to lie and pretend that he was fine, he just gave a shrug. 'I am trying to chase up the contracts for the Grande Lucia. I think I might need to make a trip to Italy.'

'When?'

'Soon,' Alim said.

He would be courting temptation if he went back this weekend, Alim knew, yet he had to see Gabi.

'I have just held the morning meeting with your father. He thinks that a wedding would cheer Yasmin up.'

'I am not going to marry to provide a remedy for my sister's mood.'

'What about your mood, Alim?' Rina said. 'You are not happy.'

'No,' he admitted. 'But I do not need to be happy to do my work.' And there was indeed work to be done so he gestured for his mother to take a seat. 'Kaleb's thirtieth is coming up…'

But his mother was not here about that. 'I am concerned, Alim. I thought once you were home you might be happy, but it has been months now…'

'I love my land.'

'Yet you make no commitment to remain here?'

'You mean a bride?' Always the conversation led back to that. 'A bride is not the solution.'

'Then tell me the problem.'

'No.'

He did not share his thoughts, let alone his feelings, with others. In fact, until recently he had refused to examine them.

Life had always been about duty and work and solving problems logically.

Now, for the first time in his life, he could not come up with a solution to the dilemma he faced.

'Alim,' his mother implored. 'Speak to me.'

He did not know how to start.

'I might understand,' Rina insisted.

Yes, she just might, Alim thought, for there was no doubt that hers was a loveless marriage.

'Just before the diktat was invoked I met someone,' Alim said, but, even as he explained things, he knew that wasn't quite right. 'I have liked her for a couple of years but I always stayed back. Things got more serious just before I was summoned home. I left her without any real explanation and when I returned to Rome the other month…'

He didn't finish. Alim could not explain the sadness in Gabi's eyes, neither did he want to reveal the ache in his heart and the regret for the year together that had been denied them.

Alim knew it could never have been more than a year; his father would never give his approval to Gabi.

No, his bride would be from Zethlehan. In fact, his father had whittled it down to the final three—the one who would uphold tradition and best serve the country, and was deeply schooled in their ways, would be Oman's choice.

'I am thinking of going to Rome to see her.'

His mother was quiet for some considerable time and when she spoke her voice was strained and laced with fear. 'Have you broken the diktat, Alim?'

'No.'

He heard his mother breathe out in relief. 'That's good, then.'

'How can it be good?'

All that mattered to them was that he abided by the rules, no matter the cost to himself.

'There is a desert out there, Alim,' Rina said, and he stood and looked out the window; the reproach in his voice was aimed at himself, for of course he had considered it.

'Gabi will not be coming to the desert. She would never even entertain the thought.'

'She does not have to reside there,' Rina said. 'She could visit now and then and once you are married, once you have an heir…' It was a difficult conversation to have. 'Well, then the rules relax.'

And he threw his mother a look. 'Do you think I would do to my wife what my father did to you?'

The poorly kept secret was finally being discussed.

'I would never impose a loveless marriage on a bride,' Alim said, and then he closed his eyes because that was exactly what it would be, and the reason that, despite mounting pressure, still he refused marriage. 'I hate how you have been treated,' Alim told his mother.

He thought of them smiling on the palace balcony or waving and chatting as they arrived at a function.

Then the relative silence that would descend when

they returned to their private lives—his mother would retreat to her wing, his father to his.

'Do I look unhappy, Alim?' Rina asked.

He looked over. No, her features were relaxed and, as she often did, Rina smiled her gentle smile.

'You barely communicate,' Alim pointed out, but his mother shook her head. 'I have just come from a meeting with your father—we have one each working day.'

Alim accepted that, but that was for the running of the country—a private life between them did not exist. 'You sleep in a separate wing of the palace.'

'And we do so at my request,' Rina said. 'Alim, I love my country. Growing up, I always knew that I would likely be chosen and that I would one day be queen. I did my duty, I had three beautiful children who I have raised well; I continue to work hard for my country and I live a very privileged life.'

Rina knew she needed to say more.

Oh, she was very schooled in the rules, and had studied them closely.

Yes, Zethlehan was progressive in many ways, for *all* needs were served.

Save love, for it was not taken into consideration in the rules.

Still, it was a delicate topic and Rina took a moment to consider before she spoke on. 'Alim, just because I don't have a loving marriage, it does not mean that I don't know love.'

Distracted by his thoughts of Gabi, it took a moment for his mother's words to sink in and he looked up at her.

Was she telling him that she had a lover?

That the times her husband was away were not so lonely after all, that she had her own reasons for sleeping in a separate wing of the palace?

The silence between them was loaded but Rina gave a slight shake of her head. 'I am saying no more than that.'

It was as if every grain of desert sand had shifted as his mother told him without detail that she was happy. That somehow their relationship had been made to work for them.

'Your father and I have made it work for everyone…' Then she saw Alim's jaw tighten and amended, 'I do feel sorry for James,' she admitted. 'He deserves more of his father.' It was the first time his name had been spoken within these walls. 'That should have been handled better, but it is your father who makes the rules.'

Alim nodded.

'Talk to your love, Alim.'

'I did not say anything about love.'

'Talk to your lover, then. That is the one solution to all ills.'

'How?' he asked. 'She would never come to the desert.'

'I have studied this very closely.' Rina smiled and tapped the hated large, leather-bound file that sat on his desk. 'There is nowhere in the diktat that mentions phones.'

Alim smiled.

'If anyone can sort things out, it is you.'

Alim was not so sure but he knew that neither distance nor silence was working.

And it was for that reason that he picked up the phone and, rather than chase up Bastiano regarding the sale, he called the reception desk at the Grande Lucia.

'*Pronto*. May I speak with Gabi?'

'Gabi?' The female voice that answered was an unfamiliar one and didn't seem to know to whom Alim was referring.

'She is organising a wedding there,' he explained.

'Oh, that Gabi!' came the response, and it was clear that she now knew who Alim meant. 'I think she is still on maternity leave.'

'Maternity leave?'

The palace must be sitting on a fault line, Alim thought, because for the second time in an hour the sands seemed to shift.

'I think you have the wrong person,' he said, but the receptionist wasn't listening—she was talking to a colleague. Alim could hear his rapid breathing as in the background a male voice spoke and then the receptionist amended her words.

'No, no, my mistake.'

Alim didn't even have a chance to register relief before she spoke again.

'Apparently Gabi is back from her leave today.'

Alim's mind worked rapidly,

If indeed Gabi had been on maternity leave then the baby *had* to be his. It was practically nine months to the day since they had slept together and she had certainly been a virgin then.

Yet the dates confused him. Alim certainly wasn't an expert in pregnancy, but this woman was telling him that Gabi was already *back* from maternity leave.

Alim thought of the last time he had seen Gabi and she hadn't looked pregnant, but, then again, he had done all he could not to look at her.

Alim knew that he had to speak with Gabi.

Alone.

But how?

A possibility was starting to come to mind and when he spoke his voice was even and calm, for Alim rarely revealed his emotions.

'Actually, rather than Gabi, may I speak with Bernadetta?'

'Can I ask who is calling?'

'It is Alim.'

He heard her nervous gasp. 'Sultan al—'

Alim spoke over her, for his patience was running out. 'Just get Bernadetta on the line.'

He stood and, just as he had needed air the day his father had invoked the diktat, he walked out of the French windows and onto the large balcony.

Unlike then, the air was not cool, it was hot and dry, though it was calming to Alim and he gladly breathed it in, his eyes narrowing against the fierce sun as he looked out at the desert.

He could speak with Gabi there, unheard by others; only there could they discuss things fully.

There was no doubt a frantic search was under way at the Grande Lucia for the rather elusive Bernadetta and it gave time for Alim's plans to take better shape.

'Pronto,' he said when a nervous Bernadetta finally came to the phone.

'Sultan Alim…' Bernadetta attempted to purr into the phone but it was more of a croak. 'How lovely to hear from you. It's been a long time.'

'Indeed. I was wondering,' Alim said, 'if Matrimoni di Bernadetta had the necessary skills to co-organise a royal wedding here in Zethlehan.'

He heard her slight gasp. 'Of course. It would be not just an honour but a pleasure…' Bernadetta fawned but Alim swiftly broke in.

'Then I need Gabi here by tomorrow,'

'Gabi? Oh, no, I wouldn't be sending my assistant!' Bernadetta immediately responded. 'I would take care of every detail myself—'

'Bernadetta,' Alim interrupted her again. 'You have a good head for business and you hire only the best, but we both know that it is Gabi who turns a wedding into an unforgettable creation.'

He soothed her vast ego yet he got to the point.

'I want Gabi here.'

'Indeed, she's excellent, but Gabi might not be available to travel at short notice. You see, she has recently—'

Alim swiftly cut in. He did not want Bernadetta to reveal that Gabi had just had a baby. Alim was very well aware that should Gabi find out that he knew, there would not be a hope in hell of getting her to agree to come to Zethlehan.

Yet he wanted Gabi to tell him to his face.

'I don't care how busy she is with the current wedding. I do not care about her personal life and whether she has plans that she cannot change. If you want the contract for the wedding, then Gabi is to be here by tomorrow.'

Alim spoke like the Sultan he was and Bernadetta responded accordingly.

'And she shall be.'

Alim let out a breath and there followed a giddy sensation of relief that had nothing to do with what he had just discovered.

More that he would finally see Gabi.

She had been missed more than even Alim had wanted to admit.

'If, when you meet with Gabi,' Bernadetta said, 'you have any concerns…'

'I shan't be meeting with Gabi,' Alim said, anticipating Gabi's resistance to the suggestion that she come here. 'I am only making this initial contact. I don't want to be troubled with minor details. From now on, everything will be dealt with by the palace aide, Violetta.'

He gave Bernadetta a few more rapid details and then ended the call.

He looked out at the desert again and the golden sight soothed, for there solutions could more readily be found.

Alim walked back into his office, trying to take in that he could well be a father and trying to fathom all that Gabi would have been through.

He summoned Violetta.

She was more than used to dealing with scandal and had her work cut out for her in dealing with the al-Lehans.

And not just his father and James, Alim now knew, for it would seem that even his mother had a secret life of her own. One that Alim had had no clue about.

A baby.

He did not know if it was a boy or girl and Alim knew all the problems it could create.

Yet as he waited for Violetta to arrive, despite the news, his overriding feeling was relief.

Gabi would be here soon.

He looked up as Violetta came in and, without asking, she closed the door and came over to the desk.

'I require your discretion,' Alim said.

'You have it.'

Violetta, too, was brilliant at her job.

CHAPTER TEN

'GABI! GABI!'

Bernadetta was almost running through the foyer towards her.

Gabi was carrying a glass vase containing an array of Sahara roses to take up to the bridal suite.

Housekeeping should have already dealt with it but things at the Grande Lucia had got a little slack now that Alim wasn't around.

'Yes?' she answered wearily.

It was Gabi's first official day back at work and it felt as if she had never been away.

It had been hard leaving Lucia but her mother had promised to drop by with her at lunchtime so that Gabi could give her a cuddle.

Gabi could only hope there was time to actually take her lunch break!

There were so many boxes not ticked and a lot of things that should have long ago been taken care of which had been left for Gabi's return; she had just this minute come from a stand-up row with the very temperamental chef.

'I know this will come as a shock…' Bernadetta said, and Gabi stopped herself from rolling her eyes—there had been so many shocks this morning!

The cake had been confirmed for *next* Saturday, Gabi had found out.

The flowers had not, as Gabi had first thought, gone missing; instead, they had been delivered, as per Matrimoni di Bernadetta's instructions, to last week's wedding venue.

Chaos was all around.

The chef had not been informed that there were not only eighteen guests requiring the gluten-free option but that there were four vegans, two raw vegans, four kosher and five halal.

No, there was very little that might come as a shock, save that the groom had run off!

Gabi was about to be proved wrong.

'Matrimoni di Bernadetta has been invited to co-organise Sultan Alim's wedding…'

Gabi nearly dropped the vase.

What the hell was Alim thinking?

Or, more likely, he wasn't thinking, at least not about her.

His wedding needed to be organised and he had simply called on the best, without any consideration of the pain that it might cause her.

But then Bernadetta spoke on.

'Alim has asked that you fly there tomorrow and meet with his assistant.'

This time Gabi did drop the vase, for there was no one crueller in that moment than Alim.

It shattered loudly as it hit the floor and the water and crystal was strewn along with the gorgeous roses.

Gabi barely looked down and neither did Bernadetta.

'I can't,' Gabi said. 'It's impossible. I have a new baby…'

'I know that,' Bernadetta said.

'I can't leave her.' And then fear clutched at her heart because maybe Alim knew. Maybe he was planning for her to bring the baby… 'Lucia hasn't had all her inoculations.'

'Oh, for God's sake,' Bernadetta snorted. 'Do you really think I'd send you with a baby on such an important job?'

'Did you tell Alim about her?' Gabi was on her knees and trying not to cry as she scrabbled to pick up the crystal, her mind racing in fear as she thought of Alim plotting to whisk Lucia away.

Yes, Gabi was a dreamer, and some of them were nightmares.

'Of course I didn't tell the Sultan. Why would he care? This is a royal wedding he's asking us to organise.' Bernadetta was nearly shouting. 'He doesn't want to hear about your personal life.'

'I don't want to go,' Gabi said. 'Send someone else.'

'Alim wants you, though. He says you have an eye for attention and…' Bernadetta almost choked on her next words. 'He told me that he wants you adequately remunerated…' And then she told her the figure that Alim was offering just for this short trip.

Was this his way of apologising? Gabi wondered. Was this Alim's strange way of making amends?

As Sophie came over to help clear up the mess that had been made, Gabi sank back on her heels for a second and tried to make sense of things, not that Bernadetta gave her a moment to gather her thoughts.

'Gabi, if you cost me this contract, don't even bother turning up for work again. And don't think I shan't tell everyone that you were the one who blew the deal.'

Bernadetta stalked off and Gabi just sat there.

'I can mop around you.' Sophie smiled and then she helped Gabi up.

'I don't want to leave my baby.'

'Then don't go,' Sophie said. 'Tell her to get lost.'

And Gabi smiled because Sophie was Sicilian and rather feistier than she, but then Gabi's smile wavered and tears were dangerously close. 'I don't want to organise his wedding.'

She had said too much, Gabi knew, but Sophie was her dear, dear friend, though even she did not guess that Alim was Lucia's father.

'Did you have a crush on him?' Sophie asked.

Yes, he was as unattainable to the likes of Gabi as that.

Her mother, when she brought in Lucia, wasn't exactly gushing with excitement at the prospect of her daughter flying off to the Middle East.

They met in the foyer and there was only time for a very brief cuddle with Lucia as she told her mother the news.

'Gabi, isn't it time you looked for a more practical job?'

'I love my work,' Gabi said. 'I'm good at what I do.'

'Of course, but some dreams you have to let go of when you have a baby. When I found out I was pregnant with you I had to give up my studies…'

Gabi closed her eyes, she had heard it all many times before.

Only history wasn't repeating itself.

She held Lucia to her cheek and breathed in the soft baby scent.

If anything, Lucia made her want to achieve more; her love for her daughter drove Gabi to be better rather than less. And, yes, it would be hard to leave her, but the money would certainly help, as well as the boost to her career.

But more than that, so much more than that, she would be able to tell Lucia her history for she would have seen Alim's country first hand.

Gabi had grown up not knowing anything about her father; her daughter would not suffer the same fate.

'Are you able to look after Lucia for two nights?'

'You know I shall.'

Gabi thanked her mother. She knew Lucia would be beautifully taken care of, and though it was her first concern it wasn't the only one—Gabi wanted to be very sure she wasn't walking into a trap.

So, to be sure, she called the number she had been given by Bernadetta.

Violetta's voice was familiar and Gabi recalled that she had dealt with the hotel arrangements for Marianna when Mona and James had married.

Now Gabi knew why.

'Alim is concerned that his European guests will not understand Zethlehan ways,' Violetta explained. 'He said that you have a good eye for detail. We want the wedding to be seamless and all the guests' needs attended to.'

'Who shall I be liaising with?'

'Mainly me, but also the hotel manager at the venue where the commoner guests shall be housed. That is where you shall be staying during this visit, so you can work from a visual.'

'I see.'

There was no firm date yet but Violetta ran through the guest list. Some of the names were familiar. Bastiano Conti was amongst them and Gabi knew he was not just a friend of Alim's but about to be the new owner of the Grande Lucia.

It sounded legit.

Yes, it was more lavish and complex than anything she had dealt with before but, at the end of the day, it sounded like just another wedding to plan.

And so for now she dealt with it as such.

'Where will the service be held?'

'There will be two services,' Violetta explained. 'A small, very intimate gathering of family and elders, but we would take care of that. Following the formal service there will be a large reception back at the palace. We need you to help transport the guests and to ensure that they wear suitable attire.' She went through the dress codes with Gabi. 'Also, all dietary requirements from them must come through you.'

Yes, just like any other wedding!

'When you are here,' Violetta continued, 'you can speak with the palace head chef, so it might be helpful if you could bring some menu suggestions that he can incorporate. The banquet will be traditional but we want alternatives that can cater to all palates.'

'I see.' Gabi swallowed and forced herself to delve a little deeper. 'When I get there and speak to Sultan Alim I can ask him—'

'Oh, no,' Violetta quickly broke in. 'While I understand that you worked alongside the Sultan at the Grande Lucia, things are very different here. You will not have access to the Sultan; you will deal directly with me.'

And that was the real reason she agreed.

Gabi needed contacts, and not of the usual kind, and Violetta would be a very good one to have. One day she would be ready to tell Alim about Lucia and, as she was fast finding out, you didn't just call up a palace and ask to be put through to the Sultan.

And so, to Bernadetta's delight, Gabi said yes.

'You need to go home and prepare.' Bernadetta, for the first time ever, insisted that Gabi leave early. 'You have black trousers…?' she checked.

Gabi's curves had returned and she felt Bernadetta's disapproval as she looked over her figure.

'I do.'

She just hoped they would fit.

'What about this wedding?' Gabi asked Bernadetta. 'There's still so much to be done.'

'I think I can manage,' Bernadetta said, 'though if you could sort out the flowers before you go…'

Lazy to the last, Gabi thought.

Sophie found her a new vase and Gabi's hands were shaking as she rearranged the flowers. She heard an email ping in.

Gabi saw that it was from Violetta and picked up her tablet to read it. She would fly tomorrow at midday and the flight was first class.

It was all a little overwhelming.

Not the itinerary and not just leaving little Lucia but that the man she loved was getting married.

How? Gabi thought as she walked out of the office with the flowers. She did not know *how* her heart could still beat while planning his wedding.

'Hey.'

A man called out to her as she went to take the roses up to the bridal suite and, distracted, she nodded at the handsome stranger.

'Gabi!'

He called out her name.

'Oh!' She stopped when she realised that it was Raul, one of the potential buyers for the hotel, and then she remembered how he would know her. 'You were in the ballroom when Alim…' Her voice trailed off as she recalled how Alim had scolded and then dismissed her that day.

It had been the day Lucia had been born!

Oh, she had been cross, so cross with Alim, though this stranger was clearly not to blame for that!

'I'm hoping to meet with Alim.'

'Good luck!' Gabi rolled her eyes. 'He's back home.'

'Oh!'

'For his wedding.'

'I see.'

'I'm planning it, actually.'

She felt as if she was about to cry.

'Can you let him know I need to speak with him?'

'I'm a wedding planner,' Gabi said, and she let a little of her anger out before walking off. 'I don't get access to the Sultan.'

Saying goodbye to Lucia was incredibly hard.

She had already been staying at her mother's this weekend.

Going back to work yesterday and leaving little Lucia for twelve hours had seemed agony at the time but now she would be away for two days and two nights.

One day would be spent travelling to Zethlehan, then a night at a luxurious hotel followed by a day of meetings with Violetta.

The second night would be spent travelling back to Rome and then finally she would see Lucia again.

Gabi had been unable to feed Lucia herself, so there wasn't any problem with that, but it ached to see her little girl asleep in her crib and to know that she was about to leave.

'Don't wake her,' Carmel said, because she could see that Gabi was about to pick her up.

'I'm going to miss her.'

'Gabi, even if you weren't going to Zethlehan you would barely have seen her this weekend, what with the wedding and everything.'

'I know.'

Her hours were proving difficult and Gabi knew she was asking a lot from her mother just to keep her job. Carmel had raised one child alone and did not want to do it again. Right now, there were bills that needed to paid and so Carmel had agreed to help with Lucia for a few months, but after that…

'You could work with Rosa,' Carmel said.

Gabi had considered it, yet, as much as she cared for Rosa, Gabi did not want another boss. Still, it was the more practical solution and right now Gabi was beyond exhausted and could feel her grip loosening on her dreams.

Carmel went down to check if the taxi had arrived and Gabi kissed Lucia's little cheek and whispered that she was the sunshine of her life—*'Sei il sole della mia vita.'*

She wanted better for her, Gabi knew—which was part of the reason she was on her way to a new adventure.

What an adventure!

Gabi had flown before, but only within Italy and only for work.

Bernadetta, of course, would fly business class while Gabi sat way back in the bowels of the plane.

It was very different today!

Champagne was offered before they had even taken off but Gabi declined and took water as she was trying to be good. While the weight had fallen off while she'd been pregnant, Gabi had been thin for about two days after Lucia had been born and then her milk had come in, closely followed by the return of her curves.

A meal was served, then her bed prepared, while Gabi went and put on the pyjamas they offered her.

'Would you like to be woken for a meal before landing?'

It was a nine-hour flight to Zethlehan and Gabi was about to say that there was no chance of her *not* being woken, when again she was reminded that she was without Lucia.

'That would be lovely,' Gabi said.

The cabin lights were dimmed and Gabi lay there, sure, quite sure, that she would be too nervous to sleep.

Instead, she woke to a gentle shake of her shoulder and was informed that her meal would be served shortly; she had slept for seven hours. It wasn't just her first decent sleep since Lucia had been born, it was her first decent sleep since the morning Alim had so cruelly ended things.

Far from nervous, it was so nice to feel rested.

She made her way to the very nice bathroom where there was actually a shower. It felt wonderful to shower high in the sky and after she had washed and brushed her teeth and styled her hair, she took her Pill. Not that she would be needing it, but Gabi now took it every day. Not for this moment, and not to be ready for Alim, more because the absolute abandon between them that night had scared her.

In the cold light of day, she had realised that in bed with Alim she did not know her own mind.

In the deep of the night he had owned her so completely.

The absolute lack of thought and control had had her vow never to be so foolish again. No more chances.

Then she put on the heavy dark trouser suit and swore that if she ever did get her own business there would be a fitting, international choice.

Gabi returned to her seat and light refreshments and as she looked out over the ocean, Gabi amended that thought.

When she had her own business.

Sleep really was an amazing healer, and the distance from home combined with the white noise of the plane allowed her to think more clearly.

Alim had been harsh that morning when they had spoken and he had said that her mother used Gabi as an excuse. Yet he wasn't necessarily wrong.

Gabi didn't dwell on her mother's choices. She focussed instead on her own future, and her daughter's, for it was Lucia's future she wanted to improve upon too.

But first she had these days to get through.

Would she see him?

Gabi hoped so.

All the hurt, all the anger and the fact he was to marry should be enough to bury for good her feelings for him.

Yet they rose again and again, and more so since Lucia had been born, for every time she opened her eyes Gabi was reminded of the magic of him.

And the impossibility of them.

There were cross-winds, the pilot had warned them, and Gabi felt them as the plane came into land.

Her stomach lurched as she caught her first glimpse of the palace and it warned her of the might and power of the al-Lehan family.

It rose from a cliff edge, white and magnificent and looking out towards both ocean and city. And Zethlehan too was unexpected when seen from the air, for there was an eclectic mix of gleaming modern buildings that melded in with the old.

She had read up on the country's history and the royal

family's lineage that went as far back as when the country had first been named.

It was progressive in many ways—a firstborn daughter could—and had—ruled this stunning land. The desert princess's husband and children had taken the al-Lehan name. And while there were some mentions of children borne from the harem, the rulings were clear—they were not considered part of the al-Lehan dynasty.

Children like Lucia and James were simply sidelined. They were shadow families, hidden away and never formally recorded or mentioned. Lucia deserved better. So did Gabi.

And she must never lose sight of that, Gabi thought as the wheels hit the runway.

She had arrived in Zethlehan, where the time, she was informed, was five p.m.

Remembering Violetta's instructions, Gabi put a scarf she had brought over her head and shoulders but it didn't fall as nicely, or as effortlessly, as the other women's, who made it look so easy.

She opened her tablet and the first thing she saw was a message from her mother with the most gorgeous picture of Lucia attached.

She was lying on her stomach and lifting her head up and smiling widely. Oh, it was surely Gabi's favourite photo and she touched the screen and traced her daughter's beautiful smile.

Gabi was wearing heels, on Bernadetta's instructions, and felt a head above all the delicate beauties as she disembarked. A wall of heat hit her as soon as she stepped off the plane. The wind was hot on her cheeks and the air burned as she breathed it in, but soon she was in the cool of the airport and she made a quick call home.

'Lucia is fine,' Carmel told her. 'Did you get the picture that I sent?'

'I did.' Gabi smiled.

'The reception is terrible,' Carmel said. 'I can hardly hear you.'

'I'll call again tomorrow,' Gabi told her mother. 'Give Lucia a kiss for me.'

Customs was straightforward as she had a letter of introduction from the palace and, given she had travelled only with hand luggage, in no time she was walking through to the arrivals lounge.

'Gabi!'

She recognised Violetta immediately and though they had only worked together briefly it was nice to see a familiar friendly face.

'How was your journey?' Violetta asked.

'It was wonderful,' Gabi said. 'I slept most of the way.'

'Good.' Violetta nodded. 'It is good that you are well rested. We are heading this way,' she explained. 'We are taking a helicopter.'

'A helicopter?' Gabi checked.

'Of course.'

Violetta said it so casually and Gabi assumed that when you worked with royalty then taking a helicopter must be to Violetta the equivalent of taking a taxi.

The chopper was waiting and Gabi climbed in and fastened her seat belt and put on the headphones that Violetta handed to her.

'It's very windy,' she warned Gabi. 'We might be in for a bit of a bumpy ride.'

Gabi felt her stomach curl as she was lifted high into the sky.

The airport was a little way out from the city and Gabi

looked again at the amazing skyline that she had so recently seen from the plane.

The view was even more stunning than before. The sun was starting to set and the sky was such a blush pink that even the white palace in the distance seemed to have been painted rose. There was a haze over the city but then the helicopter banked to the right and she lost sight of it. Gabi craned her neck for a glimpse of the ocean to orientate herself but the view had disappeared from her window and so she turned her head to look for it on the other side.

It was way in the distance and Gabi felt her nostrils tighten as the palace faded from view.

Gabi looked over at Violetta, who was herself looking out of the window seemingly without concern.

Except even the city skyline had now faded and looking below there was only the occasional old building. 'Where are we going?' she asked Violetta.

There was no response.

Perhaps there were two cities, two palaces, Gabi told herself, while knowing that could not be right. Or maybe the pilot was diverting because of the wind?

Gabi had felt on high alert from the moment that she had agreed to come to Zethlehan but now she had her first taste of pure fear.

'Violetta,' Gabi said, more loudly this time.

Perhaps her microphone wasn't working, because Violetta did not respond to Gabi calling her name.

Now, as she looked out, there was nothing but desert. The sun was low in a burning sky and the endless sand looked like molten gold.

The ride seemed to take for ever, but finally coming into view she could see the billowing white of a desert abode.

* * *

And still Gabi fought for calm as she and Violetta disembarked.

What the hell had Bernadetta been thinking, making her wear heels? Gabi thought as she took off her shoes and then ran beneath the rotors.

'Is the service to be held in the desert?' Gabi asked, still fighting for an ordered reason, still hoping there was a sensible reason to explain why she had been brought here, but her voice was drowned by the rotors. 'Violetta?' she asked, and turned to see that Violetta was not by her side. She had run back under the rotors and was getting back into the chopper.

'Wait…' Gabi shouted.

Violetta did not.

The helicopter lifted into the blazing sky. The sand was a stinging blizzard of tiny, sharp pellets, and Gabi held her arms over her face to shield her eyes, eventually using her jacket to cover her nose and mouth. The soles of her feet were burning.

She had never felt more scared or alone, or more foolish for believing that she had been brought here for work.

And finally, when the helicopter was out of sight and the sands had somewhat settled she stood, windswept and scared but not alone.

There was Alim.

Only it was an Alim that Gabi had never seen.

Always he had been clean shaven, but not now.

Instead of the more familiar suits she was used to seeing him in, Alim wore a black robe and on his head was a *keffiyeh*; he stood utterly still, imposing and straight, and Gabi felt as if she were his prey.

She remembered his father walking through the foyer

and that moment of foreboding as she'd glimpsed the al-Lehans' power, and she felt the absolute full force of it now.

Yes, his prey was exactly what she was—he had sought her, found her and now she was within his grasp. As she stood there, waiting, they were plunged into darkness, for it was as if the desert had swallowed the fierce sun whole.

Gabi ran.

It was a rather stupid thing to do in a darkening desert but for now it didn't matter, she simply wanted to be away from him, only Gabi didn't get very far.

Alim caught up with her easily but so panicked was Gabi she shook off his hand from her arm and attempted to take off again, but she fell to the ground and lay with her head on her arm facing down, knowing that he stood over her.

Knowing there was nowhere to run.

'Gabi.'

His voice was annoyingly calm and terribly, achingly familiar.

Despite his attire, despite the unfamiliar surroundings, he was still the Alim she knew.

Gabi felt soothed when she should not, yet she could taste her panicked tears and feel the conflict for she wanted to turn around.

She wanted again to lift her face to him.

But anger won.

'You set me up,' she shouted, and thumped the ground.

'Come inside.'

'I don't want to come inside!'

Yet when he held out his hand she took it and she stood brushing herself down as the wind whipped her hair into her damp face.

So much for a sophisticated reunion!

'This is kidnap!'

'You are too dramatic.' Alim shrugged.

'Not where I come from. Your assistant told me I would not even have to see you…'

'Violetta ensured discretion,' Alim defended her. 'Don't you want a chance to be together for a while? I know that I do.' He had to shout to make himself heard over the wind. 'Don't you want a chance to speak and to catch up on all that has been going on?'

That was the very last thing that Gabi wanted!

Alim must not find out about Lucia while she was effectively stranded here.

'Come inside,' Alim said again, and the authoritarian note to his voice told her that he would not be argued with.

That did not stop Gabi. 'I don't want to.'

She shouted it but the wind whipped the words straight from her mouth and carried them into the night. Her mouth filled with sand and it was the most pointless argument ever, she knew, for she could not survive out here in this savage land.

Gabi had seen from the sky just how isolated they were.

He offered his hand to walk her back to the tent but Gabi declined it and for a few moments she stood her ground.

Alim would not stand in the fierce winds, attempting to persuade her. If she ran again he would find her in a matter of moments, for Alim knew the desert well and in her cumbersome clothes and winds such as these, Gabi would only manage a few steps.

Still, he was relieved to make it to the entrance and then turn around and sight her.

He waited, and after a short stand-off he could see that Gabi knew she was beaten.

There wasn't really a choice but to go inside and be with Alim.

The desert gave few options, she told herself.

The truth?

Gabi wanted to be with him.

CHAPTER ELEVEN

GABI WAS RELUCTANT to enter.

But for reasons of her own: she was scared she might like it.

Alim stood aside and Gabi stepped into relative silence.

She put down the shoes she carried in her hand, along with the small overnight bag, and felt him walk up behind her.

Her bare feet were caressed by soft rugs; oil lamps gave off a gentle glow that danced along the walls, though bore testimony to the fierce winds outside.

It was a haven indeed.

And she fought to keep her guard raised.

The peregrine note she had first breathed in when they'd danced was more prominent for Gabi now; it hung in the air and enveloped her from all around. It was hard to be scared with Alim so close by her side.

Gabi *was* angry, though.

'There is no one else here,' Alim informed her as he watched her walk through to the main living area.

She looked up at the high ceiling and felt terribly small. 'So there's no point screaming.'

Alim merely sighed. 'Gabi, you really are far too dramatic. What I meant when I said that we are alone is that there is no one here to disturb us and no one to overhear us when we are talking.'

He wanted to make it very clear to Gabi that whatever was said was just between them.

For now.

A baby certainly would change things—Violetta would have even more work cut out for her but at the very least he hoped by the end of this trip Gabi would leave knowing that both she and the baby would be taken care of.

Since he had found out that Gabi had been on maternity leave, Alim had been trying to find out what he could and using his best contacts to garner information.

It had proven surprisingly difficult.

Gabi did not work for the Grande Lucia; however, he had found out that indeed she had been on maternity leave. There was some recent CCTV footage of Gabi in the foyer of the Grande Lucia, speaking with a woman who handed Gabi a baby.

Alim had watched the grainy footage and had found himself holding his breath and zooming in on the image, desperate for a better glimpse of his child.

His child!

A fierce surge of protectiveness had hit him and his plans to bring Gabi to the desert had increased in their urgency.

He still did not know whether it was a boy or a girl.

And, from her silence, Alim was starting to realise that Gabi was in no rush to enlighten him with the news.

'I think,' Alim said, 'there is rather a lot to discuss, don't you?' But Gabi shook her head when he offered an opening for her to tell him.

'I have nothing to say to you.'

He was about to state that that was certainly not the case, but for now Alim chose to bide his time.

She was shocked, he accepted that, and angry too, so he offered her the chance to regroup.

'Why don't you go and get changed?' Alim suggested, and gestured to a curtained area.

'Changed?'

'Have a bath and get changed and then we can speak.'

'Alim, I'm stranded in the desert against my will and you expect me to go and slip into something more comfortable.'

'I don't like that suit.' Alim shrugged. 'And from memory neither do you.'

She just stood there.

The truth was, Gabi didn't really have anything more comfortable to put on.

Well, some pyjamas and another awful black suit and a small tube skirt and top.

Her packing really had been done in haste.

'My suits are all I've really got with me,' she admitted.

'I'm sure there will be alternatives in there.'

Again he gestured to the curtained area but still she did not move.

'Gabi, you are not stranded. If you want me to arrange the helicopter I shall do so, you just have to say the word.'

Gabi didn't, though.

She turned and walked to the area that Alim had gestured to and pulled aside heavy drapes.

It was like stepping inside a giant jewellery box.

The walls were lined with thick red velvet, which she ran her hand over, and jewelled lights dotted the ceiling.

It was a trove of exotic treasures with a huge, beautifully dressed bed in the centre.

She walked over and upon it lay a dark robe. It was

too dark to make out the colour but the fabric when she held it was as soft as the velvet walls.

There was more—a dressing table adorned with stoppered bottles. Gabi picked up one and inhaled the musky fragrance then caught sight of herself in a large gilded mirror.

She looked terrible. Her hair was wild and filled with sand and the mascara she had put on in the bathroom of the plane was halfway down her cheeks.

Gabi looked over to a screened area and curiosity beckoned her to investigate.

The lighting was subtle and it was even darker behind the screen, but she could see a deep bath and it had been filled most of the way. Gabi put in her hand, assuming that the water would be cold.

Yet it was not.

Her fingers lingered, feeling the oily warmth for a moment, and she simply didn't understand so she walked back out to Alim.

He was lying on some cushions, propped up on one elbow and completely unfazed by her rather angry approach.

'You said that there was no one else here.'

'There isn't.'

'So who filled my bath?'

He looked over to where she stood and smiled at the suspicion in her eyes and then the slight startle in them when he gave his response.

'Me.'

'You?'

'The water comes directly from hot desert springs and I added some oils that are supposed to aid in relaxation.'

A slight shiver went through her, albeit a pleasurable

one, as she thought of Alim here alone and readying the place for her arrival. But Gabi was in no mood to relax.

She wanted her wits about her, and knew that she needed to keep every one of them firing in his presence.

'Did you select the robe?' Gabi asked with a slight edge to her voice.

'No,' Alim responded. 'That would be Violetta.'

'So she lays out the clothes for your tarts?'

'Violetta has worked hard to ensure we are both comfortable and alone. We shall dine when you are ready to.'

'I ate on the plane.'

'Then there's no rush. Take your time.'

Gabi hadn't heard those words in a very long time; there simply weren't enough minutes in any day to get all she wanted to done.

Taking her time to get changed for dinner sounded like a reward on its own.

She wanted, for argument's sake, to say something scathing, but there was nothing that came to mind. Gabi wanted to point out that she was here against her wishes.

Yet her wishes said otherwise, for the truth was that she wanted to be there.

'Gabi.' He tried to capture her gaze but she would not let him. 'There is unfinished business between us.'

'I don't know what you mean.'

'Are you saying that you haven't thought of me?' Alim asked.

'I've tried everything I can not to.'

'Did it work?'

No.

Her silence said it for her, but then came the surprise when Alim spoke.

'It didn't work for me either.'

Her eyes flicked to his and she saw the burn of desire

there, and while she was angry it was tempered with relief. Absolute relief, not just at seeing him but that clearly Alim had wanted to see her again too.

Gabi had ached not only because of the sudden end to their affair but its lack of closure.

There was so much unanswered.

She'd felt as if she had been slowly going out of her mind these past months.

Not just about the pregnancy but over and over she had relived their night together, and the morning after, like a perpetual film that restarted the moment it was over, pausing, analysing and trying to work out where it had all gone wrong.

And she wanted to know.

'Go,' Alim said.

He watched her turn and disappear and he was glad of it, for there was such dark temptation between them and that did not make for sensible conversation.

In their months apart he had told himself that possibly he looked back at their time through rose-coloured glasses and that abstinence had made his memory of her grow fonder.

Not so.

And consequently he dismissed her.

She turned, and as the drape swished closed behind her it became a boudoir indeed, Gabi thought as she returned to the dimly lit cavern.

She took off her suit and top and then her underwear and there was no feeling of being rushed or concern that she might be disturbed.

Oh, there were no locks or doors but this space was so deeply feminine she just knew it had been assigned to her.

Assigned.

Gabi stepped into the bath. She did not like that word, though she knew that it was the correct one.

This mini desert kingdom was a lover's hideaway.

But she would not be his lover tonight.

Her anger at being brought here against her will served only to inflame her temper, and her blood was surely a full degree warmer as she could feel its warm passage through her veins and the weight and heat in her breasts and groin.

She wrenched herself from the bath but there were no towels or sheets to drape herself in and Gabi was certainly not going to ask him for one. And she did not put on the oils left out for her, or the rouge for her lips or kohl.

Instead, she ran a silver comb through her hair and still dripping wet she pulled on the robe over her naked body. It was a deep purple and the scooped neckline showed too much cleavage while the velvet clung to her skin. She could deny to herself her desire for Alim, but the reflection in the mirror stated otherwise.

Her eyes were glittering, her cheeks were flushed and it looked as if she had just come.

Or was about to.

Alim was sitting at a low table and watched as Gabi walked out.

The gown clung becomingly to her skin, her hair fell in one long damp coil and was twisted so that it fell over her right shoulder and dripped onto her breast.

'Oh, you didn't have to go to all this effort,' she teased as she took a seat opposite, assuming Violetta had prepared the treats and she simply hadn't noticed until now.

'Why wouldn't I?'

'I meant,' Gabi said, her voice a touch shrill, 'that clearly Violetta has been busy.'

'I selected the banquet,' Alim said. He picked up a jewelled flask and poured a clear-looking fluid into her glass. As he did so, a citrus scent coiled up in the air. 'And Violetta ensured it was all prepared, as best as it could be. However, while you were bathing I took care of the last-minute details.'

Her eye roll told her she did not believe him for a moment.

'You don't seem to understand the privacy afforded us here,' Alim said as he offered her delicacies. 'A woman is not brought here to work.'

Gabi peeled open the pastry she had selected; it was plump with succulent meat and ripe, pink pomegranate seeds. Gabi understood his words but she would not succumb to seduction. 'Why? Because you don't want her to be too tired for sex?'

He smiled that slow smile and she forgot his might, for he was Alim and they could just as easily be in the Grande Lucia, smiling across the foyer.

'Or too tired for conversation,' Alim said. 'Or too tired to lie on a clear night and look at the stars. There are many reasons other than sex to come deep into the desert. Let's explore them, shall we?'

And Gabi breathed out for he had done it again—just as she'd thought she had scored a point he trumped her.

Sex was the uncomplicated part.

'It has been a long time since we have spoken,' Alim said, inviting conversation.

'I don't think there's anything to discuss.' She gave him a smile then, but it was far from sweet. 'Apart from the reason I'm here—your wedding!' And then the bitter smile faded and for a moment she came close to crumbling and she revealed a little of her pain. 'How cruel you are!'

'Gabi, you are not here to plan my wedding. I invented that, just so that we could be alone.'

'Oh, so you ruin my career because you want a conversation…' She hesitated because the air between them was potent and she knew it was more than conversation they both craved. It was one of the reasons for her defensiveness because even after everything there remained desire. 'What is Bernadetta going to say when I return home without the contract?'

'You will think of something.'

She stared at him in anger and her lips twisted. 'You know how important work is to me.'

'As I said, I am sure you will think of something. So, how has it been?' he pushed for her to open up. 'Work?'

'Much the same.' Gabi selected a plump fig but as the questions began her appetite faded and she found that she was playing with her food.

'Is it still busy?' he asked, knowing she had just come back from leave.

'Extremely.'

She wasn't going to tell him about the baby, Alim realised. He was almost certain the baby must be his but he had to make sure.

'So what else have you been doing with your time?'

Gabi gave a small mirthless laugh before answering him. 'You've lost any right to ask about my personal life.'

'Have you met someone?' he asked. 'Is that why you are so uncomfortable to be here?'

A piece of fruit had just found its way to her mouth and he watched as she furiously swallowed, such was her haste to respond.

'I'm uncomfortable to be here because of what you did to me,' Gabi said, and she knew that tears flashed in her eyes. She wished she had found a more sophisticated answer but the fact was he had landed her in hell that morning. 'We don't all leap out of one bed and dive into the next. You hurt me, Alim, badly. I get that you might have been bored that night and just filling in time...'

'Never.'

'Don't!' Gabi said, and she stood from the table, tired of any attempt at being polite. She was glad, so glad that there were no staff and they were in the middle of the desert because she could say exactly what was on her mind and as loudly as she chose to! 'You'd had me already, Alim,' she shouted. 'I was fully prepared to leave it at that, to walk out the door and go back to being colleagues, yet you offered me a year. And a job. You made it more! And then you took it away. Did it give you a kick?'

'Gabi...' He tried to take her arms, to contain her, but she shook him off.

'And now you decide that you want to see me again. Well, tough, Alim, I don't want to see you.' Great thick tears were streaming down her cheeks, and they both knew that she lied.

It was torture not to see him and agony to be here. He did not move to hold her; instead, he drew her into his arms and it truly was the lesser of two evils because even resisting she sank into them.

'I did not set out to hurt you,' Alim told her.

He could feel her anger and the frantic beating of her heart and then she spoke. 'But you did.'

So badly.

'That morning I went for breakfast with my father and he told me the diktat had been invoked.'

Gabi frowned as she recalled a conversation that had taken place so many months ago. 'The same ruling that happened to your father and Fleur?'

'The same one.'

'Why couldn't you have told me this that morning, and saved all this hurt and pain?'

'Where?' Alim asked. 'In the hotel foyer?'

'No, you have an entire floor of the Grande Lucia at your disposal.'

'But the laws state that I cannot be alone with a woman I desire unless it is my future bride.'

Desire.

The word made her burn, it made her face feel hot and she wanted to press her cheek into the cool of his robe, so she did.

Yet she could feel the heat from his skin and the thud of his heart as he spoke.

'Even to work alongside you and want you would be forbidden. When I was showing Raul through the hotel and I came into the ballroom and you were there, I knew it was imperative that I leave or I would have broken the rules by which I have been raised. I can only take a lover here in the desert.'

'Are you camped out here, then?' she asked, and looked up. He smiled and for a moment so did Gabi. When she met his eyes, the problems of the world faded; when he smiled like that she forgot the hurt and how cross she was.

'I have been to the desert,' Alim said, 'alone.'

'Oh.'

He looked at her and her cheeks went a bit pink because she wanted to know about his alone time in the desert.

'And when I am here I think of you.'

'And the night we shared?' she asked, because when exhausted, when wretched, when aching for the memory to fade, the image of them taunted and sleep was no relief for he was there in her dreams.

'I think of that night,' Alim said, 'and I think of this.'

'This?'

'Us here together.'

He had been fighting not to bring her here for many months.

He pulled her in tighter so she could feel his arousal. His hand slipped to her back and his fingers explored the top of her spine while still his eyes held hers.

Gabi knew she should resist and not be drawn further under his spell, yet at the same time she told herself it would be the last time.

This was the only time she would be in the desert with him for she would never be tricked into being here again.

His mouth brushed hers and she tried to keep her lips pressed together but as their mouths met again she realised that the feel of him had never left her mind.

Alim's hand came to the back of her head and as he pressed her in he gave her his tongue.

She accepted. Deeply.

And she offered hers.

They tasted and claimed each other again, while his other hand slid to her breast and took its aching weight.

'Just once,' she told him.

And Gabi meant it.

This wasn't like a break in her diet, this was her absolute rule.

'Once?' Alim checked, and his fingers slid between her thighs, sliding along the velvet of her robe and then probing her softly.

He made her feel weak with the promise of more.

'I mean one night,' Gabi said as his tongue made indecent work of her ear as she amended her rules. 'One night and that's it. I shan't be your on-call desert lover, Alim.'

Gabi would be more than his desert lover, Alim thought, though he chose not to enlighten her.

With a child between them, once he married she would be his mistress.

Alim just had to tell her, though he felt no guilt withholding that information.

After all, Gabi held the biggest secret of all.

'Come to bed,' Alim said.

There, he had decided she would tell him.

Whatever it took.

CHAPTER TWELVE

THIS TIME THEY made it to the sleeping area, because Alim had decided it would be a more measured seduction.

He was not used to being lied to, or having vital information withheld from him. Not for long anyway.

Alim took her by the hand and led her there.

The wind played a seductive tune as she stepped into his chamber and they faced each other.

'Here,' Alim said, 'we are not forbidden.'

But it was a forbidden love.

His fingers traced her clavicle and moved the robe down so that her shoulder was bare, and then he did the same on the other side. Alim's hands roamed over her breasts and to the sides of her ribcage as her mouth ached for his kiss and the weight of him on her.

'I have missed you,' Alim told her.

And she could not confess to just how much she had missed him too, for that would leave her exposed and weak to his demands.

'I have thought about you,' Alim said, and he pointed to the bed. 'There, on that bed, I have thought about you a lot.'

She swallowed at the image he conjured and watched as he freed himself from his robe.

Gabi caught her breath for, to be kind, her mind had

dimmed his beauty a touch, but now it was hers to witness again.

She put a hand up and touched his chest—solid and warm. She pressed her fingers to his skin and then shared a deep kiss as her fingers pressed into the flesh of his torso.

'Have you thought of me?' he asked.

'At first,' Gabi said. 'But I'm over you now.'

'Not quite,' he said, pulling the robe down over her breasts and hips so that it fell to the floor. His hands were thorough and hungry for her body as they again felt her generous flesh.

'Tell me how you have been,' he said as he kissed her all over, gently lowering her so she lay naked on soft silks, 'since you got over me.'

'I've been…' She hesitated, and she wondered what he would say if she told him that each night she still cried herself to sleep. 'Fine.'

'Fine,' he said as he joined her and they lay with their fingers tracing each other's outlines. His muscular arms were as she remembered and his erection still responded to the trace of her finger on the hairs of his thigh. It was Alim who wavered from the sensual tracing and ran his hand along the soft insides of her thighs. He savoured them again with a teasing caress, then tortured her by halting her at the peak of the thrill.

'Did you ever think of contacting me?' he asked, and she bit on her lip in frustration. As he held back the pleasure, she became a little more truthful. 'I wanted to but, you moved to Zethlehan.'

'Not until recently.' He looked up. 'You had months when you could have made contact.'

'For the pleasure of being rejected again?' Gabi shot back, and her more honest response was rewarded by a deep kiss to her breast, one that hurt because it was so exquisite.

His fingers stroked her inside and it was his deep desire for her that made Gabi burn and want.

Yet as he removed his fingers and the deep contact of his mouth, she was reminded how abruptly he had ended things between them and as he went to part her legs, she drew them closed.

He parted them with his palm. Not even a hint of pressure, just the soft touch of his skin and she opened to Alim; he came to kneel between her calves.

She felt again like his prey.

He moved her knees and her legs up higher, and her throat was tight as he lowered his head.

'Gabi…' he said, and she felt his words in her most intimate space. 'Tell me…'

Tell him what?

That she loved him and that she was going out of her mind because she lay in the desert with a man who had brought her here on a lie? Yet she was fighting not to plead for him.

His tongue was subtle.

At first.

She considered that she might relax into the caress of his mouth and then his kiss strengthened and he moved down onto his stomach, his tongue slipping inside her. She heard the kiss and swallow of him and she moaned.

'Tell me…' he said again.

'I have thought of you.'

There, she had said it.

His tongue was making love to her and his fingers hurt her thighs but she would not have him lighten his touch, not even a fraction.

Gabi's hand was turning, searching, for a pillow, a

cushion, for an anchor but he was tasting her so deeply her fingers then tugged at his silky hair. His unshaven jaw was rough and delicious and she had never thought she would know such pleasure again.

'Alim…'

Inadvertently, as she had the night their baby had been born, she sobbed out his name.

Alim liked it.

He liked how she cried out his name as she started to come, and he drank her in, yet she frustrated him too for, even in the throes of passion she did not reveal the truth.

And so he rose from between her legs, left her in the middle of her climax, and reached for a sheath.

Gabi almost screamed in frustration at the sudden dearth of sensation. He rose over her and she ached for him to be inside her, yet he was busy taking the care he had not that first night.

'Please…' Gabi begged, and she was about to tell him she was covered, not to worry, for she was on the Pill, but it didn't matter now; he was over her and squeezing into where she was so swollen, aching and ripe.

'We don't want you getting pregnant…' he said, and she gave in to the bliss, but it was short-lived, for Gabi's eyes flew open to just one word from Alim.

'Again…'

He knew!

She was a ball of panic and he was taking her, a mire of sensation, for he was an assault on all of her senses.

His lovemaking was savage. Her pleasure he had taken care of already and now, when perhaps it should be just for him, she was taken to the edge of sanity as Alim unleashed himself.

He spoke words she did not understand but they were

harsh and scolding, yet his arms held her tight as he bucked within.

She was dragging her nails down his back and now it was Gabi's anger that was released. For he had left her, and she had had to fight to survive in a world that did not contain him.

Their teeth clashed, their bodies locked and she bit his shoulder; it felt primal and she was screaming. Her thighs burned now as her legs wrapped tightly around him, and his rapid thrusts had her high and coming so deeply as he shot into her.

'Never...' he said, and was about to tell her to never lie again, but as he came, as he felt her deep pulses drag him in, words did not matter.

He lay on top of her and they breathed in air that felt clear and cool, as if a storm had just passed.

It had.

Alim knew, Gabi thought as she lay there.

He kissed her back, a very soft kiss, for the storm really had passed.

She knew he knew now.

CHAPTER THIRTEEN

'WERE YOU EVER going to tell me?'

Alim had waited for her breath to even out before he asked her.

'Yes.'

'I don't believe you,' Alim said, and he turned his face to Gabi's. 'I gave you every opportunity and you said nothing.'

'I wanted to tell you from a distance.'

'Why?'

Gabi didn't answer that for she did not want to admit that being around him made her feel weak and that she'd been scared what she might agree to when she lay by his side.

Here, she felt they could do no wrong.

Here, in the desert, this love did not feel so forbidden, and the idea of being his desert lover felt rather wonderful, in fact.

'What did we have?'

His words said so much—that he accepted their baby as his and that the question was gently asked brought tears to her eyes.

'A little girl.'

She was back there again in those lonely hours, giving birth without Alim by her side, but now his hand found hers as she told him their daughter's name.

'I called her Lucia.'

'She is well?'

Gabi nodded for her words were strangled by tears as she heard the care behind his questions.

'You'll never forgive me, will you?'

'Gabi, I accept that the decision would have felt like an impossible one.'

Alim did not like it and maybe later he would resent the times denied to them but now was not that time; there were too many things he needed to know this moment.

'When did you have her?'

'The last time we met,' Gabi said. 'When you were showing Raul through the hotel.'

Alim frowned. 'The night I returned to Zethlehan?'

Gabi nodded.

'You didn't look pregnant,' Alim said. 'Though admittedly I was doing all I could not to look at you.'

'I lost a lot of weight,' Gabi told him. 'I've put it all back on, though.'

'Good.'

He was the most back-to-front man she knew, for he was playing with her stomach as if it was the most beautiful stomach in the world.

'I was sick a lot at first and then I was very busy with work. I was just about to go on leave when I went into labour.'

'That would have been far too soon.'

'She's done so well, though,' Gabi said. 'Lucia amazed the doctor and nurses; she was early but so strong.'

'The al-Lehans are.' One day he would tell her about the strong lineage; one day he would share in tales of babies that should not have survived but had lived to rule.

But not now.

For Alim ached with sadness that a desert princess had been born but his country would never know her name.

She did not exist as his daughter, except here in the desert.

Gabi had left the bed and had gone to her case in the hallway and retrieved her tablet.

There was something so splendid about her, Alim thought as she walked back to the bed. He knew Gabi was shy, yet here she was not and he loved how she slipped back to his side; he wrapped an arm around her as she opened up the latest image of Lucia—the one that her mother had sent her just as she had landed here in Zethlehan.

There had never been any real doubt in his mind, Alim had known she was his, but he had never expected to feel so moved by a photo.

Her eyes were almond shaped and she was a beautiful old soul, a true al-Lehan.

'When was this taken?' Alim asked.

'My mother sent it to me yesterday. I got it when we landed.'

'She is tiny,' he said, unable to take his eyes from his daughter and loathing that he could only see her on a screen.

'She's the size of a newborn now,' Gabi said. 'She caught up quickly.'

He scrolled through the images and Gabi explained each one. 'That was the day I brought her home from the hospital,' she said. 'And that's on the night she was born.'

He had been on his way here.

Alim looked at their fragile daughter and then at the mother who held her. Gabi had indeed lost weight; in the picture she looked drawn and pale, scared yet proud as she looked down at her very new daughter, and his heart twisted in fear and pain as he thought of how it could have gone.

'You have done well,' Alim said, and looked at Gabi.

She had expected him to be accusatory, to be furious for all she had denied him, yet his voice was kind and his words told her he was proud of her for the care that their daughter had received.

Yes, from the day she had met him he had enthralled her, for his responses were like no others; they threw her in new directions.

And then he turned back to the tablet and the photos of his daughter. 'That's all there are…' Gabi said.

Except there was another image that held his attention now—the one of Gabi and him dancing in the deserted ballroom.

She blushed. It felt as if he was looking through her diary and she hastily moved to play the image down.

'The photographer had left a time-lapse camera set up, there was this at the end…' She was a little embarrassed to have saved it, but how could she be when she now lay in his bed and from that night they had made a daughter?

'I'll send you the pictures of Lucia—'

'Already done,' Alim said, as he clicked on them.

They lay there in the dark with the wind an orchestra that seemed to play only for them.

'Will you bring her next time?' Alim asked, and Gabi went still, for there would not be a next time.

Nothing had changed for Gabi, except that he knew.

'Has James ever been to Zethlehan?' she asked, instead of answering.

'No.'

'In case it caused rumours to spread?'

'There are always rumours and they are dealt with by

the palace,' Alim said. 'No, James has never been here because Fleur always refused to come.'

'She's never been?'

'No. Fleur said that she deserved better than a tent in the desert so my father saw that she and James had a home in London and an apartment in Rome.'

'At the Grande Lucia?'

'No. They have only started to dine there since I bought it.' He gave her a smile. 'It is there that James and Mona met—she was there for her grandparents' wedding anniversary and Fleur and James were there with my father.'

That's right, she remembered Mona telling her that and it had seemed so inconsequential at the time.

'I don't want to be your lover, Alim.'

'You would be better than a lover,' Alim told her. 'You would be my mistress.'

He said it as if it were a reward.

'I don't want to be like Fleur,' Gabi said. 'I don't want to bring her here and…' Yet she fought with herself, for even as she said it, she lied.

There was nothing she wanted more right now than for Lucia to lie between them.

There was nothing that appealed more than the thought of visiting Alim, and their child growing up with the love of her father.

'Would it be such a terrible life?' he turned and asked her. 'I would take care of you two so well.'

She stared back at him.

'You could come here often and still have your career.'

'Career?' She gave a short, incredulous laugh. 'I seem to remember you offering me that once before; it didn't last very long.'

The hurt was still there—even recalling that moment

took her straight back to the pain he had caused her. 'Anyway, the Grande Lucia has been sold…'

'The contracts are not signed yet.'

And it didn't appease her—because Bastiano was his friend, but that meant little to Alim, she was sure.

He was ruthless and would get his own way.

Well, not in this.

'I don't want to work for you,' Gabi said, and her voice was certain. 'I want my own career.'

'And you could have it. I would see you often.'

'Where?'

'Mostly here,' Alim said. 'And once things were more settled for my country I could spend more time with you and Lucia in Rome…'

'You mean once you are married and have an heir?'

'Yes.'

And even if it appalled her, it was the life he had been born to, Gabi knew.

'You didn't approve when it was your father,' she pointed out.

'I did not know then that they had made things work.' And he told her a little about how he had found out his mother was happier than he had believed she was.

'I think we could do it even better than them.'

He made the unpalatable sweet, for now the winds buffeted the walls of the desert tent and she could almost imagine a little family here at times. But then her eyes closed on the madness that her mind proposed she consider; she saw the image of Fleur sitting taking refreshments alone; she thought of the other injured parties that an illicit love brought.

'I wouldn't do that to your wife,' Gabi said. 'And I shan't do it to our child.'

'You'd deny her a chance to be with her father?'

'Never,' Gabi said. 'You can come and see her whenever you choose.'

She was braver in words than in thought, not that he gave her a moment to think.

'I want you to move into the Grande Lucia.'

'It's about to be sold.'

'Bastiano isn't going to be kicking out the guests… you're to move there forthwith.'

'No.' He was pulling her into his world, and she would not allow it. 'I shan't be your lover and I shan't be your mistress.' She rolled onto her side and faced away from him.

'Gabi, just think about it.'

'No.' She was crying because he made her weaken. 'Haven't you heard a word I've said?'

'I heard all that you said,' Alim told her as he spooned in from behind, his hand on her stomach and his mouth at her ear, 'but I think we need to speak at more length.'

The only length she was certain of was the one that was nudging between her thighs and Gabi knew it would soon be the delicious experience all over again.

Not just now but for the rest of her life.

'No, I need to get back to my baby.'

She felt lost and reckless to be in the desert with him, and her mind was made up.

'I shan't be your mistress.'

Gabi's mind was *almost* made up but she was open to persuasion in his arms. And so she climbed out of the vast bed before she shattered again to his touch.

'Get back into bed,' Alim said.

He lay uncovered and beautiful and she had never fought harder not to simply give in to his demands. 'The only way I'll sleep with you again is as your wife.'

'Wife?' Alim's tone told her how impossible that was. 'I am offering you—'

'I don't want to be your mistress, Alim.'

'Please,' he angrily retorted. 'You want centuries of history wiped out just for you?'

A few months ago she would have backed down, almost apologised for being so bold.

Yet what they had found together had changed her, and for the better.

She had a baby to think of too.

His love, though not on offer, made her strong.

'I don't just want it,' Gabi hotly responded. 'I insist on it.'

'Oh, you do, do you?'

'Yes, and now I want to leave.'

He just lay there.

'I said—'

'I heard.'

He rolled over and the world was invading because here in their remote haven Alim retrieved his phone.

'The helicopter will be here within the hour.'

Gabi breathed out in relief, but her relief was short-lived.

'Now,' he said, 'get back to bed.'

CHAPTER FOURTEEN

OH, IT SHOULD feel wonderful to be back in Rome and to step into her mother's house and hold Lucia.

She brought her baby back to her flat and drew the drapes on the world to create her own little haven of peace.

But peace was fragile and, Gabi knew, at any moment it could be, *would* be shattered.

That much Gabi was certain of.

The days passed and she heard nothing from Alim, but the lack of contact did not serve as relief.

She knew he was working his way towards them.

Indefinable, indescribable.

Gabi just knew.

For seven mornings, the sun rose as promised in the east and for seven nights it slipped away into the west, but distance and time did not soothe Gabi. She knew that Alim kept his family close—his insistence at maintaining ties to his half-brother James, despite his father's pressure to leave well alone, told Gabi that.

And Lucia was his daughter.

Always Alim seemed a step ahead of her, and Gabi, rather than trying to second-guess his next move, decided to focus on her own.

If she was going to be strong against Alim, then she

needed a life. She needed to be able to take care of her daughter enough that she did not solely depend on him, and that started now.

'I'd hoped for something more concrete!' Bernadetta was less than impressed with the rather sparse report Gabi offered as to her time in Zethlehan.

'When is the wedding?'

'Sultan Alim is not sure,' Gabi answered, and then she looked at Bernadetta. 'I've been thinking, Bernadetta…' Except that sounded unsure. 'As you know,' Gabi amended, 'for a long time I've wanted to go out on my own…'

'Oh, not this again.' Bernadetta rolled her eyes. 'Do I have to remind you of the terms—?'

'Bernadetta,' Gabi broke in, 'I cannot hire any of your contacts for six months, I'm very aware of that, but they can still hire me.'

'Hire you?' Bernadetta gave a condescending laugh.

'Rosa would hire me in an instant. I worked for her for ages and, to be honest, with Lucia so young the thought of more regular hours for a few months is appealing. And, of course, some of Rosa's brides-to-be might not yet have found a wedding planner…' She could see Bernadetta's rapid blink but she quickly recovered.

'You wouldn't last five minutes in this industry without me.'

'I think I'll last a whole lot longer,' Gabi said. 'I guess we're going to find out, but not for a while, though. I've just returned from maternity leave so I'm legally obliged—'

'Gabi,' Bernadetta broke in, 'this is nonsense. We've got a royal wedding coming up—'

'We?' Gabi checked. It was the first time she had ever included Gabi in the business and it had taken a threat to resign to hear it. 'Matrimoni di Bernadetta has a potential contract. I have a child to raise. Bernadetta, I think we could make a very strong partnership but obviously it has to be something that would work for you too.'

'Gabi,' Bernadetta said, 'you're getting ideas above your station.'

'No.' Gabi shook her head. 'I've got ideas and plenty of them, and they're exactly where they ought to be.'

It didn't go well.

She wasn't exactly laughed out of the office, as Gabi had predicted she would be; instead Bernadetta sulked and ignored her.

In Zethlehan it wasn't business as usual either.

Violetta asked to see Alim and broke the news.

'Bastiano Conti has withdrawn his offer.'

Usually Alim would hold onto a hiss of indignation when a sale fell through at this late stage. He never revealed his emotions, even to the most trusted staff or those closest in his circle.

Now, though, he let out an audible sigh.

One of relief.

He did not want the Grande Lucia to be sold.

Alim loved that building; there had been more than memories made there and he did not want that chapter of his life closed.

Lucia.

He had to see her.

'What was his reason?' Alim asked Violetta.

'Apparently one of your chambermaids has light fingers. A family heirloom was stolen from Bastiano.'

'I will deal with that,' Alim said.

He and Bastiano were friends, and a deal falling through would not mar that.

Business was kept separate, but still he rang the hotel and asked to be put through to the head of Housekeeping to find out things for himself before calling Bastiano.

'Young Sophie…' Benita told him. 'I wanted to give her the benefit of the doubt but a ring was found when she turned out the pockets of her uniform so there was no choice but to let her go.'

Sophie was a friend of Gabi's, Alim knew.

He had often seen them chatting; in days long gone he had seen them with their coats on at the end of the day, heading out for supper.

And, on Gabi's behalf, he probed further.

'Did she admit to it?' Alim checked.

'Of course not,' Benita said. 'I've yet to find a thief who would.'

'Yes but—'

'Alim,' Benita said, 'I think there might have been something between our esteemed guest and maid.'

'Oh.'

'It's been dealt with.'

'Okay.'

Yet he could not let his thoughts of the Grande Lucia go.

He was flicking through his phone, looking at pictures of Lucia, and then he came to the photo of him with Lucia's mother.

It was a magnificent portrait of a couple gazing at each other, on the edge of a future together…

And Alim felt his heart quicken.

He reached for the leather-bound folder on his desk and read the pertinent parts of the diktat.

And then he read the rest.

Violetta brought in refreshments but instead of waving her out he had her bring him more files.

Ancient files with ancient rulings that he had been forced to learn as a child.

Alim studied them as a man now.

He read the ancient teachings and pored over the laws of his land, and as he turned the pages Alim glanced up and saw his father standing there.

They were barely speaking.

His father considered Alim to be stubborn.

'I have chosen my bride,' Alim told his father.

'That decision belongs to me,' Oman said, for he knew the laws well.

'Then you had better make sure that it is the right one,' Alim responded coolly, but his voice held a silk-clad threat, 'or there shall be no wedding.'

Oman's assessment was the correct one.

Sultan Alim al-Lehan of Zethlehan was the most stubborn man in this land.

He would not succumb to rules of old, as his father had.

Alim would work within them.

CHAPTER FIFTEEN

GABI NEVER FORGOT.

Even as she sat in her tiny flat, consoling poor Sophie, Alim was not far from her mind.

For nearly a week, Sophie had been around every day bemoaning the loss of her job and the man who had caused it—Bastiano Conti.

'I would never steal,' Sophie said. 'But if I did, I would not steal some stupid emerald and pearl ring. It would be diamonds.'

She made Gabi laugh, and in the second that the world felt lighter, Alim invaded, for her phone rang and the fragile peace was shattered.

'Why,' Alim asked, 'are you still living in that flat, when there is an apartment at the Grande Lucia at your disposal?'

She gave an apologetic smile to Sophie and went through to her bedroom to take the call.

Lucia was asleep in her crib and Gabi kept her voice down so as not to disturb her, and also because she did not want Sophie to hear.

'Because I refuse to be kept by you.'

'Your daughter has a father who will provide for her.' Alim gave in, he refused to argue on the phone when he would see Gabi soon, but there was something he badly needed to know.

'How is Lucia?'

'She slept through last night for the first time.'

'That is good. I am in Rome and I would like to meet her.'

Gabi screwed her eyes closed.

She had been dreading this, had been preparing herself for this moment. He had told her that nothing would stop him from seeing his child, and yet again Alim was a step ahead for she had at least thought there would be time to prepare for their meeting.

'When?'

'This afternoon. Is that a problem for you?'

'No,' Gabi admitted. 'I've got a couple of days off.'

'Really?'

'Bernadetta told me not to come in this weekend,' Gabi said. 'I'm not sure if I've been fired. I asked Bernadetta for a partnership…'

Alim, it would seem, had lost interest in her career plans for he spoke over Gabi. 'Can you bring Lucia to me at the Grande Lucia at one?'

She looked around her home; no, she could not imagine him here.

'For how long?'

'The afternoon,' Alim answered calmly. 'Say, until five?'

No, *that* was the part she dreaded, for Gabi knew she would have to get over him all over again.

Sophie was terribly hard to get rid of, but Gabi pulled out an excuse and, sounding like Bernadetta, told her friend that she had a migraine.

'That came on quickly,' Sophie said.

'Yes, they tend to.'

Thankfully Sophie soon left and, wishing she could lie down in a darkened room and hide from the world for a while, Gabi bathed her slippery baby and washed her hair and then she fed her.

'You're going to meet your daddy,' Gabi told her.

And though Gabi was worried for herself, and her absolute drop-knickers reaction to Alim, at least today she had the shield of her daughter. Alim would be far too besotted with Lucia to worry about other things.

And, more importantly, she was so happy for Lucia.

No, history was not repeating itself—this little girl would have a dad.

Of sorts.

And so, just before one, Gabi walked into the foyer of the Grande Lucia, as she had done many, many times, but then she stopped in her tracks.

The pillar display in the middle of the foyer was no longer its trademark red. Instead, there was a stunning display of sweet peas.

Pinks, lilacs and creams, they were absolutely stunning and she stood for a moment, enjoying the wonderful change.

'They're for you,' Gabi said to her daughter. 'He did this for you!'

Her happiness soon evaporated, though. She was met by Violetta, and it would seem that both baby and mother required preparation to enter the Sultan's world.

Pride had ensured that Gabi had dressed as well as she could for today, and little Lucia was wearing a gorgeous outfit and was wrapped in a new muslin square.

It wasn't enough.

And it wasn't just Lucia who had to be prepared.

There was a silver robe laid out for Gabi and, she quickly realised, Violetta had an assistant to do her make-up and hair.

'That won't be necessary,' Gabi said. 'I'm here so that Alim can see his baby.'

'The Sultan—' Violetta started, but Gabi would not hear it.

'He didn't tell me he was a sultan when he took me to bed,' Gabi interrupted. 'And I am not here as his mistress. I am here as the mother of his child.'

Violetta blinked, clearly more used to people bending over backwards to please the Sultan. Well, no bending over would be happening today.

'This is Hannan,' Violetta introduced them. 'She is a royal nanny of considerable standing and will help get the baby ready to meet Sultan Alim.'

'Her name is Lucia,' Gabi said. 'And she *is* ready.'

This time Violetta paid no attention.

The muslin was replaced with a cashmere wrap and Gabi bit her lip as Hannan dared check that her baby was clean enough for the Sultan's eyes.

It incensed Gabi but for now she stayed quiet.

Lucia did not.

She let out a cry of protest as her face was wiped.

'Perhaps we will wait till after she is fed so that she is content when she sees the Sultan,' Hannan suggested.

'She isn't due to be fed for another three hours.' Gabi said. 'And, given I'm due to leave at five, it would make it a very short first visit with her father.'

'Perhaps just a small feed,' Hannan suggested. 'The Sultan is not yet here.'

Gabi clutched her daughter, and already ached for her, unable to believe that Alim could be late for his first meeting with his daughter.

The wait was awful.

But finally the words were said. 'The Sultan is ready for you.'

The real question was, was *she* ready to face Alim?

His offer that she be his mistress had been met with the contempt it deserved.

Yet talking to herself was easy when Alim wasn't close.

She picked up little Lucia and held her close and when Hannan came over to check again that her baby was sweet and clean enough to meet her father for the first time, Gabi shot her a look.

Wisely, Hannan stepped back.

The small entourage walked along the long carpeted corridor and Gabi did her best not to think of the last time she had been here—being kissed up against these walls, falling together through the door that Violetta now knocked on.

Making love.

She walked in, holding Lucia to her chest, with Violetta and Hannan by her side.

Alim stood by a window in his immaculate reception room. The fire that had blazed as he'd stripped her naked was now devoid of flames and filled with an autumnal floral display.

A tamed version of itself.

Just like Alim.

He was wearing a suit and was clean shaven, and though he looked somewhat less formidable out of traditional robes, not for a moment would she forget his power.

'I apologise for keeping you waiting,' he said by way of introduction, but offered no explanation for the reason he had done so. He looked over at Violetta and Hannan. 'Excuse us, please.' Polite, in all dealings *outside* the bedroom, Alim dismissed his staff and Gabi stood, a little awkwardly, as Alim's eyes flicked down to the baby she held in her arms, though he did not approach.

'She's just been fed,' Gabi said with a distinct edge to her voice, 'to ensure that she's no trouble for you.'

'Did they feed you too?' Alim asked, implying he knew full well that it was the mother who was trouble, and he saw that she resisted a smile.

'No,' Gabi said.

'Then I had better watch out.'

Indeed he had, for Gabi made her own rules, and that, his father had pointed out, might make her an unwise choice for a sultan's bride.

He walked over and peered at the bundle that she held—their tiny baby hidden in a swathe of cashmere.

Gabi watched as his hand moved back the fabric. She heard the slight hitch in his breath as, for the first time, he met his daughter.

She had dark hair, like her parents', and her dark lashes swept over round cheeks. Her little rosebud mouth was pink and her skin as pale as Gabi's.

And she was beautiful.

Alim had been raised knowing he would one day be Sultan of Sultans, yet he met true responsibility now, for he would move mountains for his daughter and she had not even opened her eyes to look at him.

He looked up to Gabi and saw that *her* eyes were angry.

Though she held Lucia tenderly, Gabi's stance was almost confrontational, and he loved that she would do anything to protect not just her daughter but herself.

She was a wise choice indeed.

And for Gabi he *had* moved mountains.

Though Alim would tell her that later, right now he was overwhelmed to see Lucia.

'Can I hold her?'

Gabi handed him their child and it was the first awkward move she had ever seen him make.

Indeed, it was awkward at first, for Lucia was so light and she moved and stirred as she went into her father's arms, and he held her perhaps a little too firmly.

Gabi said nothing; she did not tell him to watch her head and she did not move to hush her daughter, who was starting to wakeup; instead, she walked over and took a seat.

She was close to tears, watching him hold their daughter so tenderly and witnessing the obvious love he had for Lucia.

It didn't feel fair that they could never be a family. She wanted to go over to where he took a seat, she wanted to be with the two people she loved.

His part-time lover.

The desert still tempted her. Alim always would.

Then Lucia opened her eyes.

Alim had never doubted that Lucia was his—had he, though, he would have been proved a fool, for her eyes were navy, turning to grey, and there were the same silver flecks that greeted him in the mirror each morning.

He hoped she might cry so that he could hand her back to her mother, for he had never felt more moved than now; there was guilt too for the months Gabi had dealt with this alone, and fear about how tiny Lucia was, even though she was more than three months old.

But Lucia did not cry or whimper. She looked straight at her daddy and smiled and completely won his heart.

'I could have lived my entire life not knowing about her.'

'No,' Gabi said. 'I lived my life without knowing my father so I would never do that to my child. I was going to wait till I felt a little better, and then tell you.'

'Better?' He frowned, worried that she had been ill.

'Stronger.'

'Stronger?' Alim checked.

'To say no to you.'

His eyes raised just a fraction, as if doubting she could.

'I meant what I said—I shan't be your mistress, Alim. I will always let you see your daughter whenever you come here to Rome but there will be no trips to the desert.'

'Really?'

'Yes.'

She must be stronger because she almost believed that she could say no to him.

'So you are going to be single and—'

'I didn't say that,' Gabi corrected. 'You will marry the bride of the Sultan of Sultans's choosing and I will get on with my life. I won't be like Fleur, living a lonely life with you as my occasional, discreet lover.'

'Oh, so you hope to meet someone else?'

'Yes.'

He stared at her and she tried not to meet his gaze because she just could not imagine being with another man.

Ever.

She could not imagine anyone after him, yet she had to believe it, for she would not be his mistress, neither would she be alone.

The minutes passed so slowly they were half an hour in with three more to go.

He picked up a phone and soon Hannan appeared; Gabi's lips tightened as she scooped up Lucia and took her away, and soon it was just the two of them.

'I thought you wanted to see her.'

'I don't need to stare at her for the entire visit to love her. I will call for refreshments for you.'

They made small talk as they waited for afternoon tea to arrive.

'Bernadetta is being weird,' Gabi said. 'She won't take my calls.'

He just shrugged and then told her his news. 'I have withdrawn the Grande Lucia from sale.'

'I thought the contracts were signed.'

'No. Bastiano returned to the Grande Lucia for a visit and apparently some jewellery was stolen from his suite—your friend apparently.'

Gabi wasn't going to blush or apologise for Sophie. She just gave a shrug.

'He's withdrawn his offer.'

And now Gabi rolled her eyes because Alim would be here in Rome so much more.

Her desire was safer from a distance.

Arabian teas, coffees and pastries arrived and as the maid poured Alim declined.

'Enjoy,' Alim said to Gabi as the maid left.

'Where are you going?'

'Bed,' Alim answered. 'I read that you should try and sleep when the baby does.'

Her mouth twisted into an incredulous smile when she thought of the hours she had paced the floor with her baby and snatched twenty-minute naps on the sofa.

He had not a clue!

'Half an hour of fatherhood and you're already tired?' Gabi accused.

'Months of fatherhood, had I but known,' Alim corrected. 'And months of abstinence, apart from one night in the desert.'

And he took her back in her mind to where she had been trying to avoid going.

Gabi looked ahead and tried not to think of her time in his bed.

And Alim, as he stepped into the bedroom where he had had so much planned, instead was incensed by her words.

Pride perhaps was at fault, but there was also this need to know not that Lucia was his but that *Gabi* was his—that he was and always would be her one and only.

He started to undress and then remembered he should be dressed for the planned proposal and standing when Gabi inevitably walked in.

Surprise!

Yet she did not walk in.

Alim rarely got angry, he rarely cared enough to be so.

And he was also jealous.

Gabi had riled him.

On what should be the most romantic of days she spoke of other men!

Oh, Alim wanted to prove her wrong. There would *never* be others.

So, instead of the plans he had made, Alim opened the bedside drawer and there they lay his collection of diamonds; he selected the best, then he closed the drapes and turned off the lights.

He would not be brought to his knees until Gabi was.

And so he walked out.

She sat, drinking tea.

Her foot was tapping, Alim noticed, but apart from that she seemed calm, like a guest sitting in the foyer, waiting for her car to arrive, or to be told that her suite was now ready.

Gabi was not calm.

She had been fighting with herself not to follow him in.

To 'Keep Calm and Drink Tea', as suggested.

Yet her hands were shaking and her desire was fierce and she ached for these visiting hours to be over.

For an imaginary nurse to come in and ring a bell so that she could leave.

Then he walked out.

The jacket was off, the tie gone and his shirt half-undone, as if he had been undressing and had suddenly remembered something.

Indeed he had. 'There will be others?' Alim questioned, and even though his voice was dark it held a slightly mocking edge, for he was sure there could be no other.

And what was said now would define their future, Gabi knew.

She would not be Fleur, sitting in the foyer of this very hotel and ignored. She would not be his mistress and make love and then not make a fuss when he returned to his wife.

How bloody dare he?

And so she met his eyes and she played a very dangerous game with a sultan who was already not best pleased.

'Maybe just *one* other,' Gabi said. 'Perhaps I will find the love of my life.'

'What if you have already found him?' Alim said.

'How can I have,' Gabi countered, 'when he speaks of a future wife?'

And she found out then just how strong she was because now she could look him in the eye and tell him things she would once never have dared. Now she stood her ground and it felt firm beneath her feet, for she was resolute.

She watched as he reached into his pocket and beside her teacup he placed a stone.

A magnificent one.

'You shall be kept in splendour,' Alim said, and when every other woman would reach for the stone, she had the nerve to take a sip of her tea. 'Never again speak of other men. Now,' Alim said by way of parting, 'come to bed.'

She would not succumb.

Gabi stood, walked across the lounge and looked out of the window.

A bridal car was pulling up outside the church further down the street and she watched as a bride was helped out and her dress arranged.

The little flower girl stood patiently as Gabi's heart impatiently beat for the day that it might be her.

Never the bride.

She had never been able to envisage herself as one.

And now she knew why.

A mistress was all she would ever be.

No!

Gabi was torn for as she watched the bride walk into the church she told herself that a mistress was surely better than being a virtual spinster, holding onto just two perfect nights for the rest of her life.

That was all her love life would be.

For, despite brave words she might say to Alim, in truth, there would never be another man—Gabi had already found the love of her life.

Yet agreeing to be his mistress went against everything she believed in, and if even the thought of it was eating her up, living it would be unbearable.

Neither was she cut out to keep secrets, for she would want to sing their love to the world, and she was hardly of a size that faded neatly into the background.

No, Gabi would not be his mistress, but that did not stop the door to his bedroom calling her.

Set your limits.

Alim's words now replayed to her.

Do only what you are prepared to do. What works for you...

And Gabi knew what did.

Alim.

CHAPTER SIXTEEN

GABI WALKED OVER to a dresser and took some paper and wrote down three little words.

No, thank you.

She placed them by the stone that Alim had left out for her.

Gabi would not be kept.

She would not be another Fleur, paid for in diamonds, rich in everything save respect.

Then she undressed and, naked, walked to the closed doors of the bedroom.

She would not cry and she would not be a martyr as she took those final steps, for Gabi wanted this.

Gabi stepped into darkness. The air was fragrant and sweet but there was the now familiar musky note of Alim and the pull of arousal as she came to the side of the bed.

'What kept you?' Alim asked.

'My thoughts.'

'And they are?'

'That I'll never be your mistress.'

'Then why *are* you here?' Alim asked as his hands roamed her naked body.

'I shall be your lover,' Gabi told him, and she knelt on

the bed and kissed his salty chest. 'I will be your lover in the desert at times and at others I will be your lover in Rome.'

And when once she had been demure, she was not so much now, for she wanted to intimately taste every inch of him. Gabi kissed down his stomach and between hot kisses she told him how it would be.

'I don't want your diamonds, I owe you nothing.'

And in the dark she could not see his smile, for he loved it that she stood up to him.

'But I do want the contract for your wedding,' Gabi said, and she blew onto his wet skin as his fingers dug into her thigh. 'I'm going to stand there and you can damn well watch what you're saying goodbye to, because your mistress I shall never be.'

His scent was her addiction and her undoing; she could feel him against her cheek and so she took him in her hand and tasted him.

She took him deep; his hands went into her hair and his hips rose at the bliss of unskilled but willing lips and to the heat of her tongue.

And then he pulled her up before he came, yet still she told him how it would be.

'The day your bride is chosen I'll cease to be your lover.'

Gabi had not finished school, neither was she versed in the rules, yet she, Alim knew, was as clever and as powerful as he.

He pulled her up to his kiss and as their tongues touched he lowered Gabi onto him.

The relief of him inside her was unrivalled.

A future she could now see.

He held her hips and they found their rhythm. She

danced as if free, for that was how she felt when they were together.

She wanted the light on, she ached to see him, but as she leant and reached for the bedside lamp his hand grabbed at hers. Gabi lost her stride and toppled forward. There was a tussle and he flipped her and then entered her again, and she lay in the dark, being taken.

Gabi did not bring him to his knees but to his forearms.

'Yes,' Alim said as he thrust into her. 'You *shall* be at my wedding.'

'Alim…' Gabi sobbed, for she had meant it as a threat yet it seemed to turn him on.

It was the way she said his name that called to him. Like a plea from the soul. And when Gabi said it again he came hard into her. She fought not to, Gabi really did—fought not to cave to the flood of warmth and want and the orbit of them.

She lost.

Near spent, Alim had the pleasure of the full clutch of her passion and his body pinned her as she writhed, and when she wanted to breathe it was the only need his body denied her, for he then took the air from the room.

'You shall be at my wedding…as my bride.'

She was always a little dizzy when Alim was close—for Gabi it was a constant state of affairs. Held in his arms, breathing his scent, and her body still coming down from the high he so readily gave, she told herself she had misheard him.

And then light invaded for Alim reached over and turned on the bedside lamp and his bedroom was not as she recalled it.

There were flowers.

Sweet peas.

Ten thousand of them, she was sure, and the flowers in the foyer had, in fact, been for her.

But that was not all.

A stunning portrait had been blown up and set on an easel beside the bed.

It was the image of them.

Alim had moved more than mountains, he had turned back the hands of time. For days he had pored over the rules he had studied for years, searching, discounting and trying to find a way to make it work for them.

'You and Lucia are the most wonderful things that have ever happened to me,' Alim told her.

'According to your land, we *never* happened.'

'No.' Alim shook his head. 'When the Sultan offers a commitment it is to be taken seriously…' He took her in his arms. 'I committed to you that night.'

'You offered a year.'

'I vowed fidelity.'

He had.

'And unless it has been broken, you are still mine.'

'Alim?'

'There has been no one else,' Alim said. 'There could be no one else. Had you not spoken of other men you would have walked into this room and I would have got down on my knees and asked you to be my wife.'

Gabi laughed.

Still dizzy, still confused, she laughed, because even if he had planned the perfect proposal she would not change how it had transpired.

There was nothing about them she would change.

Even now, could she go back to their first night and be on the Pill, she would not. There was nothing she would change save for the cruel rules of his land, and now her laughter died.

'Your father will never agree.'

'Reluctantly, very reluctantly, he already has.' Now it was Alim who smiled. 'I am more stubborn than he. I went through the rules and the diktat and then I showed him this image. I told my father that there had been no one else and that that would remain the case, for the rest of my life if need be.'

'I don't understand.'

'My father caved in to the Sultan of Sultans' demands when Fleur would not come to the desert. I told him that I would not.'

And still she did not understand.

'We think the same, Gabi. For the decision you reached was mine too. We would have more than made it as lovers. I would have come to Italy regularly, and brought you on occasion to the desert, and you would have remained the one and only woman in my life.'

And she stared back at him as he told her just how deep his love was.

'I told my father that if he did not choose you as my bride, then I would never marry. Kaleb is next in line, Yasmin after that, and they will one day have children. The country is not short of heirs…'

'You told him that you'd give up your throne?'

'No.' Alim shook his head. 'I would still rule, but they would be my heirs.'

He had thought every detail through and he had presented it to his father, just as he would in any business meeting.

Only this one involved his heart.

'He knows I am strong, and he knows his own regrets. He agreed.'

'And Lucia…' Gabi asked. 'What will your people think?'

'My father has been unwell, that is enough reason to have refrained from announcements and celebrations. This photo, of the night I made a commitment to you, is enough testimony of our love.'

It *was* love.

She had never truly thought she would know it.

Not fully.

An unrequited version perhaps, if she remained with Alim. Or a diluted version if she attempted to move on and meet someone else.

Yet the man she loved had changed his world for a chance for them. And he told her now why he had.

'Gabi, I never considered love important. I grew up in a loveless, albeit privileged home. I saw first-hand the pain love caused for my father and Fleur…'

He thought back to when love had first started to arrive in his heart.

'When I came to buy the Grande Lucia you were setting up for a wedding. It was the first time I saw you.'

Gabi thought back.

'No, the first time we saw each other was the day after a wedding. You had come back for a second viewing of the hotel…'

'No.'

And Gabi realised then that he had memories of her that she did not know, that the days she had felt so invisible had been days when she had, in fact, been noticed.

'Marry me?' he said, and she nodded.

'Oh, yes.'

'There is only one problem.'

And here it came, Gabi thought, the downside, for she could not remain on this cloud for ever. She braced herself for impact.

'It has to be now.'

Gabi frowned. 'Now?'

'We're already late for our own wedding.'

'You mean *now*!'

'The Sultan of Sultans has chosen. I was lucky to buy us even a few days. I have my family gathered, and I went and spoke with your mother; she has given her blessing if you say yes.'

'When did you speak with my mother?'

'That is why I was late to meet Lucia.'

Gabi was lying in bed on her wedding day when surely there was so much to be done.

'Alim…' She sat up. 'I haven't…'

There was panic, because she was a wedding planner after all and this wedding was her very own.

'There is nothing for you to do. I know you would have dreamed of this day and that it might not be quite what you had planned…'

'No.' Gabi shook her head. 'I never thought of my own.'

'There will be a bigger celebration in Zethlehan but for today everything is under control.'

Except the bride!

For instead of answering her million questions Alim got dressed and then, having read her note with a smile, he left.

Gabi sat in the unmade bed, unsure what she was supposed to do, so she called her mum.

'I am so happy for you,' Carmel said. 'It meant everything that he came and spoke with me…'

'You'll be there?'

'Of course,' her mother said. 'I'm at the hotel now with Lucia and we're both being very spoiled. I shall see you at the wedding.'

It seemed everyone knew what was happening except

Gabi and just when she was starting to think she must have misunderstood the bedside phone rang.

'Gabi…'

Gabi rolled her eyes at the familiar voice.

'I can't work today,' Gabi started, but then realised that Bernadetta wasn't calling her to ask her to work.

'If you'd like to put on a robe, the bridal suite is ready for you.'

'For me?'

'Gabi, I haven't been avoiding your calls. Well perhaps a bit, but I've been very busy arranging a royal wedding in Rome, with only five days' notice. Thank goodness I'm good at my job!'

Gabi had always resented that Alim seemed one step ahead of her.

She didn't today.

Yes, Bernadetta was a right royal pain, but she was the best in the business.

Gabi almost felt sorry for Bernadetta for the panic she must have had to arrange such a rapid wedding.

Almost!

CHAPTER SEVENTEEN

GABI KNOCKED ON the door of the Grande Lucia's bridal suite.

She knew it very well, but usually she was carrying flowers or had her arms piled high with a wedding dress.

Today she had nothing, not even her purse, for in the confusion she had left it all behind.

The door to the suite opened and there stood Bernadetta. Gabi's nerves didn't quite disappear but they faded as, even from a distance, Alim made her smile.

Gone was the black suit.

Bernadetta looked amazing in a willow-green and pale pink check suit—and, yes, Alim really had thought of it all.

'You have nothing to worry about,' Bernadetta said as Gabi stepped in. 'I've been working closely with Alim and Violetta and everything is under control. But first I have something for you from me.'

Bernadetta handed her a box, and when Gabi opened it she saw that they were business cards. They were the palest blush-pink with a trail of willow-green ivy and the lettering was in gold.

Matrimoni Internazionali di Gabriella.

'No.' Gabi went to put the card back in its box; this wasn't how she wanted it to be. 'I don't want Alim buying me a career.'

'Gabi,' Bernadetta said, 'I had a long think after our discussion. Of course I was furious at the suggestion, but when I had calmed down I thought about it properly. It is too much for one person. I was going to offer you a junior partnership. I don't want to lose you and when Alim called and asked if I would arrange the wedding, well, I knew I was about to so I had to think on my feet. I came up with this. Gabi, you're going to be overseas a lot and I hope back here often…'

Gabi nodded.

'We can work all the details out, but together we can make a success of it.'

And her heart started to soar because Bernadetta was right—married to a sultan, a career would be hard without back-up, but in a partnership, well, perhaps it could work for them both.

And there was something else too.

'It's been a tough few years in the industry,' Bernadetta said, 'but things have been starting to turn around and it's in no small part thanks to you.'

Oh, it wasn't just the suit, but Bernadetta looked lighter, younger and more relaxed. Maybe this partnership would take some of the pressure from her too.

But as exciting as the future was, there was really only one partnership on Gabi's mind today.

The door opened to hair and make-up artists and while they set up Gabi went and had a bath.

It was so wonderful to relax, knowing that Lucia was being taken care of and that soon she and Alim would be married. That on the day he met his daughter for the first time, a family they became for real.

After the bath she unwrapped some packages to discover the underwear was a soft white gauze and just what Gabi would have chosen.

It was subtle but terribly sexy and she was glad to hide it under a robe when she stepped out.

Gabi's hair was curled and pinned up, leaving a few long coils to fall, and then the make-up artist got to work under instruction from Bernadetta as Gabi closed her eyes.

'Not too much!' Gabi warned, because she wasn't big on make-up and it felt as if it was being piled on.

'Perfetto,' Bernadetta said, and Gabi opened her eyes. But sheets had been put over the many mirrors. 'I want you to see the full effect all at once.'

'What if I don't like it?'

'Then we keep the groom waiting until you do.' Bernadetta shrugged. 'But I know you are going to love it.'

The door opened again and this time it was Rosa, and Gabi found that she was nervous as the dress was unveiled.

There was no need to be.

Rosa had worked magic indeed.

It was a pale ivory and reminded her of the robe she had worn in the desert.

As Bernadetta did up the row of tiny buttons at the back, Gabi found she was shaking. It was starting to sink in that she would soon be Alim's wife.

The shoes chosen for her had just a little heel and then the door opened and it was Angela with the flowers.

Gabi had to fight not to cry when she saw them.

A bunch of sweet peas and all paper white.

'I wanted to add some gardenias but Alim was adamant. Do you know,' Angela said as she looked at the exquisite trail of blooms, 'I think this is the best I have ever made.'

Each bloom was so delicate and fragrant and perfect that there was nothing—not a single wisp of anything—that Gabi would add to them.

And then Bernadetta took the sheet from the full-length mirror and Gabi, who had never dared to even imagine herself as one, looked back at the bride.

'Oh, Gabi,' Bernadetta said.

And Gabi just stared. The dress hung beautifully and did nothing to play down her curves; her eyes were smoky and her lipstick pale and, no, she could not have chosen better.

'Are you ready?' Bernadetta asked.

'So ready—I would run if I could.'

'You would fall,' Bernadetta said. 'And I don't have a spare dress for you to change into.'

It was a smiling bride who turned heads as she walked through the foyer of the Grande Lucia and stood outside the double doors of the ballroom.

And then nerves caught up with her.

'Just walk straight ahead,' Bernadetta told her. 'Gabi, all you have to do is enjoy every moment.'

She stepped in and there in that ballroom was everyone she loved, and for a moment she looked and tried to take it all in.

Her mother looked gorgeous and was holding Lucia, who wore a little mink-coloured dress and showed one little dark curl.

And when she got over her joy, and when they had made love as man and wife, there would be questions—so many of them.

Fleur was there and she stood next to James and Mona

and, a couple of rows ahead, sat a very handsome, exotic-looking middle-aged man.

Oh, there were secrets in every family and mysteries too, but there was now no shame in the al-Lehans.

Alim did not want to know if this man was the reason his mother knew love.

Gabi, curious by nature, would be certain to find out!

Yes, Violetta had her work cut out with this family and, Gabi suspected, the adjoining rooms at the Grande Lucia would be creaking tonight.

Bastiano was there, and Sophie was too.

It dawned on Gabi then the reason she had been around so much these past days, she had been keeping an eye on the bride while so many plans were underway.

'You knew!' she mouthed to her dear friend as she walked past, and Sophie laughed.

The only person missing was the groom.

And then nerves caught up.

There was his errant sister and Alim's brother, Kaleb, and beside them was the queen, but most intimidating of all was the Sultan of Sultans, who, as Gabi nervously approached, stepped forward.

He spoke first in Arabic, which Gabi did not understand, but then he spoke again.

'The Sultan of Sultans has chosen.'

Gabi saw Alim then.

He wore a robe of silver, but it was the love for her in his eyes that brought tears to hers.

He took her hands and she felt the warmth of his fingers as they caressed hers; his voice was low and for Gabi's ears only.

'He chose wisely.'

Gabi always felt that she shone under Alim's gaze, and this moment was no exception.

They knelt on the gorgeous floor and were blessed, and then they rose as man and wife.

'Are you happy?' he asked.

'So happy,' Gabi said, and then she smiled. 'What if I'd said no?'

'Are you cross now at my assumption that you would agree to marry me?'

'No.'

For it told her of his certainty in them.

And as he moved in to kiss his bride Alim told her a truth.

'This is love,' he whispered, 'and it's ours for ever.'

* * * * *

SICILIAN'S BABY OF SHAME

For my wonderful editor Flo Nicoll.

Thank you for being you.

Carol xxx

PROLOGUE

BASTIANO CONTI HAD been born hungry.

And born a problem.

His mother had died giving birth to him and had never disclosed who his father was. All she had owned had been left to him—a ring.

It was Italian gold with a small emerald in its centre and some seed pearls dotted around it.

Bastiano's uncle, who had four children of his own, had first suggested that the nuns raise the orphaned baby who'd lain crying in the small maternity ward in the Valley of Casta. There was a convent that overlooked the Sicilian Strait and orphans had usually been sent there.

But the convent was on its last legs.

The nurses were busy but occasionally one would take pity and hold Bastiano a little longer than it took to feed him.

Occasionally.

'Familia,' the priest had said to his uncle. 'Everyone knows that the Contis look after their own.'

The Contis ruled the valley to the west and the Di Savos held the east.

Loyalty to their own was paramount, the priest told him.

And so, after a stern talk from the priest, Bastiano's

zio and his reluctant wife had taken the little bastard to their house but it had never, for Bastiano, been a home.

Always Bastiano had been considered an outsider. If something had gone wrong, then he'd been the first to be blamed and the last to be forgiven.

If there had been four brioches for lunch, they had not been split to make five.

Bastiano had done without.

Sitting in school next to Raul Di Savo, Bastiano had started to understand why.

'What would your parents save in a fire?' Sister Francesca had asked her class. 'Raul?'

Raul had shrugged.

'Your father,' she prompted, 'what would be the first thing that Gino reached for?'

'His wine.'

The class had laughed and Sister Francesca, growing more exasperated with each passing moment, had turned her attention from Raul.

'Bastiano,' she snapped. 'Who would your *zia* save?'

His serious grey eyes had lifted to hers and Bastiano had frowned even as he'd given his response. 'Her children.'

'Correct.'

She had turned back to the board and Bastiano had sat there, still frowning, for indeed it was the correct answer—his *zia* would save her children. But not him.

He would never be first.

However, aged seven, Bastiano was sent to collect the brioches and the baker's wife ruffled his hair and so unused to affection was he that his face lit up and she said that he had a cute smile.

'You do too,' Bastiano told her, and she laughed.

'Here.' She gave him a sweet cannoli just for brightening her morning and Bastiano and Raul sat on the hill and ate the gooey treat.

The boys should have been sworn enemies—for generations the Contis and the Di Savos had fought over the vines and properties in the valley—yet Bastiano and Raul became firm friends.

The small encounter at the baker's was enough for Bastiano to learn that he could get by better on charm.

Oh, a smile worked wonders, and later he learnt to flirt with his eyes and was rewarded with something far sweeter than cannoli.

Despite their families' protests, Bastiano and Raul remained friends. They would often sit high on the hill near the now vacant convent and drink cheap wine. As they looked out over the valley, Raul told him of the beatings his mother endured and admitted that he was reluctant to leave for university in Rome.

'Stay, then.'

It was that simple to Bastiano. If he'd had a mother, or someone who cared for him, he would not leave.

And he did not want Raul to go, though of course Bastiano did not admit that.

Raul left.

One morning, walking down the street, he saw Gino storm out of Raul's house, shouting and leaving the front door open.

Raul was gone and, given what his friend had told him, Bastiano thought he ought to check that his mother was okay.

'Signora Di Savo…' He knocked on the open door but she did not answer.

He could hear that she was crying.

His *zia* and *zio* called her unhinged but Maria Di Savo had always been kind to Bastiano.

Concerned, he walked inside and she was kneeling on the floor of the kitchen, crying.

'Hey.' He poured her a drink and then he got a cloth and ran it under the water and pressed it to the bruise on her eye.

'Do you want me to call someone?' he offered.

'No.'

He helped her to stand and she leant on him and cried and Bastiano did not know what to do.

'Why don't you leave him?' he asked.

'I've tried many times.'

Bastiano frowned because Raul had always said that he'd pleaded with her to leave yet she'd always refused.

'Could you go and stay with Raul in Rome?' Bastiano suggested.

'He doesn't want me there. He left me,' Maria sobbed. 'No one wants me.'

'That's not true.'

'You mean it?'

She looked up then and he went to correct her to say that what he had meant was that he was sure there were people who wanted her…

Not him.

She put a hand up to his face and held his cheek. 'You're so handsome.'

Maria ran a hand through his thick black hair and it did *not* feel like when the baker's wife had; this felt more than an affectionate ruffle and, confused, Bastiano removed her hand and stepped back. 'I have to go,' he told her.

'Not yet.'

She wore just a slip and her breast was a little exposed; he did not want Maria to be embarrassed when she realised that she was on display, so he turned to leave.

'Please don't go,' she called out to him.

'I have to go to work.'

He had left school and worked now in the bar that was a front for the seedier dealings of his *zio.*

'Please, Bastiano…' Maria begged. She reached for his arm and when he stopped she came around so that she stood in front of him. 'Oh,' she apologised as she looked down and saw that her breast was exposed to him, but Bastiano did not look. He was still pretending that he had not noticed.

And she would cover herself now, Bastiano thought, yet she did not. In fact, she took his hand and placed it on her plump, ripe skin.

He was good with the girls but in those cases he was the seducer. Maria was around forty, he guessed, and, for heaven's sake, she was the mother of his best friend.

'Signora Di Savo…' Her hand pressed his as he went to remove it.

'Maria,' she said, and her voice was low and husky. He could feel and hear her deep breathing and when she removed her hand, Bastiano's remained on her breast.

'You're hard,' Maria said, feeling him.

'Gino might—'

'He won't be back till dinner.'

Bastiano was usually the leader and instigator, but not on this hot morning. Maria was back on her knees but this time by her own doing. It was over within minutes.

As he left, he swore he would never return there.

But that very afternoon Bastiano made a trip to the pharmacy for protection, and an hour later they were in bed.

Hot, forbidden, intense—they met whenever they could, though it was never enough for Maria.

'We're getting out,' Bastiano told her. He had been paid and, if all else failed, he had his mother's ring. He could not stand the thought of her with Gino for even a moment longer.

'We can't,' she told him, even as she asked to see the ring and he watched as she slipped it on.

'If you love me,' Maria said, 'you would want me to have nice things.'

'Maria, give me back the ring.'

It was all he had of his mother but still Maria did not relent. Bastiano left.

He walked up the hill to the convent and sat looking out, trying to figure it all out. All his life he had wanted a taste of this elusive thing called love, only to find out he did not care for it. It was Bastiano who now wanted out.

And he wanted his mother's ring.

He stood, walking with purpose to the town below, where he saw it unfold.

A car driving at speed took a bend too fast. '*Stolto*,' he muttered, and called the driver a fool as he watched him take another bend…and then the car careered from the road.

Bastiano ran in the direction of the smoking wreck but as he approached he was held back and told that it was Gino's car that had been in the accident.

'Gino?' Bastiano checked.

'No!' a woman who worked in the bar shouted. 'I called Maria to say that Gino was on his way home and angry. He had found out about you! She took the car and—'

Maria's death and the aftermath had not painted Bastiano in a very flattering light.

Raul returned from Rome and on the eve of the funeral they stood on the hill where once they had sat as boys.

'You had your pick of the valley!' Raul could barely contain his fury.

'I went to check on her—'

But Raul did not want to hear that his mother had been the seducer. 'And you turned on that fake charm…' Raul had seen him in action after all. He knew how Bastiano could summon even the shyest woman with his eyes and melt restraint with a smile. 'I was a fool to trust you,' Raul said. 'You as good as killed her.'

Yes, he was the first to be blamed and the last to be forgiven.

'Stay away from the funeral,' Raul warned him.

But Bastiano could not.

And the next day things went from bad to worse. After a bloody fight at the graveside, it later transpired that half of Maria's money had been left to Bastiano.

Raul, once his friend, now accused Bastiano of engineering Maria's death and swore the rest of his days would be devoted to bringing him down.

'You're nothing, Conti,' Raul told him. 'You never have been and, even with my mother's money, you never will be.'

'Watch me,' Bastiano warned.

It is said that it takes a village to raise a child.

The Valley of Casta had never really been kind to Bastiano, but when the entire population considered you a cheat, a liar, a seducer, a bastard…that's what you become.

So, when a drunken Gino came to confront him, instead of taking it on the chin, Bastiano fought back, and when Gino called Maria a whore, Bastiano saw red and did not stay quiet. Instead, he gestured with his hand in the sign of horns and tossed Gino the biggest insult of all.

'Cornuto!'

Cuckold.

Bastiano, the villagers agreed, was the worst of the worst.

CHAPTER ONE

SOME NIGHTS WERE HELL.

'Bastiano!'

He heard the familiar, syrupy call of his name and knew that he must be dreaming, for Maria was long dead.

Unusually, he was alone in bed and as dawn sneaked over Rome, Bastiano fought to wake up.

'Bastiano!'

She called his name again.

When he reached his hand down and felt that he wasn't hard for her, it was a triumph, and Bastiano smiled a black smile as he silently told her she didn't do it for him any more.

Maria slapped his cheek.

She wore his mother's ring on her finger and he felt the cold metal as she delivered a stinging slap, one that had his hand move to his face for the wound was gaping. His cheek was sliced open and there was blood pouring between his fingers.

Bastiano fought with himself even in sleep. He knew that he was dreaming, for the savage fight with Raul had happened at the graveyard; the wound to his cheek had come *after* Maria had been lowered to the ground.

Everyone had said that it was Bastiano's fault she was dead.

And it was the reason that he was here, some fifteen years later—lying in one of the presidential suites at Rome's Grande Lucia hotel.

Raul Di Savo was considering its purchase, which meant that it had been placed on the top of Bastiano's must-have list.

Bastiano forced himself to wake up. He lay there in the darkness and glanced over at the hotel's bedside clock. Reaching over, he switched off the alarm. He had no need for it. He would not be going back to sleep.

Bastiano knew the reason that Maria was back in his dreams.

Well, she had never really left them, but that dream had been so vivid and he put it down to the fact that he and Raul were staying at the same hotel.

He heard the soft knock at the main door to his suite and then the quiet attempt to wheel in his breakfast trolley.

'Puzza!'

Bastiano smiled when he heard the small curse as the maid knocked into something and knew from that one word that the maid was Sicilian.

The door to the master bedroom had been left open but she quietly knocked again.

'Entra,' he said.

Bastiano was more than used to room service. Not only was he considering the purchase of this hotel but he was the owner of several premium establishments of his own. He closed his eyes, indicating, as she came in, that he wanted no conversation.

Sophie could see that he had made no move to sit up so she did not offer him a 'Good morning'.

The rules were very specific at the Grande Lucia and the staff were well trained.

Sophie loved her job, and though she did not usually do the breakfast deliveries she had been asked to do this one before her night shift ended. She had been called in to work late last night and so had missed the handover where the staff were told of any important guests, their idiosyncrasies and specific requests. Sophie, of course, knew that any guest staying in one of the presidential suites was an important one, and she had checked his name on his breakfast order.

Signor Bastiano Conti.

Being as quiet as she could, Sophie opened some heavy drapes and the shutters behind them so that the guest, when he sat up, would be greeted by the stunning view of Rome in all her morning glory.

And *what* a glorious day it was turning out to be!

It was as if the theatre curtains were opening on a beautifully set stage, Sophie thought.

There were a few clouds high in the sky that would soon burn off, for it was going to be a warm summer's day. The Colosseum was picture-postcard perfect and its ancient beauty gave her goosebumps.

Oh, it was a good day indeed for had she not made difficult choices and declined her family's desire for her to marry Luigi, today would have been the eve of her first wedding anniversary.

For a moment, Sophie forgot where she was and stood there simply taking in the view as she reflected on the past year. Yes, hard choices had been made but she was completely sure that they had been the right ones.

Oh, she was curious about men, of course she was, and though her mother would never understand it, she could readily separate that thought from marriage.

When she had tried to picture her wedding night and sleeping with Luigi, Sophie's blood had run cold. She had been out with a couple of younger men during her time in Rome but Luigi's wet, whiskery kisses had left their legacy and, though curious, Sophie had found herself ducking her head from any male advances.

Her parents imagined she was living a sinful life here in Rome.

Sadly, that couldn't be further from the truth!

Sophie was naïve, she knew that, but she was strong too.

Strong enough to say no to a man and a marriage she hadn't wanted.

'Buongiorno.'

A deep voice snapped her to attention and Sophie turned around as she realised that she had just been caught daydreaming, and by an important guest in his own suite!

She went to apologise but her flustered breath was literally taken away for there, lying in bed and idly watching her, was possibly a sight more arresting than the one she had just been feasting on. He was tall—she could see his length in the huge bed. His hands were behind his head and the sheet low on his stomach revealed his naked torso.

He really was magnificent, with olive skin and jet-black hair. The only blot on perfection was a jagged scar on his cheek, yet it only seemed to make him more beautiful. Most of all, it was his eyes that drew Sophie's. They were grey and piercing and as she met his gaze she found that her breath hitched in her chest and that she could not tear her gaze away. That was rare in itself for Sophie. In her job, she was very used to rich and beautiful men but with this one, with *this* one, she found that her eyes did not divert and, instead of an apology, her cheeks went a little bit pink.

'I was just preparing the view for you, Signor Conti,' Sophie said, and he gave a small smile in return as she made a little joke—as if she had been arranging the scenery outside specifically for him.

'Thank you.' He glanced towards the window and the million-euro view. 'You did a good job.'

And then he looked back at her.

When he had thought her to be taking her time Bastiano had opened his eyes to tell her to hurry up and leave, but there was something about her that halted his usual impatience.

And she mesmerised him now.

The eyes that met his were a very dark brown. He already knew from watching that she was as slender as a blade and wearing a pale green dress and flat shoes, both of which looked to be a little too big for her. Now he examined her face and saw that her thick black hair was worn up in a messy bun with a few long strands escaping.

She looked tired, Bastiano thought, and he guessed that her shift was just finishing rather than starting.

She had made him smile, just a little, but that was a surprise in itself given the dream he had so far failed to banish from his mind. The bedroom was rather messy and he was quite sure that the very sumptuous lounge was not much better; no doubt it was a stray bottle of champagne in the floor that had caused her small expletive on the way in.

'Would you like me to serve your breakfast?' she offered, still a little flustered and not just from being caught staring. Sophie made her way over to the breakfast trolley and lifted one of the silver domes.

'No, thank you,' Bastiano said. 'Actually, if you could bring me coffee that would be fine.'

'Would you like some water, or juice, too?' she offered, and then he saw the slight twitch to her lips and a certain knowing tone in her voice as she spoke on. 'Or perhaps you would like both?'

Again he smiled as she revealed her suspicions of his crashing hangover.

'Please.'

She brought over two glasses and Bastiano drank the cold water as she went back to the trolley and poured his coffee from the pot.

Usually Bastiano poured his own coffee for he did not like attempts at idle conversation, yet it was he who was pursuing it now.

'Sicilian?' he asked as she carried the cup to his bedside. She nodded and then, as she placed it on the table, she gave a little grimace, realising that he must have heard her swear.

'Me too,' he said calmly, and something in the delivery of his words told her that he got it, for the air was a touch bluer back home.

'What is that?' he asked, gesturing to the trolley, for despite the fact she had replaced the dome and covered the food there was now a rich, spicy scent mingling into the air.

'Shakshuka,' Sophie said. 'Middle Eastern baked eggs.'

The gorgeous guest screwed up his nose and Sophie was worried that the kitchen had got the orders mixed up so she quickly checked the paperwork on the trolley but, no, it was correct. 'You ordered it.'

'What was I thinking?' he drawled.

'I've heard that they're amazing,' Sophie said, and if the smell was anything to go by then her recommendation was bang on. 'Would you like me to take them back down and have something else sent to you?'

'It's fine.' He gave a shake of his head. 'Just leave it.'

'I hope you enjoy your day,' Sophie offered, and he gave a slight mirthless laugh and then nodded.

'You too.'

She went to close the bedroom door but he told her to leave it open.

As she left, Sophie picked up the bottle she had tripped over on her way in and put it on a tray. The room was a disaster and she would love, right this minute, to set about straightening things up, but it was not her job today and it was far too early to service a suite.

Anyway, as of now, she was off duty and so she headed to clock off and collect her things.

'What are you doing, delivering breakfasts?' Inga asked as Sophie retrieved her jacket from her locker. Just to be polite, Sophie had made a casual comment as to why she was a few minutes late coming off duty but Inga had, in her usual critical way, pounced. 'That is for the more senior chambermaids.'

'I just do as I'm told,' Sophie said, and poked her tongue out at Inga's departing back.

They did not get on.

Inga liked to deliver the breakfasts, especially to the very rich men, and though turning tricks was strictly forbidden, Sophie was quite certain that was the reason it was a designer bag that Inga had just put into her locker.

It wasn't for Sophie to judge and she tried not to.

Her dislike for Inga was simply due to the frequent disparaging comments and the endless digs that were sent her way. Sophie did her best to shrug them off but it was difficult at times. She didn't even know what she had done to incur Inga's wrath.

Still, she chose not to dwell on it. Sophie was more than ready for home—she was tired, hungry and ached for bed. Instead of heading out of the side entrance, Sophie, as she often did, decided to exit through the kitchen.

The reason was twofold.

It took her out to the alley, which was closer to the small flat she shared with two others.

And her little diversion would hopefully mean a free breakfast!

There were several chefs that worked in the kitchens, of course, but her favourite was Sicilian and he was just taking a batch of brioches out from the oven as she made her way over. Not the French brioche or even the sweet pastry those here in the north referred to; instead, these were the most delicious plain-baked buns of home. And he had made *millefoglie* too—also a bun, but with raisins mixed in and sugar on the top. Sophie guessed it was exactly the breakfast this morning's guest might wish that he had chosen.

Apart from Inga, Sophie was very well liked and popular at the Grande Lucia. She was a very good worker and always went the extra mile for guests. Signor Conti's mirthless laugh had stayed with her and so, instead of sneaking a brioche for her walk home, she spoke with the chef. He arranged a plate of freshly baked pastries and she put a small silver dome over it and then took her jacket off and, placing it over her arm, she headed back up to Signor Conti's suite.

She knocked and let herself in and then called out.

'Room service.'

After the maid had left, Bastiano had got up, taken one look at the eggs and replaced the dome.

His friend Alim, the current owner of the hotel, had always suggested he try them when they met for brunch and last night as he'd squinted at the selections it had seemed a good idea.

Not now.

There was no point him even being here.

Last night Alim had told him that his plans had suddenly changed and that he would not be able to show him through the hotel today as planned.

That wasn't all that irked Bastiano.

For once—in fact, for the first time in his life—a woman had turned him down.

In recent weeks, Bastiano had decided he would like a wife, and one with a castle in England and money problems had appeared to fit the bill.

It had seemed a decent solution at the time.

Lydia Hayward, with her breeding and porcelain looks would, he had decided, be the perfect trophy wife. It would be mutually beneficial, of course, and for his part he would help with her family's dire financial situation. He had flown her and her stepfather, Maurice, over to Rome so that he could kill two birds with one stone—view the hotel and put in an offer that would blow Raul out of the park. And maybe return home to Casta having secured a bride.

The more he had thought about it, the more he had decided that it might just be enough to rattle Raul—for Bastiano was more than financially secure, but settled… not so much.

But his plans hadn't exactly worked out that way.

Lydia had decided she would spend the evening catching up with friends and had left him hanging with the appalling Maurice.

Bastiano hadn't even attempted small talk with the man; instead, he had come back to his suite, and with his mood too dark to hit the clubs he had hit the bottle instead.

A foolish choice, in retrospect, for it had not been Lydia who had crept into his mind as he'd slept.

It had been Maria.

Fifteen years on and he could not fathom that he had ever cared for another person, for he cared for no one now.

No one.

Bastiano had a reputation for cold-hearted ruthlessness that ran from the boardroom to the bedroom.

Beating Raul Di Savo was the only thing that interested him.

He heard a knock at his door and a voice that was too cheerful for his black mood announce that room service was here.

Again!

Bastiano put a towel around his hips and walked out, more than ready to tell her to get the hell out and that, had he wanted a second delivery, he would have picked up the phone himself.

Yet she smiled so nicely as she took the lid from the plate she carried and held it out.

'Better?' she asked, as his eyes went to the plate.

Now, *that* was breakfast.

And his eyes went back to hers. No, they were not simply dark brown, they were the amber of a fox, and her smile was so bright that Bastiano could not bring himself to chide her. 'Much,' he rather reluctantly replied.

'I thought so too. Would you like another coffee?'

'That would be good.'

He got back into bed with the towel still round his hips and breakfast was served for the second time.

'You didn't have to do that,' Bastiano commented as, once in bed, she handed him the plate.

He guessed she must know that he was the potential new owner, for all the staff were walking on eggshells around him.

'I know.' She smiled 'But I also know that we have the best Sicilian chef here at the Grande Lucia. I was going to sneak a brioche for the walk home and it made me think of you.'

Perhaps she did not know that he might soon be the new owner? Bastiano could not care less about her sneaking a pastry. His staff all got meals on their shifts anyway, he made sure of that, but many owners were strict about such things.

'What's your name?'

'Sophie.' She saw him glance at the jacket over her arm. 'Really, it's not a problem—I am at the end of my shift.'

'Then would you like to stay and have some Middle Eastern eggs?' he offered, teasing her by replaying her words. 'I have been told that they're amazing.'

'No, thank you.' Sophie let out a small laugh as she shook her head. She wasn't unused to suggestions from businessmen and had declined her share over the last year. Sophie was no Inga!

'Enjoy.'

'I am.' He had torn open the brioche and as she left, the scent that reached him was the one of home and he spoke, really without thinking. 'I used to collect these from the bakery.'

'Ha!' Sophie said, turning around. 'Until I came to Rome I used to work at a bakery.'

'For how long?'

'Seven years,' Sophie said. 'Since I left school.'

And it was very easy—too easy—to speak of home. She missed it.

Oh, Sophie loved the life she had made here in Rome, but there was an ache for home at times, so for a moment they chatted, really just about the food and the stunning

Strait of Sicily. He guessed that she was also from the west. He was about to ask her exactly where but then Sophie yawned.

'Excuse me,' Sophie said. 'I really do have to go, all this talk of…' And she stopped because he had invited her to eat already and it might seem that she was angling for him to ask her again if she said just how hungry she felt.

Maybe she *was* angling?

Later she would look back and try to remember exactly how she had felt at that moment.

Happy and relaxed. It felt nice to be in his company.

'Have breakfast,' Bastiano said.

There was no motive.

That in itself was beyond rare for Bastiano, for he lived by motive, he did nothing without motive, yet all he saw this morning was that she was tired and probably hungry after a long shift.

And she heard, absolutely, the kindness in his offer and so, with just the briefest hesitation, she nodded.

'Thank you.'

Sophie could not know that kindness in Bastiano generally did not exist.

CHAPTER TWO

IT WAS AS natural as that.

The conversation between them came readily and it was simply pleasant to be with him. Sophie put her jacket on a chair and poured herself some chilled water and placed it on a tray. To that she added the plate of *shakshuka* and then looked around, wondering where she should take it to eat. First she glanced over at the chair where she had placed her jacket but it was rather full as his was there too. It was inside out so she could see the deep aubergine lining as well as a crumpled white shirt on the floor beside it. She looked at Bastiano, who was moving more to the centre of the bed, as if to make room for her to sit there, and so, instead of the chair, she made her way over to the bed.

Yes, it was as natural as that to walk over and sit on the edge of the huge bed, not too close, but alongside his thighs. She placed the tray on her lap.

The cloche had kept warm the eggs that were nestled in a rich-looking sauce, and she took her first tentative taste. It was a little spicier than expected and Sophie missed his smile as she reached for her water.

'Nice?' Bastiano asked.

She turned and looked at him and her eyes moved briefly to the scar on his cheek—Sophie would have loved to know its source—but then she looked back to his eyes. 'You know when you have wanted to try something for a very long time and then finally you do...'

Her words were not meant as provocative and they were not taken as such, for he was waiting for her to screw up her nose and to say that it was not as nice as she had thought it would be, but then she smiled. 'It is better than I expected.'

It was then that her words were provocative, though only to Sophie—for the pleasure of his company had her thoughts taking her mind to places they had never been.

He was stunningly attractive, yes, and she was no fool as to her situation, yet as Sophie looked at him her throat seemed to close in on itself and she could feel the pulse beat in her neck.

She was innocent from the lips down, and those lips had determinedly stayed as closed as they could when she had kissed her fiancé.

She had never shared a meal in a man's bedroom, or sat on a bed with a man and chatted so easily.

And neither had she ever stared so readily into another's eyes.

It truly was better than expected.

Was it the hot Baharat mix in the *shakshuka* that made her cheeks suddenly redden, or was it the first stirrings of desire?

Sophie did her best not to dwell on that thought. She tore her gaze from his and spoke on quickly. 'Apparently Sultan Alim has put a lot of new things on the menu since he took over the hotel.'

'Sultan?' Bastiano asked. He and Alim were friends. The Grande Lucia was Bastiano's favoured hotel when in Rome, and he and Alim often painted the town a rich shade of red but, despite lavish spending and wild ways, as far as Bastiano knew, Alim had always kept his royal status under wraps as best he could.

'We only found out that he was royal a few months ago,' Sophie revealed. 'His family came to stay and so of course the desk staff soon worked it out.' She thought for a moment. 'He's a good boss.'

'In what way?' Bastiano asked. He liked to hear the things that were important to staff, and knew that that sort of information could not readily be gleaned from a questionnaire or an appraisal. He didn't want to admit it, but he also just liked hearing her thoughts.

'He knows all of his staff by name,' Sophie said. 'And he is fair and kind. There was a Christmas meal and gift for all the staff who were working over the festive season.' She was silent for a moment as she thought back to that lonely day—coming to work had been the brightest part.

'How long have you worked here?' Bastiano asked.

'For nearly ten months. I've been in Rome for just over a year.' Sophie thought back to when she had first arrived and how nervous she had been, for she had never spent so much as a night away from home until then. 'It took a few weeks to find a job. I would have taken anything, but then I came for my interview and I wanted to work here so badly. I never thought I would get it as there was two months' training involved, but Benita took me on.'

'Benita?'

'The head of housekeeping,' Sophie explained. 'It is so much better than my old job.'

'I guess working at a bakery would have meant many early starts?'

'So early!' Sophie nodded and rolled her eyes. 'The shifts here are much better and the staff are really friendly. Well,' she added, thinking of Inga, 'most of them are.'

'Most?'

'There is always the odd person that you don't get on with in any workplace.' Sophie shrugged. 'I enjoy working here; I can't believe my luck really. It is, for me, the perfect job.'

'Why?'

'I like order,' Sophie said. 'I like things to be neat and tidy. When I see a suite such as yours, I itch to have it back as it should be.'

'Really?'

'Yes, really.' She nodded her head in the direction of the chair. 'I would have that jacket hanging up and that shirt put away.' Then she looked back at him. 'I would have that bed made, even with you in it…' And she hesitated. It was something that she often said as a joke to guests, usually the ones on the twelfth floor when she shooed them out to service their room.

It was not something that would ever be said to a guest such as Bastiano; he would never be shooed out, even jokingly.

It was not just that thought that had her pause, it was more a sudden awareness of their situation that silenced her.

Yet she had let the words out, and they were how she felt.

Not so much a neat bed, of course, more the thoughts that were there—an emerging awareness that made the room feel a little warmer.

Bastiano said nothing, just held her unblinking gaze until she spoke on.

'It really is the perfect job. Sometimes people ask me what I want to be, or they ask if I am working while studying, but I want only this—I'm happy now.'

'That's a very good place to be,' Bastiano said, though he couldn't fathom it for himself. The more he had the more he wanted, the more he achieved the further the goal seemed to stretch. 'Do you miss your family and friends?'

'I've made some friends…' She thought of her flat-mates and though they were not particularly close she got on well with them. And Sophie thought of Gabi, a wedding planner, who she had met on her first weekend here and had got on with straight away.

Usually Bastiano would leave it there. In fact, usually it would never have reached this point, for sitting in bed and chatting with a woman was not something Bastiano did regularly.

Regularly? Ha! Ever.

Yet he found he wanted to know her better.

'Do you miss home?' Bastiano asked, carefully re-wording his question.

'Sometimes,' she admitted. 'But if I was still there…' Sophie stopped what she was about to say and put down her cutlery, even though her meal was not finished. The conversation was edging towards topics that she usually kept closed.

Her newly made friends knew little about her. To them she was Sophie, twenty-four years old and happily single.

They had no idea how hard she had fought and how much she had given up to achieve such a small victory.

'*If* you were there?' Bastiano pushed, and now he *was* fishing—he really did want to know more about her.

She was about to stand, to end the conversation and get on with her day. Return to the real world.

Surprisingly, she found she liked this one.

Sophie liked the peace in his bedroom and the ease with which she spoke with this man.

She thought of his kind smile when she had realised he'd heard her swear. It had been a smile that had spoken of mutual understanding and a familiarity with the ways back home.

Something told her that he would…understand.

And though she had in the main been happy, it had also been a lonely twelve months.

'I was engaged to be married,' Sophie admitted. 'Had I stayed, tomorrow would have been my first wedding anniversary.'

'Had you stayed?' Bastiano verified. 'So it was you who ended it?'

'In a very mature and thoughtful way.' Sophie nodded and then she gave a small laugh that told him she was joking about handling things in an adult fashion. 'I ran away, if it is possible to run away from home when you are twenty-three. A month before the wedding I took a train to Rome and when I got here I called my parents and told them that I would not be marrying Luigi.'

He laughed at her explanation, although not unkindly—it was a deep, low laugh that was almost enough reward in itself for that awful phone call she had made to her parents.

Something told Sophie that he did not laugh easily, that what was happening this morning between them was both delicious and rare.

And then that low laugh faded, like a roll of soft thunder moving through her.

Lightning had already struck, Sophie realised.

She was here alone in his room and it was exactly where she wanted to be.

'Have you been back home since?' he asked, seemingly unaware of the dance in her mind. Sophie was terribly grateful for the resumption of conversation, and answered hurriedly for her thoughts were all over the place.

'No, it was a big disgrace. I expected them to be cross but when it came to my birthday and my mother would not even come to the phone I realised just how bad things were.'

'When was your birthday?' he asked.

'A few months after I ran away.' She told him the date. 'It was pretty miserable.'

Birthdays had always been about family and standing around a cake while having a hundred photos taken.

Not this time.

It had been the same at Christmas—and the reason she had been so grateful that Alim ensured his staff celebrated also. Her flatmates had all gone home to be with their families and so the meal and gift from work had been the only Christmas that Sophie had had.

'They must miss you,' Bastiano said, but Sophie shook her head.

'I'm not sure that they do. I come from a big family; they wanted me married so that there would be one less. You know how things are back home.'

He nodded. Bastiano did know how things were for many but then he looked at Sophie and was still sure of one thing—they *must* miss her, because from the moment she had opened the drapes it had been as if an extra ray of sunshine had been let in. 'Will you go back?'

'I'm their only daughter…' She shrugged but it belied the pain behind the inevitable decision. 'If I return then I am to abide by their rules. I don't know what will happen. For now, though, I live my dream.'

Even if it was lonely at times.

'What about you?' she asked.

'I don't have any family.'

'None?'

He shook his head and he saw that she waited for him

to elaborate. 'I was raised by my mother's brother and his wife.'

'What about your mother?'

'She died.'

'How old were you?'

He didn't answer.

'What about your father?'

'You know as much about him as I do—nothing.'

'Not quite.' Sophie smiled. 'I know that he was good looking.'

Yes, she was like sunlight because until now, when he had revealed that his father was unknown, it had either terminated the conversation or resulted in averted eyes or a derisive comment. Not with Sophie, for she turned the awkwardness around as she smiled—and possibly flirted—and the conversation was far from closed.

'What happened with your *zia* and *zio*?' she asked.

'I see them on occasion but we don't really speak,' Bastiano said, peeling off some brioche and handing it to her to mop up the last of the spicy sauce. 'They threw me out when I was seventeen.' He thought of the row they had had after the affair had been exposed and it had come to light that he had slept with the enemy—a Di Savo. 'Deservedly so.'

'So what are you doing here in Rome?' Sophie asked. 'Business?'

'In part,' Bastiano said, but knew that he was being evasive. Sophie obviously had no clue that he was considering purchasing the hotel. He didn't want to enlighten her for he knew that it would put a wedge between them. So to avoid speaking of work he told her something rather personal. 'I got dumped last night.'

'Oh!' She smiled at his revelation. 'I cannot imagine anyone dumping you.'

'Neither could my ego,' Bastiano admitted, and then he told her a bit more. 'She's English and lives in a castle.'

'Nice,' Sophie said, and he shrugged.

'It would have been a lot of work.'

Sophie frowned, not sure what he meant by that.

'What was your fiancé like?' he asked, curious about the man she had left behind.

'He was a lot older than me, more than forty years old,' Sophie said, and screwed up her face.

'Is that why you ended it?'

'Not really.' She shook her head. Looking back at that time, she remembered that moment when she had felt as if she could see her life spreading out before her, and not liking what she saw.

Sophie had never discussed it with anyone and perhaps she should not now but there was nothing regular about this morning. She had never met anyone who felt less like a stranger before. Bastiano knew more about her than her flatmates and she had lived with them for a year. More about her than Gabi, for she had been a touch elusive of late and their catch-ups had petered out. And he knew more about her than her parents, for they had never once asked for her take on things.

'Luigi came over to my parents' for dinner, as he often did…'

Bastiano said nothing, he even fought a slight eye rise, but at forty shouldn't the guy have at least been entertaining her?

Sophie glanced at him—the truth was a touch personal, but his eyes were patient and finally there was a person to whom she could speak her truth.

'That night I felt a little sick and didn't really eat much. When my mother took away the plates and my brothers and father left us alone he asked what was wrong with me. I told him that I had gone on the Pill.' She blushed just a little as she said it but far less than she had when she had told her fiancé. In fact, Bastiano seemed completely at ease with the sensitive topic.

Unlike Luigi.

It hadn't been up for discussion. Sophie had had to find everything out for herself. Even the village doctor hadn't been particularly friendly. In the end, it had been her friend at the bakery who had told her that she could skip her period entirely if she chose.

'What was his reaction?' Bastiano asked.

'He seemed cross. He said, "Why would you go on that?" Then he told me that he wanted children straight away and a lot of them!'

She pulled such a horrified face that Bastiano laughed.

And there was that thunder again, only this time she was counting the minutes, for the delicious storm drew closer with each revelation and with each passing word.

'I said that we needed my wage from the bakery and my mother came in from the kitchen. She didn't hear the part about the Pill, of course, just me saying I would put off having children so I could work, and she said she would look after them. It's not that I don't want children…'

He halted her when she tried to further explain for there was no need.

'Sophie,' he said in that rich voice of his, 'well done for running away.'

Bastiano was the first person she had really told about it and his reaction made her feel warm with pride for her choice, rather than sick with shame as her family had. 'Thank you.'

Oh, they were as natural as that, for Bastiano, who rarely bothered with conversation, was telling her some more about himself.

'I flew Lydia over from England with her stepfather, Maurice, under the guise of business. We were supposed to be meeting in the bar and then going out for dinner but when she turned up she said that she was going out with friends instead.'

Sophie gave him a quizzical look, because she really couldn't imagine declining dinner with him, but Bastiano read her frown as curiosity.

'I think she had worked out it wasn't just dinner.' He saw her cheeks darken in a blush and he further clarified that it had not been sex he was after. Bastiano had no trouble at all finding that. 'Like your fiancé, I had got it into my head that maybe it was time to settle down.'

Though his main reason had been simply to beat Raul to it.

Bastiano had everything money could buy and so too did Raul. The only thing neither had was a family.

He had decided that he would be first.

It had been as simple as that.

'Had you been going out with each other for long?' Sophie asked.

'We'd never been out.' Bastiano yawned and it really was a relief not to have to explain that romance and love were not always prerequisites for marriage back home. 'It just seemed like a good idea at the time, though not so much now.' He shrugged. 'Easy come, easy go. On reflection, I think I'm far more suited to the single life.'

'Well, with your looks and…' she looked around the lavish suite and stated the obvious '…your money, why not have fun?'

'Oh, I do,' Bastiano said.

Though lately he wouldn't describe it as fun.

He lay back on the pillow, but as their eyes met the silence was heavy. She wore no make-up, not a scrap, Bastiano noted as he took in her dark lashes. He felt her gaze move to his mouth and for once he was unsure where they were going, for usually when a woman was on his bed there was no question as to what was about to happen.

Come here, he wanted to say.

Sophie knew that.

Her perfect storm had now gathered and it would be so terribly easy to be swept into it, but she really was no Inga, even if he perhaps thought of her as such.

There was a reason the maids were told not to accept gifts.

Yet there was no air of expectancy from Bastiano.

Sophie felt no pressure as she put down her cutlery, took a drink of water and then stood.

She gave him a polite smile and effortlessly she was back to being a maid. She put her plate neatly back on the trolley.

'Thank you,' Sophie said. 'That was delicious.'

'You're more than welcome,' Bastiano said. 'So were the pastries.'

She came over to collect his plate.

It rested on his thigh and, though covered by the sheet, Sophie thought it was better that he be the one to retrieve it for she could see a black snake of hair on his stomach—as much as she tried not to look. There was desire pitted low in her stomach and an itch to pull the sheet down. Her hands shook a little and just like that she was no longer a maid. Their fingers met for a little too long and rather than pull back she lingered for his skin was warm and even that slight touch had her aching for more.

'I have to go,' she said as she fought for control.

'Of course.'

Yet still she stood there and instead of turning away

she put the plate down on the bedside table. She was not so much uncertain, more nervous of her own curiosity.

'Thank you,' she said again.

Bastiano could not read her, for he could feel her desire and yet sense her reticence so he moved things along a fraction. His index finger came up and he tapped it twice on the cheek nearest to her, the one that was not scarred.

A kiss to the cheek was still okay, Sophie thought, for she would kiss her friend Gabi on the cheek when they said farewell after sharing a meal. But even as she tried to convince herself, Sophie knew that this situation was nowhere near as innocent as that.

It wasn't even a conscious decision. It was more that she might as well have been standing on a conveyer belt, for it was as if she glided towards him.

She bent forward and moved her mouth to where his finger had tapped, the place where his rough morning shadow transitioned into smooth skin. The contrast sent shivers down her spine. The warmth of him on her lips was enticing and her tongue fought not to taste as her lips lingered.

Sophie sensed him holding his breath and hers now came a little too fast in response. She pulled her head back and moved to kiss the other cheek.

Bastiano jerked his head a little, for he did not like anyone touching his scar. He would by far prefer her mouth to meet his and usually he got what he wanted.

Not this time.

She misread the small signal and her mouth moved to his other cheek. Once on his scar, her lips lingered there, kissing him softly as if she didn't care about the damage beneath.

CHAPTER THREE

There was a gap between their chests, but so in tune was Sophie with his every move that she felt as if their bodies touched.

It was time to stay or go, Sophie knew. Even at this stage she could smooth it over and make her farewells.

Or she could meet those lips and discover bliss.

With Luigi, she had dreaded a kiss, let alone sex.

Not now.

When she had left home at twenty-three, Sophie had been considered a disgrace for her failure to commit.

She was twenty-four now and there was no disgrace to be had here.

It was better than her dreams. And so much better than the reality she had run from.

'Come here,' he moaned, and his hand came up and pulled her head down onto his.

Always she had avoided such contact, yet now she craved it.

His mouth was soft, and the dark shadow of his skin did not make her skin crawl with its tickle; instead, it was rough and delicious and matched the building desire in her.

Now, instead of resisting, she opened her lips, wanting and willing.

His tongue felt like a reward as it coiled around hers,

and then he slowly suckled the tip. They tasted each other, and they inflamed each other and not just with their mouths. He was stroking her breast through the fabric of her dress. His thumb was teasing her nipple and Sophie ached for bed.

His bed.

She pulled back, and knew that even now she could walk out having shared no more than a kiss.

'You taste spicy,' Bastiano said.

'And you taste sweet.'

'But I'm not,' he warned her.

'I'm working,' she told him, for she would get into the most terrible trouble if anyone found out.

'You finished an hour ago,' he reminded her, and then he stretched out an arm and she heard the click of a button that would turn on the Do Not Disturb sign outside.

'I'm in my uniform…'

'Good,' he said.

He thought her experienced, Sophie suspected.

Perhaps now would be the time to tell him she was not. That this morning was, in fact, a most irregular occurrence for her.

But Sophie knew that would change things. And there was nothing about this man and this morning she would change, even if she could.

Sophie wondered if she was on that conveyer belt again, for she moved so easily to be closer to him and when he guided her so that she sat on his stomach, she went readily.

Bastiano looked up as his fingers undid the buttons to her uniform and revealed a threadbare bra so sheer that her nipples could almost part the fabric and he could see the dark of her areolae. His hands cupped her breasts and he wanted her to shrug off the dress, to discard the bra and to lower her head, yet she closed her eyes in bliss as he toyed with her breasts.

'Take down your hair,' he told her, for he wanted the curtain between them when she took him in her mouth; he guided her back so that she sat on his thighs and the sheet moved with her.

She saw him erect, and since it was the first time she had seen, let alone touched, such a thing she held him in her hands.

'Sophie,' he said, for he did not want hands and tentative fingers even as he grew to them.

He was mesmerised, though, watching as she stroked.

Simply touching him was compelling. The feel of soft skin was a contrast to the strength in her palm and there was a coil of want that seemed to tighten within him as she gripped him more firmly.

'Take down your hair,' he said again, yet Sophie did not care for his orders, for the pleasure that grew was not just his. Her knickers were damp and she ached to feel him there. She wanted to stand and remove them, yet her legs felt clamped to his thighs.

She ran a finger over the tip and teased out a silver drop; the moan he gave had her rise to her knees.

He lifted the skirt of her dress, taking his own thick length and running it over her covered mound.

Sophie knelt up with her hands on his chest, biting on her lip at the exquisite pleasure he delivered. Oh, it was wrong! If she examined it, then she knew that was the only conclusion that could be drawn.

Yet there was so much that she had not even known was missing and she felt like a colourblind person able to see a rainbow for the first time.

She had for a long time dreaded sex and that dread had now completely gone. Sophie was turned on like she had never been in her life. Even in her imaginings there had never been desire such as this.

Despite the barrier of fabric he pushed in just a little way, enough to incite and make her ache for more.

He reached into the bedside drawer for condoms while she hovered and teased, and then he held a condom out for her once she had peeled off her knickers.

'Put it on,' he said, his voice ragged as his fingers met the pink lips that would soon enclose his length. 'Sophie…' His impatience was building for he had to be inside her. 'Put it on.'

And then she spoke and the words that she said stilled him.

'I don't know how.'

Bastiano's conscience had left him a long time ago.

He had thought it buried alongside Maria, for he cared nothing for anyone, but when it hit that he would be her first, his conscience made itself known once more.

Bastiano knew very well how things worked, especially in hotels, and often he didn't need to go out or even pick up the phone for sex to drop into his lap.

Sophie wasn't his usual style—an innocent conversation and a breakfast.

Sophie really was sweet.

'What the hell are you doing here, then?' he asked.

'The same as you,' she told him, and his lips pressed together as he got first hand a taste of her defiant streak.

'I think you should go.' His conscience seemed to stand in the wings and, like a prompter, told him the words he should say. 'I'm not looking to get involved with anyone. I'm back to the single life, Sophie.'

'You already told me that,' she said.

'You've been saving yourself, and a one-night stand in a hotel room—'

'It's morning,' Sophie interrupted, but Bastiano was having none of it and he tipped her from his lap and pulled up the sheet.

'Go.'

There was no air of negotiation to his tone but still she sat there.

'Out,' he told her, and Sophie climbed from the bed.

Humiliated, she stuffed her knickers into her uniform pocket as Bastiano looked at the ceiling, or rather anywhere than at Sophie.

And again she could see her life spreading out before her.

Regret.

Utter regret that her first time had not been with someone as beautiful and sensual as him.

She was twenty-four and she ached to know such intimacies.

Bastiano was exquisite.

He was male beauty personified, expensive yet raw too, with a visceral undercurrent that finally matched hers.

That was why she had waited—to find someone who was her match.

Maybe later she would finally give in to her parents' silent demands and return home. Perhaps someday she would settle and marry and pretend that it was her first time, while holding the secret that it had been him all along.

Almost.

'You're right,' she said, and went to do up some of the buttons on her uniform. 'I *have* been saving myself—for a time and a person of my choosing.'

'You can do better.'

'Please...' she scoffed.

Now he looked from the ceiling and at her as Sophie spoke.

'This time last year I was told I could do no better than the man they had lined up to take my virginity.'

'But he would have been your husband.'

'Do you think it helped to know that?' she asked, and her question was both important and urgent.

'No,' Bastiano admitted, and there was a flicker of guilt that flared because of his own quest for a trophy wife. He looked at Sophie, still doing up her uniform; in the bedroom he usually didn't need to think, yet she was clever and strong and knew her own desires.

'It doesn't matter,' Sophie said. She was starting to think of all the professional consequences of this current humiliation. He was, after all, a guest, and she was desperately trying to get back to being a maid. 'I am sorry for any misunderstanding…'

Bastiano loathed her apology.

There had been no misunderstanding.

'Sophie.'

She ignored him and headed for the bedroom door. This time she would not be returning. Her cheeks were on fire and, rarely for Sophie, she felt on the edge of tears.

He was doing her a favour, Bastiano told himself.

Yet it was a favour that neither of them wanted.

'Sophie.' This time he said it as he got out of bed.

Bastiano had never run after anyone but he called her name again just as she walked through the door. Sophie paused and turned around.

He was entirely naked; he hadn't even attempted to bring the sheet with him. The sight of him standing naked caused her to breathe as if she had taken the stairs all the way up to his suite.

He was tall, so tall that as he stood right in front of her

she was at eye level between his clavicle and one dark mahogany nipple.

'You forgot your jacket.'

She didn't look up and neither did she look down; the chair near the window seemed like a very long way away. 'Could you fetch it for me, please?'

'Are you sure?' His hand came to her chin and gently but firmly he forced her head up so that she looked at him.

'I don't understand the question.'

'Yes, you do.' For his words had nothing to do with the jacket that lay over the chair, and they both knew it. Still, he clarified. 'Sophie, I leave tomorrow morning. Maybe we could have dinner tonight...?'

And that in itself was a concession by his standards, for it was usually dinner and then bed, rather than the other way around.

Yet with his hands holding her chin she shook her head and surprised herself when she did, in fact, turn down dinner with this stunning man. 'I'm working tonight.'

And so he asked her again. 'Are you sure this is what you want?'

Not once in her lifetime had she been so certain. She wanted this man.

Decisions had all too often been made by others on her behalf.

From the friends she kept to the clothes she wore.

On her thirteenth birthday she had said that she would like to go shopping for clothes. There was a skirt she had seen and a top too, and instead she had come home from school to be told there was a surprise for her in the bedroom.

On her bed lay a new dress and sandals.

They were pretty enough, though best suited to a ten-year-old and not what she would have chosen. Even Sophie had not fully understood the disappointment and even anger that had welled inside her as she had thanked her smiling parents.

And she could well remember being told that it was time to leave school as her father had found her a job at the baker's.

And though she had smiled and worked hard and been proud to bring home a wage to help take the pressure from her family, she had always felt as if she were somehow not living her own life.

Being told that it was time to marry had proved to be the final straw for Sophie.

"He's twenty years older than me," she had said when they had told her whom she would marry.

"Then he's steady," her mother had replied. "Reliable."

The man Sophie looked at now was none of those things, yet Bastiano had not only asked if she was sure this was what she wanted, he had paused to have her confirm it.

It was indeed potent to be asked.

For once the choice was hers.

And so she made it. She would have him.

'Very.'

CHAPTER FOUR

It was Bastiano who closed the shutters and then the drapes and turned on the bedside lights.

The breakfast trolley he pushed out of the bedroom then he closed the door.

She had expected a fierce kiss, and to resume where they had left off, but Bastiano had decided that this should not be rushed.

'Are you nervous?' he asked, walking over to her.

'No,' Sophie said.

Her response was unexpected but, then, so was everything about this morning, Bastiano thought.

'Not at all?' he checked, for he could see the pulse leap in her throat as he stood in front of her and, more slowly this time, started to undo the buttons.

'I get nervous when I call my parents.' She smiled at his serious face and moved her own closer to his. 'And I get nervous when I go to pay for my groceries because I am not sure if I have enough money to cover…'

He smiled and she moved in and stole a kiss from his cheek, a kiss that moved to his ear. 'I don't feel like that now.'

He moved the dress down over her shoulders and watched it fall to the floor. Then he walked behind her and she felt his fingers unclasp her bra. Her knickers she had dispensed with earlier, and this was all that was left before they were naked together. His hands were warm over her arms as he moved the straps down slowly and then removed the flimsy garment.

He made her feel dizzy, her eyes closing as he ran a finger the length of her naked spine.

Now he turned her around and it felt as if every pore pleaded for his touch, for it was like being painted with fire as his eyes roamed her body.

'I feel like I know you,' she told him.

It made no logical sense for they had never so much as met before, yet she was not even close to feeling shy, and when he lifted his eyes to hers he made no promise with his reply.

'No one could.'

He led her to his bed and it was very different from before, for he gave no instructions. There was no point because Sophie would not follow them—that much he already knew.

'Aren't you going to ask me to take down my hair?' Sophie asked as she climbed between the sheets.

'No,' Bastiano said, for now he wanted no curtain between them.

Still she did not get the fierce welcome of his kiss; instead, she sank into a mattress that felt like a cloud and sheets and a pillow that were still a little warm from his body.

He lay on his side, propped up on one arm and looking down at her.

'Nice?' he asked as she closed her eyes in bliss.

'So nice.'

And so was the light touch of his hand on her breast. Less than a tickle and more than a brush, it made her breathe in sharply through her nostrils. His face came over hers and the kisses she had stolen as he had undressed her Bastiano now returned.

Each time his mouth met hers it was like a teasing glimpse of summer: warmth on her skin and the bliss of more to come, then the cool tease of distance.

The light touch of his fingers had her nipples harden like studs and he could read the need that spread through her. Each slip of his tongue coiled her tighter and the heat from his palm on her breast was a gentle torment. As his fingers squeezed her nipple hard she moaned, and was rewarded with a kiss.

So focused was she on the bliss that his lips delivered, she had barely registered the downward movement of his hand until it slipped between her thighs; he adored that they did not tighten but instead parted softly.

She tasted of all that was good, and he of all that was illicit.

His mouth moved down to her neck and the kiss on her tender skin at first was gentle but as skilled lips moved down his kisses deepened.

Sophie's hand pressed into his shoulder, feeling his warm skin as his mouth sought her breast. There he toyed, slowly at first, licking and teasing her nipple with his tongue. The scratch of his jaw was sublime and Sophie found her fingers digging into his shoulder when he sucked deeply.

Bastiano heard her soft moans, and he wanted to hear more of them so his fingers explored and pushed inside her.

She felt as if every nerve in her body was on fire with the source at her centre, as if she might fold over if he did not stop or that she would surely die if he did not go on. His mouth came back to hers and now his kiss was fierce as he teased and stroked her below.

She arched to his palm, her mouth opening wide, her jaw tensing as Sophie lost contact with the earth.

Bastiano wanted to kiss her all over and savour slowly each inch of skin, but feeling her beneath his fingers, slick and pouting, he felt himself driving closer to the point where he would be neither slow nor tender.

He reached for a condom, as he had before, but her words halted him. 'I'm still on the Pill.'

Bastiano would lecture her later, he decided. He knew he was safe, for he always wore protection—he trusted no one.

It was a first for them both, for he had never made love without one.

Not once.

There was slight trepidation in Sophie as his weight came over her, but it was quickly overridden by yearning.

'Nervous?' he checked.

'Never.'

Bastiano was.

The emotion caught him by surprise as he looked down into amber eyes, for she was so willing and wanting and he was so loath to hurt her.

For some reason he could not readily define, there was rare caution in him as he entered her a little way, and though he met resistance there was a warm willingness swallowing him in.

No, Bastiano did not rob Sophie of her innocence; she gladly relinquished it as she embraced the sensation of pain edged with bliss.

He moved up on his elbows and kissed her tense lips, fighting his own need.

Sophie squeezed her eyes closed for each slow movement from Bastiano delivered fresh trauma and her hand moved to his chest. It was a silent plea to take his time, but as he drew back the ache turned to need and her hips rose to him as he filled her again.

'Slowly,' she whispered, and she watched the tension in his features as he did his level best to honour that request.

She could feel him fight to keep the delicious, unhurried paced she demanded. And when the pain had left, when each stroke had her frenzied and thick desire filled her loins, Sophie removed her hands from his chest, ready to meet his fierce need to possess.

Their rhythm was intense, and he looked her right in the eyes. Her hands moved down his back to his taut buttocks as Bastiano dictated the pace.

He took her leg and wrapped it around him, positioning himself carefully with a patience her body could not return.

'Bastiano…' Sophie was suddenly frantic, her head slipping between huge pillows, but Bastiano flicked them away and rescued her head with his hand; he held her taut body, and only as she started to come did he cease his restraint and give her a glimpse.

Just a glimpse of Bastiano unleashed, but it was enough to harness the energy that built within; the ripple of her orgasm deepened and she shuddered as it swept fast through her.

In the throes of her cry, he knelt and thrust in deeper, his muscled arm scooping behind her back and lifting her body. Taking her hard, she was utterly open to him.

Sophie did not know where it ended, but she knew she came again to the final bucks of his desire.

He was looking down at the point of their joining, delivering those last precious drops deep within as she pulsed to him.

And it faded, for it had to.

As he released her, as he withdrew, Sophie knew that Bastiano had given her everything she could have wanted for her first time. He had taken care and brought her pleasure, he had opened her mind to her body, and it was in those dying seconds that she felt robbed.

Not of her virginity—she had been more than willing in that.

But of time.

There was so much more to Bastiano that she now ached to see.

CHAPTER FIVE

SOPHIE AWOKE MIDAFTERNOON, wrapped in Bastiano's arms.

If bliss was a place, then she had found it.

She lay there examining her needs and wants, only to find she was entirely content.

Oh, she needed the loo, but apart from that there was nothing, not a single thing she required. Sophie did not want to get up because she did not want to wake him, and because she did not want reality to impinge just yet.

Today, she decided, was her day and she intended to make it last!

She wriggled out of his arms, picked up her uniform and underwear and headed into the bathroom. It was sumptuous indeed, themed like a Roman bath with stone walls and a deep alabaster soaking tub that took centre stage. The windows were designed so that the guests could lie in splendour and gaze out on Rome with their privacy assured.

Only Sophie wasn't here for that—lazy days spent lying in an alabaster bath were not for the likes of her.

Turning on the tap and with a somewhat mischievous smile she threw her clothes in the sink. Not just to be sure that her uniform would be fresh for tonight but to make certain she would not be leaving any time soon!

Then she looked again at the bath that seemed to beckon and asked herself, Why not?

At her flat there was a small shower, and more often than not a flatmate waiting their turn.

Sophie knew she would never get a chance like this again.

And so, once she had hung her clothes over the towel warmers, rather than clean the bath, as Sophie so often did when she serviced a suite, instead she ran the deepest one and added everything that she possibly could to it—oils, salts, bubbles. All the lovely bottles that she usually replaced each day were now tipped into the steaming, fragrant water and then she climbed in herself.

This, she decided as the warm water engulfed her, was indulgence at its finest. As she lay there feeling utterly pampered, and with a body sated by his touch, Sophie knew that she would never look at this view again and not think of this wonderful day.

And that was how he had made her feel—simply wonderful.

There was no guilt about this morning's events, though perhaps that would come.

Had she done the right thing by her family's standard, her first time would have been a year ago and it would have been something to forget rather than remember. This was how it was supposed to feel, she knew that now.

She lay there and smiled, and closed her eyes to picture Bastiano better.

And that was how he found her when he came in, up to her neck in bubbles and half dozing.

'Why are there clothes hanging everywhere?' he asked. 'It looks as if the gypsies have arrived.'

Sophie opened her eyes and smiled, for he stood there

gorgeous and naked, frowning at her dripping uniform and underwear.

'If you must know, I washed them because you are a gentleman and I know that you would not send me out in wet clothes.'

'I admire your cunning,' Bastiano said. 'However, I am not a gentleman and if I wanted you gone then, wet clothes or not, you would be.'

'Nope.' She did not believe it of him, for in Sophie's eyes he was perfect.

She held out her hand for him to join her, but he hesitated because he generally didn't really care for such tender intimacies. He told himself that it was the fragrant, foaming water that seemed so inviting before climbing in at the opposite end, with his back to the view. Sophie rested her feet on his chest.

Certainly, Bastiano thought, if he did get into the bath with a woman then it was not to lie there half dozing, but that's exactly what he found himself doing.

For a while, at least.

But then her heels pressed into the wall of his chest.

He ignored her.

'What?' he asked, when her heels nudged him again.

'Rub them.'

He was too relaxed to decline, and so he got right into the soles with his thumbs, enjoying her moans of pleasure.

'Your posh English girl does not know what she's missing,' Sophie said.

She assumed him the kindest, most thoughtful person, Bastiano realised, and he chose not to enlighten her.

'Are you sore?' he asked, not meaning her feet.

'A little bit,' Sophie admitted, and then her lips twitched

provocatively as she met his eyes. 'Though not sore enough not to do it all again.'

Yes, Sophie decided, Lydia really did not know what she was missing because Bastiano massaged her calves as if he knew how they ached, and he made her feel as if there was nowhere else he wished to be.

'For skinny legs,' Bastiano said, 'you have a lot of muscle.'

'Because I am on my feet all day, climbing stairs.'

Not today, though.

Sophie accepted that they only had this day, but for the times ahead when she thought about these precious moments and her mind drifted to this intriguing man, there were things she would want to know.

And she was curious enough to ask.

'What happened to your cheek?'

It was rare that he was relaxed enough with anyone to answer.

'I got into a fight.'

'How old were you?'

'Seventeen.'

'Was the fight with your uncle?' she asked, because he had told her it was at that age he had been kicked out.

'No.'

'Seventeen was a busy year for you, then!'

'I guess.'

'Who was the fight with?' Sophie asked, and she ignored the warning in his eyes to leave it because she was too immersed in the sensual feel of his hands, though they stopped working her calves as he answered her.

'A man I hate to this day.'

Sophie looked over at the change to his tone. It did not unnerve her in the least; she just waited for him to go on, yet Bastiano revealed no more.

Always that type of conversation was marked out of bounds, yet he had opened up a touch and he found himself curious about her.

'What were you doing at seventeen?' he asked.

'I told you, I was working at the bakery…' And then she thought back to that time and she let out a small laugh. 'I was in love. Or at least I thought I was.'

'With whom?'

'A man who used to stop in on his way to work.'

'Did he stop by to see you?' Bastiano asked, assuming that to be the obvious case. 'I'd have been stopping by morning and night and again for cake at lunchtime.'

'Ah, but then you'd have become as fat as the baker.'

'I'd have worked it off,' Bastiano said, taking her legs and pulling her closer so that they both sat up and her legs wrapped around him. Together, they made an alternative reality where it *had* been Bastiano who'd stopped by in the mornings, and between teasing kisses she told him how it had been.

'It was nothing like that. He was married! I just had a crush and he very politely ignored it.'

And Bastiano wondered what her reaction would be if he told her his sins. Not that he had any intention of doing so.

She lay back down and closed her eyes, looking utterly at ease, as if she had not a care in the world.

Sophie didn't.

Not a single care.

'Usually I am cleaning this bath,' she sighed. 'Once I had to bring into this very bathroom a bucket of ice and its stand along with a bottle of champagne. That in itself is not uncommon, but on this occasion the couple were sitting in the bath.'

'Well, it wasn't me,' Bastiano said, his response dry.

'Of course not, you are too polite for that.'

He was about to correct her and say he really didn't give a lot of thought to sparing the maids' blushes—more that he tended not to indulge in romantic baths.

Yet here he was.

'What else have you seen?' he asked.

'So much.' Sophie smiled and leant back on the headrest, closing her eyes as she recounted. 'There are lots of weddings here and I enjoy them the most. There is always something wonderful going on. I don't often deliver the breakfasts, but some mornings I do, and some couples have champagne at seven a.m….' She had questioned it the first time, but now she smiled at the romance of it. 'I've seen so many different sides to life, working here. I've never even tried champagne, let alone first thing in the morning.'

'Would you like me to call for some?' he offered.

'No,' Sophie said with her eyes still closed but then, as she had done when waking in his arms, she examined her wants. There were no needs—they had been more than taken care of—but there *was* a tiny want. 'I thought I wasn't hungry,' she said.

'And are you?'

'Not really,' Sophie admitted, but she was determined to make use of the good life while she had it. 'But I could *just* manage a gelato with a shot of hot espresso…'

He groaned as another of life's simple pleasures now became a necessity and Bastiano reached out for the bath-side phone. He gave his order, telling them they could override the Do Not Disturb sign on this occasion and leave the dish in the entrance to the suite.

Ten minutes later, Sophie lay in the bath with her hand clapped over her mouth, trying not to laugh as Inga wheeled their treats through to the lounge.

Bastiano was in a towelling robe and he didn't even close the doors so his conversation with Inga drifted through from the lounge and Sophie could hear every word that was said.

'Is there anything else I can do for you, Signor Conti?' Inga asked, and Sophie knew that she was not speaking out of turn because the suite looked as if they had visiting rock stars *in situ* and was in serious need of a full service.

'That is all,' Bastiano responded.

He came back into the bathroom and Sophie screwed up her nose. 'I cannot stand her,' she admitted.

'Why?'

'Just…' Sophie shrugged, suddenly a little awkward, for after all, wasn't she doing the same as Inga?

No, she decided, for this had nothing to do with money or designer bags. Instead, it was a promise that she had made to herself long ago—that her first time would be because she wanted it and was ready for it—and that promise to herself had been fulfilled. Still, Inga and thoughts of home were soon forgotten when she realised that he had come into the bathroom empty handed. 'Where's my gelato?'

He didn't answer. Instead, Bastiano came over and lifted her out of the bath, carrying her dripping wet back to the bed. She laughed and protested and he found himself smiling as he dropped her onto the bed.

'Here.' He propped her up on the pillows and poured a shot of hot coffee over the gelato and then handed her the dish. Sophie had a taste and gave a purr of pleasure. It was deliciously cold after the warm bath and the flavour, both sweet and bitter, was perfection.

She looked over as Bastiano took off his robe and then picked up his own dish but he did not add the espresso.

'Where's your coffee?' she asked.

'I don't think you'd like it,' Bastiano said, and then took a large scoop of ice cream and held it in his mouth, so that his tongue and lips were almost blue with cold.

'What are you doing?' Sophie asked as he knelt on the bed and parted her legs.

'Kissing it better.'

Yes, she had found bliss.

It was a day in bed spent hidden from the world.

A day spent making love, dozing, laughing and talking, and Sophie never wanted it to end, though of course she knew that it must.

Wrapped in his arms, Sophie woke and did not want to look at the bedside clock.

The drapes and shutters were heavy enough to block out every chink of light, but there was a certain stillness to the air and she knew that it was night.

Sure enough, when she lifted her head from Bastiano's chest and read the time, she saw that in less than an hour her shift would commence.

And they would end.

She slid out of his arms and went back to the gorgeous bathroom. This time she had a shower and then did up her hair and dressed in her dry clothes.

She walked back into the master bedroom and there lay Bastiano, asleep.

No, she would never regret it.

She had heard her friends speak of their first time and some of them had sounded dismal, some had been described as good at best.

This had been perfection. He had taken such care of her, both in and out of bed.

For the first time in her life she had been spoiled and

adored but she knew that the world they had built this day had not been one designed to last.

Sophie ached to wake him, but she did not know how to say goodbye without tears and that certainly wasn't a part of the deal they had made.

And so, instead of waking him, instead of fumbling through a goodbye that she did not want, Sophie went to the bureau in the lounge, took out a piece of paper and wrote him a little note.

Mai ti dimenticherò mai.

I will never forget you.

And if it was too sentimental for Bastiano, she didn't care, for she never would forget, Sophie thought as she quietly let herself out of the suite. Though sad to leave, as she headed to the elevator and awaited its arrival, there was the complete absence of guilt.

Her mother, if she knew, would never forgive her and that was no idle thought—it was fact. And neither would Benita, the head of housekeeping, if she were ever to find out.

Yes, to others it might seem wrong, but to Sophie everything felt right with the world and she hugged the memory of them close to her chest.

It had been the best day of her life without a doubt, and if it were possible to float in an elevator, then that was just what Sophie would have done as she made her way down to the foyer.

She actually didn't start work for another ten minutes but knew that her friend Gabi was working on the plans for a wedding being held tomorrow.

No, she wouldn't tell even Gabi about what had happened—some things were too precious to share. But she couldn't find her friend; Sophie put her head around the ballroom doors and saw that she wasn't there.

In fact, there was no sign of her.

It felt as if Gabi might be avoiding her because usually they caught up all the time, but for the past couple of months Gabi had always been too busy or tired.

Sophie headed through the foyer and to Reception, where Anya was on duty.

'Have you seen Gabi?' she asked.

'Gabi!' Anya said, and gave a dramatic eye-roll. 'I have more than seen her! I had to call an ambulance earlier on. She went into labour.'

'What do you mean?' Sophie asked, unable to take in what she was being told. 'Gabi's not pregnant…' But even as Sophie said it, Gabi's avoidance of her in the last few months and the new distance between them was starting to make sense.

'She's more than six months gone,' Anya said. 'I had no idea either until her waters broke. I think the baby will come tonight.'

'Is there anyone with her?' Sophie asked, while knowing that there was nothing she could really do.

'I think she was going to call her mother once she got to the hospital.'

It was a rather distracted Sophie that went in for the evening briefing. Here she would be told where she would be working tonight, though it didn't really matter to Sophie. She just wanted to know what was going on with her friend.

'Are you listening, Sophie?' Benita checked.

'Of course,' Sophie said, and forced herself to at least look as if she was paying attention.

'Could you help with the set-up of the ballroom for the wedding tomorrow? Things have fallen rather behind.'

Sophie nodded and wrote the instructions down in

her notebook as Benita spoke on to the rest of the gathered staff.

'Sultan Alim has had to fly home unexpectedly,' Benita continued, 'which makes things a little easier on this busy night. Laura, you and I shall service his floor when there is a moment to breathe. Now, in Presidential Suite B we have Signor Conti...'

Sophie felt her heart soar and her cheeks warm at the sound of his name.

'He's an important guest at the Grande Lucia,' Benita carried on. 'Today he has declined to have the suite serviced. However, should he change his mind, Inga and Laura, could you see to it promptly, please?' Benita's voice was sharp and sometimes Sophie was rather sure that Benita knew what Inga got up to. 'Please remember that Signor Conti is a serious contender to purchase this hotel. He may well be your boss in the future, so please be on your best behaviour. Remember that he is here to observe the staff and glean as much information as he can about the running of the hotel.'

Sophie felt as if the floor had shifted beneath her. The handover continued but Sophie heard not a word. She wanted to call out, to ask Benita to explain further about Bastiano. Still drenched in horror, she could not quite take in what had just been said, but Benita was wrapping things up and gave her team a smile. 'Let's get to work, then.'

It was a shaken and tearful Sophie who did her best to work through the night.

Gabi's boss, Bernadetta, had been called in to accomplish overnight all the work to be done. She was a poisonous woman at the best of times, and on this night she worked the fragile Sophie hard.

The ribbons she had her tie over and over, the chairs

she had her lug and move, and she screeched at Sophie to concentrate as for the umpteenth time she had to lay the place cards according to the table plan.

Finally, *finally*, around two in the morning, Benita popped her head in the ballroom and told Sophie it was time for her break.

'Is everything okay?' Ronaldo, the doorman, asked as Sophie stepped outside the kitchens for a breath of air. Ronaldo was also on his break and having a cigarette.

'I'll be glad when it is morning,' Sophie admitted. 'It is awful working with Bernadetta and there is all this talk of the hotel being taken over.'

'I know! Let's hope it's Di Savo,' Ronaldo said. 'He has a hotel here in Rome.'

'What about the other one?' Sophie fished.

'Conti?' Ronaldo said, and raised his eyebrows. 'He's a risk taker, a loose cannon.'

'In what way?'

'In every way. He and Di Savo are sworn enemies. Security was told to be on high alert, what with the two of them staying here at the same time.'

'Really?'

Ronaldo nodded. 'Especially because last night Di Savo was entertaining Conti's guest.' He gave a knowing eye raise. 'We just have to hope that Di Savo wins the bid as well as the girl. Bastiano Conti's a cold-hearted bastard—that much I know.'

'How do you know?'

'I'm the doorman,' Ronaldo said. 'He often stays here as he and the sultan are friends. Believe me when I say I see all that goes on. I wouldn't let my sister within a mile radius of him.'

'They're friends?' Sophie checked, recalling Bastiano's skilled questioning—he had acted as if he was surprised that Alim was a sultan.

'Good friends.' Ronaldo nodded. 'Though I thought the sultan had better taste.'

It was bad enough that she had slept with the potential new boss, but it was utterly humiliating the way she had been taken in by him. Bastiano had had her opening up and speaking to him as if they were lovers.

That was what she had thought they were.

What had taken place had for Sophie been so wonderful, but now it was tainted.

She had thought he'd been asking all those questions to find out about her, but instead he had been playing her all along.

Thank goodness she hadn't told him that she thought Inga was up to tricks. Sophie did not like her, but neither did she want to get her into trouble—it was a dismissible offence.

And one that she herself had committed.

Oh, whatever way she looked at it, she was in trouble.

Her job was the biggest and proudest achievement of her life. Sophie loved coming to work each day, she loved her colleagues and the friends she had made.

And at any moment now it might all be taken away.

By morning, the ballroom was somehow ready for the upcoming wedding but Sophie was no less frantic. When Benita asked if someone could go and help out with the breakfast service, Sophie did not put up her hand.

She simply did not know how to face him.

Bastiano was more than ready to face Sophie, though.

He had woken at around midnight having had the best sleep he had known in a very long time.

It had taken a moment to register that she had gone. Bastiano had even gone to the bathroom, half hoping to find her lying up to her neck in bubbles as he had earlier in the day.

Recalling what Sophie had said about liking order, he had called the butler and asked that he send someone to service the room.

To his disappointment it was Inga, the woman who had brought the *gelato*, who'd arrived, along with another chambermaid.

'You were working this afternoon,' Bastiano commented.

'They asked me to do a split shift.' Inga smiled.

He placed his breakfast order.

Shakshuka for Sophie and Sicilian pastries for him, only this time he asked for summer berries and a bottle of champagne to be served with the juice.

Finally morning arrived and there was a knock at the door; he heard the trolley being wheeled in and then another soft knock on his bedroom door.

'Entra,' Bastiano said.

He had been in the industry long enough to know Sophie would have no say where she was assigned, yet as he sat up to a soft *'Buongiorno...'* he lay back down when he realised that it was not Sophie.

The curtains were opened and the shutters too, but Bastiano deliberately closed his eyes.

'Can I serve you breakfast?' Inga asked, when protocol dictated she should leave rather than speak.

'No.'

'Is there anything else I can do for you, Signor Conti?'

He opened his eyes and though imperceptible to many, Bastiano knew the ropes well and could both hear and see the veiled offer; yes, Inga would love to be in bed with the boss.

'You can leave.' His voice was curt and with a flick of his wrist he dismissed her.

Inga left and the minutes dragged by ever more slowly as Sophie failed to appear.

It edged close to seven and still Sophie did not arrive. Bastiano knew only too well how bad it would look if he were to call down to the front desk and ask after her.

There was nothing he could do except wait.

And, when the morning was already misbehaving, Bastiano got up and poured his own coffee, but by then it was far too cool. He flicked open the newspaper and suddenly his day got a whole lot worse.

There was an image of Raul Di Savo, his nemesis, sitting in a café, one Bastiano recognised as being opposite the hotel. And he was holding hands with Lydia Hayward.

So she hadn't been catching up with friends after all.

Bastiano and Raul both had colourful reputations and both knew how the other worked.

Raul must have found out that Lydia was a guest of his, Bastiano surmised. Hostilities had just increased tenfold, and he screwed up the paper and tossed it to the floor.

His phone rang. It was Maurice, spluttering his apologies that Lydia remained unavailable and asking when they might meet to speak about the castle.

But Bastiano had no interest in Maurice's draughty old building now.

'We shan't be meeting, Maurice. And when you see your stepdaughter, tell her that the reason for Raul Di Savo's interest in her is simply to get back at me. There is no more to it than that.'

He was in no doubt that Maurice would indeed pass

the message on and, he hoped, at the very least, that it would cause Raul and Lydia to have a major row.

Next he called down to the front desk and asked that his bags be packed and his transport arranged.

Forget Rome! Forget fragrant baths and spiced Sicilian pastries! And most of all, forget Sophie!

Bastiano was back to being a bastard.

CHAPTER SIX

SOPHIE HAD SIMPLY not known how to face Bastiano.

It wasn't just that she was frightened for her job, Sophie felt angry and humiliated—sure that he had been silently laughing at her all along.

And so, after the longest night at work, instead of heading to his suite she headed for home. Once there, she called the hospital to find out what she could about Gabi but they gave out little information.

'Can I visit?' she asked. After learning the hours when she could see Gabi, she decided that she would go in the evening, before the start of her next shift.

She felt sick at the thought of walking into work and positive that she was going to be in deep trouble.

Perhaps he wouldn't buy the hotel, Sophie thought as she tried to sleep. Though there was little solace that that would contain things, for she now knew that Bastiano was a personal friend of Sultan Alim.

And as nice as Alim was, he had a fierce reputation with women too.

Sophie lay there with visions of Bastiano thanking Alim for the *nice surprise* sent to his suite.

And yet for all her worries there remained the absence of regret.

Today, Sophie knew, could so easily have been her first wedding anniversary.

And so that evening, as she walked onto the maternity ward to visit her friend, she knew full well that it could easily have been her sitting pale in the bed, having just given birth, with Luigi by her side.

No.

She might have to suffer the consequences work-wise, but her first time would always be as she had wanted it to be.

Even if she lost her job.

'Sophie…' Gabi started to cry as soon as Sophie walked in.

She had bought her a bunch of flowers and a little lemon-coloured bear for the baby, who was nowhere in sight.

'It's okay,' Sophie said, taking her friend in her arms and not really knowing what to say. 'Is the baby okay? The nurses wouldn't tell me anything.'

'I had a little girl,' Gabi said. 'Lucia.'

'And how is she doing?'

'She's in the nursery. She's very early but they say that for her size she is doing really well.'

'I bought this for her.'

Sophie handed over the little bear and Gabi smiled when she saw her baby's first toy.

'I can't believe she's here,' Gabi said.

'Believe me…' Sophie's eyes widened '…neither can anyone! All the staff are in shock. Why on earth didn't you tell me that you were pregnant?'

'It seemed wrong to be telling everyone when I haven't even told her father…' Gabi admitted.

Sophie waited, but Gabi shook her head; clearly she still wasn't ready to reveal who the father was.

It didn't stop Sophie from trying to work it out, though!

'Ronaldo?' Sophie asked, because she often saw them chatting.

'Oh, please,' Gabi said, and then through her tears she started to laugh. 'Ronaldo?'

'Well, he is good looking.' Sophie shrugged. 'And you two are friendly.'

'I talk to Ronaldo because he knows all the gossip,' Gabi said.

Not *all* the gossip, Sophie hoped.

She stayed for a little while and promised to come in and visit again, but all too soon she was heading to work, terrified of what awaited her yet conflicted, for she knew she secretly hoped to see Bastiano again.

Benita gave her a smile when a blushing Sophie joined the group for the briefing.

'The wedding is in full swing,' Benita said, and took them through the plans for the night ahead. 'Signor Conti checked out early this morning.'

Nobody heard as Sophie's heart dropped.

She stood, staring at her pencil poised over her notepad, and there were tears in her eyes as Benita spoke on.

'The staff have been busy all day and have not been able to service the presidential suite. Sophie, could you make a start, please, and I'll come and help you as soon as I can, then you can go and help with the clear up once the wedding guests have left.'

The workload was so heavy that Benita suggested she didn't stay for the rest of handover and so, with a heavy heart, Sophie made her way up in the elevator, the same one in which she had once floated back down to earth.

Each presidential suite had its own butler's pantry and its own cleaning supply room so there was no trolley to collect. She let herself in and saw that it was a lot neater than when she had left it.

Sophie walked through the vacant lounge to the master bedroom. On a silver trolley stood an untouched breakfast. She lifted the domes and saw the pastries and *shakshuka*, but there were summer berries too. What brought tears to her eyes, though, was that there was an unopened bottle of champagne standing in a bucket of water, and she knew he had ordered it for her.

It was the most romantic thing that had ever happened to her.

Or, rather, that had never happened.

Maybe she had been too hasty, Sophie thought.

There was the expensive scent of him in the air and the memory of them in her mind.

Sophie was quite sure she was going to be fired anyway and so, just for a moment, she lay on the bed where he had slept and tried to tell her heart to slow down.

Please, let her job be safe!

Which meant she had better get on and do it, for Benita might well be here soon and so she peeled herself from the bed.

First she wheeled out the breakfast trolley and did a little pick up of rubbish. There was a screwed-up newspaper on the floor and when she smoothed it out there was a photo of Raul Di Savo and a pale blonde beauty, sitting together in the café opposite the hotel.

It was Lydia, Sophie was sure.

This must have been the reason that Bastiano had checked out early.

His rapid departure had nothing to do with her—Sophie knew she didn't wasn't so much as a pawn in his games.

She had been nothing more than a diversion—that was all.

Sophie scrubbed the bath where they had lain smiling and chatting; it hurt to recall him joining her and then carrying her through to the bed that she now stripped back and remade.

To service a presidential suite to standard took ages. Benita had said that she would come and help but, of course, she was too busy and so it was Sophie who had to make sure that it was done to perfection.

And it hurt.

It was some considerable time later that Benita arrived with her check list and together they went through the suite.

Ornaments, decanters, glasses, furniture, all had to be gleaming. Every feature down to the last detail was checked and ticked off.

Two pairs of eyes were needed as generally, though inadvertently, something was missed.

Not on this night.

She had erased every last detail of them.

'All ready for the next guest.' Benita smiled. 'Very well done, Sophie—Signor Conti always leaves a storm behind him.'

'Really?' Sophie couldn't help but fish for details.

'He likes the women and knows how to party.' Benita gave a tight smile. 'You have done an excellent job,' she said as she flicked off the lights. 'You would never know that anyone had been here.'

Now Sophie just had to tell her heart the same.

CHAPTER SEVEN

REALLY, HER BIRTHDAY was just another day.

Sophie got up late and had coffee with her flatmate, Teresa, who then headed off to her waitressing job.

It had been Teresa's birthday last month and Sophie had stopped on the way home from work and bought a cake.

It shouldn't hurt that Teresa made no mention of the date.

She made too much of things, Sophie told herself. She pulled on a top and skirt and left a little earlier than usual for her twilight shift at the Grande Lucia.

She unlocked the mailbox in the foyer of her building and there was a small wad of mail; Sophie found that she was holding her breath as she flicked through it.

Nothing.

There had been no phone call this morning from her parents and now not even a card.

Her oldest brother had called the other week and told her that Luigi still came for dinner each week, only now he hit the wine.

'Do you think that makes me want to come home and marry him?' Sophie had said and ended the call.

They didn't get it.

Bastiano had.

Even after all these months just the thought of him could stop Sophie in the street.

Just the memory of that day was enough to make her smile—a little gift she could open and treasure on a day when she felt forgotten and small.

There was still a little while before her shift commenced and Sophie decided that she would drop in on Gabi and see how she and little Lucia were doing. It had been a while since they had caught up. Gabi had only been back at work for a couple of weeks and had already been on an international trip to help organise Sultan Alim's upcoming wedding while her mother cared for Lucia.

It all sounded terribly glamorous to Sophie.

'Sophie!' Gabi gave her a tired smile as she opened the door. 'It's good to see you!'

Little Lucia was crying and Sophie was more than happy to hold her as Gabi made them a quick lunch. 'What time is your shift?' Gabi asked.

'I start at two,' Sophie said. 'How was your trip overseas?'

'It was…' Gabi gave a tight shrug. 'It was hard leaving Lucia.'

'But what was it like?' Sophie asked. She had never been out of Italy, let alone flown to the Middle East! But then she remembered that Gabi had had a bit of a crush on Alim and guessed her questions might be insensitive. 'How was Alim?'

'I didn't really see him.'

'So you don't know who's buying the hotel?'

Gabi shook her head.

'Everyone is worried for their jobs,' Sophie sighed.

'It should be okay,' Gabi tried to reassure her. 'Raul

Di Savo has many hotels, one of them is here in Rome. I am sure there wouldn't be too many changes.'

'What about if the other one gets it?'

'God help us all then,' Gabi sighed. 'Conti takes over old buildings, guts them and then modernises them…' She pulled a face. 'Sultan Alim has spent the past two years restoring the hotel. Conti will ruin all that…'

'He might not,' Sophie countered, though she recalled him talking about Lydia and the castle that she lived in and how much work it would have been.

Was it all just business for him?

'Apparently, he turns all his acquisitions into upmarket rehab facilities,' Gabi said. 'I can't imagine there would be many weddings being held at the Grande Lucia if that is the case.' Then she gave a tight shrug. 'Not that it will matter much to me. I am not sure I can hold on to this job.' Gabi explained things a little better. 'My mother wants me to get a job with more regular hours.'

'Is she still cross about the baby?'

Gabi nodded. 'She has started to come around—at least we're finally speaking. In truth, I wouldn't be able to work without her support.'

'What about Lucia's father?' Sophie asked.

'I'm not ready to talk about him,' Gabi admitted.

'Fair enough,' Sophie said, and glanced at the time. 'I'd better go. I'll come and see you both soon.'

'Make sure that you do.'

And so her birthday went unnoticed again, and of course Sophie didn't blame her friend. Gabi had enough on her mind as it was.

Sophie walked the back streets, down the alley and entered the hotel via the side entrance, then walked through the kitchen and to the locker area.

There was a pile of clean uniforms with her name

on that were freshly starched and uncomfortably tight and scratchy when she put one on; quickly, she re-did her hair.

The hotel was very full, they were told at the briefing.

There was a high turnover of rooms to make up and no time to waste if they were to get everything done.

Benita gave out assignments for the day. 'Sophie, you are on the twelfth floor, odd numbers.'

Sophie nodded. The twelfth floor housed the cheaper rooms, all without any landmark views and were just plain hard work.

'Oh, and, Sophie,' Benita added, and Sophie waited to be told that when she had finished she was to go and help out Inga, who always seemed to be running behind, but instead there was some surprising news. 'You have a delivery to pick up at Reception.'

'A delivery?'

'Yes. Is it your birthday or something?'

Sophie nodded and her heart started to beat fast, wondering if maybe, just maybe, her parents had sent her something here.

She was almost bouncing on the spot for the briefing to finish and when it did, instead of heading straight up to the twelfth floor, she went straight to the reception desk.

'There is a delivery for me?' Sophie said to Anya.

'Indeed there is,' Anya said. 'Lucky girl.'

Even as she came out of the cloakroom, Sophie knew that the flowers Anya held were not from her parents, for this was not the type of gift they would ever give.

It wasn't a big bouquet; in fact, it was a small posy that Anya handed to her, wrapped in cream tissue paper and exuding understated elegance.

The flowers really were exquisite.

Perhaps a hundred miniature roses in the softest

creams, all edged in the palest green. Each one looked as if it had been individually painted with the most skilled brush, and the scent when she drew the bouquet close to her face was like inhaling summer.

'It's stunning,' Anya sighed. 'All the staff have been coming in and out for a peek.'

And as if to prove her point, Inga came over.

'They're nice,' she said.

'I think Sophie has an admirer,' Anya teased. 'Come on, open the card.'

'Who are they from?' Inga asked, but when Sophie opened the card it was blank.

'I don't know,' she lied.

Or was it the truth?

For the Bastiano Conti everyone spoke of did not send flowers and was guaranteed to forget.

Had he remembered?

Or was this an elaborate gift from Gabi?

Even an expensive gift from a stressed, broke, new mum made rather more sense than it coming from Bastiano, yet her heart knew they were from him, and each bloom felt like a tiny kiss to her soul.

'They need to go in water,' Anya told her. 'I can do that for you and you can collect them when you go home.'

'Thank you,' Sophie said, but she was reluctant to let them go and so she selected one and coiled it into her messy bun.

Oh, the twelfth floor had never seen such a smiling maid, for even if the roses weren't from Bastiano, it was simply nice to know that someone had remembered.

And yet the flutter in her heart told her that that someone was him.

'Benita's looking for you,' Laura told her. 'She wants to see you now in the staffroom.'

There was still that slight edge of dread, Sophie thought as she took the elevator down. Still that fear that she was about to be found out.

But it had been months ago, she consoled herself.

Three months, in fact.

And, Sophie knew, Bastiano had stayed a couple of times at the Grande Lucia since then, though never when she had been working. Sadly, she wasn't privy to the guest list and tended to find out about these things after the event.

But surely, Sophie thought, if word was going to get out then it would have happened by now.

Her palms were just a little slippery as she opened the door to the staffroom.

'Buon Compleanno!'

'Happy birthday' was being called out to her and there was even a cake with candles and jugs of soft drink.

'Your favourite chef made this for you,' Benita told her. 'He says next year a little more notice would be nice. You should have told us!'

The chef had made her *torta setteveli*, or seven veils cake. Layers of chocolate mousse, hazelnut, praline, cream and sponge, all topped with a chocolate glaze.

It was the last thing that Sophie had expected. To have her colleagues gather and wish her a happy birthday meant everything and she thanked her lucky stars for the day she had been given a job at the Grande Lucia.

The cake tasted like chocolate silk and was a mouthwatering slice of home.

'Actually,' Sophie admitted, 'this tastes better than any I have ever had.'

'Well, don't have too much,' Benita teased, and gave a little pinch to her waist as Sophie went for a second slice. 'Or you will be asking for new uniforms.'

Sophie laughed; the cake was decadent and rich indeed but that would not stop her from having a second slice. Soon, the staff who had gathered drifted back to their responsibilities and the remains were left in the fridge for Sophie to take back to her flat.

She sailed through the rest of her shift. The flowers and cake had lifted her, yet home would have to wait for as her shift neared its end she was offered an hour of overtime.

'Sophie,' Benita called her, 'we have an important guest arriving. Are you able to stay back?'

'Of course.'

Overtime was always welcome, and it was also nice to be asked.

They raced up to the presidential suite—though cleaned, it had not had the finishing touches for an important guest.

It was always hard to be up here, but Sophie did her best not to show it, to carry on as if it was just another room that she was preparing, rather than the site of her magical day with Bastiano.

'Why don't these stars give a little more notice?' Sophie asked as the champagne and flowers were brought in and she and Benita turned back the vast bed.

'Because they don't have to; they know we will always jump to their tune,' Benita said as she turned down the silk sheets. 'Anyway,' she added, 'it's not some famous rock star coming to the Grande Lucia tonight, it is Signor Conti, the soon-to-be…' She paused, because the news had not yet been confirmed.

And Sophie just scrunched the sheet in her hand as, unwittingly, Benita let her know that not only was Bastiano due to arrive tonight but that soon he would be taking over the hotel.

'I should not have said that,' Benita admitted.

'It's fine,' Sophie answered. 'It shan't go any further.'

'Make sure it doesn't. The contracts have not yet been signed and Alim wants to leave any formal announcement until they are.' Benita let out a long sigh, but now that Sophie knew, Benita admitted to a little of what was on her mind. 'Really, I wish it had been the other. Conti is bad news.'

'Bad news?' Sophie said, and while she usually acquiesced to Benita, suddenly she saw red. She was sick of hearing everyone bad-mouth Bastiano.

'I doubt he got to be a billionaire by accident,' Sophie said tartly to her senior. 'I think the Grande Lucia would be very lucky to have someone as astute as Signor Conti as its new owner.'

Benita raised an eyebrow as Sophie sprang to his defence but decided against saying anything further about her potential new boss!

'The room looks perfect,' Sophie said, blushing a little at having spoken her mind to her senior.

She put a slip of paper by the bed, informing him about the weather tomorrow—she wanted to add a heart.

Benita went to close the shutters and drapes so that all the esteemed guest had to do was peel off his clothes and drop into the sumptuous bed.

It seemed a shame to block out the view but that was how things were done during turndown.

The lights were dimmed and the room ticked off on the service sheet, and then Benita did one more sweep of the drawing room and lounge before exiting to the corridor.

And Sophie stood there, her heart hammering, uncertain what she should do.

Oh, she wanted so badly to speak to him—she simply had to find out if she was about to be in trouble, but more than that she needed to see him again.

And then Sophie knew how to let Bastiano know that she was thinking of him.

She walked over to the drapes and opened them, pushing back the shutters, and remembered that moment when her heart had found him.

It truly felt as if it had.

Not the man everyone spoke of so ominously, more the man who had smiled and made her melt.

She looked out on Rome at night and recalled turning to his smile.

'What were you doing?' Benita asked when Sophie joined Benita in the corridor.

'I was just checking that I had written the weather down for tomorrow. Everything is looking perfect.'

'Then you can go home now, Sophie. When are you back on?'

'In the morning, at six.'

'Well, go and get some sleep.'

Sophie walked slowly down the corridor and, instead of taking the elevator to the basement, she went to the foyer, hoping for what, she did not know.

A glimpse of Bastiano perhaps?

But he had not arrived.

Benita had already told her that she would be on house duties tomorrow and working in the foyer. Certainly she would not be up in the presidential suites.

Sophie knew she had to speak with him.

But how?

Her voice might be recognised, or perhaps he would not take the call.

As Sophie reached Reception she thought about hanging around to wait for his arrival.

'Sophie?' Inga stopped as she walked past. 'What are you hanging around for?'

'I had some overtime,' Sophie said, 'but I think I dropped my notebook...'

And in that moment she made up her mind and turned for the elevators.

It was wrong; she could well be fired for what she was about to do, and Sophie's heart was hammering as she pressed the buttons that would take her to the floor from which she had just come.

She had to use her staff pass as the presidential suites had limited access.

He might bring a woman back with him, or a friend, Sophie suddenly thought in panic. The butler would be there, and also there would be the bellboys delivering his luggage. There were a million things that could go wrong, but she simply had to speak to him, to thank him for the beautiful roses.

If Bastiano was to be the new owner, then she was probably about to lose her job anyway, so she let herself into the suite.

The lights were dimmed and there was soft music playing to welcome him.

She touched nothing.

Sophie sat on a chair by a writing bureau and waited as the moments ticked by, but then finally there were voices.

Voices!

She stood from the chair and went into a small alcove where the staff would be unlikely to venture.

Sophie stood in the dark, her heart hammering, realising the foolishness of her actions and anticipating his anger...yet there was also excitement curling in her stomach for finally she would see him again.

'I have no luggage…' She heard his deep voice tell the butler that there was nothing to unpack, and then a terse, 'I can pour my own drink!'

Bastiano simply wanted the man gone.

The butler closed the door and finally there was silence.

What the hell was he doing here?

What was he doing, putting in an offer for a hotel he didn't even want, just to score a point over Raul?

Raul didn't want it either.

He had paid Bastiano a visit the other day. At first Bastiano had assumed he had come to argue over the hotel.

Instead Raul had asked for Lydia's address.

Bastiano's price?

The return of his mother's ring.

This morning, just as he had finished speaking with the florist to arrange Sophie's birthday surprise, a packaged had arrived.

Bastiano hadn't yet opened it.

Now, all these years on, he gazed at the ring, remembering Maria trying it on and holding it up to the light.

Yet memory was not kind.

Now that he held the ring in his hand, long-buried memories were starting to come back.

'Give me back the ring, Maria.'

He could hear his younger voice attempting to hold on to his temper as she had claimed his mother's ring as her own.

A couple of hours later, still wearing it, she had died.

He placed it on the gleaming table, for holding it kicked up black dusty memories that were best left undisturbed.

Bastiano stood and poured a cognac. Looking around the suite, he remembered the last time he had been here, reading the paper, finding out about Raul and Lydia, but then he remembered the hours before that, the bliss of a day away from the world, and so clear were the memories that for a moment he was sure he could recall the scent of Sophie.

He could.

Bastiano opened his eyes and wondered if it was Sophie who had prepared the room; as he filled out the breakfast order, he wondered if she might be the one to serve it.

He hoped so.

And then he heard a movement.

Her intention had been to call out, to step out, but now she stood in the dark, terrified by the predicament that she had placed herself in.

'Sophie?'

She heard her name, he knew she was here and she knew she had to reveal herself.

'I didn't know how else to see you…' she started as she stepped from the shadows and walked towards him.

Her presence was enough for Bastiano to know that this was the real reason he was here in Rome. Sophie was the reason the contracts were unsigned, and that he'd had his lawyers stringing things along, for while he did, there was a chance to see her again.

'If you had wanted to see me then you should have come back that morning,' Bastiano said.

'I was scared I was about to lose my job!' She could hear that her voice was raised. There was fear mixed in with desire for, yes, the months that had passed had dimmed her recall of his absolute power. 'You never told me you were thinking of buying the place. Why did you lie?'

'I never lied.'

'You did.' Sophie raised an accusing finger. 'I would have never told you the things that I did—'

'And I knew that,' Bastiano hotly responded. 'I wanted to keep us the same.'

'We're not the same.' She came right up to his face, and all the hurt and anger she had held in these months flooded out. 'You're the rich man and I'm the maid, how could we ever be the same…?'

'You know that we are.' He too was nearly shouting. 'In here we are.'

Weeks and months of denial and anger met now and she loathed his absolute beauty, that, even now, had absolute power over her. And in turn he loathed the chink in his armour that bore her name, because he could not forget and he could not move on.

He kissed her hard and she fought with herself not to kiss him back.

'What happens when you own it?' she asked. 'My job is everything to me…'

'I'm not buying the hotel.' He stole more kisses and when she pulled back her mouth he simply found it again.

'So why are you here?'

For this.

He didn't say it, but now his mouth did.

Today had been hell and he craved oblivion. Their teeth clashed as their mouths met once again, and his tongue tethered her fury as she returned his fierce kiss.

Bastiano went for her uniform and she heard the rip of the buttons and she was kissing him back and crying as she tasted him again.

'Now we are the same,' he told her as very deliberately he removed her uniform, pushing it down her arms and then past her hips so it fell to the floor.

'No.'

For he was still the rich man in his expensive suit and she stood in drab underwear, but soon he was removing that too.

He turned her and kissed her so that her back was to the wall and his suited body pressed against her naked flesh.

Sophie closed her eyes and drank in his scent, recalling her silent desire to know this man less restrained. And now she knew, for the sound of his zipper and his ragged breath in her ear turned rage to desire, and it was she who held his head now, kissing him back hard as he wrapped her leg around his waist.

'Never let me down,' she begged, and her words were nonsensical for even as he drove into her, even as he consumed her, Sophie knew she was opening herself to hurt, and that tomorrow the countdown would resume and abstinence must surely start over again.

He placed one hand on the wall behind her while the other dug into the cheek of her buttock. He was as coarse in delivery as her violent need required. She did not understand how the woman who had trembled and hidden only a matter of moments ago now coiled naked around him.

Now they were the same.

Matched in desire and lost in lust.

'I thought of you…' he told her, and whether or not she believed him those words tipped her.

He felt the shift and lifted her other leg, so she was wrapped firmly around his hips and their kisses were intense as he spilled deep inside.

'You're going to get me fired,' Sophie whispered as their bodies began to relax and now, slowly, he let her down.

'Never,' Bastiano said. 'Are you supposed to be working now?'

'Not until morning.'

'Good,' he told her. 'Then we have all night.'

CHAPTER EIGHT

'YOU PREPARED MY SUITE,' Bastiano said as they stepped into the master bedroom and he saw the gorgeous night view of Rome.

'I did.'

Sophie did not feel disadvantaged at being the one who was undressed, for indeed she got to slip straight into bed and to lie watching as Bastiano got undressed.

'I wanted you to remember me when you came in.'

'I don't need a view to remember you.' It was undoubtedly the most romantic thing he had ever said but she appeared not to notice its significance. In fact, Sophie thought she was being fed a line and lay there sulking as he went and had a quick shower.

'You got my flowers.' He could see the tiny rose that was now knotted in her hair but as beautiful as her flowers had been, Sophie was not going to let him off that easily.

'Three months late.'

'You were the one who didn't come back,' Bastiano pointed out, taking his time to dry himself.

'And you were the one who failed to tell me you were thinking of buying the place. Can you imagine how it felt to find out?'

'I meant to tell you before you left for work,' he admitted.

'I was scared for my job and I kept thinking of all the things I'd told you.'

'Sophie, I was hardly sitting taking notes.' He got into bed and the soapy clean scent of him was divine. 'I wasn't even thinking about the hotel, I was just…' And it was he who was quiet then because now he allowed himself to look back properly at that perfect day.

'I thought you were staying for another night,' she said. 'You were booked in until the Monday.'

'I left angry,' he admitted. 'I found out…' Bastiano shook his head, not wanting to bring up the feud with Raul.

He was tired of it.

But Sophie had long since guessed the reason he had walked.

'You found out about Raul and Lydia?'

He looked over and gave her a slow smile. 'Nothing gets past you.'

'With the right education, I'd have ruled the world.' Sophie smiled and then told him how she knew. 'I saw their picture in a screwed-up newspaper, I guessed you had seen it.'

'I had.'

They lay together and he pulled her close so that she lay in the crook of his arm, and it was such a nice place to be.

'He came to see me the other day. We hadn't spoken for fifteen years. I thought it was to argue over the hotel but he wanted to find out where Lydia lived.'

'Did you tell him?'

'For a price,' Bastiano said, and thought of the ring.

'Why do you two hate each other so?'

'We always have,' Bastiano told her. 'Our families have always been rivals.'

It was the easy version of the story.

It was too complex a conversation for ships that passed in the night, yet they lay there and stared out at the view, Sophie nestled in the crook of his arm. This was more than a casual encounter, Bastiano knew.

Sophie had arrived with no warning.

She had stepped onto the stage of his life, but there was so much debris, so much damage, and he did not know how to clear it. He told her a little of the complicated version.

'We used to be friends,' he admitted. 'When we were growing up our families frowned on it but we didn't care, and as teenagers we thought we could take on the world. Then Raul left for university.'

'What did you do?'

'I worked in my uncle's bar.' There was no point prettying it up—he and Raul had been enemies for a reason. 'After he left I slept with his mother.' He awaited her recoil or the uplift of her head and narrowing eyes but she just lay there. 'We had an affair, and when it was exposed she died in a car crash.'

'How old were you?' Sophie asked.

'Seventeen. I wasn't exactly innocent before that, though. In the end I tried to persuade her to leave her husband and come away with me but she refused. Raul believes I as good as killed her.'

'Were you the one driving?'

He frowned at Sophie's question.

'No.'

'Well, then, how could it be your fault?'

Sophie lifted herself up on her arm and he glimpsed again her absolute refusal to simply acquiesce.

'Her husband had found out about us.'

'How old was she?'

'Thirty-four,' Bastiano said. He had thought Maria closer to her forties at the time but really she had not been much older than he was now.

Sophie's lip curled. *'Poutana.'*

'Hey!' He rose to Maria's defence, as he always had. 'We were in…' Bastiano halted but a little too late, for Sophie knew what he had been about to say.

'In love?' she sneered, and then shook her head. 'That's not love.'

'How would you know?' he demanded.

'I know what love isn't,' Sophie responded hotly. 'I left home because, for all my lack of experience in the matter, I believed that love should make you smile.'

'Perhaps—if you live on the cover of a chocolate box.'

'So, if it was love, why didn't she leave her husband?'

'She was very religious,' Bastiano said. 'When Maria was growing up she wanted to be a nun.'

Sophie gave a derisive snort. 'Why wasn't she one, then?'

'Because at sixteen she got pregnant with Raul.'

Bastiano reached over and turned out the light but, far from annoyed at her scathing assessment of Maria, he was actually touched that somehow, on rather black evidence, she was defending him.

They lay in silence but far from sleep.

It was difficult to speak of that time but it was also hard to hear.

'It was Raul you fought with?' she asked.

'After the funeral.' Bastiano nodded. 'That was the easy part—the next day we found out she had left money in her will to be divided between him and me. He thinks I knew that she had money…'

'Did you?'

'No,' Bastiano said. 'Raul told me he'd watch me go under, he said I was nothing without her money.'

'So she left you enough to buy the Grande Lucia?'

'No.' He gave a low laugh at the thought. 'I bought a derelict building…' He thought of how the Old Convent had been then. 'There were no roads to access it. There weren't many tourists then in the west and I bought it for a song. I've bought a few more since then.'

'You could have blown that money,' Sophie said. 'Instead, look at all you have done.'

She did not know the scope of his wealth, just that he could consider the purchase of this hotel, which told her how much Bastiano had done with the start he felt he had not deserved.

In Sophie's mind he had earned every cent.

'Last month,' Sophie said into the darkness, 'when I called home, my brother told me that Luigi had taken to drink.'

Bastiano said nothing.

'It's my fault apparently.' She turned and saw his strong profile and that his eyes were open but he did not look at her. 'As I said to my brother, I'm quite sure there was a problem long before he had me to blame it on.'

'You certainly take no prisoners.' He looked at her then and she heard rather than saw his smile. 'Were you always tough?'

'I had to learn to be,' Sophie told him, 'and fast. I have five brothers and all of them would be perfectly happy to have me pick up after them. I pick up after myself, unless, of course, I am being paid.'

Bastiano slept, but Sophie lay there awake, troubled by her own words on the subject of love.

He made her smile.

Oh, not in a chocolate box way.

Just the thought of him, and the memory of them, had elicited more smiles in the last three months than she had collected in a lifetime before that.

And the world turned too fast when they were in bed, for when she reached for water, Sophie could make out the outline of the Colosseum when before it had been wrapped in darkness.

As she lay back down he pulled her in so that her head lay on his chest and she watched the sky, willing morning not to come.

His hand was on her arm and she toyed idly with the snake of black hair that had entranced her when she had gone to reach for the plate that first morning.

There was no reason now not to move the sheet, no reason left to be shy, and so she slipped her hand lower, feeling him grow hard under her fingers.

Her face felt warm on his chest and his hand was still on her shoulder as she slid down.

She had no real idea what she was doing, but he rose to her palm as if to greet her. She felt the warmth nudge her cheek and as she kissed just the tip and then knelt and ran her tongue down the side, he grew to the length of her face. This she knew, for she worked her tongue up and down, absorbed in the task at hand.

Bastiano moved the hair from her eyes.

And then as she ventured deep he took her hair and coiled it around his hand, just so that he could see her.

Usually he preferred a curtain of hair, but with Sophie he liked watching the stretch of her jaw and then the tease of her tongue.

He liked watching while she closed her eyes and they were lost to each other, utterly oblivious to a world waking up outside.

So oblivious that the sound of the main door opening went unheard.

Bastiano moaning her name did not.

'Sophie…'

One hand was stroking her bottom, the other wrapped in her hair, and she was lost in the moment as he came to her mouth.

And Inga stood there, jealousy rising like bile as she saw Sophie's uniform a puddle on the floor.

Sophie, always sweet and smiling, and yet so judgmental of Inga, was at it too.

And with their soon-to-be boss—Bastiano Conti.

Oh, the two of them were not quite finished yet and remained oblivious to her arrival in the suite, but Inga's eyes lit on a ring, and she knew exactly how she would punish Sophie for her hypocrisy.

She slipped the ring into the pocket of Sophie's discarded uniform and quietly wheeled the trolley back out, then she took out a pen and changed his breakfast order to seven.

'Hey.' Inga wheeled the trolley back to the kitchen and spoke with the chef. 'Signor Conti's breakfast is not due for another hour. Luckily I noticed.'

Very lucky.

For some.

Explain that, Sophie!

CHAPTER NINE

'I'M GOING TO be late,' Sophie warned as they showered together.

'Don't go to work today.'

'You might have some sway if you were the new boss...' She laughed. 'No, I am going in so I can be guilt-free on my days off.'

'How long are you off for?'

'Two days and two nights.'

She quickly dressed and, yes, she was going to work but with conditions attached.

'This time you're to come back,' he warned, taking her in his arms. 'Tonight we'll go out, somewhere nice.'

And she frowned because, yes, it was an age-old problem but Sophie truly had nothing suitable for a date with Bastiano Conti. Luckily, he read her concern.

'I'll take care of everything.'

As she left, Bastiano was ready to plan their evening.

More than that, he was considering flying her home.

Never had he had any inclination to bring anyone back to the Old Convent, but telling her his history, finally having someone on his side, for the first time he wanted to explore his past...

With her.

Bastiano cared for no one and had been raised not to do so, yet he knew now the real reason he was back in Rome.

Sophie.

Maybe the return of his mother's ring was a sign that things were starting to turn around. For the first time he believed that maybe, just maybe there was more to life than revenge.

He walked out and looked over to the table where he had placed the ring last night, yet there was no ring there. He had left it there, Bastiano was sure.

In fact, he could remember precisely the moment he had put it down for it had been then he had become aware that Sophie was near.

And he tried not to think that she too might have seen him with it.

He looked at the floor beneath the table.

Unlike the last time he had been here, the room was immaculate and after a few minutes of fruitless searching it was very clear that the ring had gone.

He recalled her expression when he had told her they would go out tonight.

Perhaps Sophie had decided that she needed something to wear.

Had she taken some notes from his wallet he would not have cared, but he'd only just got his mother's ring back.

Bastiano was still scanning the floor and the surfaces as he dressed, still going over last night's details in his mind as he pulled on a shirt and impatient fingers did it up, but he didn't even attempt to tuck it in.

And that was how she saw him.

Sophie had just come from the morning's briefing and instead of house duties she was to work in the foyer, ensuring that all surfaces were gleaming, including the brass revolving doors.

It wasn't her favourite job but it was not an unpleasant one. She could observe the guests and chat with Ronaldo the doorman. It was not an easy shift either, for there were many lounges and there were always guests leaving coffee rings and crumbs. But today she could have been anywhere, she was so happy.

They had shared something so precious last night, Sophie knew it.

And then she saw him and it was not the Bastiano she knew.

Immaculately dressed or deliciously naked, she knew only those two.

Now he looked dishevelled, his clothes thrown on, his shirt barely done up and he wasn't even wearing shoes.

'Sophie…'

His hair was tousled, his jaw unshaven but most disconcerting was his impatience, for she could feel it as he strode up to her.

'Can we speak?'

'I can't.' She tried to smile and address him as if he were just another guest. 'Bastiano, not here…'

'Yes, here!' His voice was low but so clipped that Ronaldo and a couple of guests turned their heads. 'Do you have something of mine?'

'Bastiano…' She was nervous. His eyes were blazing, his lips were pale and tense and she could feel his anger. 'I don't know what you're talking about.'

'Just give it back now and we'll say no more about it.'

Yes, he got that he had never paid her, and he got that she probably thought she deserved something after two nights in a rich man's bed but, hell, *not his ring*!

'Problem?'

Inga perked up and came over. Sophie found she was holding a tense breath but she forced herself to speak. 'No, there's no problem.'

'Sophie...' Bastiano was livid, even his scar seemed to be jumping to the pulse in his cheek, but he waited until Inga had turned around before he spoke again. 'Give me back the ring.'

'I don't know what you're talking about, Bastiano,' Sophie said, relieved that Inga had walked off. 'Can we please speak when my shift ends?'

Only Inga had not merely drifted off but had fetched Benita, the head of housekeeping.

'Can I help you, Signor Conti?' Benita asked.

'It's nothing,' Bastiano said, and he did all he could to rein his temper in. This was her job after all.

But things were already out of hand.

'Signor Conti seems to think that Sophie might have his ring,' Inga said.

'I am sure there is a misunderstanding.' Benita smiled. 'Did you drop it?' She looked around the foyer. 'It might already have been handed in.'

'No, I didn't *drop* it,' Bastiano answered curtly with his eyes firmly fixed on Sophie. 'I'll go to my suite and check again, I'm sure it must be there.'

'Sophie only prepared your room,' Benita patiently answered. 'You weren't even in residence when she did...' And then her voice trailed off as she looked at Sophie's flaming cheeks and then Bastiano, who had clearly just come from bed. And as realisation hit, Benita's eyes briefly shuttered.

It happened, everyone knew that, but Benita had expected better from her, Sophie knew.

'Could you come to my office, please, Sophie?' Benita smiled at Bastiano. 'I shall get to the bottom of this.'

It was awful.

Occasionally staff were caught stealing and Sophie knew only too well what would happen.

'I have to go through your locker with you, Sophie,' Benita said. 'These are very serious accusations, though I'm not just concerned with theft. Have you had any dealings with Signor Conti since he checked in?'

'I did not take his ring.'

'That doesn't answer my question, Sophie,' Benita said, though Sophie's flaming cheeks had already done just that—of course she had had dealings with him.

'You won't find anything in my locker.'

'Then you won't mind me checking.' Benita was firm. 'And if there is nothing to worry about then you will be more than willing to turn out your pockets for me now.'

Bastiano had decided he would be the one to best deal with this. Although he now had no intention of buying the hotel, Benita didn't know that so he walked into the office, ready to take control, just in time to see Sophie pulling from her pocket his mother's ring.

'I don't know how it got there…' She shook her head at the impossibility and then turned and there was Bastiano. 'I didn't take it,' she pleaded.

'Are you saying that you've never seen this ring before?' Benita checked, though there was a slightly mocking edge to her voice, for the evidence was clear.

'Yes,' Sophie said. 'I've never…' And then she halted for to say she had never seen the ring would be an outright lie. Last night, as she had stood nervous and trembling in the alcove she had, after all, watched as Bastiano sat staring at the small piece of jewellery for the longest time before putting it down.

And he would know that she had seen it.

She turned to him and her eyes implored him to believe her. 'Bastiano, I didn't take it.'

Bastiano said nothing.

He wasn't even disappointed in her.

Instead he was disappointed for *them* and scornful of himself—for a moment there he had started to believe in the possibility of them.

Not now.

'Could you wait outside, Sophie?' Benita said, and though her request was polite her voice was pure ice.

Sophie did as she was told.

She leant up against the wall and heard snatches of the conversation; she heard Benita mention the police and knew he was being asked if he wanted formal charges made.

'No,' Bastiano said, but he could see that Benita was tempted to so he pulled rank. 'It would cause more trouble for me than the ring is worth. I have it back now.' His head was pounding; he did not want to be standing here, speaking with the head of housekeeping, though he did so, for one reason only. 'There is no need for Sophie to lose her job, it was a one-off—'

'Signor Conti,' Benita broke in, 'I think we both know that I have more than one reason to fire Sophie.' She gave him a tight smile. 'You own plenty of establishments yourself, you will know that liaisons between staff and guests are an ongoing issue.' She shook her head. 'I will deal with Sophie and, of course, I shall brief Sultan Alim…'

'There's no need for that.'

But Benita wasn't just cross with Sophie.

She was cross with the very esteemed guest for the havoc his libido had caused.

'Unlike Sophie,' Benita tartly responded, 'I value my

job so I shall deal with things by the book. I trust you accept that from the head of housekeeping?'

'Of course.'

He walked out and there Sophie stood, pale in the face with her back against the wall, but she still met his eyes with confidence.

'If you needed money you should have just said…'

Sophie hurt.

Unbearably.

'I was never there for money, Bastiano,' she said, but he was walking off and that incensed her. 'It was about more than that, you know it was.'

'Please…' He raised one hand and flicked it in the air, dismissing her absolutely. Sophie was incensed.

'Why did you send me flowers for my birthday, then?' she called out.

Bastiano halted and then turned and walked back to her.

She had only ever known him nice.

Oh, she'd been warned he could be otherwise, but the Bastiano that other people painted so darkly was one she had never seen.

Until now.

'Your birthday?' He frowned. 'Who said anything about your birthday? I sent flowers so you would know I was in residence and would know to come to my suite. Accordingly, you did.'

Bastiano waited—for an angry slap perhaps, or for Sophie to tell him that she'd always known what a bastard he was, and how he had finally proved it.

Her words cut far deeper though.

'I don't believe you,' Sophie said. 'You're better than that.'

Benita came out then. 'I've got this from here, thank you, Signor Conti.'

She waited until he had walked off and then turned to Sophie.

'Signor Conti doesn't want the police brought in, but I'm left with no choice but to fire you.'

Benita was not cruel in her dismissal—her disappointment was the part that hurt Sophie the most.

'I didn't steal the ring.'

'Sophie, what were you doing to even give him the opportunity to think that you had? We serviced the room and left together, long before Signor Conti arrived.'

She had no answer to that.

'I thought you were better than that,' Benita said. 'It would be bad enough with any guest, but he is the future owner of this very hotel.'

'I didn't know that when we first—'

'So there were other times?' Benita said, and shook her head. 'Come on.'

It was not a pleasant morning.

Her room pass was handed over as well as her uniform. All she had in her locker were some shorts and a strappy top. Having dressed, she emptied it out entirely.

'You had a good job here,' Benita told her. 'You know what this industry is like and how word spreads. You will struggle to find work in a good hotel…'

It was true.

Everything Benita said was true.

But as scared and upset as she was, that was not what hurt.

It was the look he had given her, the black smile that had told her he had expected no less.

No trial by jury.

There wasn't even a trial.

Dario, the head of security, had been summoned and she did not get to leave by the trade door but was escorted out the front to serve as a warning to all staff what happened if caught.

And Bastiano saw it all unfold. He watched as the staff on Reception, the doorman and the maids all paused and turned to watch a rather dignified Sophie walk out.

'Sophie,' Anya called out. 'Your flowers...'

And she almost crumpled.

Sophie looked at the perfect blooms and remembered the joy in her heart when she had received them, and then she glanced over to where he stood. 'I wish I'd never laid eyes on them,' she said, while meeting his dark gaze.

'Likewise,' Bastiano mouthed for her eyes only.

He headed up to his suite but everything he touched turned black. He thought of her, feisty and sunny and smiling when they had met, and how much she had loved her job.

And now she had been fired.

He looked at the ring in his palm and it felt as if it scalded his skin; he was pocketing it when there was a knock at the door.

'Room service.'

Not the type he wanted.

It was Inga with breakfast, and she lifted a silver dome and offered to serve.

'No.'

'Would you like—?'

'Out!' he barked, and when the door closed he picked up the dome himself and saw those bloody baked eggs he had ordered last night while, yes, secretly hoping for Sophie.

He hurled the plate and it slid down the wall.

No, there were no rock stars in residence at the Grande

Lucia, but when the staff came to service the room a few hours later and saw how it had been trashed, it was decided that there might just as well have been.

CHAPTER TEN

THANKFULLY HER FLATMATES were at work when Sophie arrived home and she was able to let go of the tears she had been holding back.

Yesterday had been the happiest day of her life.

Today felt like the worst.

For three months Sophie had lived with the knowledge that she might lose her job over what had happened between her and Bastiano. But the scenario had evolved in the most humiliating, painful way imaginable. And still she had no explanation for how the ring had got into the pocket of her uniform.

She had been branded a thief and a whore, not just by her boss and peers but by Bastiano himself.

Worse, though, even worse was the damning look in his eyes—almost as if he had expected nothing less from her.

It had been her first glimpse of the man that everyone said he was—ruthless and cold—but it was not the Bastiano she knew.

As Sophie stripped off her clothes and pulled on a T-shirt in which to sleep, she flicked out her hair and felt something knotted amongst the strands.

A flower.

The stem was bent and twisted, yet somehow the tiny bloom was still perfect.

Recalling his words—how the flowers had been left to let her know that he was in residence—Sophie was tempted to screw up the rose and toss it into the trash, yet she could not.

It was all she had left of them, the only tangible reminder of a time when life had felt very close to perfect. And so, instead of discarding it, Sophie put it in her journal, pressing the pages together and then placing the journal under her mattress and doing what little she could to preserve the fleeting beauty.

Things did not look any better in the morning.

If anything, in the days ahead, things started to look considerably worse.

The Grande Lucia had been an amazing place to work and Benita was right—getting a job in a hotel of its calibre was going to prove difficult, if not impossible.

The phone calls she made went unanswered or she was told to provide a résumé and references. Sophie knew she had to get to the library and use a computer but even that felt daunting.

'Any luck?' Teresa her flatmate asked when Sophie returned after another fruitless search for work.

'No.' Sophie shook her head. 'Even the cafés aren't hiring.'

Summer really was over.

'You have a message,' Teresa told her, 'from a lady called Bernadetta. She asked you to call her—maybe it is about some work?'

Bernadetta?

Sophie frowned as she read the message and then made the call. Bernadetta was Gabi's boss and the one who had run her ragged in the ballroom that night.

Maybe she had heard and was calling to offer her work.

It was a futile hope and a very fleeting one because two minutes into the conversation it became apparent that Bernadetta had indeed heard the news about Sophie being fired and was speaking to her only because she had to.

'Sultan Alim has asked me to contact you,' she explained tersely. 'I told him that I'm not sure you can be trusted with something so confidential but he insisted.'

'I don't understand.'

'Matrimoni di Bernadetta has been asked to organise his wedding.'

'His wedding? Who is he marrying?'

'Gabi. She just doesn't know that yet.'

Sophie stood there gripping the phone, completely stunned.

'Gabi?' Sophie checked, but Bernadetta had already moved on.

'The wedding is to be this Saturday at the Grande Lucia. As Gabi's close friend, the Sultan wants you there. He also needs you to ensure that Gabi is home on Saturday when he calls her.'

'She doesn't know?'

'It's a surprise.'

Sophie's heart was beating terribly fast. Gabi, *her* Gabi was about to be proposed to by Alim. 'Does that mean Alim is Lucia's father?'

But Bernadetta wasn't calling for a chat. 'Are you prepared to ensure that Gabi is home on Saturday?' she asked.

'I'll do my best,' Sophie said, her head spinning as Bernadetta relayed instructions. Alim, it would seem, had thought of everything, even down to providing an outfit for Sophie that was suitable for a royal wedding.

'You are to go and see Rosa. She is making Gabi's dress, and will put something together for you as well.'

'Rosa?' Sophie swallowed. Rosa might be a friend of Gabi's but her designs were completely out of Sophie's league.

'It's all covered,' Bernadetta practically whistled through gritted teeth. 'If there are any problems please let me know and I must reiterate that you are to say nothing to Gabi.'

'Of course I shan't.'

It was the most exciting, breathtaking, happy news and there was no one to share it with.

First she called Gabi who, after offering her commiserations about Sophie losing her job, then asked if there was anything she could do to help.

'Could you help with my résumé?' Sophie asked. 'I don't have a computer and I tried at the library but I don't know how to make margins.'

'Of course. Come on over.'

'I'll come on Saturday,' Sophie said, and then she remembered something. 'I have to go to the doctor's at nine, I'll come after that.'

It wasn't a lie. Sophie did indeed have to go to the doctor's for a prescription for her Pill. With a royal wedding to go to on Saturday, she rather wished she had been a little bit more organised and had some more Pills so that she could avoid having her period that day!

The wedding should prove a wonderful diversion from her current problems but her heart felt heavier with each passing day. Even walking into an exclusive boutique for a private fitting, it was an effort to smile.

Still, her smile did come a little more readily as Sophie found herself for once spoiled for choice.

'This one would be perfect on you,' Rosa said as she held up a dress that seemed little more than a slip.

It was a gorgeous silver-grey and it actually reminded her of Bastiano's eyes.

'Try it on,' Rosa said. 'And slip on the shoes so you get the full effect.'

Sophie went into a very lavish changing room and pulled off her skirt and top and then tried to put the dress on over her head before discovering a concealed zip.

'Is it on?' Rosa asked.

The dress was amazing. It hung beautifully and gave Sophie curves when she usually had none, but for Sophie there was a concern.

'Isn't it a bit much for a wedding?' she asked as she stepped out, but Rosa had thought of that.

'Indeed, but I have a light overdress that goes well with it in a sheer chiffon. I'll just get it. What size shoe do you take?'

Sophie told her and, left alone, she lifted her hair and was trying to decide whether she should wear her hair up or down when she turned and looked at her silhouette.

She had a bust.

Oh, there was no doubt that Rosa was a miracle worker with fabric but there was also no denying that her small bust was a touch fuller.

It was because of the Pill, Sophie told herself.

'Here,' Rosa said, holding out a sheath of pale fabric that Sophie slipped on over the dress before adding the shoes. It was gorgeous and worked amazingly well, although it did dim the beauty of the dress just a fraction. 'You look wonderful.' Rosa smiled. 'I cannot wait to see Gabi's face when she finds out all that Alim has arranged.'

'Are there many guests?' Sophie asked a little later as, for the first time in her life and long overdue, she splurged on some gorgeous underwear.

'Just family and close friends.'

It was her first inkling that Bastiano might be there. Sophie knew that he and Alim were friends.

She watched as Rose wrapped her new silver knickers and lacy bra in tissue paper, and Sophie vowed to herself that Bastiano wouldn't be seeing them.

Yet, though the thought of seeing him would usually have consumed her, Sophie awoke on the morning of the wedding with more than the possibility of seeing Bastiano on her mind.

In the bathroom, having showered, she tried to quash the gnawing of anxiety in her stomach, for her period still had not arrived.

Stress can delay things, Sophie told herself.

Not that she really knew, but she had heard it said amongst friends, and so at her appointment at the doctor's that morning she suggested the same.

The doctor just handed her a jar.

'I've taken my Pill every day,' Sophie said when she returned with her specimen and the doctor ran the test.

'Do you take it on time?'

'Always…' Sophie said, and then swallowed as she thought back to the other morning when she had been fired. 'I had an upset the other day, I might not have taken it until lunchtime.'

'The other day?' The doctor frowned. 'Sophie, you are pregnant.'

'I don't think so.' Sophie shook her head. She had come here to be reassured, to be told she was mad to worry, but the doctor just looked at Sophie as the news started to sink in. 'I can't be.'

As the doctor examined her Sophie's fear only increased.

'I would say that you're more than twelve weeks.'

'How could I not know?' She started to cry, but this doctor was far kinder than the one back home and took some time to gently explain that not all women had symptoms.

'People have commented that my uniform was getting tight,' Sophie said. 'I just never gave it much thought.'

It was a lot to take in, an awful lot to take in, and Sophie left the doctor's more bewildered than she had ever been in her life.

But she had to get to Gabi's.

'Hey.' Gabi gave her a smile and then when she saw Sophie's puffy eyes she drew her inside. 'You'll get another job.'

'I loved that one, though,' Sophie said. It was easier to let Gabi think that her tears were about losing her job and Gabi soon set to work, typing up her friend's résumé.

'You really need a reference,' Gabi said. 'Why don't you put me? I can say you've helped me organise some weddings.'

'That's stretching it,' Sophie sighed.

'Well, why don't you put me as a personal one for now?'

Gabi made it all look so easy, and soon she had printed off several copies of Sophie's résumé, but as she handed them over, curiosity got the better of Gabi and she asked what Sophie had been doing in Bastiano's room.

'Oh.' Sophie was immediately on the defensive. 'So now you think I stole his ring?'

'Of course not!'

'I would never steal,' Sophie said. 'But if I did, I would not steal some stupid emerald and pearl ring. It would be diamonds.'

Gabi laughed and just as she did the phone rang and she went to answer it. Sophie watched as her friend's face paled and she excused herself and went into the bedroom.

It must be Alim!

A few minutes later Gabi emerged, declaring that she had a migraine.

'That came on quickly,' Sophie said as she was ushered out.

'Yes, they tend to.'

They promised to catch up soon but as Sophie walked off, though happy for her friend she felt terribly lonely too. Gabi had struggled with being a single mother, yet she had a job and her mother lived here in Rome.

And now she had Alim.

Sophie couldn't help but wonder what hope there was for her when she had none of those things.

She had nothing, save for her Sicilian pride, though even that was going to be hard to find today.

Sophie tried, though.

She got ready and she wore make-up through necessity rather than choice. Just a little, but enough to ensure that no one could guess she'd been crying. And for once she wore her hair down, though more because it would hopefully hide some of her blushes when she walked into the hotel.

The dress was a dream but, now that Sophie knew she was pregnant, it seemed terribly obvious, for her bust was certainly fuller and there was a soft curve to her stomach. Sophie was very grateful to add to her outfit the sheer fabric that hid even a tell-tale hint that her body had changed.

And so to the Grande Lucia.

She took a cab, which was a treat in itself for Sophie, and as it pulled up Ronaldo jumped forward to let the passenger out.

'Benvenuto...' he said, but then Ronaldo's warm welcome petered out as he realised who it was, and now his greeting was both awkward and curt. 'Sophie.'

'Ronaldo.'

She climbed out of the cab and took a second to seemingly fiddle with her dress, though really she was trying to summon the courage to walk inside.

Through the brass revolving doors she went and into the familiar foyer.

It didn't feel familiar, though, for instead of hearing her name called and the regular smiles and waves as she walked through, her ex-colleagues all pretended to be busy and looked the other way.

All that she could handle, Sophie thought as she stood outside the ballroom and gave her name.

The sly glances and whispers, and even being downright ignored, all hurt, but it was a manageable hurt.

What her heart couldn't deal with, though, as she walked through the entrance doors of the ballroom, was the certain knowledge that Bastiano was here.

Even without sighting him, Sophie knew that he was.

There was a current that ran through her whenever he was close and she could feel his eyes on her as she again gave her name so that she could be guided to her seat.

He was here, she was certain.

Yes, Bastiano was there.

He had withdrawn his offer for the hotel and would gladly never have set foot in the place again, yet business was business, he had told Alim.

And they were still friends.

So, having offered his best wishes to the surprisingly nervous groom, he was just taking his seat as they awaited the arrival of the bride when Sophie appeared.

She looked stunning, Bastiano thought.

He watched Sophie momentarily falter as she was guided to the seats near his.

'I am a friend of the bride,' she said to the woman who was ushering her towards where he sat. 'I should be on the other side.'

But this was no ordinary wedding, and she went where she was guided, away from the side where all the royalty had been seated.

'We commoners sit together,' Sophie said as she took her place beside him and Bastiano gave a tight smile.

'For now,' he responded, looking ahead rather than at her.

As soon as the service was over he would move away, Bastiano decided. She might just as well have spilled a bottle of perfume over herself for her fragrance overwhelmed him, yet he knew she had not. The scent was pure Sophie and for now he had to breathe it in, aware of every flicker as she sat supremely still beside him.

And then as the ballroom doors opened they stood and Sophie turned, seeing her friend but all the time feeling Bastiano's eyes boring into the back of her head.

'You knew!' Gabi mouthed as she caught sight of her, and Sophie smiled for her friend; as Alim kissed little Lucia, Sophie did her level best not to break down.

She wanted to tell Bastiano about the baby, she wanted there to be hope for them.

But there was none.

There never had been, she now knew.

It had never been going to end well.

She wanted to be happy for her friend, yet to stand broken-hearted at a wedding, next to the man who had shattered her happiness, was a very private hell and too much to sustain.

Gabi and Alim were in love, it was plain to see.

It just seemed to magnify the hopelessness of her situation as she stood next to Bastiano.

'How long does the service go on for?' he asked at one point.

'How the hell would I know?' Sophie responded and she felt rather than heard his slight mirthless laugh.

It truly was agony.

Finally, though, Gabi and Alim were husband and wife.

As the chairs were moved away and the guests went to take their seats at the tables for the celebratory meal Sophie looked at the place cards and saw she would be seated by him.

It was a hell she chose not to sustain.

'Gabi...' She kissed her friend and congratulated her and then she struggled how best to say what she had to.

Gabi said it for her. 'You're going to go?'

'I just...'

She felt sick.

Oh, maybe it was all in her head and simply because she knew she was pregnant, but suddenly she felt light-headed and nauseous and utterly out of place.

'I understand, Sophie,' Gabi said, for she had heard all the rumours and could have thought of nothing worse than being forced to sit next to Alim when her own world had fallen apart.

'I'm so happy for you,' Sophie said. 'I honestly am. I wouldn't have missed the wedding for the world.'

It was the reception that she could not tolerate.

'Here.' Gabi swiped Sophie's place card from the table and wrote something down. 'That's Alim's private number. Put him down as a reference.'

'I can't.'

'Yes, Sophie, you can.'

'I'll only use it if I'm desperate.'

Desperate was how she felt, though not about work.

She wanted to walk right up to Bastiano and plead her case. She wanted to tap him on the shoulder right now and tell him that she did not take his stupid ring. And she wanted to tell him what she had found out just a few hours ago.

Her eyes scanned the room and immediately she saw him—talking to some leggy blonde. Or rather she was talking as Bastiano's restless eyes scoured the room and found Sophie's.

She turned and walked away and headed for the restrooms, but she didn't get that far.

Sophie looked over to Reception, where Anya stood—once they would have chatted, but now Anya could not meet her eyes.

And there was Inga, polishing the brass doors and chatting to Ronaldo.

Everyone ignored her.

Once she had belonged but, like it or not, she no longer did, so Sophie left.

Not just the wedding.

It was time to accept that there was nothing for her here in Rome and to return home.

Her disappearance did not go unnoticed.

'Excuse me,' Bastiano said to the leggy blonde.

He had no idea who the woman was but that was nothing new.

The difference today was that anonymity held no charm.

He wanted to speak to Sophie, to find out how she had fared. He wanted to know that everything was okay in her world and then he could walk away more easily.

Bastiano could not find her.

As he took his seat the place card next to his had gone, though Bastiano being Bastiano had already checked and knew full well that Sophie had been placed next to him.

Perhaps she had asked to be moved, Bastiano decided when the table filled and the space next to him remained empty.

Wise choice, he told himself, though that did not sit right.

But then the lighting dimmed and it became increasingly clear that Sophie hadn't just moved tables, she had left the venue.

'Where's Sophie?' he asked the happy couple, having sat through the meal and endless speeches.

'I expect it got a bit too much for her,' Gabi said, and she looked straight at Bastiano. 'It would be hard to be here, labelled a thief by everyone and the subject of painful gossip. I'm just grateful she made it to the service.'

And later Bastiano could not help but have a word with Alim.

'I think Sophie might have been dealt with a bit harshly.'

'Oh, so you're in the practice of hiring thieves?' Alim asked, raising his brows, but then he saw his friend's concern. 'She'll be okay.'

'She won't get work.'

'Not true. I've just been informed that I'm to act as a reference.'

And with Sultan Alim of Zethlehan as a reference, Sophie would be okay.

Bastiano could relax now and put the unfortunate incident behind him.

Except he couldn't.

There were beautiful guests galore and yet he was in bed before the bride and groom.

Alone.

And he woke, as he always did, before the sun.

'Entra!' he called, when on the dot of six his breakfast was delivered and he closed his eyes to indicate he did not want conversation.

Some things never changed.

Except they had.

'Would you like me to serve?'

He opened his eyes to the pale blue ones of Inga, the maid that Sophie did not like.

'Out,' he told her, and struggled to contain his anger, for Bastiano had worked out what had happened.

It took less than an hour to prove his hunch.

He stood over Dario, with Benita by his side, looking at old CCTV tapes.

'My breakfast is served at six every morning, except on that morning.'

'You ordered it for seven,' Benita said, looking at the paperwork.

'No.'

Of that he was certain.

The only variance to his breakfast order had been the occasional *shakshuka* and that had either been eaten by a sexy maid or flung against the wall.

His breakfast was always at six.

There it was, right on time, being delivered by Inga.

And there it was, not two minutes later, being wheeled back out.

Sophie was not a thief.

Most disconcerting to Bastiano, though, was that he

had cared enough to find out and pursue justice for his little maid.

'She will get her job back now?' Bastiano checked, but Benita gave an uncomfortable shrug.

'Sophie wasn't just fired for stealing.'

'If turning tricks is the criteria for firing maids at the Grande Lucia,' Bastiano responded tartly, 'then the unemployment rate in Rome is about to skyrocket. Would you like me to name names?'

Benita closed her eyes for a moment before responding. 'That shan't be necessary.'

'Good,' Bastiano retorted! 'So you will be rehiring Sophie?' Bastiano checked, and Benita nodded.

An hour later Bastiano boarded his helicopter for home with his conscience clear.

Almost.

Not.

CHAPTER ELEVEN

SOPHIE HATED HER JOB.

She tried not to show it, of course.

But no matter how thoroughly she cleaned the sleazy bar on the edge of her home town, the surfaces did not gleam and the carpets were still sticky.

Still, Sophie far preferred the cleaning duty when the bar was closed to the hours when it was open.

It was a job and a roof over her head, she told herself, though not for much longer. Pino, her boss, had made it clear when he'd hired her that the live-in post was a temporary one. Now, at six months pregnant, she was still no closer to working out where she would live when the baby arrived.

It would not be at her parents'.

Sophie had left home in disgrace, returned in shame, and after a lot of heartache they had asked the priest to speak with her. She had been told of couples who were desperate for a baby and would be able to provide a wonderful home.

An argument had ensued when Sophie had told her family that she would be the one to provide for her baby and she had barely seen them since.

Gabi's mother might have come around once little

Lucia had arrived, but Sophie knew that it would not be the case with her own parents.

And she could not stay there.

Even if Pino did keep her on, she wouldn't want to raise her baby in a room over a bar such as this.

And Pino gave her the creeps.

Which was why, instead of, as she usually did, working through her rare day off, Sophie headed upstairs to her small bedroom.

'Where are you going?' Pino asked. 'It's time to open up.'

'It's my day off,' Sophie reminded him.

'Well, I need you to work.' Pino shrugged and went to open the main door, clearly not expecting a discussion.

'I have an appointment in town today,' Sophie said, 'at the hospital. It's my six-month check. I cannot miss it.'

It was a lie.

Sophie had had just a couple of visits to her old family doctor but she didn't tell Pino that. Instead, she headed upstairs and washed as best she could in the small bathroom she shared with Pino and then pulled on a black dress and boots and a thin jacket.

As she came down the stairs she could hear Pino chatting to one of the regulars and hoped she could slip out unnoticed.

'Sophie!'

Just as she got to the door he called out to her.

'Make sure you're back for five.'

That would be pushing it.

Casta was three hours away and three back, and she had no idea how long it would take to get to the Old Convent from the railway station, or how long the interview would take.

For the first time in months she had hope.

A woman who dropped off some deliveries to the bar had told her about the Old Convent in Casta. It was an upmarket health and wellness facility and they were looking for live-in chambermaids.

'It's gorgeous,' she told Sophie. 'They take only the best produce…' She sneered in the direction of Pino. 'He takes the dregs. You should call them. A woman called Karmela runs the housekeeping. My niece worked there. They took her on when she was pregnant and she carried on working there for two years after the baby was born.'

'She lived there with the baby?' Sophie's heart had started thumping so fast it must have woken her own baby up because she felt its little kicks.

'Yes. She worked hard, mind you, but she loved it. Look your neatest, though, it's very posh.'

The telephone interview had gone very well and now, as the train went through a tunnel, Sophie dug in her bag and found a comb.

Oh, she would love to make more of an effort, Sophie thought, but she had nothing to make an effort with.

She did have Alim's number!

Sophie took the place card from the wedding out of her purse and looked at it for a long moment.

She hadn't used it yet. The type of jobs that she had been able to find had not required a reference, certainly not one from a sultan, and she would not use this gift lightly.

Yet she needed it today.

Sophie couldn't wait to meet her baby, but she was nowhere ready to. Her parents' suggestion of adoption had very quickly taught Sophie just how much she wanted her baby.

Yes, the circumstances were far from ideal, but her baby was already much loved.

The train pulled out of the tunnel and into the belly of the valley of Casta. It was the first time she had ever been there and the scenery was breath-taking. Ahead was the ocean, with a hill either side of the valley, and now the train turned seemingly on a dime and ran on stilted tracks that hugged the rocky hillside.

Sophie dared not look down so she closed her eyes and rested her head against the window.

She should have stayed in Rome, Sophie thought. At least there she had had friends.

She ached to contact Gabi but did not know what to say—after all, her friend was now married to royalty. Would it sound as if she was begging for help when she told her she was pregnant?

But it wasn't just that.

Alim was a friend of Bastiano's.

With the best will in the world Sophie knew that Gabi would be worried if she found out her predicament and would end up telling Alim.

Would he tell Bastiano?

Sophie guessed that eventually he would and Bastiano's reaction to the news…

Sophie did not want to know.

Oh, he would be aggrieved and cross and no doubt decide she had set out to trap him.

His anger she could deal with.

Almost.

What she couldn't cope with, though, was the sense of duty that would surely ensue.

Bastiano was right—they were the same.

Beneath the glamour of his life, beneath the fearsome reputation and his playboy ways, he was as Sicilian as she.

Bastiano Conti forced into a duty marriage was something that Sophie could not bear to think of.

She had run from one after all.

As she stepped out of the train Sophie breathed in the salty air; the wind whipped her hair and she pulled her jacket tighter.

'I am looking for the Old Convent,' Sophie told a woman behind the station desk, and she was informed that there was a bus due in fifteen minutes.

'Though it only takes you to the base.'

Sophie nodded. She had been told on the phone that there was a gated entrance and once she arrived she had been told to buzz and a car would be sent to collect her.

The bus took her through Casta and then inched its way up the hill, but Sophie was too nervous to take in the view. She was let off, seemingly in the middle of nowhere, but Karmela's instructions were good and soon she pressed a buzzer on the gate and gave her name and said she was there for an interview.

Soon a car arrived and she was driven down a long driveway with overhanging trees on either side, and then they arrived at the Old Convent building.

The grounds were sumptuous. There were fountains and pretty walkways and, far from foreboding, as she stepped into Reception there was a tranquil air to the old building.

'Sophie?' The receptionist was friendly and greeted her by name. After filling in a few forms, she was shown through to her interview.

Karmela, the head of housekeeping, greeted her and asked her to take a seat, wasting no time before getting the interview under way.

'You said on the phone that you had experience in a five-star hotel.'

'I worked at the Grande Lucia in Rome for a year.'

'Can I ask why you left?'

Sophie told the truth.

In part.

'I had some issues with my baby's father.'

'Well, he would have trouble creating issues here. The security is tight, there is limited access and it is gated.'

It wasn't that type of trouble Sophie had been having, of course, but she gave Karmela a smile.

'You would have to sign a confidentiality clause. Some of our guests are very famous and we do not want staff speaking out of turn.'

'We had many famous and titled guests at the Grande Lucia.'

'I understand that.' Karmela nodded. 'Here, though, a lot of our guests are…' She hesitated. 'Shall we say, recovering from a life lived in the fast lane.'

'Oh.'

'Does that concern you?'

'Not at all,' Sophie said.

'You're currently working?' Karmela asked as she read through her paperwork.

Sophie had updated it by hand.

'I am.'

'Would you be happy for me to ring for a reference?'

Sophie's throat went dry and it took a moment before she could respond. 'I think that might make things rather awkward for me.'

'How much notice would he require?' Karmela asked, and she looked up from the paperwork at Sophie and watched as she struggled to reply.

Oh, she did not know how best to put it. 'He would not take it well if I told him I was leaving.'

Karmela seemed to get it immediately.

'What about your previous role?'

'Sultan Alim is my reference—he's the owner of the Grande Lucia. He gave me his private number to use.'

'May I contact him?'

'Of course,' Sophie said, and wrote down the number.

The rest of the interview went very well and soon Karmela was speaking as if Sophie already had the job!

'You will be required to service the rooms and to provide a turndown service. We encourage guests to eat in the restaurant but on occasion you would also be required to deliver meals to their suites. Some of our guests can be rather demanding, but I am sure you are used to that.'

Sophie nodded and decided that now was the time to address the obvious.

'I know that I might only be able to work for a couple of months, but I am very good at my job and when I've had my baby I will work harder still.'

'Sophie, we're very used to single mothers here. There is room in the cells for both a bed and a cot.'

'Cells?'

'We have kept the names of old. The cells are where the nuns would sleep but don't worry, they have been modernised. They are basic but very comfortable. In your case the timing works well—there's a two-month period where you'll be entirely supernumerary and trained to our standard. Signor Conti has a very strict vision for the place that has worked well…'

'Signor Conti?'

'Sì.' Karmela nodded. 'Bastiano Conti. His facilities are world renowned. This gorgeous old building was a dilapidated shell when he first bought it. Now guests fly in from all over the world to retreat here…'

Sophie didn't hear the rest of what was said.

The Old Convent was owned by Bastiano.

There was no way she could work here now, Sophie thought as hope was snatched away.

As soon as he saw that she was pregnant…

Sophie closed her eyes as she pictured Bastiano finding out that the thieving maid who had delivered far more than breakfast was now pregnant with his child.

Sophie simply could not bear to face it.

She was too busy trying not to break down as Karmela wound up the interview.

'The driver will take you directly to the train station,' Karmela told her as she saw her to a waiting car. 'I'll be in touch soon.'

Karmela was as good as her word and the following morning Sophie took a call informing her that the role was hers.

To both women's regret Sophie politely declined.

CHAPTER TWELVE

'Buon Compleanno!'

'Grazie,' Bastiano responded mechanically as his PA wished him a happy birthday.

She was new and from out of town and, of course, did not know that there was no such thing as a happy birthday for Bastiano.

It had been the day his mother had died after all.

He rather hoped she would leave things there, but given that he had been gone for a few days there was much to catch up on.

'How was your meeting in Rome?' she asked.

'Fine.'

He had been back three times since the wedding and though he was no longer vying to purchase the Grande Lucia, he had told his PA to book him in there on business.

Certainly there had been no pleasure.

Rome had felt empty.

There was no sign of Sophie and, given all that had happened, he had been loath to enquire as to her whereabouts.

Bastiano did his best to ignore the date and dealt with the essentials, but by lunchtime he gave in and pressed on the intercom.

'Call for my car.'

A short while later he drove down the private road he had had built when he had taken over the convent and headed into the small town.

He parked by the church and walked down the gravelly side to the graveyard.

He came here rarely now.

He had used to visit Maria's grave, more out of guilt than grief, but he was not here to visit Maria today.

As a child, he would visit his mother's grave on certain occasions, but there were no memories to draw on and there had never been any comfort to be had.

Again, there was none today.

Just guilt.

He had been raised on it.

It was a pervasive guilt that time did not ease, for his very existence had robbed her of life.

Logic tried to tell him otherwise.

His mother had told no one about the baby she carried, and had done all she could to avoid showing—skipping meals until she had fainted one day. She had arrived at the convent hungry and weak.

The Old Convent might no longer be consecrated but for Bastiano those rules of old still applied, hence the policy of support to single mothers who wished to work there.

If only his mother had gone there sooner.

'I have your ring,' he told her, but there was no sudden rustle in the trees and the birds sang just as they had before.

There was no sign that she had heard.

He took it from his pocket and thought back to when Raul had come to visit to ask for Lydia's address, and the opportunity had arisen to ask for the one thing that was precious to him.

It did not feel so precious now.

He stared at the emerald and the tiny seed pearls but instead of beauty he saw only its curse.

Both of the women he'd loved had been wearing it when they had died.

And then he thought of Sophie, turning out her pockets and holding it in her palm, along with the cruel words he had hurled at her.

Of course the flowers had been for her birthday; at the time it had felt easier to lie than admit to caring.

He had lost her for this ring.

What once had been vital was meaningless now. Bastiano took the small ring and tossed it, for it had brought no peace; all it signified was destruction and pain.

He had to know for himself how she was.

Bastiano simply had to know that Sophie was doing okay.

He was the *stulto* now as he drove back up the hill, for he took the bends far too fast and was impatient at the gate, leaving his car with the engine still running.

'Park it,' he told the doorman.

Through the convent he strode, and before he could change his mind he delivered instructions.

'I want to speak with Sultan Alim,' Bastiano said. 'I'll take the call in my office.

'Of course.'

Zethlehan was three hours ahead of Sicily but even though it was late afternoon there Bastiano knew it might take some time to be put through as Alim would likely be busy.

It wasn't Alim he wanted to speak to, though, but Gabi.

Bastiano just had to know how Sophie was.

It felt as if it was taking for ever to get hold of Alim.

He paced his office and looked out at the view of the strait but it did nothing to soothe him, as it usually it did.

At seventeen, when Maria's will had been read, he had scaled the convent walls just to get away from the toxic gossip in the village.

As Raul had started his ascent in Rome, Bastiano had remained in Casta.

His rise had been slower than Raul's.

Bastiano had seen the potential of the building and his low offer had been accepted; he had taken a loan and renovations had commenced.

The first clients had trickled in and then a B-list actor had moaned to the press about the cost, saying that it was prohibitive.

In response to the best publicity he could have hoped for, Bastiano had tripled the rates.

Now there was a waiting list to get in, though they kept two places on constant reserve should a young royal or such need urgent respite.

Though he had several more exclusive retreats under his belt this was his base and served as his platform to the world. Thanks to his famous guests, Bastiano was a name on the most coveted guest lists. He travelled frequently and partied hard but it was here that he chose to return.

Yet lately these walls no longer felt like home.

'I have Sultan Alim on the line.'

Bastiano picked up the phone.

'How are you?' Alim asked.

'I am well,' Bastiano said. 'Very well. Have you sold that hotel yet?'

'It is off the market,' Alim replied. 'Why, have you changed your mind?'

'No.' Bastiano was rarely awkward. 'Actually, I was

hoping to have a word with Gabi. I wondered if she had heard anything from Sophie.'

'Sophie?'

'The chambermaid…'

'I know who she is. I thought you were back in touch.'

'Why would you think that?'

'Because your head of housekeeping called a while back for a reference. I gave her a glowing one.'

Sophie had been here?

Bastiano made a few noises and said a few words but in less than a minute he had ended the call. He rang Reception and asked that Karmela meet him in his office.

All this time he had been worrying and wondering, only to find out that Sophie had passed through.

'Is anything wrong?' Karmela asked, looking worried as she came in.

'Nothing is wrong,' Bastiano said. 'You interviewed a young woman a couple of months ago…'

'I interview many people.'

'Sophie,' he said. 'She used to work at the Grande Lucia.'

'Ah, yes.'

'She wasn't offered the position?' he checked.

'Indeed she was. Sophie was an excellent candidate and her references checked out, but when I rang to offer her the job she said that she had accepted another position.'

'Where?'

'I didn't ask that,' Karmela said. 'I was disappointed and also cross that she had wasted so much time. I had even told her that there would be no problem when the baby came…'

'Baby?'

'You have always said that so long as their children are kept out of earshot you don't mind if we employ single mothers.'

'I meant, are you saying she was pregnant?'

'Yes, about five or six months along,' Karmela recalled. 'She said she'd had to get out of Rome because she was having some issues with the baby's father.'

The words were like knives.

'Bring me her résumé.'

He was sweating.

Even in the blistering heat of a Sicilian summer Bastiano was so fit that he barely broke a sweat. Even when held by the throat by Raul and accused of causing the death of Maria, he'd stayed cool.

Not now.

He cast his mind back to the wedding and the last time he had seen her. If what Karmela was saying was correct, then Sophie would have been about three months pregnant then.

He would have known. They had made love the night before!

Yet the fast, frantic sex had been the result of pure need and as for the morning…

Karmela brought him the paperwork and though Bastiano wanted to be alone, there were questions he needed to ask.

Most of it was typewritten but her most recent employment was written by hand.

'What is this address?'

'A bar, and not a particularly nice one,' Karmela said. 'I didn't bother to ring them for a reference.'

'Why not?'

'Sophie told me it was a live-in job but she didn't feel particularly comfortable there and it would be made worse if her boss knew that she was considering leaving. I rang her previous employer instead, Sultan Alim.'

Bastiano waved his hand to dismiss her, for he needed to digest all he had just been told, but as she reached the door there was something he had to know, something that could not be gleaned from the pages he held in his hand.

'How did she look?'

Karmela held out her hands and gave a somewhat helpless shrug, unsure what to say. 'Signor Conti, it was a couple of months ago…'

'How did she look?' he asked again. Bastiano did not care if his questions led Karmela to think that the baby was his, for his only concern now was Sophie.

'Tired,' Karmela said.

'And?' Bastiano pushed.

Karmela thought for a moment. 'Relieved. She seemed terribly relieved to have found this place. I got the distinct impression she was struggling where she was, which was why I was so surprised when she turned down the job.'

And Bastiano knew why she had.

Sophie had thought him wonderful when they'd first met—a gentleman who would not have her leave his suite in wet clothes.

She had seen only the good in him.

Until he had proved himself to be otherwise.

In the throes of love making she had pleaded for him never to let her down and he had.

It was time, Bastiano knew, to put things right.

'It's time to open up,' Pino called as he rapped loudly on Sophie's bedroom door.

'I'll be right there.'

It was late on a rainy afternoon and she was exhausted and had a headache to boot.

Lately she had been unable to sleep. She was simply too uncomfortable or too nervous with Pino prowling around, but this afternoon the baby was asleep and Sophie wanted to close her eyes and join it.

It wasn't an option, though.

She hauled herself from the bed and pulled on her shoes. Running a brush through her hair, she braced herself for another long shift behind the bar and then cleaning glasses late into the night.

Sophie knew only too well she could not work for much longer. The baby was not due for another six weeks but her body was telling her that she needed to rest.

Where, though?

She had been so defiant when she had told her parents and the priest that she would provide for her baby but the truth was she had saved little. Her job covered board and meals but the wages after that were tiny.

As she walked out of the bedroom, there in the hallway was Pino.

He gave her the creeps the way he was always hanging around.

'I've been thinking,' he said as she headed down the stairs and he walked behind her. 'You're a good worker, perhaps you can stay on once the baby comes.'

'Stay on?' she turned at the bottom of the stairs and for a second, maybe two, she actually thought that Pino was being nice as he moved past her and unbolted the door.

'You can move your things into the front bedroom at the weekend. It's warmer there.'

It was the middle of January, and not cold as such, but it was wet and the building was damp—though it was not for that reason that Pino would have Sophie move her things.

The front bedroom was his.

Never.

But now the fight was over.

Sophie knew she would have to contact Bastiano.

Oh, she was more than aware that it took two to make a baby and he had responsibilities.

It was the extent to which he might meet them that broke her heart.

Sophie walked into the bar as the patrons trickled in. She knew most of their orders without asking, which was just as well for her mind was too busy for conversation.

Sophie knew that she had to leave.

And soon.

'Sophie!' Her name was being called from several directions and she poured their drinks but did not serve them with a smile.

There was an impatient drumming of fingers coming from the left.

He could wait.

Sophie had perfected ignoring an impatient patron until she was ready to serve.

'Can I help you?' Sophie finally asked the drumming fingers, yet before she had even looked up she was on high alert.

His nails were neat and manicured and there was an expensive scent that in this place was non-existent rather than rare.

Her eyes slowly lifted, taking in the tie and dark suit, and then she met the eyes she had ached to see yet had sought to avoid.

'Bastiano...'

Her mind was moving slowly, trying to tell her that it was possible that he had been passing by and had just stopped in for a drink, while at the same time knowing this place was light years away from anywhere that he would frequent.

'What can I get you?' she asked.

'I'd like to speak with you in private.'

His olive skin was pale and the scar on his cheek was so livid it looked as if it had been freshly seared into his flesh.

Sophie could taste his fury and she felt her chest constrict as his eyes looked down at her swollen stomach.

What she did not understand was that his fury was not aimed at her.

Bastiano had been observing Pino—standing with his arms folded behind the bar and watching Sophie work. Not only had Pino's laziness incensed Bastiano, he had also seen the roaming of his eyes.

He wanted Sophie out of here.

'I'm working,' she told him, playing for time, for, even after many months preparing for a moment such as this one, still Sophie was none the wiser as to what to say, and so, of course, she said the wrong thing. 'What can I get you?'

'Sophie!' he warned. 'I want to speak to you now, outside.'

'She already told you—she's working.'

Bastiano did not even look over as Pino spoke on. 'I think it's time for you to leave.'

The bar fell silent.

Pino's voice signalled danger and, after all, there was a stranger in town.

A slick, suited stranger and she watched as Pino looked out of the window at Bastiano's rather flash car. It was clear to all that he did not belong here.

'I'm not going anywhere,' Bastiano said, and as he did so he looked right into Sophie's eyes. 'Until we have spoken.'

'Bastiano…' she attempted, and her voice came out a little high and strained. 'Not now.'

She wanted to warn him not to make a scene here, for she had seen more than her share of trouble within these walls.

'You heard her,' Pino said, and then made an already tense situation a hundred times worse for he came over and put an arm around her shoulders.

Sophie shrugged him off but the damage was more than done.

To Sophie, apart from on that terrible morning, Bastiano had always been kind, but she saw the other side to him now.

He did not explode; instead, it was far worse. It was as if the bar had been placed in refrigeration.

She could almost see the white of Bastiano's breath when he spoke for his words were pure ice.

'Sophie,' he said. 'Go and wait in the car.'

She would be angry with Bastiano later.

Right now she simply wanted out.

But she wanted him to follow her out because she knew how rough the bar's patrons could be.

'We'll speak outside,' she suggested.

'No,' Bastiano corrected her, though his eyes never left Pino's face. 'You go and wait in the car and I shall collect your things.'

Bastiano lifted the flap of the bar and Sophie walked out. The patrons parted as the one lady present left; when she was inside his vehicle, with a bleep, Bastiano locked her in safely.

He was angry with good reason for he knew she had been too scared to give this man as a reference.

Bastiano knew *exactly* his type.

Uninvited and most unwelcome, he walked behind the bar and into the hallway.

Pino followed him.

Bastiano climbed the stairs and found the cupboard Pino called a room—and no doubt charged Sophie half her wages to live in.

It took two minutes to clear it.

There was an old wooden wardrobe that held a couple of skirts and a bag that felt like it held some shoes. The chest of drawers contained just as little and Bastiano had soon packed her things. He went into the bathroom and picked up her brush and make-up and pulled down all the underwear that dripped over the bath. Not because Sophie would be needing them, for soon she would have much finer things, more because he could not stand that Pino had seen them.

He went back to the room and looked under the bed and found another pair of shoes and then he lifted the mattress and found her purse and a small leather journal. He had been poor once too, and he knew all the tricks.

'She owes me two weeks' notice.' Pino was at the door, watching his every move.

Bastiano said nothing, but as he stuffed Sophie's belongings into the bag the journal fell open and there, pressed between the pages, was a rose. *His* rose.

'I said…' Pino continued, but that single rose was Bastiano's undoing and he pressed the man against the wall.

'You make me sick,' Bastiano told him, and then he told him something else. 'Lucky for you she has her own room because if I find out you have so much as touched her, I suggest you sleep with one eye open.'

Pino seemed to recognise the ferocity in Bastiano's threat, so he put his hands up and Bastiano let him go.

He walked down the steps and out through bar with her bag over his shoulder; there were many fools present but not one game enough to speak out.

Or rather there was one fool.

From the safety of the top of the steps Pino had the last word.

'At least I gave her shelter. Where were you?'

Sophie watched from the car and she waited for the sound of a fight yet it was all eerily quiet and then, to her confusion, as calm as anything, Bastiano walked out.

He unlocked the car and climbed in, throwing her bag into the back and fighting to contain his temper as Pino's words replayed in his head.

'You had no right to charge in—' Sophie started, but Bastiano broke in.

'Is it my baby?'

'You know it is.'

'Then I had every right.'

He wanted to pull off hard, to leave some rubber in his wake, yet he had never driven with a pregnant woman beside him before. 'Why didn't you come to me?' He didn't get it, he truly did not, and was doing his best to contain his temper as he drove. 'You came to the Old Convent looking for work and yet chose to return here. Why?'

'Because I found out you owned it,' Sophie said. 'I didn't want you to know.'

'Why?' Bastiano demanded, but then gave in. Now was not the time for a row. He wanted her in Casta, he wanted her rested and fed.

'We'll talk back at the Old Convent.'

'What will your staff think when I arrive?'

'I have no idea,' Bastiano said, 'neither do I care.'

'Well, I do,' Sophie retorted, and now she too was angry. 'Are you intent on ruining every job I get?'

'Don't worry, Sophie, you will never have to work again.'

'I never used to worry about going to work,' Sophie said. 'I loved my job.'

She had, Bastiano knew that.

'Why didn't you come to me?' he asked again. 'I know I'm a bastard…'

'I never said you were.'

She hadn't.

They were coming to the stretch of road where he had witnessed Maria's crash.

The convent was visible in the distance as they drove in angry silence.

'It's beautiful,' Sophie commented as they passed a humble little church in golden limestone with a small bell tower.

Bastiano glanced over—pretty certainly wasn't the word that came to his mind as they drove past, for behind the church was the graveyard that held only dark memories for him.

'I'm glad you think so, given we'll be there in a couple of weeks.'

'Excuse me?'

'We should marry before the baby is born…'

Should.

That single word said it all.

She would be his wife by duty and nothing more.

It was the real reason that she had chosen not to tell him and had done her very best to go it alone.

Bastiano was right.

They were the same.

She had known exactly what his response would be.

Sophie looked over at him, a man who, when she'd met him, had been considering marrying a woman he had never even dated.

'You would take more care choosing an apple from the tree than in choosing a wife.'

'I don't pick apples.' Bastiano shrugged. 'They come to me peeled and sliced.'

'You know what I mean.'

The car was approaching the entrance to the convent now and Bastiano did not need to buzz. The gates sensed his car and slowly opened as they approached.

'You don't have to marry me, Bastiano,' Sophie said as the car idled, and she did not meet his gaze as he turned and briefly looked at her then offered his response.

'Where we come from, Sophie,' Bastiano responded as the car moved off, 'I do.'

CHAPTER THIRTEEN

THEY BOTH CHOSE to leave it there.

It was dark and late and, though she did not say it, there was certain relief as the car came out from the tunnel the trees provided and the Old Convent loomed close.

The old building really was a comforting sight.

'Where are we going?' Sophie asked as the car veered away from the main convent and took a cobbled path that led towards the ocean.

'Did you think I would put you in the cells?'

A small laugh, which Sophie hadn't known she had left in her, escaped. 'I honestly wouldn't mind.'

'Well, instead you are being sent to seclusion.'

'Sounds good to me.'

The car pulled up at the front of a large sprawling building and she thought of days gone by when the nuns must have come here on retreat. Thankfully nobody jumped out to open the car doors. In fact, Bastiano fetched her bag and carried it to the main door, which he opened.

'This is where you live?' Sophie checked as she stepped in for, even before she had properly looked, it was clear that this was a home.

'It is.'

'I thought you said I was being sent to seclusion.'

'This used to be it,' Bastiano told her. 'It is my favourite space.'

She could see why; it was, for want of a better word, stunning.

The stone walls held all the charm of yesteryear and there were unspoiled views of the ocean from the huge lounge and likely most of the rooms too. The furnishings were modern, though they blended in with the surroundings, and there was a huge leather couch that Sophie ached to simply stretch out on, but she was far from ready to be living with him.

'I want to be alone.'

'I thought you might. In fact, I was thinking of putting you into one of the more secluded suites we keep for royals and such.'

'Then why didn't you?'

Bastiano answered with a question. 'How long until you are due?'

'A couple of months—the end of March.'

'That's only six weeks away.' Bastiano said. 'And time apart doesn't seem to serve us well.'

She was exhausted, he could see, and it was not fair to discuss it tonight.

'I'll show you to your room.'

Sophie eyes widened, just a fraction but enough for Bastiano to see.

'I'm not a complete bastard, Sophie.'

'I never said you were remotely one.'

She never had, Bastiano recalled, as she followed him down a long corridor.

'You really can relax here,' he explained. 'You have your own pool…'

'Did the nuns used to swim?'

'No,' Bastiano said. He was in no mood to smile at one of her jokes, yet he almost did. 'I had them put in.'

It was such a far cry from anything she was used to.

Oh, it might once have been a place for deep contemplation and it would serve as the same now, only with a bed that looked like a cloud and a bathroom so huge that she might need a map to locate the exit.

'Do you want to eat with me?' He offered her a choice.

'No.'

'Then I shall have Karmela bring you supper and come and unpack your things.'

'I think I can manage that,' Sophie said. 'There's not much.'

'We'll sort that out soon.'

'I don't want you dressing me.'

'Fine.' Bastiano shrugged. 'Is there anything you need?'

'No.' Sophie shook her head and then, when she guessed he might feel it was his job to entertain her, she gave a tight smile. 'I might just have a bath and go to sleep.' There was, though, one question that she had for him. 'How did you find out,' Sophie asked, 'about the baby?'

'I told you, I found out you had come here looking for work.' He omitted to mention the frantic feeling that had prompted him to call Alim.

'I wanted something that was live-in.'

'How did your parents take it?'

'As I expected them to. We haven't spoken for a long time but last week they asked me over for dinner…'

'That's good.'

'Not really. The priest was there to tell me about a lovely couple who would give my baby everything that I couldn't.'

He didn't need to guess what her response had been.

'I'm tired, Bastiano.' She really was. Yes, tonight she was supposed to have been working, but now she felt as if she had been unplugged from a fading battery and her energy had simply run out. 'Can this wait until morning?'

'Of course.'

To show Sophie how it all worked, he clicked on the intercom and was put straight through to Karmela.

'Could you send a light supper to the guest room?' he asked.

'Of course,' came the response. 'Anything else?'

'I'll just check.' He looked at Sophie, who shook her head. 'That will be all.'

'She'll be over soon,' he told Sophie.

'Thanks.'

'We can speak tomorrow night.'

'Tomorrow night?'

'I have to work. I lost a day today.'

'Sorry about that.'

Her sarcasm was wasted, for he had already gone.

It wasn't just Sophie who needed to be alone.

Bastiano too wanted to process the events of today. As soon as he had found out about the baby he had jumped in his car. The usual three-hour trip had taken two and he had been more focused on the practical—getting her out of the hell hole where she had lived and, yes, putting things right as speedily as could be arranged.

He poured a drink and lay on the bed, trying to wrap his head around the fact that he would soon be a father.

And that, had he not found out for himself, he might never have known.

He heard a car pull up outside and guessed that Sophie's supper was there.

Bastiano had no appetite.

A baby!

He had never considered fatherhood. When he had vaguely considered taking a wife his thought process had halted there.

In fact, he had heard a few weeks ago that Raul and Lydia were expecting and had silently thanked his lucky stars for the escape.

Bastiano lay there brooding for an hour at least, watching his bachelor life disappear before his eyes.

A knock on the door had him look up and there stood Sophie, her hair wet from a bath or shower and wrapped in a guest robe.

'Did you pack my pyjamas?'

'I packed everything that was there.'

'No, my pyjamas were under the pillow.'

'Well, I didn't go looking under your pillow! Who the hell wears pyjamas anyway?'

'I shared a bathroom with Pino,' Sophie said.

'Fair enough.' He nodded to his wardrobe. 'Take a shirt if you want one, though I've got my own bathroom and I shan't be peeping through the door.'

She smiled.

And not for the first time today.

But, then, that was what she did. Even in the middle of a row, there were some smiles.

And he returned it.

'I meant a clean one,' Bastiano said as she picked up his shirt from the floor.

'This will be fine. I hate starch.' And then she asked him something. 'It's your birthday?'

'How do you know?'

'Karmela said something when she brought my meal. You should have said.' Sophie gave a sweet smile. 'I'd have sent you flowers. But then again it might have given a mixed message.'

'Ha-ha,' Bastiano said, but as she walked off he had a parting shot. 'There will be no mixed messages from me.'

Good, Sophie thought, because sex was the last thing she needed to complicate things.

'Buon Compleanno.' Sophie shrugged and turned for the door, but it was Bastiano who had the last word.

'I still want you.'

No, he didn't deal in mixed messages.

To his own surprise, Bastiano's desire for her remained.

CHAPTER FOURTEEN

SOPHIE HAD NO excuse for not sleeping well.

The supper had been delicious, her bath relaxing and the bed, when she had finally lain down on it, had felt like a cloud.

It was Bastiano who had unnerved her, though in the nicest of ways.

It had never entered her head that this far into pregnancy, and with so much to sort out, there would be such fierce attraction between them.

Sophie swung her feet to the floor and instead of cheap lino she felt the warmth of a thick rug. His home was so warm that there was no need to pull on a robe.

It was early, just before six, and she decided to go and get some milk and bring it back to bed.

She didn't expect to find him in the kitchen, dressed only in trousers and waiting for the percolator to fill.

'I thought you'd have your coffee brought to you in bed.'

'Not when I am here,' Bastiano said. 'I hate conversation in the morning.'

Sophie helped herself to some milk.

'How much prenatal care have you had?'

Always he surprised her. Sophie hadn't thought it the type of question he would ask so casually.

'I thought you didn't like conversation in the morning?'

'Some things have to be checked.'

'Not much,' she admitted.

'We have a doctor that visits daily. I'll get him to call in on you, though I think you should have the baby in Rome.'

'Rome?' Sophie gave an incredulous smile at his suggestion. 'Isn't there a hospital here?'

'Yes but you're not having the baby in Casta.' Bastiano shook his head.

'*I'll* decide where I'm having my baby.'

'*Our* baby,' he countered, but then he halted. He did not want to descend into a row but there was no way she was having the baby here. 'I'll have the doctor visit.'

'Well, let me know when,' Sophie said. 'I want to go into Casta. I need a few things for me as well as the baby. I was thinking of going to the market today.'

'In Casta?' He gave her an appalled look but Sophie just shrugged.

'You're turning into a snob, Bastiano.'

'I turned into one long ago,' Bastiano said. 'You are not dressing my baby from the Casta market. We'll speak tonight.'

He really didn't like conversation in the morning, Sophie thought, because without another word he took his cup and left her alone in the huge kitchen. Sophie headed back to bed and lay there watching the morning arrive over the ocean.

Yesterday's rain had gone, revealing a mild Sicilian winter's day.

Her favourite kind.

It didn't matter that she had hardly anything to wear because the morning was spent wrapped in a thick white robe.

The doctor came and he put her at ease straight away.

'It is busy over there!' He gave an eye-roll in the direction of the main building as he examined her. 'It is nice to have a straightforward pregnancy to take care of.'

'It doesn't feel very straightforward.'

'There is one baby, a healthy mother and a nice-sized baby. That's good news to me.'

She was thrilled to find out that the baby was a good size given her meals had been somewhat sparse.

'What do you deal with over there?' Sophie asked as he took blood to test. Since Karmela had mentioned a confidentiality clause, she had been dying to know what went on over at the Old Convent, but the doctor wasn't about to reveal anything.

'That would be telling tales. Believe me, young Sophie, you don't want to know.'

'But I do.'

After he had taken some blood, they discussed her having an ultrasound.

'Bastiano asked me to refer you to a colleague in Rome.'

'I haven't decided where I'm having the baby yet.'

'Well, without stating the obvious, I suggest you both work it out because babies keep to their own schedules. You could go into labour tonight and then the choice will be out of both your hands.' He gave her a lovely smile. 'Don't worry if you do, though, I've delivered a lot of babies.'

'It would be you who would deliver me?'

'It would be my privilege to.'

Sophie liked him.

He had salt-and-pepper hair and was patient with her endless questions; he didn't make her feel stupid or small.

And he was the first person who seemed genuinely pleased about the baby.

The rest of the morning was spent being pummelled by the resident masseuses, after which she sat on a lounger by the pool, so warm in her robe it was no surprise that she dozed off.

'Hey.'

She woke to his voice and looked up to a suited Bastiano.

'Is there no such thing as privacy?' Sophie asked.

'Privacy is not going to get us very far,' Bastiano said. 'I'm not going to be back until late tonight; work has piled up. What did the doctor say?'

'That everything is going very well.'

'What else?'

'He took some blood.'

'And?'

Sophie knew exactly what he was there for. Bastiano wanted to ensure that his instructions had been carried out.

Well, two could play at that game.

'He said that I am to go for an ultrasound in Casta tomorrow and that he would be thrilled to deliver me.'

She was surprised that he laughed.

So was he.

'You are such a liar.' Bastiano said.

He idly picked up the tie of her robe and as he did, the back of his hand brushed the baby bump beneath and then he turned so that his palm rested on the thick fabric.

'Sophie, please don't have the baby here. I couldn't stand it if anything went wrong.' He could feel the swell beneath his palm and then he looked up at Sophie and knew he simply could not bear it if something happened to either of them. 'If I can wrap things up here we can move into a hotel for a few weeks. Get married there...'

'In a hotel?'

'It's just a formality.' Even Bastiano knew he had said the wrong thing and he cursed himself as she removed his hand. The closeness that had almost appeared slipped back like the tide. 'Okay, we can get married in a church, I'm sure there are a few to choose from in Rome! I just don't want it to be born a bastard.'

'It's the twenty-first—'

'I'm aware of the century,' Bastiano interrupted. 'I want us married before the baby arrives.'

'I don't want to marry you,' Sophie said. 'I don't want a husband who doesn't love me.'

And she loathed that she fished, that she actually threw him a line, one that she hoped would see him pull her into his arms and tell her that of course that wasn't the case.

But Bastiano had long ago decided that his love was a dangerous gift and so he was rather caustic in his reply. 'It stopped being about you when you forgot to take your Pill.'

'Why couldn't I get pregnant by some bastard who just wrote me a cheque?'

'Do you really see us co-parenting, Sophie?' he asked. 'Do you think I am going to smile and nod at your new lover when I pick my child up for an access visit?'

'You could try.'

'If you wanted that then you should have found some new-age guy. I'm traditional. I'm Sicilian, for goodness' sake!'

'I want our child to grow up in a loving—'

'I can be loving.'

'I'm not talking about sex,' Sophie said.

Bastiano was.

He wanted to break the embargo and peel off her robe. Quite simply he was certain this was a dispute best settled in bed.

It was black-and-white to him.

'I want more from marriage,' Sophie said. 'I ran away because it wasn't love…'

'You ran away from a man who relied on your mother to cook for him,' Bastiano said, 'and now you have to settle for a virile billionaire. Boo-hoo.'

He stood and she lay there staring out at the ocean rather than look at him.

They were getting nowhere, Bastiano knew.

He had tried reason, he had tried religion, now he decided it was time to fall back on ways of old.

'How about we go out for dinner tonight?'

'I thought you had work.'

'I'll cancel it. We're going to go out tonight.'

'Are you asking me or telling me?' Sophie checked, and she saw the tightening of his jaw.

She was acting like a sulking princess, Sophie knew.

'We never did have our night out.'

'No,' Sophie said, 'I was too busy stealing your ring…'

'Sophie…' He halted but then he pushed himself to speak on. 'I know you didn't steal it.'

'Do you, now? And how's that?' She desperately wanted him to reply that it was because he knew she would never do that kind of thing. But he didn't.

'We'll speak tonight at dinner. I have a lot of work to get through but I should be through by five so be ready.'

'Five?' Sophie frowned. 'So early?'

'If I could have my PA reschedule the sun I would,' Bastiano said.

'Meaning?'

'I'll see you at five,' he told her. 'And please,' he added, 'do not buy anything from the market to wear! Your regular rags will do!'

He left her smiling.

In her worst mood, somehow he had made her smile.

And, he made her skin prickle.

Oh, the attraction had not faded for her, not a fraction, yet surely it must have for him.

It didn't feel as though it had.

A car drove her down the hill and it was indeed market day, for Casta was busy and it was nice to wander around.

There were signposts for the infirmary, where Bastiano was adamant that their baby would not be born. She passed a school and smiled at the sound of children's laughter.

There was the old courthouse, where Bastiano had told her Maria's will had been read.

It really was gorgeous, with an old hotel that had seen better days and a street lined with shops and cafés.

And it was exciting too because there were a couple of famous faces behind dark glasses in the café that Sophie went into, no doubt on day release from the Old Convent.

The owner greeted her warmly. 'Passing through?'

'No, I'm staying at the Old Convent.' Sophie smiled.

'Ah, a guest of Signor Conti.' The owner smiled. 'Then we need to find you a nice seat.'

He called to a waitress and she was guided to a table near the back. 'For you,' the owner said, and he brought her a large glass of hot blackcurrant without Sophie even looking at the menu. 'It is our house special and good for you,' he told her. 'And don't worry, no one will trouble you here, we'll keep an eye open.'

It took a moment or two to register that they thought she must be a *client*.

Bastiano really had done wonders, Sophie thought, for, unlike home, the town was a buzzing and happy place to be.

Sophie headed over to the church that had caught her eye when she had first passed through town.

It must be here that he had fought with Raul, Sophie guessed, and she slipped around the back to the graveyard and read the inscriptions on the tombstones.

Gino Di Savo.

Raul's father, Sophie knew, and saw that he had died some ten years ago.

Next to him lay Maria, and Sophie wondered about the mind of a woman who would seduce a seventeen-year-old.

And then she turned and Sophie found what she was looking for. There she found out Bastiano's mother's name.

Philomena Conti.

Sophie felt her nostrils tighten when she saw the simple grave.

And then she saw the date of her death and Sophie did not even try to hold back the tears.

Philomena had died on the day that Bastiano was born.

Had Karmela not let on that it was his birthday yesterday, she might never have known. She understood the man a little more, and he was kinder than even she had given him credit for—even in their rows about their baby he had not scared her by telling her that his mother had died giving birth.

It was a sobering thought indeed.

And it was time, Sophie knew, to stop fighting.

She did have something to wear.

One thing.

Sophie stood in the little silver knickers she had purchased on the day Rosa had persuaded her try on the dress.

The over-dress she could not even get over her bust, but the silver-grey underdress slid on.

It clung to every curve, yet somehow it revealed little, for it fell to just on her knee and there was barely even a glimpse of cleavage.

It was incredibly seductive, though.

For the first time in months Sophie added heels and though she had very little make-up to work with, she melted her mascara under a hot tap in order to reach the last dregs and used a pen to dig out some lipstick.

Soon she saw his car approaching and Sophie was suddenly nervous. She felt overdressed for Casta and the small restaurants there.

Hell, she felt overdressed for five o'clock in Rome.

'Sophie!' Bastiano called out.

He wondered if she'd plead a headache to avoid dinner, but instead she stepped out confidently.

Bastiano had thought her like the sun on the day they'd met.

Now a silver star emerged before the sky had even darkened.

Her dress clung tightly to the baby they had made and her legs seemed too fragile.

'Where are we going?' Sophie asked when he bypassed the car.

'We're walking.'

Along the cobbled path on very high heels there was little choice but to take his arm.

It was nice to walk.

'Am I overdressed?' she asked as they approached the convent.

'Perhaps,' he said, 'but only because I prefer you in nothing.'

It was nice to flirt, but as they headed towards the restaurant nerves caught up.

'Will there be a lot of people?'

'I have twenty guests in residence,' Bastiano said as they walked in. 'And on my instruction, all are dining in their rooms tonight.'

Oh, it was heaven.

The tables were all candlelit and each candle had been lit for her. Even the stone walls were softened with thick white pillar candles but Bastiano steered her to the balcony. It had been dressed with care and a single table had been set up just for them.

'It is cool,' Bastiano said, 'even with heaters…'

'You're not eight months pregnant,' Sophie countered as she took a seat. 'I've forgotten what it is to be cool.'

'There's no wine list,' Bastiano said as he ordered bitter lemon for them both. 'My regular guests have no restraint.'

He made her laugh.

And then he made her want to cry.

'I owe you an apology,' Bastiano said, and he was suddenly serious. 'I was wrong to accuse you of taking my ring. I overreacted that morning. It was my mother's ring, it meant everything to me, and I had only just got it back from Raul.'

'From Raul?' Sophie frowned. 'Why did he have it?'

'I gave it to Maria.' He felt uncomfortable admitting it. 'She was wearing it when she died and all her jewellery was left to Raul. I don't think he even knew it was mine.'

'How did he find out?'

'When he asked for Lydia's address I said I would only give it to him if he returned the ring.'

Now she better understood his reaction that morning. It must have been hell to get it back, only to lose it.

'It was Inga who put the ring in your uniform.'

'Inga?' Sophie frowned. 'Did she confess?'

'Please,' Bastiano sneered, 'she has no conscience, she was still blaming you as they escorted her out.'

And he told her how Inga had shouted and sworn as she'd been walked out, remembering Sophie's quiet dignity in the same situation.

'I had Dario and Benita go over the CCTV footage. Inga must have…' He hesitated. He didn't want to embarrass her because he had realised that Inga would have heard them making love so he softened it a touch. 'She would have seen your uniform on the floor.'

It *was* cool outside; despite the heaters there was a chill from the ocean but the air suddenly seemed to blow warm on her skin as she recalled that morning and met his eyes.

'Do you think she heard us?'

'Who cares?'

'I do,' Sophie said, completely appalled. 'Though I shouldn't—she sleeps with guests.'

'That's shocking.' Bastiano pretended to shudder and then laughed. 'Thank God for the Ingas of the world.'

'You're terrible, Bastiano!'

'Oh, indeed I was.'

And instead of being cross, Sophie smiled and then she laughed because her name had been cleared, and it was the best feeling in the world.

Or amongst the best of feelings, because he was looking at her in that way again, a way that made her feel warm, a way that made the tiredness disappear and her body feel sensual and alive.

A waiter came out with a loaf of *mafalda*, which they tore and dipped in oil.

'The Contis and the Di Savos should have focused on making oil rather than feuding over wine,' Bastiano told her as they dipped their bread. 'They would have made their fortune.'

'The Contis and the Di Savos need to stop feuding, period,' Sophie said, referring to him and Raul.

'I agree.'

He was tired of it.

'Lydia is expecting too,' Bastiano told her.

'Your *almost* wife.'

She looked at him and knew that unrequited love was such a curse.

'The bread is fantastic,' Sophie said, to change the subject. She wondered if this would be her life, moving from topics to avoid hurt. Discussing the weather and the food on the table, rather than the hole he had shot through her heart.

'You can't get better than here,' Bastiano responded.

'Not true,' Sophie said. 'The chef at the Grande Lucia made the best…'

'Can I tell you something?' Bastiano said, and leant closer. She met his eyes and she knew she was in the path of a seducer, for his mouth had that smile and his eyes made her burn, and instead of fighting him Sophie let herself be played, for there were worse things she could think of than being seduced by Bastiano.

'Tell me,' she said, and tore another strip of bread.

'I stole the chef from the Grande Lucia. He is the one cooking for us tonight.'

'You stole Alim's chef?' She started to laugh.

A real laugh, because so skilled was she that at times she forgot his game.

'Of course. When I withdrew my offer I had my PA contact your chef with an offer he could not refuse. Now, instead of feeding the hordes in Rome, he has a maximum guest list of twenty-two to cater for. Staff too…'

'Your staff get meals?'

'Of course.'

'Five-star meals?' Sophie asked, as in front of her was placed a dish of *busciate*, Sicily's finest pasta dressed in a light almond sauce.

'Everyone deserves to be looked after,' Bastiano said. 'Not just the guests. That is why my retreats work so well.'

'It's amazing,' Sophie said. 'You should be very proud.'

'I am,' Bastiano said. 'People accuse me of bulldozing treasures but that is because I don't allow the interiors to be photographed—I don't need the publicity. The retreats I offer are for the guests to enjoy.'

And tonight that pleasure was exclusive to Sophie.

Tiny lights started to dance as dusk fell and she found out what he had meant about not being able to reschedule the sun, for it had turned to fire and was mirrored in the ocean.

'Dance?' Bastiano said as soft music came on.

It had been months since they had been in each other's arms, and so much had changed, yet they melded together like they had never been apart. Sophie wrapped her arms around his neck, swaying in his arms.

He looked right into her eyes and then she closed her eyes to his kiss.

She had forgotten the taste of perfection.

How with that mouth he made magic.

How the heat from his palm in the small of her back made her fingers press into the back of his head. And how the feel of him aroused her and could make her forget her cares.

She felt feverish, being held by him, dancing with him, being seduced by him.

His kiss was perfection.

It made her crave him and it made her feel weak.

'Why do you resist us?' Bastiano asked.

In his arms, she didn't know the answer to that.

'Come on,' he told her. 'I'm taking you home.'

CHAPTER FIFTEEN

THEY WALKED IN the dark but the moon was bright and the stars lit the night. They held hands as if they had been lovers for life.

'I love it here,' she said, because it was far safer than saying 'I love you'. She kept things light, determined not to reveal the ache in her heart. 'I went to one of the cafés in town and they thought I was one of your clients,' Sophie admitted, and she started to laugh. 'I'm trying to work out what they thought I was in rehab for.'

'They would have thought you were the partner of an errant actor,' Bastiano said. 'We sometimes have wives and girlfriends take a little holiday while their husbands straighten out.'

'Really?' she asked, as they reached the door and he gave her a light kiss, but one that made her toes curl.

'Really.'

'Who?'

'I can't tell you that,' Bastiano said.

They were stood at the door and she could hear the waves, and she knew that this was the moment.

'At least not until you marry me.'

Bastiano did it by the book.

Well, he didn't go down on bended knee but he took

out a black box and her throat was tight as he opened the clasp.

And there it was.

The proof that he did not love her.

Oh, the ring was stunning.

A diamond so huge that if she reached out and plucked a star from the sky it would surely sparkle just as brightly.

And in that moment she knew she would never matter to him the way she wanted to, because it wasn't the ring that meant everything to him.

'Isn't there something missing here, Bastiano?'

He knew exactly what she was referring to.

'Do you know why people think I'm such a bastard?' he said, and when she didn't answer he told her. 'Because I don't say things that other people want to hear.'

It was a terrible proposal because a big salty tear fell to her cheek. 'Sometimes it's kinder to lie,' she said.

'Not in this.'

If they were going to be honest, she would tell him how much this hurt. 'You gave Maria your mother's ring.'

'And look how that ended up!' He did not understand that she would choose his mother's cursed ring over the diamond he had selected with such care. 'I threw away the old ring,' Bastiano told her. 'It was bad news.'

And he was so cold, Sophie thought, that he could dispose of the thing most valuable to his heart.

Where the hell would that leave her and their child? But then he told her something, something honest and true.

'I will do everything to make our marriage work. I will read every book so that I can be the best father I can possibly be…' Yet still he saw tears. 'Sophie…' He told her the real truth. 'Believe me, you don't want my love.'

With a sob, she brushed past him and rushed straight to her room.

Believe me, she wanted to shout out, *I do*.

Instead, she stood with heart hammering and a body still alive from his touch and his kiss, loathing this one-sided love while knowing it was time to step up.

Of course they would marry.

Bastiano would be a wonderful father and even without his love it could be a wonderful marriage too, for she knew he cared for her.

He had proved it today, for even when arguing he looked out for her—not once had he hinted that his mother had died giving birth.

Bastiano was kinder and fairer than he knew and she knew she loved him.

And there was desire.

Such desire.

So she was stuck with the virile billionaire.

Boo-hoo!

Even with a heart breaking, just the thought of him made her smile. She wanted a slice of that dark, guarded heart, even if it could never be hers to own entirely. Sophie was starting to understand that there was a side to Bastiano she would never be allowed to know.

That privilege had been Maria's and she was through trying to compete with a ghost.

All she could be was herself.

And she would make her own rules.

She kicked off her shoes because they hurt, but it meant that her approach to his room was silent.

Bastiano lay on the bed with his hands behind his head, just as she had first found him, only he was dressed and sulking now.

'If we marry,' Sophie said, and Bastiano looked over to

where she stood at the door, 'it is to be here. If our child is going to be raised in Casta then I want to be married in the church. It is more than a formality to me.'

'Sophie...'

'Let me finish. If we are to marry then there is to be compromise. We can fly out straight after the service. I know it will take a couple of weeks to arrange...'

'I'll sort it,' Bastiano said.

He would.

'You just need a dress and to turn up.'

They would be married in the next forty-eight hours if it meant they could get the hell out of Casta and to the shiny equipment and slick obstetrician he had planned.

'I'll move out tomorrow,' he told her.

'Move out?' Sophie gave a laugh. 'It's a bit late for that.'

'In that case, come here.'

And there was a burn in his eyes that made her both excited and nervous at the same time. 'Should we wait for the wedding?'

'Do I look like Luigi?' he asked.

'No.' Sophie smiled and came over.

She sat down on the bed, as she had on the morning they had met. His hand found hers and then he felt the ripe swell of her stomach.

He could feel the kicks their baby gave and it was both mind-blowing and then calming because while inside her their baby was safe.

'I'm going to take such good care of you both.'

His voice was husky and thick with emotion and even if it wasn't love she knew his words came from the heart.

'I know that.'

Just as she had on that very first day, she leant over only this time she went straight for his mouth.

It was a deep and sensual kiss but an unhurried one, and he guided her so that she sat on his stomach.

'Back again,' he told her.

Only now there was a baby between them and a wedding to arrange. It was both the saddest and happiest night of her life.

Sophie could see the glint of her ring as she undid his tie and opened his shirt. She bent her head and they kissed long and slow, his hands sliding over the silver dress.

'I found out I was pregnant on the day I got this,' she said as he found the tiny, invisible zipper she had failed to spot when she had first tried it on.

He slid the zipper down and then pulled the dress up and over her head. Her breasts were full and encased in lace, and he stroked them through the fabric, then tipped her forward so he could taste with his mouth.

His fingers unclipped it and with it hanging on her arms his mouth met her flesh. It was the touch of a tongue that could make her weep and the nip of teeth that could have her beg.

So wanting was she that her sex was on his hands as he dealt with his belt and zipper and then there was the giddy bliss of him guiding her on.

'You and me,' he said, but did not finish.

Not because he did not want to say things at night that would fade with the dawn but because his love, Bastiano was sure, was a toxic curse.

But when they were together, life seemed to work.

And right now they were together.

Sophie could feel the gentle guidance of his hands as he held her hips and the dig of his fingers in her buttocks as he fought to hold back.

Her thighs gripped him and she ground down, causing a shiver to run through her body, but it felt like fire as she met his eyes.

He thrust up into her softly engorged grip and she leant her hands on his chest. Now there was nothing to hold back, for he knew of her love and so she cried his name when she came.

And he moved her then at whim and shot high into her.

It was deeply intimate and the most intense climax of his life, laced as it was with her name.

They lay there afterwards with his hand on her stomach and she felt it roam across her bump.

'It's asleep,' she told him, and soon so was she.

In the deep of night the baby awoke.

Sophie didn't notice.

Bastiano did.

He felt the wave of movement beneath his palm and then an unmistakable kick and he knew he was holding the future.

Not just the baby's but Sophie's too.

And he would do all he could to give his baby's mother the wedding she deserved.

CHAPTER SIXTEEN

'*BUONGIORNO, SIGNOR.*'

Bastiano did not answer the cheery greeting.

The best room in the best hotel in Casta was nowhere close to the twelfth floor at the Grande Lucia. The maid ignored the flick of his wrist to dismiss her and instead set about opening the drapes.

'It's a beautiful day to get married,' she told him.

Thank goodness it was today!

Bastiano had been away from the Old Convent for two nights and he itched to get back.

Not literally.

The Casta Hotel wasn't that bad!

He missed home.

Only that wasn't right, because as soon as the wedding was over they were flying to Rome and he was looking forward to that.

It was being so close to the street that irked, Bastiano decided.

Bastiano had never missed anyone in his life, so he had not worked out yet that he simply missed his future bride.

The pall that had hung over him for months was back and surely it was not how a groom should feel on his wedding day.

A trophy wife would be easier, Bastiano thought as

he showered in less than sumptuous surroundings. Yes, a nice trophy wife would have demanded a high-class wedding instead of the local church.

He pulled on black jeans and a jumper but found that he was grinning as he wondered how Sultan Alim and Gabi were faring down the hall.

Certainly this was no palace.

Though he had agreed to a low-key wedding, Bastiano had decided that Sophie deserved more than the basics.

Her family would be there but so to would Gabi and Alim.

And it would seem the entire valley would join them too.

Word was out and the joy at the upcoming nuptials was genuine.

As well as that, a couple of A-list guests at the Convent had applied for day leave.

It was turning into the wedding of the year and Sophie had no clue.

He took a walk down to the baker's rather than think about why he was doing all this for her.

The church was dressed for the occasion with flowers and ribbons and, out of sentiment more than habit, Bastiano walked around the side to the cemetery.

Even if it was just a formality, it was, after all, his wedding day.

But as he turned the corner a man looked over and Bastiano felt his hackles rise.

Raul Di Savo.

Here, after all that had passed between them.

But this time Raul did not leap across tombstones to attack him; instead, he stood stock-still as this time it was Bastiano who made his way over.

'I'm guessing that you're not here for the wedding.'

'No, I only just heard about that.' Raul gave a tight smile. 'Today is my mother's birthday.'

'Oh,' Bastiano said, and his first thought was that Sophie might freak if she found out he had arranged that they marry on Maria's birthday.

Bastiano hadn't known, though.

He looked at the tombstone, just as he had many times, and sure enough Maria's birthdate was etched there.

'I hear you are soon to be a father,' Bastiano said, and Raul nodded.

'Lydia is back in Venice. She's due in a few weeks.'

'Sophie too.'

Bastiano turned and walked away and stood for a moment at his own mother's grave.

There was no peace to be had here.

Had she even known she had a son?

Today it mattered, because a few weeks from now he would have a child of his own and there was a sudden need to put things right, to end feuds of old. He could hear the crunch of gravel as Raul walked off, and then the more rapid crunch of his own footsteps as this time it was Bastiano who strode towards him.

'Raul!' he called out, and watched Raul's shoulders stiffen before he turned around.

'Why did you refuse to hear my side?' He stared at the man who had once been a friend. 'Was it because I wasn't family?'

For a moment Bastiano thought history was about to repeat itself, that he would again meet Raul's fist, and he had a brief vision of trying to explain why he had chosen today, of all days, to confront his nemesis…

Except there would be no fighting today.

'Not here,' Raul said. Together, they walked up the hill

and sat on the ground outside the convent, where as boys and young men they had wasted many days.

They sat at first in silence, but it was Raul who finally spoke. 'I didn't *want* to hear your side. It was easier to blame you…'

'I guess,' Bastiano said. He had learned from the cradle that family came first.

'I always covered for her.'

Now the trees rustled, now the bird song seemed to fade as Bastiano learned there had been others.

Many others.

And beneath his feet the earth seemed to shift and then resettle as he chased the thoughts around his mind.

'I know now you didn't go there to seduce her,' Raul said. 'I just wasn't ready to hear it at the time.' And then he looked Bastiano right in the eyes. 'I apologise. When I found out she had taken your ring…'

Bastiano was about to correct him, to say that she hadn't taken it, he had given it to her, but that had been a trick of his mind. A trick Maria had played well.

'If you love me you would want me to have nice things.'

It hadn't been love.

Maria had told him that it was, and with nothing with which to compare it, he'd believed her.

'My mother had many lovers. I don't even know if Gino was my father,' Raul admitted. 'He married her just because she was pregnant…'

'He did the right thing at least.'

'No.' Raul shook his head. 'He resented the hell out of us. No one should marry because…' He halted, perhaps unsure of Bastiano's circumstances.

'I love Sophie.'

He knew he should have told her first, but he had only just realised it himself.

Love *did* make you smile.

Because on the morning of his wedding, as he reshuffled the truths of his past, just the thought of her was a comfort. It was Sophie he missed, Bastiano knew, not the walls of home.

'I'm sorry,' Raul apologised again. 'I wasn't insinuating that you didn't love. I was just saying how things sometimes—'

'No,' Bastiano broke in. 'You're right. I haven't told Sophie.' He looked over to the Old Convent and thought of her preparing for her wedding and not knowing how he felt. 'In fact,' he told Raul, 'I told her that I never could love her.'

'Then you need to call her now.'

'Merda!' Bastiano said as he tossed his phone, and they might have been teenagers again, for Bastiano had his foot in Raul's hands and was trying to get a leg up to scale a wall, but there was glass and wire at the top—his security was good enough to keep out even the hungriest press. He had to get to Sophie.

'You need to get changed,' Raul said, when Bastiano had no choice but to give in. 'You get married soon.'

To a bride who didn't know he loved her.

CHAPTER SEVENTEEN

BASTARD!

Sophie sat in the back of the bridal car with her father and watched as the priest signalled for them to go around.

He was late for his own wedding!!

Perhaps that was why he had been calling, Sophie thought, trying to fight the tears that were threatening.

To call things off.

She took a deep breath as the car slowly drove up the hill and she wasn't sure if it was the tightening in her stomach that made her gasp or the sight of a very dishevelled groom running towards the church with, Sophie was sure, his nemesis beside him.

The priest was now all smiles since the groom had arrived. But as she stepped out another pain hit.

Thankfully both her father and the priest thought it was nerves and that she was merely composing herself when she reached the church door and stood silent for a moment.

The church was full, that was all she saw.

And she was in labour.

If Bastiano could be late for his own wedding Sophie was quite sure he would be only too willing to call the whole thing off if he knew.

And she wanted to be married now, before the baby arrived.

Which meant she just had to grin and bear it!

The pains weren't too bad, and they were ages apart; first babies took a long time, the doctor had told her.

So she walked down the aisle, and blinked as a very famous actress gave her an encouraging smile, and a rap artist too.

What was going on?

And there was Gabi and Alim, and her heart was on fire as she walked towards the man she loved and always would.

She let in the sun, Bastiano thought as she walked towards him.

Here, in this church, where there had been so much darkness and pain, it was awash with colours and smiles.

It was way too late for white, so her dress was cream, with pale mint-green edging, just like the tiny roses she wore in her hair.

She had chosen her dress and flowers as if all this time he had loved her and wooed her.

And so badly he did love her.

And when he said his vows they were heartfelt and right, and Bastiano knew he could never have made it with a trophy wife, for it would have been over with by now.

'I will love you all the days of my life,' he told her, and he stared deep into her eyes, but Sophie's were slightly narrowed with suspicion.

'I really do love you,' he whispered, as he slid the ring on her finger.

Please, don't lie, Sophie thought, for his words sounded heartfelt and she couldn't bear the illusion, not on her wedding day. Her words were the same, though she paused midway as a pain hit and he gripped her fingers tight.

Bastiano knew.

He had seen her standing at the entrance and had read the pain behind her smile. His instinct had been to call off the wedding, but he knew how important it was to her.

'Perhaps,' he said in a low voice to the priest, 'we can do the shorter form…'

It was indeed a quick service and the bells rang out in Casta as the bride and groom emerged.

The past was gone, Bastiano knew.

Almost.

He looked over to the cemetery where his mother lay and he wanted them out of the valley now and into the waiting helicopter.

There would be no cake for the bride and groom.

'Look!' Gabi was holding up a ring. 'Look what I found in the gravel!'

Was it a sign?

His mother's blessing?

Sophie certainly seemed to think so for she slipped the ring on her finger, and though he smiled and shook hands with the guests, Bastiano felt as if he had been drenched in ice.

'We'll go to the chopper,' he told her, but Sophie shook her head.

'I don't think there's time.'

'Sophie…' Fear clutched at his heart and all he could see was that damn ring on her finger, not the wedding band or the engagement ring he had given her but the one that meant death.

'Why don't you go to the infirmary and let them check her?' Gabi suggested. She was used to drama at weddings and keeping things under control. 'If they say there is time to transfer then you can go from there.'

'Good luck,' Raul said, and shook his hand. 'You deserve it.'

A car drove them through the valley and the short distance to the infirmary but Sophie had plenty of questions on the way.

'You were late.'

'I was trying to get to you.'

'How come Raul was your best man?'

Oh, how she wanted to know, but there was so much pain she gripped his hand tight and knew the world was going to have to wait.

The scent of the hospital made him feel ill.

They walked through the maternity unit and past the nursery where babies cried and to a very small delivery suite where it seemed a cast of thousands was gathered.

Well, actually, there were four, Bastiano counted, but he was not about to say what he had to with this audience present.

'Could I speak to my wife alone, please?'

'I'm having our baby here,' Sophie shouted, because she was so pleased to see her salt and pepper doctor and his kind smile. 'I don't want to go to Rome!'

'Signor...' A midwife who introduced herself as Stella asked if she could have a word outside.

She was elderly and kind as she told him there was no question that Sophie be transferred.

'She is soon to have the baby,' Stella said. 'Your wife is ready to push. You need to stay calm for Sophie.'

'I am calm,' he told her.

Bastiano was.

No one knew him.

No one really could.

For he had never allowed anyone to get close. It was a strange and unfamiliar sensation to want to draw Sophie close now.

Bastiano had accepted back in the car that their baby would soon be here and he was not about to add to the drama.

The midwife seemed to think otherwise.

'Bastiano,' Stella said, 'I was here when you were born and so I understand why you are worried for Sophie, but there isn't time to transfer her now...'

'There is time for me to speak with my wife alone, though?'

'For a moment, yes.'

'A moment is all I need.'

Sophie watched as he walked in and the doctors and nurses were called out and then Bastiano closed the door.

'I love you,' he told her.

'Bastiano...' she begged. 'Please, don't do this. You loved Maria.'

'No, she told me that I did and I had nothing to compare it to, and so I believed her. You were right, I was seventeen, and I had no idea what love was.

'I love *you*,' he said. 'Like I never have before or ever could another.'

He would never say such a thing to please someone else, Sophie knew that.

And so she knew it was the truth that she heard.

It was love, and she could feel its fierce embrace, a grip stronger than the pain that engulfed her.

Stella's encouragement was needed, for despite Sophie's slender frame it would seem that she grew big babies.

Bastiano's support was needed too, so he looked not at an emerald and seed pearl ring on her finger but deep into her eyes and told Sophie, when she was sure that she couldn't, that, yes, she could, and that with one more push their baby would be here.

'Make that two,' Bastiano said.

Yes, she grew big babies.

With broad shoulders and a long frame.

And Bastiano watched as his son unfurled and was delivered onto Sophie's stomach, his lusty cries filling the room.

'His father was the same.' Stella laughed as their baby refused to settle. 'I used to stay at the end of my shift to give him a cuddle.' She smiled as she helped Sophie to feed her baby and then there was calm.

He was such a beautiful baby, with long lashes and straight black hair, and finally the shock of his early entrance to the world turned to peaceful slumber in his mother's arms.

The hell of the last few months was gone.

'*Complimenti*, Signora Conti,' a domestic said as she brought in a very welcome meal.

'I can't get used to my name.' Sophie laughed as Bastiano held the baby and she ate brioche and drank warm milk laced with nutmeg.

'There are two names you have to get used to,' Bastiano said, gazing at his son. 'Have you decided on his yet?'

'No.'

She had never known such happiness and later in their little room on the maternity ward they watched the sun set over Casta on their wedding day and the birth day of their son.

'Here.'

Bastiano cracked open a bottle and Sophie had her first, long-awaited taste of champagne, smiling when Stella came in to check on them.

'You have had a lot of phone calls,' Stella informed then. 'There is a big party going on in town.'

'What time do you finish?' Bastiano asked.

'Midnight.'

Sophie handed Bastiano their baby, who was now content, and she watched as he placed him in the little Perspex cot.

'I'm tired,' Sophie said.

'Sleep.'

'You'll stay?'

'Of course.'

It was an exhausted sleep that she fell into and it was after midnight when she woke and there was a frantic moment because neither her baby nor Bastiano was there.

Sophie put on a gown and headed out, past the delivery suite, and she came to the nursery and saw Bastiano sitting there, their baby in his arms, talking with Stella.

She heard a cry from her baby and watched as Stella held out her arms and Bastiano handed him over.

They were talking, deep in conversation, and Stella looked in no rush to go anywhere, despite the fact her shift was over.

Something told Sophie not to approach. For Bastiano to be sitting talking so intently made her certain that Stella was saying something he might just need to hear.

She went back to her room and lay watching the moon drift across the sky and the surf crash onto the rocks. She hoped that there could be some resolution for her husband, for he had made his peace with the past, but there was so much still missing.

'Hey.'

It was a long time before he came back and his face was like marble in the moonlight, his scar vivid, and she could hear the strain in his voice, though he carried on as if everything was normal. 'He is hungry again.'

She fed their not so tiny baby and tried to work out a name for him.

'I can't decide,' Sophie said, when they had nailed it down to the final two. He slept in her arms and made little contented noises, barely murmuring when Bastiano took him and placed him in the cot.

Then he came back to the bed and took her in his arms, breathing in the scent of her hair, and a world that had gone off kilter tipped back to delicious normality again.

'Stella was with my mother when she had me.' He told her of the conversation he had had. 'I always thought she died giving birth but it wasn't until after…'

'So she knew she had had a son?'

She felt him nod and they held each other. 'She chose my name. It means respected man, and that was what she wanted for me, even though she was not married.'

'She chose appropriately,' Sophie said, for Bastiano was very respected in Casta now.

'Apparently, she had a heart attack, her blood pressure kept going up. During the birth she kept calling out for my father…' He was the closest in his life he had ever been to tears, but he fought them, and then he told her the truth he had just learnt. 'He couldn't come, of course, as he had a wife and son. I've just found out that Raul is my brother.'

She peeled herself from his arms and during a conversation where there were no smiles to be had, Sophie found one.

'Half-brother,' she said. 'There is a very important half, for Maria was not your mother.'

'No.' He smiled. 'Certainly not.'

And he told her what he had gleaned, for his mother had cried through the long delivery with the young student midwife.

'She and Gino were dating a little but she wanted to save herself for marriage. Maria decided she wanted Gino and gave him what my mother refused to. Maria got pregnant so he married her, but it would seem he had loved my mother all along. She gave in and slept with him and an affair commenced, but by then he had a wife and a son. He loved her, I think, he gave her this ring…'

'What about you?' Sophie asked. 'Did he love you?'

He let out a long breath. 'He blamed me for her death, and apparently he took one look at me and walked out.'

'Do you think Maria knew?'

'I think she seduced me the same way she seduced my father,' Bastiano said. 'I think I reminded her of him and to get back at her husband for not loving her, she left her money to his son…'

'And look what you did with it,' Sophie said.

For he had fought his way back to respect, and turned ruins into beauty.

They shared a kiss, and there was peace when he lay on the bed beside her. They stayed up to watch the night disappear and light fill the sky.

'Call Raul,' she told him.

'It's too early.'

'I would think this news is thirty-two years late.'

So she lay there and listened to Bastiano as he told Raul the news. That they were more than friends, and even as enemies they had been tied to each other and unable to walk away, for they were brothers.

Which meant there were more questions as they worked their way back into each other's lives.

'Yes,' Bastiano said, 'we have a name.' And he looked over at Sophie as he said his son's name out loud. 'Rafael.'

They had chosen appropriately for it meant God has healed.

He had.

EPILOGUE

THERE WAS NO place nicer for afternoon tea than at the Grande Lucia and Sophie did not have to be asked twice before she said yes.

Lydia and Raul were coming in from Venice and Gabi and Alim were in residence, so what better excuse than to fly to Rome and catch up with friends?

Ronaldo greeted them warmly and Anya waved. What bliss to sink into a leather chair and eat the pretty cakes and to laugh and catch up.

Raul and Lydia had a daughter, Serena, just a few days younger than her cousin Rafael, and little Lucia was a delight, the boss of the babies, they all agreed.

Oh, Sophie loved being back here.

There was a soothing familiarity to the place and she was thrilled that Gabi had persuaded Alim not to sell it.

It was almost a second home.

She looked over at Bastiano, who was holding their son, and to see him laugh at something Raul said made her heart swell.

Yes, Sophie was a thief for she had stolen his heart and she treated it with such tender care, as he did the same for hers in return.

Familia.

Absolutely.

They had been born to love each other, she was certain of that.

'Are you staying?' Gabi asked.

'Of course.' Sophie smiled. 'I just wish they hadn't fired Inga and she could serve me breakfast in bed.'

Oh, that would be perfect, but she could more than live without it.

It was a wonderful catch-up and afternoon tea stretched into dinner, so it was late in the night when Bastiano took Rafael through to the nursery and placed him in his crib while Sophie got ready for bed.

'Sophie,' Bastiano called to her, for she was taking ages and now that the baby was asleep it was time to crack open champagne.

'One moment.'

He poured two glasses and placed hers by the bed. The turndown service had been in and he was just about to get up from bed and open the drapes and shutters for the view when Sophie emerged from the bathroom.

She was wearing her old uniform and her hair was up in a messy bun. She always made him smile.

First she opened the drapes and the shutters and stood a moment to take in the view, and to take in her life, for it was everything she had hoped for and more.

'Get over here,' he told her.

'I'm just preparing the view for you, Signor Conti,' she told him, and turned around and smiled. 'Then I am going to make the bed...with you in it.'

Yes, the words were out, and she had let them out, and they were how she felt.

They loved each other so.

* * * * *

For the Ashprington Crew

Peter, Alice, Jo, Lyle and Io

I

He kneels before me like a penitent, face to the stone wall. The bag over his head means he can't see the indentations in the rock face, the last marks made by those ancient masons so long ago. Their chisels built these caves, a million million strikes chipping away at the slow sandstone, revealing the secrets of their innermost thoughts in the patterns that stretch all around us. There is history here for anyone who takes the time to read it, prophecy too.

'This is the dark place, the warm and the wet. We are here unborn. Waiting.' I pitch my voice higher than normal, occupying the character I've created for this little game. He doesn't answer. Can't answer. His mouth is taped shut. I used the same roll on his wrists, tying them together behind his back. And the funny thing is he let me.

'We await our birth here. Bound and gagged by our previous lives.' I push his head forward, firmly but not roughly. He resists for a moment, but soon bends low to the gritty floor. A channel cut in the rock dribbles a stream of water, leached in from the city up above us. The men who built it knew the secrets of the earth, planned this place so that it would never flood. There are channels throughout, all carefully worked to drain into a sump. From there, the water goes straight down to hell.

'Are you ready to be reborn? Are you ready for the mysteries to be revealed?'

The faintest twitch by way of a nod, felt through my hand rather than seen in this almost total darkness. We brought candles, my new friend and I, but they are over on the far side of this carved room. I look briefly back at them. See mine still burning straight and true, his almost out as it devours the last of the wax, burns out the cotton wick. Not much time left.

'Come, stand, and begin your journey of rebirth.'

I help him to his feet, steady him as he sways a little. He's been kneeling a long time on the cold stone, legs weak. The rope around his neck is too thin for a proper hanging, and too short. A symbol like the many others in this ceremony. I take it up, pull him around.

'The way is dark. The way is not easy. Trust is the only way. Trust in your friends. Trust in your brother.'

The words are nonsense, of course, but they are what he wants to hear. This whole ceremony is for him and no one else. I lead him down the narrow carved passageways, taking care to avoid the lowest parts of the ceiling. Most of them, at least. It's important he suffer a bit, here at the last.

There is a narrow path around the pool, so I can stay dry. For him, the experience is less pleasant. One moment he is shuffling forward, slowly gaining in confidence, the next he is up to his armpits in cold water, struggling to stop himself from going under.

'Do not falter here, at the last.' I tug on the rope and he flounders for a moment before getting his footing, surges up and out of the pool like a performing dolphin in expectation of a fish. His mouth is taped, so he cannot shout, but I can hear his breath forcing its way out of his nose in terrified snorts. He moves his head from side to side as if trying to see where he is. I pull him forward a couple of steps until we are back where we started.

'Come, brother.' The knife is as sharp as I can make it, blade thin and pointed. I slide it out of its sheath and slice the tape holding his wrists together. His hands go immediately to the sack over his head, whipping it off to reveal wide, staring eyes. A glance over to the carved stone table, and I see his candle gutter once, then expire with a little flicker of blue light. It is the sign I have been waiting for.

'Welcome to the brotherhood,' I say as he reaches up and starts to peel the tape from his mouth. In that instant I know that he is ready, his soul shriven and pure. Only corruption awaits, or salvation. Before he can free himself, I run the blade swiftly across his exposed neck, just above the rope. Hard through skin and artery and the crunchy cartilage of throat. Blood wells as he opens his mouth to speak, finds himself unable even to ask why. I can see it in his eyes though, that question writ large. It is not for me to answer him as he sinks slowly to the floor, his life force mingling with the water in the carved stone channel. He goes swiftly to a far better place and all I can do is watch, hope, pray that my time will come again. And when it does that I will be found as worthy as he.

2

'You got a minute, Inspector?'

Detective Inspector McLean slowed his stride more in surprise than from any desire to talk to the person who had appeared, as if by magic, beside him. He'd been hoping to have a chance to clear his head of work-related thoughts before his meeting. Fate would appear to have had other ideas.

'Ms Dalgliesh. Thought you'd be down at the Parliament. Isn't there supposed to be some new angle on the independence vote today?'

'Today and every day. Doesn't sell papers, so my editor's no' interested.' Dalgliesh wore her trademark long leather coat despite the muggy afternoon heat. An unlit cigarette dangled from her mouth, which meant she wanted something from him. Had it been lit, then chances were she was just paying a courtesy call before digging the knife in.

'Heard you'd caught that gang of scallies pickpocketing all them tourists come for the Festival.'

'That more interesting to you than politics?'

'Anything's more interesting to me than politics. Word is they was mostly Eastern Europeans. People love it when you throw in a bit of racial tension. No' just over here stealin' our jobs, but plain stealin' our cash and all.'

'Sorry to disabuse you of your casual racism, but the gang we lifted were all home-grown. There'll be a press conference tomorrow, maybe Thursday.' McLean quickened his pace, hoping to get to his destination before the rain came on. And before Ms Dalgliesh could pester him any more.

'Truth is, Inspector, that's not really what I'm after. Can't abide all that nonsense myself, but you've gotta do what the editor says or no bylines and no cash.' Dalgliesh sped up, keeping time with him, though every third or fourth step was a skip.

'What do you want then?'

'A favour.'

McLean stopped so suddenly, Dalgliesh was a few paces on before she realised. She wheeled around and trotted back as he stared at her, incredulous.

'A favour? Are you serious? Why would I even think of—?'

'Well, I'd owe you, for one thing.'

McLean studied the reporter, looking for any sign that she was taking the piss. Hard to tell when her perpetual expression was of someone who'd been pulling a face when the wind changed. It was true he despised almost everything she did and stood for, but on the other hand the goodwill of a journalist, particularly an investigative journalist with questionable ethics, was not something to be passed up idly.

'I'm listening,' he said, and was rewarded by a lengthy pause. Whatever it was that Dalgliesh wanted, she was finding it hard to ask, which had to mean it was important.

'Ben Stevenson. You know him?'

McLean nodded. 'Another one of your lot, isn't he?'

'Aye. You don't need to be so sniffy about it. Ben's all right.'

'I'm not sure everyone would agree with you. Seem to recall he's not been all that nice about my boss in the past.'

'Dagwood? There's nothing worth digging up on him. Might be a buffoon, but he's one of the straightest coppers I've met.'

'I was thinking more about Jayne McIntyre, actually. She might've been Assistant Chief Constable if your friend Ben hadn't run that piece about her family life.'

'Aye, well, there is that.' Dalgliesh had the decency to look embarrassed, for all of two seconds. 'Still, she'd've bin wasted up there at the top. Some folk're just meant to be detectives.'

'You're all heart, Ms Dalgliesh. And so's your ghoul of a friend. Goodbye.' McLean turned down East Preston Street, heading towards the remains of his old tenement block and his meeting with the developers trying to renovate the site.

'He's gone missing,' Dalgliesh called out after him. 'Ben. He's disappeared.'

McLean stopped. Hardly surprising that a journalist might go off the radar for a while; it was the nature of their job, after all. That Dalgliesh was concerned enough to come to him made it far more serious.

'What do you mean, disappeared? He gone on holiday and forgotten to tell anyone?'

'Ben's not had more than a couple of days off at a time in five years. He lives the job, can't stand sitting around doing nothing.'

'So he's chasing a story.' McLean knew he was only saying it because he didn't want to get drawn in. He also knew that it was too late for that.

'Chasing a story, aye. But it was here. In the city. Told me it was going to be big, too.'

'He say what it was about?'

Dalgliesh leaned against the wall as she lit her cigarette. Took a deep drag and held on to the smoke for a few seconds before letting it go. 'And let someone like me pinch it? Don't be daft.'

'So how do you know what he was up to?' McLean glanced across the road, where a shiny black car had just double-parked. No doubt his developer arriving for their meeting.

'I'm a journalist, aren't I?' Dalgliesh said. 'Sticking my nose in other people's business is what I do.'

'So you reckon Mr Stevenson's got himself into trouble, then?'

'Well, he's no' bin seen at work for almost a month. He's no' answerin' his phones. He's no' bin home and his ex hasn't heard from him in six weeks.'

'His ex? Why would she care?'

'Coz he's meant to have custody of their wee girls alternate weekends. No' like him to miss that, apparently.'

The car had disgorged two suited businessmen who were even now donning hard hats and being shown in through the front door.

'I'll look into it as soon as I can, OK?' McLean dug out his phone, jabbed at the screen until it brought up the notebook function and tapped out a badly misspelled note to remind himself. 'Right now I need to be somewhere else.'

Dalgliesh smiled, a sight so alarming McLean thought for a moment her head was going to crack open and reveal something rotten inside. 'You're a star, Inspector. I'll send over all the stuff I've got already.'

Visions of his desk, legs already buckling under the weight of unattended paperwork. He really didn't need more piling up.

'I'm not promising anything, mind,' he said. 'And if this friend of yours turns up with a tan and a new girlfriend, you'll owe me double.'

He'd been avoiding the place. Hiding from the emotional turmoil it represented; that's what Matt Hilton would say. Perhaps he'd be right, but mostly it was just that his old flat in Newington was a long way down the ever-growing list of priorities. Of course, that didn't explain why he'd not done anything about the letters from his solicitors or from the developers trying to acquire the site, why he'd been ignoring calls about the matter for weeks now.

It was a simple problem. He owned a share of the site because he'd owned one of the tenement flats that had been destroyed by the fire. A sharp development company had managed to buy out most of the other shares, but they couldn't do anything without his say. They'd offered him money, quite a lot of money, for a quick sale. There really wasn't any reason why he shouldn't have taken up the offer and walked away from the place. But he couldn't bring himself to do that.

The senior partner from his solicitors had come to the station in person, waited for an hour in the reception area with the drunks and the vagrants and the just lonely, until McLean had come back from a crime scene. That more than anything else had finally persuaded him of the serious nature of the matter. It wasn't something that would go away if he just ignored it long enough, and other people were being inconvenienced by his inaction. His grandmother would have been appalled at his rudeness.

And so he was here, back in Newington for an on-site meeting to discuss the redevelopment. Perhaps the builders thought seeing what they had planned would sway his mind. Certainly seeing the facade still there, shored up with scaffolding, its windows empty eyes on to the sky behind, brought everything into focus. The front door was the same, too. The paint faded a bit, the number gone, but it was even propped open with a half-brick, just like the students downstairs had always done in times past.

'Detective Inspector McLean?' A voice behind him. McLean turned to see a man in a dark suit, black shoes polished until it was almost painful to look at them. He was wearing a hard hat, but otherwise could easily have been mistaken for a banker or accountant.

'That's me. Mr . . . ?'

'McClymont. Joe McClymont.' The dark suit held out a hand to be shaken. McLean took it, surprised at how firm the man's grip was. His skin was rough to the touch, too. Hands that did more work than pushing a pen around.

'Sorry I've been a bit difficult to pin down. Only so many hours in the day.'

'Well, you're here now. Why don't we go in and have a look at the plans.' McClymont didn't try to pretend it was no big deal his project being delayed months, McLean noticed. He just headed into the building, assuming he would be followed.

Apart from the lack of roof, the entrance hall was remarkably similar to how he remembered it, possibly a bit cleaner. Rain had washed the large flagstones, and the extra ventilation had managed to remove almost all trace of a hundred and fifty years of cat piss. At the back of the hall, the staircase only climbed a dozen or so steps now, the rest of the building having been cleared away beyond the top of the ground floor walls. McClymont stepped through an opening that would have been Mrs McCutcheon's front door, then down a set of new steps where the back wall had been and into the communal garden. A couple of Portakabins had been craned in to form a site office, but McLean took a moment to turn and look up at the back of what had once been his home. All he could see was the inside of the front wall, held aloft by massive steel pillars and braces. Individual flats were marked out by the different coloured walls, and there at the top on the right, the bay window of his front room still with a bit of skirting board hanging on like a drowning man. He'd stripped paint off that board, sanded it until it was smooth, and varnished it. He'd spent hours, days, years in that room, staring out the window or just sitting on the sofa, listening to music, reading a book, sharing pizza and wine with friends, cuddling up with one in particular. The rush of memories made him dizzy.

'We have to keep the original frontage. That's part of the deal with the council. Much easier if we could knock it down and start again, but it wouldn't be the same, aye?'

McLean turned back, seeing another dark-suited man, this one without a hard hat. He was older, grey-haired and thick-set, eyes cracked with lines set deep in leathery skin.

'Joe told me you were here. Come on in the hut and I'll show you what we want to do to the place.'

3

'The front stays the same, but we're going to extend out here into the back by three metres on the first four floors. Fifth will have a balcony looking out towards Salisbury Crags and the top two storeys will be twin-level apartments.'

Joe McClymont had A1-sized plans splayed out on a large table in the Portakabin, and a scale model of the development stood in one corner. The old man had turned out to be his father, Jock. Whilst he let the youngster talk, he was quite obviously in charge. McLean couldn't say that he took much to either of them. Despite their outwardly professional appearance, the well-polished shoes, the suits and the expensive car, these two screamed dodgy to him. A third person hovered in the back of the office, a middle-aged lady McLean hadn't been introduced to. She was working at a slim laptop computer, but every so often would look up and eye him with ill-disguised hostility.

'Hang on. Balcony on the fifth and two storeys at the top?' McLean counted on his fingers. He'd not really been paying too much attention, but that detail suddenly hit home. 'You're building a six-storey block here?'

'That's right. Six storeys, aye. Three flats each on the first four, two big apartments spread over the top two floors.'

'How's that going to work? The building's only four storeys high.' McLean glanced over at the model in the corner, then studied it a bit harder. From the front it looked just like the building he knew of old, but then of course it would have to. No way the council would let anyone demolish it if they could make life difficult by insisting it be preserved. No matter that half of the street didn't match anyway.

'See those steps you came down from the ground floor?' Joe McClymont jerked a thumb over his shoulder towards the remains of Mrs McCutcheon's flat. 'We had to underpin all the old walls, front and side. Meant digging down the best part of three metres. You've no idea how much that lot cost, by the way. But it means we've space for a couple of basement flats below the original. They won't get much light from the front, but the backs'll open out on to the gardens. Be great for kids.'

'They'll still be communal, though? The gardens?'

McLean didn't need to be a detective to see the shifty look that passed between the two developers. 'Something like that, aye,' Joe eventually said.

McLean looked back at the plans, paying a bit more attention now. It certainly looked impressive, but he couldn't help thinking the rooms were rather small, the ceilings low. He turned fully and studied the model a bit more carefully this time. The frontage was as it ever had been, but the floors didn't line up with it any more. The facade was just that, and a much more compressed living experience was being created behind it.

'Seems to me you've already done quite a bit of work.'

'Site like this doesn't come up often,' Jock McClymont said. 'You can't sit still in this game.'

'Which brings us to the point of the meeting, really.' This time it was Joe McClymont who spoke, but it was obvious that the two of them had rehearsed their pitch.

'You want me to sell you my share in the site. I know.' McLean paused for a moment, watching the expressions on the faces of the two men. Now that he knew, he could see that they were father and son, but where old Jock had an avuncular look, his face filling out with the years, Joe was thin and hungry. Of the two, he looked the most dangerous, but McLean had been around long enough to know that if he had any trouble it would come from the old man. Behind them, the woman was muttering strange words under her breath as if on the phone to a foreigner. They made his head ache slightly, so he tuned her out as best he could.

'What if I don't want to?'

A distant siren underlined the long moments of silence that followed. Even the woman stopped speaking.

'I don't understand.' Joe's face was creased with genuine bewilderment, as if no one had ever refused to be bought before. 'Why wouldn't you? I mean, what's the alternative?'

'I was rather hoping you might be able to tell me. I mean, it seems a bit presumptuous starting work when you don't actually own the site, doesn't it?'

'We own a controlling share, laddie.' Jock McClymont's gruff but cheerful voice changed to a low growl. 'We've been playing nice so far, what with this being your home an' all. But there's only so much slack we can cut you.'

Interesting choice of words. He didn't really need the hassle all this was going to create, but he also knew better than to fight his own nature. 'What if I just want my flat back?'

Jock's eyes narrowed. 'You want one of the apartments.'

'No. I want my apartment. Top floor left. Shiny blue door. Three bedrooms, proper bathroom and a box room a hard-up student would be happy to live in. I want a kitchen where I can look out over the garden and see Arthur's Seat if I crane my neck a bit. I'll pass on the rusty bicycle frame chained to the railings on the stairs outside, and if there's no lingering smell of cat piss in the entrance that would be a plus.'

Both McClymonts stared at him, their expressions nearly identical. Joe was the first to speak again.

'But the plans—'

'Are a bit rubbish, aren't they?' McLean cut him off. 'Six storeys? Really? How the hell did you get that past planning? All you're doing is leaving the front wall and building a crappy modern box behind it. You really think that's what the city needs?'

'What the city needs is unimportant.' Jock McClymont's growl was even more menacing now. 'We've a lot of cash tied up in this place. More besides. We're not going to let it go just because of you. Top-floor flats are going to cost way more than your share's worth. If you'll no' take the money we've offered . . .'

'I think you misunderstand me, gentlemen. I appreciate the time and effort you've put into all this.' McLean swept an arm around the general area of the Portakabin. 'But what you're proposing . . . I can't begin . . .' He picked up the top sheet of plans, spun it around on the table. 'You need to come up with something a lot better than this if you want me to help make it happen. Now if you don't mind, I've important work I need to get back to.'

McLean stood outside the front door, took a deep breath and looked around the street. It was as familiar to him as his skin, a place he had lived for fifteen years and more before that terrible fire. But that was then and this was now. He had a house, far too big but just as difficult to part with. It wasn't that he needed a place nearer to work, he could have bought one if he wanted. No, it was something much less rational, a feeling that the people who'd lived and died in that tenement block somehow deserved better. More than that, was a growing dislike of McClymonts senior and junior. And finally, the nub of it. He'd been taken for granted. They wanted him to sell up, thought that throwing a little more money at the problem would make it go away. They should probably have made the effort to get to know him a bit better first.

Head down to avoid making eye contact with passers-by, he set off on the walk back to the station, hoping for a chance to get his thoughts together. When his phone started to buzz in his pocket, it wasn't one of the ring tones DC MacBride had programmed into it that he knew he had to answer, and yet something about the trilling gave it an urgency he couldn't ignore. Fishing it out of his pocket, McLean stared at the screen. An international number. No doubt someone trying to sell him some scam financial scheme or get him to part with sensitive passwords for his computer. Intrigued, he thumbed the accept call icon and held the slim handset up to his ear.

'Hello?'

'That's not Gordon. Shit, have I dialled the wrong number?' McLean recognised the voice even though it was far too long since last he had heard it, and couldn't help the smile that turned up the corners of his mouth.

'Seems so, Phil. How's things?'

'Wait . . . What? Tony? Jesus mate. How are you doing?'

'Oh, same old same old. Busy. You know how it is.'

'Tell me about it. Place is running me ragged. American students. They're so . . . what's the word?'

'Committed?'

'Yeah, that's it.' Phil laughed. 'Either that, or they should be.'

'How's Rae? You two not going to be asking me to be godfather any time soon, I hope.'

'Rae's . . .' Phil paused a little too long, out of practice at talking to his old friend the detective. 'Rae's fine.'

'Not taking to California then?' McLean slowed his pace, eking out the time before he reached the station and had to end the call. Then he realised he was in the wrong street, stopped, looked around. He'd started walking home without realising it.

'Damn. Forgot who I was talking to. Yeah. She's not really enjoying it all that much. And truth be told, she does want kids. Just not sure this is where I'd want to raise them, you know.'

McLean didn't say 'and you think over here's any better?', even though he wanted to. It surprised him that Phil would even consider having children, but then it had surprised him when his old flatmate had got married too. People change.

'Might be better off coming home. Who knows? Could be an independent nation in a month or two.'

'Don't joke about it, Phil. The whole thing's a bloody nuisance.'

'You don't think Scotland could go it alone?'

'Could? Aye, course it could. Should? Well that's a question for a long evening of beer and pizza. Probably a bottle of whisky to round it all off.'

'Sounds like a date. Next time I'm over. Listen Tony, it's been great chatting but—'

'You still need to phone Gordon. Whoever he is. Yeah, it's good to hear your voice, Phil. Should call more often. And you know you can, any time, right?'

'Yeah. I will. Maybe see you soon, too.' And with that the phone went dead.

McLean stood at the edge of the Meadows, watched the afternoon walkers, the students lazing on the grass or playing kick-about football. A couple walked past, their young daughter holding one hand each. She swung crazily with every third or fourth step, totally trusting in their grip, certain she could come to no danger. Such innocence was both touching and troubling. Bitter experience had made a cynic of him, but that didn't mean it had to be the same for everyone. He shook his head at the strange thought and the even stranger circumstance that had brought it. A glance at the clock on the corner of the old Dick Vet building told him it was late enough to consider not going back to the station, heading home for a well-deserved evening off.

But that was never going to happen, was it.

4

They always pick on the little ones.

They'd pick on me, only I know the teachers have been talking. Telling everyone about mum and dad. I can see it in their eyes, the way they won't look at me, or speak to me. They want to bait me like they did last term, but something stops them. They still talk about me behind my back, though, just quiet enough that I can't really hear. Johnson and Bain and Cartwright, they know they can't be mean to me, and that just makes them want to do it more.

So they take it out on the little ones.

This boy's new. His folks live in the big house around the corner from mine. Just moved back from overseas, wherever that is. The bullies have been working at him for a week now, and he just won't rise to their bait. That's not good. I learned the hard way. Ignoring them doesn't make them go away, just makes them crueller. He'll learn, but how long will it take? And how badly will they hurt him?

He's in the corner now, surrounded by them. Johnson's maybe a year older than me, Bain and Cartwright my age. They're all big, and stupid. The new boy's tiny. Like he's only four or something. He doesn't really stand a chance. And he lives just around the corner from Gran's house, which is maybe why I step in.

'Leave him be, aye?' My voice wavers as the words come

out. As I realise what I've done. Never draw attention to yourself, that's the first rule.

Johnson turns slowly, his piggy little eyes searching to see who's interrupted him. At first I think he's going to hit me. Won't be the first time, won't be the last. But then he sees who it is, and his face changes. A hint of uncertainty in his frown, a hint of fear?

'What's he to you, McLean?'

'Nothin'.'

'Aye, right. Nothin'.' Johnson pauses for a moment, then slaps Bain on the shoulder, his frown breaking into a grin, making him look like the idiot he is. 'Hey everyone, McLean's a homo. He's got a new boyfriend.'

Bain and Cartwright laugh like it's the funniest thing they've ever heard. 'Homo! Homo!' And they run off down the corridor in search of someone else to pick on.

'You OK?' I ask the boy. He says nothing. Just nods. Eyes still wide.

'Best keep away from them. You're Bale, right?'

He nods again. 'N . . . Norman.'

'I'm Tony. I live just round the corner from your place. You know the old lady who used to live in your house died in her bed? They didn't find her for months.'

It's not true. Well, not entirely. Mrs Leslie did die in her bed, but my Gran was there with her when it happened, and they buried her in the churchyard a week later. 'Hey. I wonder if that's your room now?'

Norman's eyes widen even further, the colour draining from his face.

'Y . . . You think it might be?'

I'm about to answer, tell him it's unlikely, but the bell cuts me off. 'Gotta run. Maths next.'

It's only when I'm in the classroom and opening up my exercise book that I realise I've probably been just as cruel to him as Johnson, Bain and Cartwright.

5

'Hurry up, Constable. I haven't got all day.'

McLean held open the back door to the station, waiting for Detective Constable MacBride to come in. Heavy rain spattered off the tarmac of the car park, bouncing up as high as the constable's knees as he ran from the squad car he'd just vacated. It didn't matter; by the time he reached the door, he was just as soaked as if he'd walked. Or maybe fallen into a swimming pool.

'Bloody hell. Where'd that come from?' MacBride shook himself like a dog as McLean let the door swing closed. Water sprayed liberally around the entranceway, soaking the already slippery floor tiles, the grubby walls and the detective inspector.

'Cheers. That's just what I needed.' McLean slapped his damp folder against his legs, trying to wipe the worst of the rain off it. He'd missed the downpour by seconds, counting himself lucky that seniority meant MacBride had been driving and had to lock up.

'Sorry, sir.' MacBride dipped his head like a serf before a nobleman, then ran a damp hand through wetter hair. It was long, McLean couldn't help noticing. Perhaps a bit too long for regulations, though he wasn't about to say anything. Things were a bit more lax in plain clothes anyway, and there was that other matter . . .

'They still giving you grief about your scar?'

MacBride's hand stopped mid-run, a familiar red tinge blushing his cheeks. McLean could see the mark quite clearly, despite the long fringe of thin ginger hair. If anything the attempt to hide it just brought it more to everyone's attention.

'You know what policemen are like. Bunch of wankers the lot of them.' MacBride patted down his fringe, not quite managing to hide the livid red scar on his forehead. The result of a near miss from a piece of glass blown out of the window of an exploding mental hospital, it formed a perfect lightning-flash mark. Even more so now the tiny dots where the stitches had been had faded.

'Still calling you Constable Potter, I take it?'

'And worse. Like bloody children.'

McLean tried not to laugh. DC MacBride looked like he wasn't long out of school himself.

'They put a cloak in my locker. Must've nicked it from some university professor or something.'

'Could be worse. Knowing this lot they'd probably have hidden a black cat in there if they could find one.'

MacBride looked at him like he was mad. 'A black cat?'

'You know. Witchcraft, covens, that sort of thing.'

'You've not actually read the Harry Potter books, have you, sir?'

McLean shook his head. 'I think I caught some of the film on the telly a while back. Might have fallen asleep before it finished.'

'There were eight films, sir. Not sure even you could've slept through all of them.'

'Is that so?' He tapped the folder against his leg again. 'Well, at least they've got something harmless to focus on.

Pete Robertson gets called all manner of nasty things and he broke his back, poor bugger.'

McLean didn't add that both accidents had taken place on his watch. He knew all too well what the junior detectives and uniforms called him behind his back. Couldn't really say he didn't deserve it half of the time.

'Aye, well. If they put half as much effort into the job as they do taking the piss . . .'

This time McLean did laugh. 'You've been hanging out with Grumpy Bob too long. Beginning to sound just like him.'

'Did I hear my name being taken in vain?'

Both McLean and MacBride turned to see Detective Sergeant Laird approaching from the direction of the station canteen. He had his paper under one arm, a large Styrofoam cup of coffee in his hand and looked like a man in search of an empty incident room in which to snooze.

'All the time, Bob.' McLean held out the folder for the sergeant to take. 'Here. Make a start on collating this lot, will you? I've got to go see Dagwood.'

Grumpy Bob looked nonplussed for a moment, then managed to shift his coffee into the other hand and take the folder. 'Done something wrong, have you?'

'Christ, I hope not. Mind you, with Dagwood you never know.'

'Hear you caught those pickpockets working the Old Town.'

McLean stood in the familiar position, the wrong side of Detective Superintendent Duguid's desk, in the large office on the third floor that had once belonged to Jayne McIntyre. That Dagwood hadn't torn him off a strip as soon as he'd entered put him on edge. It was unusual to be called before the boss for anything other than a dressing down. Mostly he was ignored if he did things well, abused only when he cocked up.

'I'd hardly take credit for it myself, sir. DC MacBride coordinated the operation along with DS Laird. And if anyone deserves praise it's DC Gregg. If she ever gets tired of working here, she'll make a fine actress.'

Duguid stared up at him as if the names only vaguely meant anything at all. It hadn't been that momentous an operation as these things went. Gangs of thieves appeared every year as the city swelled with tourists come to see the Festival and the Fringe. This lot hadn't even been all that well organised; stupid enough to all be staying in the same squat, interested only in the cash and smartphones they nabbed. A tiny tracker beacon in the detective constable's bag had led a team of uniforms right to their door. McLean's total involvement had been approval of the plan and allocation of the budget.

'You'll not get far with that attitude, you know.' Duguid slumped back into his chair, its springs squeaking in protest.

'Far how, sir? In case you hadn't noticed, I've not really been pursuing promotion. I'm happy where I am.'

That brought a ghost of a smile to Duguid's thin lips. 'Happy?'

'Poor choice of words, perhaps. Put it this way. I don't fancy a chief inspector's post, let alone anything higher. Don't suppose I'd get very far even if I did.'

'Aye, well. At least you know your mind.' Duguid fell silent for a moment. McLean was about to ask him what he wanted when he finally spoke again.

'You know I'm retiring. End of the year.' Neither sentence was voiced as a question.

'Yes, sir. You told me back in the winter. At the hospital. When—'

'When those buggers stole my car. Still not found them now, have you?'

It was true. Far more man-hours had been sunk into that investigation than it could possibly justify, and yet no single clue had emerged. It was as if whoever had boxed the detective superintendent in, hauled him out of his beloved Range Rover, given him a swift, sharp kicking and then stolen the car had never existed. Given the other events that had happened that fateful night, DC MacBride's wizard scar the least of them, McLean couldn't help thinking that might well be the case.

'I'm sorry. We tried. Chances are it's in the Middle East now, or Africa. China maybe. Sad to say, but high-end motors get nicked the whole time. Hardly anyone smashes windows to steal a purse or rip out a stereo for the drug money any more, but you park something worth a hundred grand in the street . . .'

'Do I need to remind you it wasn't parked?' Duguid's voice dropped an octave.

'No sir. You don't. But we did what we could, and I've passed what little we found on to the NCA. Something like this is nationwide, not local. We have to let them deal with it.'

Duguid did something that might have been the bastard child of a shrug and a nod, and let out a noncommittal grunt at the same time.

'Was that all you wanted to see me about, sir? Only—'

A knock at the open door interrupted McLean, and he turned to see DC MacBride.

'Constable?' Duguid asked.

'Erm, sorry to disturb you sir. Only I thought you'd want to know. There's been a body found. Out at Gilmerton. Suspicious circumstances.'

As if on cue, McLean's phone chimed. He pulled it out of his pocket to see a text from the control centre at Bilston Glen.

'Looks like they want my unique expertise on the matter, whatever that is.' He held the phone up, angling the screen so Duguid could see it. The detective superintendent shook his head as if he didn't want to know. Or didn't care.

'Go on then. Get out there and see what all the fuss is about.'

McLean said nothing, just turned and headed for the door. He expected Duguid to say something right at the last minute, just to make him stop, but for once he was quiet. As DC MacBride fell in alongside him and they both walked down the corridor in silence, he couldn't help wondering what Duguid had really wanted to tell him. Not about the stolen Range Rover for sure, which meant it had probably been about his retirement, his replacement. Well, there'd been speculation enough, and it wasn't as if he had a say in the matter. Whoever it was, McLean would have to work with them as best he could. It was either that, or a job at Vice.

6

With its commanding position on the hills to the south of the city, overlooking the Castle Rock, Arthur's Seat and the Firth of Forth, Gilmerton ought to have been a fine place to live. No doubt in the past, when the big estates at Burdiehouse and the Drum had been built, the rolling countryside would have lent itself to long walks and summer picnics, at least for the gentry. Now it was a busy intersection on the Old Dalkeith Road, funnelling commuters into the city, or out towards Midlothian and the Borders. Rows of grey-brown houses blocked the best of the views, and a brutal 1970s prefab block housed a couple of boarded-up shops and a library. The only place with any life in it was the betting shop.

DC MacBride hadn't said much all the way out, piloting the car with a grim determination that suggested he was still angry about his scar. Coppers could be as stupidly cruel as kids, McLean knew all too well. Chances were the detective constable had been the brunt of bullying at school as well.

'Park up round the back there.' He pointed to a small opening at the end of the block, and MacBride turned swiftly, gaining himself an angry blare of the horn from a car coming towards them. A couple of squad cars were already hogging the space at the far end of the car park, behind the library.

‘Someone said something about a body?’ McLean spoke to one of two uniform officers who were leaning against a nearby brick wall. The smell of cigarette smoke still lingered in the air around the one who pushed himself upright, then came over to the car.

‘Aye sir. Round the corner past the bookies.’ He made a half-hearted attempt to point, a motion that made him look like a one-armed man doing the breaststroke, only without any water to swim in.

‘It’s a bit casual, isn’t it?’ McLean asked. ‘Shouldn’t you be setting up a perimeter? Keeping the public away?’

The constable shrugged. ‘It’s no’ as if anyone can see him, sir. I’ll take you there.’

MacBride parked, then the two of them followed the constable back out of the car park and around the corner. Another constable stood by a nondescript black door that McLean might have taken for someone’s home. He nodded once, then stepped aside to let them in.

Inside was a dark room with posters hanging on the walls, a small shop counter just past the door. It took McLean a moment to realise that this wasn’t a house or a shop, but some kind of visitor attraction.

‘What is this place?’

‘Gilmerton Cove, sir,’ the uniform constable answered. ‘You telling me you’ve never heard of it?’

‘Can’t say as I have.’ McLean peered at the posters on the walls. They were like those in many modern visitor attractions, a series of historical pieces explaining what the place was all about. He had just started reading about the Covenanters when a familiar voice came from the back of the room.

'Had a feeling this would get punted your way, Tony. You do seem to get all the odd cases.'

Angus Cadwallader, city pathologist, stood in an open doorway dressed in his white overalls and, rather incongruously, a hard hat and green wellies.

'I could say the same for you, Angus.' McLean knew better than to shake Cadwallader's hand, especially at a crime scene.

'Ah, but I get to choose my cases. Not have them handed to me by some dispatcher in Bilston Glen.' Cadwallader paused a moment, looked down at his feet. 'Not sure whether that's better or worse.'

'Maybe I should have a look-see and make up my own mind.' McLean peered past the pathologist, seeing an even smaller room than the first. 'No forensics team yet?'

'Oh, they're here. It's just there's not a lot of room. Or air for that matter.' Cadwallader must have seen the bemusement on McLean's face. 'You've really no idea what this place is, have you?'

McLean shook his head. 'Nope.'

'Well, come with me and discover the mysteries of Gilmerton Cove.' Cadwallader stood aside to let McLean step into the small room. 'Might be best if we leave young MacBride behind, though.'

Gilmerton Cove, it turned out, was a series of caves and underground passages, just beneath the pavements and crossroads. For all that Cadwallader had said there wasn't much space, it was surprisingly large. Even more so when McLean was told that it was all man-made.

'No one's quite sure who first carved it all out. Some say

Covenanters, some the Hellfire Club. There's similar caverns up Roslin Glen way, underneath Hawthornden Castle. Probably loads more still waiting to be found.'

McLean listened to the potted history as he climbed into a pair of standard-issue white overalls and slipped paper covers over his shoes. They had descended some steep steps carved into the rock and were now in an arched cavern, piled high with battered aluminium cases filled with forensic equipment. Further on, along a narrow passageway, bright arc lights flooded what would normally be a dark and claustrophobic space. No doubt that way lay the victim, as well.

'Who found the body?' He asked the question before realising that his tour guide for the day was Cadwallader, and not the first officer on the scene. 'Sorry. Habit.'

'I've just been studying it, Tony. Why don't we both go and have a look, eh?'

Cadwallader led the way down a confusing collection of passageways, through strangely hewn rooms, rough rock tables and benches carved from floor and wall. The ground was littered in fine gravel except where water channels had been carved in the bedrock, leading to a sump that drained down to God knows where. Or maybe the Devil. A heavy cast-iron grille covered up the hole, four channels dropping into it from four points, like the points of a compass. Water ran through all of them, fed no doubt by the recent rain. A distinct dampness in the air lent a chill, unpleasant note to the caves. Three of the water channels were uncovered, little rivulets of murky water trickling along them and into the well. The fourth was mostly hidden by a temporary raised walkway installed by the forensics team.

Given the walkway, McLean was sure they must be close to the body, but Cadwallader carried on, through a metal doorway that wouldn't have looked out of place in a submarine, then stooped as the passageway they were following became lower and lower. There were rocks to either side too, as if this area had only just been opened up. Or the ceiling had fallen in recently. McLean had to crouch right down for the last bit, the weight of the rock crushing in on him as if he were Atlas, bringing with it a deep-seated fear that was hard to suppress. Stepping out into the final cavern was a relief. At least for a moment.

The body lay close to the far wall from where he and Cadwallader had emerged. McLean could see that it was a man, a bloody gash ripped from the front of his neck. Another floor channel led from his prone form to a nearby sinkhole, filled with dark, still water. In the half-light, it looked like blood, but no one body could have produced such a volume.

'I'll say this much, it would have been quick.' Cadwallader stepped carefully over to the body and knelt down with an uncomfortable popping of knees. Two white-suited forensic scientists had been carefully examining what looked like another entranceway, piled up with rubble and rocks, nearby. They had stopped what they were doing as soon as McLean had entered and were even now watching him, waiting for him to put a foot wrong so they could tell him off. Even behind their face masks and paper hairnets he could see their scowls. As if anyone as lowly as a detective could hope to glean anything from a crime scene.

'We got an ID yet?'

'Again a question best put to the first officer on the scene. Unfortunately he had to be taken off to hospital.'

'Hospital?' McLean moved closer, keeping his feet firmly on the temporary walkway. There was something horribly familiar about the white face, half mashed into the fine grit of the cavern floor.

'Yes. He threw up, fainted and banged his head on the rock over there.' Cadwallader pointed back towards the door, and as he did so, McLean saw the blood.

It was smeared all over the back wall of the cavern in great swirls and patterns. Sticky black whorls, glistening under the harsh spotlights like the trails of demonic slugs. Stepping backwards to get a better look, McLean let one foot slip off the raised walkway, then caught himself as a harsh intake of breath reminded him he was being watched.

'Are those words?' He tilted his head, trying to make sense of it, failing.

'Best you let us photograph it all. We can use some trick filters to bring it all out nice and sharp.' One of the SOCOs lifted up the camera slung around her neck, just in case he wasn't sure how it was done.

'Good point. Sorry.' McLean bobbed his head, walked carefully back to the body and hunkered down beside Cadwallader.

'Want to hazard a cause of death?' the pathologist asked.

'Thought that was your job. But I'm guessing this.' McLean pointed at the mess that had once been the man's throat.

'Judging by how far the blood's gone, there's probably not a lot left in him. Unless it's been mixed with something to make it run. We'll get a sample for analysis.'

'Killed here though.'

'Best guess, yes. And quite a while ago. Days, maybe weeks. Difficult to judge when the conditions for preservation are so good. I'll know better after the post-mortem. Any idea who he is?'

McLean leaned back, twisted his head around until he could take in the face. Scrunched into the gravel, almost white skin. One eye was obscured, but the other one stared ahead unseeing, glazed over. Fair hair cropped short, light build, difficult to gauge height whilst he was lying crumpled on the ground. He could have been anyone, really, but there was something about the face. He'd seen it recently. No he'd been reminded of it recently. Hadn't seen the man for a while.

'I wish I didn't, but I think I do.'

7

'Nobody's been in there. It was all locked up.'

They'd commandeered the library just around the corner from the little house that hid the entrance to the caves. Soon everything would be moved down to the station, where DC MacBride and Grumpy Bob were busy setting up a major incident room. For now, McLean wanted to get the few witnesses interviewed as soon as possible.

'Locked up? What do you mean?' He was sitting in a small alcove formed by the bookshelves. Across a wobbly table from him, the tour guide from the visitor centre looked nervous and pale, picking at her fingernails and occasionally sliding her spectacles up her nose.

'Do you know anything about the cove?' she asked. McLean shook his head. 'Well, it's an old site, goes back at least a couple of hundred years, probably a lot more. There's passages leading off in all directions from the main complex, but they're all collapsed, or filled with rubble. We'd love to excavate them all, only, well, money's not exactly free-flowing for something like that. And being off the beaten tourist track, we don't make as much as we'd like. There's the problem that some of them go underneath the main crossroads, too. The engineers get nervous.'

'But you did open up that cavern. The one where we found the body.'

'There's a team from the University Archaeology Department. They've been coming out for a while. Using the place to test kit, that sort of thing. They got some money together and were going to do a survey of the blocked tunnels. They opened up that cavern a couple of months back, put the metal door in to keep it sealed off from the public until we could work out if it was safe or not.'

'So no one could get in there?'

'Not unless they had the key. And they'd have needed other keys to get into the caves in the first place.'

'So who has the keys?'

The tour guide pushed her spectacles up her nose again. 'I have a set for the visitor centre and the caves. My son's got one too, and there's a spare set at home. I don't know which of the archaeology team had their keys, but I've never had one. They couldn't get to the door without me or my son letting them in first.'

McLean glanced over to where the archaeology students were sitting. They didn't look old enough to be at university. But then when he'd been that age he'd not looked old enough to be at university either.

'I'll be speaking to them next,' he said. 'But I'm trying to put together a timeline. When were you last open?'

'Us? It's the peak season. We've been open every day over the summer.'

'What about that cavern, then?'

'No, that's been locked, and the archaeology team's been off for a couple of months. Don't think anyone's been in there since June. Well, apart from . . .' The tour guide swallowed hard, her face going pale.

'Could someone have come down on a tour, hidden and

stayed in after you locked up for the night?' It was a long shot, McLean knew, but he had to ask.

'I don't think so. We do a head count, same number in and out. And I always take a walk around the caves last thing, before we lock up and go home. There's nowhere down here you could hide, really.'

'Except that locked cavern. If you had a key.'

'I guess so. Was he there long, do you know?'

The question brought McLean up short. It was the nub of the investigation, after all. Rigor mortis had been and gone, and the core body temperature was the same as the cave, which meant the death hadn't occurred in the last few hours, but beyond that Angus had only offered the vaguest of guesses. Given the conditions in the cave the poor bastard could have been lying there weeks.

'We'll find out soon enough. In the meantime, I'm afraid we're going to have to shut you down for a while. At least until forensics have processed the scene.'

'I guessed as much, soon as I heard what they'd found when they opened up the door.' The tour guide's face told the story eloquently. It was a small tourist attraction and this was peak season. The loss of income would hit them hard.

'I'll try to get them to go as quickly as possible,' McLean said, although he knew he wouldn't. 'Just one last thing. You were first in this morning, right? Before the archaeologists turned up?'

A simple nod by way of answer.

'Did you notice any blood on the floor? Any sign that anyone had been there since you left last night?'

'Blood?' The tour guide's face turned pale. 'No. I don't

remember any blood. Just the poor wee lad running out down the passageway. He was sick in the well, you know.'

It didn't take McLean long to work out which of the archaeology team had thrown up down the well. His name was Eric and he still had a stain of vomit down the front of his T-shirt. Should really have been sent home to clean himself up. His pale face had a sheen of sweat on it that made him look only slightly more healthy than the dead body even now being carefully removed from the cavern somewhere beneath their feet.

'You were the first into the cave, am I right?'

The student swallowed, his Adam's apple bobbing like some alien life-form trying to escape through his neck. Had anyone thought to offer this lot a mug of tea? McLean looked around the library for a constable to send off in search of something suitable, but could see no one close by.

'Was dark in there. Smelled bad.'

McLean's attention was drawn back to the young man. 'Stale? Like it hadn't been disturbed for a while?'

'No. It was like bin bags. Rotting. Something else, too.'

'There were no lights in there?'

'No. We only opened the cave up recently. Hadn't had time to survey it properly. Got some temporary arc lights in there, but we took them away with us for the summer. I was rolling out the extension cable so we could set them back up again.'

'When did you see the body?'

'The body. Yes.' The young man's eyes went out of focus for a moment, the alien trying to burst out of his neck again. McLean thought he was about to be sick, readied himself to get out of the way. It wasn't necessary.

'Couldn't work out what it was at first. I mean, there wasn't meant to be anything in there. Wasn't when we left it. If it'd been a new cave I might've expected a skeleton, maybe. There's a story about old man Paterson being buried somewhere in there.'

'Paterson?' McLean wrote the name down in his notebook.

'Oh yeah. That's right. You've never been to the cove before.' Eric seemed to recover some of his composure once he had a task to concentrate on. 'Tradition was it was built by a blacksmith, name of George Paterson, back in the early eighteenth century. He lived in it, for sure. Used it as an illegal drinking den for a while and claimed he dug it all out himself. But it's much older than that. He probably found it, cleared it out and used it. No way he actually built it, though.'

'So who did?'

'Well that's the mystery, innit? No one knows right enough. There's all manner of weird conspiracy theories. Why we were digging out that tunnel, wasn't it. Trying to put a bit of science behind it all.'

'So, the body.' McLean nudged the interview back on track.

'Yeah. It was weird. And the light wasn't good. Thought it was a rock formation or something. Anyway, Ali was coming up the tunnel behind me with the big lamp, so I had to go in properly.'

McLean wondered whether that was correct protocol when exploring caves just a few feet beneath houses and a busy street, but kept it to himself.

'He plugged in the lamp. Shone it up at the ceiling like I'd done, then over to the body. I'd got a bit closer to it by then, and when the light hit it I could . . . oh God . . . his throat.'

McLean was on his feet quickly, but not quickly enough. Someone obviously had given the archaeology team tea, and biscuits too. Second time around they didn't look anything like as appetising. Even less so spattered over his shoes.

8

'His name's Ben Stevenson. He's a reporter with the *Tribune*. Sometime colleague of our old friend Jo Dalgliesh.'

McLean stood in Detective Superintendent Duguid's office, and not for the first time wished there were more chairs in the place. The afternoon sun shone through the long glass window wall, making everything uncomfortably warm and humid. Duguid had his jacket off, draped over the back of his expensive leather executive's chair, shirt-sleeves rolled up. McLean had just walked from the car park at the back of the station, up several flights of stairs. He was short of breath, and sweat was beginning to trickle down his back.

'And someone cut his throat open, eh? Going to be hard narrowing down the list of suspects for that one.'

McLean ignored the attempt at humour. Duguid's mood had lightened considerably since he'd announced his retirement, but it was still hit and miss. 'The thing is, Dalgliesh approached me just a couple of days ago. Wanted to know if I could look into his disappearance. Seems he was on to some big story, then just disappeared.'

'Dalgliesh asked you for a favour?' Duguid grinned in an oddly simian manner. 'Which part of her anatomy did you tell her to shove that into?'

'Actually I said I'd see what I could do. Was on my way to an important meeting, so anything to get rid of her, really.'

'Well it's not going to be so easy next time. You'll need to speak to her, get as much detail as you can about what this Stevenson fellow was working on. Trace his movements over the past few weeks.'

McLean suppressed the urge to remind Duguid that he knew how to carry out an investigation.

'You want me to work with her, sir?' Just asking the question was enough to send a shudder down his spine.

'Makes sense. She came to you, after all. And you've got history.'

'If you mean by history she wrote a book about the man who killed my fiancée and I've hated her ever since, then I guess you've got a point.'

'Don't be such a drama queen, McLean. She's a useful asset for the investigation or she's a pain in the arse making life difficult for us. Which would you rather have?'

Put like that McLean had to admit that the detective superintendent had a point; that old saw about keeping your friends close and your enemies closer. It didn't make it any easier to accept, though. Still, if Duguid was going to make life awkward for him, he could just as easily do the same.

'You going to be Gold on this one, sir?'

'Christ. You think it's that important?'

As excuses went, it was a bit rubbish. So Stevenson was a reporter, and one who'd gone for one of their own when he'd exposed lurid details of Chief Superintendent McIntyre's private life that were, as far as McLean could see, none of anyone else's business. But even so, he'd died violently. There was no denying it was murder, and there was nothing domestic about it either. Protocol dictated that it be classed as a major incident.

‘You’re right, of course. It’s got Cat A murder written all over it. I’ll have to take charge, I guess.’ Duguid ran an over-large hand through his sparse hair. ‘Still, keep it as low-key as possible for now. Not that it’s going to be easy, him being a journalist and everything.’

‘Grumpy Bob and MacBride are setting up the incident room.’ McLean turned to leave, was almost at the door before Duguid spoke again.

‘You’re going to make it complicated again, aren’t you McLean?’

‘A body with its throat cut, hidden in a secret cavern underground and no obvious idea how it got in there?’ McLean stood in the doorway, enjoying the faint breeze wafting in from the corridor outside. ‘I don’t think even I could make it any more complicated than that.’

It was always cool in the city mortuary, but that was about all it had going for it on the positive side. Cool and dry. Summer had been warm, but the past three weeks had seen almost endless, miserable rain. McLean thought he might have been starting to grow gills, and he couldn’t remember a time when his feet hadn’t been damp. Of course that was mostly his own fault for insisting on walking everywhere.

The silence in the mortuary was a plus, too. He had to admit that as the doors swung closed behind him, cutting off the splashing roar of traffic from outside. There was only the gentle swish of air through the ductwork, the occasional far-off clatter of a dropped specimen tray or the squeak-squeak-squeak of an un-oiled trolley wheel as another departed soul was taken from the cold store to the place where all their most intimate secrets would be revealed.

He took his time walking to the examination theatre. The journey from the station had been leisurely, too. McLean liked to think while he walked, helped by the rhythm of his feet on the pavement, but this time it had been difficult to focus. A man had been murdered, of that there was no doubt. He needed justice, deserved it as much as anyone. And yet this man had been a thorn in the side of many a police officer over the course of his journalistic career. He was part of a pack more interested in salacious detail than important fact, favouring spectacle and hype over solid investigative journalism. He was a hack and proud of it – or rather, had been a hack and proud of it. It was hard then to drum up any great enthusiasm for catching his killer.

McLean had seen it in the eyes of the junior officers at that morning's briefing, and in the eyes of some of the more senior officers during informal meetings the night before. It annoyed him that they could be so childish, these professional grown men. And it annoyed him that he got annoyed at what he'd known he would face, as soon as the identity of the dead man was confirmed. So the thoughts had gone around in his head, always bringing him back to the wrong questions, stopping him from focusing on the killer rather than the victim.

'Ah, Tony. You made it then.'

McLean looked up, surprised to find he was already at the examination theatre. Angus Cadwallader stood on one side of the table, his ever-present assistant Tracy on the other. Between them lay the mortal remains of Ben

Stevenson, already well into the post-mortem examination process.

'I wasn't sure if I really wanted to.'

'Well, you don't have to attend, you know. Dr MacPhail's here to verify my findings and it'll all be in the report.'

Cadwallader sounded almost hurt as he spoke. McLean wondered if he, too, was upset at the imposition this man's murder had put upon him. Then he realised just how stupid that sounded, shook his head to try to rid himself of the malaise he'd picked up at the station. It helped, a bit, although it got him a strange look from the pathologist.

'You know I prefer to get the news first-hand, Angus.' McLean stepped a little closer to the examination table, saw that Stevenson was already open, stopped before he could see what was inside.

'Well, we'd better get stuck in then.' Cadwallader grinned at his pun, then added to it by reaching into the dead man's torso and carefully lifting out something slippery. Tracy was ready with a plastic container that looked suspiciously like it might once have contained ice cream. Newly filled, she placed it on a nearby set of scales and noted something down.

'You've done the exterior examination already, I see,' McLean said. 'Any clues you might want to share?'

'All in good time, Tony.' Cadwallader pulled out something else and handed it to Tracy to weigh. 'I need to finish this. Then we can discuss what happened to the poor fellow.'

McLean opened his mouth to reply, then shut it again. Cadwallader was right, of course. If he'd arrived on time, then he could have listened as the pathologist detailed his examination for the microphone hanging above the table. Coming in late and expecting his old friend to stop, switch off, talk about what he'd already just talked about and then start all over again was really a bit much to ask. And besides, if he was busy pulling stuff out of the poor man, there couldn't be all that much longer to go.

'Cause of death was almost certainly the cut to the throat. It's very deep. Almost took the poor man's head off. He'd have lost consciousness very quickly, bled out in a matter of minutes.'

Half an hour later and they were sitting in the shared office that opened on to the examination theatre. Cadwallader had taken off his gore-smeared scrubs and was even now climbing into a new, clean set, ready for the next body to be wheeled in. Outside, Tracy was busy putting the removed organs back into Ben Stevenson's torso and sewing him up with her large, neat stitches. Dr MacPhail had wandered off in search of some lunch.

'What about ligatures? Was he tied up?'

'There's marks around his wrists, but they're very light. He never fought against them. And there's nothing around his ankles, so he wasn't tied up. He could walk.'

'Forced at gunpoint, maybe?'

'It's possible, I suppose. That's your department, though. I'm more interested in what I could find on him.'

McLean said nothing, just leaned against the desk and waited for Cadwallader to decide his audience was ready.

'First off, his knees were marked where he'd been kneeling on the ground for a while. He was wearing trousers, but the rough surface had puckered his skin before death. There were similar marks on his forehead.'

'So he knelt right down, put his head to the ground. Praying?'

'That sort of posture, at least. But he'd have had to have knelt that way for some time. Ten, fifteen minutes. Maybe more.'

'There was blood on the cave wall. Do we know if it was his?'

'It was, yes.' Cadwallader reached for a sheet of paper on his desk, picked it up and waved it around as if that made everything clear.

'So that would have been done by the killer. After Stevenson was dead.'

'If not by the killer, then by someone with him.'

'Let's not complicate things any further, shall we?' McLean said. 'Bad enough we've got a body in a cave and the only way in is through a locked door with only one set of keys.'

'Yes, well. You'll have to puzzle that one out, I guess. There's one thing you might find interesting though.'

'There is? What?'

'He was wet.'

'Wet?'

'Soaked right through. His hair's quite short, but it was damp at the roots. It was damp in the cave, of course. The whole bloody city feels like it's underwater. But damp air wouldn't soak him through.' Cadwallader paused a moment as if trying to remember. 'No, it was Tracy who noticed it first. When she was taking off his clothes and bagging them up for the forensics people. They were damp as well, you see. His trousers were almost dry, but his underpants were still wet. Like he'd been starting to dry out. His body heat would have driven most of the moisture off eventually, but of course he started cooling down the moment his throat was cut.'

'How long was he down there? Can you hazard a time of death?'

Cadwallader smiled, that evil glint in his eye that McLean knew meant nothing but trouble.

'Difficult case, you know. The temperature down there was cool, and very stable. No rodent damage either, and very little insect life on him.'

'So it was recent?'

'That's what I thought at first. Oh, a few days, of course. Rigor mortis had been and gone, and what little blood he had left had settled on the side where he was lying. But there's a few other tests we can do, and they all suggested he'd been there longer.'

'Longer?' McLean felt the familiar unpleasant cold sensation in his stomach that always came when things were about to get weird.

'Best guess is about three weeks,' Cadwallader said. 'Could be four, but certainly not less than eighteen days.'

9

It's remarkably easy to pose as a doctor. Hospitals are so busy, their staff turnover so rapid, all you really need is a white coat, a stethoscope, a smattering of medical jargon and you're there.

The hard part is keeping it up for any length of time. Sooner or later someone's going to ask you to do something you don't know how to do, or ask you a question you can't answer. That's when you need a quick-exit strategy.

I don't really like hospitals. I died in one not so different from this. And yet here I am. Drawn to this place like a moth to a flame. Goodness flourishes here, amongst the wickedness and despair. It is a place where ordinary people do extraordinary things, a place where souls are redeemed. That's why I keep on coming back. God's work, my sacred duty demands it of me. It is my refuge and my hunting ground both.

Everyone needs to eat. Watch them eating and you'll see more of them than they'll ever tell you themselves. I start with the staff canteen. Check out the late lunch crowd. It's easy to spot the groups, the med students who've been in it together since first year, the trainee nurses who'll probably head into the private sector as soon as they graduate. These are not special people. They shine with a dull light at best. Given time and effort I might coax the goodness out of them, but time is a luxury I have never had. No, somewhere in here there is one who is almost pure. I can feel him like an angler feels the gentlest of tugs on his baited line. It is not sight or smell or touch that brings me to him; I do not taste the air like a snake, or listen to the voices clamouring all around. Instead this is a different sense, a knowing that guides me away from the crowd, off towards the edges of the room. God's hand.

And there he is, alone by the window, playing idly with a plate of congealed spaghetti bolognese, drinking occasionally from a stained white mug of cold coffee. His obsession oozes from him like a disease. Maybe that's why his colleagues shun him. Whatever the reason, he is perfect. I can see his secrets writ large across his face. I know he is the one.

'You mind?' I ask as I sit down opposite him, slide my tray on to the table until it neatly lines up with his own. His look is startled, wary, but I can see the interest there as well. He doesn't know me, but that means he hasn't been scorned by me yet.

'New here, aren't you?'

'Aye. First week. Crazy place.'

'A and E?'

I shake my head. 'Geriatric care.'

'Lots of that here. I'm in oncology. Specialise in terminal cases, lucky me.' He holds out his hand. 'Jim,' he says.

I wipe my own hand on my purloined white coat hurriedly before taking his. The touch is warm and dry, the grip firm. I sense the aura of near-perfection about him and know he will be saved. 'Ben,' I say. 'Ben Stevenson.'

10

'You seen Dan Hwei about?'

McLean looked across the incident room, hoping to spot the press liaison officer at one of the media desks. They were all empty, as was much of the rest of the room. Only Detective Constables Gregg and MacBride were in attendance, along with a half-dozen support staff. So much for a major investigation.

'Think he went off to DCI Brooks' briefing.' MacBride dragged his eyes away from his computer screen, and scanned the room as if only just realising there was almost nobody there.

'He does realise this is a murder investigation?' McLean asked. 'What's he briefing about, anyway?'

'Some big drugs operation, I think. Been working with Serious and Organised, or the NCA or whatever it's calling itself this week.' DC Gregg didn't even look up as she spoke, just continued jabbing at her keyboard with two fingers. Obviously not happy at being left out of the action. Either that or she really was rubbish at typing.

'Ah yes, I remember now. Thought we were getting a busload of detectives over from Strathclyde to work on that.'

'Chance'd be a fine thing.' Gregg abandoned her typing and finally turned to look at him. 'They keep dragging us over there to fill numbers. Not saying they don't need the help, mind. But we're not exactly overstaffed as it is.'

McLean held his hands up in mock surrender. Sandy Gregg wasn't someone to mess with at the best of times. 'You'll not find me arguing with you, Constable. Not much I can do about it, either. I was just looking for Dan.'

'Anything specific you needed him for, sir?' MacBride asked.

'A phone number for Jo Dalgliesh, actually. Words I never thought I'd hear myself say.'

MacBride grabbed his mouse, clicked a couple of times, then scribbled a string of digits down on a Post-it note and handed it over. 'It'll be on your phone anyway, sir. She's always calling you, after all.'

McLean retreated to the quiet of his own office before placing the call. Not that the incident room was exactly overcrowded, but something about the act of talking to the press made him feel strangely guilty. Using his office phone meant that he could at least pretend he wasn't giving Dalgliesh his mobile number, too. MacBride was right though; he'd changed it once before and she'd still managed to get hold of the new number in a matter of days. Hours, possibly.

'Aye?' Dalgliesh's telephone manner was in keeping with her general demeanour. McLean imagined her sitting at a cluttered desk, unlit cigarette dangling from her lip, leather coat still on despite being indoors.

'Ms Dalgliesh?' McLean asked.

'Aye. Who is this?'

'Detective Inspector McLean.' He almost added 'Lothian and Borders' but managed to stop himself at the last minute.

'So it is. Well, well. What an unexpected surprise.' Dalgliesh paused for a moment, the line crackling with gentle static. When she spoke again, her voice was flat. 'You found Ben.'

'Is it that obvious?'

'Can't think of any other reason why you'd phone me. He dead?'

'I think it'd be better if I spoke to you in person. It's . . . complicated.'

'Shit. No' that body you found up at Gilmerton Cove?' Dalgliesh muffled the receiver at her end, but McLean could still hear a string of colourful words. It stopped him asking her how she knew about the body long enough for him to realise it would be a wasted question. Guarding her sources, particularly within the ranks of the police, was second nature to the journalist.

'You want me to come round the station?' she asked after the air had cleared. 'Only I've a meeting set up for this afternoon's taken me months to arrange. Really don't want to cancel it.'

McLean glanced at his watch. Almost noon. 'No. I'll come round to your office. I could do with stretching my legs a bit. Give me fifteen minutes.'

Never having been a fan of the press, McLean hadn't spent much time in the offices of the *Edinburgh Tribune*. He knew where they were though, just a short walk from the station, down towards Holyrood and the parliament building. A hot sun and humid air meant he was sweating by the time he got there, but the reception area was well air-conditioned, bright and surprisingly modern. He gave his name to the receptionist, then waited while she phoned up to the floor where all the hacks lived. Sooner than he was expecting the lift pinged and Jo Dalgliesh bustled out.

'Fifteen minutes on the nose, Inspector. I'm impressed.'

McLean didn't know what to say. He was taken aback by Dalgliesh's appearance more than anything; couldn't recall a time he'd seen her not wearing her trademark battered leather coat. Even more unsettling was seeing her in a skirt, cut just below the knees, calf-length suede boots and a blouse that looked like it might have been fashionable in the 1980s. She even had a red silk scarf tied loosely around her neck. The only thing suggesting she might be a journalist with questionable ethics and not some well-to-do middle-aged lady off to tea at Jenners was the fact that she was carrying a battered notebook. That and the severe crop to her greying hair.

'Going to a party?' McLean asked.

Dalgliesh paused a moment. 'What? This?' She half-gestured at her blouse. 'Important meeting later this afternoon. Got to look my best.'

McLean let the obvious comment slide; scoring points off Jo Dalgliesh wasn't why he was here, after all. 'There somewhere we can go and talk?'

'Sure. This way.' She led him through a security door that took them into a large, open-plan office. This was more the type of thing McLean had been expecting to see – a busy, barely organised chaos as dozens of journalists clattered away at keyboards or clustered around large screens discussing how best to frame their more lurid stories. He recognised a few of the faces and some even smiled at him, warily, as he followed Dalgliesh through to a small meeting room.

'So, Ben,' she said once she'd closed the door behind him and wound down the blinds covering the window that looked out on to the main office. 'He's dead.'

'Yes. He's dead. I'm sorry.'

Dalgliesh cocked her head to one side like a confused puppy. 'You really mean that, don't you? I'm sorry too. He could be a pain in the arse at times, but he was . . .' She broke off as if unsure what he was.

'Do you know what he was working on?'

'Not a Scooby, Inspector. Ben's . . . Ben was very secretive when he had a project on.'

'OK. What sort of things interested him? What might he have been working on that would take him out to Gilmerton Cove?'

Dalgliesh leaned back against the conference table that dominated the room, ran a scrawny hand over her face, frowned as if the effort of thinking needed to be shown on the outside. McLean was fairly sure it was all an act, the pauses just a little too dramatic.

'He loved a good conspiracy theory, did Ben,' she said eventually. 'Secret societies were his thing. Last time I saw him he was babbling on about the Beggar's Benison and the Hellfire Club. But I got the impression his project was something different. How did he die?'

Always the journalist. Well, she'd find out sooner or later. 'He had his throat cut. Ear to ear. Deep, too.'

If she was shocked, Dalgliesh didn't show it. But neither did she immediately scribble down notes in her book.

'And you found him in a cavern behind a locked door. Least that's what I heard.'

'One of these days I'll find out which constable is talking to you and he'll be spending the rest of his life directing traffic on the Gogar Roundabout.'

'What makes you think it's a he? Or just the one?' Dalgliesh gave him a shark's smile.

'True enough. And you're right. Yes, we found him in a cave behind a locked door. How he got in there is one question, but perhaps more pertinent is the fact that he appears to have gone there of his own volition, and died without a struggle. And his killer left behind a little message for us, too.'

'He did? Are you going to tell me what?'

'That depends on whether you're just going to print it all, or help us with our enquiries. If it's the former, we're done here. The latter and you'll get an exclusive.'

Dalgliesh tried to look casually uninterested, but McLean could see that he had her attention now. Her back was straighter, her eyes bright, even though they were narrowed in a suspicious frown. 'What's the catch?'

'You don't publish anything until we let it out.' McLean saw the protest coming before Dalgliesh could even open her mouth to voice it. He raised a hand for her to wait. 'I don't mean you can't write anything at all. You'll get a story, and before anyone else out there. I just need to control how the details are released. Don't want our killer getting tipped off as to how close we are. Or how far-off.'

Dalgliesh considered for all of ten seconds. 'OK. What do you want me to do?'

‘I want you to try to find out what he was investigating, who he was talking to, where he’s been the last few weeks.’

Dalgliesh stood, crossed the room to where McLean was standing. ‘Deal,’ she said, and stuck out her hand to be shaken. For an irrational moment, he thought of refusing to take it. She was someone he would have happily seen hung upside down in chains in a dungeon, after all. But she was also as close to an answer to this case as he was going to find. Swallowing his pride, he took her hand, finding it both warm and surprisingly small.

‘You hold anything back, I’ll find out,’ she said.

‘Likewise, Ms Dalgliesh.’ McLean let go of her hand, resisted the urge to wipe his own on his trouser leg. ‘Enjoy your meeting. Good luck with the promotion.’

‘How did you . . .?’

‘All dolled up like that? And the man who owns this paper’s in town for a couple of days. First visit he’s paid to Scotland in a decade?’ McLean shook his head to suppress the smirk that wanted to spread across his face. ‘You’re not the only one good at finding out things, you know.’

11

'How are we getting on down there?'

McLean stood in the entrance hall of the tiny cottage that served as a visitor centre. The posters telling the history of the place still hung on the walls, but all available floor space had been taken over by the forensics services and their endless piles of aluminium cases. There were more downstairs, with a steady stream being brought back up from below.

'Almost done in the caves. And no, I'm not going to tell you what we've found so far because I don't want to be rude.' Jemima Cairns stood with a clipboard, noting down the numbers on the battered cases, checking them all before they were taken outside and loaded into the big van. It was somewhat menial work for a forensic scientist of her experience, skill and pay grade, but someone had told McLean in passing that she wasn't overly fond of enclosed spaces. She'd been down once, apparently, then taken an uncharacteristic interest in the paperwork.

'That little, is it?' McLean asked.

'Might have got more if the scene hadn't been disturbed by a herd of elephants.' Dr Cairns' normal expression was a scowl, but it wasn't often this deep. 'Don't know what they're teaching archaeologists these days. I thought they were meant to be all about preserving evidence. The way they tramped around that cave and scuffed up all the ground . . .'

'I don't think they were expecting to find a body in there,' McLean said. 'Well, at least not one quite so fresh.'

'Still makes our job almost impossible. Nothing but the body, and the blood on the cave wall. Can't even tell how he got in there. No sign the lock's been tampered with, so whoever did it must have had a key.'

'OK if I go down and have a look?' McLean asked.

'Knock yourself out. We're pretty much done. You can even skip wearing the bunny suit. Unless, you know, that's your thing?'

McLean smiled at the joke, left Dr Cairns ticking off boxes. He was about to tell Grumpy Bob to join him, but the old sergeant was busy reading one of the wall-mounted display panels and seemed happy enough.

'I'll see you down there,' he said and headed for the narrow stairs that descended into the cave complex.

On a second viewing, it seemed somehow smaller, and yet also more impressive. Whereas before he had been led straight to the scene, this time he was able to take a moment to look at the way the sandstone had been carved, the many alcoves and rooms leading off the passageways. It was cool down here, a welcome relief from the humid heat of the day outside, but it was also damp and smelled like a small army of SOCOs had been working in it for days.

Lit up with arc lights, the cavern where Stevenson's body had been found was an impressive sight. Almost perfectly round, the walls rose vertically for about ten feet, before curving elegantly into a dome. There was nothing else in the place except for the markers where the body had lain, the channel dug into the rock floor to divert water to the sinkhole, and the sinkhole itself.

McLean walked over to the spot where Ben Stevenson had met his end, noting the soft, gritty floor as he did so. Dr Cairns was right; it looked like a herd of elephants had been practising dressage on it. No chance of finding a footprint that could be matched to a potential killer. Of course, forensics weren't as careful in leaving as when they arrived, so the state of the place might have had something to do with them. It didn't matter, there were no answers here.

Looking up at the wall, he squinted to try and see any pattern to the blood smearings. Like the other caves, this one had been hewn from the rock with sharp-pointed chisels, leaving a rough surface. The arc lights cast shadows that seemed to leap and writhe as he tilted his head this way and that. It made his eyes ache just looking at it, not helped by the rivulets of water seeping through the rock and smearing the blood as they travelled slowly to the floor. He gave up and turned his attention to the site where the body had lain.

Ben Stevenson had bled out into the drainage channel, his blood mingling with the rainwater and flowing unimpeded to the sinkhole. The channel was smooth and clean, curving almost perfectly with the arc of the walls. McLean followed it around until he was standing at the edge of the sinkhole.

It was about four feet in diameter, oval-shaped and cut into the floor with a slightly raised edge all around except where the channel met it. The water inside reflected the arc lights, perfectly still and mysterious. He wondered how deep it was, whether the water was stagnant or connected to an underground stream somewhere. He knelt against the low stone lip, peering into the blackness as if that was a good way to find the answers.

Which was when the lights went out.

'Oi! I'm in here.' McLean shouted the words over his shoulder, slipping as he did so. He shot a hand out to steady himself, missed the edge and plunged it into the water. He was fully expecting to follow it, wondering how he was going to live down the inevitable jokes, but after a couple of inches, his hand hit solid rock.

Relieved at not having an impromptu swim, it took him a while to realise that it wasn't a very shallow well, but a step carved into the side, perhaps a foot wide. He rolled up his dripping sleeve a bit before feeling further. Another step. After that it was too deep. In the gloom, with very little illumination spilling from the entrance at the other side of the cavern, he thought he could see beyond the reflective surface of the water, down to where something white reflected in the darkness. He pulled out his torch, flicked it on and pointed it straight down. Sure enough, maybe ten feet below at the bottom of the well there was something pale and foreign. Out of place.

'Still in here,' McLean shouted, his voice echoing in the darkness. A couple of seconds later the lights came back on again. He squinted, surprised at how quickly his eyes had become accustomed to the darkness.

'I'm sorry sir. Thought everyone had left.' A young SOCO shuffled through the opening, then stood up tall. He was the complete opposite of his boss, Dr Cairns. Wiry-thin and at least six foot four. Completely the wrong build to be down here in the tunnels.

'It's no matter.' McLean stood up, rolling his jacket

sleeve back down and feeling the dampness in it. Soaked right through. 'Has anyone checked out the well?'

'How do you mean? We took a sample of it, but . . .' The young SOCO looked puzzled.

'We'll need to get a remote underwater camera. There's something down there.'

'You know, I don't think it's a well at all. Think it might be another passage.'

All the arc lights in the cave had been gathered around the well. Pointing downwards, their glare reflected off the surface of the water, but enough penetrated into the depths to show a series of steps spiralling to the bottom. With the extra light, McLean could tell that the white object wasn't a fallen rock or something old. It looked like a discarded shopping bag, moving back and forth ever so slightly as if tugged by an invisible current.

'Could be. We're heading in a downhill direction so it'd make sense to go deeper if you were digging tunnels further.'

The unusually tall SOCO's name was Karl. He had managed to find a telescopic pole with a hook on the end, but it wasn't quite long enough to reach all the way to the bottom. McLean watched from the other side as he leaned over the short parapet, arm up to his elbow in the water. A couple of shorter forensic experts looked on, one with a camera on a strap around his neck, the other holding a clipboard that, as far as McLean could tell, had no paper attached. He got the impression they were there more out of idle curiosity than any kind of professional pride. Only Grumpy Bob was paying no attention to the well. The old sergeant seemed to find the cavern walls far more interesting, peering up at the vaulted ceiling as he wandered around muttering to himself.

'How far do you think they go?'

'Ah, now that's a question for the archaeology boys. I've heard there's caves like these up Roslin Glen way, and the city centre's full of hidden passages and stuff. Could be it all links up.'

From where he was standing, McLean couldn't tell whether Karl was being serious or not. He knew about the caves at Hawthornden Castle though, and there was the small matter of the subterranean world underneath Rosskettle Hospital that had come to light recently. Mine workings and tunnels lay undiscovered all over Midlothian, dating back to Roman times and earlier. It wasn't so far-fetched to think that these mysterious caverns might spread further than anyone realised.

'If it's not a well, then why's it full of water?'

'Looks like it's blocked at the bottom. There's a jumble of rocks and stuff. All the rain we've had the past few weeks, wouldn't surprise me if it just got flooded out. Ah, here we go.' Karl leaned even further into the water, his chin just a fraction of an inch above the surface as he extended his considerable reach. He'd stripped off to the waist, and McLean couldn't help but shiver at the thought of how cold he must be.

'Got it?' he asked.

'Yup.' And slowly Karl pushed himself away from the low stone parapet surrounding the hole, with first his shoulder, then his arm and finally the long telescopic pole emerging from the water like Excalibur.

'Get some plastic sheeting down, can you? And turn that floodlight round.'

The SOCO with the clipboard frowned at McLean, but did as he was told. Soon Karl was pulling the end of the pole out of the water, a sodden mess of something fabric drooping from its hooked end. He manoeuvred it, dripping, over the stone parapet and on to the freshly laid sheet, rivulets of water flowing away from it as it took on a more recognisable shape. A pale white jacket.

McLean slipped on a pair of latex gloves as he approached the newly fetched plastic sheeting where Karl was laying out the coat as if he were the best man setting out the groom's suit before the big day. The SOCO with the camera was busy taking photos, the flash making it hard to focus on any detail.

'Doesn't look all that old to me. Craghoppers. You can buy them in pretty much any outdoor clothing shop. Got one myself.' Karl opened up the front of the coat, fingers working slowly down the line of the zip, checking the pockets. McLean wondered if he was going to get dressed any time soon, felt it best not to say anything.

'Sort of thing a journalist might wear?' he asked.

'Sort of thing anyone might wear. Ah, here's something.' The SOCO put his hand carefully into one of the pockets and pulled out a damp notebook and pen. 'Bag, please.'

His colleague bustled over with an evidence bag, sealing up the notebook before it could disintegrate any further.

'Can I see that?' McLean put his hand out.

'We need to get it to the lab. We can dry it out properly there.'

'I'm not going to open it. Just want to look at the cover.'

A short pause, then with obvious reluctance, the SOCO handed his bounty over. McLean turned the notebook around very carefully. He could feel how sodden it was, and the water pooling in the bag was grey with pulped paper. It was cheap, spiral bound, the sort of thing you picked up in packs of six for a pound from the local supermarket. There was nothing written on it, no useful name or address, but there was a crude symbol, etched in biro across the cover.

'That what I think it is?' Grumpy Bob loomed over his shoulder, blocking out the best of the light. 'Aye, it is. Isn't it?'

'Yup.' McLean handed the notebook carefully back to the SOCO, taking one last look at the compass and set-square. 'Bloody Masons. Dagwood's going to be happy as a clam.'

12

If I were a kind man, I'd tell him to improve his home security. I'm not though, at least not like that. So I won't.

It takes thirty seconds to get in through the front door, and I don't even have to try all the entry buttons until someone buzzes me in without asking who it is. The lock is old, the electro-mechanical release mechanism worn enough that a couple of well-timed shoves spring it open. Inside, the city noise drops away, leaving me with a smell of foreign bodies, bin bags left out too long, cat piss. Upstairs the only way of knowing I've got the right place is a torn-off strip of paper with a name written on it in biro, taped underneath a bell-push that has long since been painted solid. Security here is no better, just a Yale lock that yields to a supermarket loyalty card, and I'm in.

I know these tenement flats are small; I posed as a buyer for the one being sold next door so I could get a look at the layout of the place. Even so, the sense of being in a cave is almost overwhelming. A narrow skylight darkened with many years of city grime is the only source of illumination for the tiny hallway, filtering down from high above and setting me at ease. I take a moment to gather my wits about me, listen for any sound that the flat is occupied even though I know it won't be. He has no family, no life beyond his work. This is his lair, but it is no more than a place to sleep, occasionally to eat. And to feed his obsession.

The kitchen is barely more than a cupboard; the cooker, sink, fridge and cupboards squeezed in with commendable ingenuity. An empty bowl and mug sit by the sink, waiting to be washed. From the smell of sour milk it's been a day or two since last he had breakfast. Black grounds in the bottom of a one-person cafetière are the only sign of sophistication. I move on.

The shower room – no bath here – is at least tidy, although limescale pastes the glass enclosure and black mould is feasting on the grouting between cracked white tiles. The medicine cabinet over the basin holds no surprises. He may be a doctor, but he doesn't self-medicate. Not that desperate. Not yet. It's the pile of reading material beside the toilet that interests me most. Some medical texts, printouts from the teaching hospital library, slipped between copies of *Scientific American*, *New Scientist* and a couple of more obscure medical research titles. They are well thumbed, the pages stained with toothpaste and saliva where he's read them whilst brushing his teeth. The articles are about new techniques in stem-cell therapy, off-licence drug treatments, alternative medicines of a kind far removed from the homeopathic. I begin to see a picture of the man emerging.

The bedroom is tidy, which surprises me. I expected more scientific papers, clothes thrown across the bed, signs of the hunger that gnaws at him, that has honed his soul to such a fine edge. I find them instead in the living room to the front, overlooking the street, and the depths of his obsession become apparent.

This is where he lives when he's not at the hospital. The other rooms have functions that can more or less be circumvented; who needs to sleep in a bed when there's a couch? There are no pictures in the whole flat, that's one of the first things I noticed. The decor looks as if it was left behind by the previous owner. But the walls in the living room are covered in papers torn from medical journals, printouts of emails from research scientists across the globe, newspaper cuttings and other snippets of information. This is what I was looking for, what I saw in him the first time we met in the hospital canteen. This is what drives him to the exclusion of all earthly temptations, what shrives him.

This will be the key that opens him up.

13

McLean stared at the pile of reports, folders and other general detritus strewn across his desk and stacked precariously alongside it. Just looking at the mess made him weary; the thought of tackling it, doubly so. He'd managed to grab a bite to eat once he and Grumpy Bob had returned from Gilmerton Cove, but had completely failed to find either Detective Superintendent Duguid or DCI Brooks. There were other officers in the station who were Freemasons, but those two, and Duguid in particular, held senior enough positions to be of use. Not that he really thought the Masonic link was anything other than a hoax, a diversion maybe, but it was a lead that would have to be followed. He rubbed at tired eyes, not looking forward to having that conversation with either man.

When the phone rang, at first he couldn't work out what it was. The handset on his desk normally lit up when a call came through. Then McLean realised it was his mobile, hidden under a folder containing transcripts of the interviews with all the archaeology students. Yet another dead end in the investigation. He snatched up the phone and managed to hit the right button on the screen before it switched to answerphone.

'McLean?'

'Aye, so it is. Thought I'd get you on this number rather than go through the station.'

McLean took a moment to recognise the voice. The short, round, senior forensic scientist. 'Dr Cairns?'

'The very same. We've processed the crime scene photographs from the cave. Thought you might like to see them.'

McLean looked around his office again, disappointed to see that it was just as full of unnecessary paperwork as it had been five minutes ago. His laptop was folded up and buried under the mound somewhere. 'You want to ping them over in an email?'

'Aye, well, I could do that. But then you'd only see what you wanted to see. Better if you come over and I show you what we've got.'

He didn't really need an excuse, even if the paperwork would still be waiting for him when he got back.

'I'll be right over.'

'You said you had something to show me?'

It had only taken him half an hour to get from his stuffy little office to the fresher, air-conditioned labs of the forensic services across town. Dr Cairns had been passing the reception desk when he'd arrived. She had taken him straight through to the room with all the computers in it, where the photographic image manipulation was done. He couldn't help looking over at the desk where Emma had worked, pleased to see that no one else seemed to be using it. The last he had heard, she was somewhere in North Africa, but he hoped that she would come home soon. Seemingly the forensic service hoped so too.

'You wanted to see the photos from the cave.' Dr Cairns broke through McLean's distraction. He dragged his gaze from the empty desk back to her, catching the merest hint of a grin on her normally taciturn face.

'I did, yes.'

'Well Benny's been running them through the image analysis software. Reckon we've got something that makes a bit of sense now.'

Dr Cairns led McLean across the room, past a half-dozen casually dressed technicians hunched over computer stations, each of which probably cost more than the entire IT budget for his station. They all had enormous flat screens, two or three per operator, and he couldn't help but feel a twitch of jealousy even though he had no real need for anything more sophisticated than a laptop that actually talked to the network.

'You got the Gilmerton Cove file up, Benny?' Dr Cairns pitched her words loud to the scruffy fellow sitting in front of the largest screen in the whole room. Earphone cables snaked away from his long, ginger and slightly greasy hair, and he peered through spectacles so thick McLean had to consider that they'd given him the big monitor because he couldn't see anything smaller. His ears must have worked though, as he reached up, unplugged his earphones and turned to his boss, eyes flicking a quick glance in McLean's direction without any hint of alarm.

'Just finished it now.' Benny tucked his earphones carefully into the top pocket of his shirt before reaching for the mouse and clicking up a screen full of thumbnail images. 'You want me to print it out?'

'And waste our budget on ink? No, you can email the whole file over to the incident room. Let them pick up the tab. Come on, shoo.' Dr Cairns flicked her hands at the technician until he slid, reluctantly, off his stool. Standing, McLean could see that he was at least as tall as Karl, shoulders and back hunched in the habitual pose of a man who doesn't really enjoy standing out in a crowd. Dr Cairns scrabbled up on to the vacated stool, and grabbed at the mouse in a lunge that nearly saw her topple to the floor.

'Bloody hell. D'you no' get altitude sickness up here, Benny?' she said, before clicking through a series of images too quickly for McLean to see. Finally she stopped and he peered close, trying to make something out through the pixellation. The overall impression was blue. Early Impressionist.

'What am I supposed to be looking at?'

'This is your cave wall. Blood reflects a narrow band of the light spectrum, so we've run a filter to cut out everything else. See?' Dr Cairns clicked once more and the scene changed. It was a bit like one of those old parlour magic tricks McLean remembered from when he was a boy. The blue deepened, but a series of lines, letters and words leapt out at him in glowing yellow.

'Is this the pattern, then? What was written in Stevenson's blood?'

'Written?' Dr Cairns turned on the stool, lifting a single eyebrow in his direction. 'You ever tried to write in blood on a sandstone wall?'

'Not recently, no.'

'Well, it's not easy. Let me tell you that. Our man here's tried to write some words. You can see them here.' Dr Cairns highlighted an area of the screen, then zoomed in on it. The lines looped around each other in a way that at a casual glance might look like letters, but the more McLean stared, the less he could see.

'I don't . . .' he began.

'Perhaps it'll make more sense if I do this.' A couple more clicks and the image shifted, widened out, stretched. 'See?'

McLean tilted his head, just about seeing the letters now. 'Does that . . .?'

'"Seek not Baphomet and the Brotherhood, for all are brothers in death." Isn't it charming how misogynous these secret societies are?'

'The Brotherhood? Never heard of it. Baphomet sounds familiar. Can't think where, though.'

'Me neither.' Dr Cairns shrugged, then clicked the mouse a couple of times to bring up a new image. 'Might have something to do with this, though.'

McLean peered again at the large screen, unsure what he was looking at for a moment. And then he saw it. Not words any more, now the lines formed a pattern, a drawing, roughly sketched out over ten feet or more of cave wall.

'You managed to do anything with that notebook we found?' McLean asked. In response, Dr Cairns turned and gave him a teacher's best smile.

'Top marks for the detective. And before you ask, no, it's still drying out. We won't be able to do anything with it for at least a week.' She clicked the mouse again and the screen split into two images. One side showed what had been there before, the other a photograph of a very soggy notebook in an evidence bag. The pattern drawn on the wall with Ben Stevenson's blood was hard to make out – impossible without the aid of many thousands of pounds' worth of computing and image processing equipment – but it was undeniably the same as that scrawled in biro on the front of the notebook. The Masonic compass and set-square.

A pile of empty boxes stood outside the office on the top floor, waiting to be filled with the detritus of Detective Superintendent Duguid's mercifully brief stint in charge. No one manned the desk beside the open door, so McLean rapped on the jamb, peered inside.

'Hello?'

There was no reply, so he stepped inside, looked around. The desk was strewn with reports and folders piled almost as haphazardly as in his own office. The large executive chair on the other side was empty, though. He was about to turn and leave – the old schoolboy fear of being caught in the master's study alone never really left you after the first thrashing – when a cough behind him suggested it was already too late.

'What do you want, McLean?' Duguid pushed past him on his way to the chair, trailing a waft of stale tobacco. A lot of the hardened smokers were using e-cigarettes these days, at least until someone in HQ found out and put a stop to them vaping indoors, but Duguid had always been a high-tar, twenty-a-day man. Nothing was going to stop him now, least of all technology.

'About the Ben Stevenson investigation, sir. Something's come up that . . . well . . . you have a greater knowledge of these things than I do.'

Duguid slumped down into his chair, slapping his hands against the desk to keep from tipping over backwards. 'What on earth are you talking about?'

'This, sir. Was hoping you might be able to have a look at it.' McLean reached forward with the slim folder he'd been partially concealing behind his back, held it up for Duguid to take. The detective superintendent eyed it suspiciously before finally conceding. He opened it up as he slumped back once more into his treacherous chair, pulled out the photographs nestling within.

'This some kind of joke again?' The growl was back, McLean noticed. That almost always happened when the subject came up.

'Far from it. We found that mark on Stevenson's notebook, and daubed on the cavern wall in his blood. I believe it's the Masonic compass and set-square.'

'Of course it's the bloody Masonic compass and set-square. Any idiot could tell you that. Same as any idiot could have drawn it. Doesn't mean the Masons are out there cutting people's throats.'

McLean took a step back to avoid being burnt by Duguid's sudden rage. It was always thus when his beloved Freemasons came up.

'Did you ever write your name on the wall when you were a boy?' McLean asked, then added, 'Sir?' The effect was as he'd hoped, calming the detective superintendent's anger with bafflement.

'What the fuck are you talking about?'

'I didn't. Wrote other boys' names a few times, to see if I could get them into trouble though. Never worked.'

'No. You've lost me completely.' Duguid shuffled the photographs back into their folder.

'Would someone involved in Freemasonry paint the

most recognisable symbol of their organisation in the blood of their victim at the crime scene?'

Duguid looked a little embarrassed. 'Oh, I see.'

'Exactly. This isn't about the Masons. It's about someone pretending to be something to do with them, or someone deliberately trying to send us off in the wrong direction. There's plenty of you on the force, sir, but not many senior detectives, and not many at your level within the organisation. I'd appreciate your input on that.' McLean nodded at the folder and its photographs.

'DCI Brooks would have been able to help you with this. If you'd asked him.'

'I know, sir. But I chose to ask you. Thought I might actually get somewhere that way.'

Duguid took the compliment, he had at least that much sense. 'I'll ask around, show it to some people. Looks phoney to me, but if your man Stevenson was a Lodge member I'll find out.'

'Thank you, sir. There was some writing on the wall, too. A mention of something called the Brotherhood. Capital B. Does that mean anything to you?'

McLean studied the detective superintendent's face as he flicked through the photographs and came to the enhanced image of the writing. He was looking for any telltale flicker of recognition. There was nothing for a moment, then a weary shake of the head.

'Sounds like utter bollocks to me. I mean it's a male institution, no women in the order, but I've never heard of something referring to itself as "The Brotherhood".'

'Well, if you could ask around I'd be grateful. Not sure

this will go anywhere, but we've precious few leads to work on.'

'That bad?'

McLean looked past Duguid, through the window and out into the darkening city beyond. Another day gone, the trail to the killer that little bit colder. Who was he kidding? It had been stone cold the day they discovered the body.

'Worse,' he said, then turned and left.

'Detective Inspector McLean?'

He had thought the street empty. It was certainly late enough as he walked out through the gates to the parking lot at the back of the station. He'd looked in vain for a squad car to cadge a lift from and was resigning himself to a long walk home, perhaps via a pub and a curry. Looking around, he saw a woman standing just a few feet away, no obvious shadows to explain how he'd missed her before.

'Can I help you?' As he asked the question, he realised he'd seen her somewhere before. It took a moment, then he placed her. Tapping away at a laptop computer in the site office around the back of his tenement building. She was short, slim, and with her severe, grey hair might have been thought frail were it not for the way she carried herself. Back straight, eyes clear as they fixed their gaze on him without the aid of spectacles, she exuded an inner strength quite at odds with her appearance.

'Violet Grainger. I work with Joe and Jock McClymont.' She held out a hand. McLean wasn't surprised to find her grip firm, was surprised at how cold it was. She fixed him with the stare of someone who has heard about being friendly but hasn't yet mastered the skill. 'Wondered if I might have a word. About the development in East Preston Street.'

'Not sure if there's much more I can say.' McLean released his grip, but Ms Grainger still clasped his hand, enveloping it with both of hers.

'It means such a lot to them, you know. That site. They've put everything into it.'

'Isn't that a bit presumptuous? I mean, they don't even own it all.'

Ms Grainger stared straight at him, her pale grey eyes unnerving in the half-light. It felt like he was trapped. A small animal in the headlights as the truck came bearing down on him. For an instant he knew the old fear, from his childhood. The monsters lurking under the bed, the troll in the attic, the ugly, half-formed creatures that roamed the graveyard beyond his garden in the hours of darkness. He knew them then, and would have done anything to escape them, escape that feeling.

'Not yet, no. But they own most of it. You could sell them your share, you know. Take the money and walk away. Then everyone would be happy.'

McLean tugged his hand away from the old woman's cold grasp. Something about her words, particularly that last one, rang hollow. Only one person would be happy in this arrangement and it wasn't him. Neither was it Joe or Jock McClymont. He knew that as clearly as if it had been written across Ms Grainger's face. Instead, a fleeting confusion filled her eyes, then she pulled herself together. Drew down a mask of blankness over her face, pursed her lips before speaking again.

'But I can see you're not a kindly man.'

Her petulance burst the surreal bubble that had surrounded the whole meeting. 'I've made my position clear on the matter,' McLean said. 'My old flat, or as close to it as modern building regulations will allow. You can have the rest of the building for all I care, but that's my price. Now if you'll excuse me, Ms Grainger, it's been a long day and I'd quite like to get home before it ends.'

He walked back towards the station. He'd call for a taxi if there were no squad cars heading out. Turning at the entrance, McLean looked back to where the old woman had been standing. The street was clear, straight in both directions for a hundred yards or more. But she was nowhere to be seen.

14

Mrs McCutcheon's cat stared up at him from its favoured place in the middle of the kitchen table as McLean let himself in through the back door. Another long, frustrating day and all he really wanted to do was crack open a beer, order a pizza and put his feet up.

'You and I need to have a chat about hygiene sometime soon.' He dumped his folder down on the table, getting nothing more than a suspicious stare from the cat in return. He couldn't bring himself to shoo it out of the way. It wasn't as if he spent a lot of time preparing food at the table. Or eating at it, for that matter. It was nice just to have someone to talk to when he got home, really. And Mrs McCutcheon's cat was a good listener.

The heat of the day was dissipating quickly, evening fading to night, but the air in the hall was still and humid, cooked by a long day under the sun. He would have liked to have left windows open, let the place ventilate properly during the day, but with just the cat to keep an eye on things, McLean knew that was a bad idea. If the local community support team found out how lax his security was, they'd give him hell. Or worse, use him as an example to all the other officers. There was an alarm system, of course, but the house had been built at a time when there was always someone at home, and burglary was very much a minority sport. It wasn't an easy place to make totally secure.

A little pile of flyers, catalogues and brown envelopes lay on the mat. He scanned them from a distance, hoping to see the slim form of a cheap postcard. McLean couldn't help it, every day was the same. It was over a year now since Emma had left, gone off on her mad quest. At first the postcards had been fairly regular, the places she sent them from at least vaguely familiar. More recently though, they had become sporadic, sometimes two in a week or even on the same day, then months of nothing at all. The last one had shown a picture of a stone fort in Ethiopia, and had travelled to Edinburgh through at least six different countries if the blurred franking marks obscuring most of her words were anything to go by. He'd pinned it up with all the others, on a large map of the world taped to the dining room wall, charting her progress in the hope that she might head back towards home soon. But if anything she was getting further and further away, and as the months rolled past, so his memory of her shifted from something urgent and vital to yet another sad loss. One of so many it was hard to care about any of them any more.

Crouching, he scooped up the pile of mail, flicking through it swiftly as he stood up again. Nothing immediately of interest, he was turning back to the hall and the kitchen, thoughts of that beer and pizza at the forefront of his mind, when the doorbell rang.

It wasn't a foreign sound, but he heard it so infrequently these days that it took McLean a moment to realise what it was. He shoved the post down on the old wooden chest to one side of the porch, then set about the task of unbolting and unlocking the door. Finally it swung open, let in a waft of cooling evening air and revealed a large figure on the doorstep. He couldn't have said who he was expecting to see, since he'd not been expecting anyone and hadn't received any visitors in weeks. Of all the possibilities though, this was quite a long way down the list.

'Madame Rose?' McLean looked up into the large face of the transvestite medium, esoteric antiquarian bookseller and part-time fortune teller. 'Umm . . . Hello.'

'Oh, Inspector.' Madame Rose clutched a large hand to her bosom in a gesture of well-timed theatricality. 'I'm so sorry to bother you. But I couldn't think who else to turn to.'

'It's been a nightmare. You just wouldn't believe the trouble I've had.'

Back in the kitchen and McLean was busying himself with the making of tea. Madame Rose had settled into a chair at the kitchen table and almost immediately Mrs McCutcheon's cat had leapt into her lap. The medium looked haggard, there was no other way McLean could describe her. Normally tweedy to the point of ridiculousness, done up like the most old-fashioned of Morningside grandes dames, now she clasped a slightly tatty old overcoat around her as if the summer heat were no more than a memory. Her hair was a mess, grey the dominant colour, but it was her face that was the most shocking.

'Trouble?' McLean asked, trying hard not to stare. How long had it been since last he'd seen her? Around about the time Emma had left, at Jenny Nairn's funeral. She'd been sombre then, but larger than life. Now for all her great size, she seemed small. She'd lost weight, noticeably, and where once her skin had been a flawless mask of foundation and rouge, now she wore barely any make-up at all. She even sported a dark hint of stubble around her chin.

'I've always tried hard not to be judgemental.' Madame Rose scratched at the side of her nose with a fingernail rimmed with dark grime. She let out a little laugh. 'Could hardly be, could I? Not the way I am. Live and let live, that's always been my motto. Shame I can't say the same about other people.'

'Who's been giving you grief?' McLean fished teabags out of the two mugs, poured in milk and carried them over to the table. It was perhaps more telling than anything that Madame Rose didn't make any comment about the lack of teapot, loose-leaf tea, proper cups with saucers. She just cupped the mug between both hands and lifted it to her mouth.

'Who hasn't?' she said after taking a long sip. 'I had to close the shop, you know. Regular customers who'd been coming for years. They were getting shouted at in the street. Old Mr Jeffries was shaking with fear the last time he came for a reading. Took him almost an hour to calm down. I offered to walk him out, but he didn't want to be seen with me in public. He's been coming to the shop for twenty years.'

McLean leaned back against the Aga, cradling his own mug of tea un-drunk. Any minute now he expected Madame Rose to break down in tears.

'You've still not told me who they are. I take it they've a problem with what you do, who you are?'

'I really don't know what their problem is. If I'm being honest, I'm not really sure who they are, either. That's a large part of the problem. Oh the people doing it are Neds, mostly, I guess. I'm no stranger to a half-brick through the window. Worse shoved through the letterbox sometimes. Do you know how long I've lived in that house, Inspector?'

McLean recalled a room, larger than he'd expected to find at the back of a Leith Walk shop front, filled from floor to ceiling with antiquarian books, esoteric objects, things that could only really be described as 'things', and cats. Lots of cats. Curiously he didn't recall it smelling much of anything. 'I've no idea.'

'Before you were born, that's for certain.' Madame Rose took another long drink of tea.

'I'm really not sure—'

'What I'm saying, Inspector, is that I've lived in this city, in that particular part of this city, for a very long time. By and large people have been at the very least civil. Not much outward hostility, even given my . . . condition. Oh, there's been the odd person who'd have a go. There's always bullies, wherever you are. But mostly I've been left to live my life the way I chose.'

'So what's changed?'

Madame Rose looked at him for a moment before answering. McLean could see the lines around her eyes and mouth, the skeletal nature of her neck. He'd never really considered her age, but it was possible she could be in her sixties, he supposed. Older, even. Still, to have lived in the city so long?

'Everything, Inspector. And nothing. Things have been getting steadily worse since the eighties. But now it's like the bullies are being organised. Like there's an invisible hand behind their actions. They're hounding me out of my house and home. Driving away my livelihood. They even killed one of my cats.'

At these words, Mrs McCutcheon's cat, which had been curled up in Madame Rose's lap, purring gently, stood up and nudged the medium's hand. Without thinking, she began to scratch its ears.

'Have you been to the police?' McLean asked.

'Of course. But what can they do? It's never the same faces I see outside the window. That's if I see anyone at all.'

'But you said you thought they were being organised. I'm not saying you're wrong, but if you've not seen them, how do you know?'

Something of Madame Rose's former slightly imperious self came to the fore as she drew herself upright and stuck out her faux bosom so that Mrs McCutcheon's cat was almost trapped beneath it. 'I'd have thought of all people you would have understood. The likes of you and I, we deal in intangibles, gut feelings.' She swirled her mug, put it down on the table with a solid thunk. 'The portent in the tea leaves.'

'But you must have some idea—'

'If I knew who it was, I'd put an end to it. I am not without resources, my protections. This isn't the first time my place in the city has been challenged, though I have to admit I've not seen such a sophisticated attack in many a year.' Madame Rose stared back at him with some of her old vigour returning. Despite appearing less like a dowdy spinster and more like a man dressed badly in drag, McLean found himself referring to the medium as 'her', thinking of her as the gender she so obviously felt happiest being. She'd helped him, possibly helped Emma too, though that seemed to be a work in progress. And now something had upset her so much she had to come to him in return.

'I'll look into it. Can't promise anything, but if someone's organising a hate campaign, well, we have laws against that these days.'

Madame Rose's smile almost split her head in two. 'Thank you, Inspector. Tony. You have no idea how much that means to me.' She lifted Mrs McCutcheon's cat off her lap, placed it carefully on the table in front of her, stroked it once, left her ample hand resting on its head. 'There was one other thing.'

'Go on.'

'I'm not looking for a place to stay. They'll not drive me out of my home that easily.'

'But?' McLean held Madame Rose's gaze, almost certain he knew what he was going to be asked next.

'Just for a little while, maybe a month until I've dealt with this . . . delicate situation . . . I was wondering if you might have space in this lovely home of yours for one or two more cats?'

15

It never ceases to amaze and amuse me how easy it is to fool people. They hear what they want to hear, see what they want to see, and if you know what that is then the rest is child's play.

Child's play. I allow myself a small smirk of amusement at the realisation of just how appropriate that is. I am in the Royal Hospital for Sick Children, after all. The Sick Kids, as it's universally known. Not as easy to get into as you might think, which is a good thing, I suppose. No problem if you know how. If you've spent as much time here as I have.

He's here, though. Jim. He consults in the oncology ward two days a week, often more if he allows himself to get too attached to a case. I've been watching him a few weeks now, noting the simple patterns to his life, working out where his strings are and how to pull them. Today is a special day. Today I bring him one step closer to apotheosis.

'Ben?' His voice is hesitant. I have my back to him, head slightly turned so he can recognise me as I converse with one of the nurses on reception. He's three minutes late, which is annoying. The nurse was beginning to bore me.

'Jim?' I turn, let a second pass before smiling. 'What on earth are you doing here?'

'Could say the same about you, Ben.' He crosses the hall

with a weary step, the gait of a man who doesn't see his bed often enough. To my side, the nurse looks at him with an expression that suggests she wants to mother him, if only he'll let her get close. He hands her the clipboard he's been carrying, exchanges a familiar greeting before turning back to me. 'So what brings you to this neck of the woods?'

'Not in front of everyone.' I tap the side of my nose in a conspiratorial manner, lead him away from the nurse who is so obviously looking for some gossip to spread around the hospital. Across the hall it is quieter. I can lower my voice. This is serious business that should not be overheard.

'We're hoping to set up a trial for a new leukaemia therapy. All very hush hush at the moment. You know what people are like if they get a whiff of a possible cure.'

'I . . . how don't I know about this? Are you using differentiated stem cells? Nucleic refactoring?' His eyes go from tired to ablaze in an instant, the questions coming thick and fast. I never realised it would be this easy. Takes away a lot of the challenge, really.

'Please, keep it quiet.' I lay a hand on his arm, squeeze gently until he stops. 'It's early days. Might not even get approval.'

'I want to show you something. Someone.' He pulls away from my hold, starts to walk back across the hall. I don't move, and when he turns to see why, I mime looking at my watch.

'I can't. Already late for the meeting. Maybe another time?'

His impatience is a beautiful thing to see. Such a mind

that can heal the sick and not know what is wrong with itself. He is so close, if he could just see the simple step he needs to take.

'Tomorrow,' he says eventually. 'Meet me here at eight, OK?'

I nod, say nothing, move another piece on the game board.

16

'Thank you for coming in. I know this must be a very difficult time. For you and your daughters.'

Interview room three had been redecorated recently, which meant that it didn't look too shabby or intimidating. There was a powerful odour of paint though, and the window didn't open. On a warm August morning that made for a somewhat uncomfortable meeting. McLean had taken off his jacket and hung it over the back of his chair. Beside him, Grumpy Bob slumped like a man half asleep. Across from them the object of their interview looked fresh and well by comparison.

'It's not easy explaining to a child that daddy's not coming back ever again. But in some ways it's better they deal with it at such an early age. The young mind is so plastic. So malleable.' Charlie Stevenson wasn't exactly wearing widow's weeds. She was dressed for summer in a flowing floral dress that was so thin it revealed rather more than it hid. She was perhaps early thirties, well tanned and even better toned. A fashionably large pair of sunglasses was pushed up into her long straw-blonde hair, itself piled up in a loose knot on the top of her head. She had piercing grey eyes that fixed on McLean as he spoke and wouldn't let go.

'You and Mr Stevenson were recently divorced, I understand.'

'Yes. The papers finally came through about six months ago. Of course we'd been apart for a couple of years by then.'

'How long were you married before that?'

'Ten years.' The ex-Mrs Stevenson gave a little theatrical frown. 'No, I tell a lie. It was eleven. Give or take a month.'

'And you had two girls.'

'Lucy and Clare, yes. Lucy's five, Clare's seven. Is this relevant, Inspector?'

McLean paused before answering, holding that grey-eyed stare. She was undeniably good-looking, but something about the way she carried herself put him on edge.

'I'm trying to get a picture of Mr Stevenson's mental state over the last few months. You are . . . were closest to him.'

'That's debatable. Not since Lucy was born, at least.'

'Mr Stevenson had custody of the girls at weekends, I think.'

'Twice a month, yes. And he'd take them for longer if I needed to get away. He wasn't a bad father, Inspector. Ben doted on the girls.'

'What is it you do, Mrs Stevenson?'

'As I said, the papers came through six months ago. I've not been Mrs Stevenson in a very long time. I'm Miss Christie again now.'

'Of course, I'm sorry. What do you do, Miss Christie?'

'Do?'

'Work. What's your business that you occasionally have to get away for, for longer than a weekend?'

An angry scowl flitted across Miss Christie's face at the question. 'Again, I'm not sure how relevant that is. I'm not a suspect, am I? Only I've not got a lawyer or anything.'

'No, Miss Christie. You're not a suspect.' McLean clasped his hands together to keep from fidgeting, leaned his elbows on the table. Miss Christie uncrossed her legs, then crossed them over the other way, leaning forward herself.

'I'm trying to get some idea of Mr Stevenson's state of mind leading up to his death. You say you've been separated a couple of years, but you probably saw him as often as his colleagues at work, and you've known him longer than anyone. So tell me, when was the last time he had the girls for more than a weekend? When was the last time he had them at all?'

Miss Christie didn't answer straight away. It might have been that she was genuinely trying to remember, but McLean got the impression she was acting. She uncrossed and crossed her legs again, like a little girl desperate to be excused. He gave her all the time she needed, confident that Grumpy Bob wouldn't butt in. The silence was probably only twenty or thirty seconds, but it felt like a small ice age.

'He hasn't had the girls over in eight weeks. Maybe three months.' This was obviously a source of great annoyance to Miss Christie.

'But he saw them? Every so often?'

'He'd drop by my house sometimes. Pick them up from school and bring them home, maybe. But he'd never stay long.'

'Did he say why?' This from Grumpy Bob, the first he'd contributed to the conversation so far.

'He was working on something big. I know that much. It was like when he had that scoop a few years back. You remember, the corruption scandal in the council? Backhanders and nepotism and God only knows what else. That was Ben's last big story. I kind of got the impression he was on to something similar. As big, anyway.'

'But he didn't discuss it with you.'

'Not even when we were married. Ben was always very protective of his work, his sources. He often said he'd rather the story didn't get published than he betray a confidence. Took that very seriously. Too bloody seriously if you ask me. Like these narks, whatever they were, were more important than his wife and children.'

'So this new thing. It started about three months ago, then?'

'I reckon so, Inspector. That's when the girls started complaining, anyway. They love going to stay with their daddy. Kids are so innocent that way. Can't see the faults in us adults.'

McLean leaned back into his chair, as much to get away from the eye-catching view of Miss Christie's décolletage as anything. He'd scribbled a few notes down, but the main questions Mrs Stevenson – Miss Christie, he corrected himself – could answer, she had done.

'I think that's all for now. Thank you. Detective Sergeant Laird will see you get home OK.'

They all stood, Miss Christie gathering up the large canvas bag she'd brought with her, as Grumpy Bob went to open the door. She was about to leave when McLean thought of one last thing.

'You have a key, to Mr Stevenson's flat?' he asked.

'Of course. It was my home once.' Miss Christie hefted her bag as if to fetch something out of it.

'I'd be grateful if we could have it. Just until we've finished with the forensic investigation. I'm sure you'll keep away if we ask you to, but I'd hate for it to fall into someone else's hands.'

McLean held out his hand, maintaining eye contact all the while. There was a pause, and then Miss Christie shrugged, reached into the bag and pulled out a key ring. 'Fair enough,' she said as she handed it over. 'But I'll be wanting a receipt.'

The CID room was quiet, with most of what little action there was taking place in the major incident room up the stairs. McLean had gone there in search of DC MacBride, or at a pinch DC Gregg. He needed someone to come along with him when he visited Ben Stevenson's flat, and Grumpy Bob had disappeared after escorting the late journalist's ex-wife away from her interview. He didn't expect the pale, freckled face topped with an unruly mop of straggly red hair that stared up at him from a desk that had been empty for a couple of months now.

'Didn't think you were back until next week,' he said, then realised how rude that sounded. 'Sorry. It's good to see you, Kirsty.'

Detective Sergeant Ritchie's initial frown turned to a smile. 'I was going stir-crazy, sir. Cooped up in that wee basement flat.'

'You could have gone out, you know. Enjoyed the Festival, taken a holiday, rested.'

'Oh, I did plenty of that, but it gets a bit dull after a while. There's only so many books you can read before your brain starts to go all mushy.'

'That a fact?' McLean wished he had the time to put that theory to the test. He'd love the opportunity to lose himself in a good book for a change. Instead he had overtime rosters and reports so dry they made his eyeballs shrivel.

'Thought I'd do a bit of background reading. Bring myself up to speed before I start back proper on Monday.' Ritchie pointed at the computer screen in front of her, just in case he didn't know how she might do such a thing.

'I've got a better idea. Fancy a stroll up to Marchmont?'

'What's up there?' Ritchie was already out of her seat and lifting a lightweight fleece jacket off the back of her chair.

'A journalist's flat. Come on. I'll tell you all about it on the way.'

It took rather longer to walk there than he'd anticipated. DS Ritchie might have been declared fit for work by the doctors, but a fortnight in a hospital bed followed by a couple of months recuperating had left her frail. Walking more than a few hundred yards made her short of breath, and she couldn't match his normal pace at all. Not for the first time McLean was reminded of just how close to death she'd come, and all because of a kiss.

Ben Stevenson's address was a surprisingly large tenement flat in Marchmont. As McLean and Ritchie walked up the street towards it, he couldn't help thinking either that journalists were paid far more than their whining and complaints might suggest, or that Stevenson had a sideline in bank robbery. Then again, maybe the man had inherited money. It wasn't unheard of, after all.

''Bout bloody time. What took you so long?' As they

approached the front door, McLean noticed a figure standing by the door. It didn't take long for him to recognise Jo Dalgliesh, and he was relieved to see that she was back in her normal gear – scruffy jeans, Doc Martens, tattered leather coat and a canvas bag big enough for a fortnight's holiday. The pavement around her feet was littered with dog ends. Clearly she'd been waiting a while.

'What's she doing here?' DS Ritchie asked.

'Should have told you. She's working with us on this one. Sorry.' McLean had phoned the journalist before he'd gone in search of a constable to accompany him to Stevenson's flat. He'd been so surprised to find Ritchie in, he'd quite forgotten about it.

'Thought I'd have a quick fag.' Dalgliesh checked her watch. 'Didn't think I'd get through the whole packet.'

McLean ignored the jibe, unlocked the door with the key Charlie Christie had given him and entered the hallway. He remembered these tenements from his student days. Not Stevenson's block, but one or two along. They were bigger than the Newington flats, the communal stairs more opulent. This one was well kept, too. No students living here now, if the lack of broken bicycles and discarded pizza boxes was anything to go by. No half-brick to prop open the front door, either. And a complete absence of the stench of cat.

'You been here before?' McLean asked.

'No' fer a wee whiley. Used to come round a lot when Ben and Charlie were still together.'

'Charlie being the ex-wife?' Ritchie asked. She'd been eyeing the journalist suspiciously from the moment she'd first appeared.

'Aye. Never really liked her, if I'm being honest. Ben must've though. They stuck together long enough.'

'And they had two children.' McLean started the climb up to the top floor, glancing out of the window on to a neat communal garden behind the building.

'Two wee girls. Ben dotes on them. Doted, I guess. Poor wee things are going to miss their daddy.'

He stopped mid-step. The concept of empathy from the likes of Dalgliesh was so alien to him that he simply couldn't walk for a moment. This was the woman who, after all, had written a book dissecting in minute detail the final hours and violent, terrifying deaths of ten young women, without a thought for what the sharing of such information would do to the relatives of the dead.

'Top floor, Inspector.' Dalgliesh pushed past him on to the next landing. McLean stared at her back for a moment, realised that his mouth was hanging open. He shut it with an audible click, then followed her up the stairs.

17

From what little he recalled of the man whilst he was alive, McLean had been expecting Ben Stevenson's flat to be an untidy place, piled high with bric-a-brac, probably smelling faintly of carry-out and unwashed plates. The reality was a stark contrast to the slightly scruffy reporter's work persona.

They stood in the open doorway, looking over a large, wide hall. Doors led off to various rooms yet unrevealed, and an iron spiral staircase wound its way up into the attic. Everything was tidy, the furniture he could see a mixture of antique pieces and a more modern sideboard.

'Best you put some of these on before you touch anything.' McLean took a pair of latex gloves out of his pocket and handed them to Dalgliesh. 'And don't touch anything without asking me first, OK?'

She nodded, pulling the gloves on with far too much dexterity to suggest it was something she hadn't done many times before. McLean forced his hands into another pair, snapping them tight around his fingers. Behind them, Ritchie reached the top of the stairs and the front door with an audible sigh of relief.

'You want to take the back of the flat to start with, Sergeant?' McLean asked.

'Just give us a minute to catch my breath, aye?' Ritchie leaned heavily on the railing. Her normally pale face was almost white now, just the beige spread of freckles to give her any colour.

'Take your time. Not meant to be working today, anyway, are you?'

Dalgliesh raised an eyebrow, but said nothing, shadowing McLean like an obedient spaniel as he stepped into the hall. He didn't go far, just turned slowly on the spot, trying to get a feel for the place and the man who had lived here. Even from this viewpoint he could tell the tenement was huge and airy. Christ only knew what it was worth, especially if there was a second storey.

'We looking for anything in particular?' Dalgliesh asked.

'Anything that points to what he was working on, I guess. Did he have a study?'

'This way.' The reporter led him down the wide hall and through the living room. McLean noticed a familiar-looking Linn turntable, nestling in front of a wall filled with shelves of vinyl LPs. He thought he'd amassed quite a collection himself before the fire in his Newington tenement had turned them all into puddles of black liquid, but Stevenson made his efforts seem positively amateur.

'If I'd known journalism paid this well I might've gone into it myself.'

Dalgliesh let out a snort of laughter. 'Ben came from old money. He was good, but no' that good.'

Through a door at one end of the living room was what might once have been a maid's room. It was relatively small, but still big enough to hold a large desk dominated by an enormous computer screen. Bookshelves and filing cabinets lined three walls. The fourth, facing the main road, was mostly taken up with a sash window.

'Behold, the inner sanctum.' Dalgliesh lifted up both arms and turned on the spot. 'This is where Ben worked, when he wasn't at the paper.'

McLean walked around the desk, casting his eyes over the books on the shelves. Stevenson's reading tastes seemed eclectic and his filing system was haphazard. Autobiographies of famous footballers nestled cheek by jowl with crime fiction; political diaries snuggled up to scientific and economic textbooks. There were quite a few conspiracy theory books, too, but they covered a broad range of subjects.

'You worked with Stevenson on a few big stories. Seem to recall your byline on that piece about the independence referendum a few months back.'

'Oh aye, Ben 'n' me were thick as thieves, Inspector.' Dalgliesh didn't try to hide the sarcasm in her voice.

'But you worked with him. You came here? Discussed stories you were writing?'

'Sat just there.' Dalgliesh pointed at an armchair in the corner by the window. 'Me with my laptop, Ben on his Mac. Get the right story and we could be quite the team.'

'The right story?'

'Aye, well. There's times when collaborating's fine. Other times you just don't want another journo snooping around what you're doing.'

'And Stevenson's latest story was one of those times.'

'I asked him, sure. You could always tell with Ben when he had something on the go. But this one was personal. He wasn't going to share.'

McLean pulled out the chair and sat down at Stevenson's desk. It was uncannily tidy, just the computer, keyboard, touchpad instead of a mouse. A couple of hard-bound notebooks sat to one side, but when he opened the first, it was blank. The desk itself was a thick sheet of smoked black glass on a couple of chrome trestles. No drawers in which to hide things. To his right, a low, wheeled cabinet stood just within reach. The sort of thing artists used to store paints and brushes in the studio, it had a few small drawers and a big hinged flap on the top. Opening them revealed an assortment of pens and pencils, a couple more notebooks with nothing much written in them and a bar of expensive dark chocolate from Valvona & Crolla.

Swinging round in the chair, McLean put his hand out to the nearest bookshelf, just within reach of a long-armed man. The books here were the same haphazard mix of novels, biographies and historical texts, but there seemed to be something of a pattern. Two thick hardbacks were histories of the Freemasons. Alongside them, a couple of thinner paperbacks claimed to reveal the mysteries of the Knights Templar. A third was simply called *Head*, but when he pulled it from the shelf and looked at the front he could see that it had a subtitle: 'Baphomet, the Brotherhood and the Temple'. He frowned at the word 'Brotherhood'. Too much of a coincidence for his tired old cynicism to accept. McLean had never heard of the author, but when he flicked open the cover he saw that it had been signed and dedicated 'for Ben, a true believer'.

'You know anything about this?' He held the book up for Dalgliesh to see, wondered if she knew about the words daubed in Stevenson's blood on the cavern wall. She leaned over the desk, took it from him, peered at it myopically.

'Oh aye. I remember this one.' She laughed, then handed the book back. 'Dougie Ballantyne. Wee nutter that he is. Got this theory about the Templars and the Masons and Rosslyn Chapel and all that stuff. How they worship this severed head or something. Supposed to be the secret society to end them all, you know. Batshit stuff.'

'Seems Stevenson took it seriously enough.' McLean opened up the book again, looking at the signature. He flicked through the pages briefly, saw that the text had been marked in places. Damn, that meant he was going to have to read the bloody thing.

'That might well be it, then. What he was working on,' Dalgliesh said. 'That's his current project shelf, after all.'

McLean leaned back in the chair, hefted the book a couple of times. It wasn't a thick volume, but he reckoned the contents were going to make his head hurt more than the whisky it would take to read them. 'You want to help find who killed him, right?' he asked Dalgliesh.

'Aye, anything I can do.' She nodded.

'I'll get this computer to our IT bods. No point me messing with it here. But if you really want to be helpful, you can find out all there is to know about this.' McLean held up the book. 'See where he was going with it, and maybe we'll get a clue as to why someone wanted him stopped.'

They were heading for the door, McLean with the book clasped in one hand, when DS Ritchie's voice broke the quiet.

'Sir? I really think you ought to see this.'

McLean turned on the spot, almost knocking Dalgliesh

flying. He looked around for the detective sergeant, unable to see where she had called from.

'Up here.' Ritchie appeared at the top of the spiral staircase, crooking her head so she could see them without taking too many steps down. McLean started towards her, then realised Dalgliesh was following him.

'Stay here, OK?'

She scowled at him, but hung back as he climbed the stairs. They opened on to a surprisingly spacious attic, neatly converted into a master bedroom suite.

'I thought these places usually had communal lofts,' Ritchie said as she stepped out of McLean's way.

'Usually. Depends how the titles were drawn up when the place was built. Dalgliesh said Stevenson came from old money. Chances are this place has been in the family since the start.'

'Well, it's been done up recently if that's the case. Here, look.'

Ritchie headed off across the room, leaving McLean to follow. It was difficult to get a sense of the size of the apartment below, where the party walls were. The bedroom was magnificent though, under the pitched roof, with the ceiling rising to a high point maybe fifteen feet overhead. Facing the road, there were two small skylights designed to look like the original fittings, but at the back much larger dormer windows opened on to a narrow balcony and a view out across the Meadows to the Old Town that made him stop and stare.

'Through here, sir.' Ritchie stood beside what looked like a built-in wardrobe that surrounded the bed and filled the end wall of the building. McLean dragged himself away from the view.

'What is it?'

By way of an answer, Ritchie slid open the door. Instead of a row of suits hanging over drawers of socks and shirts, there was a narrow doorway that led into a small, hidden dressing room.

'Think this might have been where he was doing most of his work recently.' Ritchie nodded at an old dressing table pushed up against one wall. It had been cleared of the usual contents and was now piled up with books, notepads and maps. The notepads were the same type as the one they'd found in Stevenson's jacket, only dry. The mirror that would have been attached to the dressing table had been carefully removed from its frame and placed in the corner a few feet away. The wall behind it was covered in newspaper cuttings, pages torn from books, photographs and all manner of other papers, pinned up and with coloured strings running across everything as if a drug-addled giant spider had taken up residence.

'Aye, Ben could get a bit obsessive like that sometimes.'

McLean and Ritchie both turned to see Jo Dalgliesh standing just outside the dressing room, looking in.

'Thought I told you to stay downstairs.'

'What, and miss all the fun? No way Jose.' The reporter crossed into the room, peering up at the wall and its seemingly random collection of images. She pointed to one close to the centre, an elderly man with a massive, bushy white beard. 'See him. Is that no' the chappie wrote that book?'

McLean still clasped it in his hand. He looked at the cover, then turned it over to see the back. Sure enough, there was a tiny photograph of the author. It was possible there might be two people with such a distinctive beard. At the right time of year there would likely be hundreds in department stores and shopping malls all across the land. Only one Santa Claus lookalike was on Ben Stevenson's wall, though.

'Douglas Ballantyne the third.' He read out the name on the book, then followed a long thread of red woollen string across the wall to a page torn out of a magazine, an interview with the very same man. 'Think we might have to have a word with him.' He tapped a finger against the thin card of the book cover. 'If he's still alive, that is.'

18

'Heard you took that reporter off to Stevenson's flat. What the hell were you thinking doing that?'

McLean stopped mid-stride, not so much because of what Detective Chief Inspector Brooks had said as because of the podgy hand that had grabbed his arm. He'd been hoping to slip from the back door of the station up to his office without being noticed, but today it would seem he was out of luck.

'I'd have thought that would've been obvious, sir.' He shook his arm free of Brooks' hold, then perhaps a little over-ostentatiously adjusted his jacket. The DCI rewarded him with a scowl, same as ever.

'It's a potential crime scene and you go marching in there with a civilian. I don't see anything obvious about it at all. Bloody irregular if you ask me.'

McLean tried not to shake his head, but may have failed a little. 'Ben Stevenson died in the cavern where we found him. His flat was never a crime scene, but it could yield clues. Dalgliesh went there regularly; she knew the place better than anyone. Knew Stevenson better than anyone. Without her I'd never have picked up what he was working on when he died.'

'That still doesn't answer my question though. Since when did you start hobnobbing with the press?'

'I can think of many people I'd rather hobnob with

than Jo bloody Dalgliesh. She came to me in the first place, before her colleague turned up dead.'

'And you don't think that's suspicious? You think it's a good idea bringing her in on the investigation when she might be a suspect? Christ, it's no wonder they turned you down for the DCI job. Surprised you even made it to inspector.'

'If you really think Dalgliesh is a suspect in the violent, ritual murder of her colleague, then I'm not sure there's anything I can do to help you, sir. As you're well aware, I have less reason to like her than many people in this station, after that book she wrote all about how my fiancée was abducted and murdered. Remember that?'

McLean paused a fraction of a second, just enough for Brooks to start his reply, then cut in. 'As it happens, I'd rather work the case without her getting in the way, but she knows Stevenson, knows his work and more importantly she's agreed not to publish anything we haven't cleared.'

'Chance'd be a fine thing. She'll be making shit up about how useless we are and spreading it around like she always does. She's a menace, and you of all people should know that. I want her cut out of this investigation. You understand?'

McLean studied Brooks' face. He was a fat man; there was no charitable way of putting it. He liked his food and was less keen on exercise. He wasn't a bad detective when he put his mind to it, but lately most of his effort seemed to have been going into pushing for promotion. If the rumour mill was anything to go by, he would be scrabbling up the greasy pole into Detective Superintendent Duguid's office just as soon as the man himself had retired. The prospect filled McLean with weary gloom. True, he'd be rid of Dagwood, but he'd learned over the years how to deal with him. Brooks was a different matter altogether.

'As SIO for this case, I think that's my decision to make actually, sir. And the suggestion to work with her came from the superintendent, so it's not something I've done without consultation anyway.'

Brooks reddened, his jowls wobbling as his anger rose. It was usually possible to gauge when he was going to explode, as sweat would shine his forehead. That hadn't happened yet, but it was only a matter of time.

'Fine,' he said after perhaps ten seconds of escalating tension. 'Use her. Or try to. She'll stab you in the back though. It's the story with her kind. Nothing else matters. You mark my words.'

He turned away, marching off with a sideways rolling motion like a sailor not long off the sea. McLean watched him go, trying hard not to admit that, annoying idiot though he was, the man was probably right. Well, Dalgliesh had kept her end of the bargain so far. Only time would tell how long that could last. Shaking his head with weary resignation, he began the long climb up the stairs to the major incident room.

'My office. Now.'

McLean glanced up from the report he'd been checking with DC Gregg to see Detective Superintendent Duguid standing in the doorway. As far as he could remember, this was the first time Duguid had visited the major incident room since the first briefing on the case, days ago.

'Get that over to forensics. See if they've got anything

from the notebook yet.' He sent Gregg off before addressing Duguid.

'Is it important, sir? Only I've got a mountain of actions to get through.'

'Of course it's bloody important. You think I'd come down here looking for you if it wasn't?' Duguid turned away from the door, forcing McLean to follow. He said nothing all the way up the stairs and along the corridor to his office, waiting until he was seated and the door was closed before finally speaking.

'You asked me if Ben Stevenson was a member of any Masonic Lodge. Well the simple answer is no. He wasn't.'

McLean stood in his usual position in front of the desk, hands clasped behind his back. He bobbed slightly on his feet, waiting for the detective superintendent to get to the point. Unless that was the point and Duguid had dragged him all the way up here for no good reason.

'The simple answer?' he asked after a moment's silence.

'You're not a Freemason, McLean. Can't expect you to understand. There's a lot of nonsense written about us. Lurid speculation by the gutter press, disdain from the broadsheets. You'd be surprised to know how much good we do. How much money we raise for charity.'

'I'm sure it's all a bit of harmless fun, sir. But someone cut Ben Stevenson's throat open and then daubed your most recognisable image on the wall in his blood. I know whoever did that isn't a Freemason, or if he is he wasn't doing it for anything other than his own sick reasons, but this is a legitimate line of enquiry, don't you think?'

Duguid glowered at him for a moment, and McLean

wondered if he'd pushed a little too far. The detective superintendent was notoriously prickly about his precious Lodge, and secretive too. Not one of the reformers who wanted to drag the whole organisation kicking and screaming into the nineteenth century.

'If you'd let me finish. I asked around and Stevenson wasn't a member of the order. His father was, but Stevenson was considered—' Duguid paused a moment as if choosing the right word. 'Unreliable.'

'You thought he'd spill the beans as soon as he knew anything important.'

'Oh, we fully expected that. It happens far more often than you'd think. No, we weren't worried about that so much as the damage he'd do digging around for secrets that didn't actually exist. Like your reference to the Brotherhood, capital B, and Baphomet, the talking head.'

'You know about these things?'

'I know of them. Stupid conspiracy theories with no basis in fact. One of the more idiotic accusations made against the Knights Templar was that they worshipped a demon in the form of a disembodied head. That was Baphomet, apparently. Truth is there was no Baphomet, no conspiracy. The Templars were rich and the king of France owed them a lot of money. He persuaded the pope to accuse them of witchcraft and demon worship. It was a power grab, simple enough, and it happened seven hundred years ago. The Freemasons have been about for less than three hundred. You do the maths.'

'So why does it keep coming up? Why the reference to Baphomet in the cave?'

'Search me. It's like a bad penny. Always there when you least need it. But I can tell you this much. That gobbledegook that went on down in that cave's got fuck all to do with Freemasonry.'

'An elaborate hoax then.' McLean remembered the book he'd found in Stevenson's flat. 'Or maybe a trap.'

It was Duguid's turn to look surprised. 'A trap?'

'Do you know a chap called Douglas Ballantyne?' McLean didn't have to wait for the answer; Duguid's face said it loud. 'Stevenson had his book. It was inscribed "to Ben, a true believer".'

'Ballantyne's a nutter. Grade A conspiracy theorist. Take anything he says with a bucketload of salt.'

'Oh, I intend to. Don't worry about that. But if Stevenson really did believe him, what if he were looking into his claims? Maybe kidding himself he could bring a journalist's open mind to them?'

'Don't tell me you think he might have found something and been killed for it. I already told you there's not a shred of truth in that nonsense.'

'No, I don't think that. But someone may have used that to lure him in. You can't tell me this murder wasn't planned meticulously, after all. The killer's put a lot of effort into it. They had to have a reason even if it wasn't anything to do with Freemasonry or this non-existent Brotherhood.'

Duguid said nothing for a moment, as the implications percolated through his brain. McLean could see their progress written on the detective superintendent's face.

'Who would want Stevenson dead?' he asked eventually.

'That's the wrong question. Chasing down his enemies isn't going to solve this case.'

'How no?' Duguid ran long fingers through straggly greying hair.

'Because it's too elaborate. Too contrived. No, it's not who wanted him dead we should be asking, but why.'

19

The squad car had dropped him half a mile from home before executing a tyre-burning U-turn and disappearing at speed to an urgent call-out. McLean didn't mind, really. It was late, but there was still plenty of light left in the day. That was the great thing about the summer so far north. You paid for it in the winter, of course.

Walking up the street to his house, he noticed something odd about the silhouette of the church, and paused to work out what it was. Somewhere in the back of his mind he'd noticed the arrival of piles of scaffolding, portable site huts and building machinery in the street. He'd made a donation to the roof restoration fund a while back, and the minister had told him they were only waiting for the good weather before starting. Judging by the steel fingers reaching up into the evening sky, the good weather was here. It looked like a massive hand, clawing its way out of the ground in a bid to grab the church and drag it down to hell.

Shaking his head at the strange image, McLean was about to set off again when a voice broke the rumbling silence.

'Inspector. Tony. What a pleasant surprise.'

He turned to see the slender form of the minister emerge from the shadows in the graveyard, like some hapless spirit bound by the iron railings that stopped the dead from escaping. She was wearing her usual black, just the white smile of her dog collar underlining her pale face and grey shoulder-length hair, so that she was for a moment just a floating, disembodied head.

'Minister, I—'

'Mary, please.' She emerged fully into the light, and McLean could see that she was wearing gardening gloves, a pair of secateurs in one hand. A clump of what looked like dead brambles hung limply from the other.

'Doing a spot of weeding?'

'It's never-ending at this time of the year. So much nutrition in the soil.'

McLean glanced around the graveyard. None of the headstones looked to be less than a hundred years old. Not much in the way of nutrition left, surely. Then he noticed the smile crinkling the edges of the minister's eyes.

'I see they've started on the roof.' He changed the subject before it turned to the recently interred.

'They have indeed. I know you're not a praying man, Tony, but if you felt like asking for a nice dry fortnight or so . . .'

'I could always ask my boss. He seems to think he's got a direct line to the Almighty.'

'Probably best you don't.' The minister rolled her eyes, looking upwards. 'We don't want to piss him off, after all.'

'Good point.' McLean shifted on his feet. It had been a long day and he was hungry, anxious to get home. On the other hand, he didn't want to appear rude.

'I've been running a series of evening meetings. If you're interested.'

He started to protest, but the minister interrupted him.

'Oh, don't worry. They're not prayer meetings or anything. Just informal discussions over a cup of tea or a beer. They're quite popular, you know. There's a surprising number of single folk around here, too. Young professionals like yourself. Too busy at work to make friends. Not enough hours in the day.'

It seemed an odd thing for the minister to say. McLean knew that he wasn't the most sociable of people, but that suited him just fine. He had friends, could always go out for a drink or a meal if he wanted. True, they all tended to be fellow police officers or closely linked to his work, but that wasn't so unhealthy really, was it? So much easier to make conversation if you weren't constantly having to second-guess whether the other person was going to be horrified by something you might say.

'We also have poker evenings once a month. With a face like yours I'd love to play a few games. Might even raise enough to finish the whole roof.'

'I'm sorry. I know you mean well, but it's really not my thing. And card games leave me cold.'

'Fair enough. But bear us in mind if you find yourself rattling around in that big old house. Can't be easy all alone there. Especially after . . . well.' The minister dropped her gaze to her hands, fiddling with the dead brambles. It was a good act, McLean had to admit. She'd have been great at interrogating suspects. On the other hand, it was hardly a year since the house had been full of life. Bizarre, unpredictable life, but life all the same. Now it was just him and the cat. The cats, he corrected himself. He had to admit there were times when a little human company might have been nice.

'I'll think about it,' he said, knowing that he wouldn't.

'Speak to your colleague. Kirsty. She'll tell you what we get up to. There's no happy clappy stuff. Just a chance to chat. Or listen.'

'Ritchie?' McLean couldn't help looking up at the scaffold-clad church. The sky was darkening now, orange sunset fading to the deep blue-black of night. 'She's been coming here?'

'Oh yes. About two months now. Didn't she tell you?' The minister looked a little worried, as if she'd betrayed a confidence.

'No. She's only just come back to work. She was off sick. I'll ask her about it though. Tomorrow.'

'You do that, Tony. And mention me to her, won't you?' She nodded a quick goodbye, turned and walked back into the gloom.

He was so wrapped up in his thoughts that he almost walked straight past his entrance gate. On the face of it, there was no logical reason why Ritchie would have gone to that particular church and that particular group; she lived halfway across the city. He was surprised to find that she was religious-minded at all, if he was being honest with himself. It wasn't something that had come up in conversation, and she wasn't the sort of person to disappear on a Sunday morning when there was work to be done.

But there was the illogical thought that wouldn't go away. She had been touched by evil in the form of the enigmatic Mrs Saifre, saved by a blessing from the font of that church. That was a connection he really didn't like to think about; the ramifications were too much.

'What the—?' Something twined itself around his feet as he crunched up the gravel driveway. He'd not left any lights on in the house, and under the trees it was as dark as night, branches whipping at his arms as he tried to stop himself from falling over. 'Bloody cats!'

The offender skittered off into the bushes, then stopped and turned to watch him. Its eyes glowed faintly in the dying light and he could just about make out enough of its shape to see that it wasn't Mrs McCutcheon's cat. She was smooth-coated and this was a great shaggy beast of a thing. One of Madame Rose's perhaps, or the local pride that seemed to have decided he needed protection.

'I can look after myself, you know.' McLean stalked off to the back door and let himself in. Through to the kitchen and he flicked on the lights. At least a dozen pairs of eyes looked up at him from well-chosen positions about the room. It had been like this every evening since his visit from the old medium. In the main he didn't really mind. They were all house-trained, as far as he could smell. Mostly they kept to the kitchen and the garden, too, with only Mrs McCutcheon's cat venturing into the rest of the house. How long that would last, he had no idea. Same as he had no idea how long the cats would be staying. He'd try and remember to ask Grumpy Bob to have a look into it. The old sergeant had friends at Leith nick who might do him a favour.

'Don't get up on my account,' he said as he passed through the room. Mrs McCutcheon's cat was the only one to ignore his command, stretching from her favoured spot in the middle of the kitchen table before leaping down and following him out into the hall.

A small pile of uninteresting mail waited on the mat by the front door. Some bills, some junk, and a letter from his solicitors. He slid a finger under the seal, tore it open as he headed to the library. The typing was dense, its content a bit too dry for his frazzled brain to take in. Something to do with the tenement block in Newington. An offer from the McClymonts that would probably be easier to understand with a dram of the Scottish Malt Whisky Society's finest.

McLean dropped all the letters on the side table, then fetched his prize. He considered putting some music on, but found he wasn't in the mood. Looking over at his turntable and the meagre collection of LPs he'd managed to amass since the fire just reminded him of Ben Stevenson's collection. What would happen to that?

Mrs McCutcheon's cat leapt into his lap as soon as he sat down, nuzzled at his free hand until he scratched her behind the ears. She had taken the arrival of Madame Rose's cats well, but seemed determined to remind him at every opportunity that she was the first.

He took a long sip of whisky, feeling the burn on his tongue, then reached for the pile of letters. Sooner or later he was going to have to make a decision about the flat. Logic argued he should just take the money and run, but there were always more important things to do.

As he lifted the letters towards him, a slim card slipped out of the pile, landing picture side up in his lap. The cat sniffed at it, then batted it with a paw before he managed to pick it up. The photograph showed a slightly out-of-focus image of the Taj Mahal, and when McLean turned the card over he recognised the untidy scrawl of Emma's handwriting.

Not many of us left now, but it's getting harder to follow the trail. Heading east again soon. Missing you. E. XOX

McLean stared at the words, turned the card over and peered at the picture again, studied the smudged postmark as if it might give him some clues. He sniffed the card, and imagined he could catch the faintest hint of her scent even though he knew that was impossible. Mrs McCutcheon's cat nudged at his hand once, then curled up in his lap and began to purr. He took another sip of the whisky, placed the glass down on top of the letter from his lawyers, and just sat in the quiet, staring at the postcard.

20

'It's for your own good, Anthony. That school's just holding you back.'

The library is Gran's serious room. I don't normally go in there. The books are older even than she is, dusty and dry and covered in cracked leather. Some of them are written in foreign languages like French and Spanish and Auld Scots. It's where she has her writing desk, and the hidden cupboard with the whisky in it that she thinks I don't know about. And it's where I am summoned when I've done something wrong.

'But all my friends are there.'

'You'll make new friends. There'll be plenty of other new boys. The Grove is a fine prep school. Good enough for your grandfather and father both.'

The sun is shining outside. It's been a long hot summer so far and I'd really rather be out there playing than in this stuffy old room.

'Dad went there?' It's been two years now since they left and never came back, mum and dad. I can still remember them as clearly as the moment they waved goodbye with promises they'd be home soon. It's hard to imagine my father as a boy my age.

'He did. And he made lifelong friends there.' Gran has been sitting in one of the high-backed armchairs, but now she comes across and sits next to me on the sofa. 'Oh, Tony. You're so like him. You'll do well there, believe me.'

'But my friends—'

'Will still be here when you come home for the holidays. And there's plenty of those left. Term doesn't start for another month yet.'

A month seems a very long time. Too far in the future to really worry about. And I'll be going to a place where my dad went. That has to be pretty cool.

'Go. Play outside a while. It's far too nice a day to be cooped up indoors.'

I don't need to be told twice. It's only when I'm at the door that I think to ask, 'Can I go round to Norman's?'

'Norman Bale?' Gran frowns in that way she has. 'Yes. I suppose so. It's not far. Just be careful going up the road.'

I nod my understanding and rush out the door before she can change her mind.

21

A terrifying scream woke McLean from dreams of his childhood. He tried to sit upright, then realised he already was, wedged into the high-backed armchair in the library. Mrs McCutcheon's cat was long gone, Emma's postcard fallen to the floor where his sleepy arm had dropped it. The windows were dark, just the light from the table lamp casting a small glow around him like a protective shield. The echo of that scream unsettled him, even if it was just in his mind. He strained to hear anything but the low, constant hum of the city and the occasional creak and groan of the old house settling around him.

Then it came again, different now that it wasn't being warped by sleep. A wailing, hissing noise from outside. Caterwauling, there was no other word for it. With a heavy sigh, McLean hauled himself out of the chair and went to see who was fighting whom.

A glance at the old clock in the hallway showed that it was ten to four in the morning. He'd not thought himself so tired, but he must have been asleep in the armchair almost five hours. It didn't bear thinking about that his alarm was going to go off in another two.

The kitchen was empty as he walked through it, then out the back door. The night was warm, a gentle breeze ruffling the leaves all around him as he let his eyes adjust to the darkness. Whatever had been screaming had stopped for now, but as the night noises began to filter in, McLean could hear something unusual from the end of the driveway, where it opened out on to the street.

Gravel crunched under his feet like explosions in a quarry as he tried to walk as quietly as possible in the direction of the noise. It sounded like someone was cursing under their breath, or having an argument with themselves, and for a moment McLean wondered if a tramp had decided his gateway was a nice warm spot to kip for the night. He wished he'd brought a torch, then remembered he was still wearing his work suit. It wasn't brilliant, but he always carried a pen light in his jacket pocket.

Green light reflected back off the dark, rubbery rhododendron leaves, the occasional flash of blue eye reminding him that wherever he went in his own home, he was never far from a cat these days. McLean played the torch around the end of the driveway, trying to see into the shadows cast by the far-spaced street lamps in the road beyond. Something much larger than a cat let out a muffled 'fuck' and then a dark figure burst out of the bushes. For an instant it stood in the gateway, facing him, and McLean could see a pair of startled eyes peering out from a black balaclava. Then the man turned and ran. McLean made a half-hearted pursuit out into the road, but he knew when he was outclassed. Whoever had been hiding in his bushes would have given a professional sprinter a run for his money. In no time at all he was at the road end, not stopping or looking back before he disappeared around the corner.

McLean stood in the gateway for a moment, staring at the empty spot where the running man had last been. His hand went to his pocket of its own accord, pulling out his phone. He had brought up the speed dial screen and was about to call the station when he was distracted by something rubbing against his leg. Mrs McCutcheon's cat was standing beside him, looking pleased with itself. It looked up at him, blinked slowly, then sauntered off into the bushes. Well, he could take a hint.

The rhododendron leaves were thick around the outside of the bush, but they soon gave way to a cave-like interior. McLean remembered it well from his childhood, the best of dens for a lonely child thrown out of the house to get some fresh air. Under the meagre light from his torch, it seemed smaller than his memory, and there was a pungent odour of human excrement that he wasn't expecting. Careful where he put his feet, he swept the torch back and forth until he located the source.

'Seriously? Some drunkard took a dump in your garden and you think it's important enough to get forensics involved?'

There hadn't been much point in trying to get to sleep after the incident. McLean had made himself a large pot of coffee and sat in the kitchen until the forensic expert had turned up somewhere near six. She was new; he'd not met her at a crime scene before. But obviously someone higher up the chain had warned her about him. Still, she'd understood the importance of the task, collected up the stool and promised him it would be analysed for DNA. Amazing how much information you could get from shit, had been her exact words as she left.

Getting into the station early, McLean had hoped he'd be able to immerse himself in the Ben Stevenson case, plough through the mountain of useless actions the investigation had thrown up so far. Unfortunately DCI Brooks was also an early riser, and he appeared to have daily updates from the forensic service fed directly to his brain. There was no other way he could have known, surely.

'Half-three in the morning, dressed completely in black, with a balaclava over his head?' McLean shook his own; this man was going to be in charge soon. Things never change.

'If you thought there'd been a crime, McLean, you should have reported it. Not used your personal hotline to the forensic services to get you ahead of the queue.'

Pinching the bridge of his nose didn't usually help relieve the stress of dealing with superior officers, but McLean found it did at least stop him from resorting to violence. That rarely went well, and besides, Brooks had a reputation as well as bulk on his side.

'I did call control, sir, and I also told them it was low priority. I've spoken to my neighbours, no one's been burgled recently. If someone was casing the area, they've had a nasty surprise. Will probably try their luck somewhere a bit more downmarket. Grange or the likes.'

Brooks' nostrils flared at the insult. McLean knew perfectly well where the DCI lived and how it fitted into the complicated hierarchy of the city's social-climbing classes.

'And just how does a forensic analysis of this crap help, then?'

'Believe it or not, sir, they can get a good DNA sample from human excrement. Especially if it's fresh, and I can assure you this one was very fresh. If this man's on the database, we'll know who he is.'

'And then what? You going to try and do him for damage to your property because he shat in your bushes?'

'No, sir. But I will make a note of it on file. Should he come to our notice again. Besides, I don't think the crap was meant for my bushes.'

Brooks stared at him as if he were mad. 'What on earth are you talking about, man?'

'I'd have thought it would be obvious. You want to shove shit through someone's letterbox, you don't really want to be carrying it around for too long. Well, not in a bag anyway.'

'Letterbox?' Brooks lumbered to a slow realisation. 'You mean this was meant to be a warning? What the fuck for?'

The idea had come to McLean in the wee small hours, and he'd turned it over and over ever since, unable to let it go. 'That's what bothers me. I don't know.'

'Well you've pissed off enough people, I guess. Policemen tend to be a bit less direct, mind.'

'Yes, I've found that. Was thinking of someone else who had shit shoved through their letterbox recently.'

'Oh yes? Anyone I know?'

McLean hesitated. He'd not had time to ask Grumpy Bob to speak to Leith station about Madame Rose, and the more he thought about it, the less keen he was on sharing anything about the medium with DCI Brooks. 'It's probably nothing, sir. I'll let you know if anything comes of it.'

Brooks narrowed his eyes until they almost disappeared in the folds of flesh that made up his round face. Perhaps he thought doing so would help him to read McLean's mind, or maybe he was just trying to squeeze out a reluctant fart. Either way he seemed to fail.

'You do that, McLean,' he said after a while. 'And don't go blowing the departmental budget on petty vandals. Bad enough chasing whoever did this.' He waved a pudgy hand at the major incident room.

McLean thought of Ben Stevenson's daughters and how pleased they would be to hear that the police were doing their utmost to bring their father's killer to justice. He bit back the retort he wanted to give, just nodded an acceptance of his superior's crassness. Sometimes that was all you could do.

'You got a moment, Bob?'

It was a stupid question, really. McLean had spent ten minutes searching the empty offices and unused incident rooms until he'd found the detective sergeant. Grumpy Bob was sitting in the corner of the CID room, feet up on his desk, head wedged against the wall and giving his newspaper very close attention indeed. He slowly lifted it off his face, folded it and placed it on the desk before answering.

'I could probably find some space in my hectic schedule, sir. What did you have in mind?'

McLean cast an eye over the rest of the CID room, looking for other officers lurking in the corners. It was empty, but this early in the morning that was hardly a surprise. Even so, he felt uncomfortable letting too many people in on this particular piece of business.

'You still on speaking terms with the duty sergeants down in Leith station?'

'Some of them, aye. You looking for something in particular.'

'Madame Rose. You remember her?'

'Him, if I'm not mistaken. But yes. Has that shop down the Walk. Peddles fortunes and deals in old books.'

'That's the one. She helped out with Emma last year. Came to me yesterday asking if I could look into a little local problem she's been having.' McLean told Grumpy Bob the whole story, noting as he did that the old sergeant took his feet off his desk, sat upright and started to pay attention.

'They killed a cat?'

'Left the poor thing just inside the front door. Gave one of her regular customers a terrible fright when he turned up for his weekly tarot.'

'So what do you want me to do?'

'Well, I know she's spoken to someone at Leith a couple of times, but whoever's doing this is being very cunning about it. Seems it's never the same faces twice. Difficult for us to take it seriously.'

'You sure he's not just being paranoid. I mean, he's not exactly dealing from a full deck, right?'

McLean slumped against the wall, the weariness of too little sleep fighting with his patience.

'She, Bob. You've been on the equality and diversity training, right? Madame Rose might've been born a man, but she's happier being a woman. She wants to be a she, who am I to tell her she can't?'

Grumpy Bob paused a moment before answering. 'Aye, you're right. I was meaning more about the whole fortune-telling thing, mind. Unless you're telling me you believe in all that stuff too, now?'

'You know me and belief, Bob. But this isn't about me. It's about Rose. She's helped me more than once now, the least I can do is return the favour.'

'You mean the least I can do?' Grumpy Bob grinned. 'You want me to have a word with someone at Leith?'

'My guess is no one takes her seriously because of what she does, how she dresses. Sure they'll have taken down her complaint, it'll be in someone's PDA. But no one will have done anything about it. See if you can't change that, will you?'

'Consider it done.' Grumpy Bob picked up his paper, and for a moment McLean thought he was going to drape it over his face and go back to sleep. 'Tomorrow soon enough? I'll be seeing old Tam Sykes then anyway.'

'Tam's still working? Surely they put him out to pasture years ago.'

'Aye, they did. But you know what us old coppers are like. He's been helping out with some cold case reviews. Tam'll have a word if I ask him, and it'll be better coming from him.'

McLean recalled his strange meeting with the medium a few nights earlier. The more he thought about it, the more her secondary request – the almost afterthought that he might be able to give a home to her cats for a while – seemed to be the thing she really wanted from him. Chances were the attacks on her house were not something the police would have much luck looking into.

'Tomorrow's fine. Just returning a favour really. And I get the feeling Rose can look after herself anyway.'

22

'Got an address for that conspiracy nutter of yours, sir.'

McLean looked up from his desk to see the thin but smiling face of DS Ritchie peering around the door jamb. The bags under her eyes had faded a bit, her pale complexion perhaps a little more coloured than it had been a few days earlier.

'My what? Oh. Right.' His brain caught up with his mouth just too late. Poking out from underneath a series of reports that appeared to have been written by someone with English as very much a second language, he could just see a corner of the book taken from Ben Stevenson's study. McLean fished it out, staring once more at the cover.

'That's the chap.' Ritchie committed herself fully to the office as she saw the book. 'Douglas Ballantyne the third. He's been away in the US, apparently. Travelling since May, so I guess he's not a key suspect. Happy to see us any time we're passing. Soon as he's back.'

McLean flipped it over and scanned the blurb again. He'd been meaning to read the actual book, but there was never enough time. Or maybe it was just that he didn't want to have to wade through what would inevitably be a load of old rubbish dressed up as historical fact.

'You want to read it?' He held it up for Ritchie to take, but she backed away, hands raised to ward it off as if the words might somehow corrupt her soul.

'No thanks. My head's messed up enough as it is.'

McLean said nothing, although he may have raised a quizzical eyebrow. Ritchie took it as an invitation to shut the door, only then realising that there was no other chair for her to sit on. She leaned back against the wall opposite the desk, gathering her thoughts before she spoke.

'I know what happened to me, sir. Back . . .' Her words tailed off.

'You got sick. A nasty flu bug. People die of the flu you know.'

'Old people maybe. Babies, invalids. I'm thirty-two, fit. Well, I was fit.' She gave a little cough. 'Now I'm a fucking wreck. You saw what I was like after climbing three flights of stairs.'

'Give it time, Kirsty. You nearly died. Takes a while to come back from that.'

Ritchie wiped at a forehead suddenly damp with sweat. 'You make it sound like you've got experience.'

'In a way, I guess I have. Not like you, of course, but I've been there. Down so far you never think you'll make it back up again.'

'How did you? Make it back up again, that is?'

'Friends, mostly. And time.' McLean shifted in his seat, trying not to make it look like he was uncomfortable with the conversation. He was, of course. Just a little. But in a way it was his fault Ritchie was the way she was; he owed it to her to do his best to help her. Would have done even if it hadn't been.

'You have many friends out of the job?' It was an innocent question, he could see that, but it was also barbed.

'A few. Maybe not as many as I'd like.' And the closest,

the one who really helped him out through the bad days, was half a world away in California. McLean remembered the quick and unexpected call from Phil just the other evening, the memories it had sparked. He made a mental note to give his old flatmate a call back some time soon, filed it away with the large pile of mental notes he'd already made to the same effect.

'Didn't have many friends in Aberdeen anyway.' Ritchie continued as if she hadn't heard his answer. 'None of them have bothered coming to visit in the – what is it? Two years since I transferred down?'

'Christ, is it that long?'

It was a small thing, the slightest wince at the word. Unless he was being over-sensitive. Or maybe remembering the conversation he'd had with the minister.

'You'd think a city this size it'd be easy to make new friends, but when does a detective have the time, eh?'

'Well, policemen aren't all that bad.'

Ritchie laughed, which was a nice thing to see. 'You know what they say about doctor and nurse relationships, right?'

'There'll be all sorts at your evening meetings, though. Up at the church?'

Ritchie's face coloured slightly, the blush of a child caught doing something that wasn't strictly wrong, but might not be right either.

'You know about that?'

'Bumped into the minister the other night. She's been trying to get me to come along for months now. Might have let slip that I'd maybe see a familiar face there if I did.'

'You should come. It's – well, it's helped me come to

terms with what happened. I know who that woman really is now, what she did to me.'

McLean leaned back in his chair, said nothing. He didn't need to ask who 'that woman' was or what she had done to Ritchie. It was just hard to tally that knowledge with being a rational, logical person.

'Never really been one for sharing,' he said eventually. 'You know that. And I'm not that comfortable with belief, either. It's too lazy. Thanks for the invitation, but I'm fine with the friends I've got.'

'OK.' Ritchie nodded her acceptance. 'But I think you're ducking the issue. There are things that don't easily fit a rational explanation. Sometimes you have to believe something will work, otherwise it won't.'

'I prefer to look at it as thinking outside of the box. If I can't find a rational explanation, then I'm using the wrong definition of rational. And talking of work—' McLean peered at the book where he'd dropped it on to his desk. 'Douglas Ballantyne the third? Where's he live?'

'Down in the Borders. Near Peebles.' Ritchie stood up straight, once more the businesslike detective sergeant. She unpeeled a Post-it note from the top of the pad she'd been playing with throughout their conversation, stuck it down over the Santa Claus lookalike author image. McLean picked up the book and note together, glanced at the address. It sounded expensive, which suggested there was a ready market for idiot conspiracy theories.

'Give him a call, will you? Arrange a time. We're all one big happy Police Scotland now, so it's not as if Borders can complain if we spend an afternoon on their patch.'

'I'll get on it.' Ritchie pushed herself away from the wall, opened the door. 'And thanks.'

'For what?'

'For listening, I guess.'

'Any time.' McLean pulled the reports he'd been deciphering out from underneath the book. Held them up for Ritchie to see. 'It's got to be better than all this rubbish.'

Lunch in the station canteen was something of a novelty for McLean. He rarely had time for anything more sophisticated than a sandwich at his desk, and lately going into any place where a lot of junior officers congregated was uncomfortable. Probably more so for them than him; he didn't really care all that much what they thought about him as long as they did what they were told. Nevertheless, the speed with which any table he sat at emptied itself was at best impressive, at worst rude. It was true there were some officers who didn't mind sharing a coffee, muffin and blether, but then if McLean wanted to eat quickly it was best not to get caught in a conversation with DC Gregg.

Mercifully she was nowhere to be seen, and the few faces that looked up at him as he entered didn't immediately radiate hostility. Conversation continued its muted buzz unabated. Better yet, the canteen itself yielded a plate of ham sandwiches that looked like they might have been made sometime that week.

He'd barely sat down when the canteen doors burst open, and DC MacBride came rushing in. At almost the same moment, McLean's phone buzzed in his pocket, the harsh klaxon ring tone announcing that the control centre in Bilston Glen had need of his services. From the look on the detective constable's face as he scanned the room, it didn't take a genius to tell that the news was likely to be the same from both sources. McLean ignored the phone; they'd send him a text message anyway.

'I take it from your lack of breath that something important's happened?' He picked up his limp sandwich and eyed it ruefully. To bite, or not to bite?

'Call just came through, sir. They've found a dead body. A young woman. Out by Fairmilehead.'

McLean dropped the sandwich back on to the plate, pushed it away as he stood up. Probably for the best; he'd only end up with indigestion.

The lane had already been cordoned off by the time he arrived, which at least meant someone with half a brain was in charge. McLean had hoped DC MacBride would have commandeered a pool car, but the detective constable had been called away to another case. In the end, he had cadged a lift from the nearest squad car. The moment he'd clunked the passenger door shut the driver had executed a perfect reversing J-turn and sped off, which rather begged the question of how he was going to get back to the station once he was done. Not for the first time he realised he couldn't put off getting himself a new car much longer. If only people would stop dropping things on them.

'What are we looking at, Constable?' He showed his warrant card to the fresh-faced uniform who had been tasked with keeping the public on the right side of the blue-and-white tape. It wasn't a difficult job, really. Not this far out of town. Fairmilehead didn't exactly attract passers-by. Not on foot, anyway.

'Dead body, sir. That's all anyone's told me.' The constable lifted the tape to let him on to the site.

'Forensics here yet?'

'Over there.'

McLean headed in the direction he had been pointed, arriving at a cluster of white Transit vans and a couple of squad cars pulled up in a courtyard formed by three semi-derelict stone buildings: part of a farm that had long since succumbed to the ever-expanding housing estates that grew like cankers alongside the main roads branching out of the city. Through trees lining the lane, he could see a green field dotted with horses and then the seething mass of the city bypass. How long before the horses were evicted too, their grazing given over to yet more semi-detached boxes?

'Tony. You're here. Excellent.'

McLean didn't need to look to know who was speaking. He'd known Angus Cadwallader at least half his life. The city pathologist was already wearing a full-body forensic suit, the hood pulled down to reveal thinning grey hair. Judging by the gore smeared across the front of it, he'd examined the body, too.

'You've had a look, I see. Any thoughts?'

'Probably best if you see for yourself,' Cadwallader said. 'Wouldn't want to colour your judgement.'

McLean gave his friend a quizzical look, but the pathologist was obviously giving nothing away.

'I guess I'd better go and find myself a romper suit then.'

*

His initial impression was of something that had been thrown away because it had ceased to be useful. At first it was difficult even to tell that it was a body he was looking at, let alone a woman.

She had been dumped naked into a large metal bin, the sort of thing used to store horse feed and other items you didn't want the rats and mice to get at on a livery yard. Dumped was the word, too. This was no careful placing, so much as a body simply tipped in. She lay awkwardly, head staring sightlessly upwards from where it was squashed into the corner. She looked almost like a discarded mannequin, only one with real blood. And she was young. That much he could see despite the damage to her neck and the mess all over her face.

'Judging by the relative lack of bleeding, I'm going to guess she was killed elsewhere and brought here.' McLean dragged his eyes away from the grisly sight to Cadwallader standing beside him.

'Cause of death?'

'You have to ask, don't you Tony?' The pathologist ventured a grin, but it was a humourless effort. 'You'll be wanting a time too, I've no doubt.'

'When you can.' McLean gave his old friend a light slap on the arm. 'I'll go speak to the forensics team. See what they've got.'

He left Cadwallader with the body, and followed the marked-out pathway back to the forensics van where he'd borrowed his white overalls. They didn't fit, bunching up in his crotch and under his armpits in a manner that made walking difficult if you didn't want to look like a sumo wrestler. The scene of crime officers seemed to be able to move unhindered in theirs, which suggested they kept a special batch of ill-fitting ones just for detectives.

'Inspector McLean. We meet again.' The short, round figure of Jemima Cairns appeared around the corner of the nearest van. She wore the expression of a genius surrounded by fools, a near-permanent scowl on her face as she constantly scanned the scene for evidence of anyone doing things they shouldn't. Her quick up-down appraisal of his overalls suggested that he'd at least got that much right.

'Dr Cairns.' McLean nodded a greeting. 'How's the crime scene?'

'In a word, bloody impossible. No, that's two words.' Dr Cairns didn't seem to really mind. 'You couldn't have picked a worse place to leave forensic evidence if you'd tried. There's horses, goats, pigs, chickens, humans.' She said this last one as if she felt that was where humans should come in the pecking order. 'Christ only knows what else. The place is dusty as hell, and that wind isn't helping.'

McLean followed the forensic scientist's gaze across the small courtyard. A group of scene of crime officers were inching their way over towards the central building, studying the ground with commendable intensity, but every so often the wind dropping down off the nearby Pentland Hills would whip the dust up into eddies, covering up anything that might be a clue, or worse, moving it back to a place they'd already looked at.

'All we need now is some rain and we'll be buggered sideways till Tuesday.' Cairns looked up at the sky, pale blue and cloudless at the moment, but you never knew.

‘So you don’t hold out much hope of getting anything from here, then,’ McLean said. ‘Apart from the body, of course.’

‘Chance’d be a find thing. This place is too contaminated by far. We might get something and never even realise. Or there might be nothing to find.’

‘You think that’s deliberate? Why the killer chose this place to dump the body?’

Something like worry flitted across Cairns’ face at the idea. McLean could understand her concern. No one liked to be outsmarted. Not like this, with the stakes as high as they were.

‘Nobody’s that good,’ she said eventually. ‘We’ll find something. You can trust me on that.’

23

'Subject is female, Caucasian, early twenties at a guess. In generally good health from her outward appearance.'

Another day, another visit to the city mortuary. McLean had hardly slept the night before, his dreams filled with the silent, pleading, nameless face of the dead woman. He'd risen with the dawn, then paced about the house drinking too much coffee until just before six. Even after walking to the city centre and stopping for yet more coffee, it had been a full hour after he'd arrived that the post-mortem was scheduled. Fortunately for him, Angus Cadwallader wasn't much of a sleeper either. They'd managed to find another insomniac pathologist to witness the examination and started early.

'What little blood was left in her has pooled around the shoulders and upper back, which is consistent with the way she was found. There was very little blood at the scene though, which would suggest she was killed elsewhere, then dumped.'

Cadwallader inched his way around the body, exposing the dead woman's most intimate secrets. A final indignity to add to the violence already done to her. McLean fought the urge to turn away. It was important he witness this, and not just so he could get the information he needed as quickly as possible.

'There's no obvious sign of her having been restrained. No bruising around the arms.'

'She knew her attacker, then.'

'That would be my best guess.' Cadwallader fell silent again whilst he studied the body some more. 'No sign of sexual intercourse, so she wasn't raped.'

'She was naked when we found her,' McLean said.

'Yes. Yes, she was. That doesn't necessarily mean any sexual motive though.'

'No. You're right. That would be too easy. Have you managed to narrow down time of death? I think we know what killed her.'

'Don't jump to conclusions, Tony. She could have been poisoned and her throat cut after she was dead.'

'Was she?'

'No. Well, I can't be sure until the tox screening's done. We've results for alcohol already, but the more esoteric poisons take time.'

'Alcohol? She'd been drinking?'

'Not a lot. Couple of glasses of wine maybe, but not long before she died.'

'Food?'

'I'm getting to that.' Cadwallader picked a scalpel off the tray of torture instruments his assistant Tracy had brought over. McLean turned away, like he always did at this point. The picture began to form in his mind. Young woman, finished work and off for a drink. Was she on her own or with friends? Where did she go, and who saw her? Actions for the investigation dropping into place. She meets some-one she thinks she knows, but it turns out he's not the friend she thought he was. But why didn't she try to defend herself? Unless she didn't know what was about to happen. If so, it must have been quick, premeditated. And the method of disposal, so casual and yet at the same time so well thought out. It wasn't by chance that she'd been left somewhere so difficult to investigate forensically. Wasn't by chance she'd been stripped of all identification.

'Ah. Now that is interesting.'

McLean turned to see what Cadwallader was talking about, then wished he hadn't. The pathologist had opened up his patient and removed what was probably her liver. He turned it over and over in his blood-smeared hands, peering closely at it and prodding it. McLean was no expert, but even he could see it was diseased.

'Cirrhosis?'

'Quite advanced. Sad to say, but we're seeing it more and more, especially in young women. I'd guess this one's had a bottle of wine a day habit for quite some time. Probably binges on spirits at the weekends.' Cadwallader ploiped the liver into a plastic specimen tub and Tracy took it off to weigh. 'Poor girl would probably have been showing clinical symptoms soon. Heading for complete liver failure in a year or two if this hadn't happened to her.'

'Some silver lining,' McLean said. 'But it's not really relevant to her death though, is it?'

'No, but it's interesting.' Cadwallader gave him a pained look. 'I suppose you want me to look at her throat now.'

He pulled the overhead light towards the young woman's head, illuminating the mess that had been made of her neck. 'The wound's deep, right through to the vertebrae. It's been done with a very sharp knife. Probably quite a large blade. I'd have to get a second opinion, but I'd hazard a guess he stood behind her, reached around with his right hand, swept from left to right.'

A chill formed in the pit of McLean's stomach, only partly at the horrible image of execution and the dead body splayed out on the examination table in front of him. 'You seen anything like it before?'

'If you're asking me was this done by the same person as did for your journalist, I really can't say.' Cadwallader prodded the fleshy mess around the dead woman's neck with the tip of his scalpel. 'If you're going to cut someone's throat, there's only so many ways you can go about it. Same if you're cutting your own.'

'This wasn't a suicide, Angus. Even I can tell that.'

'Not saying it was. Just saying it's not enough to jump to conclusions. There's a few tests I'll run that can shed some light on it, but these things are coincidence, occasionally.'

McLean looked again at the dead woman's pale face, eyes closed, features relaxed in a manner that belied the violent nature of her ending. He shook his head gently, partly at the terrible waste of life, partly at his friend's words.

'You know me, Angus. I don't believe in coincidences.'

'Her name's Maureen Shenks. She's a paediatric nurse. Works at the Sick Kids.'

McLean looked up from his paperwork-strewn desk to see Detective Sergeant Ritchie standing in his open doorway clutching a sheet of paper that smelled as if it was fresh from the printer. A few days back at work and she was looking much better, seemed to have more energy. He wondered where she was getting it from and if there was any going spare.

'Maureen Shenks.' McLean repeated the name as if doing so might give any meaning to her death. 'We know anything about her?'

'Apart from this? No.' Ritchie flicked the sheet of paper with a finger, then stepped into the room and handed it over. The top half of the page was a photograph, quite obviously of the woman whose body they had found in the bin the day before. The rest was a brief summary of her life. Edinburgh born and raised. Twenty-three years old. Nothing on record with the police.

'Family?'

'Not sure. MacBride's working on it. She's young enough her parents could be still alive. This came from Missing Persons, though. She didn't turn up to work three days ago. Flatmate phoned it in.'

'I guess we'd better talk to the flatmate then.'

'I've given her a phone. She's on duty. Works at the Sick Kids too. Want me to bring her in when her shift's done?'

'I think this is probably serious enough to interrupt her shift, don't you?' McLean grabbed his jacket from the back of his chair. The wall directly opposite his window was painted bright with sunshine. 'And it's too nice an afternoon not to walk.'

'It's not like her to just up and leave like that. I mean, she loves the kids. Lives for them. Some of them get really upset if she doesn't see them every day.'

Maureen Shenks' flatmate was a mousy young woman called Adele. 'Pronounced like the penguin,' she'd said when they had first arrived at the hospital. She'd been hesitant about abandoning her duties, but as soon as McLean had identified himself as detective inspector her attitude had changed. Now they were huddled together in a small room at the back of the main building, which judging by its contents was a place old cardboard boxes went to die.

'I asked about. You know, just in case she'd gone off on a date and . . . well . . .'

'Did she do that often? Stay out overnight?'

The internal struggle in Adele's mind was writ large across her face, the conflict between telling the truth and protecting the reputation of her friend and flatmate. 'Not often.' The stress fell tellingly on the second word of her answer.

'Did she have a boyfriend, then? Someone she was seeing steady?' DS Ritchie asked the questions; they had decided it would be better that way on the walk over from the station. McLean's earlier idea that it was too nice a day not to walk had lasted almost ten minutes before the searing heat and his dark wool suit had persuaded him otherwise. It was refreshingly cool in their makeshift interview room, but his shirt was still clammy against his back.

'There was a bloke. Tommy something. But that was a year or so back. They went out for almost three months before she broke it off.' Adele paused in her flow long enough for Ritchie to start to ask another question, then added: 'Tommy Adshead. That was his name. Knew it would come to me eventually.'

'What about family?' Ritchie asked again.

Adele looked momentarily puzzled, as if she couldn't quite understand the link between ex-boyfriend and relatives.

'Her parents. Where are they?' McLean asked.

'Oh, right. Mo never knew her dad. All her mum would say was he was her worst mistake and Mo was her best. That's sweet, isn't it?'

'Have you spoken to her about Maureen? Her mother?' Ritchie had a pad in front of her and had scribbled 'boyfriend' and 'mother' so far. Nothing else. She'd already put a line through 'boyfriend'.

'Oh, no. Jane's away with the fairies. Half the time she doesn't even recognise her own daughter, let alone me.'

Ritchie ran a line through 'mother'. 'She's senile?'

'Early onset Alzheimer's. She's in a home in Corstorphine.'

'And there's no one else? Brother, sister?'

'Why do you . . . Oh.' Adele fell silent, her gaze going from Ritchie to McLean and back. The full implication of there being a detective inspector involved beginning to sink in.

'She's not . . . you've . . . I mean, she's OK isn't she? You've found her?'

'You reported her missing this morning.' Ritchie glossed over the questions with her own. 'How long had Maureen been gone by then?'

'I've been on days and she's been on nights, so we've not seen each other that much lately. But she usually lets me know if she's going out. I missed her completely yesterday, but I could tell she'd not been in when I got home last night. I got a call from here to see where she was. She never turned up to her shift, you see. Thought she might have been . . . I mean . . . I called you lot when I got in this morning and she'd missed another shift.'

'That was unusual, was it? For her to miss a shift?'

'Don't think Mo's ever . . .' Adele's voice tailed off as her eyes widened in realisation. 'You've found her, haven't you?'

'We think so, yes.' At McLean's words, Adele looked up from her nervous fingers. He held her gaze, waited until she had calmed down. 'Am I right in thinking Maureen had no immediate family other than her mother?'

'That's right,' the nurse nodded, seeming much younger than when they had first met.

'And how long have you known her?'

'Me? Since we were little. Six, maybe? Earlier?'

Damn, there was no easy way to do this. 'Well, I'm very sorry to have to tell you this, Adele, but Maureen's dead. We found her body yesterday afternoon.'

'Dead?' The nurse's voice had been squeaky to start with. Now it notched up another octave. 'How?'

'That's what we're trying to find out. All I can say at the moment is it wasn't natural, and it wasn't an accident.'

'She . . . she was killed?'

'I'm afraid so.' The nurse was fidgeting with her hands again, wringing them round and round each other. McLean reached out and took a hold of one, gently. 'Adele, I'm sorry. This must be a terrible shock, but it's very important I know as much about your friend as I can.'

She looked up at him, eyes wet with tears. When did adults start looking so young? Had he been like that, back when he first joined up? It seemed unlikely.

'Of course. Anything.'

'Thank you.' McLean patted the nurse's hand, then sat back. 'There is one thing. You're not family, so you can say no if you'd rather not. But we need someone to positively identify the body.'

Adele looked up sharply, the ghost of an idea flitting across her face. McLean had seen it all too often before, that tiny spark of hope. Maybe it wasn't her friend lying on the cold slab in the mortuary. Maybe it was someone else who just happened to look similar. Sometimes that spark flared, became a lifeline, and that made the crushing reality all the harder to accept. This time it died quickly; the rational, nurse's mind winning the battle. She wiped at her nose, sniffed.

'I've seen dead bodies before. Children, mostly. This place . . .' She trailed off.

'I'll have a word with your boss. See about getting you the rest of the day off. DS Ritchie will organise taking you to the mortuary.'

Adele's boss was a harassed-looking woman about McLean's age. He could see that she wasn't happy at losing yet another nurse for the day, but she took the news of Maureen Shenks' death in her stride. McLean had been going to ask her to come to the station; he'd have to interview her as part of the investigation. One look at the bustling busyness of the hospital, though, was enough to persuade him it would be better to set up something there instead; possibly the box-filled room at the back of the old building. Losing one of the nurses in such a terrible fashion was going to be disruptive enough without all the staff being dragged off across town at hourly intervals to talk to the police.

'We all done here?' He turned away from the reception desk to where DS Ritchie was standing, mobile phone in hand.

'For now, aye. Just sorting a car. I take it you want me to go with her?' She nodded in the direction of Adele, sitting on a chair in the waiting area and staring into the middle distance in the manner of someone trying to come to terms with news that's too big to comprehend.

'Please,' McLean said. 'I'll head back to the station and bring Dagwood up to speed. I've a horrible feeling this is another Category A, though.'

They were both walking across the reception hall, McLean for the door, Ritchie for the nurse, when she stopped in mid-stride, and turned so suddenly McLean felt her hand brush against him. He followed her gaze to where a white-coated doctor was disappearing through a door.

'You all right?' he asked.

Ritchie shook her head. 'Sorry. Just thought I recognised someone. Didn't expect to see him here.'

'Oh yes? Something I should know about?' McLean raised an eyebrow and grinned to let Ritchie know he was only kidding. He must have struck a nerve though, as her freckles darkened in embarrassment.

'No. It's nothing like . . . I mean . . . No. Just someone I met at a . . . meeting.'

'None of my business anyway, Sergeant.' McLean gave her a slap on the arm, as much to cover his own embarrassment as anything. He'd meant it as a joke, but it had clearly backfired. 'I'll see you back at the station, aye?'

He left her standing in the middle of the hall, resumed his walk to the door. He had an idea he knew what the meeting was that DS Ritchie meant, but couldn't quite work out why she was so uncomfortable talking about it.

24

'Jon's been coming here since he was six. Can you imagine that?'

I let him stew a fortnight, kept away from both hospitals, disappeared as if I'd been no more than a figment of his imagination. It was wise to keep away while the police were asking questions, too. She had to go, the nurse. She was too much of a temptation to him, and I couldn't risk him falling when he's so close to perfection.

It hasn't hurt to keep him waiting, though. If anything his righteous zeal has grown. When I appeared in the reception hall just after his shift end, he fell upon me like a starving man on a meal. No admonishment for missing our earlier engagement, no asking me where I'd been. He simply guided me through the building to an intensive care ward, pausing only to make sure we were both kitted out in sterile gowns and face masks, even though we will come no nearer to the object of his concern than a pane of glass away.

'What's the matter with him?'

It's fairly obvious, given the state of the boy. He lies sunken into plump white cushions, surrounded by machines, connected to them with wires and tubes. His face is mostly obscured by an oxygen mask, but what little I can see of it has a pallor associated more with the very old than the very young. His eyes are panda-like, dark and sunken as he dozes. He has no hair, not even eyelashes, just sweat-shiny skin the colour of rancid custard, splodged here and there with darker patches.

Jim reaches a slow hand up to the glass, splays fingers on the surface. 'What's right with him? Most of his organs are barely functional. Every time we think we've got it beaten, the cancer just comes back again. He's on chemo at the moment, but honestly, it's not going so well. It's a brutal way to treat a child, anyway.'

'What if we could try something different?'

'There is nothing different. Unless you mean prayer.' He looks at me. I can see the reflection of his head in the glass as he turns, but I keep my eyes on the boy. 'Trust me, if I thought that'd work I'd try it.'

'Actually I was thinking of something a little more . . . scientific? You'll be aware of cell line therapy. Individual cultures, DNA reprofiling?' I rattle off the words, all gleaned from the papers I found in his flat. Fascinating stuff, if you're into that sort of thing. His reflection drops its head, his hand coming away from the glass as his young patient continues to die a long, painful, drawn-out death.

'It's all too new. Too experimental. It takes too much time.' He rubs the grit from tired eyes. 'Jon doesn't have time. Not any more.'

'You know I work mainly on the research side these days, right?' I finally turn to meet his gaze. 'Can't remember the last time I actually treated a patient, if I'm being honest.'

'I did sort of wonder. See you about a lot, but never round the wards or in theatre.'

'Always think that by the time you've got there, it's

usually too late. I'd much rather have the body heal itself. Just maybe give it a little help.'

'You reckon you can help Jon?'

I make a show of studying the boy through the glass, even though I couldn't care less what happens to him. He is flawed. There is no point trying to save something as flawed as that. The silence feels right though, makes it look as if I am thinking.

'I don't know,' I say eventually. 'But I can try.'

25

'Why is it that of all the officers working out of this station, you are the only one who doesn't seem to understand the chain of command?'

Late afternoon, Detective Superintendent Duguid's office. Having cooled down at the hospital, McLean was once more hot and sweaty from his walk back. He could have gone straight to his nice cool office at the rear of the building where the sun never shone, but that would only have been a delaying tactic.

'I always find I get better results this way, sir. Every time I take something to DCI Brooks he sends me straight to you anyway. Thought I'd cut out the middleman, save us all some time.'

'With that attitude it's no wonder no one will take you seriously. You do realise they'll probably give Brooks my job when I leave, don't you? What're you going to do then?'

'I'll cope, sir. Same as always.'

Duguid made a sound halfway between a snort and a harrumph. 'So what's so important you had to bring it straight to me this time?'

'The young woman we found yesterday afternoon, out Fairmilehead way. We've got a name for her, a bit of background information. My first impression is this isn't going to be easy. There's no obvious suspect, no jealous boyfriend and no sign she was raped.' McLean summed up the facts of the case he'd uncovered so far.

'So what you're saying is we've got another major incident on our hands.' Duguid ran spidery fingers over his thinning scalp, slumped back into his seat. 'Fucking marvellous.'

'I'm sure Maureen Shenks is over the moon about it.'

That got him a sharp look. 'What are you on about? She's dead. She couldn't give a fuck. I'm more concerned about the sick bastard killed her. That's the difference between you and me, McLean. You're all about justice for the victims. I'm more interested in making sure the guilty are caught and locked up so they can't do it again.'

'Wasn't aware there was a difference, sir.'

'Course there's a bloody difference, man. You keep prattling on about ideals. I'm interested in results.'

McLean wasn't aware of any recent prattling, but he kept silent on the matter. 'You want me to lead on this one, sir? I've already got Grumpy Bob and MacBride organising the incident room.'

Duguid made a play of shuffling through the folders on his desk. Most of them were closed, some still tied up with string. McLean knew a fidget when he saw one.

'I want you to pass the case on to Spence,' the detective superintendent said eventually. McLean's first instinct was to complain, but then reason kicked in. He was already senior investigating officer on one major incident; the last thing he needed was another.

'Control assigned me the investigation, but I can see the sense in that. I'll get everything we've found so far drawn up into a report for him. Grumpy Bob can hand over to

DS Carter once he's done all the difficult stuff, and I've no doubt Spence will be pinching all the DCs anyway. Is Brooks going to be Gold on this one?'

Duguid gave him the sort of stare you got from a wary sheep. 'You don't mind?'

'How I feel about it's not really important, is it, sir? Just as long as we catch whoever did this, right?'

The tiny office, tucked away at the back of the station, was a small haven of coolness in the heat of mid-afternoon. McLean didn't much enjoy the mountains of paperwork that the job seemed to create on a daily basis, but when the temperature outside was hot enough to melt the tarmac, and the major incident room smelled of parboiled detective, it was nice to have somewhere he could escape to. Of course, it would be freezing in the winter, but that was a worry for another day.

Signing off overtime sheets was relatively mindless, and it wasn't too hard to justify the expenditure, not with two dead bodies on their hands. It gave him a chance to let the investigation percolate in the back of his mind, let the few facts settle and see what new connections might appear. The intervention of his telephone ruined whatever insight might have come. It took McLean a while to find the handset, buried under a spreading mound of folders. The flashing light told him the front desk was calling, but he knew from bitter experience not to believe it all the time.

'McLean.'

'Thought you might be there, sir. There's a bloke down here wants to see you about a car? You buying another one? Only after what happened to the last two . . .' Pete

Dundas was the duty sergeant that afternoon, it would seem.

'This one of your tiresome pranks, Pete? Only you can't pester me for the overtime sheets and send me off on wild goose chases.' It had been a while since anyone had tried to pull a fast one on him, but McLean was ever wary of the so-called humour of his fellow officers. Usually it involved costing him money and wasting the time of innocent bystanders.

'Honest as the day, sir.' Sergeant Dundas did a passable impression of a man offended at the very thought he might not be telling the truth.

'OK. Tell him I'm on my way.' McLean hung up, shuffled the papers into something resembling a child's idea of order and squeezed his way around the desk. He knew nothing about buying a car beyond that he'd been thinking about it. Unless he'd suddenly developed some kind of psychic ability, chances were this was some kind of prank. He just hoped it wasn't an expensive one.

It clicked when he saw the man waiting in reception. McLean had only met him a couple of times, the last being when he'd brought a flatbed truck to the garages of the forensic services and loaded the old Alfa Romeo on to it. McLean had thought the car beyond repair, its roof crushed under the weight of a falling body, but Alan Roberts had just looked at it, sucked his teeth and said it would be expensive. There had been a few telephone conversations since then, and McLean had written a couple of eye-watering cheques, quite probably more than it would have cost him to go out and buy an identical car. Lately it had been mostly silence, though now he thought about it, there might have been an email, buried quickly under a mountain of others.

'Inspector. Sorry to disturb you at work. Reckoned I had a better chance of catching you here, though.'

'Mr Roberts.' McLean shook the man by the hand, noticing his spotlessly clean brown overalls, like a mechanic from a bygone age. In many ways that was what he was. 'This about the Alfa?'

'It certainly is. Got her back from the body shop last week. We've just been finishing off the mechanical work. She's all done now. Good as new. Better really.'

McLean checked his watch. Too early to call it a day, and there was the small matter of a major incident investigation requiring his attention.

'That's great, thank you. But I don't think I'll be able to pick it up until the weekend. It's a little busy here.'

'Aye, that business in Gilmerton with the journalist. I heard.'

'You did?' Mr Roberts worked out of a busy little garage in Loanhead, which wasn't all that far from Gilmerton. Still, it surprised McLean that he'd take much of an interest in the case.

'Thought you'd be a bit too busy to come and collect, so I brought her over for you.'

Parked on the street by the front entrance to the station, Alan Roberts' flatbed truck had begun to attract quite a lot of attention from public and police alike. Partly this might have been to do with the double yellow line, but mostly it was the gleaming red classic sports car on the back.

McLean remembered his father's old car fondly. He'd

found it hidden away at the back of the garage after his gran had died, had it fixed up and driven it around for a year or so before Detective Sergeant Pete Buchanan had fallen several storeys on to its roof. Before that accident, the car had been tidy, but not exactly new. Its paint had been glossy and red, just a shame about the several different shades where individual panels had been resprayed down the years. Now it looked even better than it must have done in the showroom, sometime in the early 1970s.

It was still red, gleaming in the hot afternoon sun like something wet and dangerous. McLean didn't think he'd ever seen it so clean. Any car so clean, for that matter. Roberts set about undoing the straps holding it down to the flatbed, while yet more underemployed police officers wandered up to see what was going on.

'You got her fixed. That must have cost a bit.' McLean didn't need to turn to know it was DS Ritchie who had spoken.

'I couldn't see it scrapped,' he said as Roberts tilted the flatbed back hydraulically until it formed a long shallow ramp to the road. They both watched as the mechanic fished a key out of his pocket, unlocked the car and climbed in. The noise it made when he started it up was not what either of them were expecting.

'Didn't used to sound like that, did she?' McLean thought the question, but it was Ritchie who asked it.

'Not as far as I remember. They did say they were going to do a bit of mechanical work on it. Bring the brakes and cooling up to modern standards. Stuff like that.'

A bit more rasping exhaust noise and the little red Alfa Romeo inched backwards down the ramp, on to the road.

The cluster of police officers thickened around it, all peering in through the windows, so that McLean almost had to fight his way through them. Mr Roberts had turned off the engine and was climbing arthritically out of the low-down seat when he and Ritchie made it to the kerbside.

'Your keys.' Roberts handed them over. 'You'll want to take it easy for the first few hundred miles. Let the engine bed in a bit.'

'I thought you were just fixing up the bodywork and giving it a bit of a service,' McLean said. He ran a hand over the warm, smooth surface of the roof. The shine was so glossy it was almost painful to look at.

'That was the first cheque. We had that conversation about making a few improvements, remember?'

McLean thought he might have done, vaguely. Mostly it had been messages on his answering machine informing him of progress, or lack thereof. He'd not been too bothered, or rather he'd been too busy to worry about it. Roberts had a good reputation, the rest was just time and money.

'It's all in the folder there, Inspector.' Roberts reached in to the passenger seat with much popping of joints, and came back holding a large black ring-binder. Inside were many, many receipts, and photographs in neat plastic wallets. 'Oh, and there's this as well. Never did have much truck with technology, but there's a couple of thousand photographs on here.' He dug a hand into the pocket of his overalls, coming out with a small black memory stick.

'I . . . um . . . thank you.' McLean took it, dropped it into his own pocket.

'No. Thank you, sir. There's not many's prepared to

spend the money keeping these old girls alive. She's been a pleasure to work on. Just try not to break her again, eh?' Roberts gave him a grin, then walked away. McLean watched him as he started to pack up the flatbed, ready to leave. When he turned back to his car, DS Ritchie was on the other side, peering in through the window. She crouched down, ran a hand along the curve of the bonnet, then went to the front and looked back along the side.

'This must have cost you a fortune, sir. They've done a beautiful job.'

McLean looked at the gleaming chrome door handle and the trim around the window edges. They had been tarnished before, pitted by age and road salt. Now they were like new. The door itself had never quite sat right on its hinges, the gap at the front noticeably larger than that at the back. He couldn't see that now. It was almost as if they'd given him a different car.

'Hop in then, Sergeant.' He opened the door and smelled a heady mixture of leather cleaner and oil.

'What?' Ritchie stared at him over the roof.

'I said hop in. I think we should see what Mr Roberts has done, don't you?'

26

He had to wind the window down to keep cool; there was no air-conditioning in the little Alfa, of course. Even so McLean reckoned he must have had an idiot grin plastered all over his face as they drove south from the city centre. Traffic was mercifully light and they made good speed, the temperature gauge on the dashboard rising swiftly to the middle and then sticking there.

'Don't think I'll ever get tired of that noise,' DS Ritchie said, as they pulled out of a side turning and McLean put his foot down. The exhaust crackled and popped and the car surged forward like a terrier after a rat. Whatever Alan Roberts and his mechanics had done to the thing, it was a different beast indeed from the car he'd found tucked away in his grandmother's garage after her death.

A chuckle from the passenger seat brought him out of his musing. He glanced sideways to where DS Ritchie was sitting, a smile on her face as the breeze from her open window played with her short red hair. 'What?'

'I've not seen you look this happy in . . .' Ritchie paused a moment, her smile turning to a thoughtful frown. 'Can't really say I've ever seen you so happy, actually.'

'Thanks,' McLean said. 'I think.' He wrapped his fingers around the thin steering wheel, suddenly self-conscious. The moment's simple enjoyment had gone, the bubble burst. It was still a damn fine day though, and a great way to be spending it driving a classic sports car.

'Where we going, anyway?'

'Nearly there.' McLean dropped a gear and sped forward to make it through a set of lights before they changed. The Alfa did exactly what he asked of it, chirping its rear wheels with a little spin. He had to admit he'd missed the thing. A couple of hundred yards further on and they slowed for another crossing.

'Gilmerton Cove?' Ritchie peered through the windscreen as the lights turned green. McLean indicated right, then dropped the clutch and spun the wheels trying to get across the turning before the car coming towards him. He didn't care about the blaring horn and rude hand gesture the manoeuvre got him. The car brought out the long-suppressed adolescent hooligan in him.

Parking in the lot behind the library at least meant they were off the street and largely out of sight. It still left him with a dilemma. Part of him wanted to make DS Ritchie stay and act as a guard. It would be too terrible to come back and find key marks in that lovely gloss-red paintwork. But that was just paranoia, and besides, she was a trained detective, not some junior uniform constable to be set menial tasks.

McLean still turned back and gave the car one last long look before he walked round the corner and out of sight.

'She'll be fine, sir. Don't worry.'

'You're right. I'm just being stupid.'

'Mind you, I don't think I'd dare leave something like that in a public place. Who knows what some little toerag'll do to her?'

‘Not helping, you know.’ McLean looked across at the detective sergeant, saw the smile on her face. She was recovering well from her brush with death, her cheekbones less prominent, eyes less sunken, but she still had a way to go.

‘We going to the crime scene then, sir? Only I thought forensics were all packed up and away now. Place is meant to be opening to the public again soon.’

McLean stopped at the edge of the road. Somewhere under his feet, give or take, Ben Stevenson had met his gruesome, violent end. He had gone willingly into the caverns, perhaps in search of higher truths, lured by someone with motives he couldn’t begin to understand. At least not yet. Going down there again himself would serve no purpose.

‘There’s only one way into those caves, right?’

‘Pretty much. Well, there’s two, but they both exit on to the road up there.’ Ritchie pointed up towards the entrance to the visitor centre. ‘There may be others, but they’ve been filled up with rocks for centuries. Stevenson and his killer had to have come past here at some point before he died.’

‘And yet we got nothing off any cameras.’ McLean pointed at the CCTV on a nearby pole. They’d already spoken to all the shops in the area, trawling the footage for the slightest glimpse of anyone who might have looked like the dead reporter. For a backwater suburb, Gilmerton was surprisingly well covered by cameras, but they’d found nothing.

‘Half of them had been scrubbed by the time we got to them. Some weren’t even working, just for show.’ It was nothing McLean didn't know. That wasn't why he'd come out here.

'You can't always trust the cameras, anyway. But someone will have seen our man on his way here.' McLean turned away from the road, walked the short distance to the door to the betting shop on the corner. 'You just need to know how to ask.'

There were bookies and there were bookies. Some places you wouldn't go into without a stab vest and a fully armed back-up team. Some places you'd get a hard eye and a cold shoulder but certainly no answers to any questions, however civilly you put them. And then there were bookies that were simply businesses trying to keep afloat in the face of twenty-four-hour online poker, smartphone apps that made it even easier to lose your shirt, and a population increasingly too simple-minded to manage anything as difficult as studying form. McLean had noticed this one, part of a national chain, the first time he'd come to Gilmerton Cove. He had no doubt that some detective constable had been in, armed with his PDA and some questions, to quiz the owner about the night Ben Stevenson had died. There would be a transcription of the answers on file somewhere in the major incident room, and probably backed up to the cloud too, wherever that was. They weren't the sort of questions he was interested in now, and certainly not the right answers. It was always better to do these things yourself, anyway. And besides, he'd needed an excuse for taking the car out.

Inside, the bookies showed just as much promise as expected. The smoking ban had long since cleared the air, but a yellow nicotine stain still clung to the ceiling and walls. Burning tobacco would probably have been preferable to the medley of aromas that assailed his nose as McLean stood in the doorway and surveyed the scene. It wasn't exactly a hive of activity, just a couple of old men in opposite corners staring up at old-style bulky television screens screwed to the walls, a spotty-faced youth behind the counter. One other punter stood at a table in the middle of the room, tongue protruding from the side of his mouth as he concentrated on the tiny print in his *Racing Times*.

'What're we . . .?' Ritchie began to ask, but McLean quieted her with a wave of his arm as he stepped fully into the room. One of the old men looked at him with a distrustful glare, but the other one didn't take his eyes off the television. He walked up to the punter at the table.

'Got any tips?'

'Eh?' The man looked up, surprise widening his eyes.

'What's on this afternoon? Ayr?'

The man's eyes narrowed for a moment, then his gaze softened. 'Ayr, aye. Not much of a turnout, mind.' He folded up his paper so McLean couldn't see the horses he'd picked, then turned and walked away.

'Friendly,' Ritchie whispered.

'Doesn't want to chance his luck, does he?' McLean smiled at his own joke, headed for the counter and the spotty youth.

'The boss in?' he asked before the lad could speak. The youth looked up at him, startled, then saw the warrant card McLean had pulled out of his pocket.

'I . . . I'll just get him.'

He scurried off, disappearing through a door at the back just as McLean felt a presence by his side.

'He going to be long?' It was the punter with the *Racing Times*, now rolled up into a tight tube and clasped in a nervous hand. 'Only the race starts in five.'

McLean looked at his watch. 'Shouldn't be a problem. You got your runners all picked out then?'

'Yeah. Reckon.' The punter tapped his rolled up paper against his arm. He was short, wiry. A face like a shaven ferret. Malnourished might be the right word. It wasn't hard to see where most of his money went.

'Can I help you?' The manager had arrived, shadowed by the spotty youth. 'Only I already spoke to youse lot last week.'

'Take the man's bet first, aye?' McLean stood to one side, letting the punter in with his slip. Money changed hands, and then the man sidled off, the faintest nod of thanks as he went to find a stool from where he could see his luck run out on the racecourse. McLean watched him go, then turned back to the manager.

'Anywhere quiet I might have a word?'

27

The manager's office had the dubious honour of making the run-down betting shop beyond it look well kept. There was a desk, not large, and covered with a stack of paperwork that could give McLean's own one back at the station a run for its money. A couple of tall filing cabinets filled the back wall, a broken printer balanced precariously on top. Boxes cluttered most of the available space. There was certainly nowhere to sit other than the chair behind the desk, which the manager dropped himself into like a man whose legs have had enough. Given his size, McLean could only sympathise with them.

'Don't really know how I can help you, Inspector. It is Inspector, isn't it?'

'It is, yes. Mr . . .?'

'Ballard. Johnny Ballard.' The manager made the most minimal of efforts to get up, almost raised a hand to shake, then collapsed again into his chair.

'Well, Mr Ballard. I know you're a busy man, so I won't waste too much of your time. Like you said, you've already spoken to one of my constables.'

'Aye, young lad, scar on his forehead like that chap in the film.'

'You're not that busy today.'

'Today, every day.' Ballard rocked back in his chair,

making room for his gut behind the desk. 'Who needs a bookies when you've got the internet, eh?'

'People looking to be paid in cash, I'd guess.'

'Now look here . . .' Ballard would have sprung to his feet, McLean was sure of it. Had his belly not been in the way.

'Calm down, Mr Ballard. I'm not here to make life difficult for you. Quite the opposite. I imagine business has been even slower since our lot set up in the caves downstairs. Not much of a betting man myself, but I'd wager the two old blokes don't spend more than a fiver at a time, and the lad whose brew money you just took probably doesn't bring in any more.'

'Keith's all right. Even wins a bit now and then. Just enough to keep him going.' Ballard slumped back into his seat again. 'And you're right enough. Business isn't exactly booming here, but that stuff with the journalist? Well, let's just say it's not helping.'

'Sooner we're gone, the better?'

'Wouldn't hurt, aye.'

'So tell me then, Mr Ballard. In the month up to the body turning up in the caves. You notice any new people through the door?'

'What d'ye mean? We get new customers every day.'

'You sure of that? Every day?'

'Well, maybe not—'

'You have a core of regulars. Don't worry, I'm not interested in them. I'm looking for anyone who might've come in more than once over the last month or two. Maybe asking questions, maybe just looking around the place.'

Ballard furrowed his brow in a good impression of a man who found thinking hard. McLean knew it was an act, even if just a subconscious one. You didn't get to run a bookies in this part of town without having an above-average intelligence and a way with people.

'Kind've hard to remember it all. What, two months back? That'd be when they were working on the drains, digging up the road down the hill a bit. Had a few of the workmen come in. Not big spenders, and one of them cleaned up on a three-way accumulator if I remember right.'

'Roadworks down the hill?' McLean looked across at DS Ritchie, who was leaning against the wall by the door. 'Why've I not heard about this before?'

'No idea, sir. I'll find out.' She pulled her phone out of her pocket and started tapping at the screen.

'There was a bloke, now I think about it,' Ballard said, dragging McLean's attention back. 'Strange little fellow. Came in with the road crew sometimes. On his own others. Not sure he ever placed a bet though.'

'He speak to anyone? Meet anyone? Bookies is a good place to arrange to meet someone if you don't want to go to the pub.'

'Aye, could have been that, I guess. Bit bloody cheeky, mind.' Ballard furrowed his brow again, his eyes almost disappearing in the folds of skin around his face. 'No. Thought I could remember what he looked like, but it's gone. Just got an idea of a person, nothing more.'

'Well, it's better than nothing. We can speak to the road crew, see if any of them remember.' It wasn't much – probably wouldn't come to anything – but it was more than anyone else investigating the case had managed so far. 'I'll send an e-fit specialist up to see you too, if you can spare a half-hour from your busy schedule.'

'Never had you as a betting man, sir.'

'Can't remember the last time I put money on anything. And my knowledge of horse racing could be summarised neatly by the phrase "bugger all".'

'But . . .' Ritchie half-turned towards the now-closed door to the bookies.

'Bullshit with confidence, Sergeant. That's the trick.' McLean set off in the direction of the car park, anxious to get back to his precious Alfa before someone could drop something on it from a great height.

'No way that was bullshit. How'd you know all that stuff about Ayr racecourse? Not exactly your home turf, is it?'

McLean stopped mid-stride. Turned back to face Ritchie. 'I was three years on the beat, Sergeant. Not like some of you fast-track youngsters these days. Most of that time I spent with old Guthrie McManus. No one else had the time of day for him, but he was OK once you got to know him. Helped if you weren't completely useless at the job too, I guess.

'Thing is, Guthrie was fond of a flutter. I must have followed him into pretty much every betting shop in the city back then, watching while he placed his bets, claimed his occasional winnings. You don't do this job if you're no good at noticing things, so I picked up enough to get me by. Learned another useful thing, too. See Guthrie liked a bet now and then, but he also knew a good source of information. Wasn't a bookie out there he couldn't tap for answers if he needed. And he was good enough to more or less make it pay.'

Ritchie stared at him, jaw slightly slack, but McLean's attention was caught by the man exiting the bookmaker's, head down with the despondent weight of someone who's just lost the weekly food money on a horse that was a dead cert to win.

'Stay there a minute,' he said to the sergeant, then raised his voice to the ferrety little man. 'It's Keith, isn't it?'

At the sound of his voice, Keith stopped walking, looked up with that familiar guilty expression, mixed with confusion.

'It's OK. You don't owe me anything.' That seemed to relax the man, at least a little.

'What then? Only I'm—'

'Busy? Aye, I noticed that. So I'll not keep you long. You go in there a lot, I reckon. Make a bit, lose a bit?' McLean had positioned himself so it was difficult for the young man to move on without being obvious about it. Now he spoke more quickly than normal, giving him little room to get a word in.

'What's it to—?'

'Reckon you notice stuff, too.' McLean nodded at the tightly rolled-up *Racing Times* Keith was clutching as if it still held the secrets to all happiness. 'You look for the patterns, am I right?'

'I . . . yeah. Do my best.'

'And you like that. Noticing stuff, aye? Like when the road crews were in a few weeks back. When the police came round after they found that body in the caves.'

'Who are you?' Keith finally looked up at McLean's face,

took in his dark suit and began to reach a conclusion. Maybe not as observant as he thought he was.

'I'm Tony,' McLean said. 'And I'm trying to find out who killed that reporter.'

'You're polis.' It wasn't a question, and Keith finally seemed to understand something of his situation. As he moved to step past, McLean took a hold of his arm, as lightly as he dared.

'I'm not here to bother you, Keith. I'm looking for help, and if you can help me maybe I can help you in return.' He looked up, past the young man's head towards the door to the betting shop. Keith's head twitched involuntarily as his eyes started to follow, a haunted look on his face.

'What you want then?' he asked eventually.

McLean let go of the arm. 'Like I said, I reckon you notice things. See the patterns. You'll have noticed the road crews coming in and placing bets from time to time, and I reckon you'll have noticed someone else come in over the past couple of months. Someone who didn't quite fit in. Maybe didn't even place any bets.'

'Like someone casing the joint?'

'That's the one. Maybe even just hanging around to see who comes and goes and when.'

Keith shook his head. 'I dunno. Can't really think of anyone, right enough. I mean, there's always folk coming and going.'

'Well, give it some thought, OK?' McLean dug into his jacket pocket for a business card. There was a folded ten pound note in there too, another of Guthrie McManus's tips. He pulled both out together, hiding the money under the card as he handed it over like a magician. 'Give us a call if anything sparks a memory.'

'You think that was wise, giving him cash like that? He'll only lose it on the horses. Come back for more.'

They were making slow progress back towards the station, traffic backed up along Clerk Street by an accident, or just too many buses. McLean found it hard not to keep his eye on the temperature gauge, waiting for it to tip into the red like it always used to, but so far it had held perfectly steady in the centre of the dial.

'It's a risk, but you never know. If I were a betting man, I'd lay you a tenner he calls me in the next couple of days saying he thinks he remembers someone. I'll get him to do an e-fit, same as the manager. If we get two different people, we've just lost a bit of time and ten pounds. If they both come up with something similar . . .' It was thin, and McLean knew it. But then the whole investigation was thin. The harder they looked, the less evidence there was that anyone at all had killed Ben Stevenson. No forensics in the cave, nothing at his home but the all-too-obvious signs of his obsession, no motive, not even the slightest hint of a suspect.

'We're really clutching at straws, aren't we, sir?' Ritchie summed up the hopelessness in a simple cliché.

'Still one or two to go.'

'There are?'

'Oh yes. There's Douglas Ballantyne for one.'

'Douglas . . . oh, aye. I'd forgotten about him. The conspiracy theorist.'

'The same. He should be back from the US by now. Think we should pay him a wee visit tomorrow.'

'And you really think he'll be able to help us?'

'He was in contact with Stevenson. At the least he should be able to tell us what he was working on. Jo Dalgliesh has been looking into that, too. If we can piece together Stevenson's movements and motives leading up to his death, then maybe we can have a guess at why someone might want to kill him.'

The traffic started moving again, and McLean eased the car forward to keep with the flow.

'Straws,' Ritchie said as the acceleration pushed her gently back into her seat. 'Clutching.'

28

I gave the child a week. If it hadn't died by then I would have helped it along, but it only managed three days in the end. I'd have preferred five, if I'm being honest. That would have given me a little more time to prepare. But God's will cannot be gainsaid, and the child however flawed was one of His creations too. He has set me this task to perform. It is not for Him to make it easy.

People fall apart in surprisingly predictable ways. Jim, for all his years of medical training, had allowed himself to get too close, too emotionally attached to his patients. Losing them felt to him like failure, as if it were somehow his fault that the child had got cancer in the first place. This child was particularly special to him. I've no idea why. Maybe he had a friend who suffered a similar fate; that might explain his interest in medicine. The whys are unimportant, only the hows matter.

I find him where I expect him to be, at the glass wall where we had our little chat just a few days ago. He looks unwell, like a man who's not slept in days. He stares through at the empty bed as if he thinks that staring might make it unhappen.

'I'm so sorry. I just heard.' Not true, of course, but timing is everything. He turns at my voice and I can see the red around his eyes and nose, the tears threatening to come back at any moment. He wipes a sleeve against his face, sniffs hard. Says nothing.

'I tried,' I say. 'We might have been able to do something, if we'd had a little more time. There was a trial, but . . .' I let the words tail off, leave the next step to him.

'It always takes too long. Endless committees wringing their hands. If I could just bring them here. Show them this.' He slams an angry palm against the glass, making it wobble. A passing nurse starts to scowl, then realises who it is, bobs her head and hurries away.

'It doesn't have to.' I pitch my voice low and quiet, but he still hears. I can see the change in his posture. This is what he's been waiting for.

'You don't mean—'

'Not here.' I reach into my pocket, pull out the card I wrote earlier. An address, my assumed name. Nothing else. 'This evening at eight. There's some people I'd like you to meet. Some things you might like to see.'

I hold his gaze as he takes the card from me, slips it into his pocket. He nods once, just the slightest tip of the head, but it's enough. If he takes this step, he will be free. His redemption will be complete. Now only time can tell.

29

If his house was anything to go by, then making stuff up for a living was very lucrative. At least if you were as convincingly creative as Douglas Ballantyne. McLean had tried wading through the book that he'd taken from Ben Stevenson's flat, the mad ideas wrapped up in a plausible presentation of carefully selected facts. Like so many others, Ballantyne was obsessed with the Masons, the Knights Templar and all the associated nonsense that clung to them like body odour to a teenage boy. It was a rich market of paranoia to feed.

Nestling in a quiet glen about a half-hour's drive south of the city, Ballantyne House was surrounded by acres of parkland. Scraggy-looking sheep sheltered under ancient trees, doing their best to escape the withering summer sun. A small herd of deer peered nervously at the car as McLean navigated a narrow driveway that took him and DS Ritchie away from an already minor road and brought them finally to the house itself.

'Remind me to get started on that misery memoir when we get back to the city, sir.' Ritchie's gaze didn't shift from the building as she climbed out of the car and closed the door behind her. Even McLean had to admit it was impressive, as Scots Baronial piles went. Three storeys of red sandstone and harling radiating in the afternoon heat. It was almost picture perfect, although he reckoned it would be a bugger to keep warm in the winter.

‘Any sign of our man? He knows we’re coming.’ McLean looked around, half-expecting to see a stout, bearded fellow with a couple of spaniels cavorting at his heels, striding across the fields to greet them. Instead, a low, menacing growl raised the hairs on the back of his neck.

‘Oh bloody marvellous.’ Ritchie reached very slowly for her car door, clicked it open again. ‘I really don’t like dogs.’

‘You and Grumpy Bob both.’ McLean tried to pinpoint the source of the growling, finally locating it as two Rhodesian Ridgebacks appeared from around the corner of the house. They didn’t bark, didn’t run snarling and slavering towards him. That was perhaps even more scary, in some ways; that someone had control over them even though they were clearly desperate to kill.

‘Aubrey! Campion! Sit!’ The voice was oddly high-pitched, and McLean thought for a moment that it must be a woman’s. Whoever it was, the dogs obeyed with machine-like precision, settling on to their haunches in a manner that said quite clearly they were still ready for the chase. Bred for hunting lions in the African veldt, McLean recalled reading somewhere. He was no huge fan of dogs, having grown up in a house with few pets, and those mostly feline.

‘Don’t mind my boys. They won’t bite unless I tell them to.’ Again that high-pitched voice, but at about the same time as he saw who was speaking, McLean heard the masculine undertones in it. And sure enough, the man himself appeared, patting one of the two dogs on the head as he walked past them.

Douglas Ballantyne was a bit older than when he’d been photographed for his book, but it was undeniably the same man. His beard exploded from his chin and neck in a ruddy-grey mass that must surely be home to small nesting birds. He was dressed in loose-fitting jogging bottoms, with a dark velvet smoking jacket over a faded rock band tour T-shirt, making for a rather incongruous ensemble. The heavy-framed spectacles and ornate-topped walking cane didn't exactly help the image.

'What a lovely creature.' Ballantyne stared past McLean, then did a double-take as he noticed DS Ritchie. 'The car, I mean.'

'Of course you do. Mr Ballantyne, I presume.' McLean held out his hand, receiving an odd look from the writer.

'Yes, yes. And you're the policeman. McLean. Heard a lot about you.'

'You have? All good, I hope.'

'At least not bad.' Ballantyne relented and took McLean's hand, tried one of the Masonic holds. A test McLean must have passed by not acknowledging. 'Come on in. I'll make us some tea.'

The interior of the house was pleasantly cool after the fierce heat outside. Ballantyne had led them around the back; McLean suspected that the front entrance was probably locked and had been for years. A couple of small rooms opened on to a kitchen best described as lived in. There was no sign of a Mrs Ballantyne, and McLean doubted one existed. Nor was there any sign of staff. No PA, no cleaner, just the man himself and his two dogs. They'd calmed down once they realised neither he nor Ritchie was a threat, and slunk off to scruffy-looking beds in the far corner of the room as soon as they entered.

'Tea?' Ballantyne grabbed a heavy iron kettle, shook it

to see if it contained water, then clanged it down on the hotplate of the huge range cooker. He stared at it for about ten seconds, then took it off again. 'Idiot. I always forget it gets put out in the summer.'

He started again, this time with an electric kettle, then busied himself finding mugs and teabags. The kitchen was cluttered, busy, the large table strewn with papers, a laptop and piles of books, but it was by and large clean. Not unlike his own kitchen, McLean couldn't help noticing. Only bigger.

'You wanted to talk to me about Ben Stevenson, I understand. That's what the constable on the phone said, anyway.' Ballantyne spoke over his shoulder as he went from cupboard to cupboard, hopefully in search of biscuits.

'Detective Constable MacBride. Did he tell you why?'

Ballantyne gave up his search. 'Sit, Inspector, Sergeant. Please. Don't mind the mess.' He made a half-hearted attempt at clearing the table, mainly piling everything into a big heap in the middle, the laptop balanced precariously on top. 'He said something about him dying.'

'He was murdered, Mr Ballantyne. In the caves at Gilmerton Cove. You know the place?'

'Know it? I wrote a book about it. Fascinating place. All that talk about the Covenanters, Masons and God knows who else linked to it. All wrong, of course.'

'Oh? Who do you think built it, then?' DS Ritchie asked.

'Something far older than all of them.' Ballantyne was about to say more, but the kettle clicked off its noisy boil, distracting him while he poured water into mugs.

'Was that what Stevenson was looking into?' McLean asked once tea had been handed out and biscuits found.

'Ben?' Ballantyne laughed. 'No, Ben was still a novice. He was obsessed with the link between the Knights Templar and the modern Masonic movement. Textbook conspiracy theory stuff.'

McLean tried to remember the contents of the book he'd skim-read. It had seemed pretty much textbook conspiracy theory to him, but then maybe he, too, was a novice. 'So you don't think there's a link, then?'

'Oh, of course there's a link. It's as plain as the day when you know what you're looking for.' Ballantyne took a slurp of tea, leaning forwards over the kitchen table in his enthusiasm for the tale. 'But it's not what all the books say. Not what you'll find if you look it up on Wikipedia.'

'Let me guess. The Brotherhood?'

Ballantyne's eyes gleamed with excitement. 'So you have read my book. I'm impressed.'

'I read Stevenson's copy. The one you wrote the dedication in. It was well thumbed.'

'Was it? Was it indeed?' Ballantyne looked genuinely surprised. 'And I thought he just bought it to humour me.'

'I think he was rather more interested in your theories than you realise, Mr Ballantyne.'

'You do?'

'Yes. And I think he got too close to something. Maybe a true secret, or maybe someone who didn't want the world to know there was no secret.'

'And they killed him for it? I see where you're going, Inspector, but I very much doubt Ben would have uncovered anything worth killing for.' Ballantyne paused for a moment, as if a thought had interrupted his flow. 'You say he was killed in Gilmerton Cove? And you found his body, obviously, otherwise you wouldn't be here talking to me about it. Tell me, was there a ritualistic nature to his murder?'

'I'm not really at liberty to discuss that kind of detail,' McLean said. 'Why do you ask?'

'Well, it occurs to me that if poor old Ben really had uncovered something worth killing for, then you'd never have found him. You'd probably never have realised he'd gone missing in the first place.'

'Why do you say that?' McLean had a sinking feeling that he already knew the answer.

'The Brotherhood control the media, Inspector. Every aspect of it. The news, the television, films, books. Yes, even my efforts.' Ballantyne waved an arm in the direction of the precarious pile of papers. 'It may look like we're revealing long-hidden secrets, but it only happens because they let it. Much as it galls me to admit it, I am just an instrument in their greater plan.'

'And that is?'

'Oh, I've no idea. Well, that's not strictly true. I've an idea, but it's not something I'd dream of divulging. Not yet at least. Maybe there'll be a time I can write that book. If it serves the purpose of the Brotherhood to have it revealed.'

'So what if Stevenson had this same idea but wasn't prepared to wait?'

'That's the nub of it, Inspector. If he'd done that, then they'd have sent the Adrogenae after him. And if they had done, then he simply would never have existed.'

30

'The expression you're looking for is "stone bonker", I think.'

The road back to Edinburgh was relatively clear, just the occasional caravan to overtake with a satisfying surge of acceleration. It occurred to McLean after a couple of high-rev manoeuvres that Mr Roberts had told him to take it easy for the first few hundred miles. He backed off as they approached an articulated lorry, slowing to match its pace through the bends around Silverburn and Habbies Howe.

'Nut job does it for me. I was almost with him up until the point where he mentioned those weird supernatural assassins. What did he call them, Androgen-something?'

'The Adrogenae. Yes. I'd forgotten. He mentions them in the book. Apparently they're one of the reasons no one's ever heard about the Brotherhood until now.'

'I didn't really understand what it was they did, though. Do they go back in time and kill your grandfather or something?'

'Search me. I don't think making sense is high on Douglas Ballantyne's list of priorities.'

'So we wasted an afternoon then.'

'A bit, maybe.' McLean dragged his eyes away from the road briefly, looked across at the detective sergeant. Ritchie stared out of the window at the grubby back of the truck. Someone had written 'Danny takes it up the arse' in the grime, and then rather incongruously drawn a large pair of breasts. It didn't say much for the cleanliness of the logistics wing of a major supermarket chain.

'I'm not seeing any positive side to the whole thing. Apart from getting a ride in your car.'

'Well, the way I see it, Ballantyne's so full of shit you could plant flowers in him. But I've read his book. He has a way with words. His arguments are plausible because he's selective with the facts. It's an old trick, true, but he does it very well.'

'Every age has its snake-oil salesmen, I guess.'

'And willing idiots to buy it, too. Like Ben Stevenson.'

'You think he fell for that?' Ritchie hooked a thumb back over her shoulder in a vague approximation of the direction of Douglas Ballantyne's country estate.

'Hook, line and sinker. He was obsessed. You saw his secret room, the connections he was making.'

'But he was a journalist. Surely he'd have some kind of bullshit filter.'

'Recently divorced, missing his kids, not had a big story in almost five years?'

Ritchie didn't answer immediately, thinking things over. The road straightened out and McLean took the opportunity to overtake the lorry. For a gut-clenching moment he thought he'd overcooked it, the next corner arriving much more quickly than he'd anticipated. A dab of the brakes pushed him hard against the seatbelt, Ritchie's hand going out to the dashboard to steady herself. Mr Roberts had worked his magic on the braking system too, it seemed.

'You think that's enough to lose your mind?'

'I've seen people lose theirs over less.'

'Still doesn't get us any closer to finding out who killed him, though.'

'Maybe. Maybe not. It does tell us that he was very suggestible.'

'You think someone led him on? He wasn't on to anything at all?' Ritchie asked.

'I don't know.' McLean paused, drumming his fingers on the steering wheel as he tried to put into words the slippery thoughts he had about the case, the way it was beginning to feel to him. He needed a good long walk, really. That usually helped.

'It just doesn't stack up as some secret society trying to silence him before he could spill the beans. Ballantyne might be a loony, but he's right about one thing. If that were the case, if his Brotherhood or whatever he calls it really existed, really was all-powerful and really didn't want the cat let out of the bag, then Ben Stevenson would have just disappeared. Or he'd have committed suicide, had a tragic fatal accident. Anything but being slain in some mock-Masonic ritual and his blood smeared all over the walls of a cave where he was always going to be found.'

'So you think chasing the story he was working on is a waste of time?'

'Not quite. It was his obsession, and it was probably what led him to that cave. But I think we're asking the wrong questions.'

'So what are the right ones?'

'I wish I knew, Kirsty. I wish I knew.'

Traffic built up as they approached the city, as if cars were flies and Edinburgh a particularly ripe piece of rotting meat. McLean glanced at the clock on the dash, surprised at how late it was. Summer in the north meant long hours of daylight and with them the tendency to work well past the end of the shift. Not that he had shifts, but Ritchie did and technically she'd already put in an hour and a half's overtime.

'Think we need to have a recap at tomorrow's morning briefing. Get a better feel for where we are with this case. I'll have to speak to Dalgliesh, too. See if she's got any further on Stevenson's story.'

'Can't be easy, working with her.' Ritchie stared out the windscreen, one hand toying absentmindedly with her pendant, the little silver cross that she'd taken to wearing lately.

'Possibly the understatement of the year.' McLean slowed the car as they approached the junction with the bypass.

'She's not a bad journalist, when she puts her mind to it.' Ritchie looked away from McLean as she spoke, so he couldn't tell whether she was joking or not. He hoped she was.

'You heading back to the station?' she asked as he took the Burdiehouse turning.

'That was the plan. You can have the rest of the evening off, even after that last comment. I thought I'd head home, see how much damage the cats have done whilst I was away.'

'Cats? Plural? Thought you only had the one. She's not had kittens, has she?'

The thought of Mrs McCutcheon's cat giving birth to anything was so strange, McLean almost drove into the back of a car that had braked to turn into a side street. 'Christ, no. I'm looking after Madame Rose's cats for a while.'

'Oh, that's right. Grumpy Bob told me. Sounds horrible what's happening to her. Any idea who's behind it?'

'Haven't had time to look into it, to be honest.' McLean realised it was a while since he'd heard from the medium. Yet another thing to add to the to-do list.

'Well, if you're just going home you can drop me off at your church. I've got my bag, don't need to go back to the station.'

'The church? OK. I take it tonight's another one of Mary Currie's Bible classes.'

'Bible class?' Ritchie laughed. 'Hadn't really thought of it that way. No, we don't all sit around discussing the Gospels. It's more about tea and sympathy.'

'Still not selling it to me. Always been more of a beer and curry man.'

'Yeah, well sometimes there's beer. If Eric's remembered to bring any. He works in an off-licence in Morningside, gets all the bottles that are past their use-by dates. Sometimes he brings wine for us to taste. It's been very educational, even if Norman doesn't approve. Mind you, Norman doesn't approve of much. He'd be more for studying the Bible and maybe sharing a cup of water and a dry biscuit.'

McLean couldn't help but notice the change in Ritchie as she spoke. Her hands came up out of her lap as if they had a life of their own; her voice was more animated than he'd heard it in ages. Much more like the enthusiastic detective sergeant who'd transferred down from Aberdeen.

'Why'd you go in the first place?' he asked after a while. 'Never had you pegged as the religious type.'

'Didn't really think I was. Oh, I went to Sunday School when I was a kid, used to love singing hymns, carols at Christmas, all that stuff. But I grew out of it. Thought I'd grown out of it, anyway. I mean, it's hard to have faith when your mum goes senile. She was a genuinely good person, kind. Wouldn't hurt a fly, worked in a charity shop when she wasn't out earning enough to keep a roof over our heads. I kind of saw through the whole God thing then.'

'So what changed?' McLean asked the question even though he knew the answer. They'd had this conversation before.

'I nearly died is what.' Ritchie's hands dropped back down into her lap. McLean was concentrating on the road ahead, but he could see in the corner of his eye that she had turned to face him. 'And whatever the doctors say about that, all their talk of Spanish Flu and blood poisoning, none of them had a clue what was wrong with me.'

'And you do.' McLean knew he was pushing where he shouldn't, somehow couldn't stop himself.

'Too bloody right. You do too. Otherwise you wouldn't have come and visited me that night.'

'Which particular night? I visited as often as I could.'

'I had nightmares, you know? More like hallucinations, maybe. Visions of hell. People burning, screaming in agony. Their faces melting away. And sitting in the middle of it all, smiling, was that bloody woman.'

McLean realised he'd slowed down almost to a crawl, checked in the rearview mirror to make sure he wasn't causing an obstruction. They weren't far from his house and the church now, but he didn't want the journey to end until Ritchie had finished talking.

'Mrs Saifre?'

'Like you need to ask. And you know as well as me that's not her real name. Its real name.'

'I . . .'

'It's all right, sir. I know you see the world differently. Rational explanations and all that. Not going to ask you to name it, or anything. But you knew. You helped. Mary knows what you did, won't tell me, but I'm a detective so I'll find out sooner or later. Or maybe I won't. Doesn't really matter. All I know is I was ready to die and I was going to that place. She had me, plain and simple. Then you turned up in the dead of night, and the nightmare went away.'

They had reached the church now, for all McLean's attempts to drag the journey out just a little longer. He pulled in to the kerb, left the engine running.

'You had a high fever, Kirsty. Things can seem very strange when—'

'Don't.' Ritchie stopped him by reaching out and placing a single finger over his lips. He couldn't recall her having touched him before, apart from a handshake when they'd first met maybe. It was a strangely intimate gesture, for all that it was fleeting. Before he could protest, or say anything more, she had unclipped her seatbelt and stepped out of the car. She grabbed her bag from the footwell and slammed the door shut with just the necessary amount of force. McLean watched her as she crossed the pavement and half-jogged down the wide stone path, through the graveyard and into the open door of the church.

31

'Wasn't sure I'd got the right place. It's a bit off the beaten track, isn't it?'

I've been waiting for five minutes longer than I expected, was beginning to wonder if I'd made a mistake with this one. But no, here he is, and only a little late.

'It has to be. The work we do here is . . . close to the edge. We can't do it at the hospital, never get it past the ethics committee for one thing.'

The building is a faceless modern warehouse on the outskirts of town, part of a development of twenty or so identical units. Most house small start-ups, builders, storage units for internet shops. This one's been empty for several months now, all but forgotten by the letting agents. It's been a challenge to prepare, cleaned down and dressed as the set for the final act in this passion play. The effort will be rewarded, I am sure. He is so close to perfection, this one. Just needs to accept what God has ordained for him.

'I almost didn't come,' he says as I usher him in through the door. 'Jon's death, well, it hit me hard, you know. Then the police were round asking questions about Maureen. You know Maureen?'

'I'm not sure I do,' I say as I continue to walk down the corridor. He has to half run to keep up.

'Thought everyone knew her. She's a nurse at the hospital. Specialises in chemo.'

'So many hospitals, so many nurses. It's hard to keep track of them all.' I push open the door into the main room at the back of the building, moving to one side to let him pass by. He takes two steps in, then stops. I can't see his face from where I'm standing, but I'm sure his mouth is hanging open.

'What are you hoping to trial here?' He walks slowly into the centre of the room, runs a hand along the edge of one of the ICU beds, peers at the monitors, all switched off and silent for now. His eyes are everywhere, soaking up the detail. He is weighing the possibilities, considering the implications. I shudder at the thought of what is to come, drink in the tension as he turns back towards me. 'Is this even legal?'

'This isn't a licensed research facility, if that's what you mean. But then I think you already knew that.'

'I don't get it. Who do you work for? This isn't the university or the NHS. Big pharma?'

'Come. Let me show you something.' I head to the anteroom, confident he will follow. There are microscopes, centrifuges, machines that look like they might somehow read your DNA, though in truth they're nothing more than glorified ice-cream makers. The benches are spotlessly clean, the racks of glassware, pipettes and other paraphernalia shiny and new. Arranged along the back wall is a line of tall freezer units, humming gently to themselves. I sense him behind me as I stop at the first.

'In here are the cell lines that could revolutionise the treatment of at least a dozen different cancers. They've all worked well in animal studies, but they need trialling in humans.' I turn and face him, see the questions written large across his face. So very easy to read.

'Your young patient Jon might have benefited, had we been able to get him here. A therapy tailored to the specific DNA of his cancer. Pluck out the faulty genes and replace them with good copies. Self-replicating too. Our goal is a one-shot treatment that basically would've cured him.'

'You can do that? But I thought . . . I mean . . . That's years away, surely?'

'If you play by the rules, yes. But you and I, we know better, don't we?' I step to the side, feeling the moment build. 'You want to look?'

He hesitates, at the last. It's almost as if he knows that to open the door is to cross a line. As if coming here hasn't been. As if the endless nights of research, the furious quest for knowledge that will help him save those barely worth a second glance, wasn't a long slippery slope he'd been sliding down towards this point for years. But in the end he reaches for the handle, twists it, pulls the door open. Just as I knew he would when I first started to tug gently at his puppet strings. In that act he is committed. In that act he is pure.

'Wha—?' His last word is unfinished, the needle slides into his exposed neck, poisons pumping into his blood-stream and shutting him down like a child's toy with its batteries removed. I time it so my hand, shoved into the small of his back, tips him forward as his knees buckle. He kneels into the empty fridge like a man at prayer, weak hands struggling to slow himself as he plunges into the darkness within.

32

There were no cats to be seen anywhere when he drove the car into the old coach house that served as a garage. Nor could McLean see any lurking in the bushes or stalking across the lawn as he walked the short distance to the back door. The reason soon became apparent; they were all in the kitchen, clustered nervously around the figure of Madame Rose. Only Mrs McCutcheon's cat looked unperturbed, glancing up at him with an expression at once unreadable and obvious in its meaning.

'Rose—'

'Inspector. I'm so sorry. I didn't know where to turn.' The medium looked up from her seat at the table, and McLean almost didn't recognise her. The stubble he was just about prepared for, after their last encounter. What he hadn't expected was the heavy bags under the eyes, the tired creases dragging down the corners of her mouth, the lifeless greasy curls of greying hair and the general air of despondency. Even her clothes looked somehow as if she'd slept in them for a day or two.

'I gave you a key, remember? That kind of suggests it's OK for you to drop in when you want.' He went over to the Aga, heaved the kettle on to the hob. If ever there was a time he needed a beer, this was it, but tea would have to do.

'I thought that was just so I could look after the cats.'

Madame Rose stroked one particularly fluffy creature that had curled up in her lap.

'They don't need much looking after, really. Keep to themselves. Barely eat any food. I reckon most of the neighbours are getting through a lot more than usual, mind you.'

That brought the ghost of a smile to Madame Rose's face, but the effort of maintaining it for any length of time was clearly too much.

'You're too kind. You know that?'

'People mention it, from time to time.' McLean dropped teabags into mugs, poured boiling water over them. 'Tell me what's happened. We might as well start from the beginning.'

Madame Rose gathered herself together. She was tall, at least six foot two, maybe more, and sitting up straight she presented a formidable figure. Still, McLean couldn't help but notice the cracked nail varnish as she raised a hand to tidy her lank hair around her shoulder.

'They set fire to the fish and chip shop downstairs. Gianni's been there since the war, you know.'

McLean didn't, but he assumed Madame Rose meant the Second World War. Although knowing her, it could always have been the Boer War, or maybe even the aftermath of Bannockburn.

'Worse, they'd deliberately parked trucks all along the road so the firemen couldn't get easy access. It wouldn't have helped. By the time they arrived the place was going like a . . .'

'House on fire?'

Madame Rose scowled at him, but there was a spark in her eyes that hadn't been there before.

'I tried to get into my house, but they wouldn't let me. The street's cordoned off. It's chaos.'

'Hang on.' McLean tried to remember the last time he'd been to visit Madame Rose at her place in Leith Walk. The entrance was a single door opening on to stairs, sandwiched between a bookmaker's and a chip shop. He could see it now. 'If the chip shop's on fire?'

'My home is safe, Inspector. It will take more than a bully with a Molotov cocktail to burn me out.'

There was something in the way she said it that left McLean in no doubt as to the truth of her words. There were things about Madame Rose he didn't begin to understand; things he didn't want to understand, if he was being honest.

'What's going on here? What's really going on?'

'I don't know who's behind this, or why they're attacking me. And that's the worry, Tony. I really don't know.'

McLean resisted the urge to toot the horn outside the church, instead climbing out of the car and leaning on the roof in the vain hope that would make things happen more quickly. He'd phoned Ritchie, asked if she could help him with Madame Rose's problem. She'd asked for fifteen minutes and he was early, so technically she had another five before she needed to be out on the pavement waiting for him.

When she appeared it wasn't from the church itself, but from the gate further up the road that led to the rectory. That made sense, he supposed. The church only had half a roof at the moment, the rest covered by tarpaulin that snapped in the breeze like gunshots. Maybe tooting the horn wouldn't have been so bad after all.

She wasn't alone, that was the first thing McLean noticed. A young man, dressed in sober black, accompanied her to the gate. He looked like he was going to leave her there, but then saw McLean's car. The two of them came up together. McLean had been trained to be observant, but he didn't need that to notice they were arm in arm.

'You must be Inspector McLean.' The young man held out his free hand. 'Daniel Jones. Dan. Kirsty's told me a fair bit about you.'

'Has she indeed? All good, I'm sure.' McLean took in the dark-coloured shirt under a loose fitting jacket, white clerical collar just visible in the fading light of the evening.

'Daniel's working with Mary at the moment,' Ritchie said. 'He helps out with the discussion group.'

'Won't keep you. Just wanted to say hi.' Dan let go of Ritchie's hand. She nodded, then stepped off the pavement and went round to the passenger door.

'Nice to meet you,' McLean said, slightly confused as to what was going on.

Dan just smiled. 'I'll give you a call in the morning,' he said to Ritchie, then he turned and walked back towards the church.

'So that's why you've been looking so much chirpier lately,' McLean said as they both climbed into the car. He was rewarded by a flush of colour to her freckled cheeks.

'Sorry. None of my business.' He started the engine, pulled away from the kerb.

'It's OK. I don't mind.' Ritchie struggled with her seatbelt for a moment, head down so McLean couldn't see whether she was lying or not. By the time she'd sorted it out they were at the end of the road.

'Daniel's not long been ordained. He's working with Mary at the moment, looking for a parish of his own.'

'A minister?' McLean tried to hide the surprise in his voice.

'Is that a problem?' Ritchie didn't try to hide the defensiveness in hers.

'Not with me, no. None of my business, like I said.'

The evening streets were relatively clear of traffic as they drove back across town in the direction of Leith Walk. McLean told Ritchie about Madame Rose, the harassment she'd been receiving and now the fire. The detective sergeant listened, but didn't say much, and he began to wonder why he'd not come on his own. If it was serious there'd be plenty of police presence, and plain clothes would be called in once the fire was out. No real need to see what was going on just now.

He had to pull over to let a couple of fire engines pass, and when they hit North Bridge the extent of the chaos became apparent. It was mostly buses and taxis, but they still managed to block the northbound carriageway. At the end of the bridge, by the North British Hotel, he could see a cordon set up and a couple of traffic cops in hi-vis jackets trying to impose a semblance of order. No point driving to the scene, then. McLean made a quick U-turn and headed for the station.

'Think it'll be easier if we walk,' he said.

Alongside him Ritchie nodded her agreement. 'Not sure how much help we'll be, if it's that serious.'

It took half an hour to get the car parked and then walk

to Madame Rose's place. They needn't have rushed; there were still plenty of fire engines at the scene, and ominous black smoke billowing from windows to either side of the medium's terrace house.

'Who's in charge?' McLean flashed his warrant card at the first uniform he found, a dour-faced constable given the unenviable task of keeping the smartphone-waving gawkers at bay. No doubt the fire was being live-tweeted and posted to all manner of unsavoury websites.

'Sergeant Bain's senior officer at the moment, sir. But it's the fire service in charge for now.'

Service, of course. No brigades or forces any more. McLean thanked the constable and left him to his hopeless task.

'See if you can't find Bain. Find out what happened.'

DS Ritchie nodded her understanding and headed off into the melee. McLean turned up his collar as he picked a route past fire trucks. Night was falling in that half-hearted way it did in the city at this time of year, the street lights only really deepening the shadows. Half a dozen fire trucks were lined up on the street, blocked from the pavement by a number of badly parked cars and elderly Transit vans. They were a nuisance to the firemen rather than a difficult obstacle to overcome, but McLean could tell just from looking at them that the number plates would be clones, the vehicle identification numbers filed off. If they could be matched to any database, it would almost certainly be a list of stolen motors, all missing at least a couple of months.

'What's going on?' he asked the first fireman he found

who wasn't obviously busy. The young man looked at him as if he were mad, or perhaps a hallucination, until McLean showed his warrant card again.

'Two empty flats on fire. We're keeping it under control best we can, but it's not like any fire I've seen.'

'How so?' McLean looked past the trucks and abandoned vans to the shop fronts, cracked and blackened. There was nothing recognisable left of the chip shop, and the bookies on the other side of Madame Rose's door was a mess of billowing black smoke.

'It's spreading all wrong.' The fireman pointed to the tall houses set back from the shops that had been built in what would once have been front gardens. McLean could see what the fireman was on about. Hoses pumped water at the sandstone walls to either side of Madame Rose's place, beating back the smoke that poured from cracked windows, but the middle house had not caught fire at all.

'How's that even possible?' McLean asked.

'Beats me. Not complaining, mind.' The fireman rubbed at his face with a black-gloved hand, transferring soot to his chin and nose. 'Makes our job a bit easier.'

'You any idea how it started?'

'Best bet's the chip shop. Reeks of accelerant, so I doubt it was an accident. Let's put it out first, aye? Then you can go poking your nose in.'

McLean found Sergeant Bain at the back of one of the fire trucks, cradling a mug of tea and chatting to DS Ritchie. Alongside them was perhaps the last person he expected to see.

'Ms Dalgliesh? How did you get past the security barrier?'

'Nice to see you too, Tony.' Jo Dalgliesh scribbled something down in her notebook, closed it and slipped it into the large bag hung over her shoulder. 'Arson at the local chip shop. Just doing my job.'

'Didn't get the senior reporter's position then? Sorry to hear that.'

Dalgliesh pouted. 'Actually, I did. Doesn't mean I'm above a little local news. Besides, the mess you lot are making of the traffic, this'll probably be in all the nationals tomorrow. I'm surprised the telly crews aren't here already.'

'Oh, they are,' Sergeant Bain said. 'I managed to keep them to the other side of the street though.'

'Well, I guess that's something. And since you've obviously got everything under control, perhaps you can bring us all up to speed.' McLean remembered Bain from his early days as a beat constable. He'd be about the same age as Grumpy Bob, looking to his retirement and probably coasting a bit. He'd been a good copper, so maybe he deserved it. The sergeant looked somewhat sheepishly at his tea, searching for somewhere to put it down. He didn't quite have Grumpy Bob's nonchalance.

'Fire was reported a couple of hours ago, sir. Control sent me out to supervise the traffic and coordinate with the fire service. Didn't realise they'd assigned any plain clothes yet.'

'They haven't. I heard from one of the residents.'

'Madame Rose?' Dalgliesh asked.

'Who is none of your concern, Ms Dalgliesh.'

'Aye, but he lives there, don't he?' The reporter pointed

at the unburnt house, sandwiched between the two still merrily ablaze.

'Do we know what started the fire, Sergeant?' McLean wanted to tell Dalgliesh to piss off, but he needed her on his side, needed information from her about Ben Stevenson. So he decided the easiest thing for now was to pretend she wasn't there.

'Not sure yet, sir. Looks like it's probably arson though. These cars and vans . . .' Bain pointed at the abandoned vehicles. 'And there's a reek of petrol round the door now they've got that bit out. But who'd want to burn down a chippy?'

'That's assuming it was the target, of course,' Ritchie said. 'Madame Rose was getting harassment. Maybe this was meant for her.'

'Why'd anyone have it in for a barmy old transvestite fortune teller?' Dalgliesh asked. So much for ignoring her.

'I don't know. Maybe because the tabloids keep on drumming up hatred for people like her?'

Dalgliesh gave him an old-fashioned look, but didn't press the matter. No doubt she knew when she was outnumbered and could be marched off the scene at any moment. McLean turned his attention back to Sergeant Bain.

'Those two houses either side. We know if there was anyone in them when the fire started?'

'Both empty. No furnishings. Lots of building materials, piles of timber, paint pots, that kind of stuff.'

'All very flammable.' McLean watched as the firemen switched off the hose on the nearest building. Only steam was rising from its windows now. They'd have the other one out soon, by the look of things. 'I don't suppose for a moment that's a coincidence.'

He knew it wasn't, of course. Someone was trying to get Madame Rose to leave. Killing her cat hadn't worked. Pushing shit through her letterbox hadn't worked either. So now they were going to burn her out. Looking up at the house, it was clear that hadn't worked out quite the way they had intended. Which left the question hanging: what would they try next?

33

'Control decides who attends a crime scene. It's not up to officers to pick and choose where they go. You know that as well as I do.'

'With respect sir, control hadn't even worked out they needed to assign anyone from CID. I wasn't there as an investigating officer.'

'Well why the hell were you there then? And why did you have to drag DS Ritchie along with you? Her shift was over, for fuck's sake.'

Early morning, up in front of the beak again. McLean wondered whether DCI Brooks would move into this office, assuming he got the detective superintendent job once Duguid had finally taken his leave. The detective chief inspector's own office was only marginally smaller than this one, and had a better view from its window, facing out towards Salisbury Crags rather than over the rooftops towards the castle.

'Are you even listening to me, McLean?' Duguid's question cut across his musing.

'Sorry, sir. Just trying to work out the best way to explain it. I know the owner of the middle house. She came to me a while back complaining of harassment. Someone killed one of her cats.'

'She report this to the police?'

'Of course. It's Leith's patch, so they looked into it. Not much they could do, by all accounts.'

Duguid's permanent frown turned into a scowl. 'This wouldn't have anything to do with the nuisance Grumpy Bob was making of himself at Leith nick, would it?'

McLean said nothing, wondering who'd been telling tales and why. It was highly unlikely Grumpy Bob would have upset anyone enough to warrant a complaint.

'This isn't your own private police service you know, McLean. You can't go off investigating things just because you feel like it, or your friends ask you to. And you can't pull other detectives off their active cases just to look into things for you.'

McLean clenched his fists behind his back. Not because he was particularly angry, but to stop himself from making the obvious retort. He couldn't begin to count the number of times Duguid had abused his position in exactly that way.

'I'm sorry, sir. Didn't think asking Bob to have a word on his way home would bother anyone.'

'You never do, McLean. Think, that is. That's your problem. Always trying to be the white knight, rushing gallantly in to save the fair maiden.'

That brought an involuntary smile to McLean's face. Of all the ways Madame Rose might be described, fair maiden was not one.

'I'll leave it alone then, sir. Plenty for me to be getting on with on the Stevenson investigation anyway.'

Duguid's face creased even further and for a moment McLean thought he was going to cry. Then he realised that the detective superintendent was grinning. 'No. You won't leave it alone, McLean. I've squared it with control. You stuck your nose in, you can have the bloody case.'

It was probably for the best. McLean knew himself well enough to realise that he'd just pester whoever else was running the investigation. Duguid did as well, which was annoying. It meant that while he'd got what he wanted, the shine was rather spoiled by the knowledge that Duguid had too. And there was the small matter of the rest of his workload to cope with.

He cadged a lift in a squad car over to Leith Walk. Only one fire truck remained, a few firemen clearing up the last of the operation. It was a mess, but then fires always were. At least they'd managed to tow away the parked vehicles and get the traffic moving again.

'Fire investigator here?' McLean asked of the first fireman he could waylay. The startled young man said nothing, just pointed a heavy-gloved hand in the direction of Madame Rose's front door, where a tall, stout man was crouching down and staring at something. He wore a bright yellow hard hat that appeared about two sizes too small, perching on the top of his large head in a manner that suggested it wouldn't give much protection if anything should fall on it.

'Mr Burrows. We meet again.' McLean picked his way through debris pulled out of the shop fronts as the fire investigator stood and turned to meet him. Jim Burrows had investigated the fire out at Loanhead in which McLean had nearly died. That one had been put down to burning underground coal deposits and firedamp seeping up through cracks in the concrete. He was intrigued to hear what the investigator made of this unusual scene.

'Inspector.' He held out a hand the size of a dinner plate. McLean shook it, then pointed to where the fire investigator had been staring.

'Find something?'

'Yes and no. See here?' Burrows pointed at the door to Madame Rose's house. The street door, McLean corrected himself. There was presumably another door around the back somewhere. This was familiar from his previous visits, the rather faded sign above it still advertising the telling of fortunes and reading of tarots. The top half of the door had been glass, but someone had taken a brick to it fairly recently. The sheet of plywood in its place was spray-painted with the words 'faggot' and 'peedo'.

'What am I looking at?'

'All of it. Paint, wood, glass. Look here.' Burrows took a few steps down the hill to the remains of the empty betting shop. The window frame had been painted white some time in a previous millennium, and the heat of the fire had bubbled and browned it at the edges.

'It was hot enough here to partially melt this glass, see?' Burrows bent down and carefully scraped a few shards from the pavement. 'You wouldn't have been able to stand here while the blaze was going. Even if you could've breathed, the heat would've burned your skin right off.

'And yet here.' Burrows took two admittedly long strides back to Madame Rose's door, then stopped. 'Here there's no sign of scorching at all. There's even some paper still stuck through the letterbox.'

McLean pulled latex gloves from his pocket, snapped them on, then plucked the paper out. It was a flyer for a local meeting. '!!!Stop the Developement!!!' misprinted in bold script across the top of the page, a badly reproduced photograph just below. There was no sign of singeing on it at all, but there was no way someone could have pushed it through the letterbox after the fire. He folded it carefully and slipped it into his pocket for later perusal.

'So what stopped it then?' he asked.

'Search me. Never seen anything like it before.' Burrows walked uphill while he spoke, coming to a halt in front of the charred remains of Gianni's Chip Shop. 'I mean, the wall's brick between the shops, so that might've stopped the fire spreading. And there's a gap between the back of the chippie and the front of the house. That'd go some way to explaining why the fire didn't spread back like it did with the other two.'

McLean studied the facade of Madame Rose's house, the stonework darkened only by a couple of centuries' exposure to Auld Reekie and more recent car exhausts. To either side the neighbouring houses were smeared with soot, black tears streaking upwards from every burnt-out window.

'You been inside yet?' he asked.

Burrows shook his head. 'Won't get inside those two. The roof's going to come down any minute, could take the front wall with it. Only safe way's to bring it down with machinery from the outside.'

'Won't that be a risk for the other houses?'

'Those ones, maybe.' Burrows pointed up the hill, then down. 'But they'll probably be OK. Engineers know how to shore them up. That one,' he pointed at Madame Rose's house. 'That'd probably stay standing if you dropped a bomb on it.'

34

'Got you working on this one too, have they?'

McLean had been looking for a squad car to give him a lift back to the station. It wasn't far, but the heat was oppressive. The city centre would be crowded with tourists come for the Festival and the Fringe, too, which always lessened the joy of walking. A quick search of the cordoned-off part of the street had revealed nothing but a short reporter, clad in a leather overcoat that must surely have been too warm to wear.

'Ms Dalgliesh. Back again, I see. I'd have thought you'd send a cub reporter to a job like this.'

'You're very stuck up, Tony. You know that? Some might even say repressed. Public school education, I guess.'

That stung. It was possible Dalgliesh was just guessing as she tried to wind him up, but it was just as possible that she had dug as deep into his background as she could and knew the names of both expensive and exclusive schools his grandmother had sent him to.

'I take it you're writing a piece about the fire.' It was feigned interest, but it seemed to do the trick of diverting her from talking about him.

'Just a puff piece, really. Apart from the traffic buggery last night, it's not much of a story. This part of town's been crying out for some regeneration for ages. Maybe this will kick-start something. Get the council off their arses.'

McLean's hand went unbidden to his jacket pocket, the 'stop the development' flyer he'd pulled from Madame Rose's letterbox. He stopped himself before Dalgliesh noticed, flexing his fingers into a fist and out again as if relieving an arthritic twinge.

'Actually, I was going to give you a call.'

'You were?' Genuine amazement spread across the journalist's face.

'Ben Stevenson. Could really do with an update. You found out what he was working on yet?'

'It's your lucky day then.' Dalgliesh gave him a broad grin that made her look like some kind of demented, wizened shark. 'But you'll have to buy the coffee.'

It came in a ridiculously large mug, more like a cereal bowl with handles than something designed for drinking from. On the plus side, the cafe they went to also sold large slices of very good chocolate cake. McLean had missed breakfast in his hurry to leave the house, so a mid-morning indulgence was, he thought, perfectly justified.

'First off, Ben Stevenson was a fine journalist.' Jo Dalgliesh brushed ginger biscuit from her moustache as she spoke, taking a mouthful of coffee as she chewed. Fortunately swallowing before she spoke again. McLean was too fascinated by her appalling manners and utter lack of self-consciousness to say anything himself.

'Oh, I know you lot think we're all vicious hacks churning out rubbish just to make life difficult, but actually it takes quite a bit of work sometimes.'

'Making life difficult? And here's me thinking it came naturally.'

'You know, for someone who wants my help you can be a right sarky bastard at times.'

McLean took a small bite of his cake to stop himself replying too quickly. Dalgliesh was right, of course. He needed her help. It was just difficult to put aside the loathing of years, harder still to sit across a table from this woman and not think about the hatchet job she'd done on him and the families of Donald Anderson's other victims.

'OK. Fair enough. Sorry.' He raised both hands in a mock admission of defeat. 'I'm not going to pretend I like you, Dalgliesh, but I'll try to be civil.'

'Aye, well.' Dalgliesh studied him as if trying to work out whether or not he was taking the piss. He must have passed the test, as she pulled out her notebook, laid it out on the table between them.

'Took a wee while to piece it all together, but I'm fairly sure I know what Ben was working on when he . . . you know.'

'The Brotherhood?'

Dalgliesh raised an eyebrow. 'Aye, that. Bunch of shadowy figures pulling the strings. The secret world government behind everything bad that's ever happened right through history. Fingers in all the pies. Even own the bloody pie factory. Make the illuminati look like amateurs.'

'And Stevenson was on to them?'

'Oh, he thought he was. Contacts here, secret meetings there. But it's all bollocks, aye?'

'It is?'

'Pure bollocks. You'll have talked to Dougie Ballantyne? Daft wee shite that he is.'

McLean nodded, remembering the trip down to the Borders. Tea and gibberish.

'What did you make of him?' Dalgliesh picked up her coffee, took a drink while she waited for McLean to reply.

'Delusion on a grand scale. But he's smart. Very good at seeing patterns, connections between things that you wouldn't think were connected. Most of the time that's because they aren't, but he makes a plausible argument.'

'If you only take his evidence, and only the way he presents it, sure. My job, yours too I guess, is to see all sides of an argument. Check the facts. Look for verification, a second source. You start doing that with Ballantyne's theories and they all fall apart soon enough.'

'But Stevenson believed him. I thought you rated him as a journalist.'

'Aye, I did. Ben was one of the best, when he put his mind to it.'

'So—?'

'You know what Ballantyne says about himself? How he justifies his rubbish?'

McLean thought back to the conversation. It had only been a couple of days, but rather more than he'd hoped for had happened in the intervening time. 'Something about being a messenger?'

'That's the one.' Dalgliesh slurped some more coffee, looked at her biscuitless plate with something akin to regret, rubbed a nicotine-stained finger in the crumbs and stuck it in her mouth. 'He reckons he can get away with revealing secrets because they're feeding them to him. All part of some strategy to come out from the shadows. He actually believes the Head talks to him and tells him what to write.'

'Ritchie's expression was "stone bonker". I think that just about sums up Douglas Ballantyne the third.'

'And yet, for all we can see him for the loony he is, Ben thought he was on to something.' Dalgliesh tapped the closed notebook lying on the table between them. 'He really believed there was a Brotherhood. Maybe even a disembodied talking head that ruled them all.'

'From what I've heard, Stevenson was under quite a lot of pressure. Workwise he'd not had a decent story in years. And his home life was hardly stable.'

'Ah. Youse lot have talked to Charlie then.' Dalgliesh's face was rarely a closed book, but even so McLean was surprised at the flash of anger that spread across it.

'Ex-wife of a murdered man? One of the first people we interviewed.'

'Aye, well. Did she tell you how she came off in the divorce? Did she tell you she was the one playing away from home?'

She hadn't, of course, but it didn't really change anything. 'All the more reason to suspect that Stevenson wasn't perhaps concentrating on the job as well as he should have been.'

Dalgliesh shook her head. 'You don't know Ben. That's not his way. If anything the pressure would have made him more careful, more – what's the word? Conscientious.'

McLean was surprised Dalgliesh even knew what it meant. 'You saw his secret room. That wall. Didn't look all that conscientious to me. Looked like the last stages of madness.'

'Actually, I'm glad you mentioned that.' Dalgliesh rummaged around in her shoulder bag, coming out with a handful of A4 colour prints. The first was a photograph of the room off Ben Stevenson's bedroom, the wall covered in photos, magazine cut-outs, Post-it notes. Everything linked together with endless lines of coloured string. At this scale it was almost impossible to make anything of it other than a bad piece of modern abstract art.

'Resolution's not too good on the printout.' Dalgliesh smoothed out the creases with a leathery hand, placed a couple more photographs alongside the first to make something of a montage. 'But I've got the whole thing on my computer and you can zoom in enough to see what's what. What's interesting is there's nothing here that's particularly Masonic. See, there's stuff about the Hellfire Club, Beggars Benison, all that nonsense. The Guild of Strangers gets a mention, there's some Templar writings. There's even some stuff about Police Scotland I'll have to look into at a later date. But there's no set-square and compass, no reference to any Grand Lodge or High Poobah. It's almost as if the Freemasons were deliberately excluded from what he was looking into.'

McLean pulled the first photograph across the table, swivelling it around so he could see it better. It didn't really help much, all the details too small to make out properly. The original was still in place, locked up after the forensics team had been through Stevenson's flat. He'd have to go over and have another look soon, but in the meantime he could take Dalgliesh's word for it.

'So he wasn't really looking at the Masons, then,' he said.

'Oh, he started there. Everyone does. But then he got

Ballantyne's book and went off in a different direction. See?' Dalgliesh prodded a yellowing finger at the photographs, sliding them over each other and obscuring half of the picture.

'Not really, no. I thought you said Ballantyne was nuts. Surely Stevenson saw that too?'

'Oh, aye. He saw that. But then something else caught his eye. Someone else.'

'Who?' McLean pulled one of the pictures closer, peered at the blurred lines as if they would magically clear just by squinting.

'That's what I'm trying to find out.' Dalgliesh flicked a final photo on to the table. This one was a close-up of the wall, a blurred image of a man standing underneath a street lamp in the dark. Impossible to make out any features, but Stevenson had scribbled over it in red marker. 'Who is he?'

35

The walk back to the station had, as predicted, left him clammy with sweat and bruised from the elbows and backpacks of the milling masses on the Royal Mile. It had also given McLean some time to think about Dalgliesh's research. It annoyed him that she had a detailed photograph of the wall in Ben Stevenson's flat, but since he'd not yet given it proper scrutiny himself, it was perhaps just as well someone had. The implications were clear. Stevenson had begun pursuing a conspiracy, and ended up finding something else entirely. Someone else entirely.

He needed to see the wall again, and not just a high-resolution photograph of it. He should have studied it more closely the moment they'd found it, obvious now that it was going to be crucial to unlocking the case. McLean couldn't quite understand why he hadn't done so, but then Dalgliesh had been with him, and Ritchie hadn't been well, and before he knew it they'd found the dead nurse, Maureen Shenks. Where the hell had all the time gone? And when had he become so distracted? Round about the time he'd stopped getting more than a few hours' sleep a night, perhaps. Or maybe when Duguid took over. He shook his head to dislodge the unhelpful thought, headed for the major incident room. DC MacBride was the first useful person he found.

'You busy, Constable?'

As questions went it was pretty stupid. MacBride was surrounded by a crowd of uniform constables and sergeants as well as several admin staff. He wasn't the most senior officer in the room by a comfortable margin, but he was quite clearly in charge.

'Just need to get this lot handed out, sir. Be with you in a moment.'

McLean left him to his task, heading over to the wall with its map, whiteboard and blown-up photographs. There were a few of Stevenson himself, sprawled on the ground in the damp cave. One of the room at his home that wasn't much clearer than Dalgliesh's. He stared at it unseeing as he tried to gather his thoughts.

Apart from the fact that Jo Dalgliesh knew a lot more about the details of the case than she should have done, the point she had raised was a valid one. Whoever had killed Stevenson had made it look Masonic, that much was clearly evident from the sigils daubed on the cavern wall in his blood. But the flavour of Freemasonry those clues pointed at was hardly secret knowledge, its exposure not really the sort of thing that would get you killed even if you were a Mason sworn to secrecy. And according to Duguid, Ben Stevenson wasn't and never had been a member of any Lodge. The more he thought about it, the more McLean convinced himself that the Masonic angle was a diversion, a feint to get them all looking in the wrong direction. The only problem was, there was no other direction to look in. No forensics, no CCTV, no clues at all.

'Just had to get rid of those actions. Sorry about that, sir.' DC MacBride appeared at McLean's side. He had a weary, hangdog look to him at odds with his usual unflappable cheeriness.

'Everything all right?' Yet another stupid question, but somebody had to ask them.

MacBride let out a long sigh. 'Could be better, sir. I thought Dagwood was meant to be Gold on this investigation, but I don't think I've seen him in here once. You're SIO, but apart from the morning briefings you're mostly out and about with DS Ritchie. Grumpy Bob seems to have disappeared completely and all the other CID officers are running around after Brooks in the hope he'll be nice to them when he gets the top job.'

'Meaning you've been left to run a major incident room on your own.'

'I wouldn't mind so much sir, only . . .'

'You're a detective constable and it's way above your pay grade?'

'That and the jokes.' The detective constable's hand went up to his forehead, unconsciously brushing at his fringe to spread it out over his scar.

'Still getting called Potter?'

'That would be fine, to be honest, sir. If that was as far as it went. But Christ, people can be dicks at times.'

McLean knew all too well what the constable meant. 'And policemen even more so, right?'

'There's times I wonder why I even bother. Plenty other lines of work I could be in.'

McLean gave MacBride what he hoped was a friendly slap on the shoulder. 'It's not that bad, Stuart. Believe me, they'll get bored and move on soon.'

‘Really?’ The look on MacBride’s face suggested he’d take some convincing.

‘Really. Now grab your coat and come with me. We’ve a crime scene to investigate.’

He knew as soon as he slid the key into the front door that something was wrong, paused before pushing open the door.

‘Who secured the scene?’

‘Er . . . Not sure, sir. You and DS Ritchie were the last ones here, I think.’

‘Forensics haven’t been?’

‘Let me check.’ MacBride tapped away at his tablet computer, holding it up close to the window, presumably to get a better signal. McLean wondered how the detective constable had managed to get his hold on it; uniforms had been using digital notebooks for a while now, but this was much more sophisticated.

‘Scene was photographed and processed for fingerprints four days ago. Nothing else. Dr Cairns signed it off. Someone must have returned the keys to us.’ MacBride nodded at McLean’s hand, still hovering by the lock.

‘That all?’

‘That’s all the computer says. You want me to call forensics and check?’

‘No. I guess we didn’t ask them to do any more than that. Something here doesn’t feel right though. You got gloves?’ McLean pulled out a pair of his own, squeezed his hands into the tight-fitting latex as MacBride did the same.

‘Right. Stay close and don’t touch anything if you don’t

have to.' He didn't really need to say it, and the look on MacBride's face told him he'd struck a nerve. Well, there were times you just had to take it as it came.

The key caught slightly in the lock as he twisted it, as if it was reluctant to let anyone in. Beyond the doorway, the hall looked much like he remembered, bright and wide. McLean could imagine it being a warm family home, the sound of children playing in one of the other rooms, the smell of cooking from the kitchen to welcome the weary journalist on his return from work. That was the picture Stevenson's ex-wife had painted, but he knew now that it was a lie. And the odour that reached his nostrils was far from welcoming. Something rotting, overlaid with a smell he couldn't immediately place but which brought hazy images of childhood and grazed knees. Antiseptic, that was it. Only somehow different.

'Eww. What is that?' DC MacBride said.

'Not sure I really want to know.' McLean breathed through his mouth in the hope that it would help. It didn't really, but the gentlest of breezes from the landing outside made it just about bearable. He'd not wanted to spend very long in the flat, just enough time to look at Stevenson's wall, but now he was going to have to search the whole place. There'd be an awkward conversation with Jemima Cairns too, if she'd been the last person in.

The dreadful smell seemed to linger in the hallway. Through in the living room it was much easier to breathe, and in Stevenson's study there was nothing at all. It didn't look any different to how McLean remembered it from his first visit. Nothing on the main floor did. There was no obvious sign of where the stench was coming from, either.

'It's . . . I don't know. Almost like rotting apples or something?' DC MacBride was still pacing slowly around the hall when McLean emerged from the kitchen. The constable sniffed the air, took a few steps, sniffed again, his head tilted forward as he tried to pinpoint the source. Quite how he could do that without gagging, McLean didn't know.

'Well, you can let me know when you've found it. I'm going upstairs.'

The bedroom appeared no different to when he, Ritchie and Dalgliesh had been there a few days earlier. The smell diminished as he moved away from the top of the stairs, almost as if it were anchored to the front door. All thought of it vanished from his mind as he stepped into the small dressing room beyond the bedroom, though.

The wall was clear. No maps, no printouts, no photographs. For an instant, McLean wondered if the forensics team had taken it all down to recreate in their lab. That's what he should have asked them to do, but the tangle of coloured strings strewn over the dressing table gave the lie to that idea, as did the drawing pins spread lazily around in the carpet like so many traps for the unwary bare foot. There was no way a scene of crime officer would take down the photographs and leave the string. It was either all evidence or none of it was, which meant someone had been in here after Dr Cairns had sealed the place up.

'Think I've got it, sir.' DC MacBride's voice echoed up from the hallway below. McLean took one last look at the desecrated room before heading back down. He found the constable squatting by the front door, the Persian rug pulled back to reveal polished floorboards underneath. Closer still, and McLean could see that MacBride had pulled up one of the boards, revealing a hidden space beneath. The smell was overpowering, so much so that he had to cover his mouth and nose with his jacket. MacBride had done the same, his eyes watering slightly as he looked up.

'Felt the floor move as I was pacing about.' His voice was muffled by jacket and handkerchief. 'Found this. Not quite sure what to make of it.'

McLean came closer still, peering down into the space between the floor and the ceiling of the flat below. It had been lined with tin foil, more of which had been stapled to the underside of the floorboard, and inside lay something he couldn't immediately identify. It was red and shiny, with flecks of black and green. Tiny little white things wriggled around in it, and as he focused on them, so realisation began to dawn.

'Cover it up, Constable.' McLean took a step back, then another, pulling his phone out of his pocket as he went. The number was on speed dial, the call answered swiftly. Even so he knew that the time he'd have to spend waiting for the team to arrive would be far too long.

36

'Now there's something you don't see every day.'

Angus Cadwallader knelt in Ben Stevenson's hallway, leaning over the hole left by the removed floorboard. Returning scene of crime officers had set up spotlights that shone over the scene, leaving little doubt as to what someone had placed in this little hiding hole.

'It's a heart, isn't it?' McLean was unfortunate enough to have encountered one before. 'A human heart.'

'In the middle, yes. Not sure what all this greenery is around it. Not exactly my area of expertise. Some kind of nest I'd guess. Think that's where the worst of the smell's coming from, too.'

McLean stepped back from the edge and out on to the landing, breathing deep after too long of trying not to breathe at all. The smell was still strong in the hallway, even after the windows had been forced open. What he still couldn't quite work out was exactly what the smell was. Not rotting flesh; that, sadly, was another odour he'd encountered all too often in his career. No, DC MacBride was closer to the mark when he'd suggested rotting apples. There was a sweetness to the aroma, along with a harder, sharper edge, like vinegar maybe, or even—

'Embalming fluid.' Cadwallader joined him on the landing, pulling his long latex gloves off with a satisfying snap. 'Old-fashioned stuff. Not come across it in a long while.

We don't use it in the mortuary any more. I think it's reacted with the vegetation, or maybe the tin foil. It's not actually made of tin, you know.'

'Yes, I think I was aware of that, Angus. Anything else you can tell us about our somewhat macabre find?'

'Not a lot I can do here. Have to get it back to the mortuary and run some tests. It's a man's heart though. Adult.'

Lightning flashed and popped as the crime scene photographer recorded every moment while a couple of technicians tried to work out the best way of getting the heart, vegetation and foil out all in one piece. It reminded McLean of why he and MacBride had come to Stevenson's flat in the first place.

'Let me know what you find will you, Angus?' He gave his friend a gentle slap on the arm as he headed for the stairs.

'You not hanging around to watch them take it out?' Cadwallader asked.

'That's what underlings are for.' McLean pointed to the pale-faced form of DC MacBride, still stuck in the hallway with its fetid air. 'I need to find a crime scene manager.'

He found the woman he was looking for out in the street. Jemima Cairns was overseeing the return en masse of the forensics team, her normally dour face thunderous. It didn't improve when she saw him approaching, darkening even more if that were possible.

'Could you no' have left well alone?'

'It's not as if I put it there myself, you know.'

'Aye, well . . .' Dr Cairns muttered something under her

breath he didn't quite catch. McLean was all too aware that she could be caustic at times, which didn't make the next question he was going to ask any easier. Still, in with both feet at the deep end, that's what his grandmother had always said.

'You signed it off, right?'

The glare might have killed someone not ready for it. 'If you think—'

'That you missed something like that? Course I don't. I might be slow sometimes, but even I know better than that.'

Dr Cairns still glowered at him like a child whose favourite toy has been confiscated, but McLean could see a grudging acceptance in there too.

'So why d'you need to ask then?'

'Someone broke in after you'd left, but you were the last person to see the place before they did. That means I have to talk to you about what the place looked like. What you'd done. That wall display in the upstairs bedroom, for instance. You left it intact?'

'Aye, left it there right enough. Would've liked to have taken it down carefully. Find out what order everything got put up. You can tell as much from the way a thing's done as from what it is.'

'Why didn't you, then?'

Dr Cairns' scowl deepened again. 'That's your department, isn't it? Working out the puzzle from the clues left behind? I'm a forensic scientist, not a shrink. Besides, there wasn't the time or the budget. I asked, but was told no.' Realisation dawned on her face. 'It's gone, isn't it?'

'Yes.' McLean kicked at the ground with his foot,

reluctant to admit what had happened. As if not saying it would make it not so. Then the forensic scientist's words filtered through. 'Wait, what? You were told no? By who?'

'By whom, Inspector.' Dr Cairns couldn't resist the dig, obviously. It brought a brief smile to her face, which was better than the scowl. 'The request will be on file somewhere, I'm sure. And the response, although I think that was from a detective sergeant if I recall correctly. No idea who actually made the decision. I assumed it was you, since you're SIO on the case. Could've come from Detective Superintendent Duguid, of course. Or someone else higher up. Could've just been the DS who responded.'

McLean ground his foot harder into the pavement, trying his best to suppress his anger. The effort raised a slight twinge of pain in his hip, the last echoes of the broken bone reminding him that he'd never be quite as fit as before he'd fallen off that precariously balanced chair in his attic. Might have been better if he'd actually hanged himself. At least then he wouldn't have had to deal with incompetence on a grand scale.

'Judging by your face, this is the first you've heard of it?' Dr Cairns had lost her scowl now, showing not so much enjoyment at his discomfort as concern.

'Exactly so. If you'd asked me I'd have said yes. That wall is crucial to this case, I know it. And now someone's destroyed all the evidence tied up in it.'

Dr Cairns gave him a friendly pat on the arm, smiling at last. 'Just as well we took lots of photographs then, aye?'

The office was a haven of relative cool after the muggy heat of the walk back from Ben Stevenson's flat. McLean could have cadged a lift – there were enough squad cars milling around – but he needed time to think, a space where he wasn't being pulled this way and that by conflicting demands. And so he'd left the SOCOs to go over the flat, DCs MacBride and Gregg to interview the other residents of the tenement block, and set off back to the station on his own.

It hadn't helped. The pain that had flared up in his hip was a constant niggle, and he couldn't stop dwelling on the stupidity that had left a valuable piece of evidence open to tampering. As to what the hell was going on with the heart under the floorboards, he couldn't even begin to imagine. Had it been there all along? Not if Dr Cairns was to be believed, and she wasn't someone he'd have expected to miss something like that. Which meant that someone had gone back and taken down the evidence wall, then carefully placed a pickled human heart under the floorboards.

Whose heart was it? Where did you get a hold of a human heart? Why was it there? The questions kept whirling round and round in his head until he realised he was already back at the station, slumping into his office chair. No memory of the walk at all.

There was paperwork; when had there ever not been? But at that moment the idea of wading through something as dull as overtime sheets had a certain appeal. Perhaps if he immersed himself in something completely brainless then his subconscious could go to work on sorting out all the complicated stuff. As he flipped open the brown card folder, however, McLean saw that this wasn't the latest staff roster, but something else entirely.

Someone had cocked up on the filing and left him the

post-mortem report on the dead nurse, Maureen Shenks. McLean was about to get up, take it to the incident room where DI Spence was conducting that investigation. He'd not had a chance to find out how it was progressing, and it was always useful to know these things. A chat with his fellow detective inspector might be useful and enlightening. On the other hand, he'd witnessed the PM himself. There'd been similarities in the method of killing used on the nurse and Ben Stevenson. And if he asked Spence to see the report he'd get grief from Brooks, at best told to mind his own business, at worst a complaint to Duguid that he wasn't concentrating on his own cases. Perhaps this was a lucky chance to get ahead of the game.

And there was always that natural inquisitiveness, of course. He couldn't deny that. McLean rolled off the elastic band that had been holding the folder closed, leaned back in his seat and started to read.

37

He comes out of the coma slowly, exactly as it should be. It helps that he's connected up to all the machinery; means I can monitor him waking as the poisons are filtered out of his blood. I imagine he'll have the mother of all headaches right now, but that's a small price to pay for what awaits him on the other side.

'Wh . . . wha . . . where?' The question is barely a whisper, almost drowned out by the hum of the life-support systems. I hover out of sight, observing as he slowly comes to terms with his situation. The muscles around his eyes twitch, but they don't immediately open. As if the eyelids are stuck together with glue, the eyeballs dry inside. There is sweat on his skin, tiny beads forming around his temples and slicking his thin hair.

'Is . . . is anyone there?' And now he tries to move his head. He can't, of course. The bed is designed for epileptics, the restraints soft but very secure. His arms and legs are strapped down, too. In a minute or so he will realise just how helpless he is. As he should be when meeting his maker.

'You are blessed, Jim. You have a certainty about you few possess.'

I can almost see his ears twitching as he tries to pinpoint my voice. He opens his eyes now, but all he can see is the ceiling high overhead.

'Ben? Is that you?'

'Ben has gone on before you.' I reach out, stroke the side of his cheek with the back of my finger. 'Ben is already in heaven.'

'What's going on? Where am I? Why can't I move?' His voice is growing stronger, even as the panic rises. The machines tell me this, but I can read him without them. The same way I can see the readiness of his soul, free of the stains of life.

'I envy you. That's my downfall, you understand. You have found such a state of grace I can never hope to achieve. I can only pray that when it is my time to be judged He will look upon these works of mine favourably.'

'I . . . I don't understand. What are you—'

'Shhh.' I place my finger over his lips, silencing him. His eyes lock on to my face now, and I can feel the tremors that shake through his body, smell the fear rising from him. God is near, ready to take this perfect soul to his bosom. But this can't be a swift and violent end. Not like the journalist. I could feel him slipping back into sinful doubt almost from the moment he reached apotheosis. His end was always going to be quick or risk the loss of such a perfect prize. I knew that the moment I first met him, confirmed it over the weeks I fed his obsession, led him to the secret knowledge he so craved.

This one is different. He is scared, but he is also ever hopeful. I can taste it on him, see the colours of it playing in his aura. This one put his faith in medicine, science, technology. Only fitting then that his beloved machines hasten him toward his salvation.

'Go now, Jim. Do your great works. Heal the sick like our Lord Jesus healed them.'

He's ready, has been ready for hours now. Still, I want to savour this, feel the presence of the Lord when he comes to collect this soul. I reach over to the machine, flick the switch. The motors whirr and the ceremony begins.

'What's happening? What are you doing? Ben?'

'Don't panic. It will all be over soon.' I pick a careful path through the tubes and wires as the precious fluid drains slowly from his body. The litany is silent, the words flowing through my mind as I take up my perch on the stool by the door and watch.

38

'You got a minute, Spence?'

The detective inspector was holding court in the middle of his incident room, his thin, pointy head rising up over the gaggle of junior detectives surrounding him. McLean couldn't help noticing that there were more uniforms and admin in the incident room for the Maureen Shenks murder than he had working on the Ben Stevenson case. Indeed quite a few of the officers who were meant to be working with him seemed to have been poached. Some things never changed.

'Not got enough to do, you have to come sticking your nose in here, McLean?' Spence ambled across with all the urgency of a sloth. The look he gave McLean was one of a headmaster wearily dealing with an awkward boy, which given he was only two years McLean's senior seemed a bit much. Nothing he wasn't used to, though, and if Brooks got the promotion to detective superintendent that everyone expected, the chances were good that Spence would have his DCI job. That would be fun.

'Just thought you might have been looking for this.' McLean held up the PM report. 'Someone stuck it on my desk by mistake.'

'What is it?' Spence made no move to take the folder.

'Missing piece of your puzzle, if that board's anything to go by.' McLean gestured over to the whiteboard on the far side of the room. Several questions had been written on it in teacher's handwriting, but there were few answers as yet. How long had it been since Spence had taken over?

'What the hell are you doing here?' McLean turned in the doorway to see DCI Brooks lumbering up the corridor. Just once in a while, he thought, it would be nice if people could be civil.

'Afternoon, sir. I was just dropping off the PM report on Maureen Shenks. It got shoved in with my filing by mistake.'

'Maureen . . .?' For an instant Brooks looked like he was going to ask who, but he rallied with a noncommittal 'Oh'.

'You might want to read it sir. There's some alarming similarities in the method used on the nurse and on Ben Stevenson.'

That got McLean the full angry grimace, and at the same time he felt the folder being tugged from his grasp.

'You've read it?' DI Spence held the report at arm's length, as if it had been sullied. Either that or he needed his reading glasses.

'Of course I've read it. I attended the post-mortem, remember. Before you were assigned the case.'

'So you have nothing better to do than stick your nose in? Ben Stevenson's killer behind bars, is he?' DCI Brooks pushed past on his way into the incident room in a manner best described as brusque. The busy hum of activity that had filled the air when McLean arrived had dropped into a tense silence now.

'It's not a pissing contest, sir. I'm not trying to take over your investigation or steal your glory or whatever you think's going on. I'm just pointing out that there are similarities between two Cat A murders currently under investigation. If nothing else, it's a line of enquiry worth pursuing, don't you think?'

'I'll be the judge of that, McLean.' Brooks pulled the report from DI Spence's weak grasp, flipped it open and went straight to the back.

'Take your time,' McLean said. He fought back the urge to make a sarcastic comment, knowing full well how counterproductive it would be. 'You know where to find me if you need me.'

'Brooks tells me you've been sticking your nose into his investigation.'

As conversational openers went, it was much to be expected from Duguid. McLean was surprised at just how quickly the complaint had been made though, and how petty it was. It threw him, too. This wasn't the reason he'd come to see the chief superintendent.

'I was just giving them their PM report. Someone filed it in my office by mistake.'

'Oh, I know all that.' Duguid waved away the excuse as if it were a particularly annoying fly that wouldn't leave him alone. 'You didn't have to read it.'

'No, I didn't. True enough. I bet you're glad I did though.'

Duguid stopped swatting the fly, arched a fading ginger eyebrow at him. 'Glad?'

'You know as well as I do neither of these investigations is getting anywhere, sir. Forensics have found bugger all at either scene, background checks are coming up with nothing. There's no obvious motive for either killing. Category

A murders are rare as rocking horse shit. Makes sense to compare notes, at the very least.'

Duguid slumped back in his chair like a man defeated. 'Christ but I hate the complicated ones.'

'Couldn't agree more, sir.'

That got him a frown in return. 'Could've fooled me, McLean. What did you want to see me about anyway? I assume it wasn't to complain about Brooks telling you to piss off.'

'No, sir. It wasn't. I wanted to have a word with you about DC MacBride actually.'

'MacBride?' Duguid furrowed his brow in a fine impression of a man confused. 'What's Harry Potter moaning about now?'

Don't rise to the bait. Count to ten. 'Do you think that sets a good example, sir? Calling him names behind his back?'

'Thought it was quite clever, really. What with that scar of his. Wish I'd come up with it myself.'

'Really? You enjoy being called Dagwood behind your back do you, sir?'

Duguid's face reddened, a muscle ticking at his temple. 'It's just a name.'

'No, it's not. It's a sign of disrespect. It's officers thinking they know better than you and can go do what they please.'

'They do that anyway. Names never hurt anyone, McLean. Surely you learned that in the playground of your posh private school.'

And then some.

'You're missing the point, sir. It's not just name-calling.

MacBride's being systematically bullied by a small faction in this station. Under your command. He's trying to man up, as you might put it, trying to ignore them, but they're persistent buggers. It's affecting his work and if it doesn't stop soon I'm worried he'll quit. He's too good an officer to lose.'

Duguid stared up at McLean from his chair, mouth slightly agape at the outburst. All the redness had drained out of his skin, leaving him deathly pale.

'For God's sake, man. He's a detective. Dealing with nasty shit is almost his entire job description. If he can't take a little good-natured ribbing, maybe he'd be better off in a different job.'

McLean said nothing. He wasn't really sure there was anything he could say that wouldn't get him in even deeper shit than he usually was. He'd tried. Sometimes that was the best you could do.

39

The Good Lord moves in mysterious ways, His wonders to perform.

I've long since given up trying to second-guess my sight. His gift to me. Not everyone's soul is visible on the outside, and even fewer are close to pure. What is purity, anyway? A strict adherence to the teachings of a discredited church? I don't think so. Neither is it as simple as just being good. We all want to be good, after all. It's just that we almost always fall too far short. Some, and they are precious few, strive for one thing above all else. They approach purity simply because they let all the normal distractions fall away, the wants and needs, the lusts and the thousand thousand petty desires. They have found a focus, and in that focus lies their redemption.

But I don't know when I will see them, or where. Sometimes months go by, years before one crosses my path. And sometimes they appear in quick succession. Almost as if they are being sent my way. Which, of course, they are. For is this not the Lord's work that I do?

Which is why I shouldn't be surprised. But it's been a long time since my sight brought to my attention someone I already know.

I have watched him, of course. Studied him as he speaks and when he prays. Seen the people he associates with. They are lost causes, their souls dark almost to be invisible.

I had thought him the same, but now I can see I was wrong. Or maybe he has changed, found that purity of purpose so few ever find. It doesn't really matter. The sight has shown me; who am I to question it?

He has faith, this one. It has been tested, but he still clings to it. Despite all he has seen, all he has read about, he still holds to those discredited old teachings. He is searching for a higher truth though, and he is certain, so certain, that he is close to it. That is his focus, I see it now. That will be his undoing.

And his deliverance.

40

'Is that Detective Inspector McLean?'

Late evening, and he really should have gone home a long time ago. McLean had been wading his way through a particularly badly written report, not helped by a complete inability to stop his mind from wandering. The telephone was a welcome distraction.

'It is. Who's speaking?'

'Oh, yes. You won't remember me. I'm from the forensic services. Amanda Parsons. Dr Cairns said I should call you.'

McLean raised an eyebrow even though there was no one about to see it. 'She did? Why?'

'I've been running the DNA analysis on that . . . um . . . sample of yours. Not yours yours, obviously, but—'

'Sample?' McLean interrupted before the caller went off at a complete tangent. He couldn't recall sending any samples off for DNA analysis, but his brain was full of too many other things.

'The . . . the stool sample? Human excrement? From the bushes outside your house?' The voice on the other end of the phone sounded young, no doubt a junior technician given the task no one else wanted. At least McLean remembered now. The man in the bushes at the end of his drive. Of course. And the young forensic scientist who had come in the wee small hours to collect it.

'You've got a match?' he asked, knowing it was never as easy as that.

'Umm . . . no. Nothing on the database at all. A couple of close ones, but they didn't work out when I ran the full analysis.'

McLean stared sightlessly at the opposite wall of his office. It wasn't very far away. 'And you felt the need to call at this hour to let me know? Couldn't it have gone in an email?'

The technician didn't reply immediately, the static silence on the phone making McLean feel bad for his outburst. If it had been an outburst.

'Sorry, it's been a long day,' he said. 'I take it there's more?'

'Yes, there is. See, there's no match on the database, but, well, I get given a lot of . . . that's to say—'

'You get all the shit jobs, is that it?' McLean couldn't help but smile as he said it.

'Exactly so. Shit, mucus, skin samples, semen. Christ, you wouldn't believe what people leave behind at a crime scene.'

'Trust me, Amanda. I would.'

'I . . . Yes, I suppose you would. Sorry. I get a little distracted sometimes. But your sample. It wasn't on the database, like I said. Would have written it up and emailed you the results, but something bothered me about it and I couldn't work out what.'

'I take it you did work it out though, eventually?'

'Oh yes. Quite pleased with myself, really. You see, it wasn't on the database, but I recognised the profile. Ran a couple of close matches, no joy. But then I remembered we'd had another shit sample in recently. Hadn't got a match on that one either, and it hadn't made it on to the database either. Ran the two side by side and bingo. A perfect match. Well, as close to perfect as you'll get in this game. Whoever shat in your bushes did this one as well.'

McLean found he had leaned forward, hunched over his desk with the phone clamped to his ear, interest finally piqued. 'So where did this other sample come from, then?'

'Nasty one, that. It was shoved through a letterbox down Leith Walk about a month back.'

The drive home was quick, traffic light at what was really a very late hour to be still at work. McLean wondered what the young forensic scientist was doing at her lab, but it was always possible they had shifts to cope with the endless demands put on them. He'd have to thank Jemima Cairns the next time he saw her at a crime scene. Thank Amanda Parsons too.

He hadn't needed to ask any more details about the earlier sample. Leith Walk might be a mile long, but he couldn't imagine that many letterboxes along its length having excrement shoved through them in the past month. He should probably have brought it up as part of the fire investigation, but that had barely started, and if he was being honest with himself he'd forgotten. With the Stevenson case at an advanced stage of going nowhere, it was nice to have something he could get his teeth stuck into. A puzzle it might actually be possible to solve.

A couple of cats scurried off the drive and into the bushes as he arrived home. Light spilled out from the kitchen window, and as he pushed his way in through the back door he could smell something spicy cooking.

'I thought you were never coming home. It's not healthy, you know. Working such long hours.'

Madame Rose was back to her normal self. Face immaculately made up, hair arranged on top of her head in a greying bun, she had found an apron somewhere and was leaning over the Aga stirring a pot of something that bubbled and steamed. A couple of her cats were curled up at her feet, basking in the heat from the oven even though it wasn't exactly cold outside. Mrs McCutcheon's cat was nowhere to be seen.

'I find it easier to get stuff done at night. Not so many people distracting me. I can actually get some thinking done.'

'Well park your seat in a chair and get some eating done.' Madame Rose pulled a plate out of the warming oven. It was already heaped with rice, and she ladled a hefty portion of something that looked suspiciously like chilli con carne on top before sliding the heavy load on to the table. 'There's grated cheese in the bowl, sour cream in that wee jug.'

McLean noticed the two sitting in the middle of the scrubbed kitchen table, where Mrs McCutcheon's cat usually slept during the day.

'You don't need to do this for me,' he said, as the medium pushed the plate towards a place already laid out with cutlery.

'Nonsense, it's the least I can do. You helped me in my hour of need.'

He had done, McLean had to admit. But then she had helped him and Emma both. He pulled out the chair, slipped his jacket off to hang it over the back, then remembered what he'd been meaning to do all along.

'Well, it smells delicious but it'll have to wait two minutes.'

Madame Rose gave him something halfway between a scowl and a questioning look as he headed swiftly out of the kitchen. McLean had put on a clean jacket that morning, the previous one smelling rather too much of the Leith Walk fire. What he'd forgotten to do in the rush was transfer the contents of his pockets. It wasn't usually a problem; he had a few pairs of latex gloves and some small plastic evidence bags in all his jacket and coat pockets, except when they were fresh back from the cleaners.

This one hadn't made it that far yet, and he hauled it out of the growing pile in the corner of his bedroom, fishing in the pocket for what he wanted before returning to the kitchen and the unexpected meal. When he arrived, it was to find a glass of beer poured and waiting beside his plate, Madame Rose seated across the table with her back to the Aga.

'Not having any yourself?' McLean asked as he tucked in to one of the best chillis he had tasted since Phil had finally moved out of the flat in Newington.

'Had mine earlier.' Madame Rose glanced up at the clock on the kitchen wall, but said no more. There followed a silence while McLean ate for a while, then he unfolded the sheet of paper he had fetched, smoothing out the creases.

'What do you know about this?' He pushed the paper across the table. Madame Rose picked it up, read it through.

'First I've heard of it,' she said after a while. 'Where'd you get it from?'

'The door to your shop. It managed to survive the heat of the fire, too. Somehow I don't think that's on account of the paper.'

'I tried to get back in today but they wouldn't let me. Said it needed to be signed off by Health and Safety. It's my house and they won't let me in.'

'Standard procedure after a fire. I'm sorry.' McLean took back the flyer whilst spooning another mouthful of chilli into his face. It was cheaply produced, a line drawing of a shouting man with an exclamation mark in a speech bubble above him. Below it, the words '!!!Stop the Developement!!!'. Bad spelling apart, it was easy enough to see what it was about. Plans had been lodged to knock down the empty shops and redevelop some of the tenement blocks. Remembering the general air of run-down seediness about the place, McLean couldn't help thinking it would only be an improvement, but obviously enough of the locals disagreed.

'Your place on Leith Walk. You own that, right?'

Madame Rose nodded.

'And has anyone approached you about buying it?'

'Buying it?' The look of horror on the medium's face was enough of an answer.

'So you've not had any offers recently.'

'No. I don't think anyone's ever asked. And I wouldn't sell even if they did. It's my home. No, it's more than that.'

An image of the house, untouched by the fire and yet surrounded on all sides by destruction, swam unbidden into McLean's mind. Much more than a home, it would seem.

'Well, I've an idea I might know why you've been getting grief recently. Why they shoved shit through your letterbox and killed one of your cats.'

'You do?' Madame Rose clasped a large be-ringed hand to her ample chest.

'I don't know who. Not just yet. But I suspect the why is a rather crude attempt to soften you up. Someone's waiting for you to get the hint and put the place on the market. Then they'll swoop in and buy it at a knockdown price.'

'But who would do such a thing?'

McLean picked up the flyer again. At the bottom was a name, a contact email address and a mobile phone number. 'Right now I don't know. But I've a suspicion there's someone who might.'

The needle crackled quietly on the vinyl as it spiralled into the centre of the record. McLean sat in his favourite high-backed armchair, a glass of whisky on the table by his side, and let the repetitive hiss-thunk hiss-thunk wash over him. It wasn't often he had a chance to sit and think these days, even less so with a stomach pleasantly full of good food. A shame really that he had to go back to work the next day.

'Your grandmother had a keen eye.'

McLean opened his, only then aware that he'd closed them and was drifting off. Madame Rose had come in silently to peruse the bookshelves. She reached up and pulled out a hefty leather volume, one large finger caressing the spine like a lover.

'Can't be sure that wasn't one my grandfather bought. Might have been in the family for generations.'

'Yes, of course.' Madame Rose extracted a pair of half-moon spectacles from her ample bosom, where they were dangling on a fine silver chain. She slid them on before opening up the book. McLean reckoned it must have weighed at least a couple of kilos, and yet she held it as if it were no more substantial than a slim paperback collection of poetry.

'Did you ever get around to cataloguing them all?' he asked. He knew Madame Rose had begun the task, with Emma helping, but events had conspired to put a stop to that. And then Emma had left.

'I barely scratched the surface.' Madame Rose laughed as she closed the book and put it back where it had come from, lining it up perfectly with the others on the shelf. 'We made a start on this room, but there's plenty more in the old study, and boxes up in the attic that look like they've not been touched in a century. This whole house is a treasure trove.'

'It's too big and costs a fortune to heat in the winter. I really would be better off selling it and moving someplace smaller. Maybe more central.'

A look of horror spread across Madame Rose's face. 'Sell? Surely you can't mean . . .'

'Don't worry. I'm not serious. Selling and moving would be far more disruptive than staying here. And it's not as if I can't afford the bills.'

'It's more than that, though. Isn't it? This is your home,

same as it was your grandmother's before you. It would have been your father's too, had he not . . .' Madame Rose hesitated.

'Died? Abandoned me? It's OK. I don't mind talking about it. It was a long time ago.'

'And yet a part of you is still back there. Stuck in the past.'

'Isn't a part of all of us?' McLean took up his whisky, needing the fortification if this was going to turn philosophical. There wasn't much left in the glass, but pouring another one might not be wise.

'We are all defined by our past. That's not the same as living in it. You can move on if you want to. There's nothing holding you back.'

McLean downed the last of the whisky, hauled himself out of the chair and went to the record player. 'I'll take your word for it,' he said as he lifted the needle carefully back into its rest and switched everything off. 'But now I think I'd better get some sleep. I've a feeling it's going to be a busy one tomorrow.'

Madame Rose took another book from the shelf, caressing it as she had the first. 'They always are, Inspector. They always are.'

41

'I'm going to my dad's old school soon. It's gonnae be cool.'

We're sitting under the old cedar tree in his garden, Norman and me. I like his garden better than Gran's. It's smaller and the trees are older, like the house I suppose.

'You're not coming back to our school then? Next term?'

'Nah. Going down to some place in England. Near London, I think.'

'England? Wow.' Norman says it like it's someplace far, far away, and for the first time since Gran told me the news I realise that it is. It's further than I've ever been before. Further than I can really imagine.

'Come on. Let's go see if we can get to the top of the tree again.' Always easier to be doing things than thinking about them. And the view from the top's brilliant.

'Race you.' Norman scrambles to his feet, but I'm quicker. Stronger too, he's always been a bit weedy for his age. He goes for the lowest branch while I try to shimmy up the thick trunk. The trick to climbing the old cedar is getting to the first fork. Then it's easy. You can get there along a branch if you can jump up and pull one down far enough. Or you can shove your hands in the cracks and haul yourself up the trunk like those men Gran let me watch on the telly, climbing the Old Man of Hoy.

I'm almost at the fork when I hear a loud crack. Norman doesn't scream, but then maybe the solid thud of him hitting the ground has winded him. I'm not that high up, really. Looking round I can see a thick branch, a pale hand poking out from under a thick blanket of dark green needles. I jump down and hurry over, terrified that he might have broken his neck.

'Norman, you OK?' The branch is heavy, thick as my thigh where it's broken under his weight. It's a silly detail to notice, but I can see where something has attacked the wood, sticky sap oozing around a deep wound. That'll be why it's broken; Norman's not that heavy, after all.

He groans as I haul the branch off him, reaches up to his head. For a moment I think he's fine, and then I see the cut on his hand. It's deep, dark red blood flowing freely, smearing on his face as he pushes needles out of his hair.

'Shit. That looks bad.' He winces at the rude word, same as he always has. It gives me a thrill saying it though. Even if I know Gran would clip me round the ear if she heard me. I reach out and take his other hand, haul him to his feet. He sways, stunned by the fall or my cursing, it's hard to tell with Norman.

'Come on. Better get you back to the house. Get that cleaned up.'

'Mum's gonnae kill me.' Norman looks at his clothes, bloodstained and torn. His face is very pale, more so even than usual.

'No she won't.' I try to sound reassuring, even though I know how different Mr and Mrs Bale are to my Gran, to how I remember my own mum and dad. 'Well, maybe a little bit.'

42

'You know anything about common repairs, Bob?'

The tiny room they had commandeered for the fire investigation was a sharp contrast to the two major incident rooms a floor down. As was the manpower available for the job. Grumpy Bob made up the entire team at the moment, and he looked up from his desk at McLean's question like a man who had only just got comfortable enough for a quick nap.

'Tenements and stuff like that?'

'Aye. Used to be the council would serve a repair order. Not sure if they're doing it still. You know, when all the residents in one block couldn't agree what needed doing. Had it happen to my old place in Newington a good while back, but there's been nothing from them this time around. I wasn't sure if it still happened.'

'You'd be better off asking the lad. He'd have an answer for you in a couple of taps on that wee screen of his.'

'Didn't really want to load him up with any more work. He's already doing too much as it is.'

'Fair point. He's been looking a bit run-down lately.' Grumpy Bob scratched at his chin where the morning's razor had missed a bit. 'Doesn't help that he's so keen. Shows all the other constables up.'

'Christ, Bob. He uses his brain, shows some initiative,

and people think that's keen? It's the bloody job, isn't it? Least it was when I signed up.'

Grumpy Bob sat up straight, his face reddening slightly at the rebuke. 'Just telling it how it is, sir.'

'Sorry. Didn't mean to snap at you. It's just . . . this place, sometimes. People get an idea and run with it. Never seem to know when enough's enough. Like all those stupid pranks they played on me last year.'

'You got a nice car out of it. And a couple of suits.'

'Not helping, Bob. And you know that's not the point. I'm thrawn enough to weather it out, but MacBride's not coping so well.'

'Aye, I know. Been keeping an eye out. He'll get over it, mind. He's tougher than he looks.'

The door opening behind him put an end to the conversation. McLean spun around, expecting to see the object of their discussions. Instead it was DS Ritchie who shuffled into the room backwards, an awkward box under one arm, coffee in the other hand.

'Here, let me.' McLean thought of relieving her of the coffee, but took the box instead. 'Anything interesting?'

'Depends what you find interesting. It's mostly just photos from the scene.'

'Any news from the fire investigation team?'

'Report's in there, too.' Ritchie nodded at the box, then took a sip of her coffee. 'Sorry. Didn't think there'd be anyone in here yet.'

McLean put the box down on the nearest table and started leafing through the contents. The report was a thick sheaf of paper, densely packed type giving him a headache before he'd even started reading it. He flicked through, looking for the executive summary, gave up and turned to the photographs. These had been printed on glossy paper, which probably meant the budget for the investigation was blown already. The problem with digital cameras was a tendency of crime scene photographers to rattle off a dozen or more pictures of exactly the same thing. Fortunately someone had already been at this lot and only printed up a few duplicates of each.

'Definitely arson then?' Grumpy Bob had picked up the discarded report and begun flicking through.

'Double arson, if you're being technical,' Ritchie said. 'Someone shoved lighter fluid through the letterboxes for the betting shop and chippy both. They're not sure how the fire spread to the two houses either side of number twelve but left it untouched. Most of the report goes into technical details about stone wall thickness, safety gaps, stuff like that. To be honest, I think they're scratching their heads on this one.'

McLean took a series of wide-view photographs and pinned them to the wall. One taken from the far side of the street showed a line of vehicles parked in front of the burnt-out shop fronts and houses. 'We get anywhere with the vans?'

Ritchie guddled around in the box and came out with a handful of papers. 'Some of them are local. Had every right to be parked there. These three are untraceable as yet.' She handed the sheets to McLean, who scanned them for salient details. Two Ford Escort vans and a Fiat Doblo. Common enough that finding out who owned them without proper identification would be a pain.

'Let me guess. These were right outside the door to number twelve. Madame Rose's place.'

'That's the one. Forensics have got them all back at their labs. Might be able to get something useful from them. The plates are clones though, and they've all had their VINs removed. Might get lucky with the Fiat. Apparently some of the parts are individually numbered and they can cross-reference with the actual vehicle build number. They'll get the VIN from that and then we'll know who owned it.'

'Sounds technical,' McLean said.

'Well, you know me and cars, sir.' Ritchie smiled, took another sip of coffee.

'I presume this will take some time.'

'Could be a couple of weeks. Depends a lot on who we speak to at Fiat. Even then it'll probably turn out to have been stolen from down south a year ago.'

McLean fished the flyer out of his pocket, unfolded it and pinned it to the board next to the photographs. 'We'll have to try some other avenues of enquiry then.'

About five minutes into their questioning, McLean realised that Dudley Sanderson and Douglas Ballantyne had probably been separated at birth. They didn't look much alike, and Sanderson was a good ten years younger than the bearded conspiracy theorist, but the two of them shared a world-view with remarkable exactness.

He'd asked DS Ritchie to call the number on the flyer, hoping that she would take up that strand of the fire investigation and run with it. Mr Sanderson had volunteered to come in to the station immediately and answer all their questions. That should have set the alarm bells ringing; McLean was well experienced in nutters and could usually spot them before he had to interact. Perhaps he was more tired than he realised, tired enough to agree to sit in on the interview at least.

And so here they were, stuck in a hot and stuffy interview room three. It still smelled overpoweringly of fresh paint, and the hot sun shining through the small, high window was just enough to cook all the goodness out of the air.

'So what you're saying, Mr Sanderson, is that numbers ten and fourteen are owned by two different development companies. Number twelve is, of course, owned by the individual who lives there.'

Sanderson dragged his gaze away from Ritchie, or at least Ritchie's chest, at which he had been staring almost constantly for the whole interview. The expression on his face was almost as if he had forgotten McLean was there, which was perfectly possible given the rambling nature of his monologue. There was a hint of irritation in his eyes, too. Clearly not a man used to being interrupted, although that might have been because nobody ever listened to him at all.

'That is correct, Detective Inspector. Brightwing Holdings owns the freehold of number ten, and a company called Wendle Stevens owns number fourteen. They—'

'So if two different companies are involved, what makes you think there is any development in hand? These are big houses. Most of them have already been split into flats. I'm sure they're going to do the same to these, but that's not what you're claiming, is it?'

Sanderson left a short pause before answering, as if he were checking to make sure McLean wasn't going to say anything else.

'As I was trying to say before I was interrupted, Detective Inspector, the two companies are both registered with the same firm of solicitors. They both filed plans at the same time and they're using the same architects.'

'So you think they're actually the same organisation acting under two different names.' Foolishly, DS Ritchie asked the question. Sanderson's head snapped around, his attention once more fixed on her chest. McLean suspected that he was less fascinated with her breasts than embarrassed at looking into a woman's eyes. He could have been wrong though.

'I don't think it, Detective Sergeant, I know it.'

'You have proof? A paper trail?'

Sanderson's gaze dropped momentarily to the table. His hands were clasped together in front of him as if in prayer, and he fidgeted with them for a moment.

'It's not . . . They're very clever these people, you know. Companies within companies. Always hiding from view. I don't really know why they do it. Tax avoidance, probably.'

'So you don't have any proof.' McLean dragged the man's attention back to himself.

'Not as such, no.'

'Well what do you have then? What exactly is this development you so desperately want to stop?'

'It's there in the plans, Detective Inspector. If you just know how to look at them properly.' Sanderson's hands clasped together again as he warmed to his theme. 'Oh, they look like simple flats, splitting up the houses floor by floor, but you can see that's not what they want to do. Not really. It's just a ruse to keep the council happy.'

'And what is it they really want to do, Mr Sanderson?'

'Why, knock the whole terrace down and build a block of flats in its place, Detective Inspector. Somewhere they can fill with immigrants getting their rent paid by hard-working tax payers like you and I.'

With hindsight, McLean could see that the signs had been there all along. The more excited Mr Sanderson became, the redder his face grew. Little flecks of spittle arced from his mouth, spattering the table so that DS Ritchie had to lean back or suffer an involuntary shower.

'Where exactly do you live, Mr Sanderson?' It was a question he should have asked at the start of the interview, really.

'I'm not sure how—'

'Jock's Lodge? Restalrig maybe?'

'Newhaven, actually.'

'But not Leith Walk. Not, in fact, Leith at all.'

'Well, no.'

'Then why are you so concerned about what happens there?'

'They can't be allowed to get away with it. Knocking down all the best bits of the city and throwing up cheap boxes filled with foreigners stealing our jobs and prostitutes giving us their exotic diseases.' Sanderson lingered on the last two words as if the thought excited him somehow.

'Of course not. That would be terrible. But surely you should be looking out for your own patch? Let the people of Leith Walk decide what happens there.'

'Ah, but how can they do that if they don't know it's happening, Detective Inspector?' Sanderson dragged his gaze from Ritchie's bosom.

'And that's what you were doing with these leaflets, I take it.' McLean pushed the offending article across the table towards Sanderson, who picked it up and studied it closely, a triumphant smile spreading across his face as he did so.

'Exactly. Looks like it worked, too.'

43

McLean watched DS Ritchie escort Dudley Sanderson from the interview room and back towards the reception area at the front of the station. His head hurt from too little sleep and trying to get into the mindset of someone who saw evil intent in the most simple of things.

'Get anything useful from him?' Grumpy Bob sidled up with a mug of coffee in one hand, a newspaper rolled up and shoved under his arm.

'Rather too many nutters around these days, Bob.' McLean eyed the detective sergeant's spoils. 'You heading for an empty room and some quality time, then?'

'I don't know what you mean, sir.' Grumpy Bob gave his best deadpan face, then took a slurp of coffee, swallowing loudly before adding, 'Was just heading back up to the fire incident room, actually. Figured if you and Ritchie were interviewing, it'd be as quiet as anywhere else in the station.'

They set off for the stairs together, McLean filling in the details of the interview as they walked. It always helped to go over these things, but the more he spoke about it, the more he came to the conclusion that Dudley Sanderson was a deeply troubled man.

'So he's got no evidence. In fact he's got evidence to the contrary, and yet he still believes someone is trying to knock down an entire block of Leith Walk and redevelop it on the sly?'

'Exactly, and he doesn't even live there. Doesn't even live in Leith for that matter. I'm not sure I ever quite worked out what his interest in it was, if I'm being honest. Maybe Ritchie will have a better idea.'

'Still, it's a bit odd,' Grumpy Bob said. 'Even if your man isn't dealing from a full deck.'

McLean paused mid-step. 'What do you mean?'

'Well, the fire's been set deliberately. There's no doubt about that. Unlikely it's Gianni the chip shop owner, and the rest of the block was uninhabited. The two houses that burnt down were empty. Just Madame Rose's place there in the middle. And yet he was the one being targeted for abuse beforehand.'

'She, Bob.' McLean couldn't help himself correcting the detective sergeant. He wondered when it had become important to him. And why. Grumpy Bob raised a quizzical eyebrow, but said nothing else.

'We interviewed them all though? Gianni? The builders in numbers ten and fourteen?'

'Spoke to Gianni myself. He's either a bloody good actor or he genuinely has no idea how the fire started.'

'You ask him if anyone had offered to buy the place off him?'

'One of the first questions. He's a proud old bugger, make no mistake. Told me he'd been working there since his old man first set it up just after the war. Apparently he was a POW, Gianni's old man. Decided he liked Scotland so much he wanted to stay.'

'And he owned the shop outright?' McLean shook his head. 'No, I knew that already. Rose told me. What about the builders? Developers, whatever. The other two houses that burned down?'

'Still waiting for the lad to get back to me on that, sir.'

'MacBride? I thought he was busy with the Stevenson enquiry.'

'Aye, he is at that. But there's no one else here I'd trust to ferret out the information. Not in less than six weeks, anyway.'

'So we've not actually spoken to them yet.' They had reached the incident room and found it empty.

'Not as such, no.'

McLean rubbed at his forehead, found it didn't really do much to relieve the pressure. He could feel the case slipping away from him. Too many things to concentrate on and not enough time.

'OK. Speak to Ritchie when she gets back. Dudley Sanderson gave us the names of the developers. Should save us a bit of time searching them out. Set up some interviews, find out if they stand to gain anything from the fire.'

'Believe it or not, sir, I have done this before.' Grumpy Bob grinned as he spoke, and McLean realised just how annoying he was being.

'Sorry, Bob. Force of habit. I'll let you get on with it and keep well out of the way. Not as if I haven't got anything else to do, after all.'

'Stevenson?'

'For one thing, yes. Trying to coordinate with Spence on the Maureen Shenks case too, and you know how well he plays with others.'

Grumpy Bob placed his coffee mug carefully down on

the nearest desk, laid the paper alongside it. 'Don't much envy you that.'

'Aye, well it'll be even more fun when he gets made up to DCI. Think I might put in for a transfer then. I've heard Vice is nice and quiet these days.'

'The whole thing's a fucking mess if you ask me.'

DCI Brooks paced back and forth in the Ben Stevenson murder enquiry room, creating a small clear patch in an otherwise crowded space. All around, the uniforms, detectives and support staff were keeping themselves studiously busy, keen not to be drawn into the impromptu meeting. McLean could only sympathise with them; he too had better things to be doing than pointing out the obvious to people who should have known better.

'I'm not going to disagree with you there, sir. But that's not helped by everyone having to run up and down the stairs between two different incident rooms.' McLean didn't add that it wasn't helped by one enquiry constantly poaching staff from the other.

'Oh good Christ, you're not still suggesting these two are linked are you? They've absolutely nothing in common.' Brooks stopped his pacing for a moment, just long enough to give McLean his best 'you're an idiot' glare.

'Nothing? You mean apart from the fact that both had their throats cut from behind, left to right with a sharp, narrow-bladed knife? Apart from the complete lack of any forensic evidence? Apart from the fact that the likelihood of two Category A murders within weeks of one another not being connected is so vanishingly small it's hardly worth considering?'

McLean watched the detective chief inspector's reaction to his words, his fat face reddening with each new suggestion. It was easy to guess when Brooks was going to interject; he stopped pacing just an instant before opening his mouth.

'You—'

'Of course, I'm not jumping to conclusions.' McLean interrupted before Brooks could get his objection in. 'I think it's wise to treat the two as separate cases, even if they do end up being the same killer. I just think we can save a lot of time, and money, if we merge the admin and data processing of both enquiries. And if we're all working from the same incident room we're in a good place to spot any obvious connections should they appear.'

'If the press get hold of the idea we're linking the two cases . . .' Brooks left the obvious conclusion hanging. The idea of a serial killer would have the tabloids salivating, but it was unlikely they'd care much about the reputation of the police in pursuit of a juicy story.

'Quite frankly I'm more concerned with catching Ben Stevenson's murderer, and Maureen Shenks' too, than what the tabloids want to write about me,' McLean said.

'All right for some. You don't have to worry about getting sacked, do you?' DI Spence muttered the words under his breath, but it was easy enough to hear them.

'Neither would you, if you actually did your job, Mike.' McLean didn't bother to hide his scorn.

'What the fuck do you—'

'Enough.' Detective Superintendent Duguid had been silent up to this point. McLean wanted to think he was acting swiftly to avoid the demoralising effect on the investigation team of seeing two senior officers bicker in public, but it was more likely that he just wanted to get back to his comfortable, quiet office.

'McLean is right, difficult though that is to admit. There are too many similarities to ignore, and the cost of running two major incident enquiries side by side doesn't bear thinking about. Spence, I want you to bring your team in here. Any spillover can go into the smaller rooms across the corridor.'

'Would it not be easier to—'

'Up here, Spence. This enquiry has been going on longer. And it's less far for me to walk.'

McLean almost smiled at the joke, though it would have been funnier if Duguid had ever actually been in the incident room before. But the thunderous faces of DI Spence and DCI Brooks, Little and Large, were enough to kill any humour in the situation.

'Grumpy Bob's running the room at the moment, ably assisted by DC MacBride. They'll get you sorted for desk space and workstations.' McLean checked his watch, even though he knew exactly what time it was. 'I've got to run.'

'What?' Brooks rumbled the single word out in a low growl.

'Interviewing a possible witness. I'll let you know if anything comes of it.'

'How long have you been working on the Leith Walk site?'

If the offices of Wendle Stevens were anything to go by, the razing to the ground of their building by fire could only be a good thing. McLean sat in a room that was too small for the three desks squeezed into it. Too small for the three sweaty bodies too, judging by the smell. Still, it was a new company, with fresh hopes and making the best of what little it had. And anything was better than being stuck with Brooks and Spence.

'The building was auctioned in January. We probably paid a little more for it than we should, but that's the nature of the game, right?'

Jonathan Wendle was an infectiously enthusiastic man. Probably still in the first half of his twenties, he made McLean feel old and tired just by the energy bubbling off him. Stevens, the other half of the partnership, was out visiting another potential site, which was probably for the best. McLean didn't think he could have coped otherwise.

'And you'd started on the work a couple of months ago? What were you doing to the place?'

'Gutting it and starting again, Inspector. Not much else we could do, really. Place was a disaster. Some idiot had split it up into flats in the seventies, and we all know that's the decade taste forgot.'

McLean bit back the retort that he had fond childhood memories of the time. Wendle wouldn't even have been born much before the end of the eighties anyway.

'But things were going OK?' he asked. 'You were on schedule with the renovations, keeping to budget?'

Wendle waggled a large hand back and forth in an easily understood gesture. 'More or less. But it's the biggest project we've taken on so far, so we've got quite a lot of leeway built in.'

'What about the other buildings, number ten and number twelve?'

'What of them?'

‘You weren’t trying to buy them, then? Knock them all down and put up some cheap flats in their place?’

Wendle paused before answering, the thoughts writ clear across his young face as they knitted together. McLean had already decided the young man wasn’t involved in the arson; his enthusiasm was still too great. Someone driven to burning their assets to claim the insurance money would have been far more desperate.

‘A little bird’s been tweeting at you, hasn’t it, Inspector?’ Wendle made little beak-closing motions with his fingers. ‘I can’t tell a lie, we’ve been approached about selling the site. But Bill and me bought it with our own money. We had a plan and we mean to stick to it. Of course, I’m not sure exactly what we’re going to do now. Have to wait and see what the insurance assessor has to say. The engineers too.’

‘But someone did try to buy the place off you? Before the fire?’

‘Quite a few developers, actually. You’d be surprised how often sites change hands before someone rolls up their sleeves and actually does the work.’

‘Anyone put pressure on you to sell? Get any threats?’

Wendle frowned as if the question surprised him. ‘Not really, no. I mean, you get some unpleasant characters who don’t like being told no, but . . . no, can’t say as I have.’

44

'Gods. You wouldn't believe the number of people who've asked me that.'

Basil Temperly was perhaps the exact opposite of Jonathan Wendle, despite them both having chosen the same profession. Where Wendle was young and enthusiastic, Temperly stooped low as if the weight of the world was on him. What little hair he had left was grey and thin, the skin on the top of his head spotted here and there with brown. It looked like he'd spent too much time under the flight paths of Edinburgh's seagulls and forgotten to wear a hat.

'Has anyone been particularly insistent? Have you had any threats?'

'Threats?' Temperly scratched at his chin and leaned back in the rickety chair on the other side of the table in interview room one. McLean had thought to visit the man at his offices, the same as he'd done with Wendle, but Ritchie's phone call had found Temperly visiting one of his other sites, just around the corner from the station. Ten minutes was perhaps not ideal for preparing the interview, but you couldn't have everything.

'There's a rumour going around someone wanted to buy up that whole block, numbers ten, twelve and fourteen. Knock them down and build cheap flats in their place. I imagine you could probably double the accommodation if you did that?'

At her question, Temperly moved his head slowly in the direction of DS Ritchie. It wasn't that he hadn't noticed her already; she'd escorted him from the front desk on his arrival, after all. But there was no mistaking the look of distaste on his face. For a moment McLean thought that she might have hit on something, perhaps come close to some truth. Maybe he was the one who'd been trying to take over the whole block, and had torched it when he found himself thwarted. Then he realised it was just simple misogyny. A man like Temperly might agree to be shown around by a woman, but he certainly didn't expect her to ask him questions.

'Have you been talking to that dreadful man Sanderson?'

'We've been talking to everyone involved in the sites. This is a very serious case of arson, Mr Temperly.'

'Well Sanderson's a pain in the arse and nothing to do with my building site, or those upstart teenagers over the other side. You'll have spoken to that nonce at number twelve too, I expect. He'd not sell up even if everyone else would.' Temperly shifted his gaze back to McLean, where he was obviously more comfortable. 'And no, I wasn't about to sell up. Prime spot like that? Sure, I might make some easy money passing it on, but the real profit's in renting these days.'

'What about now? If someone were to offer you a good sum for the plot?'

'You mean soften me up first, then make an offer?' Temperly narrowed his eyes. 'Sneaky.'

'Very. But you didn't answer the question. What are you planning on doing with the site now it's just a burnt-out shell? There's a lot more work involved now. Might just be easier to cut and run. Take the insurance money, leave the heavy work to someone else?'

'I see where you're coming from, Inspector. And it's a tempting prospect. But no, I wouldn't sell up now. Who knows, the job might even be easier without planning making everything difficult.'

'Which, of course, would be a good motive for torching the place. That and the insurance money.'

'Oh come on!' This time Temperly rounded swiftly on Ritchie. 'I came in here of my own volition. Would I do that if I'd torched my own building? Am I a suspect? Because if that's the case I probably ought to call my lawyer.' He reached into his pocket and pulled out his phone, just in case they weren't sure how he was going to do that.

'You're not a suspect, Mr Temperly. No.' McLean cut in to defuse the sudden tension in the small room. Across the table, Temperly slowly pushed his phone back into his pocket. 'You're helping us with our enquiries. Nothing more. If I thought you had anything to do with the fires, you'd be under caution and you would, as you so rightly pointed out, be fully entitled to have your solicitor present during all questioning. I've a feeling neither your firm nor Wendle Stevens wanted this fire to happen. It was set by a third party, and I'm trying to find out why. Then I can hopefully find out who.'

'McLean. My office. Now.'

McLean was barely out of the interview room, watching as DS Ritchie escorted Basil Temperly from the station, when the all-too-familiar voice boomed out down the corridor. He turned slowly, knowing full well who it was had shouted at him.

'Is it urgent, sir? Only I was hoping to grab something from the canteen before they ran out of lunch.'

Duguid stared at him with puzzled, piggy eyes for a moment, as if the idea of someone not immediately jumping to attention at his command was inconceivable.

'Yes it is bloody urgent. Now get your arse up to my office. There's someone needs to talk to you and you really don't want to keep him waiting.'

Trying hard to keep his sigh inaudible, McLean closed the interview room door and headed in Duguid's direction.

'Who wants to see me, sir? Why?'

'Not here.' Duguid growled the words as they climbed the stairs. As far as McLean could tell, there wasn't a soul within earshot, but he'd long since given up trying to understand Duguid's moods. He'd find out soon enough.

Three flights up and they reached the door to Duguid's office. It was closed, the admin desk just outside it unmanned. Duguid reached for the door handle, grasping it before finally speaking. 'This had better be a huge misunderstanding, McLean. I'm not covering for you if it isn't.'

Bemused, McLean was going to ask what he was talking about, but without another word, Duguid opened the door and ushered him inside.

Two men were waiting for him, one in uniform and sitting in Duguid's expensive leather executive chair, the other in a dark suit and with his back to the door, staring out at the view. McLean had met the deputy chief constable a few times before, generally speaking when he'd done something wrong. The other man he didn't recognise, not from behind at least.

'Ah, Detective Inspector McLean.' The DCC leaned back in his purloined chair, swinging it gently from side to side. 'So good of you to join us.'

'Sir. Is there something I can help you with?'

'Very possible, Detective Inspector. Very possible.' The suited man turned from the window. McLean still didn't recognise him, but the English accent, cheap suit and general demeanour meant it wasn't hard to guess. He'd met enough detectives from Serious and Organised, or whatever they were calling themselves these days, to know one when he saw one.

'Tell me, how are your friends the McClymonts these days?'

'I'm sorry. Who are you?' McLean asked.

'Answer the question, McLean.' The DCC growled the words, irritation creasing his face.

'Happily, sir. When I know who I'm being interrogated by.'

The DCC's scowl deepened and he was about to speak when the other man butted in. 'Fair enough. Tim Chambers.' He held out a hand to be shaken. 'I head up the drug task force. NCA. We've been watching your friends the McClymonts for a while now.'

McLean took the proffered hand, stared Chambers in the face. He was perhaps early fifties if the lines were anything to go by, but fit, hair showing only the faintest of grey in among the dark brown. If he was National Crime Agency and accompanied by the deputy chief constable, then chances were he was a chief superintendent at the very least, which made the implicit accusation all the more serious.

'Sorry to be so defensive, sir. It's just that's twice you've referred to people I don't know as my friends. That kind of puts my back up.'

'Really? You're telling me you don't know Joe and Jock McClymont? But you had a meeting with them just a few weeks ago. You're listed as a partner in their latest development here in Edinburgh.'

'I . . . what?' McLean looked to the DCC and Duguid who was still standing by the door. He genuinely had no idea what Chambers was talking about. And then the penny dropped.

'The tenement block in Newington.'

'Ah, so now he remembers.'

'But that's mad. I'm not a partner in that. Well, apart from the fact I own a share of the site. And as for the McClymonts, well, yes I've met them. Just the once. I didn't like the plans they'd drawn up for the site, told them as much. Haven't heard anything back since, but then I've been a bit busy investigating a couple of rather unpleasant murders.'

Chambers raised a single eyebrow, Roger Moore style. He pulled a slim smartphone from his pocket, swiped it on and tapped the screen once, lifting it to his ear.

'The file on McLean. How many meetings?' A pause, during which his face darkened visibly. McLean had been on the receiving end of Duguid's anger before now, but he reckoned whoever had briefed Chambers was going to get it far worse when the man himself got back to HQ.

'One. That's it? And the documents lodged with planning. They're signed?' Another pause, then without another word, Chambers cut the call, slid the phone back into his pocket.

'I owe you all an apology, gentlemen. Particularly you, Detective Inspector. I was led to believe you had a long-standing relationship with the McClymonts. It would seem that's not the case.'

'You could have just asked.'

Chambers managed a thin smile. 'You know that's not how we do things.'

'Well, for the record, as I said, I've met them just once, didn't care for them or what they're trying to do to my old home. What've they done that's brought them to your attention?'

Chambers said nothing for a while. McLean knew he was supposed to think this was the senior officer deciding whether he could divulge operational secrets or not, but he also knew it was just for show. He stood and waited; some people couldn't help but fill a silence.

'We've had our eyes on them for a while now. Suspected they were bringing cocaine and other nasties into the country, using their development company to launder the proceeds. They were a canny pair though, almost like they knew what we were doing and when. That's why we got very interested when your name turned up on a planning application amendment document they submitted a couple of months back.'

'They what?' McLean found he'd clenched his fists, struggled to relax them. 'So that's how they got their planning permission. Christ, the cheek of it. When I get my hands on them . . .'

'That'll be difficult, I think,' Chambers said.

'You've arrested them, have you? I'll settle for that. For now.'

'No, we haven't arrested them. We won't be arresting them any time soon, sadly. Not ever. They're both dead.'

45

'Just why exactly do we have to do this?'

McLean stared out over the steering wheel at the road rumbling north towards Inverness. They'd left Perth long ago and were stuck behind a truck struggling to go faster than walking pace. Beside him in the passenger seat, Grumpy Bob had dispensed with his newspaper, finished the cup of half-decent coffee he'd managed to find at the last service station and was now fidgeting like a schoolboy needing to be excused.

'I have to do it, apparently, because I've dealt with the McClymonts before. And probably because the deputy chief constable was pissed off at being dragged away from his comfy office. Makes no bloody sense. Not when I'm meant to be heading up a murder investigation, but when the DCC says jump, it's a question of how high.' McLean gripped the steering wheel tight, his knuckles whitening in frustration. 'You're here because you weren't quick enough with an excuse and I didn't fancy making the trip on my own.'

The road opened up into dual carriageway and he dropped a gear, ready to overtake. Before he'd even checked his mirror the peace was shattered by a loud blaring of horn as the car behind squeezed through the narrow gap, one set of wheels on the dead zone where the central reservation began, the driver gesticulating wildly in his rush to get past, get on.

'Bloody hell. He's in a hurry to kill himself, isn't he?' Grumpy Bob made a rude gesture as McLean looked over his shoulder, checking there were no other idiots about before overtaking the truck in a less hurried fashion, pulling back in just before the dual carriageway ended again.

'You want to go after him?' he asked. They were in an unmarked squad car, complete with blue flashing lights hidden in the grille and not-so-discreet siren under the bonnet.

'Nah. It's not our patch, after all. Maybe just make a note of his number and have a word with someone when we get there.' Grumpy Bob fished his notebook out of a pocket and scribbled something down. 'There'd be a weird kind of justice if we passed that car upside down in a ditch a bit further up the road, mind you.'

'Don't joke about it, Bob. This road's a bastard. Sooner it's dualled the whole way, the better.'

Grumpy Bob said nothing in return, and McLean went back to his musing. This whole trip was a complete waste of time, a punishment detail if ever he'd seen one. He just wasn't sure why he was getting it in the neck for a cock-up on the National Crime Agency's part. They had been the ones watching the McClymonts, the ones who'd not managed to actually pin anything on them in months of investigation.

'Why aren't Serious and Organised doing it?' Grumpy Bob voiced the question that hadn't been far from McLean's mind all the way.

'And spend some of their own budget? Christ only knows. Sooner we get there, the sooner we can get back to some serious work.' He accelerated, safely overtaking the next lorry, pushing the car up over the speed limit while the road was clear.

'Still seems a hell of a waste of time.'

'You won't find me arguing with you there, Bob. The whole thing's a complete fiasco.'

It took another hour to get to Raigmore Hospital, park and then find their way to the mortuary. Grumpy Bob moaned all the way, and McLean began to plot ways of leaving the curmudgeonly old sergeant behind. He would probably have preferred a train ride back to Edinburgh anyway.

'DI McLean and DS Laird. We're looking for a Dr Gilhooly?' McLean showed his warrant card to the receptionist, but before she could reply he was interrupted by the sound of someone clearing their throat behind him.

'Detective Inspector, eh? Your men in there must be important.'

McLean turned to see who had spoken, noticing for the first time a little waiting area tucked in behind the door he had just entered. A uniformed officer had been sitting there, and now he unfolded himself, standing so tall he almost had to stoop under the ceiling tiles.

'Sergeant Tanner, sir.' He held out a hand the size of a glutton's dinner plate. 'Was told you were coming. Anything you need, just ask.'

'Thank you, Sergeant. Seeing the bodies will probably be enough. Sooner I can get this done and stop wasting all of our time, the better.'

'Of course. Follow me.' Tanner raised his head a little

and spoke to the receptionist. 'Buzz us through will you, Janice.'

The mortuary was perhaps not as well equipped as Angus Cadwallader's den down in the Cowgate, but it was functional enough. Sergeant Tanner had to stoop through each doorway, but he moved with a slow gait that was at least easy enough to keep up with.

'Hear they're some kind of criminal masterminds, these two,' he said.

'Hardly,' McLean replied. 'All I know about them is they're a couple of property developers who've likely greased a palm or two over the years. NCA's had their eyes on them a while though, suspected drug-running, but they've not been able to pin anything on them.'

They had reached the examination theatre, a much smaller space than McLean had been expecting. The table in the middle of the room was already occupied, a body covered in a heavy white sheet.

'You'd be the Edinburgh police then?' A man in a white coat approached from the other side of the theatre, meeting them in the middle. He was slight, a fact made even more obvious by the looming presence of Sergeant Tanner. 'Was expecting you an hour ago.'

'Dr Gilhooly, I presume.' McLean didn't wait for an answer. 'This one of our crash victims?'

'Certainly is, and you're welcome to him.'

The doctor pulled back the sheet to reveal a man's head and shoulders. McLean had seen more than his fair share of car crashes, and they rarely left a body unscathed. The man he looked down upon had been badly cut across one cheek, almost losing an eye in the process. His nose had been flattened to one side and he was smeared in blood. His shoulders sat all wrong, suggesting worse to view under the rest of the sheet. The doctor was about to reveal more, but McLean reached out a hand and stopped him.

'That's OK. I've seen enough. It's Joe McClymont all right. This his dad?' McLean pointed to a gurney by the wall, another body covered in a white sheet.

'Reckon so.' The doctor pulled back the top, revealing the much less badly damaged face of Jock McClymont. He looked strangely peaceful in death.

'Yup, that's the old man.'

'Well I could've told you that. Saved you the trip.'

'I know. But there's a procedure has to be gone through. Talking of which, is the van here?'

'Ready and waiting,' the doctor said.

'Then we'll take these bodies off your hands. Get them back to Edinburgh where they belong.'

Dr Gilhooly walked back the way he had come, stuck his head through the open door and shouted something McLean couldn't quite make out to someone beyond. A moment later they were joined by two orderlies with a trolley. Joe McClymont was swiftly transferred from the examination table, then one of the orderlies fetched his father from his spot by the wall.

'Sign and they're yours.' The doctor produced an official-looking form attached to a clipboard, handed it over as the orderlies wheeled the bodies out of the examination theatre. McLean scribbled his signature, took the top copy.

'Now, if you don't mind, I've a ton of PMs to do this afternoon.' And with that Dr Gilhooly turned and left.

'He always like that?' McLean asked as they retraced

their steps back through the hospital, Sergeant Tanner leading the way.

'Pretty much. Can't be fun, dealing with dead bodies day in, day out.'

McLean was going to say that it didn't seem to have done his friend Angus Cadwallader any harm, then realised it would be lost on the sergeant. 'What happened to the car?' he asked instead.

'What's left of it's down the yard. Forensics are sending a covered truck up to fetch it back to their labs. Should be with them by the end of the day.'

'What's left of it? How bad was the crash?'

'As bad as a car hitting a rock at eighty miles an hour can be. Fire crew had to cut the roof off to get the bodies out. The younger one had most of the engine in his lap, poor bastard.'

McLean looked out across the car park to the pool car he had driven up in, remembering the idiot overtaking him and the long, monotonous hours stuck behind slow-moving lorries. Suddenly the train seemed like a much more sensible idea.

'You want to see it? The car?' Sergeant Tanner asked. 'It's not far to the lock-up from here.'

Grumpy Bob looked at McLean with a questioning expression, no doubt hoping it wouldn't be necessary. He wished it were so, but the one thing Detective Chief Superintendent Chambers of the NCA had asked was that he inspect the car and see that it wasn't tampered with before their forensics team could get a crack at it. For some unaccountable cloak-and-dagger reason, Chambers hadn't wanted anyone else to know that was what he was doing.

Almost as if he didn't quite trust the old Northern Constabulary. Rude, and a waste of time, but then a favour done was a favour owed by the NCA. That might come in handy some day.

'Better had. Since we came all this way.'

It was a struggle getting Sergeant Tanner into the back of the pool car, but he didn't complain. McLean drove, unable to see anything in the rearview mirror but face. At least the journey was short, ending up near the waterfront. Security fencing surrounded a compound filled mostly with half-wrecked cars, making it look more like a breaker's yard than anything.

'Your man's car's inside. Trying to keep it as clean as possible for the forensics boys.'

McLean didn't have the heart to tell him that most of them seemed to be women these days. He wasn't too keen on leaving the shiny new pool car parked so close to so many wrecks, either, but he locked it up and followed Sergeant Tanner into the large workshop anyway.

It wasn't exactly a hive of activity. Sound fizzed in and out of static from a radio, badly tuned into some pop station. There were half a dozen bays, each with a vehicle lift much like a well-stocked garage anywhere in the country. Two squad cars were undergoing repairs, various important-looking bits of machinery piled up around them. Three other bays were empty, and the last one held a large flatbed trailer with a tarpaulin hiding whatever it was that lay beneath.

'Aye, Boaby. How you doing?' A short man in greasy overalls appeared from the far end of the workshop, rubbing black-stained hands on an equally manky piece of rag.

'Got some detectives from the big city come to see that wreck, Tam.' Tanner gestured over to the tarpaulin as the mechanic eyed up McLean and Grumpy Bob. He must have found them worthy as he gave them a curt nod, then walked over to the trailer and began rolling back the cover.

'Bloody hell!' Grumpy Bob backed up the words with a low whistle of surprise. It wasn't hard to see why. McLean knew a bit about cars, and he was fairly certain this had been a 5 series BMW. It didn't look much like the manufacturer had intended though. There was no glass, for one thing, and the roof had been balanced precariously back in place, upside down, after being cut off to remove the bodies. The front end had folded in on itself so completely it was hard to tell where it had all gone.

'Do we know how it happened?' he asked, walking slowly around the wreck and trying not to imagine the horror of the crash. Had the McClymonts known they were going to die? Or had it all happened so quickly they'd not had time to consider it?

'Idiot was driving too fast, wasn't he.' Tanner's normally cheerful voice dropped to an angry growl. 'They all do it. Buy these stupid powerful cars and think they're Jim Clark or Stirling Moss. And we're the ones have to pick up the pieces. Least this bloke didn't take anyone else with him. Apart from his dad, of course.'

McLean crouched down and studied the back end of the car. It was new, not more than a few months going by the registration number. BMW M5, so very powerful indeed if he had his facts straight. DC MacBride would be able to find him the exact specifications, but it wasn't all that important.

'You think he just lost it going too fast, then? No evidence of foul play?'

'Nothing obvious at the scene, no.' Tanner turned back to the mechanic. 'You see anything obvious, Tam?'

'Not looked at it, have I. Told us not to. This one's for your big city forensics boys.' There was perhaps an edge of bitterness in the old mechanic's words, as if he felt the job of teasing out the car's secrets should have been left to him.

'I think they're more interested in the interior.' McLean studied the shut line, trying to work out if the boot had been opened. The rear end of the car was almost completely undamaged, but the release mechanism would be somewhere in the mangled remains of the front, so chances were that it hadn't been.

'Not much we can tell from here anyway.' He straightened up, feeling a twinge in his back that told him he would probably not enjoy the four-hour drive back to Edinburgh. 'Apart from the fact that he was driving too fast and met something that wasn't going anywhere. RIP Joe and Jock McClymont. Don't suppose you'll be much missed.'

'What were they doing up Inverness way?'

Cruising back down the road they had driven up that morning, McLean realised he'd been keeping his speed slow, not more than sixty even on the dual carriageway, slower when it dropped to single lane even though traffic was mercifully light. They'd dropped Sergeant Tanner off at his station, declined the offer of lunch in the canteen, and headed south as soon as was politely possible.

'What?' McLean risked a sideways glance, taking his eyes off the road for long enough to see that Grumpy Bob was searching his paper for anything he'd not already read.

'The McClymonts. They're Edinburgh property developers. Seems a bit odd the two of them heading up this way.'

'Maybe they were thinking of branching out. Property's expensive in Edinburgh these days. Might have thought it'd be easier to make money up here.'

'You don't believe that, do you sir.' Grumpy Bob didn't phrase it as a question.

'Nope. And neither do the NCA.'

'So what was young Joe doing hooning up the A9 then?'

'That's the big question. There's a lot of drugs come in through the west coast ports. All those old wee villages and hidden bays. Could be they were going to meet up with some of their suppliers. If they were running drugs at all, of course. No one's managed to pin anything on them so far.'

'That why you were so interested in the car boot then?'

'You noticed that?' McLean raised an eyebrow but kept his gaze on the road. 'Didn't think I was being so obvious.'

'That's my sharply honed detective skills at work.'

'Yes, well. That chief superintendent from the NCA, Chambers, wanted me to make sure the car was OK. It'll be interesting to see what forensics get from it. My guess is not much.'

'Should we have stayed with it until the truck turned up?'

McLean paused before answering, let another mile of road disappear under his wheels. 'Reckon that's what Chambers wanted me to do. Probably would have had me in the truck all the way back, just in case something went missing. Not sure where he gets his paranoia from.'

'How long have they been after the McClymonts, then?'

'No idea, but probably years. You know what they're like when they get an idea stuck in their little heads. Hadn't found anything enough to pin on either of them, though. That's why I didn't think there was any point staying with the car. Even if the suggestion that Inverness can't be trusted is a bit shitty.'

'Aye. Shitty. And a waste of time.'

McLean looked out at the scenery as they sped past Pitlochry and south towards Perth. Back at the station was a tiny office filled to bursting with paperwork, a major incident room going nowhere fast. A detective constable he couldn't afford to lose on the brink of quitting due to overwork. A boss who was getting demob happy. 'I don't know. There's worse ways to spend the day, Bob.'

46

The night air was warm and heavy as McLean climbed out of his car, then reached back in to fetch out the bag of takeaway curry he'd picked up on the way home. He ached from the long drive to Inverness and back, a wasted day. It wasn't until he reached the door, saw the light pouring from the kitchen window, that he remembered his house guest. Well, there was probably enough Rogan Josh to go around.

He needn't have worried. Madame Rose was leaning against the Aga when he came in, wearing the apron once again. He could tell just by the smell of the room that she'd been cooking.

'You don't need to feed me, you know,' he said by way of greeting. The medium merely nodded her head at the carrier bag.

'I can see that. You're quite the chef, it would seem.'

McLean put his carry-out on the table and went to the fridge for a beer. It took a while to find, hidden behind bags of vegetables and other unfamiliar produce. He was fairly certain it hadn't been that full the last time he'd looked.

'You went shopping.'

'Ah, the detective inspector's keen observation.' Madame Rose pulled a large saucepan out of the oven and put it on the hotplate. Steam billowed past her head as she pulled off the lid, letting it go with a clatter and a 'bugger' as the realisation dawned that its handle would be very hot. McLean suppressed a smirk, but obviously not well enough.

'It's not funny.' She blew on her fingers, flapping them past her lips in a fanning motion. 'I could have burnt myself.'

'Sorry.' He fetched a glass from the cupboard, poured the beer in, took a deep draught. 'But really, you don't need to go to all this effort. I'm used to looking after myself.'

Madame Rose fetched a plate from the warming oven, ladled what looked like a mountain of stew on to it, then juggled a baked potato bare-handed to the table.

'The least I can do, really.' She lifted the potato on to the plate with one final deft move, then slid the whole thing over to where a place had been set. The butter dish, salt and pepper were already waiting in the middle of the table.

'Well, thank you.' McLean sat down and contemplated a somewhat more substantial meal than the curry he'd thought would do him a couple of nights and maybe breakfast as well, if he had time for breakfast. 'This looks . . . interesting.'

'It's a recipe I picked up on my travels in North Africa. Mutton stew. Of course the Berbers would have served it with couscous, but I couldn't find any in your cupboards.' Madame Rose gave him a look that suggested this was perhaps the most egregious of his many failings. As he looked at her, McLean realised that she was fully back to her old self now. Perfectly presented, even with the apron around her waist. The dark stubble and darker eyes were gone, her hair still grey, but recently washed and neatly arranged about her head. And she held herself upright, not stooped under some impossible weight like she had been directly after the fire. Clearly her fortunes had taken a turn for the better; he just hoped that his would follow suit.

He speared a piece of meat, smeared thick sauce over it with his knife and popped the whole thing in his mouth. The flavour was rich, with subtle hints of something flowery. Then he bit into the meat and tasted something that took him straight back to childhood.

'Where'd you get mutton from?'

A worried frown spread across Madame Rose's face. 'Do you not like it?'

'Actually, it's a lot better than I thought it would be. A lot better than I remember it being from my schooldays, anyway. I suspect this isn't scrag end of neck from a toothless old wether, though.'

'Everyone wants lamb these days, but you can't beat a good bit of mutton for flavour.' Madame Rose pulled out a chair and sat down opposite him. McLean took another forkful and shoved it in his face.

'Not having any yourself?' he asked perhaps a little too soon for politeness.

'I'm more of a six o'clock supper person.' Madame Rose glanced up at the clock and McLean couldn't help but follow her gaze. It was well past ten, even though the sky wasn't really dark outside.

'Can't remember the last time I had supper at six. Probably back when I was at school.' McLean cut open his potato and shoved a generous wedge of butter in it. He could, he realised, get used to having someone cook for him. But then it occurred to him that he always had someone cook for him; the chef at whichever takeaway he chose to dine from that evening.

'You hear anything from the building control people?' he asked.

'It's like dealing with children.' Madame Rose's frown deepened. 'The engineers won't go in until the frontage is secured, the scaffold crews won't do anything until they know who's going to pay them, and I can't go home until the others are secured. Round and round in circles. It's not even as if my house is unsafe.'

'I'm not even going to ask how you did that, by the way.'

'Did what?' Madame Rose's face was a mask of feigned innocence. Or it might just have been the heavy layers of foundation.

McLean shook his head, scooped up another forkful of stew. 'Well, you're welcome to stay here until it's sorted. Not as if I'm ever here myself.'

'Thank you, Tony. It's not everyone would be so kind. Quite the opposite, in fact.'

'About that. The hate campaign. You've still no idea who might be behind it?'

Madame Rose kept silent perhaps slightly longer than was wise when answering a policeman. She had a look on her face that suggested she thought the question double-edged. It hadn't been, not when he'd asked it. But it occurred to McLean in that slight hesitation that Madame Rose had always appeared in control of any situation when he'd met her in the past. She gave an impression of having hidden knowledge, perhaps even power. That was part of her act, of course, but he couldn't quite convince himself there wasn't more to it than that.

'It left me very puzzled,' she said eventually. 'And that in itself was a worry.'

'How so?'

'Can I be frank with you, Tony?'

McLean hesitated, another forkful of food halfway to his mouth. 'Have you ever not?'

That got him a pout that looked rather ridiculous on Madame Rose's face. 'There are forces at work in the world most people are not prepared to accept.' She paused.

'Go on.'

'Mostly that's fine. The sort of things I'm talking about rarely interact with the mundane lives of everyday people. They don't care if they're not believed in. But some of us are more sensitive to them. Some of us attract their attention, and some of us are charged with mediating. We keep the balance in check.'

McLean chewed and swallowed as Madame Rose fell silent once more. A part of him had been expecting this conversation for quite some time. Another, larger and more rational part of him had been wondering how he would react. A couple of years earlier and he would have scoffed, told the medium to stop trying to scare him with ghost stories. Now he'd met some of those ghosts, and they weren't all pranksters under white sheets.

'You're sceptical, and that's to be understood. You were raised by your grandmother to question everything. Don't stop on account of me. Just entertain the possibility that the answers to those questions won't always necessarily fit into her beloved science. There's far more to the world than that.'

'And what happened to you, the attacks, the fire, they're

all part of some . . .' McLean searched for a word that didn't sound silly. Failed.

'Call it a power grab, if that helps. A very subtle one at that or I'd have seen it coming a mile off.' Madame Rose considered her chubby hands for a minute, as if she too were searching for the right words. 'You and me. We try to maintain a balance. In our different ways. But there are others out there. Other sensitives who look to use that to their advantage. I believe such a one was behind what has been happening.'

'Do you have a name? I can get them brought in for questioning. If there's any possible evidence of a link to the fire—'

'Ah, Tony. Ever the White Knight.' Madame Rose leaned back in her chair, clasping a hand to her ample bust. 'There won't be any evidence. Not that your forensic scientists would be able to gather, anyway. But it doesn't matter. I am not without my own resources, and they have been brought to bear on the problem. I only needed time and a refuge to recover from the initial ambuscade. This house and your generosity have renewed me, given me the space to marshal my forces. The battle is already joined and my enemy is on the run.'

McLean looked down at his plate of mutton stew, half eaten and still delicious, and yet his appetite had deserted him. 'Sounds rather like you're taking the law into your own hands. Not sure how I feel about that. At least about being used to help it.'

Madame Rose let out a heavy, theatrical sigh. 'I am sorry you feel that way. It's not how I view it at all, and I wouldn't dream of so abusing your hospitality. Ours is a different law, an older law than the one you uphold as a policeman, but it respects society's rules. I won't be getting my collar felt any time soon.'

'Then why tell me at all?' McLean put his knife and fork down side by side at the edge of the plate, reached for his beer in the hope that it would help the sour taste that had appeared so suddenly in his mouth.

'Because it's only fair you know. Because things will happen soon that will seem to make no sense. Things may already have begun to happen. I feel a shift in the currents. The tide is turning once more in our favour.'

McLean looked again at the medium and saw that she was completely back to her old self now. In total control and weaving an aura of mysterious otherness around her like a fog. On balance, he thought he preferred the older, more vulnerable version.

47

'You ever get the feeling you're being pulled in too many different directions, Constable?'

DC MacBride looked sideways from the driving seat as he navigated through the endless rush hour traffic. 'You really want me to answer that, sir?'

'Stupid question, sorry,' McLean said. 'You probably do twice as much work as I do, and sometimes I wonder why I even bother having a home to go to.'

MacBride said nothing, but it wasn't an awkward silence. McLean let him concentrate on getting them to their destination, a fairly modern industrial estate in the arse end of Sighthill. McClymont Developments had its offices and stores in an identikit brick and steel warehouse, the same as eleven others clustered around a large tarmac parking area. Most of the units bore large, shiny signs, names of companies McLean had never heard of. A couple had estate agents' 'To let' boards nailed to their doors, the few front-facing windows boarded up, heavy iron roller doors closed with rusty padlocks.

'We know which one we're looking for?' McLean peered through the windscreen as MacBride drove slowly around the car park. 'Ah, there we are.'

It wasn't quite the most run-down of the units, but it wasn't far off. A small plaque screwed into the wall beside the main entrance read 'McClymont and Son' in flaking paint. MacBride parked right outside the large warehouse door, rolled down and padlocked like most of the others on the estate.

'Is there anyone here?' he asked, leaning forward, hands draped over the steering wheel as he stared at the building.

'Should be. Ritchie phoned ahead. The secretary should be here to let us in.' McLean popped open the door, heaved himself out of the car seat and into the heavy heat of the afternoon.

'What are we hoping to find?' MacBride slammed his door closed behind him, plipped the key-fob to lock the car.

'I'm not really sure. Was hoping we might know it when we saw it.'

If the outside of the building was unprepossessing, it was nothing compared to the inside. They were met by Ms Grainger. McLean remembered the time she'd approached him in the street, asked him to sell his flat, called him unkind. If she remembered it too, she didn't mention it. Her greying hair was swept up into a tight, conical bun and her pinched mouth gave her the look of someone who's run out of lemons to suck. She had a spinster's air and a Morningside twang to her accent, which made McLean suspect that a lifetime of not quite living up to expectations had worn her to this sharp point.

'It's a terrible business. Terrible.' Ms Grainger shook her head as if that might dislodge the fact of her employers' demise and so make it not have happened.

'It can be a treacherous road. I'm very sorry.' McLean

allowed himself to be led down a narrow passageway and into what must have been the nerve centre for McClymont Developments. A sizeable open-plan office, it had two large desks facing each other at one end, a smaller reception desk by the door. A couple of drawing tables stood side by side in the opposite corner, paper plans laid out on them, their corners curling slightly. Everything smelled of dust and mildew, the heat outside only just beginning to penetrate the walls. Ms Grainger crossed the room to a small kitchen area, filled a kettle and switched it on to boil.

'Do you know why they were going north?' McLean asked while she busied herself finding mugs and teabags.

'Old Mr McClymont liked to shoot the grouse. He had a gun at some place up on the west coast. Near Ullapool, I think it was.'

'And Joe was into that too, was he?'

'Young Mr McClymont didn't care for the shooting, no. He liked his deep-sea fishing. Used to take a boat out from Achiltibuie and catch the mackerel, out in the Summer Isles.'

'Business must have been slack, if they could spare the time.'

'There's never so busy you can't take a couple of weeks off in the summer. Old Mr McClymont never missed the start of the season, no matter what was happening. Besides, most of the workmen take their leave around now.'

'So it's booming, then?' McLean had wandered over to the drawing tables and was peering at the plans. He recognised some of them as the designs for redeveloping his old tenement block. They didn't appear to have been changed in the light of his objections.

Ms Grainger didn't reply immediately, occupied as she was with the preparation of tea.

'They'd be better if the Newington site wasn't held up.' She handed McLean a chipped and stained mug. The milk had curdled on the surface, forming an unpleasant scum. She hadn't at any point in the conversation asked whether he actually wanted tea, or what he took in it.

'Perhaps if they'd consulted me first, before starting work.' McLean put the mug down on the nearest available surface, making a brown ring mark on a yellowing building plan. 'Tell me, Ms Grainger. How many other projects are the . . . sorry, were the McClymonts working on?'

Ms Grainger gave him a cold look. 'They had a few things at early stages, but the East Preston Street site was the biggest thing they'd ever taken on. Put everything into it, they did.'

'Would it be all right if I had a quick look around the building?'

'There's nothing here. A couple of vans, some machinery, scaffolding. Most of the plant gets hired in these days.' Ms Grainger sat down at her desk, and that was when it hit McLean. She had a small old-fashioned computer monitor, keyboard and mouse, but there was nothing at any of the other desks. Most places nowadays did everything using CAD software. Even the scruffy offices of Wendle Stevens had been dominated by large flat-screen monitors. McClymont Developments, in contrast, looked like it belonged in the 1970s.

'It won't take long. Then we'll leave you in peace.'

Ms Grainger's face soured even more at the word, but she didn't move from her desk. 'Suit yourselves. I've got to get all the accounts in order for the bank and the lawyers. Just as soon as youse lot release the bodies we can start winding up the company.' She gave a heavy sigh, the veneer of respectability falling away.

'How long have you worked for Mr McClymont?' McLean asked. Ms Grainger looked up at him in surprise.

'Since I left school. When I was sixteen. Used to run messages for old Jock Senior. There was a character. He taught me how to do the books. I was always good with numbers, just couldn't do the sums in the exams.'

'There's no Mrs McClymont, I take it. Joe's mother?'

'She died what, twenty years ago now. Broke old Mr McClymont's heart at the time. Cancer, it was. Probably something to do with the forty-a-day habit she had. Catriona. Och. Haven't thought about her in years.'

'Any other family?'

Ms Grainger didn't answer straight away. McLean supposed that she'd not really had time to come to terms with the news. Sudden death had a habit of doing that to people. They rationalised, of course. They told themselves everything had changed, their loved one, colleague, parent, whatever, was gone now and never coming back. But then they just carried on doing the things they'd always done, not realising that there was a hole that wouldn't be filled. Not until they stumbled into it.

'Young Mr McClymont had a girlfriend, but I wouldn't have called her family. They were always breaking it off, getting back together, breaking it off again. I don't know if she even knows he's dead.'

'Do you have contact details? I'll send a liaison officer round to break it to her gently.'

Something akin to relief spread across Ms Grainger's face at the thought she wouldn't have to perform that particular duty herself. She opened a drawer and pulled out a black leather address book, flicking through the pages until she found what she was looking for. She wrote something down in meticulous script on a yellow Post-it and handed it over. McLean read the name and couldn't help but raise an eyebrow.

'Thank you, Ms Grainger. You've been very helpful.'

'We looking for anything in particular, sir, or just being nosy?'

They had left Ms Grainger in the office, going about her business. Not for the first time McLean wondered why Serious and Organised, or the NCA as they liked to think of themselves nowadays, hadn't closed the place down for a full forensic investigation. But then there was nothing to suggest the car crash that had done for the McClymonts was anything other than a tragic accident, and despite their suspicions, they'd never managed to find anything that could link the builders directly to the drug trade. Even the car had been clean, at least after preliminary analysis. It was still in the yard at HQ undergoing a more thorough examination, but if it had been used to transport any kind of narcotic, they would have found it by now.

'Nothing wrong with being nosy, Constable.' McLean found a panel of light switches by the door into the main warehouse, flicked them on to a hammering of fluorescent tubes. Light flooded the large room, augmenting the meagre illumination that had penetrated the grubby roof windows high overhead.

As Ms Grainger had said, there were a couple of panel vans parked in the middle of the warehouse, side by side. White, and getting on for ten years old if their registration plates were to be believed, they were exactly the sort of thing builders all over the country used. One of them had 'McClymont and Son' stencilled on the front in fading red paint, but the other was unadorned by anything other than rust spots. The front wall was taken up by the roller doors; the other three were clad with industrial-strength shelving, except where a set of steps led up to the space above the office. The higher shelves were filled with cardboard boxes, piled randomly. McLean walked around the room, taking in heaps of scaffolding, rusty and unused, cement mixers crusted around their edges, piles of hand tools, pretty much everything you might expect to find in a builder's yard. Only a builder's yard stuck in the previous century.

'Something up here you might find interesting, sir.' McLean looked around, then up to the top of the narrow stairs where DC MacBride now stood.

'What is it?' He threaded his way between the two panel vans and climbed the rickety steps. The space was cluttered with yet more junk, empty boxes, black bin bags bulging with the heavy cloth sheets decorators used. Everything was caked in a thick layer of dust, untouched in many a year. A narrow walkway snaked through the detritus towards the back of the building, where a skylight cast mottled light on something much newer.

'Couldn't help noticing there weren't any computers down in the office. Well, apart from that old thing the secretary was using. They even had a fax machine that's probably as old as I am.' MacBride reached into the nearest pile and pulled out a shiny white box, shook it to show that it was empty. McLean recognised the brand; it was the same logo on the back of his phone.

'This is all new stuff?' he asked.

'Looks like it, sir. We've got at least a dozen tablets and phones, four top-spec laptops, a couple of high-end desktops.' MacBride stepped further into the pile of boxes, lifting and shaking to check none still had their contents in them. 'The McClymonts surely liked their Apple products.'

'And yet none of it's downstairs in the office. Interesting.'

'Could just be that they had it delivered here to run it through the business. Get the VAT back, that sort of thing.'

'A dozen phones though? There's only the two McClymonts and Ms Grainger on the payroll full time. I met them, Constable. They didn't strike me as the type to hand out top-of-the-range phones to contract staff.'

'I guess we'll have to search their houses, then.' MacBride ended his sentence with a heavy sigh, reminding McLean of just how much pressure the constable was under. Taking him out of the station on this trip was supposed to be a break from the endless admin of coordinating the multiple major incident enquiries, but now he thought about it, the work would still be there when they got back.

'Actually, it'll probably remain a mystery. Unless the NCA boys want to look into it. Come on. We've wasted enough time here as it is.'

McLean handed the box to the constable, turned back to the stairs, then stopped in his tracks. 'Those boxes, they've got serial numbers on them, right? Same as on the computers and phones and stuff that was in them?'

'That's how it usually works, aye.'

McLean pulled his phone out of his pocket, thumbed around the screen until he remembered how to work the camera function.

'Let's just take a note of them all then, shall we? I've a suspicion there's more to this than meets the eye.'

'You want me to run these through the database, I take it, sir?' MacBride tried to hide his weary resignation, but it wasn't a very good effort.

'I think you'd probably do it better than me, Stuart. It's not high priority though.' McLean peeled the Post-it note off from where it had stuck itself to his phone's camera lens, looked once more at the name he'd been given. 'Besides, there's someone I should probably talk to first.'

48

'Ah, the prodigal son returns. And about bloody time.'

McLean had left DC MacBride to park the car. He'd been intending to head up to the major incident room, catch up on the day's lack of progress and hopefully find DS Ritchie. Instead he was barely through the back door to the station when the familiar, irritating tones of Detective Chief Inspector Brooks rang out across the hallway.

'Were you looking for me, sir? Only I've been out on a case.' McLean pulled out his phone, held it up for Brooks to see. 'You should have called.'

'Don't get cocky with me, McLean. I know what you're like.'

'Was there anything in particular? Only I'm quite busy.'

'Aye, I heard that. So busy you've time to go poking your nose into NCA business. Thought you were meant to be heading up a murder investigation. Isn't that a bit more important than some idiot killed himself in a car accident?'

'I agree. It would be nice only to have one case to work on, sir. And much as I'd like to, saying no to a detective chief superintendent isn't really wise. Not when he's got the DCC's ear too. I'm sure you've had cases where you felt the same?'

Brooks' eyes narrowed, the folds on his face deepening as his anger rose. 'Two people are dead, McLean. They had their fucking throats cut. One of them was dumped in a bin like so much trash and whoever did it is still out there. I'd say that was a good bit more important than your developer friends.'

'I've been out less than two hours. And for your information they weren't my friends. I hardly knew them. If I thought the investigation into Ben Stevenson and Maureen Shenks' deaths could be helped by my pacing back and forth in the incident room, rest assured that's what I'd be doing. I don't recall it having all that high a rate of success when you've tried it though.'

He shouldn't have said it. McLean knew that as the words were coming out. Brooks wasn't Duguid, for all that he was likely to have the top job in a few months. McLean could cope with Duguid's bluster; his temper was quick to ignite and just as swift to blow over. Brooks was a different prospect altogether, needed much more careful handling. The detective chief inspector's scowl relaxed rather than deepened, as if he knew he'd scored a point in some arcane competition to which only he knew the rules.

'Perhaps if you were paying attention, you'd know that we've new forensic results on the nurse. Results that could crack the whole thing open. Need I remind you that time is critical in any murder investigation, McLean? You should have been here directing operations, not gallivanting off across the city. You delegate that shit to the sergeants.'

And they fuck it up, so you have to go and do it all anyway, wasting yet more time. McLean shook his head slightly, more at himself falling into the same old trap than anything Brooks had said. The DCI was right, up to a point, but that didn't make him any less of an arse.

'Thank you for the reminder, sir. And thanks for letting me know about the forensic update. I'll be interested to see what that's all about. There's just one small thing.'

'Aye? What?' The scowl was back, a hint of worry in those narrow eyes.

'DI Spence is SIO on the Maureen Shenks case. Not me.'

Brooks' face darkened, building up to a righteous anger.

'You're the one wants both cases investigated together, dammit. You need to be here to coordinate that. If you can't manage that then I'll have to suggest to control they assign a more experienced detective.'

The late afternoon sun baked the streets, tarmac shimmering as it melted in the heat. McLean watched the temperature gauge in his Alfa nervously as they sat in traffic heading south from the city centre. Brooks' important piece of new forensic evidence had turned out to be nothing of the sort, just an excuse for the DCI to give him a hard time. McLean couldn't see any point in pacing the incident room, getting in the way of the admin and constables who were doing all the real work, so he'd found DS Ritchie, and persuaded her to come and help him break the bad news to Joe McClymont's on-again off-again girlfriend. She was currently fanning herself with a notebook.

'What I wouldn't give for a bit of a breeze right now.'

Both windows were open, but without any noticeable forward progress, all that meant was they had the pleasure of breathing exhaust fumes.

'I probably should have kept the pool car. Shame MacBride only signed it out for the morning.' McLean inched forward as the traffic freed up, then slowed to a halt again a few yards on. 'This old girl's fun to drive down country lanes, but not exactly appropriate for this kind of work.'

'Old girl?' Ritchie raised a slim eyebrow. They'd never really grown back properly after she'd pulled him out of a burning factory a couple of years earlier. Her hair had, though, and it was longer now than he thought he'd ever seen it, cut shoulder length. Was it his imagination, or was it a deeper red than he remembered? Shinier and healthier-looking, too.

'I know. Very sexist of me. What can I say, I'm a throw-back to an earlier era.'

'No, it's kind of appropriate.' Ritchie patted the dash-board with her free hand. 'But you're right. You shouldn't be using her for this kind of work. Get yourself some-thing new.'

'And keep this for my days off?'

'Aye, well there is that.' Ritchie smiled at the joke. 'It'd be a shame if something got dropped on her again, mind. You have something of a reputation now.'

The traffic eased a little, and McLean concentrated on driving smoothly past the blockage, a delivery truck far too wide for the narrow road. He glanced nervously upwards at scaffolding clinging to the side of a modern office block as he passed, searching for any heavy objects that might be descending from on high. It was foolish, really, but then given how much it had cost to fix the Alfa, maybe something cheap and dispensable was a good idea.

'Not sure I'd know where to start. With a new car. Seems like there's always more important things to do than flicking through magazines and cross-referencing specifications.'

'You could get Stuart to do it. He loves that sort of thing.'

'I rather think he's got enough on his plate right now.'

'True. Oh well, I might have a look-see. Always fun spending other people's money.'

'Is it? I wouldn't know.' McLean turned down a side street, looking for the right number. This was an expensive part of town, decent-sized detached houses set back from the road. Almost all the front gardens had been paved over, with top-end motors parked up or spaces where they would soon be returning from work. They put him in mind of Joe McClymont's flash BMW, and sure enough there were plenty of similar models to be seen. Conspicuous affluence, or more likely just barely managing to make the payments each month.

The house he was looking for had a Range Rover outside the same year and specification as Duguid's. McLean parked in the street in a welcome bit of cool shade under a large tree. He had to wait for Ritchie to wind up her window and get out so that he could lock her door, yet one more reason why a car from the early seventies wasn't perhaps ideal as an everyday runabout and workhorse.

'You ready for this?' he asked, more for his own reassurance than hers. He wasn't entirely sure he knew why he needed to come here. The news could have been broken by a trained family liaison officer, after all.

Ritchie gave him a funny look. 'Reckon so. Just have to hope she's in.'

The look on Charlie Stevenson's face when she answered the door was enough to tell McLean that she had already heard the news. That and the smell of alcohol. Afternoon was progressing towards evening, but it was still a little early to be hitting the sauce.

'Oh, it's you.' She opened the door wide, then turned and walked away, expecting him to follow. McLean did so, Ritchie making sure the door was closed behind them. They walked through an elegantly decorated hallway, shoes clacking on polished wooden floorboards, and into a large open-plan kitchen-diner.

'The girls not at home?' McLean asked. There was plenty of evidence of them. Childish pictures pinned to the fridge door with magnets, the dining table given over to colouring books, a box in the corner heaped with Barbie dolls and plastic horses. Piles of clothes, neatly folded and waiting to be put away.

'Why? You here to interrogate them?' Stevenson slumped in a high seat, leaning against the breakfast bar that separated the cooking part of the kitchen from the dining area. A bottle of wine stood erect on the counter alongside a large wine glass that was half full.

'Sorry, bad joke. They're at their gran's. Hard enough explaining to them why they can't see daddy any more without having to tell them Uncle Joe's not coming to visit any time soon either.'

'I'm sorry.' McLean pulled out a stool and sat on it, across the breakfast bar from Stevenson. No, not Stevenson, he reminded himself. She'd reverted to her maiden name, Christie.

'Why are you here, Inspector?' Christie picked up the wine glass and swirled around the clear liquid within.

'Firstly, I came to tell you about Joe McClymont. I'll

admit, I was surprised when Ms Grainger gave me your name.'

'Bitch. She phoned me about an hour ago. Never heard her sound so happy in her life.'

'Happy?' Ritchie asked.

'Who're you then? Inspector's squeeze? Better-looking than the last one at least.'

McLean saw Ritchie stifle a smile. They both knew that Grumpy Bob had sat in on the previous interview.

'Detective Sergeant Ritchie.' She produced her warrant card, holding it up even though Christie showed no interest in it whatsoever. 'I'm sorry for your loss.'

'Really?' Christie swirled her glass, then took a long swig. Coughed as it burned its way down.

'Really. I don't know you, never met Joe McClymont, but I've had the bottom fall out of my world before. It's not nice and I'd not wish it on anyone.'

'Yeah? Well you could wish it on whoever it was ran Joe off the road. You could wish it on Ms Violet fucking Grainger.'

'I take it the two of you didn't get along.' McLean decided not to point out that the accident had not involved any other cars.

'Can see why they made you a detective.' Christie put her wine glass down with surprising dexterity. Perhaps not as drunk as she was acting. Either that or just lucky.

'How long have you and Joe McClymont been seeing each other?'

'Seeing each other. How very polite of you. Joe and me were at school together. Grew up in the same street. I'd probably have married him if I'd done the same as everyone else. Left after my O grades and got a job in Tesco. But I was cursed with a brain, Inspector. I went to university. Got ideas. Met Ben.'

'But you kept in touch with Joe, I take it.' McLean began to understand why the marriage had failed. Built on sand and hope. A childhood sweetheart just around the corner to offer a sympathetic ear, a shoulder to cry on and temptation when things got rocky.

'Joe was a good listener. Ben only liked the sound of his own voice. When it got bad, I'd go round to his place and just talk. It didn't get physical until much later.'

'But before you and Ben split?'

Christie stared at him a long while before answering. 'Yes.'

'Do you know what Joe was doing up Inverness way?'

'This time of year, probably going deep-sea fishing. He's got a cottage in Achiltibuie, and a share in a boat up there. Jock liked his shooting, but Joe just loved to be out on the water.'

'Did you ever go up there with him?'

A look of horror shuddered across Christie's face. 'Once. God it was awful. Never stopped raining, and the midges. The girls were bored out of their tiny minds, kicking up a fuss you wouldn't believe. Don't think Joe really wanted me there, either. He seemed tense a lot of the time. Only really happy once he'd been out on the boat.'

'You go fishing with him?'

'Christ, no. I'm hopeless on boats. Just spend the whole time throwing up.'

'So you only went the one time.'

'Yeah.' Christie stared into the middle distance as if the

thought had only just occurred to her. Her hand reached out for the glass and she took another long gulp before focusing once more on McLean. 'Lucky, really.'

'Ms Grainger suggested that you and Joe weren't seeing each other any more.'

'My, you are full of questions today, Inspector. Sure you only dropped round to give me the bad news?'

McLean shrugged. 'Thought you'd rather hear it from a familiar face. And I wanted to know more about the McClymonts. They were redeveloping the tenement block I used to live in, after all.'

Something like understanding dawned. 'Oh, you're that policeman,' Christie said. 'Makes sense, I guess. And yes, we were in one of our off periods, but they never lasted long. You might have had something to do with it, now I come to think of it.'

'Me? How?'

'You wouldn't sell your flat. Joe was baffled by that. The amount of money they were offering. Old Jock and that bloody harpie of a Grainger woman couldn't believe it either. Heard them talking about it one time I was round the old man's place. She kept on going on about how it was impossible you could refuse them.' Christie shook her head. 'No idea what that was about, but it fair buggered up their plans.'

She took another swig from her glass, refilled it from the bottle. Stared at it as if she were contemplating just necking the wine instead.

'Was he a violent man, Ms Christie?' DS Ritchie filled the awkward silence.

'Joe? Not really. Never hit me, anyway. Quite the

opposite. He could be very generous if he wanted to be. He gave me my car, for one thing.'

'Really?' Ritchie arched an eyebrow in surprise. 'I wish my boyfriend could afford something like that.'

Christie picked up her wine glass, drained it in one. This time when she put it down it wobbled drunkenly on the counter.

'Yeah. Me too.'

49

He didn't notice her as he drove into the car park at the back of the station, but DS Ritchie must have done. It wasn't until McLean had locked the passenger door and looked up that he saw what had caught Ritchie's attention. A short, wiry figure was leaning against the stone gatepost, cigarette dangling from her mouth and leather overcoat wrapped tight despite the lingering late afternoon heat.

'Think someone wants a word, sir.'

McLean let his shoulders slump. He'd not really been looking forward to the incident room, but a session with Jo Dalgliesh was probably worse.

'I'll be back as soon as I can.' He glanced at his watch. 'But don't hang around for me if I'm not back by shift end.'

Ritchie nodded her understanding, headed to the station while McLean walked back across the car park towards the waiting reporter.

'You've been hiding from me, Tony.'

Jo Dalgliesh looked tired, that was the first thing McLean noticed. She was more slumped than usual, leaning against the gatepost like she needed the support. She didn't stand up as he neared. The smoke from her cigarette spiralled lazily from the tip, and she spoke around it, as if the effort of taking it out of her mouth was too much.

'Ms Dalgliesh, what a surprise.' McLean hadn't meant it,

but as he got a better look at her wizened face, he found that he did. Her eyes were sunken, lines crinkling around them far deeper than he remembered. 'Everything OK?'

A thin smile spread across her face at that. 'Aww, I didn't ken you cared.'

'I don't. Just trying to be polite. Was there something you wanted, or is this a social visit?'

Dalgliesh finally pushed herself away from the wall, letting out a low 'oof' as she did so. 'No' as young as I used to be,' she said. McLean couldn't help but notice the limp. 'You gonnae buy us a coffee then?'

McLean considered the options. He could tell her to piss off, but then she'd just write something nasty about him, or worse, write something nasty about one of his colleagues and attribute it to him. He'd been out of the station pretty much all day, which meant there'd be a mountain of questions awaiting his immediate answer, none of them remotely interesting or useful. He needed to get back up to speed on the Stevenson and Shenks murder investigations in time for tomorrow's morning briefing, and there was no doubt a sea of paperwork waiting for him in his office. On the other hand, she'd come looking for him, which meant she probably had some information. Not that difficult a decision to make, really.

'Come on then.'

It took longer to get to the cafe than it should have, Dalgliesh clearly in some pain as she limped up the road just a little behind him.

'Someone give you a kicking?' McLean asked. 'Only, if you let me know who it was, I'll send flowers.'

'You're all heart, you know that, Inspector?' Dalgliesh hobbled in through the cafe door as he held it open, heading straight for an empty chair. McLean went to the counter and placed his order, trying to remember what the reporter had drunk the last time. It must have been right, or she just didn't care, as she greedily slurped at the latte he brought over to the table a few minutes later, eyeing up the pair of chocolate brownies he'd added for good measure.

'And cake as well? I must have been a good girl.'

'Thought you looked a bit peaky. And sorry, by the way. That dig about the flowers was uncalled for.'

Dalgliesh raised an eyebrow, chocolate brownie paused halfway between plate and open mouth. 'Is that Tony McLean in there, or has there been some invasion of the body snatchers thing going on and I never got the memo?'

'Old habits die hard. I'll never like you much, Dalgliesh. You've caused me enough pain as it is. But I've seen people beaten up badly and whoever did you over knew how to cause pain. Not sure you didn't do something to deserve it, mind.'

Closer up, and in the unflattering light of the cafe, McLean could see the make-up inexpertly plastered on Dalgliesh's face, not quite hiding the bruises. Her nose had always been crooked, no doubt a relic from run-ins with the subjects of her more lurid stories in the past, but now it was swollen around the bridge and spidery veins bloodshot her eyes. The hand holding the cake shook gently.

'Aye, well. That is part of what I wanted to talk to you about.'

'Last time we spoke you were looking into Ben Stevenson's story. The one that took him off to Gilmerton Cove.'

'You bought me cake then, too. Must be love.'

'Seriously, Dalgliesh. I thought you'd decided Stevenson was barking up a non-existent tree. Seeing Masonic symbolism in everything?' In truth, McLean was having a hard time remembering exactly what it was Dalgliesh had told him.

'Aye, I did. But I don't think Ben was barking up the wrong tree so much as being led up the garden path. Since you're so fond of your metaphors.'

'How do you mean?'

'Well, he'd hooked up wi' Dougie Ballantyne, aye? We all ken what a nutter he is. Ben thought there might've been something in it, but his later notes show he was beginning to suspect old Dougie was a sandwich or two short of the full picnic.'

'Wait . . . what? His later notes?' McLean struggled to remember whether he'd seen any notes at all. There'd been the single notebook they'd recovered from the murder scene, but that hadn't yielded anything other than the doodled Masonic symbol on the cover, and Dalgliesh hadn't seen it. Hadn't even been told about it.

'Aye, did you no' get the message? He'd backed up everything to the Cloud. Just took me a day or two to work out what his password was.'

'And you didn't think to tell us?'

'Aye, I told youse. Sent an email to your man MacBride about it.'

Had he mentioned it? McLean supposed it was possible, though he really didn't remember. 'OK, so what you're saying is Stevenson had decided Ballantyne was talking bollocks about the Brotherhood and all his other nonsense. There was no story there?'

'Other than a piece about how gullible folk are, no. And nobody likes to read a piece about how stupid they are.'

'So how did he end up in the cave with his throat cut?'

'That, aye.' Dalgliesh paused for another swig of coffee, her eyes falling on the second of the two chocolate brownies. McLean nudged the plate in her direction; it was a small price to pay for information.

'Ben knew Dougie was as mad as a Scottish Tory,' Dalgliesh continued through a mouthful, 'but he reckoned he knew why, too. Someone really was feeding Ballantyne information, and it really did point to something that looks a lot like his Brotherhood, only without the talking head and the supernatural assassins. Just a good old-fashioned secret society pulling a lot of the strings in the background. There's stuff in there about devolution and the referendum, like a road map as if it was all planned from the start. Scary stuff if you take it seriously. A load of old pish if you don't.'

McLean took a sip of his own coffee, trying to get the flow of ideas straight in his head before seeing where they led. It wasn't easy.

'You don't, I take it.'

'Top marks to the inspector.' Dalgliesh gave him a cheeky nod that turned into a painful wince.

'So what you're telling me is that Stevenson started off investigating Ballantyne's claims, discovered they were built on paranoia and too much late-night cheese?'

Dalgliesh nodded, her mouth full of the last bite of chocolate brownie.

'But he then found out that there was actually some basis for that paranoia in reality, and decided to look into that instead?'

'Aye, and that's when he started to get a wee bit obsessed. That's what all the stuff on his wall was about.'

The wall. He'd been hoping for a chance to speak to forensics about that. Go through their photographs and see what he could find. Better still if he'd been able to analyse the real thing, but someone had put paid to that. Someone who didn't want them knowing what Stevenson had been working on right at the time of his death.

'You think you know what was going on? You think someone was leading him on deliberately?'

'You're no' as stupid as you sometimes seem, Inspector.' Dalgliesh relaxed back into her chair a little, wincing as her shoulders sagged. 'Aye, I think someone was leading Ben on. Stringing him along, more like. The way his notes read, it's as if whoever was doing it knew exactly how to press all the right buttons.'

'Any idea who this person might be?'

Dalgliesh shook her head. 'That's where I hit a brick wall. Thought I was getting somewhere, but every lead just dissolved away to nothing. Ben was being played, Inspector, but whoever was playing him left no trace. Well, apart from a dead body in a cave. And that's no' the question you should be asking, anyways.'

McLean thought for a while before saying 'Why?'

'Exactly. Why? There is no secret society, just someone pretending there was, and doing it well enough to fool a seasoned hack like Ben. But if it was all just a wind-up, then why did he end up dead? That's no' a very funny punch line, eh?'

50

McLean expected Dalgliesh to get a taxi, or wander off back into town once they'd finished their coffee, but she walked with him back to the station, or at least limped along as fast as she could manage.

'So who beat you up, then? Thought you might have got too close to Stevenson's secret society, but if it doesn't exist I doubt it would have worked you over like that.'

Dalgliesh grimaced. 'Different story altogether. Something I've been working on a while that's none of your business. Least not for now, anyway. About a week ago I got a call, one of my sources saying they'd some info for me. Only when I got there the wee scrote was nowhere to be seen. On the way home I got jumped by two scallies up Calton Hill way. Felt like I was being mugged for my phone and money, but I know a punishment beating when I get one. Too many questions, aye? Getting too close to someone as don't want to be seen.'

'You want someone's collar felt, you only need to ask.'

Dalgliesh let out a short sharp snort of laughter, stopped and leaned against a nearby wall. Whether that was because she was tired and needed a rest, McLean couldn't be sure. He suspected it was down to what he'd said.

'That's priceless, you know. "Collar felt." Jesus, I've not heard that expression in a decade or two.' Dalgliesh wheezed a bit, then guddled around in her bag for a cigarette. It was a new bag, McLean noticed, and wondered why he'd not done before.

'You know what I meant. You've been helpful. I'm grateful for that and I'll return the favour if I can. If you don't piss me off again first, that is.'

'Aye, you're all heart, Inspector. I know.' Dalgliesh sparked up, inhaled deeply and let out a long plume of smoke through her broken nose. 'I can look after myself fine, but don't you worry. I find out who those boys were jumped me, you'll be the first to know.'

'You needing a lift anywhere?' They were just across the road from the station, and even though he really didn't want to offer, McLean couldn't help himself from doing so.

'Nah, you're all right.' Dalgliesh waved him off with the hand holding her cigarette, ash fluttering around in the still air and spiralling to the pavement below. 'Just needing a wee minute for my ribs to settle doon, then I'll head off back to the office. Don't you worry about me, Inspector. I'll be fine.'

The station was quiet, afternoon having almost turned to evening now and most of the day shift gone home. McLean went in the back way to avoid being caught by the duty sergeant and buried under the inevitable pile of messages that would have come from being out of the station for more than five minutes. He really wanted to go straight to his office and try to batter into submission all the disparate pieces of information that were flying around in his head. There was one person he needed to talk to before he forgot though, and at this time of the day there was only one place he could possibly be.

The major incident room was suffused with that air of desperation an investigation achieves after a week or more with no progress. A line of uniforms sat at desks, manning the phones though there seemed to be very few calls. Over in one corner, a printer spat out endless sheets of paper; actions to be checked, allocated, worked, rejected. Someone had stuck a couple of pins in the map of the city that adorned one wall, alongside a whiteboard mostly empty of ideas. McLean scanned the room, noticing a distinct lack of senior officers. He found Detective Constable MacBride leaning over the shoulder of one of the admin staff and pecking out commands one-fingered on the keyboard of her computer. He looked up, alerted by some well-honed sixth sense to the presence of his boss.

'Ah, sir. I was hoping I'd see you before shift change.'

McLean glanced up at the clock on the wall above the door. 'Sorry to disappoint. I got waylaid by a certain journalist. Says she sent you an email a while back.'

A look of puzzlement flitted briefly across MacBride's young round face, then realisation dawned. 'Oh, Jo Dalgliesh. Yes. She sent me all of Ben Stevenson's research. Well, links to where it's stored online, to be fair. That's what I wanted to see you about.'

'Any particular reason why you didn't share this with me earlier?'

'Erm . . . you weren't here, sir? It came in while you and Grumpy . . . DS Laird were up in Inverness. I read through it all, but there wasn't much to begin with, and the further you read the less sense it makes.'

'Pretty much what Dalgliesh told me. I'd still like to have a look myself.'

'There's a printed copy on your desk, sir.'

'Thanks. I think.' McLean turned back to the door, then remembered something. 'You get anywhere with those serial numbers we found? You know, the phones and computers at McClymont Developments?'

'All clean. Least, not reported stolen or anything. The phones were all SIM free, which is a bit unusual, and it's top-spec kit. The only thing that's really weird is that none of it was around. I asked the mortuary and put a call up to Inverness. Both McClymonts had iPhones, but previous generation. Whoever's got these new ones, it wasn't them. Neither of them had so much as a laptop with them.'

'A puzzle for the NCA, I expect. But thanks for chasing it up.' An image swam unbidden into McLean's mind then; a pair of Portakabins squeezed into what had been the back garden of his old tenement block in Newington. Plans strewn around a temporary site office. Had there been computer equipment there?

'Get back to Ms Grainger if you've a spare moment. Tomorrow morning's early enough. Find out what's going on with the tenement development and see if you can arrange a site visit, will you? We'd look a bit silly if they'd got all the kit there.'

MacBride nodded, picked up his tablet computer and started swiping at the screen. 'I'll see if we can't do a location trace on the phones. If any of them are switched on, it might be helpful to know where they are.'

McLean glanced up at the clock again, realising just how far past shift end it was. He didn't begrudge the detective constable the overtime, but the lad needed to find some work–life balance too.

'OK. Thanks. But it's low priority. Not our case, really. And do it tomorrow. Time you went and reminded yourself what home looked like.'

True to his word, MacBride had left the printout of Ben Stevenson's working notes on the top of the stack of paperwork adorning McLean's desk. It was a slimmer file than he had been expecting, and the words were printed double-spaced, often no more than short single-word bullet-point lists that made little sense. Unless you looked at it from the point of view of a mind slowly unravelling. He wondered what Matt Hilton would make of it, but the psychologist had left not long after the incident at the disused mental hospital, suddenly announcing that he'd been offered a lecturing post in Brisbane. McLean suspected that the two things were not unrelated.

There were other specialists who could be called on to give their learned opinions about the notes. It would probably be a good idea to get someone to do just that, then at least it would look as if they'd been thorough in their investigation. McLean could see after a casual flick through that they weren't going to find any clues as to the identity of the murderer, though.

He was just about to put the whole thing back in its envelope with a scribbled note to that effect, when his phone rang. He glanced up at the clock, wondering how it was already half-past seven in the evening, before grabbing the receiver.

'McLean.'

'Ah, Detective Inspector. I was hoping I might catch you in.'

He recognised the voice, but took a couple of seconds to put the name to it. The forensic scientist who got all the shit jobs, and seemed to work late shifts. 'Miss Parsons. What can I do for you?'

'I think it's more what I can do for you. I've been doing the analysis on that car you had sent down from Inverness. Nice motor, apart from the whole being written off in an accident thing. You know that engine develops more than five hundred brake horsepower?'

McLean did, as it happened, but it surprised him that Miss Parsons did too. Then it annoyed him that he was surprised. Why shouldn't she know about cars?

'I thought your speciality was interesting effluvia?'

That brought a peal of nasal laughter down the phone line so loud he had to pull the handset away from his ear. When he put it back, Miss Parsons was halfway through her explanation.

'. . . Jack of all trades, really. You've no idea what people leave behind in their cars. Saliva on the dashboard and steering wheel, nasal pickings in the upholstery, urine in the carpets, even faeces sometimes. And you wouldn't believe how much semen and vaginal secretions people spray about. You might want to think about that next time you buy a used car.'

McLean had only met Amanda Parsons once, in the early morning at the end of his driveway when she'd fetched a stool sample out of his bushes. He couldn't really remember what she looked like, but he was warming to her as a person.

'So what's so special about McClymont's BMW?'

'It's complicated.' Miss Parsons paused before adding,

'Any chance you could drop by the lab? Easier if I show you, really.'

McLean glanced up at the clock, even though he knew what time it was. 'Now?'

'Well, I'm still here and you're still there. It can wait till the morning though, if you'd rather.'

There was a pile of paperwork stretching back a couple of weeks to deal with, and technically the results of the forensic examination of Joe McClymont's car was an NCA matter, nothing to do with him. On the other hand, the paperwork wasn't going anywhere, the two murder investigations were stalled, and this intrigued him. McLean scribbled a message on a Post-it and slapped it on the envelope containing Ben Stevenson's deranged notes, then threw it into his out tray.

'I'll be with you in half an hour.'

51

The forensic services technical and engineering labs were on the outskirts of the city, beyond the airport. Evening traffic was light, and McLean made the journey in almost exactly half an hour. A bored-looking security guard raised an eyebrow at his car, but let him through as soon as he saw the warrant card, barely uttering a word during the whole exchange.

Miss Parsons was waiting in reception. 'Got to sign you in myself. Janine goes home at five and we've no cover for the late shift.'

She busied herself writing down details in the visitor book and finding a name badge, handing it over before finally remembering to introduce herself. 'I'm Amanda, by the way. We never had much of a chance to talk when I came to your house.' She stuck out a hand and McLean shook it, somewhat overwhelmed by her restless energy.

'It was . . . early.'

'Very. We met before that. Rosskettle Hospital? You probably wouldn't recognise us SOCOs, all dressed up in our overalls and face masks.'

'You were on that forensics team?'

'Everyone was on that forensics team.' She rolled her eyes like an eight-year-old. They were large eyes, set in a face just as young as McLean had been expecting. Her straw-blonde hair was held back with an Alice band, which didn't help to make her look any more mature. Neither did the loose-fitting tour T-shirt for a rock group McLean had heard of but which had probably split up before she was born. Cargo pants and heavy black DMs were maybe fashionable, or they could just have been the most suitable apparel for her line of work. To McLean they just suggested that she'd nicked all her clothes from her big brother. Or maybe her dad.

'The BMW's out in the workshop. Probably quickest if we go this way.' Amanda pushed open the front door, bustling through almost before McLean could catch it and follow. He'd not got far before she stopped.

'This is yours? This must be yours. Oh, I'd heard . . . but she's beautiful.' She stood just a few paces away from his Alfa, staring for a moment. Then as if it had taken that long to summon up the courage, she ran a hand lightly over the bonnet, roof and boot, walking slowly around the car.

'You just have to take me for a spin sometime. I love, love, love old Alfas.'

'Perhaps,' McLean said. 'But we were here to see Joe McClymont's BMW?'

Amanda gave the Alfa one last longing pat on the rump. 'Of course. Sorry. Tend to get a bit carried away. Here.' She strode off in the direction of what turned out to be the workshops.

Much like any modern garage, it was a line of roller doors set into the front of a tall, utilitarian building. Most were closed, but one was rolled all the way up, spilling artificial light out into the warm evening. Just inside, McLean could make out a heap of bent and twisted scrap metal that might once have been a BMW M5. Pieces had been removed, placed to either side as if it were no more than a plastic toy belonging to a child with insatiable curiosity and a pair of pinking shears. The roof lay upside down at the back of the workshop, all four doors stacked alongside it. The wheels were in a neat tube, one on top of another, beside the far pillar of the four-post lift holding the rest of the chassis just high enough off the ground to enable work on it without stooping.

'It's amazing how much damage hitting a rock at eighty can do. If the rock's big enough.'

'Wasn't this bad the last time I saw it.' McLean noticed that the engine had been removed, and looked around to see where it might be. He found it in the next bay, bolted to a wheeled engine stand and surrounded by the cream leather seats. The front two, he couldn't help noticing, were splattered with dark brown bloodstains.

'Forensic science can be a bit messy.' Amanda fetched a heavy pair of rigger's gloves from a workbench at the back of the room and handed them to McLean. 'Sharp edges,' she said by way of explanation.

'So, what is it you found for me? And you know this is technically an NCA investigation, don't you?'

'They're only interested in drugs, and we didn't find any traces anywhere. Nothing in the boot, no hidden compartments, not even some residue in the carpets, and you'd be surprised how much of that there is about.' She flicked at a stray curl of hair, unable to get it under control with a gloved hand. 'No I called you rather than them because this is more relevant to you.'

'Still not sure how. Are you going to explain it, or do I have to guess?'

Amanda's face reddened at the rebuke. McLean hadn't really meant it as such, but his words might have been a bit harsh. It had been a long day.

'Sorry. I do tend to go on a bit. See, here.' Amanda stepped closer to the vehicle, pointing to the spot on the twisted chassis where the manufacturer had etched the vehicle identification number. McLean peered at it, but could find nothing amiss. Not that he was an expert.

'The VIN, yes.'

'Now see this.' Amanda stalked off to the engine, hunkering down so that she could point to a similar series of numbers etched in the casting of the block.

'Engine number. I take it they don't match up then?'

'Would that it were so easy.' Amanda pulled off her heavy gloves as she crossed to the spotless workbench at the back of the garage. A computer screen, keyboard and mouse looked rather out of place among the heavy spanners and other tools.

'They match perfectly, and they're up here on the DVLA database. Same car, same colour.'

'What's the problem then?'

Amanda clicked a couple of icons on the screen, coming up with a list of incomprehensible numbers and text, the familiar BMW logo at the top the only thing McLean could easily identify.

'Put simply, it's the wrong red.'

'How so?'

'Here.' Amanda turned to the back of the car, lifting the boot lid open and pointing at a sticker with a colour code on it. 'This is the correct code for the colour on the car. I've checked. But this,' she turned back to the screen. 'This is a different shade.'

'Mix up when they entered the data?'

'This is a German car, Inspector. Not Italian.' A gentle smile spread across Amanda's face as she clicked a couple more times, bringing up a different page of equally incomprehensible data. Sooner or later she was going to get to the point, but McLean could wait. Her enthusiasm was infectious and far preferable to the oppressive misery of the station.

'The colour mismatch was just a little niggle, really, but it got me thinking and I really don't like mysteries. So I did a bit more digging. This car, electronically speaking, should be a Category C insurance write-off. Records have it as being badly damaged in an argument with a bus last October. That's before it should even have come into the country, by the way.'

'It's a ringer, then?'

Amanda treated him to another one of her coy smiles. 'Oh, it's so much more clever than that. Until your man McClymont hit that rock, this car had never seen so much as a scratch, but it's been given the identity of a write-off. And it's been done so well I couldn't tell at first. Those VIN and engine numbers are the best fakes I've ever seen. Add that to the clever fooling of the documentation, and this car's almost completely untraceable. It could certainly be bought and sold throughout its entire life without anyone ever knowing anything was amiss.'

'So where did it come from?' McLean cast his eye over the mangled wreckage. It was difficult to imagine someone going to so much effort over a car, but then new it was probably worth eighty grand or more.

'That's where it gets interesting. Waiting on confirmation from BMW, but as far as I can tell, this car was stolen from the private garage of an exclusive apartment development not twenty minutes' drive from here, about four months ago.'

'Four months.' McLean cast his mind back. He wasn't aware of any great spate of vehicle thefts in the city, but there were cars being stolen every day. Even Duguid's Range Rover had been nicked not that long ago.

'That's not important. The thing is, it's been done so well. If this car hadn't crashed . . . no, if it hadn't crashed and then been brought to this forensic lab, it would never have been discovered.'

52

He probably should have gone straight home from the forensic services garage and lab, but there were too many implications arising from the discovery that McClymont's car was stolen. McLean knew he wouldn't be able to sleep until he'd at least begun piecing together that puzzle. He drove back to the station slowly, mind working over the few facts he had without any satisfactory explanation presenting itself to him.

He needed to talk it over with other people who knew the case, but DC MacBride had finally gone home, and Grumpy Bob was nowhere to be seen. Out of desperation, he went in search of Duguid, but the detective superintendent wasn't in. Hardly surprising, given the hour. Only DS Ritchie was still about, peering myopically at her computer in the CID office.

'Evening Sergeant. Anyone else about?'

Ritchie looked up at him, pale skin washed out by the light from the screen. She rubbed a weary hand over her face before answering.

'Carter's around somewhere, and DC Gregg's keeping an eye on the incident room. It's a quiet one though. Why?'

'Just got some interesting information about the McClymonts. Wanted to run it past someone before I called Serious and Organised.'

As he explained the case to Ritchie, a few of the pieces started to come together, but it was still a bugger's muddle.

'Sounds like you need a list of all the sites they were working on; pay each one a visit and see what you find.' Ritchie turned her attention back to her screen just long enough to turn it off, whatever she'd been working on no longer important. 'Or, you know, leave it for the NCA to deal with.'

'You're right. It's their case, not mine. I've done them enough favours already.' McLean looked around the rest of the empty CID room, imagined the pile of paperwork waiting for him in his office, the running commentary on her home life he'd get from DC Gregg if he went up to the incident room.

'Heading home any time soon, sir?' Ritchie had gathered up her bag, slung it over her shoulder.

'Reckon so. Nothing much to be gained hanging around here. Why?'

'I was wondering if I could cadge a lift. Mary's having another one of her little get-togethers this evening. I'm already late, and waiting on a taxi will only make me later.'

The light spilling out over Ritchie's face as she opened the door to the rectory and stepped inside made McLean realise that it was starting to get dark. Summer nights in the city were so brief it was often much later than he thought, but the clock on the dashboard said half-past nine. The days were slowly getting shorter. Soon it would be winter again, the endless cycle repeating once more.

He sat in the car parked outside the church, and stared at nothing in particular in the street. Home was no more than a minute's drive, and yet he couldn't bring himself to go there. Madame Rose would be waiting for him in the kitchen, a hearty meal prepared, and right now he couldn't quite face dealing with her. It wasn't that she was bad company, really. Just that he'd grown used to being alone. Just him, the cat and the occasional postcard from Emma to remind him why he did what he did. Why he put up with the shit, the antisocial work hours and even more antisocial colleagues, the daily bath in the dregs of humanity.

He looked at the clock again. Twenty-five to ten. A quiet time of the evening away from the city centre. Later there'd be people coming home from the pub, or whatever Edinburgh Festival show they'd been to. Earlier it would have been the office and factory crowds heading home. Now was a lull in the night-time activity that suited him just fine.

Switching on the engine, he executed a perfect U-turn in the wide, empty road, and headed back the way he had come.

Scaffolding still clung to the front facade of the building, ungainly metal rods sticking out at all angles. Broken bones in the darkening sky. The first level of planks was too high up to jump and catch on to, deliberately so to deter drunken revellers. The uprights – standards, if he remembered the arcane builders' jargon – were smooth, and wrapped in shiny tape to make them smoother still. Even so, there were always idiots who tried, egged on by alcohol and friends who didn't know better. As a beat constable, McLean had seen more than his fair share of broken arms, legs, backs and necks from people who got building sites and playgrounds confused.

It wasn't a problem for him, though. The front door to his old tenement block was closed and locked, but he still had the key he'd used when he'd lived there hanging on his key ring. More surprisingly, it still worked. He looked up and down the street, but shadowed by the scaffolding no one would have been able to see him even if there'd been anyone about.

Stepping through the familiar front door sent a shiver down his spine. As he closed the door behind him it cut off the low roar of the city for a moment. He stood in the darkness and almost imagined that the past two years had never happened. Or the last twelve. He would climb those stairs like he'd done uncounted times before. Kirsty would be waiting for him. His Kirsty, with her long black hair and infuriating way of seeing right through him. They would share a bottle of wine, chat over whatever music he put on, fall into bed together.

A siren on Clerk Street cut through his musings. McLean shook his head, though only half-heartedly. He didn't really want to lose that tiny, happy moment, even if he knew it was madness to dwell on such things. But he'd come here for a reason. Best get on with it.

There wasn't much sign of progress on the building front. Hardly surprising, given his objections to the plans and unwillingness to sell up. What would happen to the site now that McClymont Developments was effectively no longer trading? One for the lawyers to fight out, he had no doubt. McLean stepped quietly through the front door to Mrs McCutcheon's flat, then followed the new concrete steps down to the communal garden.

It was an oasis of dark calm. To either side the lights

from the neighbouring tenements illuminated washing lines, garden furniture and unkempt vegetation, but here in the middle there was nothing. Off to the rear, the bulk of the Portakabin offices squatted like some alien spaceship. A mini digger parked alongside it looked strangely awkward in the half-light. The rest of the garden had been dug down, backfilled, the drainage points jutting out of freshly laid concrete like mafia victims struggling to break free. He clambered carefully down to basement level, testing the surface with the tip of his foot. It looked like it might be still liquid, but that was just a trick of the light. The floor was firm, the concrete set rock-solid, the tiny outlines of the planned basement flats etched in narrow blockwork.

McLean approached the Portakabins quietly. As far as he could tell, there was no one about, and it wasn't as if Joe and Jock McClymont were going to suddenly appear for a late-night site inspection, but still he knew that he shouldn't really be here. So far he'd not broken any rules. He had a key and a legitimate right to be in this place. The cabins were a bit of a grey area though, legally speaking. No, who was he kidding? This was breaking and entering, fair and simple.

Like much of the kit in the McClymonts' warehouse, the Portakabins had seen better days. The front door was locked, but the windows weren't, and a little jiggling of one had it swinging open. Clambering in was more difficult than it should have been, but McLean made it without knocking too much off the nearest desk. At least he'd remembered to put on gloves.

He was in the same room where he'd first seen the plans

for the redevelopment. They'd been pinned up on the far wall, and were barely legible in the reflected glow of the street lamps. The desks between him and them were old, basic Formica tops on metal frame legs. There were no phones, no computers, nothing more sophisticated than an elderly microwave oven sitting on top of a fridge, a grubby kettle alongside it. Nothing in here to raise any suspicions.

The door led out into a narrow corridor running the length of the two cabins. Hard hats and hi-vis jackets hung from hooks along one side. The other sported a motley collection of Health and Safety Executive warning posters, reminding the workforce what a lethal place a building site could be. Opposite where he stood, a second door should have opened into the next Portakabin, but when McLean tried it, he found it was locked. He went back into the first room, rummaged around in drawers until he found a bunch of keys. Not too hopeful that any of them would be the right one, but it was worth a try.

The darkness in the corridor was almost total now. He didn't want to turn on his torch though, worried he might be spotted by someone in the flats that looked on to the garden. He worked his way through the bunch largely by feel, sliding each key into the lock, twisting, meeting solid resistance. On to the next, then the next. And then finally it clicked. The door swung open and he peered inside.

A high window let what little light was left into the room. His eyes accustomed to the gloom, it was still as much as McLean could manage just to see the vague shapes of desks and tables. This place smelled different from the rest of the Portakabin though. Electric, charged. Over in the corner LEDs flickered on and off, green and red on the front of some kind of computer equipment. Screens lined up along one wall. McLean was about to step fully into the room, but common sense finally kicked in. This wasn't his case, just a mystery he couldn't leave alone. And if a crime had been committed, the two perpetrators were beyond the law now.

He pulled the door closed, locked it after him and returned the keys to the drawer where he'd found them. Then he cleared up all the papers he'd knocked to the floor when he came in. He considered the window, but decided it was too risky going back out that way. The front door was a Yale lock, so he could get out without it being obvious anyone had been in at all.

Back in his car, convinced he'd been watched the whole time, McLean pulled out his phone and thumbed at the screen until the number he'd been given came up. He hovered over the dial icon for long moments, knowing it was none of his business. Except that they'd made it his business, hadn't they? When they'd put his name on the planning documents. When the NCA had hauled him over the coals for something he'd not done. Sorting this mess out might not be his job, but with the McClymonts dead, the worry was nobody else would do it.

A quick glance at the clock. Late, but not so late you couldn't phone a policeman. Especially a detective chief superintendent.

53

Traffic was light on the drive back home, which was just as well as McLean's mind wasn't really on what he was doing. The conversation with DCS Chambers had gone better than he might have expected, but it had also made yet more work for him and his overstretched team. He drove slowly past the church, still shrouded in scaffolding, the rectory alongside with light shining from the front porch. Pulling over a hundred yards from his own drive, he took out his phone, jabbed at the screen until he found the number.

'. . . Can't answer the phone right now . . .' DS Ritchie's voice sounded strangely unconvincing on the tinny line, but he really needed to talk to someone. He tried Grumpy Bob's number, let it ring and ring. He was about to hang up when it was finally answered, the noise of a busy pub easily identifiable in the background.

'Evening sir. Anything I can do to help?'

Grumpy Bob wasn't a heavy drinker, not by old-school police standards, but there was a point in any pub evening beyond which he'd be unable to pull it back and be an effective member of the team. Judging by the slur in his voice, that point had long since been passed.

'Going to be a busy one tomorrow, Bob. Early start if you can be in.'

'Right you are, sir.' There was a noise much like a man rapidly downing a pint of beer, followed by a muffled belch. 'I'll head home and get some kip then. Was getting a bit bored of the company in here anyway if I'm being honest. What's up? Anything interesting?'

'McClymonts senior and junior. Seems they were up to no good after all. Briefing at seven sharp. I'll fill everyone in then.'

McLean hung up before Grumpy Bob could complain. He hovered his hand over MacBride's number, then sent a text instead. Stared at the screen in surprise when there was no instant reply.

A change in the light dragged his attention around to the rectory. The front door had opened and someone was stepping out. Another person, then another, they clustered around the doorway in that manner people have. Suddenly remembering all the things they want to say now that it's time to go. Before he'd really considered the implications, he'd snatched the keys out of the ignition, climbed out of the car and headed across the road. When he got to the gate and the short path leading up to the door, the conversation was still in full flow.

'You got a minute, Kirsty?'

DS Ritchie looked around as she heard her name. Finally saw him at the gate.

'Sir? I thought you'd gone home.'

'Almost. Just had to check something out first.'

Everyone was looking at him now, so he had no choice but to open the gate and approach them. Mary Currie, the minister, stood in the doorway, flanked by a young man also wearing the black shirt and dog collar that suggested he too was a minister, or maybe a curate. Either that or he'd come to a fancy dress party woefully ill prepared.

'You went back to your old flat, didn't you?' Ritchie met him a few steps up the path. 'Find anything interesting?'

'If you need a lift home, I can fill you in on the way.'

Ritchie looked back to the group, standing just a few paces away. 'Actually, Daniel already offered to drive me.'

McLean followed Ritchie's gaze back to the front door as the young minister stepped forward into the light.

'Tony. Good to see you again.' He held out a hand to be shaken. McLean took the proffered hand, expecting a limp wrist. He was surprised by a firm, dry shake.

'You'll know Mary.' Daniel assumed the task of making introductions as if it were the most natural thing in the world. He gestured with an open hand towards a couple who had been standing to one side looking awkward. 'This is Eric and Wanda.'

'Are we all going to stand around on my front doorstep all night?' Mary Currie cut in to the conversation. 'Only it's getting a bit chill and I wouldn't want to have to put the heating on.'

'Sorry, Mary. I'll just run Kirsty home. Won't be long.'

'You stay out as long as you want, Daniel. I'm not your mother.'

Even in the poor light, McLean saw the embarrassment blush the young curate's face. He pulled a set of car keys out of his pocket to cover it, turned to the couple. 'You two want a lift too?'

'Gotta go, sir. Unless it's really important?' The question in Ritchie's voice was unmistakeable, as was the hope his answer would be no. Seeing all these people with their life outside of work did put things in perspective.

‘No, you go home. But we’ve an early start tomorrow. Briefing at seven, OK?’

Ritchie nodded her agreement and she, Daniel, Eric and Wanda headed off into the night.

‘Should I be worried about those two?’ McLean turned as he asked the question, the light spilling from the hallway giving the minister a pale yellow halo.

‘Young love will ever run its course.’ Mary Currie smiled at him like an indulgent parent. ‘You want a cup of tea? The kettle’s not long on.’

McLean had never been inside the rectory before, and was surprised to find it not unlike any other home. It smelled old, much like his grandmother’s house, but it was warm and bright and welcoming. There were occasional reminders that this was a place where someone religious lived – a discreet cross hanging by the coat rack in the front hall, a couple of pictures that might have looked more fitting in a seminary – but by and large it was just homely.

He followed the minister through to the back of the house and a large kitchen. Judging by the mismatch of chairs arranged around an old table, this was where the evening’s Bible class had taken place. Except it wasn’t really a Bible class, he could see that now. Just a bunch of people looking for answers. Or maybe some company.

‘Roof should be finished by the end of the month. Then we can get shot of that scaffolding. Start holding services again.’

‘I didn’t realise it was that bad.’

'Oh it is. There's probably more steel inside than out. Still, thanks to your generosity it'll all be done soon.'

McLean wasn't sure why he felt uncomfortable about that. He'd given them money because he liked the building, not what it represented. 'DS Rit . . . Kirsty's doing very well these days,' he said by way of a change of subject. 'Not sure what you get up to in your sessions, but it seems to be working for her.'

'I think that probably has more to do with Daniel than me.'

'Daniel. Of course.' McLean accepted a mug of tea, noticing it had milk in it already.

'Oh to be young and in love. It's sweet, really.'

'He's all right, I take it?'

'Is that paternal concern I hear in your voice, Inspector?' Mary Currie gave him a wicked grin. 'Just teasing. And yes, since you ask, Daniel's all right. Earnest, but then I was too when I was his age. He's not long finished his training, looking for a parish to go and do good things in. The bishop already offered him a rural one, but he says he wants to work in the city.'

'Very earnest, then. I look forward to meeting him when he's in less of a rush sometime.'

'Do I detect the sign of a challenge being laid down?'

'I don't share your faith.' McLean shook his head. 'If I'm being honest it's the whole notion of faith I have a problem with. Doesn't really square with being a detective. I gave up accepting things at face value a long time ago.'

'So like your grandmother.' There was that wry smile again, as if the minister could see right through his facade. It wouldn't have surprised him.

'How's your house guest settling in?' she asked. The change of subject took him by surprise.

'Rose? Fine, I guess. Don't see much of her except in passing.'

'That's a very generous thing you did, letting her stay.'

'Not as if I haven't got the space. And she helped me when Emma was at her worst. I owe her that much. She's a good cook, too. If she stays much longer I might start getting fat.' McLean patted at his stomach. 'There'll be something wholesome and hearty waiting for me when I get in, I've no doubt. Told her she doesn't need to, but I can't exactly stop her.'

'And it beats a takeaway curry, I expect.'

McLean nodded his agreement, envying Grumpy Bob his pint or two down the pub. 'I should probably be getting home anyway. Early start tomorrow.' He stood up, the un-drunk mug of tea still sitting on the table in front of him.

'Yes, I heard you tell Kirsty. Dawn raid, is it?' The minister stood as well, accepting that their all-too-brief conversation was over.

'Nothing so glamorous, I'm afraid. Just a long day of stuff I can't really talk about.'

'Police secrets. Kirsty's just the same. You're very lucky to have her.'

'Trust me. I know. Don't think I don't appreciate it.'

'I'm sure you do, Tony. But don't forget to tell her from time to time. It's nice to have your efforts recognised.'

McLean smiled, nodded, unsure he could really say anything to that. It was true, and he was as guilty as the next man of taking his team for granted. Compliments from higher up the greasy pole were so rare these days, he'd all but forgotten how much good a little well-earned praise could do.

The first thing he noticed when he opened the back door was the absence of cats. It wasn't even as if not seeing any immediately in front of him on entering was all that strange, and yet somehow as he walked through the short passageway from the door to the kitchen, McLean knew that they weren't there. Or rather, just one was there.

Mrs McCutcheon's cat looked up at him from a spot in front of the Aga she hadn't been able to occupy for a few weeks now. McLean scanned the rest of the room, but Madame Rose's familiars were nowhere to be seen. Neither was the medium herself. The smell in the kitchen suggested she had left something edible behind, however. A quick look in the plate-warming oven revealed enough cassoulet to feed an army, and a half-dozen baked potatoes. Not exactly classic fare for a warm August night, but very welcome all the same.

'Surprised you didn't go with them,' McLean said to Mrs McCutcheon's cat, as he searched around for oven gloves. Only when he dumped the casserole dish on the kitchen table did he notice the post piled up against the pepper grinder in the middle. A couple of letters bore the ominous mark of his solicitors; someone was still trying to persuade his grandmother to take out a credit card at an eye-wateringly usurious rate of interest even though she'd been dead two years and more; and the electricity bill needed paying soon, judging by the red-printed 'final reminder' on the envelope. There were two others in the stack: a plain white letter with no stamp or postmark, just the word 'Tony' in neat block capitals; and a postcard, its edges battered and corners folded. The image on the front was of a Japanese temple and the handwriting on the back brought a gentle leap to his heart even before he read the words.

Not many with us now, and those last few are often reluctant to go. It's getting easier though. Spent some months in a monastery here. You should visit it some day. Can't get much further away, so I must start coming home soon.

It was signed with that familiar looping E, so stylised it could almost be a K. McLean propped it up against the other, unopened mail and set about spooning some food on to a plate. Mrs McCutcheon's cat looked up as the smell of sausage casserole filled the room, but she didn't leap on to the table to help herself. No doubt confident there would be plenty going spare later.

The fridge yielded a cold beer and as he poured it, McLean felt a little twinge of guilt at the mug of tea he'd left behind in the rectory. He pushed it aside, instead savouring the bitter flavour of the ale. Butter melting in his baked potato, a couple of mouthfuls of delicious stew, and then he reached for the plain white envelope.

Inside, a single sheet of paper was almost covered in dense, neatly written script. It didn't surprise him to find that Madame Rose was a fountain pen and ink person, or possibly even a freshly cut quill and ink one.

My Dear Tony, it began.

It is with a sense of deep shame that I feel I must confess to having abused your most generous hospitality. It is true that I turned to you when I felt there was no one else to whom I could turn, and it is true that I was recently attacked in a most grievous and personal manner. The danger to myself was, however, never quite so severe as I might have intimated, certainly not physically. My familiars were threatened, this is true. One poor soul was lost, as you know. My gratitude to you for giving the others safe haven knows no bounds.

But I myself was never in great danger. The fire was of course an inconvenience, a difficulty that took a little time to overcome. And that is all I really needed, time to bring my own resources to bear on the problem. It has been many years since I have been challenged in the manner I have recently been challenged – I will not name it directly as I know you yet have difficulty admitting to the existence of such things; our conversation the other night reminded me of that. Suffice to say I am not without my own resources and these have now been brought to bear. I am confident both that the threat has been neutralised, and that your generosity has been rewarded in the process.

The physical face of my troubles was a development company, run by a father and son with whom I believe you are acquainted. You will know too the fate that has befallen them. In the grand scheme of things, they were but petty criminals dabbling in affairs far greater than they could possibly have comprehended. The unravelling of their little empire will reflect well on you should you so desire, though knowing the boy your grandmother raised, I suspect you will pass any glory on to those around you.

There is one more player in this sorry tale, the one who

engineered this situation in a bid to oust me from my position in this great and ancient city. I have taken steps to neutralise this usurper and life will soon return to normal.

I thank you for my time under your roof and your protection. You do not know it, but you have powerful friends. Should you ever require my assistance, you need only ask and it will be freely given.

Yours in gratitude,
Rose

McLean stared at the letter, trying to make sense of it. One fact kept coming back as he stirred his half-forgotten cassoulet around the plate. It was the McClymonts who had been trying to get Madame Rose out of her house, develop the whole block into cheap flats. They'd killed the cat, set fire to the chippy and betting shop. Probably even shoved the shit through her letterbox, and then later his.

And now they were dead.

He pulled out his phone, tapped away at the screen until he found what he was looking for. Keyed in a message and sent it off to all the officers on his team. He'd told them the morning briefing would be at seven sharp. He hoped Grumpy Bob's head wasn't too sore to make it in for six.

54

'Doesn't look like there's anyone in, sir.'

DC MacBride stood on tiptoe, peering in through the grubby window of the offices of McClymont Developments. At seven in the morning it was hardly surprising, though there were signs of life at some of the other businesses on the industrial estate. The car park that had been more than half full when last they had come here had barely any cars in it at the moment, and most of those were police.

'Break down the door.'

'Umm . . . we don't have a warrant, sir.' Worry painted itself clearly over MacBride's face.

'I can smell fire. Sure of it. Can't you?'

The worry didn't go away, but the detective constable nodded, scurrying off to instruct a couple of uniforms. It was only a moment's work to smash the lock and force their way in.

The first thing McLean noticed was the smell. Not burning, but something rotten and mouldering. It hadn't been there the last time, he was sure of that, but now the air tasted as if it had been trapped in a bin.

'What is that?' Beside him, MacBride covered his mouth with the back of his hand, squinting as if the fetid stench was attacking his eyes.

'No idea, but it's not good. Come on.'

They went through to the offices, and McLean stopped at Ms Grainger's desk. The elderly computer was still there, and the fax machine. When he pulled open the drawers though, they were all empty. Glancing around the room he couldn't see much different, but then it had never struck him as a place actually used to conduct business. Not building development, at least.

'Go check those computer boxes, Constable.' McLean watched as MacBride scurried out of the room, then went over to the table where the plans for his tenement had been laid out. They were still there and he leafed through them, wondering again how the planning department had ever passed them. Another puzzle to add to the mix, though proving that any bribe had either been offered or accepted would be tricky. Something for Serious and Organised to worry about, not him.

Running a hand over the printed paper moved it slightly, revealing other plans underneath. He rolled away the fate that would now no longer befall his old home and peered at what the McClymonts had been planning for somewhere else. Except that it wasn't a building plan. The sheet pinned to the drawing board was a city street map, black and white, showing an area centred on Waverley station and spreading out to Leith Docks in the north-east, Cramond Brig in the north-west, Sighthill and Craigmillar in the south-west and south-east. Points on the map marked his tenement block in Newington, Madame Rose's terrace house on Leith Walk, but they weren't the only sites. Others dotted the map, and peering close McLean saw his grandmother's house among them. Faint lines traced from one point to another, scarcely visible in the poor light filtering into the office through the grubby window. He ran a finger along them, trying to make some sense out of the pattern. There was something circular about it, but jagged too. One point stood out, ringed in pencil. To the west of the city, but just inside the bypass. McLean was peering at it, trying to remember what was there, when MacBride returned.

'The boxes are still there, sir. One of the vans has gone, though.'

'Have we got an address for Ms Grainger?' McLean asked the question even though he knew that she wouldn't be there. Before the detective constable could answer, his phone rang. A glance at the screen showed a number only recently added to his address book. He took the call knowing what it would be about even before he was told. The conversation was mercifully short.

'That was DCS Chambers. I've got to go and meet him in Newington.'

MacBride didn't question, just nodded his acceptance. 'I'll get this processed, sir. Don't imagine we'll find anything, mind you.'

'I don't suppose we will. But get some of those uniforms to go door to door round the other businesses, OK? See if anyone saw the van leaving. Better yet if they've got any security cameras.'

MacBride nodded, tapping notes into his tablet computer. McLean was about to leave, when he remembered the map. He pulled it off the drawing board, spread it out between them and tapped on the point that had caught his attention before. 'One other thing. Get someone to go and have a look here. Might be nothing, but it was important to someone.'

'You really know how to complicate things, don't you McLean.'

Detective Chief Superintendent Tim Chambers of the National Crime Agency was less friendly at eight in the morning than he had been the first time McLean had met him. Perhaps being dragged along to a six o'clock briefing wasn't how he'd intended starting his day, but he'd seemed interested in the information both about Joe McClymont's stolen car and the computers. They'd agreed to hit the offices and the building site at the same time. Unlike the offices across town, the building site appeared not to have been touched since McLean had visited it the evening before.

'Not sure what's complicated about it, sir. I told you there were computers here, and here they are.'

They were standing in the middle of the Portakabin, perhaps a little closer together than was comfortable for two men who didn't know each other well. There wasn't much choice in the matter, as the rest of the room was filled with large flat-screen monitors, sleek modern computer boxes and mile upon mile of cabling. The lights McLean had seen flashing the night before were dead now, but the rack of servers that had been producing them looked very expensive. More the kind of thing you'd find in the basement of a multinational technology firm than a building site lock-up in Newington.

'You any idea what these are all for?' McLean watched as an NCA technician inspected the nearest computer.

Another was going through a pile of mobile phones, all plugged in to the server array and forming some kind of wireless network link, if he understood these things correctly. Maybe he should have stayed at the company offices and sent MacBride over here. It seemed more suited to the detective constable's expertise, somehow.

'We won't know until we've got them powered up. Whole thing's dead as a doornail at the moment.' The nearest technician turned in his seat to answer the question.

'Everything? Even that server thingy over there?' McLean nodded in its direction.

'Yup. There's power to the sockets, but nothing's plugged in.'

'There was last night. There were lights flickering.'

'How did you even know they were in here?' Chambers shook his head before McLean could answer. 'No, don't tell me. I can guess.'

'I have a key to the front door, sir. I'm probably the only person alive who owns a share of this site. I've every right to come in here.'

'Not in here, you don't.' Chambers nodded in the general direction of the Portakabin wall. 'We'll gloss over that for now. We've enough from the stolen car to get a backdated search warrant. Just need to find out what's on these computers now.'

'Umm . . . that might not be easy, sir.' The technician sitting at the monitor had turned his attention to the computer itself, pulled something out of the tiny metal box that looked more like it should have come out of a catering academy stove at the end of the first lesson. A faint whiff of singeing filled the air.

'I take it they're not meant to be like that,' McLean said.

'Nope. It's fried. Someone's got to these, and recently judging by the smell. They're all solid-state memory too. Don't expect we'll get anything off them.'

'Shit. And you didn't find anything at the offices?' Chambers turned to McLean, his anger low and threatening.

'There wasn't much there to start with. One of the vans and the company secretary's cleaned out her desk. I'm sorry, sir. This wasn't exactly high priority. If you'd wanted us to secure these places when the McClymonts died, you should have said.'

Chambers kicked his foot hard against a stained carpet tile. 'I know. That's why I'm so pissed off, really. It's not your fault, it's ours. We've been treating Joe and old Jock like a couple of country bumpkins, when they were much more sophisticated than that.'

McLean recalled Madame Rose's letter, still lying on his kitchen table. The more he considered its contents, the more he wished he'd paid more attention to the acerbic Ms Grainger. Jock and Joe McClymont were perhaps not quite country bumpkins, but they weren't as sophisticated as their operation might have suggested. Something, or perhaps someone, had been protecting them, maybe directing them, and just possibly using them to an end the NCA and Police Scotland would neither understand nor believe. He wasn't sure he believed it himself, and certainly didn't understand.

'What have you got on the company secretary, Ms Grainger?'

'Grainger?' Chambers stopped destroying the carpet tile with his foot for a moment. 'She's not a part of this.

We profiled her at the start of the investigation. Pegged her as just an employee on the legitimate side of the business.'

'Do you know where she is now?'

Chambers pulled out his phone and tapped the screen a couple of times, lifted it to his ear. It looked very impressive; McLean had a hard enough time trying to find the number pad on his so he could dial out at all. On the other hand, there was probably only one number Chambers ever had to call. He had minions to do everything else for him.

'Grainger. Where is she now?' That he didn't introduce himself or ask who had answered reinforced the idea. Chambers was a man used to being obeyed without question, and if the frown wrinkling across his forehead was anything to go by, a man not used to having things go awry.

'You're sure of that?' A short pause. 'Empty? Nothing at all?' He tapped the screen to end the call and slipped the phone back into his pocket.

'Let me guess. She's disappeared.'

'Without a trace.' Chambers scratched his head like a cartoon character baffled by the sudden appearance of a wall. 'And I mean without a trace. It's like she never existed. Computer records, surveillance photos, tax records. I've got my IT guys double-checking it's not a glitch, but . . .'

The detective chief superintendent fell silent. McLean suppressed the urge to clap him on the back and say 'welcome to my world'. He had a suspicion it wouldn't have helped.

His own phone broke the slightly awkward silence. McLean pulled it out, peered at the screen. DC MacBride calling.

'Constable?'

'Can you spare a moment, sir? It's about that site on the map you asked me to look into.'

McLean glanced around the Portakabin. 'Reckon we're about done here. Why?'

'I'm there at the moment. Think you might want to see what we found.'

He'd seen the building site many times before. You could hardly miss it, sitting behind a rotting security fence just off the city bypass. Weeds had begun to reclaim the parking area, pushing up through the tarmac like triffids. The main building itself was an unfinished mess of concrete pillars and boarded-up windows, reinforcement bars poking out at odd angles like rusty broken bones through grey-green skin. The only sign advertised a security firm, the image below the logo suggesting both cameras and dogs, although McLean could see no evidence of either as they pulled up at the gates. A uniform constable approached, peered uncertainly at DCS Chambers in the driving seat, then nodded as he saw McLean.

'I'll get the gate, sir. You want to go round the back, where the deliveries would've been made.'

The rough ground and horrible crunching noises as unidentified objects hit the underside made McLean glad they'd come in Chambers' car and not his little Alfa. They parked up in the shade of the vast building, alongside a couple of squad cars and what appeared to be a newly arrived forensic services van.

'What's going on?' McLean asked as soon as he tracked down DC MacBride. The constable was standing by a small service door let into one of the much larger roller doors that lined the loading area.

'Worked out what the mark on the map was, sir. This place was supposed to be the biggest shopping mall in Scotland, but the developers went bust in the crash and it's been like this ever since.'

'You got a warrant to search this building, Detective Constable?' Chambers asked.

'Would you believe it wasn't locked, sir? Not even the gates back there.' MacBride nodded in the direction of the perimeter fence. 'There was a chain looped round, but no padlock. And this door opened when I tried it.'

Chambers looked unconvinced, but McLean could well believe it. If this was something to do with the McClymonts' operation, then chances were it had been hidden away by something much more effective than locks and chains.

'What exactly have we got here?' he asked.

'Best look for yourselves. Just don't touch anything, aye? Dr Cairns is on her way.' MacBride stood aside to let them in. Chambers led the way, ducking his head to avoid braining himself on the low doorway. McLean followed and almost walked into the back of the detective chief superintendent, who had stopped still just a pace inside. Half-skipping to one side, McLean's eyes focused on the room, and he understood why.

It was a vast area, designed so that articulated lorries could drive in, reverse up to loading bays, unload and then drive straight out again. The roof high overhead was a lattice of beams, with clear windows in the steel roofing sheets the only source of illumination. It was enough light to see a collection of cars that wouldn't have looked out of place in the most expensive garage forecourts in the city.

'Bloody hell.' Chambers took a couple more steps until he was standing alongside a sleek-looking Bentley. He reached out to touch it, then stopped at the last minute, shoved his hands in his pockets.

McLean did a quick count, made it to twenty-four before he was distracted. All the cars were new, though some were beginning to attract dust. They were all expensive, mostly German or high-end British as far as he could tell. Their number plates were gone, and over in the far corner a couple of two-post lifts and some heavy-duty mechanic's tool trolleys suggested some kind of workshop.

'How the fuck did we not know about this?' Chambers asked the question to the open space. McLean knew better than to offer an explanation. Let the NCA puzzle that one out for themselves. A few things were beginning to come together in his mind though, and the sight of a high-spec Range Rover at the end of one of the rows of cars left him with a particularly unpleasant suspicion.

'Think we should leave this to forensics, sir.'

Chambers turned to face him. 'What? Oh. Yes. You're right. Don't want to contaminate this any more than we have already.'

'Best not to,' McLean said. 'And besides, there's someone I need to talk to. Think you should meet her too.'

55

Charlie Christie had obviously found solace in the bottle of wine McLean and Ritchie had left her with the afternoon before, but now it looked like it was getting its revenge. Her face had a pallid green shade to it, with dark bags under her eyes and no make-up to hide them. She wore a full-length towelling dressing gown, squinting as if she'd only just recently crawled out of bed. Glancing at his watch, McLean realised it was just gone ten, so chances were she had.

'You again?' Christie looked at McLean, then shifted her glance across to where Chambers stood beside him. 'Who's your boyfriend?'

'Detective Chief Superintendent Chambers. National Crime Agency.' Chambers showed his warrant card, eliciting the sort of response he no doubt had been hoping for. Christie pulled her dressing gown tight, even though it hadn't exactly been revealing anything.

'Please, come in. I've got some coffee on.'

McLean trod the familiar path to the kitchen at the back, this time with Chambers rather than Ritchie in tow. Christie busied herself with mugs and milk, pouring fine-smelling coffee from a jug that would have been enough to supply half of CID. How a lone, single mother thought she was going to drink it all he had no idea. Her hangover must have been of epic proportions.

'You're not overly fond of Ms Grainger, the company secretary,' he said after they'd all settled at the breakfast bar.

'Company secretary? That what she's calling herself these days? Witch wouldn't know shorthand if it bit her on her scaly arse.'

'Are you saying she wasn't the secretary, Miss Christie?' Chambers cradled his mug of coffee like a small kitten. 'What was she then?'

'Joe always introduced her as a partner. She turned up round about the time his mum died. Sort of inveigled herself into the business.'

'Inveigled?' McLean asked the question, but he could see by Chambers' one raised eyebrow that he'd been thinking it too.

'Mind, this was a good few years back, when me and Ben were at uni. I only saw Joe from time to time then. I remember the funeral though.'

'She was there? Ms Grainger?'

'Oh, aye. She was there. Holding up old Jock like she'd been a family friend all his life. Poor man took Cat's death hard. I didn't see either of them for maybe a year after that, and when I did, Ms Grainger was in there with her feet under the table, just about running the place.'

'You think she and Mr McClymont senior . . .?' McLean let the question tail off as a look of horror spread across Christie's face.

'Good God no. Jock would never so much as look at another woman after Cat died. Doted on his son, mind you.'

McLean was about to press further. The story Christie

was painting was quite at odds with what Grainger had told him herself. But Chambers cut in, changing the subject with no subtlety whatsoever and even less sensitivity.

'The car McClymont was driving. Had it long, had he?'

For a moment Christie was taken aback. McLean imagined it couldn't be easy thinking swiftly with the mother of all headaches.

'His car? What's that got to do with anything?' she asked.

'It's part of an ongoing investigation,' Chambers said. 'We're fairly sure it was stolen.'

'Oh.' Christie swallowed a mouthful of coffee, holding the mug up to her neck like a shield. 'Well, no. He'd not had it long. Joe never did keep his cars long. Always trading them in for the latest model.'

'Do you know where he got them from?'

A short pause before answering, as if she were trying to work out where this was going. McLean almost pitied her. 'Never occurred to me to ask. He gave me my Range Rover what, four months ago? I just assumed it came from the local dealership.'

'You've got all the documents. Registration and so forth?' McLean asked.

'Of course. Why?'

McLean looked sideways at Chambers. He didn't know the man, had never worked with him before. Wasn't really sure if this counted as working with him now. On the other hand, he was a chief superintendent, so could make life awkward if he wanted. Even more so than Duguid and Brooks.

'I'd like one of my forensic specialists to have a look at

it, if that's OK?' He decided on the less confrontational route. After all, sometimes his hunches didn't play out. Just not often.

'Umm. OK. I guess. Will they need to take it away? Only I've not got anything else to take the girls to school in.'

Or go to Waitrose for smoked salmon and organic fair-trade chocolate bars. 'She should be able to look at it here. I'll get someone to phone and arrange a time.'

Chambers had been silent through the exchange, but the expression on his face suggested he didn't like not knowing what was going on. He was about to say something, but Christie beat him to it.

'There was one thing I thought a bit odd.' She left the thread dangling. Perhaps the coffee was working its magic.

'Go on,' McLean said.

'Well, you see, Joe used to take his dad up north a lot. Every couple of months, at least that I know of. And he'd always drive those flash cars of his. I went with them once. Me and the girls. I told you about it, remember?'

McLean nodded, unwilling to break her flow now that she was talking.

'Well, we all went up in a Mercedes estate that time. I remember it was like a barn inside, and all plush leather and stuff. The girls loved it. Only, we came home on the train after a week. It was all getting too much, and I thought Joe needed his time alone.'

'So what was the odd thing?' McLean asked, sensing Chambers about to jump in.

'Well, it's . . . I don't know. I never saw that car again, and far as I can tell Joe came home by train too. Not the first time, either. I picked him up from the station a couple of times, off the Inverness train, when I was sure he'd driven north.'

They let themselves out not long afterwards, leaving Christie to her coffee and hangover. She seemed to have hit the numb stage of grief; dealing with the deaths of two people who had been close to her couldn't have been easy. McLean made a note to make sure a family liaison officer accompanied Amanda Parsons when she went round to check over the Range Rover. Quite what having her one solid link to Joe McClymont taken away would do to her didn't bear thinking about.

'What was that all about, McLean? Duguid told me you were prone to flights of fancy, but I don't think I've ever seen—'

'Do you know the story about the wheelbarrow thief, sir?'

'I . . . what?'

'I don't remember the full details, but it was something along these lines. Bloke works in a factory, and every evening when his shift's over he wheels a barrow full of straw out through the gate. The security guards knew him, and every day they'd check the barrow, making sure he wasn't stealing stuff from the factory and hiding it in the straw. He never was, so they'd let him through.

'Come his retirement, the bloke finishes his shift and leaves. On his way out, one of the guards stops him and asks: "Five years you came and went. We were sure you were stealing something, but we never found out how."

'The old man looked at the guard and smiled. "You

always raked through the straw, every evening as I was going home. The thing is, I wasn't smuggling anything in the wheelbarrow. It was the barrow itself, see?"'

'Not sure I see your point. McClymont was a drug dealer, not a wheelbarrow salesman.'

'It's just a story, sir. The idea is the old boy was hiding something in plain sight. We've been looking at McClymont the wrong way, treating him like a drug smuggler. What if he was just a car thief?'

'A car thief? That not a bit low rent?'

'Not when you're nicking stuff worth fifty grand or more. Give it a new identity, ship it overseas. I've heard there's a big market for high-end motors in the Far East. Africa's quite keen on them too. The job they did on McClymont's own motor, they could've sold it here and nobody would have known better.'

'Why take them north? Why not ship them out of Rosyth or Leith? Or drive them down to London and stick them through the Channel Tunnel?'

'I think that's something for your lot to figure out, don't you? The point is he was taking cars north but coming home by train. If our forensic expert's right, and I'm inclined to trust her, then the cars were ringers. That car,' he pointed at the all-too-familiar-looking Range Rover parked on the driveway in front of the house, 'is a ringer too. I'm fairly certain it really belongs to Detective Superintendent Duguid, as it happens. Or at least his insurance company.'

Chambers stared at the car as if he'd never seen one in his life before. 'This? But surely there's thousands like it out there.'

'Maybe. But they don't all have a dent in the back door there. I saw Duguid reverse into one of the Transit vans back at the station, six months ago? Something like that. Dent in exactly the same spot.'

Chambers said nothing for a while, just kept looking at the back of the Range Rover and stroking his chin.

'OK. Since you seem to have all the answers. Where does Ms Grainger fit into all this, then?'

'Brains of the outfit?' McLean offered, getting a sceptical look in response.

'Look, did you ever meet the McClymonts? Speak to them?'

Chambers shook his head.

'Well I did. Just the once, but it was probably enough. I didn't get the impression they were the types to think out of the box much. The plans they had for my place were unimaginative, just trying to cram as many flats into the space as possible. Probably as cheaply as possible too. For all I know, they might have been dealing drugs, might have been doing anything they could to get money. Laundering it through the development company. But the moment they died, Grainger does a runner? Sounds like she knew what they were up to at the very least.'

'And now she's disappeared completely. Fucking marvellous.'

'Ah, so you've decided to show up for work after all. You do know you're supposed to be conducting a murder investigation, right?'

McLean had barely stepped through the back door to the station before the words rang out across the hallway.

Detective Superintendent Duguid stood by the stairs, his face dark and threatening. A couple of uniforms chatting nearby looked around nervously before scurrying off, not wanting to get caught in the crossfire. McLean glanced at his watch, already knowing that it was approaching noon.

'Actually I was in at half-five this morning, sir, preparing a briefing for six. I'd have invited you along, but it was all a bit last-minute. Didn't think you'd appreciate a call that early.'

Duguid's scowl deepened, the tic of a vein on his forehead a sure indicator that someone was going to get a tongue-lashing or worse.

'What's so bloody important it takes precedence over two dead bodies?'

'My "friends" the McClymonts, sir.' McLean made bunny ears with his fingers. 'Seems there was more to their business than even the NCA suspected.'

'What are you going on about? Since when were you working on that case anyway?'

'Since you and the DCC sent me up to Inverness to ID the bodies, sir. Since I got a call from forensics and found out the car was stolen.'

'Stolen? How?' Duguid's rage bled away, replaced by bewilderment. 'When?'

'I don't have the full details, sir. As you can see, I've just got back in. I'm hoping there's a full forensic report waiting for me in my office. Once I've had a chance to look at it I can bring everyone up to speed. Oh, and I might have found your old Range Rover, by the way.'

Duguid's mouth had dropped open, giving McLean an unenviable view of the detective superintendent's chipped and yellowing teeth. He looked like he was struggling to process all the information that had barged its way into a brain fully prepared for tearing off a strip from whomever he could find.

'Wh—' Duguid began, but before he could say anything more, the back door to the station banged open. McLean turned to see a worried-looking DC MacBride tapping wildly at his tablet. At the same moment as the constable looked up, McLean's phone pinged a message. Duguid's did the same a second later.

'Sir. Ah, sirs.' MacBride looked momentarily confused, then rallied. 'I've just messaged you. Sorry. Need to get back to Sighthill. We've found another body.'

56

The building looked nothing special from the outside, much the same as McClymont Developments across the car park. Tucked into the far corner, close to the railway line, its windows were boarded up and a faded 'To let' sign hung at a drunken angle from the frontage. The only way in was through a solid metal door set into a much larger roller shutter concealing a loading bay beyond. DS Ritchie must have seen him coming, as she met him out past the edge of the police tape boundary.

'How did anyone even know to look in here?' McLean asked. He'd parked a good distance away from the squad cars and forensic vans. The car park might have been large, but the individual bays were narrow.

'Stuart had some of the uniforms go door to door round the other businesses, like you asked, sir. Overzealous constable knocked on this one even though it's obviously empty. Found it wasn't locked and thought he'd check it out before calling the letting agent. He found . . . well, I'm not really sure how to describe it. A body, for certain.' DS Ritchie had more of a spring in her step than McLean could remember seeing in a while, no doubt at the prospect of getting her teeth into a particularly interesting case. Either that or Daniel hadn't made it home to the rectory as early as might be expected of a man of the cloth.

Shaking the idea from his head, he followed her across

the car park and ducked under the crime-scene tape, almost immediately receiving a complaining cough from the nearest scene of crime officer.

'You'll be wanting to put on some overalls if you're going in there.' The SOCO herself was dressed in a full white boiler suit, hood pulled up tight over her hair. McLean could only tell it was a she because her face mask hung around her neck on its elastic string. She was sitting in the back of one of the Transit vans, munching on a sandwich, but put it carefully back in its Tupperware box before reaching around and pulling out white paper overalls and something that looked a bit like a cross between a shower cap and the bag you brought your curry home in.

'Grubby in there, is it?' he asked as he passed a pair of overboots to Ritchie.

'Quite the opposite. Place is cleaner than a Labrador's dinner dish. Doubt we'll find anything in there unless you lot traipse it in. Could do without the hassle of working out what's what.' The SOCO picked up her sandwich and took another bite, conversation over.

McLean waited until they had reached the door before climbing into the paper suit and slipping the overshoes on. He snapped on a pair of latex gloves for good measure before ducking into the darkness beyond. It was a large loading area, as might be expected for such a place. Looking around, however, he started to see what the SOCO had meant. In marked contrast to the dust and grime of McClymont Developments, it was spotlessly clean. More like the sort of laboratory where they build satellites than a storage room for a firm of electricians. Arc lights overhead reflected off a smooth floor that squeaked under his feet as he walked to the far side and an open doorway. A bunny-suited SOCO was kneeling by the door, brushing at the frame with a fingerprint kit. She looked up as his shadow passed over her, and McLean recognised the face of Amanda Parsons.

'Didn't expect to see you here. Thought you were doing the cars across town.'

Parsons grinned. 'They're no' going anywhere. And we're a bit short-staffed right now, with all these bodies you keep finding. I've got fingerprint training. Overtime's always handy.'

'Well I don't think there'll be a problem with that. The pathologist here?' McLean asked.

'In there.' Parsons cocked a head towards the entrance.

'You been in?'

'No. Not sure I want to, from what I've been hearing.'

'I'd best see for myself then,' McLean said, and stepped through.

'Good Christ. What is this place?'

McLean stood just inside the open door, staring upon a scene that might have been from a modern horror movie. Half a dozen intensive care beds were arranged in a semicircle, each attended by their own motley collection of life-support machinery. Much of the kit seemed last generation, or perhaps older, but the effect was chilling regardless, especially given the setting. This was a disused warehouse in a bad part of town, after all. Not exactly the Western General Hospital.

Of the six beds, five were obviously unoccupied, the machinery pushed neatly to the walls at the head of each.

The last bed was obscured by the city pathologist and his assistant deep in discussion about the body they were examining. McLean was about to head over and see what all the fuss was about when a voice distracted him.

'It gets better. Come have a look at this.' He turned to see Jemima Cairns, dressed in the full bunny suit so beloved of the forensic services. It never ceased to amaze him how they could recognise each other in that get-up, but somehow they managed. She led him through another door into a smaller room, fitted out like a research laboratory.

'Some of this stuff's better than the kit we've got back at HQ.' Dr Cairns picked up a microscope and peered at the manufacturer's logo on the base.

'Expensive?'

'Very. Well, some of it.' She put the microscope back, moved down the bench to where a smooth-sided box with a smoked Perspex cover sat. Clicking open the cover revealed an empty shell. 'Most of it's mock-ups, though. The sort of thing they bring along to medical research conferences.'

'So this is all a sham then?' McLean walked across to the wall freezers, reached out to open one then stopped. 'Can I?'

'Knock yourself out. They're all empty. We've dusted the place for prints, too. Only one set so far and they look like they belong to the victim.' Dr Cairns nodded at the tall freezer. 'He opened that. Doesn't seem to have touched anything else.'

'Nothing at all?'

'Not a thing. This place is as clean as I've ever seen. Surgically clean.'

'What about through there?' McLean pointed back to the larger room, where the beds were, and the body.

'Much the same. Oh, we'll keep looking, but we've not found anything yet. Got to hand it to whoever did this. They know how to sterilise a crime scene.'

'So people keep telling me, but I've not even seen the body yet.'

Dr Cairns raised an eyebrow. 'You've not?'

'Only just arrived. I was going to have a look when you dragged me in here.'

'Sorry. I didn't realise.'

'No worries. Never hurts to look at the whole scene anyway. Sometimes better to do that first, before you even look at the body.'

Cairns said nothing as McLean pulled open the freezer door. As she'd told him, it was empty. It didn't appear to be switched on, either. He walked slowly down the narrow aisle between the spotlessly clean work benches. Stuck out a finger and ran it over the nearest flat surface, then inspected his fingertip for dust. There was none.

'What do you make of it?' he asked.

'This? If I didn't know better I'd say someone was making a movie.'

McLean paused in picking up a pipette. Could it be that simple? Had they stumbled upon some film set that nobody knew about?

'It's not though,' Dr Cairns said. 'A movie set, that is. There's nowhere to put the cameras, for one thing. And then there's the body, of course. That's real enough, not a prop.'

'It's still a set though, a sham. Not a real medical lab?'

'Not one I'd want to work in. Like I say, most of this kit's fake.'

'But why would someone go to all that effort?'

'That's your department, Inspector. Not mine.' Dr Cairns scratched at her forehead where the tight-fitting hood of her overalls pressed against her skin, then gave up and pushed the whole thing back off her head. 'But if I was to hazard a guess, I'd say someone was playing some kind of con. Wouldn't be at all surprised if there wasn't big money involved. This lot must have cost a packet, even if most of it's not real.'

McLean was about to reply, but a familiar face appeared at the door. DS Ritchie's eyes widened in surprise as she saw the set-up.

'They're ready to move the body, sir. Thought you'd want to see it before they do.'

The large room was no less impressive for his having seen the laboratory next door to it. McLean wondered how anyone had managed to get all that machinery in without being noticed, wondered too where it had all come from. These and a dozen other immediate questions fled his mind as he approached the bed and the body lying on it.

He was naked, skinny like a man who hasn't eaten in months, and impossibly pale. Sightless eyes stared up at the ceiling, slightly filmed as if the eyeballs had begun to ossify. His face was cadaverous, mouth hanging open to reveal yellowing teeth. Thinning hair, lank and in need of a cut, hung from his skull and splayed out on the pillow. McLean's first impression was of someone in the first stages of mummification.

'Tony. Good of you to join us.' Angus Cadwallader stood on the far side of the bed, his assistant Tracy at his side. Two technicians hovered behind him with a gurney, ready to take the body away. It seemed a bit unnecessary; they could have just wheeled out the bed he was lying on.

'What have we got here, Angus?' McLean asked. Looking at the face he found it almost impossible to decide if the man had been young or old. His skin had an odd pallor to it, and he looked shrunken, almost as if the bed had begun to swallow him.

'Something very nasty indeed. And I say that as someone who thought he'd seen it all.' Cadwallader reached forward and gently lifted the dead man's arm. As he did so, McLean noticed that it had a cannula inserted into it, a long tube leading away to a machine at the head of the bed.

'See this?' McLean nodded, following Cadwallader's hand as he traced the tube back. It was clear plastic, but there were occasional clots of almost black material in it.

'This is a dialysis machine,' the pathologist continued. 'You'll be familiar with how it works.'

'I thought they usually had two tubes. One out, one back in again.' McLean had a terrible feeling he knew where the conversation was going. He looked back at the man's face again. Not old, quite young, really. Just drained.

'You always were quick on the uptake, Tony. You're quite right. Normally the blood would flow through the machine, which filters out all the unpleasant by-products of metabolism. Then the freshened blood is returned to the body. This . . .' Cadwallader paused for a moment, something McLean couldn't recall his old friend ever doing at a crime scene before. Normally it was a job to get him to stop talking, such was his enthusiasm at hunting down clues from the recently deceased.

'This machine's been modified. Not sure exactly how, that's something for the technicians to puzzle out. It's taken his blood and . . . well, I'm not entirely sure what it's done with it.'

'So what you're saying is he bled to death.'

'No, what I'm saying, Tony, is he was bled to death. There's a difference. This man has had almost all of the blood drained from him. And slowly, too.'

'Slowly? How so?'

'If it had been quick, if he'd had his throat cut or something, his blood pressure would have dropped fast and his heart would have stopped. Doing it slowly like this dragged it out. He's been placed on the bed very carefully, too. Everything slopes down to this point. It's impossible to drain all the blood out of a body without pumping something in to replace it, but this comes pretty damned close.'

'How long would it take, do you reckon? An hour? Longer?'

'Much longer. This could have taken half a day.'

McLean shuddered, though that might have been because of the chill in the room. 'It'd be painless though, wouldn't it? And he'd have passed out soon enough?'

'That really depends on how slowly the machine was working, but he'd have known what was happening. Jesus, what a horrible thing to do to a person.'

McLean looked from the shrunken, shrivelled body to the snaking tube, the corrupted dialysis machine and then back to the man's face. Clouded eyes stared straight up, as if pleading to heaven for salvation. He followed that gaze to the ceiling, white paint bright in the glare from the arc lights. The shadows of the metal roof beams painted a dark cross directly overhead.

57

'You realise we're going to have to draft in officers from Strathclyde to help make up the numbers? You've no idea what a mess that's going to make of the staffing rosters.'

McLean stood in his usual spot in Duguid's office on the top floor, trying hard to focus on the detective superintendent and not let his thoughts wander out the window. This meeting was a formality, a chore that had to be done before he could get on with the job. As usual there was nowhere for him to sit, and frankly he was happier standing. The same couldn't be said for DCI Brooks, whose hulking presence made the large room seem somehow inadequate.

'Hang the bloody rosters, Charles. We've got a third murder in as many weeks. Nothing simple about any of them. What the fuck's happening to the city that everyone's hacking each other to bits?'

Brooks prowled back and forth as he ranted, his shoes making odd 'chuff chuff chuff' noises on the carpet tiles. It was hot in the office, and sweat sheened the detective chief inspector's shaven head, dripping down into his eyebrows. Occasionally a bead would make it to one of his chins and then break free.

'We should pool our efforts again.'

Brooks stopped mid-turn, his anger focused on McLean.

'You're not really suggesting they're linked are you, McLean? You know how rare serial killers are?'

'It wouldn't surprise me if they were connected, actually. Like you said, three murders in as many weeks, all Category A. That's more than a statistical outlier; it'd be stupid of us not to consider a possible link between them.'

He regretted using the S-word almost as soon as it slipped out of his mouth, but he was tired and it was hot and he was finding it hard to think straight with Brooks moving around like a caged bear. McLean felt the atmosphere in the room chill, though not enough to bring any comfort.

'Both Detective Chief Inspector Brooks and I know how to run a major incident enquiry, McLean.' Duguid's voice was a low rumble like the threat of thunder.

'I'm sorry, sir. I didn't mean to suggest you . . . I only meant there are aspects of all three investigations that can be combined to save time. Like we did before. No point going over the same actions over and over again. It was true when we combined efforts with the Stevenson and Shenks cases. It's even more true now.'

'And you're volunteering to coordinate this, are you?' Brooks asked. McLean resisted the urge to suggest that both senior officers knew how to run a major incident enquiry. The irony would likely have been lost on them.

'If you think a detective inspector is sufficiently senior to be heading up such a thing, then I guess so. I'd have thought the press would expect someone a bit higher up the food chain though.'

'Oh yes. The press. Tell me, how is Jo Dalgliesh these days? I hear you two are getting quite pally.'

It was his weak spot and Brooks knew it. McLean rounded on the DCI, struggling to control the anger that flared up in him. 'If you had any fucking idea—'

'That's enough, McLean.' Duguid's barked words surprised him into silence more effectively than McLean would have thought possible. He looked back at the detective superintendent leaning forward in his chair, elbows on the desk and long-fingered hands pressed together tightly.

'John, you know as well as I do that Dalgliesh is helping us with the Stevenson case. She was the first to notice him missing, she got us access to all his research and she knows more about what he was working on than anyone.'

'She's a bloody menace is what,' Brooks muttered under his breath, but loud enough to be heard.

'I don't think any of us disagree with you there. But she's useful and at the moment she's on our side. I'd quite like to keep things that way for as long as possible.'

Brooks glowered, but said nothing. Duguid must have taken that as a tacit agreement. McLean hoped so, otherwise the DCI really was as stupid as he so often looked.

'OK. I'll front up all three investigations. John, you'll be in overall command of operations. McLean, you and Spence can coordinate. Get a team on to analysing the similarities between each murder.' Duguid slumped back in his seat as if the effort of making such a momentous decision had exhausted him. 'And let's just pray we don't get more bodies turning up any time soon.'

*

'His name's James Whitely. Friends all called him Jim. He was a consultant at the Western General, specialising in paediatric oncology. Worked at the Sick Kids too.'

Running out of room at the station, they'd taken over a corner of the Ben Stevenson major incident room to make a start on the new investigation. DC MacBride had somehow managed to find space for more computers, and a small army of uniforms and admin staff were beginning the process of kicking the investigation into life. Compared to the quiet of the rest of the room, it was a veritable maelstrom of activity.

'Who ID'd him?' McLean asked.

MacBride consulted his tablet. 'One of the pathologists recognised him. Dr MacPhail?'

'And we've had that confirmed? Next of kin?'

'No next of kin, no. But his boss confirmed it, and he's been missing from work over a week.'

McLean stared at the clean whiteboard as a uniform constable pinned a large photograph of Jim Whitely's pale dead face to it with magnets.

'He worked at the Sick Kids, you say. Same as Muriel Shenks?'

'Maureen Shenks, yes.' MacBride swiped at his little screen. 'You think there might be a connection?'

'Two people murdered? No obvious motive or killer for either? Both work at the same place and probably knew each other? I'd be astonished if there weren't.'

'What if he killed her?'

McLean paused before responding, not quite allowing himself to hope it would be that easy. 'Go on,' he said after a while.

'Well, Whitely's body, the way it was found. It's creepy as . . .' MacBride struggled for words.

'Creepy as fuck?' McLean suggested.

'Aye, that. But it could be suicide, couldn't it? I mean, he could've plugged himself into that machine and, I don't know, just let it drain all his blood away?'

McLean tried not to shudder. 'Interesting theory, Constable, and given how improbable his means of death was, it's just possible he did it himself. It had to be someone with a great deal of medical knowledge, after all.' He walked over to the whiteboard, searched around until he found a marker pen and wrote 'suicide?' close to the newly pinned death-mask photograph. All around him there was sudden silence as heads turned to look at what he'd written.

'Is that even possible?' He looked around to see that Detective Sergeant Ritchie had just entered the room and was, like everyone else, staring at the whiteboard.

'To be honest, I've no idea. But it's as good a place as any to start.' McLean addressed the collected police and admin staff, now that he had their undivided attention. 'Assume nothing, but I want this line of enquiry pursued as far as it will go. We need to trace Dr Whitely's movements over the last month. Interview all his work colleagues; I want to know about his state of mind. And talk to everyone who works in that industrial unit too. We need to know who's been in and out of there recently. If there's CCTV, so much the better.'

'You want me to get started on organising all that?' Ritchie asked. McLean could see she wasn't all that keen. Beside him, DC MacBride had already started breaking the problem down and assigning tasks to various members of the team. Most of whom were more senior than him, but seemed happy to defer to his assumed authority.

'Have we got a home address for Whitely?' he asked in a moment when the detective constable paused for breath.

'Here, sir.' MacBride tapped a couple of times on his screen. 'I've sent it to your phone.' Sure enough, the handset vibrated and chimed in his jacket pocket. McLean pulled it out, stared at the address on the screen until it blanked out again. Sciennes. Not far. Just a matter of getting hold of some keys.

'OK, you man the fort here. Get cracking on the suicide angle.' He turned back to DS Ritchie. 'You can come with me. See what kind of a person this Jim Whitely was.'

58

'I thought they paid doctors well these days.'

DS Ritchie stood in the dank hallway of an unremarkable tenement block in the back end of Sciennes, and sniffed. Getting in had been far easier than McLean had hoped; the cheap entry-phone system had long since broken, and the front door had opened to a gentle shove.

'Way the housing market's going, it's probably all he could afford.' He peered at the tarnished brass nameplate on one of the two downstairs flat doors, trying to make out the name in the half-light. It didn't spell 'Whitely', that was for sure.

'I guess it's handy for the Sick Kids.' Ritchie bent to inspect the other door, straightening up quickly when it opened.

'You want summat?' A fat, balding man stood in the open doorway, scratching at a flabby belly that strained to escape from a pair of stained pyjama bottoms. He had a threadbare dressing gown on, but it hung open to reveal rather more than anyone would want to see.

'Detective Sergeant Ritchie.' She produced her warrant card, holding it up for the man to see. 'We're looking for James Whitely's flat.'

'Jim? Top floor. Left-hand side. The blue door.' The fat man twitched his head upwards in the general direction, his jowls wobbling in time with the motion. 'What's he done?'

'You know him well, Mr . . .?' McLean stepped forward from the shadows. The fat man's eyes widened in surprise.

'Here, I ain't done nuthin.'

'I never suggested you had. I was looking for Mr Whitely's flat, but I'm also going to want to talk to everyone who knows him. Seems like you're pretty high up on that list, Mr . . .?'

'Durran. Hunter Durran. And who're you?'

'Detective Inspector McLean.' He showed his own warrant card. Mr Durran pulled his dressing gown closed and belted it up. An improvement, but still rather more of him was on show than was strictly necessary.

'How long has Whitely lived here?' Ritchie asked. Durran's eyes flicked away from McLean and back to her again.

'I dunno. Three, mebbe four years?'

'And you knew him well?'

'Wouldn't say well. Keeps to hisself mostly. Pays his rent on time. Quiet. Can't ask for much more.' Durran paused a moment, then added. 'You said knew him well. He's no' dead is he?'

'Pays his rent?' McLean ignored the fat man's question. 'You're his landlord?'

Durran rubbed a finger over his top lip, sniffed so loudly that for a moment McLean thought he was going to spit on the floor. 'Aye.'

'You'll have a key to his flat then.'

'You got a warrant?'

'I can get a warrant, if you insist.' McLean made a big show of pulling his phone out of his pocket, tapping at the screen. 'It'll take a while though, and I'll have to station a couple of uniform officers here while we wait. No one in or out until we're done. Not you, not any of the other people living in this block.'

'You can't do that. I—'

'I can do that, Mr Durran. If I have to. You're right, Mr Whitely is dead, and under very suspicious circumstances. You can't begin to understand the powers that gives me.' He stared at the fat man, locking eyes with him until he backed down.

'I'll just get the keys then.'

The smell was the first thing he noticed. It reminded McLean of his university days, those times when the pile of clothes in the corner of the bedroom was twice as big as the pile spilling out of the chest of drawers, and a trip to the laundry couldn't really be put off any longer. Unlike his student flat though, Dr Jim Whitely's tiny top-floor apartment was relatively tidy. It just hadn't been aired recently, and the clothes spilling from the top of the laundry basket in the corner of the shower room had been accumulating for a long while. Either that or they'd been breeding.

'You think he ever opened a window?' Ritchie peered through an open doorway, swiftly stepping back into the hall and shaking her head as if to get rid of some particularly unpleasant odour.

'Probably not.' McLean looked around the shower room. It was small, like so many of its kind in these blocks. Being top floor, it had a skylight over the shower. Most of the remaining space was taken up by the overflowing laundry bin, a tiny basin and a toilet you'd not be able to stand at and close the door. There was enough floor to turn around in if you had a child's feet, but only if you didn't mind trampling over all the papers strewn about the place.

Bending down, he picked one up between latex-gloved fingers. It was a scientific paper from a medical journal, that much McLean could tell. Most of the words in the title he could only hazard a guess at, though. He crouched down, shuffling the rest of them towards him. All scientific papers, all well thumbed, all about as easy to understand as the offside rule.

'You might want to come and look at this, sir.'

McLean stood up, locating DS Ritchie by the one open door off the hallway. It led into a sitting room that overlooked the street, mostly giving a fine view of the living rooms opposite. The floor in this room was strewn with more papers, expensive-looking textbooks and several lined A4 pads with scrawly handwritten notes all over them. A sofa had been pushed into the bay window, but it was covered in books. Only a single armchair offered anywhere to sit, and this was obviously Whitely's preferred place of repose, judging by the coffee mugs, empty plates and surrounding circle of yet more papers. Some of these appeared to have been organised into separate piles, though by what filing criteria he couldn't begin to guess.

'Seems Dr Whitely had a bit of a bee in his bonnet.' McLean stepped carefully over one pile of papers, finding a space of carpet just about big enough to stand in. Ritchie must have used it to stepping-stone her way to the middle of the room. She nodded at the wall beside the door through which he had just come.

'That remind you of anything?'

McLean turned carefully, aware that a misstep would

result in a cascade of paperwork that might bury them, and would certainly annoy the forensics team who would surely have to go over the place. A cheap desk had been shoved in behind the door, an elderly laptop computer and printer taking up what area of its surface wasn't heaped with yet more papers. But it was the wall that was of most interest.

It looked a little like an incident room for a particularly complicated and unusual crime. A half-dozen photographs were pinned up in a line, about a foot apart. Each showed a child or young man, each quite clearly taken whilst the subject was in hospital undergoing some kind of treatment. A couple were smiling despite their bald heads and nasal tubes. One was giving a thumbs-up to the camera, though the hope in the gesture didn't spread as far as his eyes. Around each photograph were pinned front pages and abstracts from more medical journals, Post-it notes with question marks scribbled on them, the occasional barely legible word. And running over it all and the glimpse of clear wallpaper behind, thick black lines were drawn with a heavy marker pen linking seemingly disparate ideas together.

McLean stared at it all a long time before realising that he'd been holding his breath. He let it out in a long sigh.

'I think it's fair to say Jim Whitely was a troubled man.'

'Troubled enough to kill that nurse then stage his own suicide?' Ritchie asked.

It was an interesting idea, but life was never that easy.

'No, I don't think so.' McLean took a step closer to the desk, brushing a pile of papers with his leg as he went. It slid sideways, fanning out on the floor. He ignored it, leaning over the desk until he could begin to decipher the scrawled words. He followed a line from a paper that appeared to be about cell-line therapy, whatever that was, through a single word 'blastocysts?', across to another paper about transfusions and then on up to the photograph of the young man with his thumbs up. He stepped back again, more carefully this time, shoved his hand in his pocket and pulled out his phone. 'No, this isn't the work of someone thinking of killing themselves any time soon. Quite the opposite.'

'How do you mean?'

'He's been trying to save these kids. Looking for any way possible. He's obsessed with this. It's what drives him. He couldn't give this up even if he wanted to.'

59

'Well look at you, all grown up and smart.'

Gran stands behind me, hands on my shoulders as we both look in the mirror. It's the first time I've tried on my new school uniform and it feels very grown-up. The jacket was my father's; it smells of mothballs and it's too long in the arms. But it was his. He wore it just like me, years ago when he was a young boy. I can't quite get my head around that, but I feel very proud to be following in his footsteps.

'Take it off now. I'll show you how to fold it properly.'

Gran takes my jacket from me, checks the pockets even though I've only been wearing it for five minutes. Then she does something I can't quite follow, turning it inside out, folding and tucking until it's a neat little square of shiny fabric. She puts it down on my bed alongside all the other clothes, some old, some new, that I'll be taking with me to school tomorrow. The old leather travelling trunk lies open on the floor. It has my grandfather's initials stencilled on the lid and paper tags tied to the handles, foreign-sounding destinations inked on to them in fading, ancient script.

We spend most of the afternoon packing, or at least that's what it feels like. Outside the summer is fading to autumn, but it's still warm and sunny. Ideal weather for climbing trees. Instead I learn the art of fitting things into a tiny space, as shirts, socks, underpants, trousers, jackets, towels, flannels, ties, handkerchiefs and a dozen other things I never thought I'd need are all neatly stowed away. Everything has been labelled with my name, red letters on little cloth tags. I've never needed my name on things before. It makes me feel important, but also a little scared. Is everyone else going to have exactly the same clothes?

'There. That's perfect.' Gran closes the lid of the trunk, only having to kneel on it slightly to get the clasps to fit. I try to lift one end, but it's far too heavy.

'Don't worry about that.' She laughs, and tousles my hair the way I really don't like. 'I'll get Jenkins to take it to the station. It'll go on ahead of you.'

Finished with the packing, I sense my opportunity. 'Can I go see Norman? Won't have a chance to again. Not till Christmas.'

I've not seen Norman since he fell out of the tree and cut himself. It seems a lifetime ago even though it's probably only a couple of days. His mum was so angry that time, I didn't dare go back. Not until now, at least.

'Norman's not well, Tony. He had to go to the hospital.' I can see the worry in Gran's face, but she hides it with a smile. 'Don't worry though. He'll be fine in a week or two. You can write to him from school, tell him all about it. And you'll see him in a few months.'

I never do write to him, of course. Never see him again at all.

60

'Sorry I'm late, Angus. I take it you started without me.'

'Nearly done, actually. Take a pew and I'll give you the potted history in a minute.'

McLean had left DS Ritchie in charge of sorting out forensics at Whitely's flat and questioning the neighbours about his movements over the previous weeks. He'd set out across the Meadows, past the university and down into the Cowgate where the city mortuary carried out its grisly unseen business, hoping that the walk would give him a chance to think things through. He needed headspace to try and rationalise the alarming similarities between Ben Stevenson and Jim Whitely. Not in their deaths, but in their lives, their single-minded obsession. But the heat had made it difficult to breathe, and the noise was far worse than he remembered from his days in uniform. His thoughts had been stuck in a loop, missing some crucial piece that would unlock the puzzle. The cool interior of the mortuary had come as a welcome relief, the distraction of Dr Whitely's post-mortem doubly so. Now he sat in a hard plastic chair with his back to the wall of the examination theatre, watching silently as Angus Cadwallader examined the dead man.

'Not a nice case, this one.'

McLean looked around to see Dr MacPhail, no doubt

here as witness to the proceedings should corroboration be required at any inquest into the death.

'Shouldn't you be . . .?' McLean nodded his head in the direction of the examination table. 'You know, witnessing?'

'I probably shouldn't be here at all, actually. Since I was the one identified him.'

McLean remembered then, the conversation with DC MacBride earlier that morning. 'Of course. You knew him. I'm sorry.'

'Oh, he wasn't a friend or anything. Just so happens we both went through med school at the same time. I'd see him around from time to time if I was up at the hospital. We'd nod, say hello. Nothing more than that.'

'Med school? I thought Whitely was older than that.'

'I'll take that as a compliment, Inspector.' Dr MacPhail gave him a lopsided grin and slumped into the next chair along. He smelled of dead people, with an underlying sharp scent that was familiar from somewhere McLean couldn't quite place. 'I'm older than I look, really. And what happened to Jim there. Well . . .'

'Do you remember much about him? When he was a student?'

'Now you're asking.' MacPhail puffed out his cheeks and scratched at his head. 'He was always quite intense, I guess. Bright. He never seemed to struggle with exams. Didn't talk to him much. We moved in different circles, had different friends. He went into paediatrics, too, which is kind of the opposite of my speciality. At least most of the time.'

'If you two lovebirds have got a moment to spare.'

Angus Cadwallader's loud voice echoed across the examination theatre. McLean looked up to see him staring in their direction.

'You all finished?' He stood up, feeling the sweat on his back where it had soaked his shirt and then cooled down.

'As much as I can do here. The lab results will take a little longer, but I think I can comfortably say Dr Whitely didn't take his own life.'

'Didn't?' McLean felt that familiar cold sensation in the pit of his stomach. He'd not been overly keen on the murder/suicide hypothesis, but it at least had the merit of being simple. And it would have solved two cases at the same time. 'What killed him, then?'

'Oh, that bit's easy. His heart gave out when his blood pressure dropped too low. He'd have been unconscious by then, which I guess is a blessing.'

'And you're sure he couldn't have done it to himself?' McLean crossed the room and stared at the violated, naked body.

'He could have done it to himself. Technically. It's a bit of a gruesome way to die though, and far too elaborate. So many things could have gone wrong, and then there's all that kit to lug into that warehouse. In my experience people wanting to kill themselves don't go in for that kind of spectacle.'

'No. You're right. Would just have been neater.'

'Death is never neat, Tony.' Cadwallader's scolding was friendly, but there nevertheless.

'I know, Angus. This one even less than most.'

'Yes, well. There's other reasons why I can say with a fair degree of certainty that it wasn't suicide. This, for instance. Cadwallader moved away from the head, down one arm, then picked up a hand, showing the thin, pale wrist to McLean. 'There's ligature marks here. There were straps on the table where we found him, but they were undone. He lost so much blood it was hard to see at the scene, but here it's fairly obvious he was tied down to start with.'

'He was strapped down until after he fell unconscious?'

'Or at least until he was too weak to do anything about it, yes.'

'So whoever did this would have watched him die.'

'That or gone away and then come back. But given the method of killing, the lengths he went to, I'd have to say he most probably watched.'

McLean shuddered at the thought of it, but before he could comment, Cadwallader had moved around the table to the dead man's neck.

'Oh, and there's this of course.' He pointed to a tiny mark just below the ear.

'Injection site?'

'See, you do learn things occasionally. Yes, indeed, it's an injection site. He didn't have much blood left in him, poor fellow, but we've sent some off for screening. I suspect a fast-acting sedative, something to knock him out so that whoever did this to him could get him hooked up to that infernal machine.'

McLean took a step back, staring once more at the whole body laid out on its back. After the cruel incisions of the post-mortem, and Dr Sharp's expert stitching to put him back together again, he couldn't really think of Whitely as a person any more. Or maybe it was just that he hadn't had time to build a picture of the man yet, could only think of him as this bloodless corpse.

'There's one question I notice you haven't asked me yet,' Cadwallader said.

'Time of death. I know. I was getting there.'

'Me too. The blood thing makes it difficult to be accurate, so I've sent off some samples for testing. My best estimate though is that he was in that place no more than a week.'

'That fits with when he was last seen at the hospital. Gives us something to work on.' McLean touched Cadwallader gently on the arm. 'Thanks, Angus. I'll see myself out.'

He was halfway to the door when he remembered something, turned back. 'Actually, there was one other thing.'

Cadwallader raised a quizzical eyebrow. 'Just one?'

'Well, yes. That heart, you know, the one we found at Ben Stevenson's place. Did you get round to examining that yet?'

'The heart? I think that was one of Tom's.' Cadwallader turned his attention to his fellow pathologist. 'That right, wasn't it?'

'Yes. Did it a couple of days back. You should have had the report by now.'

McLean pictured his office, tucked away at the back of the station. The image swam easily to his mind, a stack of paperwork covering his desk, more spilled out over the floor. What he couldn't remember was if he'd actually been in it any time in the past week.

'You couldn't give me the executive summary, could you?'

*

'It's human. Quite healthy, really. Belonged to someone in their late thirties, early forties. Male, given the size.'

Dr MacPhail bent over a bench in a small laboratory off the main examination theatre. McLean stood behind him and just enough to the side to be able to see the object laid out on a metal tray. The heart had been cleaned up, the strange green foliage removed from it and sent away for analysis. Now it looked unpleasantly like the kind of thing you might find in one of the more esoteric butchers' shops. The kind where you could buy all the parts of the animal never intended for eating unless they'd been finely minced, mixed with oatmeal and spices, shoved in a sheep's stomach and boiled first.

'Any idea whose it is?'

'Not a hundred per cent sure. Still waiting for the DNA match to come back. But I've narrowed it down.' MacPhail consulted the top sheet of the report he'd printed out before leading McLean into the lab. 'Judging by its condition, and the place we found it, I'd estimate it's been out of its owner's body a month.'

'Forcibly removed?' McLean stared at the organ, looking for signs of violence. It just looked like a piece of meat, the veins and arteries neatly cut a decent length from the bulb of the four chambers. He really didn't need another murder to add to the growing list.

'Depends what you mean by forcibly.' MacPhail picked up the heart as if it were nothing of great importance, turned it this way and that as he pointed out markings only he could see. 'It's been cut out, of course, but whoever it belonged to was dead before that happened.'

'How do you mean?'

‘This is a donor heart. Or it was meant to be. You can see from the way it’s been cut. Here, and here.’

‘A donor? But surely there’d be records. We’d know if one had gone missing before . . . before it could be used. Wouldn’t we?’

‘We should, yes. Though sadly not every organ harvested ends up in a new body. Things go wrong.’

McLean didn’t want to ask what. It wasn’t all that relevant anyway. ‘So do we know whose it is? Where it came from?’

‘Not yet. Still waiting for confirmation. I’ve asked around the hospitals about recent transplants too. We should have a name and a place soon enough. Thing is though, this has been preserved.’

‘That unusual?’

‘Very. Especially the way it’s been done. Far as I can tell this is embalming fluid. The stuff undertakers used to use. That’s what’s giving it this odd smell, and why it’s only partially rotted.’

61

'Right then. You all know what's happened. We've got three dead bodies all killed in the last six weeks. The chances of them not being connected are hardly worth thinking about, so we're combining all three investigations as of now.'

McLean stood to one side, listening as Detective Superintendent Duguid addressed the troops. To give him some small credit, this was the sort of job Dagwood was quite good at. Actually coordinating an investigation not so much, but being a figurehead and acting important he had down pat.

'Now I know we haven't got very far with the investigation into Ben Stevenson's murder, and the enquiry into the dead nurse isn't much better. But there's a good chance now that we can begin to analyse the patterns emerging. Start to put together some kind of profile. Paint a picture of our killer and work out his motivations.'

Straight out of a textbook, and one a couple of decades out of date if McLean was any judge. He glanced sideways at DS Ritchie, who rolled her eyes conspiratorially as she saw him looking. Most of the station was assembled in the large incident room, filling it in a manner that would give Health and Safety palpitations. Young uniform constables stood to attention near the front, some taking notes. Older, wiser heads slouched at the back, knowing a pep talk when they heard one.

'Detective Chief Inspector Brooks will be keeping an eye on all three investigations,' Duguid continued, blithely unaware of the crowd's general lack of interest. They were waiting for the assignments, the only thing that really mattered. Get a nice cushy desk job, manning the phones or even better punching actions into the computer, and all would be well. The poor saps who were going to be sent out on door to door would have a harder time of it.

'Detective Inspector McLean is in charge of the Stevenson case.' Duguid scanned the crowd until he saw McLean, motioned him to the front as if no one in the station knew what he looked like.

'Detective Inspector Spence is running the enquiry into the dead nurse.' The thin man joined them at the front, a nervous scowl on his pinched face. McLean wanted to whisper in Duguid's ear that the nurse had a name, Maureen Shenks, but he knew it would be a waste of time. The DS's unthinking misogyny was a thing of legend.

'We're a bit short of senior officers at the moment, so we've poached one back from uniform. Detective Inspector McIntyre will be looking into the latest discovery. You there, Jayne?'

There was a pause, and then a familiar figure pushed her way to the front. She was thinner than McLean remembered her, and of course no longer a detective superintendent destined for yet higher office. It seemed a cruel reversal, having not so long ago been Duguid's boss, to find herself working under him. On the other hand, she'd managed to keep her job despite the best efforts of the press. Yet another reason not to trust them.

'You've all got your teams. Assignments will be handed

out shortly.' Duguid waited until the susurrus died down, clearing his throat noisily when he realised it wasn't going to. The arrival of the old boss was probably the most exciting thing to happen in the station in days. 'I shouldn't need to say this, gentlemen, but I will anyway. Three murders is exceptional. Three possibly connected murders and you can all guess where the press are going to run with this.'

More murmuring in the ranks at the suggestion any of them would do anything so reckless as talking to a journalist off the record.

'The last thing we need is a panic. Especially at this time of year. City's bad enough as it is, full of bloody tourists and mime artists. Nothing, and I mean nothing, gets leaked to the press that hasn't been through me or one of the senior detectives first. Got that?'

There were a few noncommittal mumbles from the gathered officers. It was the same at every briefing for every investigation, big or small. Press contact was meant to be controlled, and just occasionally that worked. Rather unpleasantly, the thought of Jo Dalgliesh swam into McLean's mind. She'd played fair so far, trading the sensational story for something with a bit more depth. And possibly to help out her dead friend as well, though that would have implied she had some kind of heart hidden under that horrible leather coat. She wasn't the only player in the game though, and it was only a matter of time before the other tabloid hacks smelled blood.

'Right then. I don't need to tell you all how important this is. Go to it, teams, and let's get this sick bastard caught before he kills anyone else.'

*

'Good to see you back, Ma'am.' McLean forced his way through the throng of uniforms, admin staff and detectives milling about the major incident room to where Jayne McIntyre was staring at one of the whiteboards.

'Jayne I think, Tony. We're both inspectors now.'

'I know. I heard. Sorry.'

'Don't be. It was my own stupid fault after all. Could have done without Mr Stevenson here telling the whole world about it, of course.'

McLean looked at the whiteboard, seeing Ben Stevenson's dead face taped to the top. Most of the questions and actions written beneath it had been there since the start, testament to just how much progress they had failed to make.

'Why is this so difficult to solve?' McIntyre tapped at her teeth with a short, cracked fingernail as she scanned the board. 'Haven't forensics come up with anything?'

'Nothing that wasn't his. The other caves were too contaminated by the public to get anything useful.'

'Hmm. How did he get in there?'

'Must have had a key. The cave he was found in wasn't part of the tour, but the only way in's from the tour centre.'

'And we've no CCTV, no strange people seen loitering around?'

'Plenty. All of it useless. We've had teams running all the number plates we could identify, tracking down the people walking past the bookies and the local chip shop. They both have cameras that take in the street. Problem is, it's not a small number of people. Except around the time we think Stevenson must have gone into the caves. Then there's nothing at all.'

'What about the locals? They see anything odd?'

McLean remembered his trip to the bookies with DS Ritchie. Had anything come of that? He'd given the punter his card, so any contact would have been direct. Someone was meant to be getting the manager to do an e-fit, though.

'Should be something here somewhere.'

'No matter. I'll get a chance to catch up soon enough. I take it you reckon all three are linked?'

'I wasn't sure to start with, but I've seen a bit of how both men lived. Their characters are very similar, which might suggest a theme. Not sure how Maureen Shenks fits in, except that she worked at the Sick Kids, same as Whitely. Thought for a while he might have killed her then topped himself in remorse, but the PM doesn't support that theory.'

'What if she was unlucky and just got in the way?'

McLean stared at McIntyre as the words filtered through his brain, the horrible possibilities behind the idea.

'Go on,' he said.

'Well my old chum Stevenson was obsessed with his latest story. A nasty little character trait of his. Seems our man Whitely was a bit driven, too.' McIntyre pointed over at the far side of the room where that investigation was just starting to come together.

'Both of them were chasing a lie though. Something designed to hook them. Tuned to their particular obsession. With Stevenson it was a secret society controlling everything. Whitely . . . well, you said his flat was full of medical texts, case notes, that sort of thing?'

McLean nodded. 'If we're treating all three murders as

linked, then we're looking at one murderer. Two of these fit a pattern, the nurse doesn't.'

'But she might have been a distraction, if she were coming on to Whitely while our killer was trying to lure him in.' McIntyre shook her head as if dismissing the whole thing as nonsense. 'Of course, the nurse might be nothing to do with the other two. They might all be unconnected.'

'There's nothing to lose from exploring the similarities.'

'Such as?'

'Lack of forensics, for a start. Whoever's done this knows their way around a crime scene. Stevenson and Shenks were both left somewhere that would be impossible to process. Whitely's scene was so clean you could eat your lunch off the floor. Never seen anything like it. Jemima Cairns hadn't either.'

'Jemima?' McIntyre raised an eyebrow. 'You've been putting yourself around a bit since I left, Tony.'

'Stop it. You're as bad as bloody Dagwood.'

'Sorry. I'd missed that too.'

McLean saw the smile spreading from McIntyre's eyes, betraying her normal poker face.

'It's good to have you back, really. Even in reduced circumstances. Not sure I'll ever get used to it though.'

'Actually I don't really mind. Being knocked back to inspector, that is. Being a superintendent meant never getting outside, always sitting behind a desk, attending meetings, managing idiots and dealing with the fallout when they cocked up. It's nice to be back at the sharp end.'

As if on cue, McLean's phone chirped a particularly jaunty tune; this one was reserved for the worst of his contacts. A quick check of the screen confirmed his suspicions. Jo Dalgliesh wanted a word.

'You might want to hold that thought . . . Jayne.' He still couldn't get used to that. 'I think our friends in the press might be on to us again.'

'You're meant to be keeping me in the loop, Inspector. That was the deal, wasn't it?'

The first thing McLean noticed was that Dalgliesh hadn't called him Tony. He hated it when she did, but it didn't take a genius to realise that 'Inspector' was reserved for those times when she was particularly annoyed with him.

'I take it you're talking about the body we found in Sighthill.'

'Too bloody right I am. You any idea how many juicy stories I've had to pass up on just to keep onside with youse lot?'

For a moment McLean almost believed her. Working with Dalgliesh on a semi-regular basis had almost inured him to her presence, a bit like the way spending more than half an hour in a small space with DS Carter inured you to his overpowering body odour. At least until you went outside the room and were reminded of what fresh air was supposed to be like. Meeting Jayne McIntyre again had reminded him just what a bunch of self-serving shits the gutter press could be; a handy inoculation before he became too used to the reporter's presence and dropped his guard.

'We only found the body yesterday. We're still processing the scene, interviewing colleagues.'

‘So you’ve identified it. Him, I should say.’

‘Yes.’

‘And?’

‘I can’t tell you, Ms Dalgliesh. Not until we’ve assessed whether releasing that information to the general public would hinder our investigation or not.’

‘God you can sound stuck up sometimes. Posh bloody education I guess.’ Dalgliesh’s voice muffled at the other end of the line, overlaid with the sound of a clicking lighter as she sparked up a cigarette. Not at her desk then.

‘Look. We’re going to be having a press conference later on today. I’ll know what we can and can’t say before then, and I’ll make sure you get that ahead of everyone else. I can’t do any more than that.’

‘You reckon it’s the same bloke as killed Ben?’

‘I don’t even know if Stevenson’s killer was a man. You know as well as I do how little we’ve got on that.’

‘Aye, true enough.’ Dalgliesh paused. ‘What about that nurse? Shenks?’

‘What about her?’

‘Ha ha. You’re very funny, Inspector. She worked at the same place as your new body, aye?’

‘Why do you bother calling me, Dalgliesh? You think you know all the answers anyway.’

‘Got to check my sources though. Can’t go printing any old rumour and supposition.’

It never stopped you before. ‘If Duguid finds out which officer has been speaking to the press without sanction, he’ll be off the force without a pension. Are you going to press with this story tonight?’

'Maybe. Depends what I get that's better.'

McLean sighed, pinched the bridge of his nose in the hope that it would make all the annoying things go away. It didn't, and he knew all too well that hanging up on them wouldn't work either.

'Look, I can't confirm the identity of the body, but I don't think I need to really. You've got your sources and if you don't trust them, don't pay them. I can confirm that we're looking at similarities between all three murders. That doesn't mean we think there's a serial killer running loose any more than we think all three committed suicide. All options are on the table and we're working as fast as we can to solve this. If you stir up some moral outrage or get a bunch of halfwit politicians breathing down our necks then that'll just make our job more difficult. So ask yourself what's in the public interest: selling a few more papers, or finding the person who killed your colleague before they kill someone else?'

A stunned silence echoed over the airwaves and out through the earpiece of McLean's phone. For a moment he thought the line might have gone dead; reception was pretty rubbish in the dark corner at the end of the corridor outside the major incident room where he'd scurried off to take the call in the first place. A quick glance at the screen showed him he was still connected.

'Jeez. You really haven't got anything on this guy, have you.' Dalgliesh's tone was her normal mix of sarcasm and disdain. McLean wondered whether the silence had been her muting her phone so she could have a lung-loosening cough. It would certainly take more than impassioned words to get through to her. A pickaxe, maybe.

'Like I said. We don't even know if it's a guy. Don't even know if the three killings are by the same person.'

'Don't know shit?'

It was meant to be a joke, albeit in poor taste. McLean couldn't bring himself to laugh, though. It was too close to the truth for that.

62

If McLean thought the hospital had been depressed after the death of Maureen Shenks, it was nothing compared to the shock running through the place following Dr Whitely's demise. It was true that people seldom spoke ill of the dead, and especially not of those who had died young and violently. Even so, it was hard to square the universal sorrow and expressions of admiration with the image he had built in his head from visiting the doctor's flat.

They had commandeered the same small room at the back of the old building, and were working through interviews with all of Dr Whitely's colleagues and associates. One of the first jobs had been to draw up a list of names, but as they worked through it, so it grew.

'I never realised quite how many doctors and nurses passed through this place.' DS Ritchie flipped through her printed list, now much amended with scribbled names. 'And that's before we even get to the admin staff, cleaners, porters. Christ, it's never-ending.'

'Just as well he didn't have much of a social life then.' McLean slumped back in his seat, not quite sure why he'd decided to come and help out with the interviews. Jayne McIntyre was meant to be heading up the investigation, after all. And this kind of background stuff was sergeant work, really. On the other hand, the thought of going back to the station filled him with gloom; the Ben Stevenson investigation had gone cold and things didn't look much better for Maureen Shenks. This at least had the benefit of being a new case, even if it was beginning to look rather too much like the other two. Random, brutal, and with a disturbing lack of forensic evidence to work with. He'd leapt at the chance to take it on while McIntyre got back up to speed.

'Who's next?' he asked.

'Dr Stephanie Clark. Another specialist in paediatric oncology, apparently.' Ritchie ran a finger over the relevant line in her list. 'Sounds fun.'

'Laugh a minute, I'm sure. OK. Let's get her in.'

Dr Clark was younger than McLean had been expecting. He wasn't sure why, but for some reason he'd pictured a serious woman in her mid-fifties, greying hair cut short or tied in a workmanlike bun. But the woman who presented herself at the door to the makeshift interview room at her appointed hour was probably the same age as DS Ritchie. She was tiny, too. Not much over five foot, and proportioned like many of the children she treated. You wouldn't have mistaken her for a child, though. Her eyes gave the game away. That and the air of weariness that seeped out of her.

'Would you say Dr Whitely was under a lot of pressure?' DS Ritchie asked the question. They had established something of a routine now, with the sergeant doing most of the work. McLean would sit back and watch, only occasionally adding something. He really didn't need to be there at all.

'Show me a doctor here who isn't.' That was the other thing that gave Dr Clark away. Her voice was deeper and more mature than the teenager she might be mistaken for. She paused as if expecting some sympathy before carrying on. 'But no. I wouldn't have said Jim was any more stressed than any of us. Last time I spoke to him he didn't seem much different from every other time.'

'What about his work? Had he lost any patients recently?'

That brought a frown. 'That's a harsh way of putting it.'

'I'm sorry. I didn't mean it to be.' DS Ritchie fidgeted with her list. 'I'm just trying to get a picture of his mental state. Find out if there was anything that might have tipped him over the edge.'

'You think he committed suicide?' Dr Clark gave her a look that mothers give children who have done something particularly stupid. 'Well you can scratch that one off your list. Jim would no more take his own life than he'd take one of his patients'.'

'So we've heard, but it's always good to have it confirmed from multiple sources. Did you know he was very interested in cutting-edge research?'

Dr Clark nodded. 'That was Jim. Always had his head in a paper. He was fascinated by all the new therapies coming through. If there was one thing that got him down it was the difficulty he had persuading the board to let him trial some of them.'

Something clicked in McLean's mind. 'Not easy then, I take it.'

'Christ no. I mean, fair enough, some of the stuff he was on about has only just been trialled in the lab. You can't go using that kind of stuff on sick kids, however desperate they are.'

'Did you think he might try, though? Maybe as a last resort for someone terminal?'

'And risk losing his job? Being struck off the medical register? Going to jail? I don't think so. That wasn't Jim at all.' Dr Clark shook her head again, the faintest of smiles crinkling the corners of her eyes at some memory. Then a frown washed it away. 'Mind you, he was talking to that research chap.'

'Research chap?' DS Ritchie asked. She leafed through her ever-growing list of names.

'Yes. Last few weeks, I think it was. I saw them together at the Royal Infirmary too. Here a couple of times. Some researcher from the university, probably.'

'And does this researcher have a name?'

'I guess he probably does. Can't say I know it though. Never talked to him myself.'

'As far as I know Jim wasn't working on any research programmes. Don't think he'd have had the time, to be honest, what with his work here and at the Royal.'

The last interview of the day, or at least McLean sincerely hoped it was the last interview of the day. Whitely's boss lounged in the chair on the other side of the table from him and DS Ritchie. He was a fat man, that was perhaps the kindest way of putting it. An administrator rather than a physician, though McLean had met plenty of large doctors in his time. He burst from his ill-fitting suit as if he had been smaller that morning and mysteriously swelled with the day. Perhaps he would go home soon and explode.

‘So he wasn’t running any clinical trials? New therapies that could only be tried out on terminal patients?’

‘Good lord, no. Where did you get such an idea? We can’t do stuff like that.’

‘But he was talking to a research scientist. There’s at least half a dozen doctors and nurses here saw him.’

‘News to me.’

‘So you’ve no idea who this fellow is, then?’ DS Ritchie pitched in with the question. She had her list of names, most neatly ticked off, and was poised to add yet one more to the collection of handwritten additions at the bottom.

‘Absolutely none. It’s the first I’ve heard of it, to be honest.’

McLean leaned forward, resting his arms on the table. ‘Do you do much research here?’

‘Sure, we run trials with the major drug companies, universities. It’s all above board though. We’ve ethics committees coming out of our ears and nothing gets tried out until it’s been thoroughly lab tested.’

‘So it’s very unlikely Dr Whitely would have been involved in some unofficial work. Maybe keeping it under the radar until it could be shown to be effective. Doing stuff off site?’

‘You really don’t understand how this all works, do you Inspector?’ The fat man squeezed himself forward, risking the buttons on his jacket. ‘You can’t just set up a trial, draft in a few terminally ill kids and start pumping them full of experimental drugs in the hope they might magically get better. There are procedures. Consent needs to be given. Risk assessments. Cost–benefit analyses. And meetings – God, you wouldn't believe the amount of time I spend in meetings. Even getting agreement between two doctors working with the same patient can be a struggle sometimes. The idea that Jim might have been doing anything without approval is laughable, really.'

63

He is undecided now. I can see the change in him as clearly as if he'd painted his face. The sweet brightness of his certainty is being dulled by some terrible indecision. Have I left him too long, taken my eye off the prize?

He goes about the daily business of the church, unaware that he is watched. And perhaps that is another sign. Here, in the house of the Lord, how can one not always be aware of being watched? He is all around us, in us, even though the lines of wooden pews have been moved to the walls, the central nave filled with ungainly rods of steel.

This has always been a place of awe. Its builders understood the grandeur they were trying to capture. The vaulted ceilings echo His ineffable silence; the stained glass casts everything in hellish hues as if to remind us of the perils of sin. Yet now the windows are obscured, the arches lost in a forest of rusting steel. The echoes are muffled by heavy wooden scaffold boards.

And he is humming.

I came here to pray, as I have done every day of my life. As my mother and father did before me, my grandparents before them. We have kept this parish alive, kept faith with God in this place. It is sacred ground no matter the signs outside declaring it dangerous to enter. No harm can come to any in here save that the Lord ordain it.

At first I think it is a hymn he is humming as he attends

to the altar, but the notes distort and mutate into something that might have been playing on the hospital radio the last time I was there. This man who I had thought godly has become corrupted. So quickly, so thoroughly, it is hardly surprising I did not notice it before. And yet as I study him from my place in the shadows, I can see still that glimmer of purity, the spark that first alerted me to him as sure as the flame attracts the moth. It is not too late to save him, but I must act swiftly now. Decisively.

I study him, watch him go through the same ritual I have seen a thousand times before. No, ten thousand times. I know when he will kneel, when he will bow his head and begin to pray.

Silently I move through the shadows until I am standing just behind him. Head down, his neck is exposed, the starched white of his collar showing clearly under the black fabric of his shirt. He has a smile on his face as he prays, and I understand what has happened. His body has been corrupted, but his soul is still pure. It can still be saved.

He turns at the last minute, perhaps sensing my presence and wondering if God has come down to bless him in person. Surprise widens his eyes, but it is short-lived. Needle slips effortlessly into exposed flesh and he tumbles gently forward to the floor.

64

The ringing phone stirred McLean from a fitful doze. He'd nodded off at his desk, an all-too-frequent occurrence these days, it seemed. He wondered idly if it was just a symptom of getting old. More likely the fact that he averaged around four hours' sleep a night. And broken, troubled sleep at that.

A glance at the number on the screen meant nothing, but at least it wasn't any of the journalists he'd put in the address book for the purposes of avoiding their calls. He thumbed the answer button and held the phone up to his ear.

'Yes?'

'Is that McLean? The polis man?' Thick Edinburgh accent he couldn't immediately place. Those last words definitely pronounced separately, as if that's how the speaker would spell them.

'This is Detective Inspector McLean, yes. Can I help you?' No point asking a name if it wasn't immediately offered. The caller had his number from somewhere; might as well try to find out what he wanted first, then get to the bottom of who exactly he was.

'You lookin' for a man. Hanging around the bookies up Gilmerton way.'

The pieces dropped into place. The gambler studying the form, addicted, and not very successful by the look of him. McLean had given him a tenner and his card. No doubt the one was long gone, the other kept a hold of until it might be useful. Or he was desperate enough.

'That's right. Have you seen him?'

'Not sure. Might've done. Up at the hospital.'

'Hospital?'

'Aye, y'ken the new one over at Little France.'

'The Royal Infirmary. I know it.'

'Well, I was up there yesterday getting my scrip, ken? An' I was sure I saw that same chappie youse was asking about? Only he was all togged up in the white coat an' stuff.'

'It's Keith, isn't it? I remember now.' McLean had been racking his brain for the man's name, sure he knew it as soon as he'd placed him. The silence at the end of the phone was ominous.

'Look, you've been a great help, really.' McLean decided to go for broke. If nothing else, at least he had the man's phone number now. 'But it's possible you could be even more useful.'

'I'm no' coming anywhere near a polis station.'

'I wasn't going to suggest anything of the sort.' McLean had been, but it was obvious that wasn't going to work. 'I can meet you somewhere, but I'd really like you to sit down with an e-fit specialist. Get us a better description of this man you saw.'

Another long pause, then Keith spoke again. 'I don't know. I'm that busy, y'ken.'

Unemployed, disability benefit going on the horses. Very busy. 'We could meet up at the bookies, if that'd be easiest?' McLean didn't explicitly say there'd be another ten-pound note in it, but the offer was there.

'Aye, OK. When?'

He looked up at the clock on the wall. Half-past two. Twenty minutes to find someone trained in the software, half an hour to get out to Gilmerton if the traffic wasn't too bad. 'Say half-three?'

'No, his eyes were wider apart than that. Aye, about there no?'

The bookies was busier than it had been the last time he'd been here, maybe because the police had finally packed up and gone from the caves around the corner. McLean had tried to find DS Ritchie, then DC MacBride, but both were away on errands for DCI Brooks. Casting around for someone else with e-fit training had produced the unlikely figure of DC Sandra Gregg, which meant he'd had his ear bent about her new house and how they were struggling to persuade the insurers to cover the cost of replacement goldfish, all the way from the station to Gilmerton Cove. He felt a certain responsibility for the accident that had seen her old terrace house destroyed in a gas mains explosion at the start of the year, so listened as attentively as he could manage. Fortunately Keith had been waiting for them, no doubt hoping to get the job over and done with so he could continue his pursuit of the perfect six-way accumulator.

'He was clean-shaven. Mebbe just a hint of stubble.'

To give her her due, Gregg was quick and efficient with the software, pulling up menus and swapping facial features around with a practised ease. It was just a shame that Keith wasn't the most reliable of witnesses. He changed his mind considerably more often than his underpants if the vaguely unwholesome aroma coming off him was anything to go by.

'That him?' Gregg tapped at a couple of keys and the screen on her laptop filled with a mugshot.

'Aye, that's pretty close. Mebbe didn't look so much like a crook, mind.'

'We can tidy him up, put him in a suit. You saw him at the hospital, right?'

'Aye. Looked like a doctor wi' one of them white coats and ear thingies.'

'Stethoscope?'

'Aye.'

McLean tapped the man gently on the shoulder, dragging his gaze away from the screen. 'You've been a great help, Keith. Thank you.' As he got up from the cheap plastic chair in the corner of the bookies, McLean held out a hand to shake. He'd palmed the twenty-pound note earlier and was unsurprised when Keith took it with just the barest of nods, headed straight to the counter to get his unsatisfying fix.

'We done here, sir?' Gregg asked, starting to pack up the laptop. McLean looked past the cashier to the door leading to the manager's office. Someone was supposed to have come out here and gone through the whole e-fit process with him too, but if it had been done he'd not seen the result.

'Not quite, Constable. Someone else we need to speak to.'

*

'You sure these are the same person?'

It had taken a lot less time to run through the e-fit procedure with the betting shop manager than it had with Keith, but the results hadn't been all that promising. If you squinted at the two images painted side by side on the small laptop computer screen, and maybe smeared grease over your scratched spectacles, then there was a passing similarity between the two. Looked at more analytically though, it was hard to accept that they were even related.

'I guess DS Ritchie was right when she said this was a straw-clutching exercise.' McLean put the key in the ignition and fired up the engine. Frowned as he looked out the windscreen to find a large white splat of bird shit on the once-shiny bonnet.

'Pretty much everything to do with this case is clutching at straws, you ask me.' DC Gregg sat in the passenger seat in much the same way as DC MacBride, trying hard not to actually come into contact with any surface in case she somehow damaged it. McLean was going to have to do something about that soon.

'You know anything about cars?'

Gregg looked at him askance, thrown by the non sequitur. 'Cars?'

'You know, four wheels, engine, makes vroom-vroom noises.' McLean pulled away from their parking space at the kerbside perhaps a little too enthusiastically, underlining the point.

'Not much. That's more Ritchie's thing.'

'You've got a car, though?'

'Aye. Barry has one with the work. No' as nice as this, but it's comfy enough. Why you asking?'

'Just looking for suggestions. I can't really drive this around all the time. It's been smashed up once already and I don't want that happening again. Been a while since I last read a car magazine. There's never time to go to a garage, and frankly I could do without the sales patter.'

Gregg didn't answer, and they fell into an uneasy silence as McLean drove across town in the direction of the Royal Infirmary. He didn't know the hospital as well as the Western General at the other end of the city, neither was he recognised by any of the staff, which made tracking down someone helpful more difficult than it should have been. Eventually they were directed towards the admin offices and HR department, where a harassed-looking young woman peered at McLean's warrant card before letting out a heavy sigh.

'Aye? What is it now?'

'Wondering if you knew which member of staff this was.' McLean nudged DC Gregg, who opened up the laptop computer and showed the mugshot they'd teased out of Keith the punter.

'Have you any idea how many people work in this place?'

'He was wearing a doctor's white coat, had a stethoscope round his neck. I reckon that probably rules out most of the support staff.'

'Still leaves several hundred medical staff. Assuming it wasn't someone in fancy dress. Or a student.'

'Well could you at least look at it?' McLean could put up with only so much whining, even if he knew that antagonising human resources was never a good idea.

'OK.' The young woman sighed again and made a show of studying the image. 'Not very realistic, is it?'

'I appreciate that, and I wouldn't bother you if it wasn't important. So it doesn't ring any bells?'

'No. Sorry.'

'Right. Well. Thanks for looking. If I email it over, could you send it around everyone in the hospital? If anyone recognises him it could be crucial to solving a particularly unpleasant murder.'

That finally seemed to get the young woman's attention. The yawn she had been hiding badly disappeared in an instant, her eyes widening in surprise. 'Murder?'

'Yes, murder. So I'd quite like to get access to your CCTV footage as well.'

65

'Getting kind of frustrated with these. Is this really the best anyone can do?'

McLean held up a colour printout of the man Keith the gambler reckoned he'd seen at the Royal Infirmary. White, male, black hair and staring eyes. It could have been anyone, or no one. A half-dozen people working out of the industrial estate in Sighthill had claimed to have seen someone going in and out of the building where they'd found Whitely's body and each of them had produced an e-fit image too. Add in the one from the betting shop manager and they had eight images. Hard to imagine eight more different variations on the same basic theme.

'It happens sometimes. There's people out there with just average faces. No outstanding features. And if someone's deliberately trying not to draw attention to themselves . . .' DC MacBride sidled up from the far corner of the major incident room. McLean couldn't help noticing that the constable's hair was getting very long at the front now, like some throwback to the early-eighties New Romantic bands. Given that MacBride hadn't been born before most of them had broken up, it seemed more likely he was still getting grief about his scar.

'Don't suppose there's anything we can do about it?'

'Well, we could composite all the different e-fits together. See if that comes up with anything. But that's assuming they're all of the same person. If not, then we'll have a picture of nobody.'

'At the moment we've half a dozen pictures of nobody. More. Might as well give it a go, eh?' McLean noticed the slight slump in the constable's shoulders at the thought of yet another task. 'Or get someone in admin to do it?'

'No, I'll run it myself, sir. Quicker that way.' MacBride didn't even try to hide the sigh in his voice.

'Sooner or later you'll have to learn to delegate if you want to make sergeant.'

MacBride made no reply, but neither did he turn and walk away. McLean was put in mind of an awkward teenager, not quite sure how to broach a tricky subject with an adult.

'Everything all right, Constable?'

That brought a wry smile. 'That depends on what you mean by all right, sir. Thing is, I've been offered a job, outside the force that is. Pay's about four times what I'm earning here, hours are long but fairly predictable.'

'Why are you still here then?'

'Could ask you the same thing. And I didn't join up because I wanted to get rich. Never really fancied a nine-to-five desk job, either. It's just . . .'

'The more you hang around this madhouse the more appealing it seems?'

'Something like that, aye. I get so sick of the joke. The same joke. Over and over again as if repetition makes it more funny each time.'

'I had a word with Duguid already, for all the good it did. I'll see what else I can do, but honestly Stuart, this isn't a job for idealists. Trust me on that.'

'Thanks. I thought that's what you'd say. Problem is, people don't really listen to you, do they sir?'

'Not all the time, no. And I don't suppose Brooks will be any better than Dagwood. But McIntyre's a different matter altogether.'

MacBride raised a disbelieving eyebrow, almost missed under his floppy fringe. 'You reckon? After what she did?'

'Last I heard leaving your cheating husband for another woman wasn't a crime.'

'No' just any woman. And she broke that reporter's nose.'

McLean tried not to smile. 'You think there's anyone here hasn't wanted to do that? They only threw the book at her because he pressed charges. Sheriff ruled there was no case to answer and now Jayne's back as a DI. In charge of an important case too. Don't underestimate her. I'd bet Brooks doesn't.'

MacBride said nothing for a while, but he did look across the room to where the newly reinstated detective inspector was holding court surrounded by a gaggle of detective constables and sergeants. Probably the same detective constables and sergeants who found it so amusing to point out the similarities between MacBride's scar and that of a famous fictional wizard. Something of a smile played across his face.

'I'll get that composite image run through the program, sir,' he said.

'You do that,' McLean said. 'And remember, sergeants get to order constables around.'

'Situation report, gentlemen. Lady. Just where exactly the fuck are we with all these investigations?'

Mid-afternoon, pre-briefing meeting and McLean found himself in the unusual position of sitting down in Duguid's office. The man himself took the head of the conference table that occupied one end of the room. Beside him DCI Brooks and DI Spence formed their own little huddle. There was a noticeable divide between those three and himself. Jayne McIntyre sat directly opposite him, her gaze wandering around the room that not so long ago had been hers. She let it fall finally on him, raising both eyebrows in weary resignation before starting to speak.

'Forensics are going to be on site for a while yet, but early indications are the whole place was deep-cleaned. Whoever did it knows how we process a crime scene, which ought to be a starting point for our investigations were that information not readily available on the internet.'

'Still something worth pursuing, I'd have thought.' DI Spence's skin stretched over his cadaverous cheekbones as he spoke, his Adam's apple bobbing nervously. He'd not reacted well to the return of the old boss.

'Oh, of course Michael. Don't you worry. We'll be pursuing it most assiduously. But there are other avenues that might be more productive in the meantime.'

'Such as?' DCI Brooks asked.

'There's a lot of large machinery in that warehouse. It has to have come from somewhere, and it has to have been brought in by someone. Assuming for the moment we're looking at a lone killer, then he would have had to get help with most of the larger items.'

'Find the source, trace the person who delivered it, who signed for it, that kind of thing.'

'Exactly. Grumpy Bob's been coordinating door-to-door

around the industrial estate. We've already got some e-fits of someone seen loitering around there. Checking through CCTV to see if we can get anything from that. I've got a couple of constables collating manufacturer names, models and serial numbers, and there's teams going round the hospitals and universities looking to see if kit is missing.'

Duguid nodded his approval. Not much more they could do at such an early stage.

'MacBride's running some analysis on the e-fits. The ones we've got from the Stevenson case too,' McLean said. 'It's a long shot, but it might throw up something.'

'You still think these are linked?' DCI Brooks asked.

'You still think they're not?'

'Gentlemen, let's not get started.' Duguid leaned forward, steepling his long fingers together and jamming them under his chin. 'There's no harm in looking at the possible connections. God knows we've got nothing even remotely useful like a motive for any of these.' He turned his attention to DI Spence. 'What's the situation with the nurse?'

'We've tracked down her last two boyfriends, but they've solid alibis. Not much in the way of motive either. Current hypothesis is that she was picked up by her killer the same night she was killed. Probably a one-night stand that went wrong. Forensics haven't been able to get anything useful from the dump scene, but that's not where she was killed. We're still looking for that, and her clothes.'

Duguid said nothing, but his face was as easy to read as the front cover of a tabloid newspaper. A week on from taking over the investigation, and Spence had progressed it exactly nowhere. McLean almost felt sorry for him. It wasn't as if there was anything easy about the case.

'Where are you with the heart we found in Stevenson's flat, McLean?' Duguid asked.

'It's a donated organ. Intended for use in a transplant, but the recipient died before it could be used. They can only keep these things alive for so long, sadly, so it was scheduled for cremation. The hospital's not sure how it was lost from the paper trail, but it must have been about a month ago. Whoever took it used embalming fluid to stop it rotting.'

'All good and well, but what the bloody hell was it doing there?'

'If I had to guess, sir, I'd say it was to distract us from our investigation. Lead us up a blind alley and give whatever clues there might have been more time to go cold. To be honest, I don't think why it was there is important. It's how it got there and where it came from we should be asking. We really need to be looking at the hospitals angle.'

'Hospitals?' Duguid gave him a puzzled stare that made it look as if the detective superintendent were trying to stifle a fart.

'It's a recurring theme, sir. Maureen Shenks worked at the Sick Kids, where she would have known Jim Whitely. The bulk of the material coming out of that warehouse is old stuff, machinery that's probably been replaced in a recent revamp of some of the ICU wards. Chances are it's been dumped in an outbuilding somewhere and forgotten about. You know what these organisations are like. There's twenty years' worth of outdated IT kit down in our basements that no one's ever got around to throwing out. The heart has to have been intercepted on its way to disposal, which would have been at the Royal Infirmary most likely, and lastly whoever killed Dr Whitely must have had some detailed medical knowledge.'

'It's all a bit thin though, isn't it?' Brooks said.

'Everything is thin. We're having rings run around us by this guy. He somehow persuades people to follow him into places where they won't be found. Places he's prepared well in advance. He kills them without any obvious sign of struggle using methods that are as precise as they're bizarre. He has to have had medical training. A doctor himself, or a skilled nurse.'

'But why? Why's he doing this, and why's he picking these victims? If you're so sure we've got a serial killer on our hands, what's the link?' This last question came from McIntyre, and for a moment McLean bridled at the thought that everyone was ranged against him. Then he saw the look on her face and realised she was trying to push him into stating his case better.

'I'll leave the why till we've caught him. Let's find out how he's doing this without leaving a trace. There can't be many people with the skill and resources to do what he's done. That's where we need to be concentrating our efforts.'

'You not going to your Bible class this evening?'

McLean had wandered into the combined incident room in search of DC MacBride, hoping for an update. Instead he had found DS Ritchie sitting at one of the desks set aside for the information hotlines, tapping away at a small laptop computer.

'It's not a Bible class, sir. You'd know that if you ever came along.'

'Sorry, that was uncalled for.' McLean pulled out a chair and sat down. The whole room was quiet, far quieter than an incident room for a triple murder had any right to be.

'Don't worry, I'm not easily offended.' Ritchie's smile showed she meant it.

'But you are still here.' McLean looked at his watch. 'And normally this time on a Tuesday you're not.'

'True. We're down on numbers this week though. Eric and Wanda are off on holiday, and Daniel's gone up to St Andrews to see the bishop.'

'The bishop? Anything I should know about?'

Ritchie's ears reddened at the question, but she didn't answer. McLean knew better than to push it, and despite his discomfort at the whole religion angle, he'd rather liked the earnest young minister who seemed to have caught his sergeant's eye. There were worse choices she could have made. Far worse.

'What're you up to then?' he asked.

'Just collating some of the new information Jay— DI McIntyre's got from the Whitely scene.'

'Anything promising?' McLean peered at the screen, but it was a meaningless screed as far as he could see.

'Not especially. Unless you take the view that a singular lack of evidence for all three crimes suggests they were committed by the same person. It's all rather tenuous though, isn't it?'

'Tell me about it. And while you're at it, perhaps you can explain how someone can fill a warehouse with medical equipment without anyone noticing.'

'Maybe he was seen. Stuart should have finished running the e-fit program by now. Might throw something up.'

'Did I hear my name?' DC MacBride appeared at the door, his tablet computer clutched in one hand. The constable's fringe was pulled down low again, almost covering his eyes. Sooner or later someone senior was going to tell him to get it cut.

'You got those e-fits?' Ritchie asked. MacBride nodded, tapped the screen a couple of times and handed the tablet to her.

'Just added in the ones from the Whitely crime scene. Composite image is at the end. Not sure it's any good, mind you.'

McLean peered over Ritchie's shoulder as she swiped through the images on the tablet. They were all vaguely similar and all vaguely familiar, but that was most likely a result of the e-fit system rather than anything concrete. There were too many differences for them to be the same man. Then Ritchie got to the last image and let out a little gasp.

'Dear God. It can't be.'

'What is it?' McLean reached for the tablet, staring at the final, composite image. It looked like no one he'd ever met.

'I . . . I think I know this man. Don't you recognise him?'

'Me?' McLean peered closer at the image, getting no spark from it. 'No. Should I?'

'It's Norman. Your neighbour. Well, a couple of houses down. Could swear it's him.'

'Norman?' McLean's puzzlement was obviously written large across his face. Ritchie took the tablet back and zoomed in on the e-fit eyes and nose.

'Norman Bale. You must know him, surely?'

A cold feeling seeped into the pit of McLean's stomach, that all-too-familiar sensation of things spiralling out of control.

'How do you know Norman?'

'Thought everybody knew him. He comes to the meetings. Never misses one. He's been a regular at the church since he was a boy, too. His folks with him, until they died.'

McLean was only half listening, his mind going back to the past, that long hot summer so many years ago.

'That isn't Norman Bale.'

'But it looks just like him. The more I see it, the more I wonder how I didn't recognise him before.'

'You misunderstand me.' McLean looked into those e-fit eyes, searching for any suggestion that he was wrong. Finding none. 'I don't doubt you when you say this is the man who attends your meetings, but it can't be Norman Bale. I knew Norman Bale, we grew up together for a while. And yes, he lived with his folks in the big house at the end of my street. But Norman Bale had leukaemia. He died when he was six years old.'

*

66

The house looks the same as it always has, but it feels different. I walk from room to room, places I used to play, places I used to hide, trying to work out what is wrong. And then it hits me; the house is just the same as ever it was. It's me who has changed. One term at that terrible boarding school, twelve weeks of struggling to understand why the other boys found my accent so amusing, of trying to fit in. Three months of wondering how I'd been so misled, why I'd been abandoned in such a horrible, unpredictable place. I wasn't the same six-year-old boy who'd travelled down all alone on the train. For one thing, I was seven now.

'You want something to eat, Tony?'

Gran came to meet me at the station and we went to Jenners for tea. It felt very grown-up, surrounded by old ladies in their finery, me in my school blazer and short trousers even in December. But I couldn't help remembering the dark wood-panelled dining hall with its lines of tables and benches. Over-boiled vegetables and something that might once have been meat, slathered in gelatinous brown gravy that tasted of salt and little else. If I had one abiding memory of that school beyond the random beatings, the interminable dull Latin lessons and the overwhelming sense of bewilderment, it was the nagging, constant hunger. I polished off two pieces of cake with my tea, a rare luxury, but now just a few hours later I am ravenous again.

'Yes please, Gran.' I take one last look at the drawing room, somewhere I never really spent much time anyway, then follow her to the warmth and welcome of the kitchen. Old Mrs Johnson's cooked a hearty stew, filled with dumplings and carrots and meat that tastes right. There's mashed potato that hasn't got bits in it and bright green peas I can mush up into it to make peaple pie. And best, there's gravy that runs around the plate and smells so wonderful I finally feel like I'm home.

'There's a choc-ice in the freezer for afters.' Gran pours a glass of orange squash from the jug in the middle of the table and pushes it over towards me. Sometimes she eats with me, but not tonight. I don't mind, too fixated on the food even to make conversation. I know I need to finish it if I'm going to have ice cream, and it's been a long, long time since I had ice cream.

It's only as I'm chasing the last of the mash around the plate, soaking up the last of the gravy, that I realise Gran has been sitting watching me the whole time. She hasn't said a word, just watched me eat.

'What is it?' I ask, pausing before the final mouthful.

'You've changed, Tony. Grown. Shot up like a beanpole.' Gran smiles at me, but there's something not right. I remember that smile all too well. It's the same smile she had when she told me mum and dad weren't coming home after all. Despite what they'd promised.

'Is something wrong?' I ask, and her shoulders slump.

'Oh, Tony. You've had so much to deal with already. It hardly seems fair to add yet more.' She says nothing for a while, and neither do I.

'It's about your little friend up the road. Norman.'

The rest of it is lost as Gran describes to me something that can't have happened. He got ill, started bleeding and wouldn't stop. The doctors did everything they could, but he had a disease. Something that sounds foreign and horrid, and all I can think of is the sight of his cut hand, the deep red blood oozing out, mixing with the dry dusty earth under the cedar tree. Was that the last time I saw him? I can't remember. All I know is that he's dead. Like mum and dad. Gone for ever. And he bled to death from a cut that wouldn't heal. A cut that was all my fault.

67

'Where're we going, sir?' Glancing in the rearview mirror, McLean could see DC MacBride slumped across the rear seat, the air from the open window ruffling his fringe and making him look even more like a teenager than usual. Had he not been wearing a dark suit, he might easily have passed for an undergraduate arrived in the city early for the start of his studies. Or maybe one of the countless hopefuls come to try his luck at the Festival.

'The church?' DS Ritchie peered out through the windscreen as they turned into the street. The evening sun was low in the sky, casting the spiky steeple in dark relief. Fingers of scaffolding surrounded it like barbed wire around a concentration camp. Keeping the faithful out, or maybe keeping something else in.

'Nothing in there, if Mary's to be believed.' McLean brought the car to a halt outside the rectory. 'Go see if she's in. Find out more about this man claiming to be Norman.'

Ritchie unclipped her seatbelt, opened the door. 'What about you?'

'I'm going to have a quick look at the old Bale house. See if anyone's been there recently. We'll meet back here in twenty minutes or so.'

Ritchie nodded, clambered out and shut the door. McLean watched her through the gate, then pulled away from the kerb. It wasn't far to his own driveway, but he carried on past, looking for the right entrance, wondering how best to play this. How many times had he been to this house? It had all been so long ago, that last lazy summer before his grandmother had packed him off to boarding school in England. He remembered it as dark, quiet, not all that much unlike his own place. At six, he'd not understood the dynamics of the family that lived there; all he'd known was that there was a boy the same age as him he could go and play with. And then that boy had died from a disease he couldn't even spell, let alone pronounce.

'On foot, I think.' He pulled over to the kerb, just past a gateway into a garden so choked with mature trees that it was impossible to see the house that lay beyond. They both climbed out, feeling the heat of yet another long sunny day reflect off the street and the stone walls to either side. That was when McLean noticed the smell.

'Well, well, well. What on earth brings you here?'

He turned to see an unwelcome figure climb out of a nondescript car parked just a few tens of yards further on. Jo Dalgliesh had a lit cigarette dangling from her mouth and breathed out the words in a cloud of her own smoke.

'I'm tempted to say the same for you, Ms Dalgliesh.'

'Suspect we're both interested in the same thing.' The reporter nodded in the direction of the house. 'Norman Bale?'

'What do you know about him?' McLean tried not to make the question sound too urgent, but he could see from Dalgliesh's stance that she knew something and was playing with him.

'He's no' in. That's one thing.'

'You've been up to the house?'

'Aye, creepy place it is.' Dalgliesh took a long drag on her cigarette, stared at it for a while as if unable to comprehend why it had finished, then flicked it on to the pavement and ground it out under her foot. It was obvious she wasn't in a sharing mood.

'Look. You know how important this investigation is. Are you going to tell me why you're here, or do I need to get Constable MacBride to arrest you for littering?'

Dalgliesh let out her lungful of smoke in a long slow breath, then started to search for something in her bag. 'All right, all right. You were much more fun when we were working together, you know.'

'Thought we were supposed to be still.'

'Aye, well. If you'd been a bit freer with the sharing, maybe I'd have given you this a bit quicker.' Dalgliesh handed over a thin sheaf of papers, mostly photographs of the research wall in Ben Stevenson's flat. McLean leafed through them, but it was hard to make out details in the failing light.

'Always thought it was a bit strange, Ben falling for some conspiracy nutter.' Dalgliesh produced a cigarette packet from the depths of her bag and proceeded to light up again. 'He could be a bit stupid at times, but no' like that. When you told me someone had broken in and taken down all that stuff he'd got, I reckoned it had to be important.'

'And it led you here?' McLean asked.

'Aye. Took a while to find it, but it was there. He worked out his contact was following him, so he followed him back. Reckon he probably thought there might be more to the story than he was being told. Guess he found out the hard way how true that was. So tell me, Inspector. Why do you want to talk to Norman Bale?'

'He's not here, sir.'

McLean and Dalgliesh both started at the voice. DC MacBride appeared from the gloom, his feet barely making any noise on the gravel.

'Jesus, Constable. You're a creepy sod sometimes.' Dalgliesh gave a low chuckle.

'No one home at all?' McLean asked.

'Doesn't look like it. Door's locked. Most of the downstairs windows are shuttered.'

McLean looked up the driveway into the gloom. His eyes were adjusting to the falling darkness now, better able to make out the house. It didn't look at all changed from how he remembered it, but it felt very different. Very wrong.

'Let's just go have a closer look, eh?'

The house was dark, surrounded by trees that cut off even the minimal light from the street lamps and the darkening gloaming sky. McLean stood outside the front door and was transported back decades. He remembered that one final summer as if it had been a whole lifetime; a clarity of memory associated only with childhood. Growing up brought so many distractions.

'Are we looking for anything in particular, sir?' DC MacBride stood perhaps a little too close, and McLean could tell from his body language that he wasn't all that happy to be there. Over by the large window that opened on to the morning room, Jo Dalgliesh was poking around in the gloom like an inept cat burglar.

'Small pot. It used to live by the boot scraper in the porch. Probably a bit less obvious now.' McLean fetched his pen torch from a pocket, then shone it around the area. Sure enough, an upside-down terracotta pot in the flowerbed a few feet off yielded a rusted key. So much for security.

'Touch nothing.' He handed a pair of latex gloves to Dalgliesh, pulled a pair on himself. There were so many reasons why he shouldn't have been doing this, and yet he needed to know what secrets the house revealed. In the blackness the nods of understanding he received from his companions were minimal. He directed the torch at the keyhole, slid the key in and turned.

Inside was a smell that he couldn't place. Not mouldering or rot, but something older and darker. It put him on edge, and did the same to Dalgliesh and MacBride if the way they drew closer in was anything to go by. McLean reached out and found the light switch, lower down the wall perhaps than he remembered, but exactly where his six-year-old self would have expected it to be. He flicked it up and bathed the hallway in light.

'Warn me before you do that again.' Dalgliesh stepped away from him, her hand reflexively going to her side. McLean wondered whether she had been about to hold his, and found he couldn't blame her. There was nothing obviously unusual about the room they were standing in, but it raised the hairs on the back of his neck all the same.

'Kitchen's that way, if I remember right.' He pointed across to a door beside the stairs. 'That's where the family spent most of their time.'

'You know this nutter then?' Dalgliesh asked.

'One summer. A long time ago, Norman Bale was my

friend. Whoever we're looking for, whatever he says, he's not Norman Bale.' McLean led the way, retracing childhood steps along a corridor far shorter than he remembered, through a much smaller door still strangely covered in green baize, and into the kitchen.

'Looks like a kitchen to me.' MacBride walked slowly around the table in the middle of the room, ran a gloved hand over the spotless wooden surface. McLean remembered a room full of life, a place where things happened, food was prepared, plans made, prayers said. This wasn't the heart of the house any more. He crossed to the stove, placed a hand on the cover over the hotplate, lifted it and felt the flat metal underneath. Cold, or at least as cold as the summer heat would let it be. Certainly not lit.

'Not in here,' he said. 'Maybe this way.'

They followed him out into the hallway again, then through another door into the drawing room. This was no more alive than the kitchen, the air stale, the dust heavy on every surface. If the man claiming to be Norman Bale had been in the house, he hadn't spent any time in here.

Neither had he spent time in old Mr Bale's study, the morning room or the library. With each new door opened, each light switched on, McLean found himself transported back in time. And with each new door he also began to see how the house had been frozen in time, how nothing had changed since that long-ago summer.

And then they reached the dining room.

Perhaps he had been expecting it and given off subliminal signals. Or maybe there really was something about the place that put people's backs up. Either way, as he pushed open the final door downstairs and reached for the light switch, McLean could feel Dalgliesh and MacBride press in close behind him. The smell that had bothered him when he'd opened the front door was stronger in here, a wrongness he couldn't quite place. Until he switched on the light.

As a young, innocent wee boy, McLean had eaten lunch at that table. Guzzled down plates of jelly, Angel Delight and all those terrible things people had thought were food in the 1970s. He remembered a polished surface you weren't allowed to put your glass of squash down on, a slightly scary room where adults talked to you as if you might one day be an adult too.

'Oh my God.' Dalgliesh took his hand this time, clutching it hard and drawing herself closer to him than was perhaps comfortable. Behind him, McLean heard DC MacBride take a sharp breath, and he could hardly blame the constable. Neither he nor the reporter had ever met Colin and Ina Bale, after all.

They sat as they always had done, much older than he remembered them, but still easy to recognise. Mr Bale was at the head of the table, his wife to his right and at the side. In the artificial light it was difficult to tell how long they had been dead, but it had been a while. They looked like wax dummies, hair turned thin and straggly, faces fixed in rictus grins, eyes dried and white with cataracts. Places had been laid at the table in front of them both, empty plates awaiting food that would never come. And to the other side was a third place where someone had quite recently sat and eaten a meal.

68

'The Christian cross is a misrepresentation, of course. It looks impressive, but from a carpentry point of view it's inefficient. Most Roman crucifixes were just two bits of wood roped together in the middle and splayed to form an X.'

He is woozy from the anaesthetic, but I can see the spark in him as he awakens. Arms splayed, legs akimbo, I imagine he must be struggling to work out where he is. The drugs will dull most of the pain, but soon he will feel the nails through his palms and feet. I imagine he'll start to panic then.

'It's no matter, of course. Christian symbol, Roman torture. It's all a means to an end. Your end, as it happens. And your beginning.'

Eyes flutter under lids taped down. It will be dark where he is. His breathing is growing rapid, snot spiralling down from his nose to form a little puddle on the floor. He can't breathe through his mouth, of course. That's taped up too. We are closer here to any passers-by. I can't take the risk of being interrupted before this ceremony is over.

'You don't know just how blessed you are. How lucky. God has singled you out to be with him in heaven. Your soul is pure.'

Naked, his body is thin, ribs straining through pale skin turned orange by the light of the setting sun outside.

Greens and reds and blues mottle the flesh on his arms, low light filtering through the smaller north windows. East–west the church lies, catching the rising and setting sun through stained glass at either end of the aisle. Except that this far north, at this time of year, the sun rises far north of east and sets far north of west. It doesn't matter, truly. The perfect moment will be here soon enough.

I stand before him, watching as the light shifts and swirls over his body. Outside, the city roar has faded away to nothing. It does not exist any more. We are alone, he and I. And God.

'Our father, which art in heaven, hallowed be thy name.'

He shakes his head from side to side, cheeks puffing in and out as he tries to breathe. His arms tense, hands sliding over their slippery nails, but I've bent the ends over. He won't escape them. Blood drips from his stigmata, runs down his arms and drips from his elbows. It mingles in the dust on the floor with the blood from the wounds in his feet.

'Thy kingdom come, thy will be done on earth, as it is in heaven.'

I can feel the moment building, the tension stretching the air as if it were made of foam. I too find it difficult to breathe, awed in the presence of God.

'Give us this day, our daily bread. And forgive us our debts, as we forgive out debtors.'

I am heavy now like a sack of bones. Their weight drags me to the floor, knees settling into the dirt and the blood. And still I am ground down by that awesome presence, squeezed until my face is pushed into the mess.

'And lead us not into temptation, but deliver us from evil.'

His breathing is ragged now, the weight of his body making it almost impossible for him to suck in air, the panic crushing him even as the weight evaporates from my shoulders. He won't hang upon the cross for long, agonising hours. Death will take him swiftly, God's mercy as He gathers up this saved soul to Him.

'For thine is the kingdom, the power and the glory.'

I look up and see the golden light of the sun, piercing through the coloured glass to limn his head like a halo. For a moment I see the crown of thorns, the blood running down his cheeks, then it blurs as my eyes fill with tears, my whole body suffused with joy.

'For ever and ever.'

He is close now, and I know the perfect ecstasy of being in the presence of the divine. And yet even in that moment there is the exquisite sadness. Knowing that it is not my soul that will be gathered up. Knowing that it is not yet my time, that I must struggle still longer in this mundane, sinful world. And as I gaze up at this perfect, dying man, I feel the serpent of jealousy squirm in my guts and know why it is that I am not yet worthy.

The tears come freely now and I drop my head in supplication. Kneel before Christ on the cross and pray.

'Amen.'

69

The gloom outside the Bale house was only slightly less menacing than that within as McLean pulled the front door closed. He considered asking Dalgliesh to stay in her car, or better yet to go home and wait for him to call her, but he knew that wasn't going to happen. She was too much of a reporter to resist following him around as this juicy story unfolded.

'Get on to control will you, Constable. We need to secure the scene as soon as possible. Wait here until back-up arrives, then come and find me at the rectory.'

MacBride nodded his understanding, pulled out his airwave set and started to make the call.

'And Stuart? Don't do anything stupid. This man's very dangerous.'

'I'll keep out of sight, sir. And don't worry, I'll not try and tackle him on my own if he shows up.'

'Right. Dalgliesh, you're with me. And keep your eyes peeled. Last thing I want is to bump into this man unawares. Whoever he is.' McLean set off down the drive at a rapid pace, partly to avoid any of the inevitable questions the reporter would throw at him, but mostly because his stomach was telling him something bad was going down.

'Whoever he is . . .? You mean he's no' real?' Dalgliesh wheezed as she struggled to keep up. McLean ignored her. They reached the rectory in minutes, and he rang the doorbell. A light shone in the porch even though it wasn't yet dark, the evening sun still painting the side of the stone steeple in autumn orange. Some of the scaffolding had begun to come down, he noticed. Piles lying beside the graves. It still surrounded the old building like a canker. Engulfed it.

DS Ritchie opened the door a few moments later. Her expression was one of alarm, her free hand unconsciously reaching for her throat and the slim silver band that hung around her neck and tucked into her blouse.

'You've not found him, I take it?'

'No. Is Mary in?'

'Kitchen.' Ritchie stood aside and let them pass.

'Norman's not here, Inspector.' Mary Currie appeared from the hallway, her face pale in the shadows.

'Norman's not Norman.'

'That's what Kirsty said, but it can't be true. I've known Norman for years.'

Could he be wrong? McLean pulled the e-fit photo out of his pocket, unfolded it and stared at it again. Impossible to tell whether the badly constructed image was the same person as the weedy six-year-old boy he'd known. The boy whose parents were so religious. The boy who his grandmother had told him was dead.

'Daniel's missing too,' Ritchie said.

McLean's train of thought derailed. A horrible cold sensation forming in the pit of his stomach. 'I thought he'd gone to St Andrews to meet the bishop?'

'So did I, but he never showed up. They phoned about an hour ago, apparently. Wondering where he was.'

McLean could hear the panic rising in the detective

sergeant's voice. Controlled for now, but betraying her thoughts all too clearly. They weren't that far from his own.

'Look, why don't we all go through to the kitchen?' Mary Currie was the voice of reason. 'The kettle's on. We'll have a cup of tea and get to the bottom of this.'

'Dan's still not answering his phone. Just keeps going to message.' Ritchie paced back and forth in the rectory kitchen, doing a good impression of DCI Brooks despite her lack of bulk. She'd called the number three times since McLean and Dalgliesh had followed her into the kitchen.

'We'll find him. Find both of them.' McLean tried to reassure the detective sergeant, only realising what he'd said as the words came out.

'You think they're together? Why would they be together?'

'No. That's not what I meant.' McLean tried to convince himself, couldn't quite manage. He turned his attention to the minister, even now pouring teaspoons of sugar into everyone's milky tea.

'Mary, I'm right in thinking Daniel's living here? In the rectory?'

'Yes, of course. It's a big old house to rattle around in on my own. I'm forever picking up waifs and strays. Much like you, really.'

'I couldn't have a quick look at his room, could I?'

The minister frowned. 'Why would you want to do that?'

'Just to see if he left any clue as to where he was going.' It wasn't a good lie, but the minister shrugged.

'Well, I suppose if I can't trust a policeman, who can I?'

She picked up two mugs, handing one to Dalgliesh, who took it with a little start of surprise.

'I'll show you, sir.' Ritchie stuck her phone back into her pocket, call number four having been as unsuccessful as all the rest.

'Stay here with the minister, we won't be long.' McLean said to Dalgliesh, then realised that he'd not yet introduced them to each other. 'Sorry. Mary, this is Jo Dalgliesh. She's a reporter. You might get Detective Constable MacBride knocking on your door in a moment, too. I'm sure he'd be very grateful for a cup of tea, if you didn't mind.'

'For someone who gave so generously to the church roof repair fund? Not in the least.'

McLean nodded his thanks, then turned to follow Ritchie out of the kitchen, but not before he noticed Dalgliesh's eyebrow shoot up in surprise.

'So, you know where the curate sleeps. Should I be worried for the state of his soul?'

DS Ritchie stopped halfway up the stairs, looked around over her shoulder and gave McLean a very old-fashioned stare.

'Sorry, that was uncalled for. Especially given the circumstances.'

'It's OK, sir. I know you're just trying to ease the tension a bit.' Ritchie started climbing again, speaking to the dark landing above. 'To be honest, I've never seen Daniel's room. I only know where it is because it's next to the bathroom. Here.'

McLean followed her across the landing, stopped outside a plain wooden door indistinguishable from a half-dozen others. The gloom was only alleviated by the light spilling up the stairwell, and a faint orange glow through a pair of recessed skylight windows overhead. Silence filled the air like cotton wool as he reached out and rapped a knuckle on the panel.

'Daniel? Are you in there?' If only it were that easy.

'OK. Let's have a look then.' McLean dropped his hand to the doorknob, twisted it and pushed.

It was a large room, high-ceilinged and dominated by two tall windows in the far wall. Heavy, dark furniture looked like it must have been craned in before the roof went on, but had presumably been hefted up the stairs by stout Victorian workmen a century or so ago. By the light filtering in from outside, McLean made out a narrow single bed, a washstand in the far corner, floorboards covered by an old Persian rug. A desk sat between the two windows, but it was hard to see any great detail. Then DS Ritchie flicked on the light.

'Oh my God.'

The room was mostly tidy, that was perhaps the best way to describe it. The bed was made and everything was lined up square, the gaps between each individual item of furniture arranged so that they looked in proportion. In amongst the order, the desk stuck out like a nun at a rugby club stag night. It was piled with books, all of a jumble as if Daniel had been going through them in a rush, looking for snippets of information first from one then another, tossing them aside when they didn't yield what he searched for. Others lay on the floor in a circle around the chair, wagons drawn together against the Indian attack. On the desktop, ground zero, an A4 spiral-bound notebook lay in the middle of it all, splayed open to reveal a page of scribblings. McLean approached it carefully, not wanting to disturb anything, and peered at the words. He couldn't make anything out, and he was used to deciphering Grumpy Bob's impossible scrawl. It didn't matter; the stacks of newspaper cuttings, Post-it notes and half-read books told the story quite clearly enough.

'I never knew.' Ritchie stood by McLean's side, peering down at the evidence of an interest verging on the brink of obsession.

McLean picked up the nearest book, turned it over to reveal the title. *Urban Deprivation: Causes and Cures*. Other books followed a similar theme. No light bedtime reading here.

'We need to find him.' He put the book back down on the pile. Hoped to hell no one else had found him already.

Mary Currie and Jo Dalgliesh were chatting like old friends when McLean and Ritchie came back into the kitchen. The minister broke off, her face asking the question before she voiced it.

'Find anything?'

'Not what we were hoping for.' McLean wondered how best to broach the subject, then realised there wasn't really time for niceties. 'Tell me, would you have said Daniel was obsessive about things?'

Mary frowned. 'Obsessive? Not really. He's earnest, keen. His faith is very strong. But I wouldn't have called him obsessive.'

'He has a thing about social deprivation though.'

'Oh, that. Yes, there is that. But I wouldn't call it an obsession, really. More of a fixation. If there's a difference.'

'When was the last time you saw him?' McLean asked. 'When was the last time you saw this chap who claims to be Norman, for that matter?'

'I've not seen Norman since Sunday. We had a service at Saint Michael's across town. Can't use our own church at the moment. It's full of scaffolding and building stuff.' Mary Currie frowned as she tried to gather her thoughts. 'Dan was here for breakfast. He was meant to be getting the half-ten train to Leuchars, to have lunch with the bishop and be home in time for Evensong. He was thinking about taking him up on his offer, wanted to discuss it face to face. That's Daniel for you. Likes to be hands-on.'

Ritchie looked up from her phone at the words. 'The bishop's offer? He was going to take it up?'

'I'm not sure, but I got the feeling he was considering it. He's been torn about it for weeks now. Sometimes he prays for guidance, but it's been weighing heavy on him.'

McLean watched the exchange, not quite understanding it but sure somehow that it was important. 'I'm missing something here. The bishop's offer?'

'There's a parish in Perthshire that's looking for a new minister. Daniel was offered the post, but he always saw himself as more of a missionary. Never seen someone with such zeal before, but I think he might have been starting to reconsider.' Mary glanced at DS Ritchie standing in the doorway, clasping her phone as if it were the most precious thing in the world. 'Can't think why.'

The doorbell ringing broke the silence that followed.

Ritchie stood bolt upright at the sound, as if someone had wired her into the same circuit as the tinny electronic bell. Without a word she darted out of the kitchen and down the hall. Moments later she returned, less energetically, with DC MacBride in tow.

'Squad car's arrived and parked outside the gate, sir. Keeping an eye on things until the forensics people arrive. Bale's e-fit's gone out to all officers in Scotland. Should be hitting the news later. Oh, and Dagwood wants to know what's going on.'

'Did you tell him?'

'Thought it best coming from you, sir. He sounds hopping mad you ran off without updating him on Bale.'

'Well, he'll just have to wait. We've a missing curate to find.' McLean tried to remember what the minister had been saying before they were interrupted. 'He was praying for guidance? Where would he do that?'

'Where? What do you mean?'

'Well, if the church is off limits, where would he go to pray?'

'Oh, I see what you mean. No. We can't hold services in the church; Health and Safety won't let us open it to the public. Nothing stopping Daniel or me from going in there though. If he was looking for a little peace and quiet he might well have gone in there. But he wouldn't have spent all day there, let alone into the evening.'

'What about this man . . . Norman? Would he go there to pray too? Even if the signs said keep out?'

McLean didn't wait for an answer. He could see it dawning on the minister's face. He checked his watch, counted the hours. Too many, surely.

He put a hand on Dalgliesh's shoulder, pushing her back into her chair as she tried to get up. 'You stay here, keep Mary company.' He turned to MacBride. 'Stay with them. And get more uniforms over here as soon as you can.' And finally to Ritchie, already putting her phone away. 'You're with me.'

70

Darkness filled the inside of the church like peat water, shadows casting weird shapes in the open space. Scaffold poles marched down the aisles and criss-crossed in a tangle of metal; the untidy nest of some improbably large bird. The echo of the closing door took less time to fall to nothing than McLean had expected, muffled by heavy wooden boards overhead. He held his hand up for silence before Ritchie could say a word, then strained to hear anything unusual in the quiet.

Nothing. Not even the muted, distant hum of the city outside. The church was unnaturally still, as if something somewhere held its breath in anticipation. Treading softly, McLean stepped into the body of the kirk, all the while listening out for something louder than the thunder of blood in his veins, the racket of his heart beating.

The ancient, carved stone font squatted in its familiar place, where he had seen it scant months ago, but the rest of the church interior was unrecognisable. Piles of unused scaffold boards stacked up against the pews, themselves dragged to the walls. Looking down, he saw scuffed flagstones, some inscribed with words in memory of the mouldering bones lying beneath them, barely visible in the final gloaming of the dying day. Beside him, Ritchie was turning slowly on one heel, searching for signs of life, when she let out a low moan of horror.

'What is it?' McLean spoke the words in a low whisper, but she was already moving away from him at a run. And he could see for himself what had set her off.

At the far end of the nave, just as the low stone steps climbed up to the altar, someone had constructed a makeshift crucifix from scaffolding poles and what looked like roof beams. The first thing that struck McLean was its size, so much bigger than the crosses he was used to seeing on the few, uncomfortable occasions he had found himself in a church. The second thing he noticed was that this cross, unlike the usual Christian affairs, was a crude X. The sort of thing he remembered from school and lessons in ancient history.

The third thing he saw was the naked man, arms and legs splayed, dark marks where he had been nailed in place.

'Wait!' McLean tried to shout, but his voice caught in his throat. It was a wasted effort anyway. Ritchie was almost at the body now, reaching out for it. As she did so he recognised the man nailed there as the young minister, Daniel, and the pieces started to fall uncomfortably into place.

He took a step further into the church, straining his ears to hear anything over the low 'no, no, no,' of DS Ritchie as she tried to get to the cross and the man spreadeagled upon it. He had thought the church empty, but it was hard to tell. Too many shadows, dark upon dark in shapes that could simply be benches stacked in a corner, or a murderer lurking with evil intent. He reached the aisle, turning slowly, letting his eyes adjust as he fumbled out his mobile phone. The screen blazed light at his touch, almost painful to look at. Still he thumbed at it until the speed dial for the incident room came up, clamped the phone to his ear as he approached the crucifix.

'McLean,' he said as soon as the call was answered. 'Who speaks?'

'It's me, sir. Sandy . . . that is, Detective Constable Gregg, sir.' Well it could have been worse.

'Constable, I need a full tactical team out here as soon as possible.' McLean gave her the address as he approached the body. The cross was surrounded by a jumble of scaffold poles, precariously balanced one upon another so as to make getting within touching distance almost impossible. Instead of clearing them, Ritchie was trying to climb over, but every time she put a foot down the pile shifted under her and she had to step back again.

'I can't reach him. We need to move this.' She bent down and pulled at a scaffold pole, then let out a shriek as it rolled over, trapping her hand. McLean managed to find the end of the pole, lift it enough for her to free herself, then they both had to scramble backwards as the pile collapsed.

'What's going on, sir? Sounds like a car crash.' DC Gregg's voice sounded thin with the clattering of steel pipes still ringing in his ears, but McLean was more concerned by the crucified priest. The noise had stirred him, his head shifting so slightly it might even have been a trick of the light. Except that there was barely any light in the place now to trick them.

'I need an ambulance and a fire team. Five minutes, Constable.'

'I'm on it, sir. Only Superintendent Duguid . . .'

Whatever it was Duguid wanted, McLean never found out. Ritchie had managed to pick a path through the tangle of scaffold poles now. She reached the cross and began climbing it, looking for a way to cut her boyfriend down. The instant she touched him, the church filled with a screech like some terrible, fantastical monster roused from its slumbers.

'You must not interfere. This is God's work!'

McLean barely had time to react before a figure came flying through the air at him. He ducked out of the reach of a hand he thought was going for his throat, tripped on a coil of rope left behind by the builders and fell backwards. Sharp steel glinted in the half-light, whistling through the air where his neck had been, then his head smacked against something hard. Stars crazed the darkness, a roaring in his ears like standing in a tunnel as the train comes. He fought to stay conscious, vision narrowing to a dark-circled point that focused on the crucified priest and Ritchie's frantic attempts to cut him down.

'His soul is pure. You cannot stop the Lord from taking him.' The words were oddly distorted, like a radio dropped into the bath. McLean struggled to pick himself up off the floor, hands finding everything slippery. He lifted one up, seeing it smeared in something dark, and only then did the pain register, a cut across his palm, another at the back of his head where it had hit.

Everything was in slow motion except the man moving through the shadows. He was everywhere, flicking in and out of existence like some child's nightmare monster. The jumble of poles was no more of an obstacle to him than chalk lines on a pavement. Closer and closer to the cross, the crucified priest and DS Ritchie, that wicked shining blade blazing with fire as it caught a stray beam of light from the stained glass windows. McLean knew in that instant exactly what had happened to Maureen Shenks. And why.

'No!' The word sounded dull in his muffled ears, but there was an urgency in it that must have carried. As he scrambled to woozy feet, so Ritchie finally turned her attention away from the cross, saw her attacker at the last possible moment. She ducked away from him as he lunged, her training kicking in as she positioned herself best to deal with the blade. McLean stumbled towards her, the room still spinning in his head, aware somewhere in the back of his mind that he was unarmed, concussed and approaching a man with a knife. The nave seemed to draw away from him as he struggled towards the altar and he watched in horror as Ritchie fell backwards over one arm of the makeshift cross. The man who claimed to be Norman leapt around it, his movements more like those of an ape as he pressed his advantage. She was on her back, arms up to protect herself from the stabbing knife and still McLean was too far away.

'Norman, stop.'

Whether it was the pitch of his voice or something more fundamental, the use of that name stopped the man in his tracks. At his feet, DS Ritchie was curled in on herself, arms covering her head, the sleeves of her jacket shredded and bloody. Bale straightened, turned to meet his accuser, and McLean realised he was much closer to the cross than he'd thought. He looked up briefly at Daniel's pale face, wincing in pain as his head protested at the movement.

'Do you like what I've done, Tony?'

The voice was at once alien and hauntingly familiar. Older, true, but also just the same. Could it really be him? Had his grandmother lied to him about Norman's death? Had he really survived? Grown up to become this monster?

Norman stepped lightly away from Ritchie, the knife still sharp in his grasp. As he walked around the cross, he ran his free hand down Daniel's naked thigh, smearing the blood that had dribbled from the crucified man's hand down his arm, dripped from his armpit like thick, red sweat. A low noise stirred from the body, bubbles of spittle and blood leaking from his nose. Still alive. There was still hope. And help was surely on its way now. He just needed a little time.

'I thought you died. All those years ago. Leukaemia. That's what they told me.'

'Oh, I died, Tony. I had a disease that your precious science couldn't cure. Of course it couldn't. It was God's will that I die. He took me into his arms and told me I was chosen.'

McLean couldn't be sure whether his head was clearing or not, but he felt a little steadier on his feet. He edged slowly backwards, up the aisle in the direction of the font. The man who might have been Norman followed him, still holding that wicked sharp knife.

'Why, Norman? What were you chosen for? What was Daniel to you? What were the others?'

'You don't know? You can't see it?' Norman took a step closer and McLean could see the madness in his eyes, glinting in the last of the light. They flicked around like a bird's. Darting here and there, trying to take in everything but seeing something very different to the mundane.

'Tell me what I should be seeing.' McLean edged back another step, hoping Ritchie wasn't badly injured. Any minute now the cavalry would arrive. Surely.

'Of course you can't see it. None of them could. But I can. I can see it in them. In Daniel here, in Ben and Jim and all the others. And I can see it in you.'

Norman lunged forward, knife hand outstretched. McLean moved slowly, too slowly, his head still filled with sawdust and fireworks. A ripping sound, and he felt a tug on his jacket, a sharp pain in his side as the knife slid across his ribs. He pirouetted around, trying to get out of the way as Norman danced in the darkness, coming in for a killing strike. Something blocked him, the ancient carved stone font. He was trapped, helpless.

'Such glory in his work. Two perfect souls will go to heaven this day.' Norman stepped up close, knife held high as he made to strike. McLean raised his hands in defence, knowing it was useless, remembering the mess that had been made of Ben Stevenson and Maureen Shenks.

And then confusion. A dull thud echoed briefly in the hall. Bale's eyes shot upwards even as his knees gave way. He dropped the knife, crumpled to the silent floor. Behind him a grinning Devil's face loomed out of the shadows. Jo Dalgliesh held a short length of scaffold pole in her hand, an evil glint in her eye.

'You already killed one of my friends. Got few enough of them as it is. Damned if I'm going to lose another.'

71

He sat on the edge of a stone sarcophagus, unsure if that was even the right word for it, as a paramedic wound a pure white bandage around his hand. McLean wasn't quite sure if he was in shock or just working his way through the latter stages of mild concussion. Either way, the world had a surreal tinge to it that made some things indistinct whilst bringing others into sharp relief. It was fully dark now, the street lamps surrounded by their individual insect tribes. The trees rustled in a warm breeze and the night air brought sharp smells.

'Here, drink this.' A smiling, worried face hoved into view, bearing a mug of steaming tea. McLean took it, nodding gratefully before realising that it had been given to him by Mary Currie.

'How's DS . . . Kirsty?' he asked.

'She'll be fine once the cuts heal. They're only superficial. Going to need a new jacket, mind you.' The minister sunk down on to the stone beside him. She smelled of old classrooms, he realised. Not those where he'd been humiliated in front of his peers by inadequate teachers, but the warm, dusty, sun-filled classrooms where he'd semi-dozed and listened to wonderful stories of Roman history, Celtic warriors and adventurous ancient Greeks. The classrooms where he'd discovered poetry and realised that God was a lie. The thought brought an ironic smile to his lips.

'Norman. How terrible. And Daniel.' Mary Currie sounded like she was in shock herself. She probably was, and yet she'd still made tea for the ever-growing number of police descending on her church. The crime scene.

'He's not Norman. Norman died when he was six years old.'

Mary's face wrinkled in puzzlement. 'But he lives in the house. His parents . . .'

McLean shook his head, winced in pain. 'I don't know. Smacked my head on a pew in there. Things will probably make more sense in the morning.'

The minister said nothing more for a while. Then nodded towards the church door, wide open and with a young uniform constable standing guard outside.

'Is he . . . Daniel?'

As if to answer his question, a commotion from the church door spilled several paramedics and a couple of uniform officers out into the night, wheeling a gurney. One of the paramedics was holding a saline bag up high as they bustled past. Not something you did for a dead man.

'He was alive when we found him. Poor bastard. Going to take some healing. Mental as well as physical.'

'I'd better go with him. To the hospital.' Mary Currie stood up again, too swiftly. She swayed slightly, putting a hand on McLean's shoulder to steady herself. The contact was a reassurance, and it eased away the last of the fog from his brain.

'I'll make sure there's a constable on the rectory door.' He looked around at the bustle. 'Not that I think anyone's going to try and break in with this lot here.'

'Thank you, Tony. You're a good man.' She gave him a weak smile and trotted off after the paramedics.

'So everyone tells me,' he said, but no one heard him.

Detective Superintendent Duguid arrived long after the commotion had died down. His thinning hair was awry, and he had the look about him of a man on the edge of a nervous breakdown. McLean spotted him climbing out of his car and going to speak to DCI Brooks, which meant he could duck out of sight behind an ornate carved headstone before he was seen.

'Going somewhere, Inspector?'

Jo Dalgliesh was leaning against the headstone, an unlit cigarette in her mouth. As press, she should technically have been ushered back past the crime-scene tape that surrounded the church and graveyard. DC MacBride must have said something, as all the policemen milling around were studiously ignoring her.

'Keeping away from the boss, if I'm being honest. Not sure I can cope with a debriefing right now.'

'Know how you feel. Going to be interesting breaking this one to the office.'

'There'll be a prize or two in it for you, I'd have thought.'

'Aye. Mebbe. Ben died chasing this though. Feels a bit . . . I dunno.'

'Is that a conscience I see growing?'

'Fuck off, aye?'

McLean risked a glance around the headstone, saw Duguid and Brooks in deep discussion, DI Spence hanging around them like a needy spaniel. They didn't appear to be looking for him, which was all the encouragement he needed.

'Come with me,' he said to the reporter, then strode off towards the church and the shadows. She took a moment to catch up, taken by surprise. 'Where we going?'

'To find MacBride, maybe Ritchie if she's not gone off to the hospital with her boyfriend.'

That raised an eyebrow. 'Thought there was something more going on there than just devotion to duty. Why'd you need my help? Thought you couldn't stand the sight of me.'

'My house is just over the road.' McLean nodded in the general direction, then winced as the lump on the back of his head throbbed its disapproval. 'Don't know about anyone else, but I reckon I could do with a large dram. Figure I owe you one too. You probably saved my life back there, even if I did ask you to stay in the house with the minister.'

'Probably?' Dalgliesh pulled the cigarette out of her mouth, stopped walking for a moment as if insulted. Then she shook her head. 'Aye, probably's right enough. Probably.'

72

'He still claiming to be Norman Bale?'

McLean stood in the observation room looking into interview room one. Through the one-way glass, the man who might be Norman Bale sat silently at the table, staring into the middle distance. Detective Superintendent Duguid held a long-fingered hand up to the glass as if he wanted to reach out and pluck the man's head off.

'That's his story and he's sticking to it. We couldn't find any ID on him, but forensics put him all over the Bales' house. He's been living there a while now. Mary . . . the minister's known him as Norman for at least five years. He's a regular at the church, every Sunday without fail.'

'So it could be him,' Duguid said.

McLean squinted through the glass at that thin, pale face. Tried to square it with the boy he'd known all those years ago. It was possible, he supposed. But how was it possible?

'We've checked the hospital records. Norman Bale was admitted to the Sick Kids with leukaemia when he was six years old. He died shortly afterwards, according to the death certificate.'

'And yet here he is.' Duguid leaned against the glass, then backed off when the man at the interview table looked up at him.

'His folks packed up and went to Africa not long after

he died. Norman, that is. The real Norman. Left that old house empty for a good few years. Some kind of missionary work. My gran was very sceptical about it.'

'She was sceptical about pretty much everything, if I remember right. Religion more than most.'

McLean looked at Duguid in surprise. Of course the detective superintendent would have known his grandmother; she'd been a consultant pathologist at the city mortuary long into her retirement. Called in to comment on the more bizarre cases the city occasionally threw up. He just couldn't remember Duguid ever having mentioned her before.

'Strange, now you mention her. She never said anything about Norman to me. Or his parents, but she'd have known when they came back to Edinburgh.'

'Well, it doesn't really matter. Norman Bale or someone else. Odds on he killed them, creepy wee fuck that he is. The other three as well.'

'I've a nasty feeling that's just the start of it.'

'What?' Duguid's face drained of colour.

'Bale's parents have been dead at least five years. That's when they were supposed to have been buried. Ben Stevenson was killed just over eight weeks ago. You honestly think he's been doing nothing all that time? I'd be digging up the unsolved case files, missing persons, that sort of thing.'

If anything, Duguid went even paler. 'Don't fucking complicate things, McLean. Leave that to the cold case boys. Just get a confession out of him.'

McLean looked away from the detective superintendent, back to the interview room through the glass. Norman, or not Norman, was staring straight at him now, a slight frown on his face that sent a shiver down McLean's spine.

'Somehow I don't think that's going to be a problem, sir.'

There was something unnerving about his calmness. That was the thing that struck McLean most as he took his seat in the interview room. A duty solicitor sat beside the man claiming to be Norman Bale, his chair a little further away from the accused than was perhaps polite. Another chair was still tucked under the table, Grumpy Bob having decided that he preferred to stand by the door. No one had complained so far.

'You say your name is Norman Bale. That you're the only child of Colin and Ina Bale. And yet our records show the real Norman Bale died when he was six years old.'

'Records. You know as well as I do how easy it is to fake those, Tony.'

McLean met that staring gaze, still trying to reconcile it with the boy he'd known all those years ago. Norman had called him Tony just that way, but he still couldn't accept that this was indeed his old friend. If it was, then his grandmother had lied to him. That opened up an even nastier can of worms.

'So you're telling me your death was faked.'

'Oh no. I died. God took me to his bosom. Medical science failed. But the Lord had plans for me, and so I was reborn.'

'Straight away? Or did you spend some time in heaven before returning to this mortal plane?'

'Time has no meaning there. It is just one endless

moment of perfect bliss. You'd know that, Tony. If you just believed.'

Bale, or not Bale, flicked his eyes to the right, looking briefly up as Grumpy Bob pulled the chair out from under the table and sat down. McLean paid the detective sergeant no heed, taking the time to study the man sitting opposite. For a moment he'd been uncertain, but in that one look he'd finally accepted that this wasn't Norman Bale. Who he was would be a question for another investigation, another detective and maybe a team of psychologists. He was probably someone the Bales had taken in, a lodger or just a charity case. They had always been good people that way. Whoever this person was, he had insinuated himself into their lives, and maybe they had encouraged him. Maybe they, too, had seen something of their dead son in his eyes. Fooled themselves that he had returned.

'OK. Let's accept you are who you say you are. For now, at least. So tell me. Did you kill your parents, Norman?'

Grumpy Bob flipped open his notebook and pretended to take notes, even though the whole interview was being recorded. DS Ritchie had wanted to attend, but she wasn't long out of hospital, still on antibiotics for her cuts. And her relationship with Daniel meant she had been taken off the case. McLean wished he could beg the same favour.

'I would advise you not to answer that, Norman.' The duty solicitor's enthusiasm was almost too feeble to measure. He appeared to have written this one off as an insanity plea already.

'They were the first. The first time God showed me

what my purpose in life was to be. After he sent me back to them.' Norman's voice was calm, matter of fact. As if he understood perfectly the situation he was in, accepted it as just another day.

'Why did you kill them?'

'They were such good people. You met them, you must have known. They prayed every day, went to church on Sunday, gave money to the poor, time to charities. Their whole lives were dedicated to His service. It was only a matter of time before their souls became pure. When they did, I knew at once what had to be done. A pure soul cannot survive long in this world without becoming corrupted, after all.'

'So you killed them to save their souls?' McLean didn't try to hide the element of doubt in his voice.

'It's funny, really.' Norman smiled like a shark, turning to the duty solicitor. 'You have no hope. Your soul is a dirty thing. It will burn in eternal hellfire. You,' he nodded at Grumpy Bob, 'you'll be judged at the end. Saint Peter will have his scales ready for you. I truly hope you won't be found wanting. But you,' and now he turned his gaze back to McLean, 'you are so close, even though you don't know it, won't admit that you even have a soul at all. You are like Ben and Jim, Daniel and all the others, just needing that little push. You were to be my next project.'

'Were to be?' McLean suppressed the shudder that wanted to run through him. The way Bale spoke, the way he acted, suggested he thought of his current situation as nothing more than a minor inconvenience.

'God has other plans for me.' He shrugged. 'And for you.'

*

The electronic warbling of his phone was a welcome distraction from the enormous pile of paperwork threatening to bury him. They might have caught Bale, or whoever he really was, but three major incident enquiries still had to be wound up, overtime accounted for, staff rosters reorganised. The clean-up was always messy.

'McLean.' He cradled the phone in the crook of his shoulder, needing both hands to shore up a particularly precarious stack of report folders.

'Seems I owe you an apology, Inspector.'

'Who is this . . . ah, Chief Superintendent.' McLean took a moment to recognise the voice of Tim Chambers. 'Is there something I can help you with?'

'Oh, you have already. Ms Violet Grainger, to be precise.'

'You found her?'

'In London, yes. Holed up in the Savoy, of all places. I wanted to let you know. And to thank you for putting us on to her. All those months and years wasted chasing up the two McClymonts and we never got anywhere. Soon as we started looking at the secretary though, the whole thing fell apart.'

'The whole thing? I'm afraid I don't know what you're talking about, sir.'

'Really?' Chambers sounded sceptical. 'Oh well. It'll all come out at the trial. Good a piece of misdirection as I've ever seen. No wonder we couldn't pin anything on father and son. I wouldn't be all that surprised if they didn't know half of what was going on themselves. Except that young Joe was the wizard with the cars. His old man probably didn't have a clue what they were doing though.'

'So what were they doing?' McLean steadied the folders,

picked up a pen and scribbled on a notepad to check whether it worked or not.

'Stealing top-end motors. Giving them a new identity. Shipping some of them overseas. That was one half of it. The other half was a very slick drugs operation. All the proceeds went through the development company. Our forensic accountants are salivating over the details right now, and trust me it takes a lot to get them excited.'

McLean didn't doubt it. The very idea of forensic accountancy made him feel thirsty.

'Just wanted to thank you, really,' Chambers continued. 'If you hadn't put us on to the secretary, we'd have had to tuck this one away as unsolved. Hate having to do that.'

'Well, I'm glad I was a help.' McLean wasn't sure that he had been, but he'd take the compliment anyway.

'Yes, well. If you ever get bored of Edinburgh, give us a shout. Could use a few more detectives who can think outside the box.'

'Umm . . . thanks. I'll bear it in mind,' McLean said, but Chambers had already hung up.

Scaffolding clung to the building facades like metal ivy, yellow and black safety tape wound around it in a parody of flowers. The remains of the burnt-out shops had been bulldozed, leaving just the street door and staircase up to Madame Rose's house. It looked strangely out of place, a gimcrack addition to the building now that the structures to either side were gone.

A month on since she had left his house, taking her cats with her, and McLean had seen and heard nothing from his guest. He still had her letter with its strangely cryptic ending, and he couldn't stop dwelling on the improbable set of coincidences that had led to the discovery of Jim Whitely's body and the capture of the man claiming to be Norman Bale. If they hadn't been investigating the McClymonts, they would still be struggling to make any headway in the Ben Stevenson case, digging deep into the unhappy life of Maureen Shenks. They were all tragic deaths, but hers was the most depressing. Killed simply because she was in the way. Dumped like garbage.

He was with the psychologists now, Norman. Or not Norman. Happy to talk to anyone, it seemed. Some of the senior detectives were worried he was going to get away with an insanity plea, but McLean wasn't much bothered. It was enough that he'd been caught. There wasn't really any doubt that the man was insane, whoever he was. Perhaps spending the rest of his life in a secure psychiatric home was the best thing for him.

Shaking his head at the thought, McLean tried the door. It was locked, and a sign in the window said *'Closed during building works. Regular customers please call.'* He pulled his phone out to make a note of the number, but movement in the corner of his eye dragged his attention away for a moment. He couldn't see what it was at first, then noticed a single cat standing in one of the upper floor windows. It stared at him, blinked lazily, then jumped down from its perch, disappearing into the dark room beyond. McLean stood for a while, waiting to see if it would come back.

'Load of old rubbish that is, fortune telling. Don't waste your money on it, dear.'

He turned to see a little old lady wheeling a tartan shopping trolley down the pavement. She nodded at him as she passed, and before he could say anything she was gone. He still had his phone in his hand, ready to take down the number. There was no need though, he realised. And nothing to be gained from asking the questions he really didn't want to ask. He clicked off the phone and slipped it back into his pocket, began the long walk back to the station.

Acknowledgements

The arcane process of writing is a solitary thing, but every finished book is a team effort. I am very lucky to have a great crew behind me, polishing my grubby little words until they shine. A huge thanks to Alex and all the team at Michael Joseph for making these books as good as they can be. Thanks, too, to Katya and the publicity team who do such a brilliant job of telling the world all about me.

I am forever indebted to my agent, the inimitable Juliet Mushens. There aren't enough thanks in the world for her, but I'll keep sending the pink bubbly as a poor substitute.

I must thank Stuart MacBride too, for my continued misappropriation of his name. What started as a joke between friends all those years ago has rather grown out of control.

Thanks as ever to Barbara for keeping me just about sane. I still do some of the heavy lifting on the farm, but she pretty much runs it day to day now. Without her, this book would have taken a lot longer to write.

David Erskine provided me with much of the information about procedure and technology I have used in the book. If it's right, then that's down to him. Wrong is all me. Many others have helped me along the way. Too many to name here, but you know who you are. Thank you everyone. I owe you at least a drink or two.

And finally my thanks to the good folks at Gilmerton

Cove, who showed me round on a wet Saturday in January 2014. Yes, it's a real place, although I may have embellished it a little. Away from the beaten track of Edinburgh tourist attractions, it's something of a hidden gem, fascinating and eerie. If you find yourself in the capital looking for something to do, I thoroughly recommend a visit. You can find details at www.gilmertoncove.org.uk. Hopefully there won't be any murdered journalists down there when you go.